To Mother, "M", and Nana
HAPPY Birthd...
7 April 1977

Love.
Jay, Gay + boys

THE
SHAD TREATMENT

A NOVEL BY

GARRETT EPPS

G.P. PUTNAM'S SONS, NEW YORK

Acknowledgment is gratefully made for permission to include extracts from the following works:

"Desolation Row" by Bob Dylan, Copyright ©1965 Warner Bros. Inc. All Rights Reserved. Used by Permission of Warner Bros. Music.

"The Eagle That Is Forgotten" Copyright ©1923 by Macmillan Publishing Company, Inc. Renewed 1951 by Elizabeth C. Lindsay. Reprinted with permission of Macmillan Publishing Co., Inc. from *Collected Poems of Vachel Lindsay.*

"Easter 1916" Copyright ©1924 by Macmillan Publishing Co., Inc. Renewed 1952 by Bertha Georgie Yeats. Reprinted with permission of Macmillan Publishing Co., Inc. from *Collected Poems* by W. B. Yeats, and by permission of M. B. Yeats, Miss Anne Yeats and The Macmillan Company of London & Basingstoke.

"Mack the Knife" by Kurt Weill & Marc Blitzstein, Copyright © 1928 Universal Edition. Renewed 1955 by Weill-Brecht-Harms Co., Inc. All Rights Reserved. Used by permission of Warner Bros. Music.

"Oh Happy Day" by Edwin R. Hawkins, Copyright ©1969 Kama Rippa Music, Inc. & Edwin R. Hawkins Music Co., all rights administered by United Artists Music Co., Inc. N.Y., N.Y.

Second Impression

SBN: 399-11829-2

Library of Congress Cataloging in Publication Data

Epps, Garrett.
  The shad treatment.

  I. Title.
PZ4.E6419Sh   [PS3555.P63]   813'.5'4   76-20493
ISBN 0-399-11829-2

To my father and mother, who appear nowhere else in this book

NOTE: Readers familiar with Virginia geography may come across a number of unfamiliar names—Opechancanough County, Dillardville, Port Warwick, etc.—in this book. I hope this will serve to underscore that the events portrayed here take place only in the country of the imagination. No character or event in this book, with the exception of historical persons, is real, and any resemblance between events and characters in this book and real events or people, living or dead, is purely unintentional.

In those days they shall say no more, The fathers have eaten a sour grape, and the children's teeth are set on edge. But every one shall die for his own iniquity: every man that eateth the sour grape, his teeth shall be set on edge.

—Jeremiah 31:29–30

Hearts with one purpose alone
Through summer and winter seem
Enchanted to a stone
To trouble the living stream.
The horse that comes from the road,
The rider, the birds that range
From cloud to tumbling cloud,
Minute by minute they change;
A shadow of cloud on the stream
Changes minute by minute;
A horse-hoof slides on the brim,
And a horse plashes within it;
The long-legged moor-hens dive,
And hens to moor-cocks call;
Minute by minute they live:
The stone's in the midst of all.

—"Easter 1916,"
W. B. Yeats

"He would introduce his bills in committee, and the chairmen would always thank him. They were always very courteous. They'd say something like, 'We'll be glad to give this bill due consideration,' and of course before the session was over, they'd have chopped every one to ribbons. And finally one day when someone told him that his bill would get 'due consideration,' he let all his frustrations out. He reared up, eyes flashing, and he stuck out his finger and he said, 'Yes, Mr. Chairman, I know the consideration you'll give this bill. It's the consideration of the fisherman for the shad, Mr. Chairman,' he said. 'When the fisherman catches a shad and brings it into the boat, the poor fish flips and flops and tries to escape. And the fisherman speaks so politely to the shad, he says, "Lie still, little shad! I'm not going to hurt you. I'm going to treat you well, I'm not going to do a thing to you except cut your tail off. And I'm not going to do a thing more to you except cut your head off. And after that I'm not going to do a thing to you except cut all your bones out!"' And he pounded on the committee table and said, 'That's the consideration I expect from you, Mr. Chairman. The shad treatment, Mr. Chairman, the shad treatment! And I may have to take it, but I will fry in hell before I'll say thank you!'"

Part One

★

ONE

★

Richmond is built on the sand of a million-year-old beach. It squats at the fall line, straddling the James, in the center of Virginia. Northeast of the city, the bay and its tributaries hold sway over primitive counties where fishermen labor to bring a catch from dying waters. At the state's northern tip is the endless choking jumble of the Washington suburbs. To the west is the Piedmont, rising at the far edge of the state into the Blue Ridge Mountains. And below the river, stretching from the huge port complex around Norfolk to the Appalachian foothills, is the black dirt country, tobacco and peanut country, Southside Virginia.

Driving south of the city is like plunging underwater: a humid velvet violence tickles the senses like the distant odor of danger or faint strains of sensual music. Even inside the big blue Continental, its airconditioner whining, Mac Evans felt the change, and it made him weary. Perhaps, he thought, it was the late-summer heat he could see shimmering on the asphalt, waiting to prey on him. But more likely it was simply that he felt that the trip he was making was futile—at best a waste of time and at worst an embarrassment. He had asked Knocko that: *Why should he listen to me?*

Because you are his type of people, Knocko had answered. *I'm not, and Tom Jeff isn't. He won't hear it from us, because he thinks that the right people don't get mixed up with hooligans like us. But you, MacIlwain, me*

boyo—Knocko affected his stage Irishman's brogue and boozy grin—
*you're just the spalpeen to do this little job. You went to the right school
and the right college and you belong to the right clubs*—

I do not belong to those clubs, Mac protested angrily.

You used to, then, Knocko said imperturbably, *and you've got the right
name, which is what matters to these guys most of all, he knows who your
daddy was and who your brother was. You're just the type of young fellow
he likes to hear from.*

It's not going to do a damn bit of good, Mac had said.

Maybe not, Knocko admitted. *But I've got a hunch the poor silly bastard is dying to do it. Now I could be wrong*—Mac noted the phrase, a sure
sign that Knocko was unalterably convinced of what followed—*but I'll
tell you this: the guy may have gone out and gotten himself beat in the Senate race last year, but he's as shrewd as they come. He knows who did
what to him when the lights were out. And he's got to want to get back at
Miles Brock. That's just human nature.*

I'll tell you what it's like, Knocko had continued, warming to his words
with the enthusiasm he always brought to building rhetorical castles in the
air. *He's like a guy on the ledge outside the eighty-fifth-floor window, looking down and thinking how nice it would be to fall all the way down, flying
like a bird. Tom Jeff and me, we're two ragged kids down on the street yelling, 'Hey, mister, jump!' He won't pay any attention to us. But you,
you're different, Mac. It's as if his lawyer or priest was to put his head out
the window and say, 'Go ahead, jump, it's okay. You will not die. Angels
will bear you up lest you dash your foot against a stone.' And he's liable to
go on and do it. He's got to want to. It's human nature.*

After a little more wheedling, Mac had agreed to talk to Carrington; it
was, after all, his job. It was about an hour's drive from Richmond to
Tabbville on straight black roads across flat black farmland, past decaying
shacks where poor blacks lived and flat stucco boxes where not-quite-
poor blacks and whites lived and ranch houses and farmhouses where the
better-off whites lived. Tabbville itself was a tiny town—a gas station and
a store and a post office. When Tobey Carrington had been elected mayor
twenty years before, there had been no town hall. Carrington had built
one himself, donating the labor and renting the land to the town for a dollar a year. But he hadn't stayed on as mayor of Tabbville; he had gone on
to the House of Delegates and then to the State Senate.

He had worked hard in the legislature, arguing for his bills in calm, reasonable lawyer's tones. But nobody much had noticed him until, in his
second term, it had come time to vote on the plan to stop the Supreme

Court in its tracks by closing up any school ordered to integrate, to close every school in Virginia if it came to that. They had called it nullification, interposition, Massive Resistance. The nullifiers had been counting on Tobey Carrington: he was from Southside, from a diehard district, he was one of them by birth and training. But he had gotten up on the Senate floor and—always in calm, reasonable lawyer's tones—he had told them to go to hell. The plan had failed, and the school had stayed open, and men like Tobey Carrington had become heroes.

But nobody had expected it to last. Tabbville was Southside, after all— the blacks didn't vote, and the whites didn't hold with integration, and it was generally considered that Tobey Carrington had kissed his political career good-bye. But he had come back home and explained himself in that calm lawyer's way, and against all the odds he had been reelected, and people all over the state had begun saying, "Keep an eye on that young fellow; he might just amount to something."

Tobey Carrington had bided his time in the State Senate, and ten years later his time had come. It had come with the death of the millionaire Apple-Farmer who had been supreme boss of the state so long nobody called him by his name anymore—just the old man, the senator, himself. His death left a void in the state, and Carrington had moved to fill it. He had run for the U.S. Senate, against the Apple-Farmer's best friend, a man who had served four terms. He had campaigned in his calm lawyer's way, and he had won.

Then, for a few years, Carrington had been the man. There had been no one else. Like a dying king, the Apple-Farmer had bequeathed his Senate seat to his own son, his likeness and namesake, a quiet, studious man who had resembled his father in everything but courage, brains, and ability; he could not fill the void. Carrington could. Not that he would be a boss as the Apple-Farmer had been; the time had passed for that, and anyway, Tobey Carrington had not been the old man, for where the old man had been tough and stingy and vindictive, Carrington had been fair and judicious, with the mind of a legal scholar, a rational man, open and forgiving.

Behind him for those few years had gathered a whole generation of young and no-longer-young lawyers and politicians: the moderates, they had called themselves, who had been around for years, eating the Apple-Farmer's dust and swallowing his insults and fighting ever-so-discreetly for a little reform in the system here and there. Carrington had been their Moses, their Lincoln; suddenly they had no longer needed to be afraid— and if, as it had turned out, most of them had played the waiting game so long it had by then become a way of life they could not change quickly,

17

well, they had said, we've got Carrington in the Senate, and just wait a few years until we get one of our people in the governor's mansion, then you'll see some real changes.

Mac's brother, Lester, had been an important part of the organization Carrington had been beginning to build. Mac remembered the night Carrington had won that first primary. He and Lester and a few others had waited at Carrington's headquarters for the returns to come in by phone. It had been a long night, and in the end Carrington had won the Senate nomination by less than a thousand votes. But Mac had known the results long before the last precincts came in. Lester had told him. Lester had known every precinct in the state, knew the vote total from each district in each election for the last twenty years. As each return came in, Lester had checked it against a figure in his head and announced how many votes ahead or behind his prediction it was. Finally, in his head the figures had spelled victory, and he had known Carrington would win. He had turned to Mac and shaken him, saying, "This is it, bub. We've made it. We've busted their backs. We're going all the way."

Then Lester had turned around and gotten so drunk that his friend Deeb Grayson had convinced him to leave the headquarters before Tobey Carrington got there to claim victory; Carrington was a little straitlaced and frowned on drinking, and it had suddenly become a bad idea to displease Tobey Carrington. Lester had left the party and wrapped his Jaguar around a tree; Mac and Deeb had had to come out and give a man with a truck a hundred dollars to tow the car away before a policeman came along and saw Lester. All the way home, sprawled in the back of Deeb's car, Lester had crooned, "We've made it. We've busted them. Nothing can stop us now."

It had seemed that Lester was right, for a few years. Lester had explained it to Mac: right now the Apple-Farmer's people had the power. Besides Junior in the Senate along with Carrington, there was Miles Brock as governor: the last of the diehard nullifiers, a tough, cagey politician. "The dinosaur," Lester had called him contemptuously, and Mac had seen why: Brock's cold eyes, glaring out of his wrinkled farm boy's face, had something of the ageless, implacable malice of a reptile's—a cold, unwinking patience that meant to endure and conquer, not by wit or strength or grace but simply by outlasting the opposition.

But when Brock finished his term, Lester had explained, Tom Slaughter, Tobey Carrington's law school roommate, his best friend and campaign manager, would be governor; Lester would be lieutenant governor, and in four more years Lester would be governor. Junior and Miles Brock

18

and the rest of the dinosaurs would be out in the cold. It was all set. It was plain as day.

Except that somehow it hadn't worked out that way. Tom Slaughter had been crown prince, and everybody had known it, but when it had come time for the coronation, one man had refused to make way: Thomas Jefferson Shadwell, a young state senator, a fire-eating maverick, a tough liberal who had spent his life fighting the Apple-Farmer and all his works and who then, to everyone's surprise, hadn't really seen much difference between the old machine and the new, between dinosaurs and moderates—for there was nothing discreet, or timid, or cautious about Tom Jeff Shadwell. He had run against Slaughter in the primary, and the moderates found with dismay that Tom Slaughter, a good, sound corporate lawyer and back-room politician, was not really much of a campaigner. The two men had fought a bruising primary, and by the time Slaughter won, the party had been cut and splintered a hundred ways. Everything went wrong: the tired, pathetic little Virginia Republican Party had won the governorship, and Tom Slaughter had left the state.

But it had still been all right. Lester had been crown prince then, and the discreet moderate lawyers had still been playing it safe. They said, wait four years. Wait until Lester Evans is governor. Nobody can stop Lester Evans. He's got it made.

Which would have been true, if Lester hadn't died.

Fate hadn't finished with Tobey Carrington. The year after Lester died, he had been up for reelection; it had been a shoo-in, an easy win. The Republicans had nominated a joke, a patsy, a clown. But things had gone a little crazy that year: the national ticket had fallen apart, and the Republican clown had gotten some money, and Tobey Carrington had campaigned in his calm, reasonable lawyer's way for the last time, and against all the odds he had lost.

Suddenly it was all over. Carrington moved back to Tabbville, to the house by the old Town Hall, and tried to put his law practice together again. And because in Virginia the elections for governor take place a year after the presidential elections, by spring people had forgotten Tobey Carrington and begun worrying about the governor's race. And this year the quiet, cautious, moderate men were looking for places to hide. The only Democrat left was Thomas Jefferson Shadwell, loud and angry as ever, running for governor.

And the Republicans, having tasted power, now found they wanted it so badly they would do anything for it, and because they had no one in their ranks who could beat Shadwell, they had gone to Miles Brock and

19

begged him to switch parties, offered him their nomination. Which suited him fine: he wanted to beat Shadwell, and besides, he liked power too. He had taken their nomination with that icy gaze which seemed to say, *I have outlasted them all. They have come, and they have gone, and now I am going to triumph again.*

And this Mac—for pressing reasons of his own—was determined to prevent.

To Mac's surprise, Carrington looked the same: broad, amiable smooth face, thick dark hair shot with gray, the short, wiry body a surprise under the big head, which looked like a tall man's. Mac realized he had unconsciously been expecting to see some physical change as a sign of defeat, as if a man could not lose everything he valued and not show it somehow. He didn't know what he was expecting: a network of scars, a limp, hair turned suddenly white like a shellshock victim's.

"MacIlwain," Carrington said, extending his hand. "It's grand to see you again. How are you doing?"

"I'm about the way I usually am," Mac said as they shook hands. "It's good to see you, too. How are you doing?"

"I suppose you mean, how am I holding up in defeat?" the older man said as he led him into the house. They passed through a stiff white room where the furniture seemed to hold itself at attention, satiny-white couches and chairs and high precarious tables, vertical glass cabinets crammed with knickknacks. Mac felt the urge to tiptoe. "I'm actually doing quite well," he said. "Very well indeed."

He gave Mac a sidelong glance. *Now you just go back and tell them that,* Mac imagined him adding. They passed into the tangled male refuge of the senator's study, a bare narrow room crammed with a large wooden desk, a cracked leather sofa, an old wooden bookshelf, a big window giving onto the backyard.

As Mac settled down on the couch, dust motes flew about in the stream of light from the window. He looked at the books in the cabinet: lawyer's books, with titles like *The Murder of George Wythe* and *Judge Medina Speaks* and *Law as Literature* and *The Lawyers of Dickens and Their Clerks.* Jumbled among them were old newspapers, Xeroxed sheets, campaign leaflets, maps, and dusty bulging file folders.

"This is more like it," Carrington said. "It got so I was spending so much time away from here that I just let Sally take over the rest of the house. She turned it into a museum. I'm afraid to breathe out there. I sort of retreat in here. Cigar?" He held out a box of chocolate-brown coronas.

"No, thanks," Mac said. "I'm trying not to cultivate the habit. It's bad for the image."

The senator laughed as he sat down. "Aw, now, Mac," he said, lighting one for himself. "You're too young a fellow to worry about that. You're going to have to pick up some weight and drop some hair before you look like a real political boss. How old are you now, anyway?"

"Twenty-six," Mac said.

"Well, I've been spending most of my time in here," Carrington went on, as if he had not heard. He patted a pile of papers on his desk. "It's the first chance I've had to work on my biography of Mahone. Something I've wanted to do since I was at the University. He was a hell of a guy. Little stringy fellow—weighed less than a hundred pounds, did you know that?"

"No," Mac said, although he had.

"It's a fact. And he talked in a funny little squeaky voice, like a damn ventriloquist's dummy." Smoke shrouded Carrington's head as he puffed the cigar. "But it didn't slow him down any. He built the damn railroad, and he damn near took over the state for a while."

"They stopped him eventually, though, didn't they?" Mac said, less because he was interested than to delay the moment they would have to start talking business.

"Oh, yes, to be sure, they stopped him, and they made his name a dirty word," Carrington said. "That was because of the blacks. He organized the blacks, and they managed to get people frightened to death about it. History is a funny thing, though. You see a situation like that, and it's hard to say it wasn't a good thing, really. I guess that seems hard—"

"It sure does," Mac said. "If you were black or poor and you wanted to vote, it was kind of rough, the way they stopped him."

"Well, now," Carrington said. "I wasn't really thinking about the poll tax and so forth. All that came later. And that was bad. Although, as bad as it was, you can't really say it was all bad. Sure, it let the old man in, but there were some good things about that, too. At least it kept things honest in a difficult time—"

"We're just going to have to disagree on that one, Senator," Mac said.

Carrington looked up at him, as if remembering exactly who Mac was. "I reckon that's right," he said. "Your family never had much use for him, did you?"

"You want to blame us?" Mac asked, a little truculently. In his mind, unrolling like a player piano spool, was Knocko's perennial monologue whenever someone goaded him to fury by saying, *At least the old man kept the state honest,* which to Knocko was like a red flag, a key opening the door to his unfailing, relentless, Celtic rage: *Honest!* he would say, his face flushing and his voice rising. *Honest! Damn if I can understand how this late in the twentieth goddamn century you can still find geese to honk that old tune: the machine was clean. Sure, clean, if by that all you ask is that you not have to pay off to get a state job—sure. And not only that, if you kept your nose clean, the sheriff wouldn't rape your daughter usually, as long as you didn't be stupid enough to be black—sure, it was that honest, and sure, the old man himself never took a dime, he didn't need to, he was a millionaire.* Knocko would rear up in his chair like a hooded cobra poised to strike, whirling on his victim with an outstretched forefinger which somehow seemed to accuse whoever was at the end of it of all the corruption in the history of the state, if not the world: *You explain to me, then, how honest it was to have all that state money in the interest-free accounts, and how honest were all those hundred-dollar bills from the power company and the truckers floating around come election time, and how honest it was when, if you got out of line, your wife or your father-in-law or your brother-in-law lost his job with the county. Merciful suffering Jesus!* he would cry, throwing his arms to heaven in a gesture of disgust, *I believe on my soul the people of this state have been starved, swindled, hoodwinked, and led by the nose so long they don't know what a real honest man is anymore! Honest! An honest man in this state means somebody who believes stealing is beneath his dignity, that's all!*

"Listen," Carrington said. "I never got a chance to thank you for what you did for me last year. I wrote you a letter and all, but a thing like that needs something personal. It was a tough year to raise money, and I appreciate the hell out of what you did."

"That's okay," Mac said. "I just wish it could have been more."

"You're kind," Carrington said. He paused a moment, then said, "And I hope you understand why I never called you to do anything else. I mean—I appreciated the offer—but with the presidential thing and all—"

"Okay," Mac said. "It was your campaign, and however you decided to run it was okay with me. I had my hands full with the presidential campaign, God knows. I'm just sorry you didn't win, that's all."

Carrington smiled. "We didn't either one of us have a good year last year, did we?"

Mack shrugged.

"Politics is the damnedest thing," Carrington was saying. "People say I ran a bad campaign. But I don't know what I could have done different. The presidential thing—"

Mac politely said nothing, but Carrington seemed to sense his skepticism.

"Oh, all right, then," the senator said. "I guess I could have beat that guy. God knows he isn't much. Every time we appeared together, I got a lot of votes in a hurry. I imagine if I'd got on the phone along about Labor Day and talked tough and pleaded a little and threatened to cut some people's balls off, we might have been able to pull the whole thing together, presidential thing or not."

He took the cigar out of his mouth and looked at it fiercely, his intense, slightly cross-eyed gaze fixed on an internal landscape of lost chances and wrong decisions. "I don't know, though," he said. "I'll tell you my theory. Before I got into politics, I had this idea of what it was like. You know, a process of resolving conflicts, different interest groups reaching acceptable compromise, that sort of thing. But the real thing—it's nothing like that. All that stuff is settled long before things get into the political arena. Politics is just a sort of entertainment, I think. I mean, it's a ritual; the people believe in it. It reassures them. It's like killing the corn god so the crops will crow. That's what this election was like. There wasn't anything political about it. It was a damn ritual, was all: the people felt a little angry, a little confused, and they cut my head off. And I didn't have anything more to do with it than anybody else."

He was talking to himself now more than to Mac, and Mac sensed that he was overhearing Carrington's internal monologue, his private attempt to make some sense out of what had happened to him. It was painful, like watching a man bare his wounds. But he kept silent, because he felt he owed it to Carrington to listen.

"This campaign—it wasn't like the first time I ran," Carrington said. "That time I used to spend all day campaigning, and when it was over, I'd go to bed just bone-weary. I mean it was hard. It hurt. It was like running through cement—I've never done anything harder before or since. Last year it was different. I could do anything people wanted me to do. I could go twelve, fifteen hours a day, and I never got tired. It puzzled me at first, but along about October I realized why: it was because I didn't care anymore. It didn't make a damn bit of difference to me whether I won or lost. And I knew that the other guy cared, and in politics, if you don't care, you lose. That's a hell of a distressing thing to realize six weeks before an election."

"I can imagine," Mac said. He could. He shivered slightly, in fact, as he put himself in Carrington's place, carrying around, during the last frantic weeks of a campaign, the knowledge that he had already lost, that his will had failed him and he was politically dead.

23

"Damn it, Mac," Carrington said belligerently. "To tell you the truth, I'm well out of it. If that SOB wants to sit up in Washington and snot in a Senate wastebasket, okay, let him. I've never been one of these guys who sat awake at night just thinking about what office he could run for next. I've got a life to live. I've got a son, he's about eleven now; if I'd won another term, he'd be grown up before I even got to know him. I've been having the time of my life with him, and with Sally, and I can go on and get my law practice back and maybe even make a little money. So I've come out of it all right. Some guys, they get caught up in politics, by the time they get through, there's nothing left.''

Carrington fell silent. He stubbed out his cigar. It was time for Mac to turn the conversation to the question he had come to ask. It shouldn't have been hard; in the last two years he had sat down with dozens of men, asked harder questions, made more difficult deals. But something about Carrington held him back; perhaps it was because he had known him so long that some of his child's awe lingered, making him feel suddenly like a little boy pretending to be a grown-up. Or more likely it was Carrington's special quality, that air which Mac had admired for so long of stubborn, independent honor which had made him seem so special: something in the way he talked, and held himself, that seemed to say, *I am my own man. I make my own way. I don't play it like everybody else.*

Now Mac was going to ask him a normal political question, one which he had asked often enough in the past two years and which he knew Carrington had asked and caused to be asked hundreds of times himself. Maybe what he was afraid of was the possibility that asking the question would destroy, not the real Senator Tobey Carrington sitting before him, but the one in his mind, the one whom he had always thought of in a special way as almost a political saint, in ways that his brother or Tom Jeff or even his father had not been. So he waited.

At last Carrington himself took the lead. "Mac," he said, "don't get me wrong. I would admire to sit here and talk politics with you for the rest of the afternoon. You have a quick mind and a good heart, and it's always a pleasure. But I imagine you came down here for a reason. What can I do for you? If it's advice you want, I'll be happy to oblige if I can."

"No, it isn't that," Mac said. He took a deep breath and found himself wishing he had taken a cigar. "It's not advice," he said. "What it is, we want—that is, Tom Jeff has asked me to tell you that he wants your support this year very much. Your official, public support. We're setting up a group called Virginians for Shadwell, and what we'd really like is if you'd agree to be one of the co-chairmen—it would be purely ceremonial, we'd set everything up, all you'd have to do would be come to Richmond for

24

one press conference. You'd have no other involvement in the campaign unless you asked for it. That would be the best we could hope for. But if you don't want to do it that way—you don't want to head up the group— then we'd hope you could see your way clear to holding a press confer- ence down here any time after Labor Day. I'd be happy to come down and take care of the details of setting it up. It would just be a statement. No speeches or appearances unless you wanted to, and I promise we wouldn't be on the phone every half hour asking you to do something. But this one thing, Tom Jeff thinks—and I agree—that it would mean a hell of a lot of votes."

Carrington's face was blank for a moment, with a hint of incomprehen- sion about the eyes. Then he laughed a polite, unbelieving laugh, as he settled back in his chair and shook his head. He paused, as if choosing his words, then laughed again and shook his head with a peculiar motion like a horse clearing away insects from around its face.

"Hell," he said finally. "I suppose it's a compliment to an old broken- down ex-senator that Shadwell would seek him out at all. I suppose." He leaned back in his chair, rearing his head back on his neck until he ap- peared to be looking at Mac across a great, skeptical distance. "But I just want to know this," he said. "What in thunder makes Shadwell and Knocko think I'd want to get myself involved in this?"

Now that he had begun, Mac found it was not so difficult to talk to Car- rington about real, unsaintly politics; once he began, it was like any of a hundred political conversations he had had before. "We understand each other, I think," he said. "You know I voted for you and I admire you and I gave you a thousand dollars and I would have done more if you'd let me"—he cut off Carrington's reflexive apologetic motion—"don't apolo- gize, I'm not criticizing you, it was your campaign, and I'm not question- ing the way you chose to run it. But the point I'm making is that I'm not Tom Jeff and I'm not Knocko, and I have reasons of my own for wanting to see you do this. I think what happened to you stinks, that it's a tragedy and not even so much for you personally, though of course it is, as for the state of Virginia. And when I think about it, I just get mad as hell."

He leaned forward, almost lecturing the older man, gesturing with his two hands. "Now the point I'm making is this: we both know one guy who had a lot to do with getting you beat, and it wasn't that poor clown who ran for President and it wasn't Tom Jeff Shadwell. It was goddamn Miles Brock, and you know it as well as I do. If Miles Brock had just stirred himself, just passed the word to his friends who had the money and told them to stay neutral—that's all, not even support you—that other guy would have been out in the cold: no money, no organization, nothing.

But Brock didn't do that. And now we've lost the best senator we've had in this century, and this new guy is a baboon. And you—you're just out in the cold.

"Well, God *damn* it," he said, pounding on the arm of the couch, feeling somehow that he might, just might, be getting through, feeling the salesman's desperate urge to clinch the sale. "That's something none of us has to take lying down. Brock is running for governor now, and he's got a better chance than before because you lost. Unless you pull the plug on him. All you have to do is make this statement, that's all, and you can retire that SOB, I mean it. This is going to be a close election, and Tom Jeff thinks a statement from you would absolutely make the difference. And I agree. I'm not going to try to sell you on Tom Jeff. You two have got your own quarrels. But he by God supported you the first time, and he supported you last time. So I don't see any reason why you should take what Brock did to you lying down; that's all."

Carrington swiveled the desk chair to look out the study window. The small yard gave onto a thick stand of pines. In the center of the yard stood a shiny new-looking swing and slide set. Beyond it, standing before a thick hedge, a low white wire fence marked off a vegetable garden, sprouting thick and lush in the last verdant month of the summer. Adjoining the house was a blue flagstone patio, and in the center of this was a white metal table topped with a new blue parasol. Set about the table were three metal chairs and a plastic chaise longue. The pines caught the light of the late afternoon and diffused it through the air, so the yard had a lambent look about it, as if the light were growing out of the ground along with the trees and the vegetables.

"I don't know," Carrington said. He picked his glasses off his nose and studied them minutely for specks of dirt. At length he took a handkerchief from his pocket and wiped one lens. "I think Miles would actually have helped me if I'd asked him to," he said as he resettled the glasses on his nose. "All this business of him becoming a Republican is just a marriage of convenience to beat your friend Shadwell. Deep down he really hasn't got any use for the Republicans. And it really might have made the difference, you're right. That's the thing about Brock and Junior and that whole crowd. All they want is for you to come to them hat in hand. Once you do that they're very gracious, very polite. And they can help you a lot."

Abruptly he swiveled back to face Mac, though his eyes were only partly focused on the room around him. "The only problem is, once you ask them, that's it," he said. "You get hooked up with that crowd, and suddenly you have no balls left. By God"—he slammed his hand lightly against the top of the desk—"I never once asked those guys for anything, and I was not about to start last year. I figured, give the voters a chance. If they want me back, okay, back I'll go. If not, okay, too. I've never been one of these individuals who couldn't live without holding office."

Mac found himself unaccountably irritated. He clamped his jaws and nodded, but against his will he could hear a little Knocko deep inside him sneering, *Go ahead, then. If you want to think you're too good to succeed, go right ahead. What you really mean is you're too damn good to fight for anything is all.* But that wasn't fair, and Mac recognized it, so he nodded again and waited.

"Now, your friend Tom Jeff supported me," Carrington was saying. "There was never any question about that. It was in his interest, of course. If I'd gone back, it would have hurt the Republicans, to have won the presidential so big and still lost the Senate seat. But I honestly think Shadwell wanted me to go back. There hasn't been much love lost between us, you know, not since he cut Tom Slaughter's throat. But he supported me."

"He would have done more if you'd let him," Mac said. "Now he's asking you."

"Yeah, him and his whole crowd," Carrington said. "Knocko Cheatham—"

"All right," Mac said. "And me, too. I'm asking. It would help a lot. And I happen to think it makes a pretty damn big difference who wins this one."

Carrington had collected himself. He smiled an older man's smile of mockery. "I don't know, Mac," he said. "We had four years of Miles Brock before, and we survived."

"Yeah, we did," Mac said, snorting in disgust. "We came out with about half a party and the worst tax laws in the South. Now if we let these guys go back, they and the Republicans will lock this state up like a banana republic. I mean, think of yourself—" Carrington gave him a startled glance, but Mac plunged ahead. "No, really. You're still a young man, you were a great United States senator, and every time this new jackass opens his mouth your memory looks better. In six years, if you want it back, you'll have a pretty good shot. Unless Brock gets in."

To Mac's surprise, Carrington burst into laughter, a short, full laugh from deep inside. "Oh, no, Mac," he said. "It won't fly. Nothing personal against you. Hell, for that matter, nothing personal against Tom Jeff. I don't much like the son of a bitch, but he's honest. He tells you what he's going to do, and then he does exactly that, which is more than I can say for Miles or Junior or any of those guys. But I'm out of that now. All the way out. I was in politics twenty years, and they cut me up one side and

27

down the other, and if I'd stayed much longer, there would've been nothing left. Now I'm out, I'm doing okay, and I have no idea of getting back in for Tom Jeff or anybody else. There's something about politics—you play it too long, it ruins you, it uses you up. My God, Mac, you of all people ought to understand that."

Mac remembered his father's letters: the thin, crabbed handwriting, the dry brittle phrases. "Yes, I do," he said, "I do."

Carrington continued in a gentle tone. "Listen, Mac, I don't like to say no to you. But try to understand what I'm saying. You've come down here and offered me a chance to get back at Brock. I think the offer is kindly meant on your part. Some of the people you're working for could care less if I live or die, but you've always been a good friend. So I appreciate it. But that's the thing—there's always somebody somewhere who's done you wrong, and if you keep trying to get back, there's no end to it. If you're lucky—and I was lucky, I really was—there comes a point when you say to yourself, I'm out of it. I write it off, I'm not hating anymore. My wife asks me who did me wrong last year. And I won't tell her. Because it's over now, and I'm not going to have her hating those people for me. I'm letting go, Mac. I was up there, and they cut my head off, and now it's somebody else's turn. I'm through being a victim. All I want to do is get along and enjoy my life."

The senator was standing, and Mac realized he was being asked to go. "So you just go on back and tell Knocko I said, don't hold your breath. And tell Tom Jeff I wish him luck, because he's going to need it."

As they walked again through the stiff white breathless parlor, Carrington put his arm on Mac's shoulder. "Mac, it is good to see you," he said. "Why don't you come on down some time when you don't have business to transact? I'll have Sally make up the guest room, and we'll play a little tennis or something. I'm sure Knocko will give you a few days off from work."

All right, Mac thought. *All right.*

Carrington sensed that his barb had struck flesh. As they stood at the door, he pulled Mac around, gripping his elbow. "I'm sorry, Mac," he said. "But you know, I've never understood why you go at this thing the way you do. I mean, if you're really interested in politics, there are better ways to do it than being Knocko Cheatham's errand boy. Believe me. That bastard is riding for a hell of a fall sooner or later, and you don't need to tie him around your neck." The senator gave his elbow a slight shake for emphasis. "I'm serious now," he said. "If you're just bound and determined to mess with politics, why don't you go on back to the University and finish law school and come back to Richmond then and run for something? You're a bright fellow, you've got Lester's looks, and the name is still good, and it will be for quite a while. Lester did that."

"I don't know," Mac mumbled, embarrassed. He was thinking, *You don't understand, Senator. You think I want to be like Lester, who spent his whole life turning himself into a politician, until finally he couldn't tell the difference between himself and what he had made himself into. I don't want that. I just want to get a job done. I just want to settle some scores. I just want to win one. That's all.*

"Well, you think about it," Carrington said. "These guys are your friends, okay, I respect that. But you've got a lot of other friends who'll help you if you need it. You know that, don't you?"

"I never gave it much thought," Mac said, avoiding the senator's eyes. At that moment Mac realized how large was the gap between them: Carrington was filled with a stillness so profound and permanent that though Mac could look at him and understand why he had stopped moving, Carrington could no longer look back and understand what kept Mac in motion. In one year he had passed beyond his old life, had forgotten that brute drive which moved people forward in politics, had said good-bye to it so finally that no sympathetic trace remained.

Mac suddenly felt for Carrington a kind of bilious pity: bilious because he could not help wondering if, in the moment the older man had given up, he might not have taken the first step toward discovering some secret about being human which could not come as long as he kept going, and which would elude Mac forever unless he got rid of the thing inside him which kept him going, this mixture of hatred and grief and fury which had brought him here today and which would take him back to Richmond and through September and October and all the weary days of the dirty, bruising campaign which lay ahead. Suddenly he wanted to go, to get back to Richmond; suddenly he was frightened, frightened that he might become someday what the senator was and frightened that he might not.

"I've got to go," he said. "Have you got any message for Tom Jeff?"

"Yes," Carrington said. "Tell him good luck. It's going to be a mean campaign. And tell him to come see me if he loses. Tell him we'll play a little pool. If he wins, he won't need to see me. But if he doesn't, we might get to be friends." He laughed softly. Then the door was shut and Mac was walking back to the car.

TWO

Mac left the interstate at Axe Trail Road. Southside is haunted by the ghosts of planters and their slaves; Richmond was built by the practical men who had served them: merchants and lawyers, brokers and bureaucrats.

Axe Trail winds through their descendants' domain. Bordered by hedges and walls and manicured lawns, it dips within a block of St. Cyprian's, where their sons are schooled from kindergarten until they reach young manhood, and passes the playing fields of St. Fina's, where their daughters pursue a parallel course. Between them, on the east side of Axe Trail, sits St. Anselm's, where the sons will marry the daughters, and on the west side is the Westhampton Club, where the grooms more than likely escorted the brides to the Richmond Ball, and where the young couples will certainly hold their receptions, and where in later years they will progress from tennis and golf to bridge and Sunday brunch and weekday highballs, and where, it is to be hoped, their own sons and daughters will swim and meet for ice cream after tennis and dance and fall in love under the summer moon and the benevolent eye of the membership committee.

Mac's car wound past the sturdy gray stone of St. Anselm's and the self-assured maroon brick of St. Fina's and the blue and white hilltop clubhouse, its spotlights springing ghostly out of the darkness. He came to the end of Axe Trail and jogged right and then left and then continued on toward the James, which is the heart of Richmond and its reason for existing, but which inhabits the city like the president of a large old bank: surrounded by the estates of the rich like so many vice-presidents shielding their chief from outsiders.

Mac's house was one of the senior vice-presidents. It was separated from the river only by a narrow stand of oaks and pines and a gravel road much favored by young couples for parking on warm nights. From the woods, the broad back lawn swept up a rolling incline, past the little cottage where Mac slept and the opulent oblong of Molly O.'s rose garden, to the stone terrace Mac's father had added, built around an ornate statuary fountain his mother had brought back from Europe. At the back of the house was the glassed-in porch Lester and Molly O. had built, austerely up-to-date, stuck incongruously onto the back of the old stucco house like an enormous airconditioner.

The front of the house was a broad expanse of stone bisected by a marble patio and a portico supported by four tall pillars. Pine trees shaded the front lawn, and their fragrance and the dropping needles gave the lawn and the flagstoned walk a sheltered air, so that it had seemed to Mac as long as he could remember a sort of magically protected other world immune from weather and cold.

On either side of the wooden doorway, french windows led into the front rooms which Mac's mother had furnished in jumbled warm eclectic comfort—Chinese vases, Florentine tapestries, Persian rugs, baroque wooden chairs, overstuffed couches. Mac parked the Continental in the driveway. As he crossed the lawn, he saw a light in the east room. Molly O. was home. Even though she and Lester had furnished the new back room themselves in spacious steel, leather, and fur, now that Lester was dead she found that she preferred the musty clatter of the front rooms.

Mac stepped to the window and peered in. Molly O. was sewing and talking to Judge Anderson. Mac imagined that they were talking about gardening. Molly O. was Lester's widow. Past thirty now, she had somehow never quite given up being a girl, and somehow, because she was Molly O., she had escaped the queasy athletic rigidity which sometimes steals upon women who refuse to give up their girlhood. Perhaps this was because Molly O. was not trying to hold onto anything; she was who she wanted to be, and that self was neither complicated nor discouraged, and because of this, she had no impulse toward extra flesh, martinis, contract bridge, or any of the other soft self-destructions with which her contemporaries were introducing themselves to middle age. Molly O. rode, and knitted, and tended her roses, and supplied herself with what she needed to get along.

Her evenings she spent alone, or with the judge, who had been Mac's father's law school roommate and best friend, and who was now retired and devoted to his wisteria and dogwood and mimosas and his flowers and vegetables. He was past seventy, and almost bald, and his eyes were dim, and he divided his evenings between the bridge game at the Confederate Club and the east room at the house, where he and Lester's widow sat and talked about plants, each knowing that it was not plants that had brought them together, but the fact that each had loved an Evans and lost him.

Mac pushed open the french doors. "Hey, Molly O.," he said.

"Hey, Mac," she said, smiling slightly. "You back already? Come on in, I'll fix you some supper."

"No, thanks," Mac said. "All that driving has defused my appetite. I'll get something later." Mac disliked having Molly O. cook for him and fixed most of his meals himself over a hot plate. She had asked him once if he disliked her, and he had tried to reassure her. It was just, he had explained, that he lived alone in his little house and he lived alone inside himself, and he felt obliged to take note of that fact, as if by making a routine of eating at the big house he would somehow be beginning a pretense that there was some vital heart left to the family, that the Evanses had not been smashed and hammered and ripped apart. And though he had not been able to explain all this, she had nodded, and understood, because she had been married to his brother, and Lester also had been a man who lived deep within himself in rooms and chambers no one else could enter.

The judge took notice of him, fixing a pair of rimless spectacles on his beaked nose. "Mac I.," he said. "How's yourself? What devilment have you been up to today?" He studied Mac through the glasses with his habitual mixture of wry amusement and affectionate incomprehension.

"The same old thing, Your Honor," Mac said. "You know."

"I'm afraid I do know," the judge said, with an exasperated twitch of the head. "I'm afraid I do, yes indeed. I think you've probably been running all over creation doing *liberal* things, sowing confusion and creating mischief, and I'm afraid to ask for details because I just know they'll dismay me."

"Best not, then," Mac said. "Curiosity killed the cat."

"I should think you'd have better manners than to talk to a person of my gray hairs about death," the judge said. "I don't think it's at all polite."

"What gray hairs?" Mac said, indicating the old man's shiny head. "I don't see one."

Molly O. laughed, and the judge muttered, "The very idea."

"What are they saying at the Confederate Club these days, Judge?" Mac asked.

"About what?" Anderson said.

33

"Has Brock been in lately?"

"I haven't seen Miles in some time," Anderson said. "I guess he's out flaying the devil."

"Is it a holy war now?" Mac said. A touch of asperity was creeping into their voices, despite the good-humored tones. "A Virginia jihad? How would Oscar Wilde have put it? The intolerant being led by the insufferable, wouldn't you say?"

"In pursuit of the unspeakable, young man," Anderson said.

"Make me a promise," Mac said. "If Tom Jeff wins, I want you to take me to lunch at the Confederate Club the day after the election, so I can smoke a big cigar and tell Brock jokes."

"Young man, it is more than my reputation is worth to be seen with you at the club," the judge said. "Besides, you are liable to blow it up or set fire to the picture of General Lee."

"Right on all three counts," Mac said, and winked at Molly O. "When Tom Jeff is inaugurated, we're going to borrow a bulldozer from the Highway Department and bring it down Grace Street and raze that place with the members still inside."

"You going down?" Molly O. interrupted quickly.

"I reckon," Mac answered. "What are you going to do?"

"Nothing at all," she said. "I'll knit a while more; then we might watch Dr. Welby. Come on up if you're awake."

"I might," Mac said. "I'm pretty tired, though. Did anybody call?"

"You got two calls. Gravelier said he was going over to Hoke's. He wanted you to come on over when you got back."

"Spare me," Mac said. "Who was the other one?"

"Knocko Cheatham," Molly O. said, and although she was much too polite to let disdain creep into her voice, it was somehow obvious that Knocko was not her kind of people at all. "He didn't leave a message."

"It'll keep, I'm sure," Mac said. "Thanks."

"Devilment and more devilment," Anderson said. "Friend Cheatham is up to no good."

"Hush now," Molly O. said. "Leave Mac alone. He's had a long day."

"Thanks, Molly O.," Mac said. She gave him a quick wink of complicity. He closed the window and crossed the flagstone terrace, stepped quickly down the stone stairway, and walked past the dark glass porch to his little house. His father's governess had lived here, and when Mac was a child, it had housed a rachitic drunken black housekeeper who had died of a heart attack shortly after his twelfth birthday. It had been closed since then, until the day Mac had come home from law school and furnished it for himself. It was two rooms: a front room with large windows, where Mac kept a couch and a desk, and a tiny dark back room, where he slept. The walls of the front room had been decorated by the governess, about whom Mac knew little save that she had been Hungarian and had never married, but because she had covered the walls with voluptuous warm-colored Persian prints—angular Islamic princes wielding curved swords and wooing curved princesses—Mac imagined her spending her life there in a perpetual dream, a lonely old maid calling up an imaginary Arab lover to chase away the chill of loneliness and old age. The colors pleased him, and so he had left them up, along with a travel poster which was all that had been left by the housekeeper, Emmaline: ETHIOPIA, it said, above a picture of a young shepherd gazing at the camera, liquid dark eyes dominating a sharp hieroglyphic face. Beneath it, mysteriously, someone—the departed Emmaline?—had penciled "Rastafari" in tiny block letters. The floor was carpeted in purple and red flowers, which Mac had learned to ignore. Along the walls he had built cinder-block bookcases, and in the far corner stood a tiny refrigerator and hot plate. Beyond the appliances and the shelves and a portable television, Mac's presence had made little dent on the room. Many of his things were still stacked in cardboard cartons behind the couch. The room had an impersonal, temporary air, like a replica of a living room arranged in a deserted warehouse.

Mac folded his jacket across the desk chair, then untied his tie and draped it over the jacket. It was an aged St. Cyprian's tie, one of several Mac kept finding around the house: bright red with gray figures, stylized depictions of the saint's Episcopal crown. He turned on the radio on the desk. Then, with a sigh, he cast himself flat on the couch, hands behind his head, and looked at the ceiling. His mind was a reassuring blank of fatigue. The radio played softly; he had nothing to do until tomorrow, and he lay still in the silence, content to anticipate nothing. The digital clock-radio said 8:50. Tomorrow he would have to report to Knocko. He could not bring himself to believe that Cheatham would be surprised by the senator's reaction. Knocko had taken Carrington's measure long ago, if not profoundly, then at least competently enough to see that the other man's delicate political sensibility would leave him with equal distaste for both of the giants currently stalking across Virginia. Not only sensibility, conscience; peace of mind, too, must by now require that Carrington see himself as having been caught between a merciless Scylla and an equally malign Charybdis. Any other image would require that he see himself as everybody else did: a man who threw away the thing he loved most and was best suited for in the world because he could not make up his mind, because he could not choose his enemies or bring himself to fight.

Knocko would have anticipated it and, in his fashion, thought beyond it. His mind was dark and labyrinthine, always two jumps ahead or, at least, trying to stay that way. What had been accomplished by sending Mac to talk to him? For one thing, he had made a contact there for the Shadwell campaign. Perhaps the visit was designed to show Carrington that Tom Jeff's people were not all blacks, longhairs, Woolco managers, and muscle-bound COPE hit men. *See*, it was intended to say, *it is your type of people this year, too. Who would be welcome at any country club*, though Mac had, in fact, been expelled from the Westhampton years before.

BONG-BONG-BONG-BONG! Electronic tomtoms broke into his reverie. *"Brock says Shadwell is out of step!"* announced a portentous voice. *"Good evening, it's eight fifty-five. I'm Alonzo T. Everett, and this is the news. Former Governor Miles Brock tonight accused his opponent in the governor's race of being 'out of step' with the rest of Virginia on the busing question. Brock branded State Senator Thomas Jefferson Shadwell quote a pro-buser and a social engineer unquote."* They intercut a tape of Brock's voice: halting, magisterial, his Tidewater accent as thick and sweet as corn syrup running through a clogged drainpipe: *"The vast majority of Virginians are opposed to massive busing for the purpose of achieving a contrived racial balance. My opponent is not. And I feel that he and the other sociological experimenters must bear a measure of responsibility for tragedies when they occur, as they have in the past and will in the future unless we end this costly venture into the brave new world of big-brother-style social manipulation."*

"Brock made the charges before the annual Nansemond Spot Festival," the announcer intoned. *"Richmond police have arrested two men in connection with the shooting-stabbing murder of a ninety-four-year-old Northside woman. The two, Raoul Garrett and Ambrose Chambers, are being held—"*

The phone rang, then fell silent, and he heard the buzzer that Molly O. used to tell him to pick up the receiver. As he lurched off the couch, Mac thought, *It's early for them to be throwing their bomb.*

"Yo," he said into the phone.

"This is E.G. speaking," said a sprightly voice.

"Hello, Gravelier," he said. Gravelier—pronounced to rhyme with "grenadier"—Huntington was a schoolmate from St. Cyprian's, a wealthy young man who amused himself by publishing a weekly newspaper. "What can I do for you?" Mac said.

"I'm over at the Spottswood estate playing bumper pool and fiddling with Hoke's videotape machine," Huntington said. "We thought you might like to join us."

Hoke Spottswood, another old Saint, was an aristocratic idler whom all his school days Mac had avoided strenuously, as, indeed, had everyone else, including Gravelier, until he had discovered in Spottswood the saving grace of wealth even greater than his own. Now Huntington cultivated him assiduously, receiving as reward for his hours of boredom periodic infusions of cash for the *Sentinel*.

Mac began automatically to refuse, but an involuntary thought checked his reply for a second: maybe Spottswood would give money to Tom Jeff. And then he thought: *Good God.*

"Give me a break, Huntington," Mac said. "Call me sometime when you're off duty."

"Okay," said Huntington, unabashed. "How's the campaign going, anyway?"

"Good enough for August," Mac said. "I just got in from Tabbville and I'm kind of tired. I'll talk to you later, okay?"

"All right, then," Huntington said. "See you at the wedding."

"Okay," Mac said, and hung up. Huntington's call had shattered the leaden peace of the evening, and he was almost relieved a few minutes later when the buzzer sounded again and he heard Knocko's stentorian boom: "MacIlwain, I've tracked you down at last. What's the latest word from the sage of Tabbville?"

"It's no action, Knocko," Mac said. "Not a nibble. Carrington talks like a man who's off politics for good."

"So he won't, eh?" Knocko said without a trace of surprise.

"His words to me were: tell Knocko not to hold his breath."

"The poor frightened son of a bitch," Knocko said. "We're gonna win this one with or without him, and he's not smart enough to see it. Why don't you come on down here?"

"Now?" Mac said. "It's kind of late."

"Late?" Knocko's voice dropped into his experienced drinker's wheedle. "You young people are awful puny. It's just the shank of the evening. You eat yet?"

"No," Mac said. "I'm not very hungry."

"C'mon down to the Bosun," Knocko said. "The party will buy you dinner."

Knocko wants to talk, Mac thought. *That's my job.* "Give me half an hour," he said.

The Bosun, restaurant of the George Mason Hotel, was furnished in grandiose moderation: dark-green pile carpets, somber mahogany paneling, dull-gold drapery. The dim yellow lights gave it the air of an underwater grotto. For some reason, though the food and service were excellent,

Richmond's native gourmets had long affected to despise the Bosun, leaving it to a transitory, furtive clientele—executives entertaining salesmen and job prospects, tourists, out-of-town politicians, and legislators staying at the Mason while working at the Capitol.

When Mac entered the Bosun, Knocko was standing at the curved mahogany bar, hunkered down in conversation with the headwaiter, a squat black man whose shiny bald head reflected the dull yellow light. He was gesticulating wildly, and Knocko had bent over to bring his ear level with the man's mouth.

"How'm I supposed to deal with this stuff, Knocko?" the man was saying. "Rufus is talking crazy. I don't know any way to reason with a man like that. I mean no way at all."

"There isn't any," Knocko said, shaking his head in disgust. "That bastard is still mad because we threw him off the rules committee last year."

"What am I going to do?" the man said. "I'm the treasurer, not him. He's talking about a lawsuit. That happens, you can kiss the party goodbye in this district. It'd cut us up one side and down the other."

"There isn't going to be any damn lawsuit," Knocko said. "I'll get somebody to talk to Rufus this week."

"You going to do it?"

"Hell, no," Knocko said. "He'd go right through the roof if I called him. I mean somebody from his crowd. Don't you worry about it."

Knocko looked up and caught sight of Mac. "MacIlwain, old buddy, come on over here and meet a friend of mine," he said, grasping Mac by the elbow as he came in range. "Amos, this is Mac Evans, the secretary of the state party. Mac, this is Amos Marshall. He's on our committee here in Richmond."

"How do you do. Mr. Marshall," Mac said. They shook hands.

"Delighted to meet you, Mr. Evans," Marshall said. "Of course I know who you are. I knew your brother very well. We all miss him like the dickens."

"Thank you," Mac said. There was really nothing to add; it was true. People did miss Lester—especially Mac.

"Come on, sit down," Knocko said, steering Mac to a table in a small pool of shadow cast by a wooden partition; Knocko, fond of seeing without being seen, took the seat against the wall.

They ordered drinks: Early Times on the rocks. Knocko, Mac saw, had started without him. At first Mac had thought he had been summoned to give a postmortem on his trip to Tabbville, but now Knocko dismissed Carrington with a shrug. Mac again entertained the suspicion that Knocko had known it all along.

Knocko was tall. His hair was dark and abundant, without a trace of gray, and combined with bright mischievous eyes in a well-fed leprechaun's face, this made him look younger than his fifty years. When he smiled, he seemed even younger; it was a boy's grin, sunny, open, and oddly shy—his greatest political asset.

"How're we doing?" he asked Mac as the waiter brought their drinks. "I'll have the crab cakes with baked potato and green beans."

"Mason salad," Mac told the waiter. "Roquefort dressing. Hell, Knocko," he added as the waiter turned away, "how do I know? I'm the worst person to ask that question."

"You know more than you think," Knocko said. "You're tuned in to this stuff and you have been for a long time. What did our friend think?"

Mac studied his bourbon. In the blunt shot glass it caught the yellow light and flashed it back even darker. The amber glow was warm, deep: a repository of some Druidic mystery, an ancient corn libation which men drank to absorb the slain god's virtue. "He didn't let on," Mac said. "He said it was going to be mean."

"That it is," Knocko said. "Mean as poison. Any time you've got that whole crowd fighting on the same side it gets mean. Carrington knows that. When he ran the first time, they had it out all over the Ninth that he was a Jew and his wife was Chinese and a few other things."

Mac decided to give Knocko the needle. "I don't know if that's what he had in mind," he said. "I think he's thinking about some of the things some people said about his friend Slaughter."

"Shit," Knocko said. He finished his drink and signaled the waiter for another. Mac had pushed the right button. Knocko held his liquor well: Mac had never seen him show any obvious sign that he had been drinking, even after they had been up all night. But liquor inflamed Knocko's anger—his dark tangled resentment against the patricians who had run the party and the state for so long.

"Listen, Carrington was in Washington during that primary," Knocko said. "He was too busy being a senator to get dirtied up in the governorship. He didn't know what Slaughter's people were doing, and I mean all along, right from the start. You know what I'm talking about: 'Don't be hoodwinked by Comrade Shadwell,' that stuff. Those pictures of Tom Jeff with a sickle and hammer behind his head. And the stuff they said about Peggy would curl your hair, I mean it."

The waiter glided up noiselessly and replaced Knocko's empty glass. "Another, sir?" he asked Mac. Mac shook his head no. The waiter looked familiar; with a start, Mac recognized the face of the shepherd in Emmaline's poster: triangular face, liquid eyes, as foreign and unexpected as an ocelot in a doghouse. The waiter, his bland, deferential eyes exotic and opaque, nodded and walked away, his shoes making an almost imperceptible pop against the carpet.

"This stuff was coming out early, too, before Brock got into it," Knocko was saying. "But listen, if you really want to know why Carrington doesn't like Brock, that's why. About the first of August, Slaughter realized we were pulling away from him. He was scared to death, I mean terrified. And he started calling Washington and saying, 'Listen, Tobey, I'm in trouble down here.' And Carrington wouldn't listen. He was up in Washington, and when he would call around, everybody said it was going just fine. He told Slaughter not to worry, everything was going to be okay. Slaughter *knew* that wasn't right, so finally he called Brock and said, 'Listen, if you don't help me, Tom Jeff is going to win the nomination.' And Brock very quietly came in and took over. He ran things from then on. Carrington couldn't even get his buddy Slaughter on the telephone. And Brock turned it around for him. They came back and beat us."

Pop-pop-pop; the waiter arrived bearing the food. Knocko began eating eagerly. Mac's salad was enormous; he tasted it gingerly: the dressing was soupy, bland, redolent of mayonnaise. "Didn't do 'em much good," he said, giving Knocko his cue.

"Yeah," Knocko grunted. He chewed his crab cakes in silence for a few minutes. "Listen," he said at length, waving a forefinger in a conspiratorial gesture, as if he were about to let Mac in on a deep secret. "The Republicans would have won that year no matter what Tom Jeff said. For one thing, it was a Republican year. But everybody says *we* split the party. Hell, Slaughter's the one who did it. He made the unions mad, and he made the blacks mad. He made Tom Jeff mad, too, and now everybody blames him. I'll tell you something: the labor boys and the blacks would have gone for Hapgood no matter what Tom Jeff said. They were that mad. How's that salad?" Knocko suddenly reached over with his fork and stabbed a radish.

"Pretty lousy," Mac said. Knocko's expansiveness often included sneak attacks on his companion's dinner.

"Umf," Knocko said. "I'll say it's lousy." He wiped his mouth, then licked each tooth carefully. "Aren't we supposed to be boycotting that stuff?"

"Hell, are we?" Mac said. "Can't I boycott grapes? I hate grapes."

"No excuses, McIlwain," Knocko said. "Waiter!" He crooked his finger, and the waiter appeared as if from nowhere, his face incurious and deferential.

"Is this union lettuce?" Knocko asked.

"I don't know, sir," the waiter said. "I can ask the chef if you wish, sir."

"I'd be obliged," Knocko said. Pop-pop; the waiter padded off toward the kitchen, walking on the balls of his feet.

"Slaughter would have lost that year no matter what," Knocko continued. "There was just nothing to the guy. By the time we got through with him he just didn't know what to do with himself. Slaughter wasn't worth a damn."

Pop! The lion head reappeared. "The chef says it's not, sir."

"Not union?" Knocko asked.

"No, sir," said the waiter. He made as if to scoop up the offending salad. "Shall I take it back, sir?" he asked, looking at Mac, whose salad, after all, it was.

Duty clearly lay in banishing the scab salad. Besides, it had not been very good to begin with. But before Mac could acquiesce, Knocko quickly said, "No, thanks, leave it, please. We were just curious."

There was a brief flash of real puzzlement and irritation from the waiter's opaque eyes. Then he was gone.

"What the hell?" Mac said.

"Don't want to make a scene," Knocko said. "The Teamsters would hear about it. There're a lot more Teamsters than Farmworkers in this state. We just don't order it anymore. Go on, finish it."

The salad had by now taken on the air of a deserted battlefield. Looking at it, Mac imagined tiny Chicano pickets marching in an outraged circle around the thick rim of the bowl. "I'm not hungry," he said.

"You sure?" Knocko asked, whisking the bowl across the table. "This isn't all that bad," he said, his mouth half full of scab lettuce.

"Where did that waiter—" Mac began, but before he could finish, the waiter popped into view, turning the corner of the partition in a noiseless military turn. "Yes, sir?" he said.

"Coffee, please," Mac said. "You, Knocko?"

"No, thanks," Knocko said, chewing. He gestured at his glass. "Another of these would be fine."

The waiter pirouetted and vanished.

"You heard what Brock was saying on the radio, I guess," Mac said.

"You mean that busing stuff?" Knocko said. He put down his fork. "Yeah, I heard some of that."

"Pretty rough," Mac said.

"It's just what we expected," Knocko said.

The waiter materialized, set down coffee and bourbon with disdainful finesse, and departed bearing the empty salad bowl. Knocko took a drink. "In fact, I was kind of encouraged by hearing that this soon before Labor Day. This busing nonsense is their big issue. I figure they're scared, and they can't think of anything else to talk about."

"Maybe," Mac said. "But that stuff still hurts."

"It hurts some," Knocko said with a shrug. "But nothing like what it used to. I have this feeling that people are more concerned about the cost of food than they are about busing this year."

"You sure that's not just wishful thinking?" Mac asked.

"Who, me?" Knocko said. "Never touch the stuff."

"Good evening, gentlemen," said a voice behind Mac. He turned to see a short black man in early middle age, his head surrounded by the nimbus of a graying afro. It was Theodore Thomas, a member of the legislature from Richmond and a good Democrat. Although he was wearing a conservative gray business suit, his posture had an athlete's insouciant ease: a slightly cocky tilt of the hips, the torso carried forward, shoulders uneven. Clutching his arm was a tiny frail old white woman, wearing a fur coat and a shapeless black hat. Behind its veil her eyes were sharp and avaricious.

Knocko was on his feet at once. "Honorable Thomas, a pleasure," he said, pumping the man's hand, then quickly turned to the woman, bending down toward her in a courtly half bow, his face, from long practice, tilted just far enough away from hers to avoid breathing whiskey fumes in her nostrils. "Mrs. Dance, how do you do?" he said. "You're looking very fit. Have you heard from your grandson? How is he?"

"He's doing much better, thank you, Mr. Cheatham. It's very kind of you to remember," she said in soft, patrician tones. "I hope you're well, too," she added. "I think we're going to need all our able-bodied men to keep this horrid fellow Brock from coming back."

Knocko smiled his little boy's smile. "Yes, ma'am," he said. "But stop him we will."

"You see that you do," she said firmly.

Knocko gestured toward Mac, who had stood as well. "You know Mac Evans, don't you, Mrs. Dance?" he said.

"Of course I do," she said, putting her hand toward him in a gesture so imperious Mac found himself wondering whether to shake it or kiss it. "It's good to see you, McIlwain," she said. "The last time we met you were about thirteen. Do you remember?"

"Certainly," Mac said. He turned to Knocko. "Mrs. Dance was one of Lester's first backers," he said.

"Indeed I was," she said. "And what this state lost when we lost your brother—I can't even find the words. It's always been my great pride that I helped him in his very first campaign."

"The party couldn't get along without you, Mrs. Dance," Knocko said.

"You're very kind," she said. "But I do feel it's my duty to help out."

"Which reminds me," Thomas said, flashing the cheerfully cynical smile which was his chief charm. "Mrs. Dance and I have things to discuss."

He made as if to lead her away, but Knocko caught his elbow and asked in the hushed conspiratorial tone politicians reserve for discussions of the ebb and flow of a campaign, "How're we doing around here?"

Thomas replied in the same tone, glancing back over Knocko's shoulder as if wary of eavesdroppers, "Well, you know what this district's like. I hope black folks are going to turn out for Tom Jeff. I think they will. We're going to carry the city. But you know these white folks in the county. They'd vote for Jefferson Davis if they could." Thomas laughed and broke into a half-dance step, punching Knocko on the arm. "Am I right? Huh? You, Mac, am I right?"

"You're right, Theodore," Mac said.

Thomas put an arm around Mac's shoulders. "Mac knows what I'm talking about," he said. "He grew up with these folks. Knocko's used to Tidewater, all that federal money and liberal feeling floating around. It's a whole 'nother ball game up here, isn't that right, Mac?"

"Unquestionably," Mac said. He found Thomas's cheerful cynicism irresistible.

"A lot of these folks are living in the deep dark distant past, you know what I mean?" Thomas said. "This is one tough district, I mean to say." His voice dropped its hectoring tone, and he spoke again in a serious hush. "It's always rough, Knocko, but I think we'll hold our own. I think I'm going back. If I get some money—" He rolled his eyes silently toward Mrs. Dance and winked. "Well, listen, I got to go mend some fences here, you know what I mean?" He swooped on Mrs. Dance's elbow and was gone.

Knocko sat back down. "That old gal gives away about twenty thousand dollars every time there's an election," he said. "And you know, her husband was the biggest damn reactionary SOB you'd ever hope to meet. Ran a lumber mill. Nigger baiter, jew baiter, and I mean death on unions. She inherited his money, and she's been getting her revenge for the last twenty years."

"How's Thomas going to do?" Mac said.

"Hell, if I only had to worry about guys like him, I'd be a happy man," Knocko said. "One thing that guy knows is how to get reelected."

"Listen, I'm kind of tired," Mac said. "I think I'll run back home and turn in. What have we got on this weekend?"

"Nothing this weekend," Knocko said. "Take it off if you want. Come Monday you got a lot to do."

43

"What's that?" Mac asked.

"The candidate wants you to drive him around the Ninth next week. Wants you to take the Continental and meet him at the Roanoke airport three o'clock Monday afternoon."

"Okay," Mac said.

"Get some rest," Knocko said. "We're pulling out all the stops out there next week. We going to start kicking hell out of Miles Brock."

"That's what I signed on to do," Mac said.

THREE

★

The next day was Saturday. Mac slept past noon, then idled in bed a few hours more, leafing through magazines and listening to the local underground radio station, which on Saturdays featured a young woman who called herself Ferd. Ferd was perhaps the most inept disk jockey Mac had ever heard; she spoke in a halting spasmodic rhythm which might have been due to inexperience except for the fact that she had been on the air every Saturday morning for the last eleven months. Indeed, her show had become something of a legend, attracting a large and devoted audience; so popular was Ferd's incompetence that Mac would have suspected it of being assumed, if it had not been so heartfelt. Ferd was sincerely, excruciatingly bad, unable to concentrate on all the things she had to remember and perpetually terrified of the microphone. This was her salvation, for the management, which had found fault with and fired a string of quite competent women jocks, took great pride in Ferd and advertised her at every opportunity. In addition, the station kept her identity secret, promoting her as a mysterious audible sex symbol.

"Ahem," Ferd said, while Mac stared at the ceiling. "Oh, yeah, that was—um, let me see—Traffic with—uh—'John Barleycorn Must Die,' and now we'll hear—just a moment—why don't you listen to a commercial?—this one—hold on."

A nasal voice extolled mobile homes, while the studio mike, which

Ferd had inadvertently left on, transmitted rattles and pops as she searched for the record she had meant to play.

Mac knew the secret of Ferd's identity, which was a distinct anti-climax. She was a perfectly ordinary girl, a graduate of St. Fina's now studying elementary education at a local college.

In fact, Ferd would probably be at the wedding this afternoon. Mac would have to get up shortly and dress, but as he lay on the bunk bed in the tiny back room, with the August sunshine filtering through the azalea bushes Molly O. tended behind his window, he could think of nothing he wanted to do. He composed himself, hands behind his head, in a stillness which had little to do with boredom.

He had first learned the stillness when he returned to the University law school, nearly two years before, in the fall after Lester died. As October had worn into November, he had given up one by one the friendships and social ties he had built up at the University, finding himself more and more often alone in his room, with nothing to do, nowhere to go, not bored, not tired, just waiting for something, until finally he had come back to Richmond and back to the house. And during the year and more he had worked for Knocko, he was still waiting. A friend had given him a book: *The Incredible Thrilling Adventures of The Rock,* which began with the words, "As you'll recall, when we last left The Rock, he'd been sitting in the same spot, in the same forest, for about a hundred million years." It had pleased Mac, for he sometimes thought of himself as a stone, ossified that winter after he had buried his brother, stolid and almost motionless beside the mercurial lives of his friends, who had in the past two years fallen in love, or married, or changed jobs, or moved to new towns or joined new religions, while Mac had lived in the little house behind Molly O.'s rose garden without even taking down the Hungarian's picture of Jesus from the wall above his bed.

The commercial ended, and Ferd resurfaced, shakily announcing a Grateful Dead cut. The radio played the opening strains of "White Rabbit" by Jefferson Airplane; they were interrupted by an ear-shattering screech as the stylus skipped across the record. "Sorry, folks," Ferd said. "Blew it that time, ha-ha. What I, uh, really meant, that was the Jefferson Airplane, as some of you have guessed, ha-ha. 'White Rabbit,' right? Just wanted to see if you were paying attention." But the record now had scratched and wouldn't play, so Ferd began wearily to read the news.

Mac picked up the morning paper and glanced at the headline: BROCK CHARGES SHADWELL "OUT OF STEP" ON BUSING. Below was an account of the speech and a shot of Brock stopping to shake hands with a tiny man

46

in a chef's hat, identified as the Supreme Schoolmaster of the Order of Southside Spot Fishers. *It must gall him to have to shake hands again,* Mac thought. *He thought he was through with all of that.*

Ferd's phone rang, and she answered, "Call Ferd, what's on your mind?" It was part of a new promotion in which listeners called in to tell Ferd their problems.

"Hello, Ferd?" said a man's voice. The speaker was about forty, Mac guessed. "I listen to your show every Saturday. It's really like you're here in the room with me, you know? And you know what I like to imagine? I like—" There was a sharp click and a moment of silence. Then Ferd's voice said, "Naughty, naughty. Just for that, no more 'Call Ferd' today, ha-ha!" Her hesitant stammer had vanished, overwhelmed by the eloquence of rage.

Mac turned to the editorial page, where he read:

OUT OF STEP, INDEED

When former Governor Miles Brock has something on his mind, it behooves responsible men to listen. Governor Brock's keen intelligence and hard common sense have served this Commonwealth well in the past, and likely will again.

Certainly Governor Brock called the shots yesterday at the historic Nansemond Spot Festival, where he skewered State Senator Thomas J. Shadwell and held him to public view in all his ultraliberal splendor.

"Beneath the new rhetoric of moderation," Governor Brock soberly warned, "Mr. Shadwell has espoused an entire spectrum of positions which are repugnant to most Virginians and alien to our great traditions. . . . Indeed, the Democratic nominee is far closer to the social engineering philosophy current in certain fashionable sections of Washington and some notorious Northern college campuses than he is to the simple conservative creed we of this Commonwealth hold so dear."

Truer words were never spoken. Just as the national Democratic Party has become the plaything of the bra burners and the marijuana advocates, so, too, this state's Democratic Party, once the proud exemplar of conservative traditions, has now fallen into the hands of a tiny claque of pro-busing big-government fanatics: Senator Shadwell and his coterie of thimbleriggers and fuglemen, including the party's pixilated chairman, Patrick "Knocko" Cheatham.

Increasingly, men of conservative and moderate bent have found themselves homeless in the party of their fathers. One by one they have become independents or, like the courageous Brock, cut the Gordian knot by joining the Republican Party.

Since the tragic death of the party's last sensible moderate, Lieutenant Governor Lester T. Evans. . . .

Mac put the paper down. A regular diet of these editorials was a good recipe for ulcers. But lately he had learned to practice a sort of political

47

Zen (he had taken the idea from his friend Stephanian's definition of "Zen Communism": "We all know the sound of two classes struggling. But what is the sound of one class struggling?"). Now he looked at them, not as bits of idiotic or vicious polemic, but as *koans* whose nonsensical quality could guide him along the proper political path. "Why do you read them, if they upset you so much?" Molly O. had asked once. "Because sometimes I get tired and forget what I'm in favor of," he had said, "but they never forget what they're against, and the two sets are the same."

It was almost time to dress for the wedding. He climbed out of bed and fixed a cup of coffee on the hot plate. While he was waiting for it to brew, he saw Molly O. tending the rose garden.

"Hey, O.," he called to her, leaning out the screen door. "You going riding?"

She shaded her eyes with her hand. "You up so early?" She said. "It can't be later than two o'clock."

"Lay off," Mac said. "I've been awake since noon."

"Mac, I worry about you lying around like that on a pretty day like this," she said, half serious, half mocking. "You're going to shrivel up and turn to dust."

"Don't worry about me," Mac said. "I've been meditating. How's the John F. Kennedy?"

She looked down at the bright patch of roses. "They're all doing pretty good," she said.

"You going riding or not?" Mac said.

"Yeah, I'm going right now," she said, dusting her hands. "I got to change this minute. You want to come?"

"Maybe another time. I'm going to Train's wedding." She waved good-bye and walked toward the big house, removing her garden gloves as she went. It was time to dress for the wedding. He picked out the best suit he owned, a three-piece summer plaid he had bought to graduate in. His last spring at Harvard had been a bitter, violent political struggle. Mac had been caught up in it, and by June he found himself in a completely politicized universe, in which everything—trees and grass and stars—had political significance, everything was on one side or the other. This applied most particularly to clothes: to have worn academic regalia would somehow have been to give away something, to cross over onto the enemy's turf—dangerous, out of the question.

But something in his reserved Southern soul, which had swallowed the outlandish styles of both sides in the drama, had absorbed the apocalyptic rhetoric, had at last revolted at the idea of going through the exercises in the gaudy politicized garb which he had worn throughout that spring: slo-gan-bearing T-shirts, elaborately informal military surplus trousers. So he had quietly ordered a suit from a fashionable shop—feeling that it was only right to be formal during what was, after all, one of the few rites of passage he would ever have—and had ended up feeling isolated from ev-eryone: the reactionaries in robes, the radicals in bright colors and ban-ners.

Mac remembered how Lester had reacted to the suit. He and Molly O. had come to see Mac graduate, filling the role of surrogate parents (Mac's father had sent a long letter, which, snared by some vagary of Latin American postal service, had arrived six weeks late; his mother had sent a brief note and a check for a thousand dollars). Mac had deliberately given no warning, knowing that Lester would object to even so mild a defiance of convention. The outward forms of society had been important to Les-ter; Mac remembered the look his brother had given him after the ceremo-ny. "What's this foolishness?" he had asked, his voice elaborately hu-morous, as he fingered the lapel. Mac had put his arm on his brother's and laughed, and by that sudden rare physical gesture of affection had de-fused the moment.

Four years later, there was no question about appropriateness: the suit was just right for an afternoon wedding in August. And the emotional cir-cuit was broken: Lester was dead, and Mac remembered that awkward moment as something long ago and far away. He slipped on his St. Cypri-an's tie, which, although its maroon and gray clashed ever so slightly with the golden brown of the suit, was even more appropriate for this particu-lar wedding.

It was a stifling, windless August day. Mac ran the airconditioner in the Continental during the drive to the church. Even the short walk from the parking lot was enough to bring beads of sweat trickling down his fore-head. Once inside, shown to his seat by a St. Cyprian's classmate in a cut-away, he relaxed: St. Anselm's had a magnificent cooling system.

The bridegroom, Hank Train, had been a classmate of Mac's at St. Cyp-rian's. They had played together on the football team. Mac remembered him as a wiry, determined linebacker, weighing only a hundred and thirty-five pounds, who had overcome heavier blockers by quickness and de-sire. His football form had been textbook perfect: he had been the one the coach called on to demonstrate the correct way to tackle a dummy or block a sled. "Let me hear those pads *pop!*" and Train had popped them with dutiful savagery.

49

Train had gone on to Duke, and Duke Medical School, and now he was beginning his internship at the state hospital downtown. His bride, a St. Fina's girl, had been his steady in college and medical school.

But though Mac had known Train for the thirteen years of St. Cyprian's, he felt no real kinship with him anymore. Train had grown a fine blond mustache, and he had sprouted some liberal opinions which at first had scandalized his father, an executive of a chemical company; but his family and friends had quickly realized that these aberrations were no more than the sort of harmless eccentricity which every society permits its healers, knowing that they have been trained properly and that they will not allow opinion to guide their hands as they practice their art and live their lives.

A real defection—such as Mac's—was something more lasting and more serious.

The usher reappeared, and showed Gravelier Huntington and Hoke Spottswood into Mac's pew. He gave them a slight smile of greeting. Huntington was a small, slovenly young man, with reddish hair atop the face of an intelligent, inquisitive rodent. He was dressed in a suit that was too short for him, revealing a flash of hairy shin between cuff and socks, which had settled around his ankles in shiny puddles. Spottswood was tall and pale, livid freckles dotting his sardonic face. "Greetings, M.E.," Huntington said in the prison whisper they had perfected as boys in the remodeled gymnasium that had served St. Cyprian's as a chapel. "How goes the campaign?"

"Well as can be expected," Mac said.

"Do you really think Shadwell has a chance?" Spottswood asked.

"Yes, I do," Mac said. He was determined not to be drawn into a political argument with Spottswood; it was invariably like shouting down a well.

"I don't see how," Spottswood said. "I still think this a more conservative state than you realize."

"Oh, stick it, Spottswood," Mac said. Even Spottswood should have realized that Mac knew better than most people just how conservative the state was; his own father had plumbed that conservatism, had been a proof of it which had lasted nearly a generation. "I know that if the people you talk to every day were the only ones voting, Tom Jeff wouldn't have a chance," he said. "But fortunately there are a lot of people around who don't belong to the Confederate Club."

"I'm going to vote for Shadwell," Spottswood said.

"Good," Mac said. "Now be quiet." The organ had begun the wedding march from *Lohengrin*. The bridal party entered, and as Mac stood, a

50

Henry Morgan routine ran idiotically through his mind: *Wagner vass born by Leipzig in 1813. He grew up a liddel crazy already, but he wrote a couple good tunes.* The bride was a small blond girl; the couple's children would be fair as Vikings. The bridesmaids wore purple dresses.

The service was short and Mac paid it little attention. It was being performed by the rector of St. Anselm's, the Reverend Dr. Angus Courtenay, a man who enjoyed the confidence of his congregation as few clergymen do. Courtenay had supervised the church during its period of greatest growth, during which there had been installed a new air-conditioning system, a modern electronic organ, a religious education center, and a magnificent parsonage. He was a success with his congregation because they knew he was one of them. He had grown up in the West End of the city and had attended St. Cyprian's. The congregation counted on him to represent them faithfully before God and the Episcopal Church.

This took a delicate understanding of the church and the people who made it up, the well-educated well-bred householders of the West End; Courtenay had it. In the first year of his career at the church, a dispute had come up which had threatened to split the congregation in half. One of the oldest and most respected members of his congregation had discovered that St. Anselm of Canterbury was known as an ardent foe of chattel slavery. How, he had asked Courtenay, how could the older members of the congregation, whose fathers and uncles had fought in the Army of Northern Virginia, worship in a church named for an abolitionist? The name must be changed. But when word got out, a small group of the younger people protested that it would be wrong to change the name just because the saint had been an abolitionist; wrong, and embarrassing as well.

Courtenay had simply decreed that the church had never been named in honor of St. Anselm of Canterbury, and the next week, tiny letters had appeared on the signs at the church doors, "St. Anselm's *of Lucca*," commemorating another saint entirely. Courtenay had never mentioned the matter again, and for more than twenty-five years, neither had anyone else.

As the service drew to a close, Huntington poked Mac in the ribs and asked him in a stertorous whisper if he had seen the latest issue of the *Sentinel.*

"No," Mac whispered back. "Shh."

"Terrific story in it about some sheriff's deputies out in Opechancanough County who shot a black man," Huntington continued blithely. Heads turned in the pews in front of them.

"Shh," Mac said, looking at his shoes.

51

"This guy was working in some woman's garden, and they just came up and shot him. Amazing!" Huntington went on. "It ought to really help our circulation—"

"Please be quiet!" hissed a voice behind them.

"Sorry," Huntington muttered, but could not resist adding "—in the black community."

The organ pealed the recessional, and the procession swept out the rear door of the church. Mac turned to Huntington. "For God's sake pull your socks up, Gravelier," he said.

Huntington looked down at his bare ankles, bent ruefully to cover them. The socks stretched transparent over his shins.

"Good God," Mac said. "Those are silk socks."

"Are they?" Huntington said, fingering his tie. It was so creased and worn by ill use that it would no longer remain flush with his shirt, assuming mad pretzel patterns in the air. "They belonged to my grandfather."

"You and Miles Brock are the only two people I've ever seen wear those," Mac said.

"Brock wears 'em, huh?" Huntington said, glancing at them with fresh interest. "At least I'm in good company."

"On him the effect is somehow different," Mac said. "His stay up. I think you're supposed to wear garters with them."

"Is that what it is?" Huntington said.

They slipped out of the pew and down a side aisle. As they emerged, Mac spotted a familiar figure in a cutaway and shoulder-length brown hair: it was Justin Foote, who had been his oldest friend at St. Cyprian's and his roommate in Charlottesville. Foote was still at the University, finishing work on a PhD thesis.

"Hey, Foote!" Mac called.

Foote looked around. He was tall and thin, but he had a sleek grace which kept him from gangling. His face was lean, with features at once delicate and keenly intelligent.

"*¿Que pasa?*" Foote said. They shook hands.

"Going to the club?" Mac said.

"Yeah, let's go on over."

The four of them crossed Axe Trail Road and walked toward the clubhouse. The afternoon had cooled, and other wedding guests were also walking toward the clubhouse, where the reception would be held, the women in colorful summer dresses lending the procession a festive air. A few refused to walk even the hundred yards to the clubhouse, and their cars clogged the narrow road: Mercedes, Fleetwoods, and Coupes de

Ville, sober Oldsmobiles and Rivieras, dashing Jaguars. Some bumpers had already sprouted stickers: GOVERNOR BROCK.

The reception was to be held on the broad stone terrace overlooking the first hole of the golf course. Under the massive portico of the clubhouse, beside the huge pyracantha bushes which framed the main doors, a three-piece orchestra had installed itself. At one end of the terrace was a long buffet, and at the other a long bar. Black women with ladles stood ready to serve food, while three black bartenders were already besieged with orders for drinks. The terrace was dotted with tables topped with striped awnings, and guests were passing through the receiving line and laying claim to these.

As he congratulated the couple and both sets of parents, Mac noticed that while Train and his father were happy and relaxed, his bride was caught in the grip of some tight anxiety, and that it had communicated itself to the women in the party.

"Where have you been, Justin?" she asked Foote in a strained voice. She seemed to be clamping her jaws to prevent some genuine terror from breaking through. "We've got to take the *wedding pictures.*"

"Damn," Foote said in his deep, melodious voice. "I forgot all about that."

"Alexandra has been looking *all over* for you," she said. "Go in the clubhouse and *wait there.* We'll be right in."

"Okay," Foote said amiably. "See you gents later."

Mac succeeded in leaving Huntington and Spottswood entangled in handshakes and streaked for the bar. The massiveness of the affair had suddenly touched him with the sort of uneasy, half-real terror small children feel when standing at the base of a tall building. He felt as if at any moment some enormous weight might fall on him. He took a drink, and it subsided.

Looking about him, he saw a number of faces as familiar as the lines of his own palm: St. Cyprian's classmates like Tom Knowles, the all-time great quarterback and four-year Varsity C man, whose career at the university had been ended by a cheating scandal and whose comeback try at a small Methodist college had been ended in a more fundamental way by a blind-side tackle which had shattered his knee, talking still with his enviable athlete's self-assurance, head thrust forward from his compact stubby body as he stalked the crowd, hunting for those who might want some choice real estate; and Tucker Allen, a tiny dark young man with large, terrified eyes and hurried, nervous movements, whose father, Judge Allen, the most powerful man in Opechancanough County, had ordered him

53

to give up his girlfriend and go to law school in another state, and who had, a week after entering school, left it forever, married the girl, and joined the carpenters' union, and moved into a farmhouse in another county and sent word to the judge that if he ever came to the farmhouse, his son would meet him with a shotgun; Tim Valentine, back now after his giddy year of cruising the West Coast on a chopped Harley Sportster and safely installed in the family real estate business with no signs of wear except a slight shrinking of his once-muscular frame and a fondness for long-sleeved shirts; and, talking together, Owen Singletery, a tiny young man, for 13 years the top man in the class, now an object of admiration as the youngest assistant city manager Richmond had ever had, and Martin Moseley, the groom's closest friend, pale and sober, who, according to rumor, was no longer slated for great success at the Central Planters Bank; Harrison Lee, rising like a meteor in the tobacco business, his career certainly not damaged by the fact that he was the son of Senator Lee, chairman of the State Senate Budget Committee and Miles Brock's best friend; and Walton Redd, the tall, angular son of a farmer, who seemed perpetually angry and puzzled, forehead furrowed and a deep flush advancing and retreating over his acne-scarred cheeks, wearing his VMI ring on his right hand because he had left his left one somewhere near the Au Drang Valley.

There were also the girls he had known from St. Fina's. Most had opted for early marriage and had already settled in to a life of children and afternoons of tennis and whiskey sours at the club, and their dry accents, tanned faces, and brittle laughter had blended in Mac's mind until he no longer attempted to differentiate among them, calling them all "Peggy." And some others: Louise Whitt, whose thick curly black hair and wide mobile mouth had made her the butt of endless racist jokes in early adolescence, but who had gone off to Berkeley and come back mysteriously metamorphosed into an extraordinarily beautiful woman, but moreover also seemingly soured forever on human company, so much so that she had left Richmond and now spent most of her time alone running a crab boat on the bay; Nancy Gamble Gonzalez, who had left Sweet Briar to marry an Argentine, flustering society, and who had flustered it even more by finishing college at CCNY while her husband finished medical school and by landing a job as literary agent in New York, where her husband practiced and both of them made lots and lots of money; and Kimberley Carden, whose older sister had run away with the gym teacher at St. Fina's but who had herself finished college and law school without incident and who now worked for the state attorney general, a steely-eyed prosecutor known as "Habeas Corpus" Carden.

There were their fathers and mothers and other older people: Fritz Randolph, an enormous, ruddy, bald elephant of a man, chairman of the board of trustees of St. Cyprian's, past president of the Confederate Club, four times the recipient of the Grand Award of Merit of the Daughters of Confederate Officers, now drinking and ostentatiously not speaking to his liberal cousin, Erskine Randolph, a lean aristocrat who had been an undersecretary under Kennedy and had run for Congress four times without success, and who was now talking to Rufus O'Rourke, city Democratic chairman, an austere young lawyer with skin drawn tight over his bones like the head of a snare drum and an expression of perpetual rage, whose wife, Mary Taylor, now on crutches from a tennis accident, was as adept at packing a precinct meeting as he; and Mrs. Annie Dew, a tiny pink old woman whose late husband had been Bishop Dew and who now traveled around in a wheelchair pushed by her black chauffeur, Napoleon, himself only a few years younger than she; and her daughter, Emma Dew Warren, who had once been offered a motion-picture contract and been forbidden by her mother to accept, who though over fifty retained enough of her once-legendary beauty to make her the focus of every male eye, young or old, in the vicinity, and whose husband, Arthur, was as usual already half drunk and pestering the St. Fina's girls.

If he went forward from the bar, Mac knew, he would have to speak to all of them, and with the dull anxiety still throbbing inside him, that would be too much. He retired to the shade of a pine tree, cradling his drink and detaching himself from the scene around him, watching the crowd swirl around the bar and the buffet. As he drank, the scene seemed to diminish in size and to acquire a certain mechanical quality, until it became a sort of enormous mechanized minuet, an intricate, cunningly articulated Swiss toy scene, each of the figures moving in a predetermined pattern. Watching from his vantage spot, Mac fancied himself the toymaker, watching and waiting for the spring to wind down.

The main clubhouse door opened and, like a flock of cuckoos loosed to tell the hour, the wedding party emerged from their picture-taking session and scattered over the terrace. As if on cue, the orchestra struck up a tune and the bride and groom danced stiffly together. The bridesmaids circled about in their short purple dresses, and unaccustomed romantic thoughts suddenly swirled up in Mac's brain, images of some past era when men in white linen suits had courted women in purple on long summer afternoons, when the band played in the park and the high-wheeled bicycles circled the square. So struck was he by this wistful vision—it had burst into his brain in a giddy rush, like a sudden flock of bubbles rising from some unsuspected carbonation in his soul, some liquor-loosed yearning

55

for a world of innocence, where chaste courtship and courtly gentility had never ended and people felt as light as bubbles, which, in fact, Mac, at that moment, did—that when one of the purple dresses swirled near him and resolved itself into a pretty girl with a confused look on her face, Mac's habitual paralyzing shyness with strangers and particularly women could not stop him from acting a part in his own fantasy. "Can I get you a drink or something?" he asked her hesitantly, and although she looked surprised, she at once gratefully accepted, saying, "Yes, please. That'd be nice."

"What would you like?" he asked, restraining an idiotic impulse to bow.

She waved her hand distractedly in the air. "I don't know—anything."

He brought her, fittingly, an old-fashioned, although his wistful vision was now disintegrating under the jagged impact of the reception. More and more couples were dancing, and the dance floor had lost its clean, geometric aspect. The hum of talk was rising ominously, and by the time Mac had jostled his way to the bar and inched back, two full glasses miraculously upright, he no longer felt like a clockmaker or light as a bubble, but just his ordinary clumsy self.

He led her to a table, deftly disposing of a coat someone had thrown across it. "This is good," she said. "What is it?"

She had long black hair, reaching nearly to her waist, black-framed oval glasses, and quizzical eyes. She saw him watching them and lowered her gaze to the drink.

Speak. "It's an old-fashioned," he said. "I'm glad you like it." On rational analysis, there was no real reason for him to care whether she liked old-fashioneds or not, and he feared she would perceive the incongruity of his answer.

Instead, she waved her hand at the party swirling about them and said, "I don't know any of these people. Some guy named Justin was supposed to escort me, but he disappeared."

"That's not surprising," Mac said. Foote, a solitary soul, had never showed much patience with the arbitrary pairings of society. At that moment, Mac presumed, Justin was on the green slope behind the swimming pool, smoking a joint and mournfully watching the sun set over the fairway.

She was giving him a quizzical look. "What I mean is, he always does that," he said hurriedly. "Not anything about you, I mean." To cover the embarrassment, he dredged up a fragment of memory. "Is your name Alexandra?" he asked.

"Right," she said in a skeptical tone which was not unfriendly. "Who're you?"

"I'm Mac Evans," he said. He drank, and in his glass he found the knowledge that he liked her, or perhaps that he liked very much the idea of liking her, that a wedding was a marvelous place to meet a girl (old horny corn god out of his bottle, goat feet lusty on the flagstones to honor the bridal night!). And as he put the glass down, he realized that it had been longer than he remembered since he had met any girl at all.

She was a schoolteacher in Opechancanough County, she said, a college friend of the bride's transplanted from North Carolina by the vagaries of the federal bureaucracy as part of a pilot program in rural schools. Mac liked this fact, too, very much: a schoolteacher might have stepped full-born out of his vision.

They were interrupted suddenly by a dark, intense young woman: Cynthia Waite, who broadcast as Ferd. She was short, with jet black hair cut close to her head in an Egyptian style, and her dark mascara and black bangle earrings gave her the air of great motion, as if she were a tiny locomotive intent on whizzing right through them. "What have you done with my coat, Mac?" she asked breathlessly. In her eyes was a predatory sparkle which cut Mac's eyes like bright sunlight over snow. She had a prize in tow: a bearded English professor from her college, considerably more than half drunk; Cynthia/Ferd was in a hurry to make her getaway before anything could go wrong.

Ferd was an intrusive element, a rapacious caricature which might shatter Mac's carefully contrived mellow innocence. Silently he pointed to her coat, and she and the professor hurried away.

Mac and Alexandra talked on, and he found himself trying to explain the campaign. She seemed to find it incomprehensible; she was an outsider for whom the state's tangled tapestry of family, tribe, and vendetta was so exotic as to be inaccessible, much the way African myths seem, to Westerners lacking all context, bizarre and lifeless. There was a system which underlay the election, a history and a structure which made it comprehensible and gave value to the opposing sides. But the harder Mac tried to make that clear, the more abstract and pointless it seemed, reflected off her total ignorance.

At first he was dismayed and a little angered. But as he drank and talked, he suddenly saw that he was being obsessive; his mad attempt to bring her into the political world seemed as pathetic as a trained rat scratching at the bars of his cage after experimenters have removed the bars. It came to him that by happy chance he had ended up with perhaps

57

the only person at the wedding to whom he would not have to talk about Tom Jeff. He could hardly believe his good fortune. He stopped talking altogether and looked at her with a somewhat whiskey-ridden smile, and she, who had been, in boredom and shyness, looking down at the glass in her hand, looked up and smiled back, and there was a moment of smiling and then the bride's mother called everyone over to see the cutting of the cake.

Mac could see that the anxiety, whatever it was, had not left the bridal party: the smiles were too tight, and the bride carried herself rigidly and looked at no one. But she cut the cake and fed it to Train, and then with no break for eating assembled the group inside and threw the bouquet to her little sister.

And then in what Mac would always remember dimly as a scene from an old movie where the film speeds up until the figures move with ridiculous jerky haste, she hugged her parents and each of her bridesmaids, and she and her new husband disappeared into their car and drove away, and the wedding was over.

Mac had drunk more than he intended, and he had begun to feel the antennae of his senses withdrawing from the world around him, so that events became less comprehensible and more significant than they ordinarily would. When Foote slipped up beside him and said, "Listen, a group of us are going to have dinner and a few drinks in the grill. Why don't you come?" he could foresee the meandering evening which lay ahead. Foote said, "Invite some other people, we'll charge it to my parents," and it seemed a perfect opening. He found Alexandra and asked her to join them.

As soon as she agreed, however, he realized that he had made a mistake; sitting at the enormous round table in the club's grillroom, he knew he was right. Alexandra was the only woman in the group, which, except for Mac, was also drawn together by the fact of being old fraternity boys. The St. Cyprian's boys—Foote and Martin Moseley, the apprentice banker, and Harry Lee, the senator's son—were all old Kappa Sigmas from the University, while the others—three identical fresh-faced types whom Mac collectively called Ron—were Dekes from Duke. This caused some tension, but nothing compared to what Mac had begun to feel as he struggled to include Alexandra in the conversation.

For the others, it was as if she did not exist. Although individually each of them was a polite and decent soul, who would never intentionally snub a dinner companion, collectively each found it impossible to remember the existence of a single woman under the pressure of so many male bonds. And after dinner was over, Mac felt a guilty relief when she whispered that she was leaving.

He followed her to the door and said, "Listen, I'm sorry this turned out so—you know—"

"Don't worry about it," she said, and smiled again.

"Look—maybe we can do something or something."

"That'd be nice," she said, and was gone.

A deep pointless drunken feeling settled on Mac so quickly it seemed she might have never been there at all, an exotic purple figment of his imagination. Mac remembered how he had felt as a child when he dreamed at night of marvelous wise playmates and woke to find they did not exist and tried somehow to climb into the dream again, lying in his bed, eyes closed, summoning vainly the fading images.

Returning to the table, he drank morosely. The Duke group was arguing with the University graduates about a basketball game.

"—had you under the boards. I don't think Arnold got a single rebound the whole second half."

"What do you mean? Look at the statistics on shots. We had *you* two to one until Mahoney fouled out."

"Well, you fell apart then. That's how you win games."

"—lousy officiating is all."

Against his better judgment, he began arguing politics with Harry Lee.

Lee's mind had the consistency of cork. It gave briefly to new ideas, then bounced back to its original shape. To him the meaning of the election was absolutely clear.

"I know you're a liberal, Mac," he said. "I respect that. I mean, we're on different wavelengths, but I honestly think we need liberals and conservatives to make the system work."

"Thank you," Mac said ironically, but it was lost on Lee. He reflected that he should object to being called a liberal, for despite the fact that his cause was liberal to the core, he somehow felt himself separate from it, not liberal, but still the radical he had been in college.

"But those things shouldn't count in something like this," Lee said.

"—everybody saw Johnston crowding Mahoney but the referee."

"What do you mean by that?" Mac asked, genuinely perplexed. "It seems to me that it would count more—"

"All right, all right, you know what I mean—"

"—always blame the officiating—"

"In a *state* election it counts more—"

"I *mean*," Lee said, extricating himself with a firm tone, "that what

59

we're really talking about is: what's best for Virginia? Isn't that what this election is really all about?"

"You can put it in those terms, but—"

"Well, what I mean is, that's not a liberal/conservative issue, is it?" Lee smiled broadly, having, against all odds, dragged Mac to his point.

"What do you mean, blame the officiating? We beat you by six points in your own gym—"

"—didn't see us bellyaching about the ref—"

Mac felt pugnacity bubbling up in him as wistfulness had earlier. With an effort he unclenched his hand and retracted his head, which had sprung forward like an angry bulldog. He adopted a self-consciously reasonable, drunkenly didactic tone. "To begin with, Harry," he said, "what you're doing here is reifying the state in an invalid way—"

"Pardon?" Harry said.

"I don't know about that, but our coach didn't send in a substitute center with orders to foul your star player."

"What kind of crap is that?"

"What I mean is, you're treating something that has no real existence as if it were something like a candy bar, that you could point to."

"You can point to it," Harry said, adding nonsensically, "There's no goddamn secret about what that guy did to Mahoney."

"You stay out of this."

"Pay attention," Mac said, dragging Lee's attention back from the basketball argument, although even as he did so, he wondered why he hadn't simply taken his lapse as a chance to escape.

"I don't know," Harry said. "I can't use a lot of fancy words like reify—"

"Spare me that crap."

"But we both know what Virginia is."

"—you guys are just mad because you hadn't had a winning season in twenty years, and we spoiled it—"

"No, no, no," Mac insisted. "That's just the point. What Virginia is, is four point six million-odd people, you see, it's a social entity, and the point is how the people decide to order their affairs, you follow?"

"But that's just what I mean, Mac—"

"—listen to Joe Undefeated here."

"Please, let me finish, Harry. I mean, guys like Brock have spent their whole lives working to make sure most people didn't get a chance to say anything about the way their lives were ordered."

"What do you mean by that?"

"Have you ever heard of the poll tax is what I mean?"

"—goddamn Deke!"

"Or closing the schools? C'mon, Harry, you do know what I mean, don't you?"

But at that moment Mac suddenly found himself alone at the table. Outside, on the broad green slope leading to the swimming pool, Martin Moseley and one of the Dekes were grappling in furious silence, arms locked together, faces contorted, too closely entwined to land a blow. The others stood watching at the top of the hill.

"Come on, let's get some of this Kappa Sigma money," one of the Dekes said as Mac came up out of the grill. He turned to Mac. "Listen, Wahoo, I'll take as much as you got. I'll back Ron at two to one."

"No, thanks, Ron," said Mac, and, without waiting to see who won, went, suddenly weary, home to bed.

FOUR

★

It was a bitter harsh barren heartbreaker of a district, a remnant of the days when Kentucky and West Virginia and Tennessee had belonged to Virginia. It clung to the far western tip of the state, six hours from Richmond over narrow mountain roads. The land was rocky, treacherous, and obstinate, and in the westernmost counties were the coalfields, where every inch of shaft had been paid for in blood. It was farmed and mined by a breed of people as hard as the land itself: English, Scottish, Irish, Welsh, with very rare among them the offspring of immigrants or slaves. These mountaineers were the children of rebels who had fled the coastal strip in revolt against cotton and tobacco and peanuts and the planters who had grabbed that richer land.

Fathers bequeathed to their sons their land and their guns and their politics; each man voted as often as he could, voted as if his life depended on who won the race for circuit court clerk or sheriff, because very often it did. When the Republicans won the courthouse, they fired the Democrats, down to the schoolteachers, janitors, and sheriff's deputies, and the Democrats took it as the way of the world and waited for their chance to return the favor.

An independent, sullen Unionist outpost in a Confederate state, the Ninth District had always looked with suspicion at anything from the eastern part of the state, and their suspicion and dislike had embraced the Apple-Farmer. He had reciprocated their dislike, and as a result, the district's roads were narrow and dangerous, its schools decrepit, its towns poor, its hospitals scarce.

The Ninth played politics by its own rules. Standard political techniques did not apply: advertising and public relations, the slick tools of the pollster and flack, were useless. What counted here were people: circuit clerks and sheriffs and mayors and school trustee electors and comissioners of revenue, tribal elders who could sway their people by simply talking or failing to talk. It was a willful, unpredictable district, given to providing election night surprises. Its returns came in late and often provided the margin of victory or defeat. Only last year, Tobey Carrington had counted on the Ninth as his own key to victory; when the returns had shown a Republican sweep building up there, he knew he was finished, that he was not only beaten, but beaten badly.

Tom Jeff had lost the district four years before, because the judges and sheriffs and mayors and precinct captains and UMW business agents had held the line for Slaughter. This year he was the party's nominee, and he needed these same elders to hold the line for him; more than that, in order to win he had to excite them and convince them that their political futures depended on him. So he was trying to get his campaign moving early, before the Republicans had really begun, in order to build up the momentum which is so important.

He was taking his campaign into the hills, stopping at the country stores which still served as supply centers and social clubs for the people who lived in the mountains. It was Mac's first trip with Tom Jeff. For the last year and a half, he had worked for Knocko, and he found the contrast between that strident, cynical, furious party mechanic and Tom Jeff almost total. Tom Jeff was the apostle of grass-roots politics, a perpetual one-man fireworks display. To appreciate fully the breathless artistry of Tom Jeff's political style, Mac had to step outside himself and imagine the candidate as seen through the eyes of one of the storekeepers on whom he was unexpectedly descending. He imagined:

It is a little after nine, and the sun has not quite finished burning the ground fog out of the hollows by the roadside. The storekeeper sits in the dim cool of the store, waiting for the day to heat up. There are no customers; earlier there had been fishermen and the wives of farmers and travelers needing gas. Now there are only a few small boys poring over comic books, and he is perched atop a tall stool behind the counter amid the Red Man and the Brasso and the Nabs and the Sen Sen and the Never Fail

Four-Way Rat Traps and the fishhooks and the Confederate flag cigarette lighters.

He does not yawn; he has been up since six, and he is impervious to boredom, having taken its measure long ago. He is watching his son-in-law check inventory while his daughter, in blue shorts and hair curlers, shepherds his grandson to the toilet; the boy, in a red cowboy hat and fringed jacket, waves a toy pistol. He scratches the back of his hand and looks out through reversed letters (from outside they read RAINBO BREAD—SUNDRIES) and, satisfied that no customer is in sight, sneaks open the Bristol paper.

His world is in the store and the house behind it, and in a lifetime which has known its allotted number of unpleasant surprises—war and depression and strike and sickness and accident—he is as satisfied as he can be that, for the moment, no surprise is waiting. He begins to read.

Then it comes, and it is like the moment in the story when the fairy godmother appears or the frog speaks or the cat puts on golden boots and suddenly the world is quite another place. The clipped hair at the back of his neck tingles, for it is as sudden and outrageous as if God Almighty had put His own lips down to tree level and said: "HELLO THERE TO THE FOLKS IN F.O. BALTIMORE'S STORE! THIS IS TOM JEFF SHADWELL, THE PEOPLE'S SENATOR, CAMPAIGNING AGAINST THE FOOD TAX WITH YOU HERE TODAY!"

His head whips around: into his driveway is rolling an enormous red Winnebago van, crowned with two of the biggest speaker horns this world has ever seen and plastered with a banner: TOM JEFF SHADWELL FIGHTS FOR THE PEOPLE! and behind it comes a big sky-blue Continental with a SHADWELL! sticker on the front bumper.

And there, scrambling out of the Winnebago and hitting the ground in full gallop is the candidate himself. So fast does he move that he is inside the store before the storekeeper can stir, blinking in the dimness and striding toward the storekeeper with his hand out, and the storekeeper is shaking his hand as he thinks, yes, he is like his pictures, a squat, fat, funny owl of a man, straight black hair combed back from a ruler-edge part, Coke-bottle glasses beetling the tiny eyes, the wide, grinning mouth jutting teeth above the weak chin.

It is the grin that makes this odd, comic face work, he thinks as the lumpy little man stumps over to him, burbling, "Good morning, sir, I'm delighted to meet you," and pumping his hand. So exuberant and merry is the smile, so boisterous the squeaky voice, that the storekeeper, who has learned over hard years the instinct of keeping his face impassive, feels the corners of his mouth twitch in the beginnings of an answering smile, though for the moment that is all, the twitch, as he shakes the hand and the little man says, "I'm Tom Jeff Shadwell, the Democratic nominee for governor, and it is my pleasure to meet you. Is this your store?" He nods that it is; he is proud of it, and he feels the twitch again as the little man says, "Well, sir, it's a fine place, and I guarantee you that if anybody ever tells me that people in this country don't have pride in what they do anymore I can just send them out here and let them have a look at this store. Is this your son?"

"Son-in-law," the storekeeper answers, the first words he has been allowed to speak. But the little man is not waiting for lengthy answers; he shakes the son-in-law's hand, and the man notices that his store is beginning to fill up. Behind the little man has trooped a tall young fellow in a blue suit, with fresh razor-cut hair and a black mustache, and behind him is a big, pink, perspiring old party in a red baseball cap, writing furiously on a little pad, and behind him is a stringy little black fellow in a taxi driver's cap. And in the parking lot the loudspeakers are pumping away, blasting out about nine miles up into the hills, playing banjo and fiddle music.

And the little man by now has shaken hands with the man's daughter and offered his paw to the grandson, saying, "Is this your grandson? How do you do, young fellow, I'm Tom Jeff. Very strong little boy," he says to nobody in particular. "Look at him wave that cap pistol around."

Then he turns to face them all, and it is as if he were addressing a meeting, but still as if he were talking to each of them, so the man finds himself nodding his head occasionally as the little man says, "I reckon you know why I'm here, and I reckon you know why I'm running for governor, too. Yes, sir. I don't care about moving to Richmond and sleeping in a bed or living in a house there. I'm a lawyer and I have a house and a bed and I can make a good living the same way every other man does, which is by working just as hard as I can every mortal day of my life to provide for my family and I know that's how you get through life and it's the way of this world. But I'm running for governor to let the people send a message loud and clear that they want to get rid of this tax on food."

The little man crosses to the storekeeper and takes him by the elbow, and now he is talking as one man of affairs to another, and the storekeeper is nodding, because the little man has hit the nail on the head when he says, "Now, you're a merchant, and I don't have to tell you how unfair it is to put a tax on necessities like food and nonprescription drugs. For nearly ten years the ordinary people like you and me have been fighting to stop it, and this is the year we're going to do it. This election this year is a referendum on the food tax because this other fellow that's running is the fellow who put it on and he thinks it's just as fine as butter beans to put a tax on your food."

Then the little man beckons to the young fellow in the suit, who produces a camera, and the little man herds the whole family together with motions of his arms like a man shooing chickens, oddly crippled gestures in the air, like the movements of a puppet or an animated doll. And his daughter runs blushing to the back of the store, because the little man is saying, "I wonder if my young friend Mac here could get a picture of us together, because when people come in here and you say Tom Jeff Shadwell was in here today, they may not believe it. Smile for the camera, that's right," he says, and then before the storekeeper can even adjust his glasses, the fellow in the suit has pressed the button and the flash goes off and the little man is waving a square of paper in the air and saying, "These Polaroid cameras are the greatest thing since sliced bread, aren't they? We just wait and this little thing will develop itself, how about that?"

Then the fellow in the suit produces a sheaf of papers, and the little man looks at him and says, "While we're waiting, I wonder if it would be all right if I left some of my literature here on your counter. This is my campaign newspaper, *True Facts,* see there, that's a picture of me and there's my wife, Peggy, how about that?" and he talks so smoothly the storekeeper doesn't have time to object while he clears a space on the counter and sets the stack down where the customers will see it.

"You see," the little man is saying, "when Huey Long back in Louisiana found the press wouldn't tell his story because the newspapers were owned by the vested interests, he just started publishing his own, and that's what we've done here. Looky here," he says, sliding the paper off the Polaroid print, "that's not bad at all. Old Tom Jeff looks a little peaked, but you and your son look pretty good, and just look how clear that package of Nabs came out, you can read the label just as clear, how about that? Now, let me sign the back of it here." He whips out a pen and writes smoothly, saying, "That's F. O. Baltimore, isn't it? Here you are, Mr. Baltimore, let's just put it here by the register where folks can see it." And on the register it goes.

"Now just one more thing, if we can impose on your hospitality a bit more," the little man is saying, and suddenly in his hand is a big blue poster, saying SHADWELL FOR GOVERNOR and showing a picture of him in profile, peering into the distance so myopically that he appears to be looking at a movie playing on the inside of his own glasses. "What we're trying to do here is stimulate voting interest here in your county, because as you know, when the governor and the lieutenant governor and the attorney general read the election returns, they see where the vote is heaviest and they pay attention to those counties, so the more people voting around here, the better. So we'd just like to put this poster in your window here." And the fellow in the suit tapes it on the windows.

"See what a good poster that is," the little man says, pointing at it with his puppet's gesture. "That cost me 12 cents for each one of those. So if we can put this in your window, it'll stir up some interest. And if any Republicans come in here and ask why you don't have a picture of their fellow, you just tell them Tom Jeff Shadwell personally brought you that poster and if their fellow comes by here in person you'll put up this poster. And I'll tell you something else, I'm going to see this other fellow, he won't debate me, but our paths will cross, and I intend to tell him that if he doesn't stop by here and explain why the food tax is the greatest thing since Saran wrap he's going to lose this county, and we'll just see what happens."

Then the little man is shaking his hand again, and the group is drifting out the door, and the little man is saying, "Well, thank you, Mr. Baltimore, it's been grand to see you and your family and your store here," and he is out the door and into the van, and then the van is pulling out and that celestial voice comes out of the sound horns again, "GOOD-BYE NOW, MR. BALTIMORE AND JACK AND CHERYL ANN AND JACK, JUNIOR! Y'ALL DO GOOD FOR TOM JEFF NOW!" and then—blip—that big van is gone so quick the man blinks and wonders if it was ever there at all.

But there are the picture and the posters and the newspapers to show that it was. The storekeeper looks at them, shaking his head a little, and the first thing he thinks is that some of his customers won't like them. Maybe he'll have to get rid of them. But then he thinks of the little man and the corners of his mouth twitch, and deep inside himself he is laughing and laughing and he's not even sure why. And then he thinks, *A man's got a right to do what he wants with his own store.* And then he thinks, *Maybe I'll just leave them there awhile.*

Mac spent most of that first day cruising behind the Winnebago, alone in the Continental. Ahead in the big van were the candidate and his driver, a wiry, solemn, silent black taxi driver named Royston Reed, and a reporter, Herman Cardmore, a big, fleshy, jolly man who had been covering politics now for longer than anyone could remember.

Tom Jeff loved the van. While it was moving down the narrow roads, he sat in the shotgun seat looking down on the world, with the sound system microphone in his hand. As the big van zipped by a road crew, he might

raise the microphone and blare, "ALL THE MEN IN THE STATE DE-
PARTMENT OF HIGHWAYS KNOW THAT TOM JEFF SHADWELL
STANDS FOR A FAIR SHAKE FOR STATE EMPLOYEES!" As they
passed a gas station, he might announce, "THIS IS TOM JEFF SHAD-
WELL, THE PEOPLE'S SENATOR, SAYING HELLO TO ALL MY
FRIENDS AT GODSEY'S TEXACO!" Or, when he could find no sta-
tionary victims, he might even attack a lone car as the van came up behind
it: "A PERSONAL HOWDY-DO TO ALL THE FOLKS IN CAR NUM-
BER ATS-479 FROM TOM JEFF SHADWELL! ISN'T IT A GREAT
DAY TO FIGHT THE TAX ON FOOD?"

As they passed raucously along the narrow mountain roads, Mac felt a
powerful exaltation unlike anything he had ever felt before, not even in
those heady moments in college when he had felt himself pitted against
society and tradition and the material world and even God Himself. For in
that rebellion there had often been more terror than delight, and a certain
ritual solemnity, and underneath it all a precarious foundation of violence
and stealth, hatred and mistrust.

With Tom Jeff he felt none of these. Tom Jeff's rebellion was an expression of pure delight, of utter exhilarating confidence in himself and
the world around him, with the almost arrogant elan of the bullfighter who
snaps his fingers under the bull's nose.

It was an enormous, almost cosmic joy, and Mac's glimpses of it that
morning left him strangely envious of Tom Jeff. Long ago he had realized
that to be a truly great politician, as Tom Jeff was and his brother had
been, one would have to live so deep inside himself that all the danger and
pressure could never truly penetrate into the secret chamber where he
lived, would have to function as if his brain were packed in Freon gas.
But now it almost seemed that this exorbitant joy, this delighted reckless
abandon, might in fact be full recompense for having to leave the world
where ordinary people lived. He thought: *All things fall and are built
again, and those that build them again are gay.*

At the end of that first weary day they stopped at a tiny double-decked
slab of a motel teetering on the side of a blue mountain. Before Mac could
finish unloading the bags, Tom Jeff had hustled inside their room and
whipped off his jacket and tie. When Mac entered, he was ensconced by
the telephone in his undershirt, already dialing. Mac put the bags on the
luggage rack and poured Tom Jeff a glass of ice water from the styrofoam
pitcher on the dresser.

He handed Shadwell the glass and looked at him questioningly, pointing
at the door. Tom Jeff, eyes lost in the middle distance, signaled he had

permission to leave. But before Mac could step out the door, Tom Jeff snapped his fingers and pointed at his collar. Mac quickly adjusted his St. Cyprian's tie and buttoned the collar button. As he shut the door, he could hear Tom Jeff starting up: "Rose, my dear, Tom Jeff Shadwell. What a pleasure to hear your voice. . . ."

That first night there was a reception: two dozen men and women, political powers in their respective counties, crowded into the motel's tiny private dining room to feast on fried chicken, mashed potatoes, and smoking hot rolls. As they ate, Tom Jeff, as usual, dominated the table, commenting favorably on the food and urging everyone present to eat more. ("Finish it up, MacIlwain," he called down the table to the corner where Mac was struggling with his gravy-laden plate. "This is good country cooking, it won't hurt you." Then he explained to the table at large, "My good friend Mac went to Harvard, you see, and when he came back, he had just flat forgotten what you're supposed to do with fried chicken. I've had to teach him all over again about grits and gravy.")

But the real star of the evening was Congressman Gooch, a tiny, frail old man with thick white hair who had served two terms under FDR. Despite his age, he was the focus of the table, and the other diners watched him closely as he traded gibes and small talk with the candidate. And after dinner, when he pushed back his chair and spoke, he demonstrated that age had not robbed him of the pleasure of honest partisan hatred.

"We're delighted to see you here tonight, Tom Jeff," he said as the other diners smoked, drank coffee, and picked their teeth. "And I say that not only because you are a great American and a great Virginian, but because you are the nominee of our party, and out here, by golly, that still means something." He looked at the group combatively, a lock of white hair falling over his wrinkled face. "It seems like this year we are going to go out again and knock a few heads in order to teach some people a lesson about party loyalty, and the main person we're going to be teaching them to is that low-down, no-account, double-dealing *turncoat,* and you all know I mean Miles Brock." At the ends of the table the men pounded their fists in enthusiastic agreement.

"Now some parts of this district you don't have to worry about," Gooch said. "In my home county, I've lived there for seventy-four years in Jefferson Precinct, and you can't find a more solid Democratic precinct anywhere in this country. I remember once old Don Warfield came to hunt and he was staying at the Liberty Lodge just down the road from my house, and when I went to pay my respects, I saw he had his hunting dog up in the room with him, and I asked the manager later why he had allowed a dog upstairs. And he said to me, "T. Paul, I figured if I'd already let a Republican up I might as well not quarrel about a dog.'"

He stopped the laughter with an upraised hand. "For twenty-eight years we couldn't carry the precinct solid because there was one Republican who lived there. And for twenty-eight years we had to report one Republican vote every time there was an election. And then in nineteen and fifty-two, when General Eisenhower ran against the late Mr. Stevenson, we went to count the votes and General Eisenhower had gotten two, and we just knew somehow that rascal had voted twice, and we threw 'em both out and reported the district solid."

This time he let them laugh for a minute or two, and then he went on. "Now other parts of the district are not so promising. We've got other areas that have voted Republican since the Reconstruction days. But this year, a lot of those folks figure they're being asked to choose between two Democrats, and they don't like it one little bit. And some of them are just going to go fishing on election day. Of course, some of them are going to decide they can't live with themselves unless they vote the way their daddies did, and those folks are going to close their eyes and hold their noses and vote for the turncoat. But a goodly number of them are going to figure to themselves, 'If I got to vote for a Democrat, I might as well vote for one I agree with,' and those folks are going to go to the polls just as quiet as a mouse and vote for you, Tom Jeff."

Heads nodded up and down the table. "So God bless you, Tom Jeff," the old man went on. "We're going to do our best for you out here. You just do everything you're doing and more besides. Keep that up, and don't go talking about taxing coal, and for the love of heaven leave our guns alone, and I believe on my soul we can carry this district by twenty thousand votes."

As the group applauded, Mac saw that Tom Jeff's face was alight with glee. Afterward—after he had thanked them for coming and shaken all the hands and beamed at their promises to work unceasingly—the candidate gripped Mac's elbow, and Mac felt that he was fiercely excited. "Hear that, young Evans?" Tom Jeff asked. "Twenty-thousand-vote plurality."

"Isn't that just pep talk?" Mac asked.

"I've known that old man for twenty years," Tom Jeff said. "And I've never known him to be anything but dead serious about counting votes."

They crossed the parking lot, past the Winnebago, crouched on the pavement as silent and deadly as a warship riding at anchor. Back in the room, Tom Jeff took off his shirt and wrapped a towel around his neck. Mac poured him a glass of ice water. Watching the candidate squatting on

71

the bed, legs propped on a chair, Mac was again reminded of an enormous doll, stiff-jointed and overstuffed. He was somehow larger than life, an enormous little man. Perhaps it was not a doll Mac was thinking of, but a stone idol, some impossible hill-country laughing Buddha, the myopic gaze concealing secret knowledge.

"No, sir," Tom Jeff said, wiping his face with the towel. "If T. Paul Gooch says twenty thousand votes, he means twenty thousand. That doesn't mean we're going to get them, of course, it just means they're out there to be gotten." He laughed. "Try to sell old Miles Brock as a Republican out here! These folks are too smart for that. Out here people know about politics, they'talk politics all the time. At the store, after church at dinner, they're talking politics. And the little kids hear this, they can't wait to grow up and vote. And they do vote out here just as often as they can."

"You want to see the schedule for tomorrow?" Mac asked, offering Tom Jeff a mimeographed sheet.

Shadwell waved it away. "Don't need to," he said. "With such a fine staff as I've got, I don't need to check it, it's bound to be right. And if it isn't, you're going to hear from me about it. That's what's called trusting your staff. If they're right, you say nothing; if they're wrong, you raise the devil. Isn't that fair, MacIlwain?"

"Anything you say, Tom Jeff," Mac said. "You're the candidate."

"Don't I know it," Shadwell said. He held out his glass, and Mac refilled it. "Just me and nobody else. Little old Thomas Jefferson Shadwell from Norfolk, V-A. I've got myself out here running for governor, and rich folks are calling up to give me money, and working folks are coming around at night to make phone calls, and pretty soon we'll have the *Time* and the *Newsweek* and the CBS and the New York *Times* down here to explain what's going on so us hicks can understand what it is we're doing, and I've got young people working for me all over the state, and to drive me around in a Lincoln Continental I've got young MacIlwain K. Evans, whose father was Colonel Joshua Tutelo Evans and whose brother was lieutenant governor. Not bad for a policeman's son." He smiled cherubically, his jut-toothed face aglow like a jack-o'-lantern at harvest time. "But every now and then I get these little voices inside my head saying, 'What you doing out there, Tom Jeff?' " He turned to Mac with a challenging look, lower lip poked out combatively. "What do you think about that, young Evans?"

Being reminded of his family always nettled Mac. "I'd say you've just answered that question, Senator," he said matter-of-factly.

There was quick flash from the opaque spectacle lenses. Tom Jeff smiled. "I reckon that's fair enough," he said. "I guess it does seem that way, to hear me talk. I guess that's what a lot of folks think about me: a little fat guy who's making up for being poor and nearsighted and funny-looking, having a great time tearing around the state in a Winnebago Painted Desert motor van telling jokes and getting himself on the TV. I like for it to look that way. Folks like to think you're just a funny little guy. They like to think you're just like them. That's why most of these pretty boys never make it. Look at me, look at Brock: both of us look like we ran smack into the ugly stick. I admit it; it doesn't bother me any. And folks like to see you having a good time. Most people don't get a whole lot of fun out of life. They work hard, and they never get ahead, and every year they owe a little more, and they know that there's maybe an absolute maximum of one other person in the world that really cares if they live or die, and deep down they're scared another depression's going to come along and blow them away. So they like to see some guy having a good time. If you can get them laughing, you've got 'em. They feel good when they think about you, and they'll vote for you because you make 'em feel good." He unwrapped the towel from his neck and stretched full length on the bed.

"But you got to work to make it look that way, Mac," he said. "I can promise you that. You get into a campaign and a lot of good people stand up with you and they'll go with you just as far as they can. But that's only so far, Mac, only so far. 'Cause pretty soon the other side will start coming at you, and then it's not Mac Evans or Knocko Cheatham or Royston Reed they're talking about, it's Tom Jeff Shadwell, and his wife, Peggy, and his dog, Hugo. And then it gets to be not so much fun anymore. All of a sudden it's like those dreams you have, that you have to stand up in church with no clothes on and act like nothing's wrong. That's what politics is like, and that part is no fun at all."

He looked at Mac speculatively. "I don't reckon I have to explain that to you, though, do I, Mac? I reckon you know about this stuff better than me."

Mac chose to misunderstand. "I don't know, Senator," he said. "Nobody much ever went after Lester like that, that I can remember, anyway."

"Yeah, I can see how that would be true," Tom Jeff said, with a hint of truculence in his voice. "Your brother was one of the princes of this earth. Yes, sir, he was one of nature's noblemen."

Something in Shadwell's tone brought Mac's head around quickly, but

Tom Jeff was sincere. It was not sarcasm, but envy that had twisted his voice. Mac realized with embarrassment that Tom Jeff envied a dead man, his brother, envied him still two years after his death.

"Everybody liked him, everybody," Tom Jeff said in a wondering tone. "Maybe some people resented him a little or worried about what he would do when he got to be governor, or even some just didn't trust him, but nobody hated him. He could get along with anybody. Most remarkable thing I ever saw." He shook his head in wonder, and his spectacles flashed the lamplight in a meaningless heliograph. "But I wasn't much thinking about Lester as about your daddy," Tom Jeff said.

"Ah, yes," Mac said. "I was too young—"

But Tom Jeff cut him off. He was riding now on his own river of reminiscence, rafting back across more than two decades in politics, and Mac was along for the ride. "I guess you never really got to know your daddy," Tom Jeff was saying. "I mean to say, he was the smartest man I believe I ever met in my life. Some guy would be talking, winding up to take about a half hour to explain something, and the Colonel would just ask a couple of questions, and then all of a sudden the guy would discover he was finished without having gotten started good. There wasn't any problem that man couldn't sum up in about two sentences, just as clear—I never saw anything like it."

Watching Tom Jeff's rapt face, Mac had a sudden glimpse of the night two decades before when young Tommy Shadwell, just out of law school, had met Colonel Evans and caught from him a case of the political bug that had lasted a lifetime.

"What they did to him was a crime," Tom Jeff said. "It was a sin, and it was a shame. He was a great man, he would have been a great governor. And they got ahold of him, and by the time they got through there wasn't anything but—" he broke off.

"What would you say?" Mac said. He saw again the crabbed handwriting on the infrequent envelopes from South America. "A shell, a husk?"

"Listen, Mac, I didn't mean—"

"Don't worry about it, Senator," Mac said. "Just forget it."

"Well," Tom Jeff said, and then added quickly, the words coming in a rush, "I don't have to tell you nobody who knew anything about it ever believed one word—"

"You don't have to tell me," Mac said, heading for the bathroom.

When he came out, ready to sleep, Tom Jeff was on the phone to Knocko. "That's right, Brother C.," he was saying. "Twenty thousand, and not one vote less." He listened, and then said, "You're not kidding, it's a good sign. It's the best we've had so far." The receiver buzzed.

"Yeah, he's here," Tom Jeff said. "I'm going to take him out tomorrow and teach him to eat ham steak and cream gravy." He threw Mac a wink. "Listen, you shanty-Irish goon," he said. "Don't you be making fun of my belly. People don't vote for skinny types. That's why you never got elected to anything." The phone buzzed again. "Yeah, well, you come on and see me and I'll teach you how to be a glamor candidate." From across the room Mac could hear Knocko's laugh. "Okay, you mind the chickens now," Tom Jeff said, and hung up.

As they prepared to sleep, it seemed almost as if Tom Jeff had forgotten the conversation. But as Mac climbed into bed, Shadwell shot him another quick, speculative, almost shy look. "About your father, Mac," he said. "Do you ever hear from him? I mean, does he ever—"

"No," Mac lied quickly, and turned out out the light. They slept.

In the cold alien mountain night Mac returned to familiar dreams:

It was a warm spring night in his last year of college. Mac was sitting on the iron fire escape of Weld Hall, watching Harvard Yard in the darkness just before sunrise. The fire escape actually came from his freshman year, when he had lived in Weld. That first spring away from Virginia, Mac had frequently found himself unable to sleep, lying stiff in the anonymous iron bed, feeling attached from all sides by loneliness and apprehension and a peculiar vertigo, a feeling that he was on foreign soil.

That freshman spring, when sleep forsook him, he would crawl out onto the fire escape and wait for dawn, huddled in a blanket with a transistor earphone to his ear. The radio had played the Rolling Stones: "Can't GET no—satisFACtion." And there had been tinny newscasts about the first battles in America's brand-new war in Asia.

But in the dream it was not his freshman year, but four years later, in the roller-coaster spring when the war had come to Harvard and a student strike had ripped the University in half; it was the spring Mac had sat in a University building and a policeman had beaten him with a stick and thrown him down the stairs and arrested him and taken him to jail.

He felt again in his nerve endings that blend of fear, fatigue, confusion, and exaltation that had made that spring different from every other time of his life. In those improbable weeks Mac had suddenly felt himself at one with a great wave, a mass of revolutionaries all over the world, a select magical heroic group that was desperate, alone, outnumbered, and on the verge of impossible victory.

In his dream of that spring morning, it was that exaltation which led Mac to leap from the third-story fire escape and soar above the earth on revolutionary strength alone, flying magically above Harvard Yard.

He soared around the white building where he had been arrested and then hovered above the wide steps of Widener Library until, looking down, he saw his friend Stephanian, black leather jacket over Can't Bust'em overalls, his dark narrow face twisted in contempt.

"The Vietnamese can do much better than that," Stephanian said, and the words brought Mac down with a crash that would surely have been fatal had he not awakened at that precise instant to find Tom Jeff pulling the covers off his motel bed, pumpkin face aglow with pleasure, chortling, "Six o'clock! Up and at 'em! Let's go! Let's go! Night is over, and evil and doubt hold the sleeping land in thrall! Got to rise up and kick the bad guys around!"

Mac stumbled wearily to the shower, his eyes half closed. The dark cold motel room was a shock after the dream, and he felt a momentary disoriented panic. But as the water poured over him, the mood of the dream receded, until all that was left was the image of Stephanian's contemptuous face. Shaved and fully clothed, he emerged from the bathroom to find Tom Jeff bellowing into the phone, "Hello, Shorty? Tom Jeff Shadwell! Did I wake you up? I'm sorry, but listen, I need your help!"

Mac went to wake the others.

The next four days on the road were a blur of motion, each day different but following the same routine: salty ham and scalding coffee for breakfast, the candidate and Herman Cardmore eating nose to nose, each at 6:30 A.M. already in high spirits and top form, Tom Jeff smiling seraphically behind his bulging lenses as Cardmore, his quivering chin awash in cream gravy, parried his gibes and came back with his own.

Then out into a morning still barely light, the unlikely caravan winding along vertiginous roads which seemed to float above an infinite sea of ground fog, to an early-morning session with a deputation of mayors, farmers, miners, committeemen—stringy gray men beaten hard and flat by the harsh rocky country around them.

Then, as the fog lifted in the sun, roaring off again on an impossible schedule, Tom Jeff and the reporters riding ahead in the Winnebago while Mac brought up the rear, ferrying any dignitaries who might have come along to help the candidate on his rounds, and sometimes riding in silence while candidate and supporter conferred on matters of strategy and tactics too delicate to be negotiated in front of others; Mac for their purposes assumed to be deaf and dumb, oblivious of their discussion of whom to recruit, whom to avoid, what to promise, and what to refuse.

Mac's job was to care for local politicians and for the press corps, which grew larger as the trip went on, with two reporters from Washington and even a reporter from the Richmond papers, an embarrassed plump, balding young man with a face pink and crumpled as a baby's, the ridge of his skull perpetually damp with perspiration, sweat running into his tiny perfect blond mustache. He seemed unable to meet Tom Jeff's gaze head-on, as if traveling in the camp of his newspaper's archenemy had unnerved him, so that in all the time he traveled with the campaign party he never once asked a direct question of the candidate, confiding his questions instead to Mac, who passed them along to the candidate.

Mac was also charged with watching out for things that could go wrong and steering Tom Jeff out of sticky situations, and he was most particularly responsible for enforcing the schedule. Knocko had warned Mac that Tom Jeff would forget the clock when confronted with a human being asking for his help, and so it proved: time after time an old woman or a young couple sought him out after an appearance, confiding that benefits had stopped or license renewals had been unaccountably held up or any one of the endless list of troubles visited on small people by big governments that don't care about them and don't fear them. Tom Jeff would smile and let them know that he did care, would summon Mac over with a wave of his paw and give instructions to be noted neatly in a black spiral notebook: call this or that agency, inquire about Mrs. Ida Richardson's pension or T. W. Gamble's fertilizer shipment. And then Mac would have to step in, because Tom Jeff would now have been content to listen all day to their problems; as if he had before seen them only as votes, nameless political customers to be wooed and won, but now that they had asked for his help saw them fully as human beings like himself.

When the interview had continued past reasonable limits, Mac brought his heavy guns into play. Ordinarily he addressed Shadwell as Tom Jeff, or Senator. But when the schedule situation became desperate, Mac, followed Knocko's instructions, would steal behind the candidate and tap him on the shoulder, whispering, "Governor?" and Tom Jeff's head would turn as if by reflex. Capitalizing on this minute shift in his attention, Mac would grasp Shadwell unobtrusively but firmly by the elbow and begin guiding him toward the door, giving him time to wave good-bye and shake hands all around. If the pressure were even a fraction too light, Shadwell would simply ignore it; if it were too heavy, he would sense that he was being kidnapped and break free, and then the schedule would be truly lost: there would be no remedy but to wait in the car until he decided to come out on his own.

Mac was generally successful in keeping the procession within an hour of the schedule, stopping at country stores or for longer stops: a visit to a textile factory where the savage continual noise seemed impenetrable, except that Tom Jeff's marvelous irrepressible voice managed to make itself heard even over the incomprehensible industrial din, the candidate talking ceaselessly even though the machines had filled the air with tiny bits of lint, so that Mac coughed for hours afterward; a rally at a high school where the mayor of the town unexpectedly appeared in a white leather jump suit and introduced Tom Jeff by singing "Mule Skinner Blues" to the music of a country band, and where a pompom girl dropped her baton and stopped in the midst of the performance to cry inconsolably, her misery at last bringing the music to a stop and paralyzing the whole assemblage until Tom Jeff climbed down from the platform and put his arm around her in forgiveness; a speaking and handshaking tour of a courthouse town at the very precarious western tip of the state, where Tom Jeff, who was being shown around by the sheriff, shook hands warmly with a young man whom the sheriff promptly recognized as an escaped mental patient, who then drew a knife and had to be subdued on the hood of the Continental; a visit to a deep-shaft coal mine, where Mac caught a couple of hours of blessed sleep in the back of the van while Tom Jeff put on a miner's lamp and went down to the coal face and a party afterward at the UMW hall where one old miner who had lost a leg played the harmonica, while another, blasted by black lung, danced an odd ducklike jig he called the "black lung clog," saying, "It's got me so I can't raise my arms, but I can still use my legs for Brother Tom Jeff," and then Tom Jeff joined in, surprising Mac with an accomplished clog of his own.

At night they camped in tiny motels, and after evening speeches and late-night strategy sessions Tom Jeff would sprawl on the bed with a can of Diet-Rite Cola and watch the news. All that week it was Brock, Brock, Brock, for by coming to the far west of the state, where the camera crews were too stingy and lazy to follow, Shadwell had abandoned the electronic stage to his rival. And all that week they saw Brock's grave, weathered face intoning what had become his only message: busing—Shadwell; Shadwell—busing.

Brock's solemn face and unctuous words inflamed Shadwell. His anger would grow until it seemed to be about to burst out of the tiny hotel room. For Mac, it was the clearest hint he had gotten about the difference between Tom Jeff and Knocko. He had worked for Knocko for a year and a half and had gotten to understand Cheatham's deep, abiding anger, which was the anger of a proud man for his mortal enemies, a mixture of disdain, contempt, and deep, weary, cynical understanding, a disgusted intimate knowledge which amounted almost to sympathy—the hatred of a political professional for those who would destroy him if they could.

Tom Jeff was different; his anger seemed deeper and more fundamental, and at the base of it Mac saw the explosive fury of a small child who has been told his first lie: a direct childlike hatred of falsehood and dishonesty. Where Knocko was professional, a technician, Tom Jeff was a crusader; where Knocko was wearily amused by the antics of his enemies, Tom Jeff was insulted, not in the place where his ego and sense of himself lived, but deeper, in the place where his sense of the universe lived, his sense of the order of things which was still offended and threatened by lies and liars. Where most politicians eventually give up their sense of truth, Tom Jeff defiantly retained his, at the cost of much pain and fury.

The anger was so deep that Shadwell, who spoke mildly and would not abide cursing in his presence, seemed unable to give it voice. So as the week progressed, it became the unspoken context in which they moved, taking the form not of anger but of a vast inattention, a preoccupation on the part of the candidate. Mac sensed that he was frustrated by the campaigning they were doing. He was ready to take off his gloves, to hit Brock with everything he had. But his audiences were August audiences, still wrapped in the vague goodwill of summer, unprepared for apocalyptic rhetoric. That would come later, in the last days of the campaign, when the public juices were flowing and ready for the spectacle of two candidates, bare to the waist, chained together and fighting with knives.

By Friday night, the last night of the tour, the candidate was alone, wrapped in glum, impenetrable silence. Sitting in the motel room, Mac tried to discuss with him the night's appearance, which was a speech before the annual convention of a small fundamentalist sect called the Brotherhood of Christ the Redeemer. The week before, Mac had carefully researched the sect in order to write Tom Jeff's speech: it was small, but very active and cohesive, a Pentecostal sect which believed in the baptism of the Holy Spirit. It was made up of farming people, small storekeepers and merchants, the lower middle class; its head, Bishop Duesenberry, was a dynamic figure, a political force in his own right who reportedly could swing as many as two thousand votes in three counties.

Mac explained to Tom Jeff that he had been very careful with the speech: it was conciliatory, good-humored, and largely nonpolitical. "Let us not be, like Jonah, swallowed by the whale of unresponsive government," it warned, without specifying precisely whom that whale might represent. Mac showed Tom Jeff the mimeographed text, but he sensed that he was not holding Shadwell's attention. Finally, with a wave of his paw, he cut Mac off, and, stuffing the speech into the jacket pocket, he said, "Yes, all right, thanks, I'll remember."

The convention was being held in a great drafty parish hall which obviously doubled as a gymnasium. A tarpaulin had been spread over the playing surface, and the delegates were seated on rickety folding metal chairs. The basketball nets had been retracted, and above the wooden platform hung a huge banner: BACK TO THE BIBLE. The bishop, a hardy old man with a flossy waxed gray mustache and bushy white brows set under an expanse of gleaming pate, welcomed them as they entered. Looking at the three-hundred-odd delegates, Mac recognized them as the type of earnest believers who knocked on doors and haunted street corners, battering with the pristine force of their faith as at the portals of the disbelieving world. It was the young people who struck him. The middle-aged members of the congregation—plump prosperous couples, the men in pastel double-knit jackets and white ties, the women in harlequin spectacles, and scattered among them a few fierce, solitary old people, their lips sunk in by periodontal tribulation—seemed to have come to an understanding with their faith. But the ethereal young couples, thin and straight as cornstalks, the young men in white shirts and narrow ties, the women demure in long skirts, seemed possessed of a limitless zeal which would consume them and the world around them if it were not cooled. Mac pictured meeting a deputation of these pilgrims at his door and wondered if his doubting soul could withstand their celestial persistence.

Tom Jeff, however, found the gathering soothing; the disorderly comfortable air of the convention, with babies wailing in their parents' arms and little children running up and down the aisles, appealed to his informal soul, and he shed the distracted air which had been hanging over him all evening. When the tiny combo struck up "When the Roll Is Called Up Yonder," the electric bass throbbing until it caught the whole room in its rhythm, the singing bounding back from the cement walls, Tom Jeff joined in happily, clapping his hands and elbowing Mac, exhorting him to sing louder.

Then the bishop introduced Tom Jeff. "Brothers and sisters," he said, "before we get to the main item on our agenda, which is choosing new members for the council of elders, we have a special treat. As you know, the council invited both candidates for governor to be with us at our convention this weekend. Unfortunately, former Governor Brock had to be elsewhere"—sitting beside Tom Jeff, Mac heard him snort in disgust, for Brock had already made it plain that he would not appear with Tom Jeff anywhere at any time—"but it's a great pleasure to have with us tonight Senator Thomas Jefferson Shadwell." The mention of Tom Jeff's name brought a warm, polite spattering of applause, a friendly greeting; it was not a partisan crowd, Mac decided, but not hostile. "We all know Senator Shadwell; he's campaigned out in this area before, four years ago. He's been a member of the State Senate for about ten years now, and in that time he has made a name for himself fighting for the interests of the consumer and opposing the utility companies and the insurance companies. This year he is the Democratic nominee for governor, and I'm sure we are all very glad to welcome tonight Senator Tom Jeff Shadwell."

Tom Jeff, at the podium, beamed at them as the clapping died away. "Thank you, Bishop Duesenberry," he said, spreading the slightly crumpled speech on the podium and looking at it for a few seconds. "It's always a pleasure to be in this part of the state, to be out here in the country and speak to the real country people," he said. He was leading up to the text, softening them up with a few meaningless compliments before talking politics. "I can tell this group tonight is a friendly group of people from the fine welcome you've given me here tonight," he said. "I can tell you, not all the groups I speak to are quite so friendly. I go down to Richmond to speak to the Ki-wanis club, which as you know down there is a group of bankers and insurance executives—not salesmen, but vice-presidents and executive directors and cherubim and seraphim and what all" —there were a few laughs at this—"and power company lawyers and other big mules, and sometimes they're not so friendly. In fact, sometimes they get into such a fine frothing panic about little old Tom Jeff Shadwell you'd think I was the devil himself, which I'm not." He looked at them, and they did laugh a little at that, for these were people who knew what Satan looked like, and it was not the modest dumpy figure that stood before them.

Tom Jeff looked down at the text again, and then back at the audience, and then down at the text again, and there was a pause. And then he looked up again and said, "They've said just about everything they could about Tom Jeff Shadwell, and they've just about said that I am the devil himself," he said, and it was a different voice now from the merry after-dinner voice he had begun with, it was harder now, there was the cold steel of anger under the words, and Mac realized that Tom Jeff had made himself angry just by thinking about the big mules in Richmond, the comfortable assured money changers who had fought and despised and slandered him so long. "Which . . . I . . . am . . . not," he said again, and as Mac watched in horror, he pulled the text down under the rostrum and his fist, as if acting independently of the rest of him, very methodically crushed the typewritten sheets into a tiny ball, and dropped the ball to the floor.

"The Lord knows I am not the devil," he said again. Mac could see a few in the audience shaking their heads, as if wondering why the man insisted on denying that he was the devil. "But they've said so many things

81

about me for so long that I think a lot of people are wondering just who Tom Jeff is. And it's my honor and my privilege to be here tonight with Bishop Dusenberry and the General Convention of the Brotherhood of Christ the Redeemer to tell you just exactly who Tom Jeff Shadwell is."

Having disposed of the text, Tom Jeff now gripped the podium with both hands and leaned forward to have a good look at the audience. A few who had been shifting nervously in their seats sat up quickly to pay attention. "I am a lawyer and a state senator and the son of a policeman and I am a Baptist," he said. "And I am happy to be here tonight because even though we worship at different churches, we believe in the same things. My daddy took me to church when I was little, and he said to me, 'Tom Jeff, nothing is more important in this world than being a witness.' My daddy brought me up to witness to my faith, and I know you all were brought up to witness too. Weren't you? Are there any witnesses here?" This time he had hit them where they lived, and because they were Pentecostal, they saw nothing wrong with answering back, and a few did. "Yes, sir!" the voices said. "Yes, I do!" "Yes, I am!"

"I knew you were," Tom Jeff said, smiling broadly. He eased back on the podium. "And that's why it's good to be here tonight. It's good to be with people who know how to witness. Because that's what I'm here for tonight, to witness." Suddenly his voice took off, moving quickly now and rising in volume. As he talked, his stubby arms moved in his distinctive jerky gestures, like a crippled bird trying to fly.

"I'm here to witness tonight to who I am," he said. "I am Tom Jeff Shadwell, and for twenty years and more I have been witnessing to the same things. I have witnessed that it is wrong"—and as he said it, his mouth opened in a roar—"it is wrong for the consumer to pay more for electric power than the factories and the banks and the offices pay. And I have witnessed that it is wrong"—and he brought his fist down on the podium—"wrong for the workingman to pay more taxes so the rich and the powerful can get off without paying. I have witnessed that it is wrong"— and he bent himself almost double over the podium—"wrong to put a tax on food and medicine!"

They were listening now. It was a great show, and they weren't coughing or talking or glancing at their programs; they were watching Tom Jeff and wondering where he would go from here.

"And for twenty years and more I have witnessed that it is from the people that all power must come, from you and me and all the people of Virginia, because all power is vested in the people and magistrates are their servants and amenable to them. And for twenty years that has been my witness, and I have witnessed to it, and I have not changed one jot or one tittle of my witness because of the things they have called me, and they have called me some things I would not want to repeat here."

He looked at them, and everyone in the audience could see that Tom Jeff still felt the pain of the unjust accusations he was remembering. "They have said I wasn't a good Virginian," he said, "because I would not lie down and be still when they told me to. They have said I was not a good American because I would not wink when the utilities and the insurance corporations and the banks came around looking for ways to get their hands on your tax dollars. Brothers and sisters"—he paused now, and his voice dropped almost to a whisper, as his hands unfolded in the air to expose between his fingers the palpable injustice of the accusation— "they have even said I was not a good Christian because I said the Brotherhood of Christ the Redeemer and every other church and religious group ought to have the same rights we give to any church, and that it's wrong to discriminate against religious groups like this one because they are small or distant or because they believe in the Bible just as it was written!"

"But for twenty years, brothers and sisters," he went on, waving his arms again, "for twenty years and more, I have stuck to my witness in Norfolk and in Richmond and all over Virginia, just as Bishop Duesenberry and the Brotherhood of Christ the Redeemer has stuck to its witness out here! Because I was brought up to believe in certain things, and I believe in these things come what may! Just as I was brought up a Baptist and I will stay one until I die! And just like you, for twenty mortal years, against the scorn and persecution and the laughter, just as you have and just as Bishop Duesenberry has, brother and sisters, I . . . have . . . kept . . . my . . . faith!"

They were cheering now, and some were stamping on the floor, but Tom Jeff would not wait; he plunged ahead. "And just as I was brought up in a church and I will stay in it, just as you will stay in the church of your mothers and fathers, so we will keep our faith, and we will not say, 'I can't get the offices or the honors I want here, I can't be on the vestry or the council of elders, I can't be head man so I'll go somewhere else, I'll go to another church, I'll start my own.' We know who says that, and it's the other fellow, the fellow who couldn't be here tonight because he's too busy meeting with his friends in the Confederate Club to come and talk to the Brotherhood of Christ the Redeemer. He's the one, brothers and sisters! He's the one who was brought up in the Democratic Party, who grew up in the house of his fathers and took all that house could offer him, all the honor and preferment and the good things, until he could get no more. Until he saw that others now would get what he had had. And so he broke his faith, and suddenly he was a Republican!

"And suddenly he's saying, 'Look at me, I am a new man, I am born again, I am a new creature!' And that's all right, brothers and sisters, because we believe that a man can be born again, we believe that if any man be in Christ, he is a new creature, we believe you can be a born-again Christian. Don't we?"

And again they answered, louder this time, "Yes, Jesus!" "Yes, Lord!" "I believe!"

And then Tom Jeff was saying, "But we know that Jesus Christ alone on earth has the power to forgive sins, don't we? I tell you, I have searched the Scriptures and I have never found a single verse vesting that power in the Republican Party or the Confederate Club or the Tidewater Shipbuilding and Drydock Company. Have you? And we also know that if a man would be born again, he must repent his sins! Don't we? Well, brothers and sisters, I have been listening with bated breath and I have yet to hear that man repent one thing. Does he repent having voted for the poll tax? He does not! Does he repent having tried to close down the schools and lock the doors against little children? He does not! Does he repent having put a tax on every cup of coffee you drink and every aspirin you take? He does not! He does not repent! He does not! He says, 'I am righteous, I am your leader, I can do right, trust me, I am big daddy.' Well, brothers and sister, don't do it again! Don't put your faith in this man! He is a wolf in sheep's clothing; he is not what he pretends to be! We have kept our faith for more than twenty years now, and if we can keep it a few more months, we will do those things we have set out to do. We *will* get that tax on food off your food, and we *will* turn the government back to the people. And all we have to do is keep our faith!"

They were on their feet applauding, and the bishop had his arm around Tom Jeff, and the noise was bouncing off those cement walls, and Tom Jeff was hurrying out the door into the chill night air and into the Continental for the ride to the tiny mountain airport. Mac said nothing as they rode. He felt empty and tired and exhausted and happy. And at first when Tom Jeff said, "I'm sorry," Mac didn't know what he was talking about.

"I'm sorry about your speech," Tom Jeff said again.

Then Mac remembered the text. "Oh, forget it," he said. "It's absolutely okay."

"Well, I am sorry," Tom Jeff said mildly, "because it was a good speech and you worked hard on it. What happened was I realized those

84

folks wanted something more than a hello. They were in the mood for a revival, and I gave it to them." He smiled in self-mockery.

The smile encouraged Mac to ask the question. "That was a terrific speech," he said. "But I wanted to ask you—"

"What's that?"

"That was pretty hard stuff you said about Brock. Did you mean all that?"

There was the slightest pause, and then Tom Jeff's voice came back again with that hint of steel in it. "Listen, young man, you ought to know by now. I never say anything I don't mean. Never."

They rode on in mortified silence to the airport, and just before he climbed into the tiny plane that would take him back to Norfolk, Tom Jeff forgave Mac and thanked him for his help and wished him a safe trip back. Then he left Mac to find his way back out of the mountains, and like a steel paraclete, the tiny plane disappeared into the clouds.

FIVE

★

The Monday before Labor Day Mac suddenly found himself with nothing to do. Labor Day was by traditional fiction the formal beginning of a general election campaign, although in fact political candidates had for the last hundred years and more found it necessary to begin seeking support and traveling the state much earlier. In fact, the contest for governor of Virginia begins a few days after the election of the previous governor, continues at a low level until the presidential election, three years later, and then gets under way in earnest for the final twelve months. But the fiction holds a kernel of truth, nonetheless, because all the campaigning, organizing, and infighting which went on before Labor Day was purely preliminary: not so much an attempt to influence the voters as a race to line up money and win the help of those who earned their living by politics, or hoped shortly to be doing so. The great mass of the electorate—all but a tiny fraction of the more than one million people who might cast votes in November—were at summer's end still going about their business more or less oblivious to the election. Most of them would not tune in to the campaign until the last eight or nine crucial weeks before election day.

As Labor Day approached, Mac felt like an athlete facing an Olympic trial or an actor about to open a new play; the next two months would decide the war he had been fighting for nearly two years. Nothing else

87

seemed important; nothing else seemed real. Inside himself he was tightening up, wedging himself forward in a dark black tunnel which led only to election day. He did not mind the feeling; he did not even notice it. It seemed as natural to him as breathing. But his days were tense, skittish, and his nights dull dreamless bouts of anxiety and rage.

The Monday in question had been particularly grueling. Mac had worked through the weekend putting together an issue of Tom Jeff's campaign newspaper, *True Facts*. Shadwell workers would blanket the state with a quarter million of them starting the next week; they would be distributed in country stores, at shopping centers, at plant gates and county fairs. It was a four-page tabloid, its format taken from a number of popular commercial weeklies. AMAZING TRUE FACTS BEHIND THE UNNECESSARY TAX ON YOUR FOOD! read a huge boxed banner headline across the top of the front page. Beneath it were a column of type and a four-column picture of the candidate shaking hands with a famous race-car driver. DANGER KEEPS ME ALIVE, SAYS REMO MANZONI! was the headline beneath the photo, with an article in which the driver praised Shadwell as a good family man and a good Democrat. Across the bottom of the page was a red banner: PEGGY SHADWELL'S FAVORITE RECIPES—*see Page 3*.

Mac had been up all day and night Sunday pasting up the copy at the composing room of Huntington's newspaper. He was proud of the result, particularly an article on the second page, TRUE FACTS BEHIND GOV. BROCK'S AMAZING QUICK-CHANGE ACT. This consisted mostly of previous quotes from Brock denouncing the Republican Party and pledging his loyalty to the Democratic Party; it was designed to infuriate Democrats and Republicans alike. It also managed to suggest without saying so that Brock's best years were far behind him and that he was bumbling around the state contradicting himself at every turn. Mac had showed Tom Jeff the copy, and the candidate had laughed out loud. "Keep it up, young Mac," he'd said. "You're going to have them ready to put Brock in the laughing academy."

Mac finished Sunday morning, in time to meet the printer's deadline. He reached the plant dizzy and delirious from lack of sleep, head buzzing from the half dozen cups of coffee he had drunk to keep himself awake. At the plant, the noise of the presses and the sharp smell of ink rolled over him like a wave; he gulped for air. "Neat work," said the printer, casting a practiced eye over the flats.

"Thanks," Mac said. He focused on the man through tired, tearing eyes, and yawned broadly. "Now don't forget the union bug," he said.

"Say what?" the printer asked. He was a lean, spare man, who did not seem disposed to waste words.

"The union label," Mac said. "We've got to have the union label on it, or the whole thing's no good."

"Oh, yes," the man said. "Don't worry about that."

Mac turned to go. "We're all set now, aren't we?" he asked.

"Yes, sir," the man said. "This ought to print up right nice."

At the door, Mac paused. "You won't forget?"

"Forget what?" replied the man absently. He was measuring the page width with a pica rule.

"The union bug!" Mac said, his voice rising slightly.

"Don't worry about that, sonny," the man said. "This plant's been union since before you were born."

"I know that," Mac said. "I just have to make sure."

"Come on with me now then, and I'll put it on while you watch, if it's that important to you."

Mac felt somehow that this would be an insult to the printer, to his union, to the labor movement as a whole. "That's all right," he said, smilingly vaguely. "I just wanted to remind you."

The man shrugged, looking down at the flat again. "Suit yourself," he said.

Mac closed the door behind him and walked to the parking lot. But when he got to the Continental, he felt drawn back. For a minute he stood in the parking lot debating with himself. Then, feeling foolish, he went back inside.

"Back again?" the printer said incuriously.

"Yes, well," Mac said, coughing uneasily. "Maybe I'd feel better if I did watch you put it on."

The man laughed obscurely to himself. "Okay, Mr. George Meany, come with me now."

"Thanks," Mac said sheepishly. "Now I can sleep."

Back in the car Mac realized he still would not be able to sleep. He was tired, but tense, keyed up, quivering with nervous energy. He decided to go to headquarters and work for a few hours more.

Shadwell state headquarters was a barren, dirty warren of offices behind a decaying iron storefront on East Main Street. Farther east was the Shockoe Valley, site now of a somnolent farmers' market and a seldom-used railroad station; beyond those, on the slope of Church Hill, were the leaf warehouses of "Tobacco Row." The headquarters was on the eastern edge of the business district: a block away began a series of high-rise buildings which housed the brokerage houses, law firms, and banks which among them controlled much of the state's wealth. "We've got three-quarters of Brock's campaign fund within five blocks of us,"

Knocko said when the headquarters opened. He had ordered a garish red, white, and blue banner stretched across the street: TOM JEFF SHADWELL IS ALWAYS WATCHING. "Won't get us any votes, but it'll sure bug these rich farts," he told Mac. "Maybe a couple of them will fall down dead with heart attacks before election day."

Mac worked in the rear, a small alcove off Knocko's big office. He sat at his desk and stared at the pile of papers he had to read before writing a Labor Day speech for Tom Jeff. It was one of three the candidate would deliver; this one would be at a picnic in the northern part of the state, a bewildering suburban jumble inhabited by bureaucrats, generals, business executives, and members of the PTA.

"Can't I just go up there and talk about the food tax?" Tom Jeff had asked Knocko.

"Not up there," Knocko had snapped. "These people care about issues, Tom Jeff. You go up there without any issues, and they're liable to tear you apart."

"Heaven help us," Tom Jeff had cried in mock alarm. "Cousin Knocko's talking about issues. Run for the exits!" He winked at Mac. "This is a bad sign, Mac. Only Labor Day, and already we've got to have issues. Last time we got to October without Issue One."

"Yeah, look what happened," Knocko had grumbled.

"We didn't lose because of issues," Tom Jeff had replied serenely. "Brother Slaughter talked about issues; that's why we almost won. We could have got him talking about a few more issues, we would have won, sure enough. He was talking about issues, and I was casting out devils and healing the sick, and folks'd rather see that any day. You start talking about issues and the next thing you know you're talking about taking money out of some guy's pocket, putting on taxes, condemning land, hiring new people, building new buildings, there's just no end to it. That isn't the way to win an election. You just got to get folks to feeling involved. Brock, now, he's going to try to scare 'em. We're going to try to make 'em happy."

"Right," Knocko had snorted. "Next you'll be talking about the politics of joy, I bet. I'm telling you, Tom Jeff, if you get up there and try to get by with telling a bunch of jokes, some lady who used to be vice-chairman of the Teaneck School Board is going to pop up and say, 'Senator Shadwell, what effect is your proposal to abolish the food tax going to have on the state's debt-to-income ratio?' and you're going to be floundering. You'll look silly, and they do not go for that kind of stuff up there, believe me."

"All right, then," Tom Jeff said. "We'll do it your way, Cousin. Why don't we talk about mass transit? That's always good up there, and I can get Mac here to dig up some facts for me. That's what those people care about, how they're going to get in and out of Washington. We promise 'em that, they'll be as happy as clams."

So Mac had been assigned to write a speech about mass transit. It was no longer enough just to endorse it: the problem had become so pressing, and the solutions so expensive, that the audience would demand to know how Shadwell would pay for his promises. Mac had to spend tedious hours wading through financial projections and newspaper clippings to make sure Tom Jeff did not endorse something he could not possibly do if elected.

An hour passed as he made notes on index cards. The pages seemed to swim in front of him. Wearily he set down the file of reports and rested for a moment, head in his arms. His eyelids felt gritty, as if fine sand had become wedged inside them. He sighed heavily, and at that moment his desk phone buzzed.

He punched the button and heard the hollow distant hush of long distance; it promised disaster and anonymous bad news.

"Hello?" he said cautiously.

"Hey, Donald Duck!" cried a merry voice.

Mac held the phone away from his ear and shook it slightly, as if it were a watch that had stopped. "Excuse me," he said.

"Hey, Donald Duck!" the telephone said again.

"Who is this?" Mac said irritably. He felt like a spy who had lost his code book; he could not understand the transmission.

The voice went on. "Were you addressing me by my full name, that is, first name, Donald, and surname, Duck, or were you addressing me by my first name only, adding subsequently the imperative 'duck!'?"

It clicked. *Mad* magazine. "Hello, Arnie," Mac said.

"But you did not permit me to finish my sentence which when completed would have been, 'Hey, Donald Duck, duck!'"

Stephanian was waiting for Mac's laughter, but none came. Ordinarily Mac would have been delighted to hear from Arnie, who had been his roommate and closest friend in college, but today he felt jarred and irritated by the sudden intrusion. He looked down at the pile of papers on his desk and felt time ticking away, as if he were in a taxi with the meter running.

"How are you?" Mac said quietly.

"Pretty good," Stephanian said, his voice still merry and enthusiastic, but now a trifle tentative, as if sensing Mac's mood. "Keeping busy."

"What villainy are you on the track of today?" Mac said. "Is it the Eritreans or the Kurds?"

Stephanian lived in Boston and worked for an organization called Intervention Alert, which monitored U.S. activities abroad. He intermittently sent Mac the organization's bulletin, which was full of ominous warnings about mysterious U.S. activities in tiny countries around the world.

"Neither one," Stephanian said. "Right now there's a very serious problem shaping up in Latin America."

"Don't tell me about it," Mac said, resting his head on one hand.

"No, seriously," Stephanian said. "You should follow this situation. I really think there's a civil war shaping up, and the U.S. is in the thick of it."

"I said don't tell me about it," Mac repeated emphatically. "I got enough problems right now with Arlington and Fairfax, let alone Latin America."

"Those two areas have a lot in common," Arnie said. "You've got the CIA in each."

"Jesus, Arnie, lay off," Mac said. "We're not going after the CIA vote."

"That may be a mistake," Arnie said. "They're pretty good at rigging elections."

"We'll win this one without them, I think."

"So," Stephanian said, with an expansive pause. "How goes the fight against the food tax?"

Again Mac glanced at his watch. "Where are you, Arnie, at your office?"

"Yeah."

"They let you use the phone there?"

"We share a WATS line with some other groups in the building."

Mac had been hoping he could promise to call back and thus get back to his work.

"I read about your boy in the *Times*," Stephanian said.

"I saw that article too," Mac said. "Don't believe everything you read in the liberal Northern press."

"This guy was saying that Shadwell is going after the Wallace vote pretty heavily."

"Yeah?" Mac said. "Sure he is. What about it?"

"I was just curious," Stephanian said. "It just seems like an odd coalition he's putting together, that's all."

"Come on, Arnie," Mac said irritably. "It only seems odd if you read about it in the New York *Times*. From down here it makes perfect sense. In this state we got the ins and we got the outs. The blacks and the Wallace people, both of them are out. The state government is run by the big-money boys. Hell, Arnie, you're a radical, you ought to understand this.

We organize the outs, the little guys, to get the government away from the ins. It hasn't got that much to do with Wallace or anything else. It should have happened a long time ago."

"I suppose you're right." Stephanian's voice was dubious. "It certainly is the good old American way, coalition politics."

"It isn't just that it's a coalition," Mac said. "This is a damn good coalition, and I'm proud to be part of it, whether you or Scotty Reston approve or not."

"Well, I'm just wondering if you don't lose a lot of effectiveness by getting into this coalition-type thing."

"Right," Mac said. "Much more effective to lose elections and remain pure."

"No, not exactly," Stephanian said. His voice was taking on a vaguely professorial tone, a legacy of his years as a Harvard social studies major. "But sometimes I wonder if this isn't the way new ideas get lost in American politics. You take busing—"

"What about it?" Mac said.

"Shadwell has come out against it, so in one sense the difference between him and the other guy—what's his name?"

"Brock."

"Right. The difference between him and Brock is very slight in that sense."

"Listen, Arnie," Mac said. He found he was speaking between clenched teeth. "I don't know what you've been reading, but there is a hell of a lot of difference between Tom Jeff and Miles Brock. If Brock gets elected, he'll stall and stall on any kind of integration, he'll stand in the school door, not actually because that would be too undignified for a fine gentleman, but he will make it hard as hell for black people to get anything. If Shadwell is elected, he can't do anything about busing anyway: it's court-ordered, the localities have to carry it out, and the only thing the governor could do would be fat-mouth about it and try to make political hay and encourage people to resist. Which Shadwell would not, and Brock certainly would. Now that seems to me like a difference."

"Well, yes, but—" Arnie began.

"Let me finish. I don't know what people are thinking in Harvard Square, but around here busing is about the least popular thing since Beast Butler."

"Among the whites."

"Okay, fine, among the majority. Now I suppose it would make Shadwell a hero around the Intervention Alert offices if he endorsed busing and went around campaigning in a school bus and stood on the principle, and

93

you guys would like him, but he'd sure as hell lose the election, and then the blacks would get nothing.''

"That's very persuasive," Arnie said. "Really. I'm just interested in the way this kind of compromise affects social policy.''

"What do you mean?''

"There's another way to state it, and that's to view this kind of compromise and coalition as a sellout of some pretty important principles.''

Suddenly Mac had had enough: enough of everything, of Arnie, of the New York *Times,* of TV networks, of liberal intellectuals, of all the alien anonymous forces who always knew better and didn't try to understand because they thought they already understood. Mac let it loose. "Oh, fuck you, Arnie, just fuck you," he said. "What the hell do you know about selling out?''

"Now hold on, Mac," Stephanian said. "Maybe I used the wrong word—''

Mac cast his eyes around the room. He saw the door open; Knocko entered. Somehow having an audience made him angrier; so, for that matter, did Stephanian's voice, which reminded him that Arnie was his best friend. "You bet your cookies you picked the wrong word, you dumb Yankee bastard," he said loudly. "So don't call me again until you get some better manners, you understand?''

Mac found he had hung up the phone. The room was silent. He looked at his hands shaking with fatigue and rage and tried to figure out what had happened.

Knocko was looking at him quizzically from behind his desk. "Friend of yours?" he asked.

"Yeah, as it happens," Mac said. "My best friend. Former best friend, I guess.''

Knocko laughed. "He vote in Virginia?''

"No," Mac said.

"Well, in that case, I'm with you. Give it to the SOB." Knocko fished in his center drawer for a cigar. "You feeling all right, MacIlwain?" he said.

"Sure, yeah," Mac said quickly. "I'm a little strung out, is all. I was up late working on *True Facts.*''

Knocko said nothing. "Things getting a little rough around here, I think. It isn't healthy to be that angry before Labor Day.''

"Yeah," Mac said, abashed.

"And furthermore, I'm wondering, what if somebody calls up who isn't your best friend. You might not be so polite to them. You might actually be rude.''

"I tell you," Mac said. "I think I'll go get some sleep.''

"Good idea," Knocko said.

Mac looked over his desk and straightened his papers. Then he went to the door. "See you tomorrow," he said.

Knocko, busy with the ritual of lighting his cigar, waved for him to stop. "I've got a better idea," he said.

"What's that?" Mac said.

"Why don't you just take the rest of the week off?" Knocko said. "Rest up a little. Get some of this craziness out of your system. Come back after Labor Day. I recommend it."

Mac gestured helplessly at his desk. "I can't do that, Knocko," he said. "I've got Tom Jeff's speech to write, and then we have to get the papers distributed, and then—"

"Let me rephrase my statement," Knocko said blandly. "I do not recommend it. I am telling you to clear out."

"But the speech—"

"Forget the speech, goddamn it! We can get that done without you. It may not have as much polish. We didn't go to Harvard, after all. But we'll get it done in our own clumsy way. You just go." He pointed to the door. "Get. Go on, now."

Mac shrugged. He seemed to have no choice. Further, he suddenly discovered that he wanted to sleep. He pictured himself in bed dreaming and turned for the door.

"Just one more thing," Knocko said.

Mac turned back; he felt as if he were already asleep and Knocko had awakened him.

"When you come back," Knocko was saying, "I want you nice and calm and Ivy-League-polite. Don't want to hear any of this mess on the telephone, and if I do, I'm going to break your ass in five pieces. I am the only one around this office who gets to be a crazy son of a bitch, and I won that job through years of sweat. I don't delegate that responsibility, you understand?"

"Okay, Knocko," Mac said. He smiled. "Job's in capable hands."

Knocko grunted and waved a dismissing hand. Mac went.

For two days Mac festered in his little house. He had no idea what to do with so much idle time. He tried to read books, but he found that he was out of shape for reading, like a runner who was not worked out for many months. He could not focus his attention on the page for more than a few minutes at a time, nor could his mind absorb any but the simplest stories and ideas. He went back to his adolescence, to the moldering piles of science-fiction paperbacks in a cabinet in the big house, to find something that would hold his attention ("Look out, slugs, the free men are coming to kill you. *Death and Destruction!''*). But the reading was like scratching fly bites: the hack novels quieted his brain but left it empty, and when he put one down, the boredom fell upon him again like a tenacious predator.

The weather was fine, but Mac had never learned tennis or golf, and he lacked the patience necessary for cultivating a suntan. On Wednesday night in desperation he called Huntington, who invited him to a paralyzing evening with Spottswood and Foote, the four of them smoking joints in Huntington's apartment, three echoing bare rooms in what had once been the Huntington family stable. Mac had not smoked grass since he left college, but the effect was familiar. Where others found in cannabis a key to preternatural perceptions, or hilarity, or awe, Mac always found only cessation. The world dimmed, fell silent, became not more but less colorful, exciting, joyful.

The effect lingered like a hangover, and the next morning Mac found he could think of nothing better to do than sit in the window seat in his little house and stare into space. In his small refrigerator he had found half a can of cold chili and a Dr Pepper; from this he made his breakfast, spooning chili straight from the can and washing it down with soda. Ordinarily he liked Dr Pepper. As a freshman in college he had told Stephanian that sour mash whiskey and Dr Pepper was the most popular highball in the South; Arnie had been so horrified that Mac had asked Molly O. to crate a six-pack of Dr Pepper and send it to him through the mails; then, with Arnie watching in horrified fascination, Mac had mixed and drunk a "Dr Daniels," smiling broadly in feigned nostalgic delight.

But this morning the soda seemed to have no taste. Mac was calculating the number of hours before he could go back to work when the phone rang. Molly O. was at work; he answered it. It was Alexandra, the girl he had met at Train's wedding. He had not seen her since then, but her voice was startlingly familiar. It cut through the fog in Mac's brain.

"How's school?" he asked her.

"School hasn't even started yet," she said. "We've been having t-group sessions and learning to fill in lesson plans."

"I've been writing speeches and whatnot," he said, "but right now I happen to be at liberty."

"What about this weekend?"

"As it happens, I'm at liberty then, too."

"How'd you like to do me a favor?"

"Name it," Mac said. "Just speak the word, and it is done."

"Really?" she said, with some skepticism. "What I want is for you to come with me to Carolina for Labor Day."

"That doesn't sound like much of a favor to me," Mac said. "Sounds more like you doing me a favor."

"Appearances can be deceiving," she said. She seemed about to say something, then changed her mind and said, "My brothers will be there, and—some other people."

"Sounds like fun," Mac said. The idea of getting out of the state seemed like an inspiration from heaven; Mac wondered why he had not thought of it sooner.

Again came her skeptical tone. "It could be. Be more fun if you came."

The idea that he could make her weekend more fun seemed almost to take Mac's breath away. "My answer is yes," he said.

"Okay," she said. "That's a verbal contract in common law. You're stuck."

"Right," he said, nodding a sage two-and-a-half-year law school drop-out's nod.

"I'll pick you up after work tomorrow, if that's all right," she said. "About six."

"That'll be fine," he said. Then he had a thought. "Listen, I drive a big car. A Continental. It's a great road car. I'll be glad to drive down if you want."

"A Continental?" She seemed to find it surprising. "You drive a Continental?"

"Yes," Mac said, suddenly a little sheepish. "Yes, I do."

She whistled softly.

"I take it you don't want to go in my car," he said a bit stiffly.

"Right," she said. "One of my greatest pleasures in driving is hating all the bastards who pass me in Continentals, and I don't want to give that up."

"All right, then," said Mac, obscurely wounded.

"See you tomorrow," she said.

Mac threw the chili away, finished the Dr Pepper, and called Molly O. to tell her he wouldn't be going with her to Virginia Beach for the weekend.

"I do believe my brother-in-law has gotten himself a *girl friend*," Molly O. said when Mac told her his plans. "What I think, and I wouldn't say this if the bishop were here, is that you are sneaking off to North Carolina for illicit delights."

Mac laughed. "You'll never know, O.," he said. "Your intelligence network doesn't stretch that far south."

"That's what you think, is it?" she said. "I'll find out what you're doing, Mac Evans. You can run but you can't hide."

Alexandra picked him up in a battered gray Volkswagen squareback. They drove south on Interstate 95 in the waning daylight. She was silent, distracted, and even before they got out of town, Mac realized the coming weekend was likely to be a complicated business, although as yet he did not know why.

They passed through the miasma of the chemical plants on the south side of the James. Mac took refuge in a book: *The Last Gentleman* by Walker Percy, which he had pulled off Molly O.'s bookshelf at random, chiefly because the title reminded him of the St. Cyprian's motto: "We can't all be scholars, but we can all be gentlemen." He was reading about the hero's visit to Richmond:

> As he ate Ritz Crackers and sweet butter, he imagined how Richmond might be today if the war had ended differently. Perhaps Main Street might be the Wall Street of the South, and Broad might vie with New Orleans for Opera and Theater. Here in the White Oak Swamp might be located the great Lee-Randolph complex, bigger than GM and making better cars (the Lee surpassing both Lincoln and Cadillac, the Lil' Reb outselling even Volkswagens).

Mac laughed aloud uncomfortably, because he knew who would be the masters of those great secessionist auto plants: himself, his family, descendants of the South's mightiest industrialist, the Henry Ford of slave labor. He thought again his private heresy about the ill-treatment his region had received from history: that the South was lucky to get what it got, that it should have asked for more and said thank you when it was over.

"What are you laughing about?" Alexandra asked.

He had been lost in his thoughts and had forgotten she was there. "Nothing," he said. "I was just thinking about my great-great-grandfather."

"Who was he?" she said.

"I'm not sure I know you well enough to tell you about my great-great-grandfather yet," he said.

She looked at him curiously. "A man of mystery," she said.

He looked her up and down. She was dressed in a man's blue long-sleeved shirt, tight green flowered pants, and sandals. At the wedding, the bridesmaid's dress had hidden the contours of her body. They were rich and intricate; her breasts were full, roundly pointed like minarets, and beneath, her hips were slim, and there was a hint of cunning articulation about her thighs. Seeking to change the subject, Mac made a lucky guess. "Are you a dancer?" he asked.

She smiled, for the first time since they'd gotten in the car, brushing back her long black hair. She looked at him now with interest. "Yeah," she said. "Or I used to be, sort of. How did you know?"

Mac was grinning himself, a pleased, triumphant smile. "I don't know," he said. "You look sort of like a dancer."

"Really?" she said. In her voice was a faint echo of the skeptical tone he had heard on the phone. "What does a dancer look like?"

"I don't know," Mac said, waving a hand. "I knew a couple of dancers in school, and I guess you just reminded me of them."

"Is that right?" she said. "Did you go out with dancers?"

"Did I?"

"Yes."

"No," he said. "I didn't really go out with anybody in college."

"Come on," she said. "You look like an operator to me."

"What do you mean?" Mac said. The idea genuinely startled him.

"I don't know," she said. "I knew a few operators in school. Some of them used to hang around the dance rehearsals and pick up girls that way."

"And I remind you of them?" Into Mac's mind there flashed a picture of himself, waiting in the wings, wearing striped blazer, bow tie, straw hat, hair brilliantined, with a pencil mustache, clutching candy and flowers and leering at an innocent ballerina: Stage Door Mac. He laughed out loud. "Boy, did you guess wrong."

"Is that right?" she said again. "You are not how you seem?"

"I guess not," he said. "I never knew that was how I seemed."

They drove for a while in silence. Then she said shyly, "How about this, then. How do I seem?"

Mac considered urgently. He felt somehow a need to show himself a master of detection, the Sherlock Holmes of love. He imagined his analysis: *I perceive you are left-handed and that until recently you owned a large dog, whom you loved very much, although it annoyed you by chewing your stockings. You were once ill, but now have completely recovered, although you are still slightly prone to headache. Your first lover was an Armenian. . . .* But in fact he could come up with no concrete deductions. He shrugged. "What can I tell you?" he said. "You're a very pretty girl, and you seem nice, and I'm not really much of a judge of people beyond that. I don't know you."

"What? No judge of people? You, a professional politician?"

"I've never quite been described that way before," Mac said. "If this were a political situation, I suppose I could give you lots of educated guesses. But you don't seem to me like a political phenomenon, so I'm out of my depth."

She smiled again, even wider. "That was the right answer," she said.

"I'm glad," Mac said. "Although I really am used to dealing with political people."

"Where did you go to school?"

"Harvard."

She was giving him a speculative look. "Really?"

He nodded.

"Were you there when all that stuff was going on?"

"If you mean the strike," Mac said carefully, "yes, that was my senior year."

"Really?" she said. "Were you involved in all that?"

"Yes," he said.

"What did you do?"

Mac found himself idly fingering the crown of his skull. "I didn't do that much," he said, shrugging. "I was more done to, if you see what I mean."

"No."

She seemed to Mac to be willfully misunderstanding. "I got arrested," he said.

She looked at him curiously. "Wow," she said. "That's a surprise."

Mac was wounded again. He felt he carried his battle scars in plain view on his body somehow, indications that he was not just another fellow, professional politician, stage-door Johnny, but a veteran, a man who had passed through a great experience. "Why is it a surprise?" he said irritably.

She looked at him shyly, brushing back her hair again, then turned back to the road. "It's just the first time I've found that someone I liked was involved in all that stuff."

Mac was torn by the two messages. *She likes me,* thought half his mind, wriggling with joy like a puppy being petted; *Reactionary bitch!* screamed the other half, crouching defensively. "What do you mean?" he said.

"I don't want to hurt your feelings," she said.

"That's all right," he said. "Unload."

"Well, maybe it was different where you went to school," she said. "But I went to Chapel Hill, and I knew some radical types there, and to be honest, I really didn't like them. They seemed sort of—I don't know— evil in a lot of ways."

"Evil is a pretty big word to throw around like that," Mac said. "I can't make moral judgments for you. But myself, I always saved that word to use against the war, and the people who were planning the war. Sometimes I didn't like the kids who were trying to stop it, but I always tried to keep my own moral priorities straight."

"I was against the war too," she said quickly. "I marched in Washington and all the rest of it. But I just thought that—I don't know, it seemed

100

to me that those people were obsessed, they couldn't think about anything else. They were scary."

"There's something in that," Mac said. "I suppose they did seem like fanatics, and fanatics are scary sometimes, I can see that. But let me tell you one thing—"

"Don't get angry at me," she said quickly.

Mac calmed himself. "I'm sorry," he said. "It's just that my emotions are involved in this. I have a scar under my hairline here, it took twelve stitches to close it, from where I had an encounter with a riot baton. That kind of experience does something to you, changes you. Now those fanatics, see, I knew a lot of them, and I have a lot of respect for them, scary as they were. Because it's not easy, fighting against an unjust war, it takes a lot of commitment and courage, and it takes the kind of fanaticism that makes you keep working while other people are relaxing and having a good time, going to the movies or to dance rehearsals—"

"Dancers sometimes are trying to make things better, too," she said.

He feared he had wounded her. They drove in silence for a few miles, through the velvet twilight. Thick pine woods lined either side of the road. Mac read the highway signs: GET U.S. OUT OF U.N. EXXON. SNAKE FARM AHEAD—LIVE REPTILES NEXT EXIT. AMERICA ONLY WORKS AS WELL AS WE DO. ZION'S CHOICE CHURCH OF CHRIST THE REDEEMER.

"I really appreciate your coming with me for this weekend," she said finally.

"You keep thanking me," Mac said. "I was glad to have a chance to get away. I should thank you. It isn't often pretty girls invite me on trips."

"See," she said absently. "There you go again, operating."

Mentally he drew himself up in pride. *Well done, operator,* he told himself.

"Anyway," she said, "let me tell you why I'm glad you're coming. I mean, in a way, I guess, I'm using you a little bit."

"How's that?" Mac felt surprised, a little nervous, a little flattered. To be used implied that he was useful, and he liked the feeling.

"It's a long story," she said. "See, when I was at Chapel Hill I had this boyfriend. We went together for—I don't know, nearly two years."

Mac envied this stranger. "Did you meet him at a dance rehearsal?"

She smiled faintly. "As a matter of fact, yes, I did. But he was all right. What I mean was, he was a really good guy. You know, I've told you how I felt about the radical kids I knew—"

"Yes. Let's not go over that again."

"It's important, you see, because to me at least, this guy was different. His name was Willie. People called him Steamboat Willie."

"Steamboat Willie?"

She shrugged at his amusement. "All right, it sounds funny. I don't know why they called him that, but they did. But anyway, it seemed to me that he was genuinely different, because he seemed to want to try to help change things instead of just scream and yell and run away from cops."

Mac fingered his hairline again but said nothing.

"He was a year older than me," she went on. "I sort of looked up to him. He was studying political science, sociology, languages, really making terrific grades. I had a feeling that he was going to change things. Make them better, like I said. We were engaged and the whole bit." She stopped suddenly.

Mac prodded her gently. "What happened?"

"Well," she said slowly, "Willie was going to do a term in the Peace Corps and then come back and go to graduate school, and when he got back, we were going to get married. Which I didn't mind, because I thought it was great, it seemed constructive to me, and I wasn't worried about being away from him, because, well, I loved him, and he was the only person I had ever loved. I didn't think it would be hard to wait for him."

Mac looked up and saw her eyes sparkling with tears behind the oval glasses. He felt embarrassed, intrusive; "You don't have to tell me this," he said awkwardly. "I mean, if it upsets you—"

"I know I don't have to tell you," she said, brushing back her hair. "I want to. It's important that you understand."

He subsided, still embarrassed.

"So he went off to India at the end of my junior year. They sent him to the Punjab. Do you know where that is?"

Mac thought at once of Little Orphan Annie's turbaned protector. "No," he said.

"It's sort of in the northwest. He was going to help farmers there use these new hybrid grains, you know, the Green Revolution."

"Yes, I've heard of that."

"I was working hard my senior year, and dancing a lot, and he wrote every now and then, not often, but I figured he was busy. But then Christmas came, and I didn't hear at all for about six weeks. Nothing. And that really bothered me. I didn't know if he was all right or what. I didn't get anything until the middle of February, I got this very strange letter."

She stopped again, as if rereading the letter in her mind. With a hoot and a clatter, a big tractor-trailer swept past them, cutting back into their lane only inches from their front fender. She braked nimbly and shot the finger at the truck as it disappeared down hill.

"You'll get us beat up," Mac said.

"He didn't see me," she said. "Besides, they don't beat up girls. Anyway, here was this letter, and it was all very mysterious, but the gist of it was that he had gotten thrown out of the Peace Corps—"

"Thrown out? For what?"

"He didn't say, he just said he'd been railroaded out, and would I please come and meet him right away."

"What, in India?"

"Right," she said crisply. "And furthermore, he was very secretive and said I must not say anything to anybody, because they—I'm not sure who he meant, I guess the Peace Corps—had told him to leave the country and he was hiding out. He gave me an address in Benares."

"Jesus," Mac said. "What did you do?"

"What do you think?" she said. "I went."

"You just picked up and went to India without telling anybody?"

"Yeah."

He whistled softly in appreciation. "You have a lot of guts."

They were going uphill, and she calmly passed the same truck which had passed them earlier. The driver flashed his brights at them, then dimmed and flashed again. "I see you, mister," she said. "It isn't a question of guts, really. Here was the guy, we were going to get married, and he writes and says I'm in trouble, please come help me, so naturally I went. Anybody would."

Would anybody? Mac wondered. "So you went?"

"Yeah," she said. They were caught in the right lane behind an aged pickup truck while the trucker passed them again. She flashed her lights angrily at the pickup, and then passed, muttering, "Get a horse, grandpa!"

"How did you like it?"

"What, India?"

He nodded.

"Not so much, to be honest about it. Of course, I didn't really get a very good view of it. Probably if I'd gone under different circumstances, I'd have come home like everyone else, all spiritual and cooking seventeen different kinds of curry and all the rest of it. But I had to get to Delhi and then to Benares all alone, and here I'd hardly been out of Carolina in most of my life, and I was wondering what was going on, plus all the secrecy, nobody knowing where I was, except one friend, who I'd promised to send postcards to every week, and if they ever stopped, the idea was she'd know I was in trouble. Plus, Benares is really a strange place. It's the sacred city of India, people come there to die. Until I got there,

I'd had this idea that people in other countries were just Americans in funny suits, with accents, you know, that we were really all alike. But it's not true. They really are different. And Steamboat—''

She threw herself into her driving, racing downhill behind the truck and losing. "This damn thing's got no more pickup than a tricycle," she said absently. "Anyway. Steamboat was—it's hard to explain, but he was really a different person, almost totally."

"How so?"

"Here as long as I'd known him, he'd wanted to be in the Peace Corps, it was part of him, and I guess part of why I loved him, and now all of a sudden he was all bitter about it."

"Did he tell you why he'd been thrown out?"

"They had apparently told him he was being—what is it?—terminated early, because they'd found out he was smoking hash. But he claimed that that was just an excuse. He said it was because he'd found out that all this Green Revolution stuff was being used by the big farmers to push little farmers off their land, and the Peace Corps volunteers were helping to do that, because it was supposedly more efficient, and he'd objected. Because what's the use of producing more grain per acre if you're also creating thousands of unemployed people in the countryside at the same time?"

"Makes sense."

"I didn't know what to think, because by the time I got there, anyway, he really was smoking a lot of hash. He had met this guy named Art Baxter, an Australian, and they were living in this little hostel in Benares, which was a pretty awful place to me. But he liked it because it was secluded; they were the only people staying there. By this time he'd become convinced that there was some kind of Interpol manhunt out after him."

"Why?"

"To deport him as politically undesirable. So I kept saying, 'Let's just go. If you're so frightened, we'll go home,' you know, it didn't seem like the end of the world to me, 'so what if you get thrown out of the Peace Corps, you don't have to lay down and die.' But see, he wanted to stay, he said he had some mission to accomplish. And that was the other thing about it, why I thought he was so different. Because all the time I'd known him in college, he'd been completely rational. That was one of the things I respected about him; he was always trying to look at things realistically, without sentiment. But now he'd gotten hipped on Buddhism and Hinduism and all this stuff, which I didn't understand at all. It wasn't that I objected to it, but he was doing it in such a sort of crazy haphazard way.

I would have expected him to have gone to one of these ashrams, and moved in and studied it. If that was what he wanted, he would have done it systematically. But now he and this guy Art were sort of dabbling in it; to me it seemed they were just playing. They kept talking about Buddhism because Benares is where Buddha began his preaching—''

"What? Really? I thought Buddha was from China or somewhere."

"Wrong again," she said, smiling faintly. "Buddhism started in India, although there isn't much of it there now. There's a shrine called Sarnath about six miles out of town, which is where Buddha first, what, set in motion the wheel of the law, and they were always going out there. I've found out a little bit about Buddhism since then, and I know now they had it all scrambled up. They used to sit around and talk about nirvana, and I would get frightened, because it was obvious to me that they had nirvana mixed up with death. They were sitting around all the time thinking about dying.

"Meanwhile, here I was, little old girl from Carolina, wandering around Benares, to escape from them. They'd sit alone and talk all the time; they'd never go out to eat or anything because Willie was afraid of being spotted—''

"But he would go to this shrine?"

"Yeah, he would do all this quasi-religious stuff. He and Art used to go out every morning and bathe in the Ganges, which he claimed was a religious duty.''

"They'd go into the river?" Mac said.

"Sure," she said. "Everybody does in Benares. In the morning."

From somewhere came a memory of a book he'd read in childhood. "Did you know that there is a special kind of freshwater shark that appears only in the Ganges? A man-eater."

"No," she said. "I didn't know that."

"Yes," he said, glad to be able to add something to her story. "It's called something *Gangeticus,* and it's similar to sharks found in Africa and South America—freshwater sharks."

"To be honest, Mac, I sort of wish I didn't know it now."

"Oh," he said.

"He and Art used to like to go out and watch the cremations, too."

"Cremations?"

"Yeah," she said impassively. "They have a special place, the Burning Ghat, where they do nothing but burn bodies all day long. Because Benares is a place people come to die. And they would just sit there and watch the fires burning. It gave me the creeps. And that's one of the ways

105

I knew they were talking about death, even though they called it nirvana and similar horseshit names like that." He saw her lip curl in contempt. "So after a couple of weeks there, I got sick. I thought I was going to die, although I guess I wasn't in any real danger. But I felt awful. And I remember that I had two regrets, when I thought about dying. One was that I had given up smoking for nothing."

Mac laughed. "What, really?"

She laughed, too. "Yeah, I guess if I'd felt well enough I'd have started again, but I felt too crummy to smoke. You don't smoke, do you?"

"No," Mac said. "But I used to smoke about a pack a day."

"You gave it up?"

"Yeah, about two years ago. I got a thing about cancer."

"I'd gone through hell quitting. But anyway, the other thing was that I had lost Willie. Even though he was right there, I felt like he was hiding or that someone else had taken his place, I don't know. So while I was sick, I made him promise me that if I got well—if I got well—we'd leave. And he said okay. Which I thought meant go home, and so I felt like there was some hope. But by the time I got well I found out he and Art Baxter had planned this really terrific trip to Nepal. That was leaving."

"So what did you do?"

"I still hadn't given up on him. I felt like there was no way I could give up on him and survive myself, by this time, because we'd been through so much. So off we went to Nepal."

"You went to Nepal?

"Sure enough."

He looked at her anew: the full body, long dark hair, quizzical face. Here again was a trick played by reality; she seemed to be an ordinary girl, of the same order of creation as Mac, but she was not: she had been to places he could not imagine visiting. "How was it?" he said.

"It's a beautiful place," she said. "Getting there was not very much fun. We took a train to the border, which took about thirty hours, and most of the way there we were crammed into a compartment with eight or nine Gurkhas in battle dress, and if you don't think Gurkhas are scary, guess again. Then we got to the border, and Willie and Art wouldn't hear of waiting till the next norming for the bus to Katmandu; somebody had told them you could hitch a ride on a truck, so off we went. It's about ninety miles to Katmandu from the border, and I was scared to death. The damn road climbs, I don't know, it must be literally a mile high—or more than that, I guess. It's narrow, too, so two trucks can't pass each other very easily. I thought we were going to die right then, which seemed like a hell of a way to reach nirvana, in a Nepalese produce truck. But we got there somehow."

"How long were you in Katmandu?"

"Three weeks, a month, I don't know. We used to hang out at this place called the Tibetan Blue, which was run by some Tibetan refugees, and I really liked them. Tibetans are sort of big people, very energetic and cheerful, and they were always trying to sell us something. But the place was mostly a hangout for Westerners, hash freaks and so on. There were a lot of guys in yellow robes, as if they were Buddhist monks, but they weren't, they were just playing at it. So Art and Willie fitted right in. But I kept thinking something good was going to come of this, that Willie would come around. Mostly by now I was just scared to leave him."

"Why? What were you scared of?"

"I don't know. I guess I felt as if I'd put myself on the line so totally that if it didn't work out, there would be nothing left of me. But anyway they got worse and worse, until I couldn't talk to either of them. Finally, they cooked up this plan to go to someplace where you could see Mount Everest, I forget the name, which was two weeks' travel by cart from Katmandu, and suddenly I realized that they were getting crazier and crazier. I mean, first they would have looked at it, and then, who knows?"

"You mean they wanted to climb—"

"I don't know what they wanted, and neither did they, to be honest. I mean it was still all this nirvana crap."

"You can't climb Mount Everest—"

"I understand that, Mac," she said with some asperity. "It sounded like the dumbest thing yet to me. So I told Willie I wasn't going, and he said wait for me. And I said, no way I will. I'm going home, and if you want to be with me, you should come home, too."

"What happened?"

"Nothing happened. I think it was the saddest moment of my life. He sort of shrugged and said, okay, if I felt that way."

"Jesus." Mac looked at her, intent on the road, eyes full again. Suddenly he felt like touching her, to give her comfort, but he could not.

"That was that." she said, sighing. "Off they went, and I wired my brother for money—you'll meet him—and came on back and tried to get things going again. In the meantime, I felt awful for a long time. I went back to school, but I couldn't dance anymore."

"Why not?"

"I don't mean I couldn't, but it didn't make sense to me anymore. I did my work and stayed in my room. I didn't have many friends, because

107

somehow I felt nobody could understand what I'd been through. For a while I thought I'd hear from him, he'd write or show up, but after a year or so I figured he was dead. I felt completely alone in the world. It was like having to start all over again. So I ended up in this program, they sent me up here, and I felt like I was getting started again, making a few new friends, even dancing a little, and then—'' She slowed suddenly. In the headlights Mac could see the sneaky, dull eyes of a possum trying to cross the road. She swerved to miss it. ''Dumb old thing!'' she said softly.

''And then what?'' he said.

''About ten days ago I got a call.''

''From—''

''None other than Steamboat Willie O'Neill.''

''What? He's back?''

''Apparently so. He wanted to come see me right away, you know, up in Virginia. And that I couldn't see, because I'd spent all this time getting something for myself away from him, forgetting all that stuff he put me through, and then he wanted to show up again, and something inside me said, no, sir. He got really mad, and I compromised and told him I'd meet him down here, at our place by the beach, where my brothers would be and some other friends, maybe. But when I got to thinking, I didn't know anyone to invite. Except, well, except for you.''

Mac was startled. ''You mean he is going to be in North Carolina?''

''Right,'' she said shyly. ''He should be getting in tomorrow.''

Mac looked out the window, stunned. After hearing her story, the idea of meeting Steamboat Willie seemed absurd, like meeting Superman or Gilgamesh. He had become a figure of myth. In the velvet darkness beyond the window Mac suddenly saw the figures of her story, depthless and bright like figures in Indian painting: Willie and Art sitting at Buddha's feet, bathing in the Ganges where the sharks patrolled, then climbing the road to Katmandu, and above them brooding the dark mass of Everest, and on its summit gleaming something bright and indistinct, perhaps—who could say?—the eye of God Himself.

He heard his name being called; then he was again in the car, in Carolina under a blue-black night sky. ''Mac, are you angry at me?'' she was saying.

''Angry?'' he said. ''No, indeed.''

''I've gotten you down here without really letting you in on what it's all about.''

''It's all right,'' he said. ''Don't worry. I'm flattered you asked me.''

''Really?'' She smiled. ''Why?''

''I think it's a long time since anybody liked me enough to do something like this." He thought of his brother's call, of the two of them driving to Wakefield together, now two years and more in the past. He smiled.

"You're really not angry?"

"No."

"Not even a little?"

"Alexandra?"

"Yes?"

"Just drive on."

They were there in less than an hour.

SIX

★

It was a white frame cottage with a screened-in porch, set back from the beach behind a row of dappled dunes. The house was full of warmth and light: Alexandra's family was already there. She introduced Mac to her brothers Jason and Wallace, and Jason's wife, Alice. Jason was the elder of the brothers, tall and dark; his face was almost startlingly like Alexandra's, except for the expression. While she gave an impression of quizzical interest, Jason was friendly but detached, ironic. Mac recognized him as a lawyer, and so he was, for his face seemed to express the skeptical reserve which lawyers adopt in order to practice their art by the pit of human greed and folly without falling in. Alice, his wife, was short, slender, and lithe, with green eyes and hair the color of a wheat field. Wallace looked like Jason and Alexandra, but on him the family's dark features seemed puckish and unpredictable. Mac could not guess what he was thinking. Alexandra said he was an executive at a cement factory in Asheville.

Waiting for them also was a pot of beef stew; Alice grilled cheese sandwiches, and they ate their late supper on the front porch, in semidarkness, watching the ocean. Mac felt at once a kind of bond with Jason; he understood the other's view of the world, having tried it himself in law school; he envied Jason his lawyer's certainty, his faith in reason. Mac found himself telling Jason about the campaign; unlike Alexandra, Jason seemed genuinely interested, although his interest centered less on the question of who would or should win than on the process of winning and losing. Mac felt a bit like a tribesman being interviewed by an anthropologist.

"Do you think your man's going to win?" Jason asked.

"To tell you the truth, I do," Mac said. "I wouldn't want to make that a firm prediction, because politics is volatile as hell. And what we're doing has never been done before, which is usually a disadvantage. But I'd say that we've got a pretty damn good shot."

Jason nodded. The carefully qualified answer seemed to please him. "What will you do if you win?" he asked. "Will you be on the governor's staff?"

Mac was startled. "I don't know," he said. "I don't guess I ever gave the matter much thought."

"That's surprising," Jason said. "I would think one of the reasons people would become involved in politics would be to get that kind of job. I don't mean anything ignoble, but if you are interested in politics, it seems that you'd want to be near the levers of power."

"That makes a lot of sense," Mac said. "I'm not sure my reasons for being in politics are really that straightforward."

"I see," Jason said, although he didn't. Inside the house Alexandra, Alice, and Wallace were playing Scrabble around the big dark dining-room table. Mac stretched himself in his seat and listened to the sound of the surf. He felt admiration for this handsome family, and envy; they were what his own family might have been, had it not become wedded to failure, exile, and death. He closed his eyes and imagined it: Colonel Joshua Tutelo Evans and his wife, Mac's mother, Elaine Kuykendall Evans, enjoying an old age rich in honor and free of ideology, gathered at the beach with their son Lester, his wife, Molly O., and—why not? if the dead were brought back, why not those who had never really lived?— their baby, the infant Joshua II; or perhaps there would by now be two, Josh and little Mary; and with them also their younger son, MacIlwain K. Evans, at ease, self-assured, confident in his fledgling law practice and— why not?—in the love of his new bride, who in reverie had the supple figure of a dancer and a wealth of straight black hair. Inside himself Mac felt a stirring, the leaves of a tree of life shaking in the wind; the shivering traveled up his spine.

At the end of the evening Alexandra showed him to a small room on the second floor, fronting on the ocean. He was to share it with Wallace, who gallantly insisted that Mac take the lower bunk. He was tired from the trip and fell asleep at once.

*   *   *

In dream, his brother Lester came to him, face chalk-white in death, "Hey, bub," Lester said, smiling his infinitely charming, self-deprecatory smile.

"Hi, Lester," Mac said. He was not frightened or surprised in the presence of the dead, but awkward and embarrassed. What did one say to a dead person? "I miss you," he said.

Lester's smile twisted slightly, that bitter, cynical twist Mac had known so well. He felt the full force of his brother's personality back again: its energy and charm, its cynicism and despair. "You may miss me," Lester said, "but I'm dead. You may not miss me tomorrow, but I'll be dead for the rest of my life." He laughed quietly, at himself, at Mac, at death.

Mac struggled for words. He was crying. "Doesn't it help?" he said. "Doesn't that help—to know we miss you?"

But something was happening to Lester; he was fading and curling like an old photograph left in the sun. "How can it help?" he was saying faintly. "I don't exist."

"Lester!" Mac called. "Wait! Tell me—do the dead rise again?"

And though he had all but disappeared, though he was but the ghost of a ghost in a dream, Lester gave again that mocking smile that Mac had loved, so that he could be no one else but Lester, and said as he vanished, "Well, bub, don't hold your breath."

Mac woke, heart pounding. The sun was rising over the ocean. Above him Wallace was snoring gently. Mac had been sleeping on his right hand; it was numb and dead, and in his bones was a chill like frost on a window-pane. He shook his hand angrily, wincing as feeling flowed back into it. But he was grateful for the pins and needles; they proved he was alive.

The others woke early, and they went for an early-morning swim. The sea was slightly chill, but the sun was warm, and Mac frisked in the surf like a puppy. He felt suddenly serene and rested. It felt good to be out of Virginia. After breakfast he stretched luxuriantly on a couch in the main room of the cottage and read *The Last Gentleman* while Alexandra leafed through a magazine. The day stretched before them, serene and untouched, but Mac had forgotten the main event. It came as a shock to him when Wallace came in from the backyard and announced softly, "Hey, Sandy, your steamboat has arrived."

A tall, thin young man entered the room, lugging a backpack and a bold cardboard hitchhiker's sign: N.C.

"Hey, sorry I'm late," he said in a quiet, musical voice. "The rides were pretty slow."

"Hi, Steamboat," Alexandra said. She went up to him hesitantly, and like two children at dancing school, they exchanged stiff embraces.

"Hi, Sandy," he said.

Then there were handshakes all around. The brothers and Alice seemed to know Willie from before; they greeted him with friendly reserve, a slight suspicion.

"This is Mac Evans, a friend of mine from Richmond," Alexandra said.

Willie extended his hand. "Hi, man," he said. There was an uneasy grappling of thumbs, until Mac realized Willie was trying to give him the Movement handshake; he clasped his hand in the old sign of solidarity.

Mac looked closely at Steamboat Willie O'Neill. His dirty-blond hair was combed back from a long, squarish face. His skin hung with a touch of looseness, as if he had lost weight suddenly some time ago and still not gained it all back. He seemed somewhat sheepish and uneasy, and he cast his head slightly down, but Mac could see that his eyes were confident and defiant; they seemed to slice the world into approximate fragments. "Heard a lot about you," Mac said.

"Yeah?" Willie said curiously. "Hope I live up to it."

Alexandra showed him his room. He lugged his backpack and sign off to stash them. Mac noticed much eyeplay and elaborate shrugging of shoulders between the brothers and Alice. Then they were back, and everyone sat around a bit awkwardly while Willie asked the three of them what they had been doing in his absence. They answered briefly. Mac wanted to ask what Willie had been doing, but it did not seem his place. After a few minutes Alexandra said, "I've got to go into town for some things to cook for dinner. You want to come with me, Willie?"

"Sure enough," he said. They drove away, leaving Mac feeling abandoned.

"Think I'll hike up the beach," Wallace announced. "You want to come, Mac?"

"How far are you going?" asked Mac, vaguely interested. A short walk would clear his mind.

Wallace extended his arms, breathing deeply. "Oh, five, ten miles, maybe more," he said in perfect seriousness. "Come on, Mac! A little exercise will do you good. Maybe win the election for you!"

"No, thanks," Mac said hastily. He had not walked that far since his first year of law school; the idea appalled him.

"It's your funeral," said Wallace. "I'm off."

Alice and Jason were sitting on the porch as he disappeared over the dunes. Mac heard Alice laughing. "There goes that fool again," she said in a fond voice.

"What's so funny?" Mac asked. He sat down beside them.

Jason seemed half amused, half nettled. "My wife finds Wallace's fondness for exercise amusing," he said.

"Why?" Mac asked her.

"You tell him, Jason," she said.

"You see, Mac, when Wallace was younger, he never wanted to do anything but read books," Jason said. "A five-mile hike would have been the last thing he wanted to do. Then he went into the Marines, and they gave him survival training and so forth, and since he's gotten out, he's been fanatical about staying in shape, hikes around all the time, lifts weights, and so on."

"That seems sort of admirable to me," Mac said. "He'll probably live longer than any of us."

Alice laughed again. "Yes, but don't you see, he still doesn't want to do anything but read books. He admits it himself. He doesn't want to go hiking up the beach like that, huffing and puffing."

"I'm not sure I understand," Mac said. "Why does he do it if he doesn't want to?"

"Wallace," Alice explained, "has become absolutely convinced that our whole society is on the verge of collapse. I think somebody told him that in the Marine Corps. So he thinks only the strong will survive, and he's spending all his time staying strong. He never gets a chance to read anymore."

"I guess that makes a certain kind of sense," Mac said. "There'll be plenty of time for reading after the end of the world."

They all laughed again. Mac thought about the end of the world. *I'm ready, too,* he thought. *I can organize precinct meetings in the caves.*

Alexandra and Willie returned late from their shopping trip. Steamboat seemed more at ease; he reclined splendidly in a lawn chair on the porch, sipping a beer. Alexandra bustled around the kitchen, ostentatiously busy, preparing a dinner of chicken and rice. As they ate, Willie told them a little about his travels. Mac never found out what had happened on the expedition to view Everest, but they learned that, since leaving Nepal, the Steamboat had put in at Goa, Zanzibar, Cairo, Paris, and Kingston. Mac was awed by the itinerary; during all of Willie's travels, he had been in Virginia.

"What are you going to do now?" Jason asked Willie. Mac thought he detected in his manner something of the stern father, as if he were asking to see if Willie was worthy to see Alexandra.

But Steamboat seemed serenely unaware. He muffed the question. "I don't know," he said. "maybe I'll get some kind of job somewhere."

"A sound plan." Jason probed further. "Doing what?"

"I don't know," Willie said again. "I don't care that much what I do. I don't want to get caught up in a career or anything like that."

Alexandra leaped from the table and went to fetch more rolls. Her face was unreadable. Mac wondered what she thought of her old lover, who had been so sure of himself, so firm in his determination to do good.

After supper Mac watched television with Alice and Jason. The show was about a former policeman who had taken holy vows. A masked hoodlum was tormenting him with a switchblade. "Hey, Father," he said, giggling cruelly, "I am the Resurrection and the knife, get it?"

The priest demolished him with a timely kick to the kneecap. *You don't fuck around with the Lord of Hosts,* Mac thought.

He heard his name being called and turned to see Alexandra, Wallace, and Willie gathered around the Scrabble board.

"Hey, Mac," Wallace called. "Settle an argument for us."

"Oh, let Mac watch TV," Alexandra said.

"What's the dispute?" Mac said. "Come, let us reason together."

"We're arguing about the difference between envy and jealousy," Wallace said. "What do you think?"

"Let's see," Mac said judiciously. "I think 'envy'—you envy things other people have and you don't have, but you are jealous of what you have and they don't."

Wallace shook his head pugnaciously. "That can't be right," he said. "Because if somebody else has a new car, say, you can be jealous of that, so they're the same."

"No, I don't think they're the same," Mac protested. "I mean, you can jealously guard your own possessions, but you can't enviously guard them. I think envy applies only to what other people have, but jealousy goes both ways."

Mac noticed that Willie was looking at him closely. His pinwheeling eyes bounced the abstract definitions back at Mac in different forms, entangling him in a new geometry of relationships.

"Wait a minute," Wallace began again. He seemed to be warming to the argument, but Mac found he did not wish to be drawn further into the discussion. In matters of the heart, he was a poor cryptographer.

"I think I'll go for a walk," he said.

There was a stiff breeze off the ocean; it whipped the grass around his ankles as he passed over the dunes. The beach was deserted, and the tide was coming in. Mac took off his shoes and sat on the sand. The summer after Tom Jeff had lost the nomination for governor and Lester had won it for lieutenant governor—just, he realized, four years ago—Mac had visited his mother in Florida. At night, walking on the beach, he had seen a man flashing a giant flashlight at the horizon, until far off over the water, a tiny point of light responded. Mac had ducked behind a dune, heart hammering, until the conversation ended and the man disappeared and the sea was dark again.

He was lost in a dreamworld of spies and dope runners, and the sudden touch at his shoulder seized his heart in a fist of fear. He turned; it was Alexandra. She was wearing a light-green print summer dress; the breeze molded it to her body, and her hair lifted slightly in the wind. Mac felt a breathless, wistful wrench; the soft complications of her body compelled him like a vision of a home he had not known he had lost.

"How are you doing?" she said.

"Pretty good," he said. He turned back to the ocean. She remained at his elbow, intrusive and warm. "I was thinking about Florida."

"This can't be so much fun for you," she said.

"Hell, don't worry about me," he said. "I'm having a good time, on the whole." He turned to look at her again, and recognized the way she looked as an old friend which had come into his memory to stay. *Girl by Seashore*—from the collection of MacIlwain K. Evans. "How about you?"

She shrugged; her breasts rose and fell like the sea. "What do you think of Willie?"

"I don't know," Mac said. "I don't know what I was expecting, I don't know what he's like now. I can't tell."

"That makes a lot of sense," she said. "The scary thing is that I can't tell either."

Mac watched the sea beyond the breakers. Perhaps a whale or sea monster would sound.

"He's putting a lot of pressure on me," she said.

"To do what?" Mac said.

"He wants to come to Richmond," she said. "Get a job here, live with me, I don't know. He says he loves me. It's like hearing that from a stranger."

Am I a stranger? Mac thought. He wondered if he should say it and find out. He watched for whales and monsters.

"Poor Mac," she said, and her hand was gentle on his shoulder. "Getting dragged into the middle of all this by somebody you hardly know."

He caught hold of her arm. It was firm and strong; Mac pictured her dancing, arm cocked before her, one leg bent, whirling endlessly. "Lis-

117

ten," he said, "this weekend is the best thing that's happened to me in a long time. Don't worry about me."

Their hands met briefly. She gave his a gentle squeeze. "You want to come up to the house?" she said.

"I'll be up in a minute," Mac said. When she was gone, he watched the ocean. That night his lips tasted of sea salt.

Early that Sunday morning Wallace shook him awake. "We're all going to church," he whispered. "You want to come?"

"No, thanks," Mac mumbled automatically and dropped back into sleep. When he woke again, the house felt empty and deserted. He poured a glass of milk and carried it onto the porch, imagining them off at church taking communion. Mac wondered what faith he had. Once he had considered himself a Marxist; that spell had been brief, but he had not since then been able to find any view of the world which could displace that one brief revolutionary moment. Certainly he did not find it in religion. Even if God existed, he usually felt, He—She—It must be impersonal, distant, enigmatic—a being whose sympathy did not connect with the lives of the crazed creatures of this world. But Marxism found supreme wisdom in the blind sweaty struggles of humanity, which to Mac seemed simply the shuffling and reshuffling of a worn deck of cards with suits marked "folly," "false hope," "betrayal," and "murder." So that deity, History, was insane as well; its rituals as strong and moving as the rituals of the church, but as illusory. Mac felt the appeal of both, but to neither could his soul respond with anything but friendly skepticism. He watched the ocean and felt himself a shard of flotsam on the blind human tide.

Suddenly, from within the house, a voice broke into atonal song:

> They're selling postcards of the hanging,
> They're painting the passports brown,
> The beauty parlor's filled with sailors,
> The circus is in town.

Into the main room, hair disheveled, absently zipping his Levi's, shambled Steamboat Willie himself. He saw Mac. "Hey, Mac," he said. "I thought they'd all gone off to church."

"Me, too," Mac said. "I didn't know you were here."

Willie came onto the porch, yawning. "Yeah, man," he said. "I need my sleep."

Mac gestured to a chair, but Willie just hunkered down, resting his but-

118

tocks on his heels. "Breakfast time," he said, pulling a yellow irregular joint from his shirt pocket and lighting up.

Mac was instantly panicked. He looked back and forth for the eyes of informers or state troopers. He saw headlines: SHADWELL AIDE SEIZED IN N.C. DRUG RAID. But the cottage was secluded, and it seemed cowardly to protest.

The Steamboat smoked furiously. When the joint was half finished, he neatly pinched out the tip and put the roach behind his ear. He favored Mac with a broad smile. "You know, in some parts of Africa, people just squat and look at the scenery like this for hours at a time without saying anything," he said. "It's called a *di*. Sometimes they'll go for days without a word being said."

"Did you see this yourself?" Mac asked.

"No, man, I never got into Uganda," Willie said. "Some dude wrote a book about it." As if illustrating the concept, he began looking fixedly at the ocean, his eyes slightly glazed, wordless.

Mac finally broke the silence. "Hey, Willie," he said. "Whatever happened to that guy you were traveling with in Nepal?"

"Who's that, Art?" Willie said, surprised.

"Yeah, that was his name."

"She told you about Art?"

"Yeah."

He shrugged. "Art had some bad luck," he said indifferently. "He got nabbed in Orly Airport with a suitcase full of white powder. He's doing some hard time in France."

Mac winced at the thought. "Jesus," he said. "Were they after you?"

Willie, to his surprise, seemed wounded. "Hey, listen, man, I've got my faults, but I'm no heroin smuggler. What'd Sandy say about me? She must have given me a real talking-down."

Mac shrugged. "Not really," he said.

"But she told you all about me and her and Art?"

"Going to Nepal and so on, yeah."

Willie considered this a minute, like an African at his *di*, gazing into the distance. "Hey, Mac," he said. "What do you think she thinks of me?"

Mac was embarrassed. He averted his eyes, shrugged again. "I really couldn't say," he said. "That's between you two."

Willie nodded gravely and rocked on his haunches. "I guess that makes sense," he said. "Let me ask you this. What do you think?"

Mac looked at him for a minute. "Seriously?" he said.

The Steamboat nodded.

Mac searched for words. "Well," he said finally, "I don't know you at all, but I guess I'm fascinated by all your experiences. I've never traveled at all and I sort of wish I had."

Willie shook his head ruefully. "I'm not sure whether I'm glad I traveled all those places or not. I've been through a whole lot of stuff, you know, that I really can't express, and it makes me feel a little crazy, because here I am, and there's nobody who can understand it all. Maybe I should have just stayed here. I don't know. But then other times I think it was all worth it to find the things I did find."

"What did you find?" he asked.

"You want to know?"

"Yes, I do," Mac said.

"I'll tell you," he said, closing his eyes as if to summon up his memory. "I guess Sandy told you we were in Nepal for a while."

"Yes."

"She left and we stayed on, and we traveled around a lot in the country, and the stuff that happened I won't try to tell you because you wouldn't believe it. Hell, I don't believe it myself most of the time. But anyway, after a while Art split and I was left on my own, and I came pretty damn close to dying. About as close as you can come. I was down for a couple of months—hepatitis, dysentery, a couple of things they don't have names for. I feel like I went right up to death. Hell, I feel like I did die. Like I came back somehow, don't ask me. I have no business being here, on this planet, I mean. So I feel like I have a slightly different angle on life because of that. Like I see things clearer. And I can't explain that to you, because you haven't been through it, no offense. You see what I'm saying."

"I can guess," Mac said hesitantly. "It's a hell of a thing."

The Steamboat nodded again. "Right on," he said.

They sat again silently, like two Africans admiring the scenery. Mac found himself, almost against his will, liking this feckless counterculture Lazarus very much.

Steamboat pulled the roach from behind his ear and relit it. "You sure you don't want some, Mac?"

"Yeah, thanks anyway."

But at that moment they heard the others driving up. "Cheese it," Willie muttered. He pinched the joint out, then popped it into his mouth, chewed and swallowed. "Not a word of this," Willie muttered as the others trooped in, and he gave Mac a wink that made them, somehow, partners in crime.

That afternoon they tossed a football on the beach. Mac threw to Wallace and delighted in making him hustle to make the catch.

Alexandra and Willie were playing in the surf. Mac looked beyond the breakers for signs of marine life, shading his eyes with his hand.

"What are you looking for?" Jason said.

"Porpoises," Mac said. "You ever get them around here?"

"Not much," Jason said.

"Down in Florida, when you see porpoises, you know there are no sharks around."

"Why is that?"

"Sharks are afraid of porpoises. Porpoises are faster than sharks, and they kill sharks; they'll bump them to death."

"Really? I didn't know that porpoises could eat big fish like sharks."

"They don't eat them," Mac said. "They just kill them."

"Really? That doesn't make any sense," Jason said gravely. "I mean, what's in it for the porpoises?"

Mac laughed out loud. "Jason," he said, "I believe if I ever have any law business, I'll bring it to you."

Jason gave him a puzzled look. "Why is that?"

"I'm not sure I can explain," Mac said, "but I just think you must be a pretty good lawyer."

"Thanks," said Jason. "I guess."

At dinner that night they were subdued; the weekend was coming to an end. To lighten the mood, Alice suggested they go to a drive-in movie to see a Peter Fonda double feature. Alexandra and Willie stayed behind.

Mac sat in the back with Wallace and tried to see through Jason and Alice, who were snuggled together behind the wheel. Peter Fonda rode motorcycles in both pictures; in the first he was a gang leader, but in the second he was a college student. Wallace seemed offended by the pictures and loudly pretended to confuse the two plots. "Where's his motorcycle gang?" he asked when Fonda appeared on screen running into his art class.

"Oh, Wallace, drop it," Alice said, fondly exasperated.

"I hope there's plenty of violence in this one," Wallace said.

"There isn't," she said. "It's a sensitive story of love. I read about it in the guide to TV movies."

"Maybe a *little* violence, then," he said.

"Won't you settle for sex?" Jason asked.

"And me an ex-Marine?" Wallace said. "Not on your life."

Mac wondered about Alexandra and Willie. Was he trying to tell her

121

about death? Would she understand? Mac wondered what he would have to tell her, if she ever asked, about death or anything else. *I had a brother, who died, and parents who disappeared, and I can't ever die because I'm not really alive.*

The house was dark when they got back. Jason poured brandies all around, and Mac and Alice and Wallace joined him in a solemn toast to their weekend. As Mac lowered himself into his bottom bunk, it occurred to him to wonder if Alexandra was sleeping alone. He could not ask, of course, and his overbred St. Cyprian's tact forbade him even to think about it too closely. He was sleeping alone, which had become for him a habit, a way of life, and it was not until now, this weekend, among these people, that it occurred to him to regret it.

Monday dawned overcast, with a chill sea breeze—a blustering bully of a day. Mac woke to the smell of bacon frying; he thought of the ominous mornings of his childhood summers, when he would awaken at his mother's house to hear the radio blaring news of an approaching hurricane. Though it still had a day to run by statute, for Mac the weekend was over. Somewhere to the north his candidate would be climbing into a little plane to go to his speaking engagements.

The others were huddled around the kitchen table reading newspapers and eating griddle cakes. "Whole damn world's going to hell," Wallace was grumbling. "Yesterday Asia, today the Middle East, tomorrow it'll be Carolina, sure as we're sitting here."

"Shut up, Wallace," Alice said amiably. "Why don't you give the world a break?"

Jason offered Mac some of the paper. "Want to read about onrushing doom?" he said.

"Hell, no," Mac said. "Give me the comic section. That's where the real news is, anyway."

Alexandra was at the stove, brooding over her cooking. "You better get packed, Mac," she said. "Remember we have to leave early."

"We do?" said dull-witted Mac.

She shot him a furious wordless glare.

"Oh, ah, yeah, right, I forgot," he said.

"You all are going to leave now?" Alice said.

"Right, right," Mac said, thinking fast. "I've got a campaign dinner to go to tonight, and I've got to get back and get some work done for it."

"They make you work on Labor Day?" Jason said skeptically.

"Oh, yes indeed," Mac assured him. "The campaign never stops, you know. That's politics. I was lucky to get this weekend off."

122

Willie entered. "What, are you guys going?" he said, obviously surprised.

"Yes," said Mac. He began to wish Alexandra had not picked him to be her point man. "Got to get back."

"Listen, man," Willie said, looking at Mack. "How about giving me a ride to Richmond, and I can hitch from there?"

Now Mac looked to Alexandra for help; it was, after all, her car and her idea. "We're not going to have time," she said crisply.

"No time?" Willie began, but she cut him off.

"Hitch from here, Willie, you're such a good hitchhiker. Anybody who can get a ride to Katmandu can certainly get one up U.S. One."

Mac tried to soften the blow. "You don't want to hitchhike around Richmond anyway," he said. "They're death on hitchhikers there."

Willie looked at Mac and shrugged. On his face was an ironic smile. Caught once again in unwilling complicity, Mac found himself smiling back.

"Let's go," Alexandra said. "I want to beat the rain."

She asked Mac to drive. In the car she was silent, withdrawn. The interstate was crowded, and rain started falling after a half hour on the road; they made slow progress. Mac thought of Steamboat Willie, his cardboard sign wilting in the rain. But then he reflected that Alexandra was probably right: if he could make it to Zanzibar, he could make it up the East Coast.

"Listen," he said, "I had a really good weekend. Thanks."

She brushed back her hair and looked at him. "I'm glad," she said.

"I don't want to pry," Mac said. "Are you feeling okay?"

She considered glumly. "I feel tolerable," she said. "But I'm pretty tired and confused. I mean, I'm sorry to drag you away, but I wanted to get home and have a little time to myself. School starts tomorrow and so on."

"No problem," Mac said.

After a few more miles, she sighed and looked at him again. "That was as difficult as I expected."

"How are things?" Mac said awkwardly.

"You mean with Willie?"

He nodded.

"I don't know," she said. "It's like a different person."

"You mean than before he went to India?"

"No, I mean since then," she said. "In a lot of ways he's in better shape than I expected. I really think he wants to get back to some kind of real life, but I don't think he knows how."

123

"What does he want from you?"

"Nothing," she said with a touch of bitterness. "Nothing except for me to make it all okay again. He really wants to move to Richmond and have me take care of him, help him find work, everything. He's lost."

Mac hesitated. But he wanted to know. "Are you going to let him?"

"It scares me," she said. "I guess that's how I'm really feeling now, scared."

"I'm sorry," Mac said. "Is there anything I can do?"

She smiled at him shyly. "Just be my friend," she said. "Be around sometimes."

"You've got it," Mac said.

After a while she bunched up her jacket and used it for a pillow. Mac watched her sleeping, head against the window, tangled black hair covering her face, her dancer's body graceful even in awkward chairbound sleep. The car lurched along the wet, crowded road, and Mac wished this tortuous, rainy drive would never end. But soon enough they were back in Richmond, and Mac felt the campaign seize hold of him again. He stopped in front of his house and looked over at the beautiful sleeping stranger.

"I'm here," he whispered. "Can you drive yourself home?"

She stirred sleepily. "Yeah," she said. "Just give me a minute."

He fetched his bag and gave her the keys. She slid into the driver's seat. "Come down for dinner," she said.

"Yeah, I'd like to," he said. "I'll call you."

"Do," she said. He dipped his head to the window; their lips met briefly. He walked back to his little house in the rain, tasting sea salt again.

Part Two

★

ONE

★

Whatever it was, it had happened a long time back, before his brother or his father had been born. That, finally, was the only conclusion Mac could draw. By the time he left home for college he had been over the ground thoroughly, searched books and papers, spent hours questioning his brother and searching his own soul and imagination for the answer to the riddle of what had gone wrong with his family and where, if any-where, it might be expected to end. Sometimes he thought of himself and his brother and even of his father as automatons, blind dolls jigging to a dance piped a century or more before; more often he thought they were living creatures, but bent and twisted, separated from the human stream by some trauma which reenacted itself in new and different forms, life by life, as if each were an expression of one historical psyche, diseased in childhood, now struggling obsessively for sanity. No more than his father or his brother did Mac know why the family must remain in the dance, but he thought he knew when it had begun.

The Evanses had not started as a family with any special mark to set it off from those around it—begun, that is, on this continent. What they had been before, how the Welsh name had found its way to America, Mac did not know or care. For him they arrived in the New World washed clean of their past, as blank and empty as blue sky after a rainy morning. He knew certainly the date of their arrival: 1619. The first Evans, named Edward, had stepped ashore in Jamestown the same year as the first white woman and the first black slave.

But of that first arrival he knew only the Christian name, Edward. Of succeeding generations he knew not even that, for the names were not important to the story. One of Edward's sons had made his way up the James to the fall line, and about 1640 he had settled near Thomas Stegg's trading post, to grow tobacco and corn. There the family had rooted, immovable, while around it grew and vanished Fort Charles and Henricopolis and finally the village of Richmond. One Evans had been hanged in 1676, one of the thirty-odd to gain the honor of being the first revolutionaries hanged in the British New World. He had joined Bacon's band that marched on Jamestown against irascible old Governor Berkeley and had thereby made the family's first acquaintanceship with the consequences of defeat. Another had fought the British at Guilford Courthouse under Light Horse Harry Lee. By then Edward Evans' descendants had left the land and become artisans. They were carpenters, coopers, wheelwrights for four generations before the birth of the man who began whatever it was Mac was studying, the first Evans whose name he knew, his great-great-grandfather, Stephen R. Evans.

Of his great-great-grandfather, Mac knew many facts. In his childhood, when his brother, Lester, had taught him his family history, Mac had heard one version of his life, a story for children of happy times before the war, slavery without cruelty and war without its blundering blind savagery. Even then, however, the tale had been tinged with Lester's own skeptical cynicism, so that the South Mac saw, even as a child, was slightly different from the land of kind masters and happy slaves and noble gray warriors his grade-school teachers had told him about at St. Cyprian's. Even as a child he had known from Lester that it had been more complicated than that, and later, when he could study his great-great-grandfather's life for himself, he stepped into a history that seemed so new and strange that what he had been taught at school seemed all lies, the pathetic deceptions of people who do not themselves know where they came from and so make up stories in the darkness.

That knowledge came when Mac took what the family had of Stephen R. Evans and looked at it for himself. There were certain indisputable facts. Stephen R. Evans was born in 1813 and died in 1871, a soldier who hated uniforms and armies, a slave owner who never planted cotton or tobacco or anything else. There was a photograph, taken in 1858, framed in a heavy gold frame and marked with a dark label, "Roscoe & Richardson, Daguerreotypes, 77 Main St., Richmond, Virginia." It showed a man who, though few men smiled for portraits or photos then, still gave the impression of an unsmiling man, a man for whom life was a serious affair. He was dressed in a sober black broadcloth coat, with a high round collar over a short black cravat. His thick dark hair was swept back from his forehead and curled up slightly behind his face, which was clean-shaven, with a thin-lipped mouth, taut and wary, and thick black eyebrows over dark, dark eyes.

It was the eyes which held Mac. They were clear and deep, and they looked through the photographer into the distance, and what they saw there held them.

The eyes appeared in a reproduction of the portrait which was the frontispiece of a book called *Stephen R. Evans: Pioneer of Southern Industry,* which had been printed in Richmond in 1913, to commemorate Stephen Evans' one hundredth birthday. It was written by Stephen Evans' granddaughter Selma Evans, sister of Bishop Dabney Evans, Jr., Mac's father's aunt. Mac also had two thick heavy volumes, made in England before 1850 out of the finest rag-silk paper and bound in calfskin—made to last, Mac thought, because his great-great-grandfather had not been a stranger to the notion that future generations might have some interest in his life—and filled with small, clear handwriting. They were Stephen Evans' journals, which he had kept from 1850 until April of 1865 and which he stopped keeping when he realized that future generations were likely to take much less interest in him than he had supposed.

Born 1813: by the time the eyes first looked around and considered the future, a lot of people were concluding that there was none, at least not in Virginia. The state was near collapse, old before its time, the soil ruined by two centuries of brutal exploitation. Virginia had given up its territory to the nation, and now what was left of the state was dying, great plantations falling into ruin, the cream of its youth fleeing west to seek fortunes on soil which might stand the same treatment for another generation or two. Stephen Evans' older brother, Micah, was one of these. He left Virginia in 1832 and reared a great plantation in Arkansas and died as a major of Confederate infantry at Pea Ridge, killed when he discovered that the Indian troops of the Five Civilized Nations would not advance in the face of Union artillery, leaving his flank open. A younger brother, Paul, followed their father into the wheelwright's trade; his signature was on the document surrendering Richmond to the Union, as a member of the City Council.

Stephen Evans took a different road. He decided that his future lay in engineering, and by persistence and influence he wangled an appointment to West Point, where he could learn the trade. He was graduated as a second lieutenant in 1834 and spent the next three years poking around coastal forts as an artilleryman, including six months at Fort Moultrie in Charleston Harbor, within sight of an island which would become an important part of his life some years in the future: a pentagonal rockpile later known as Fort Sumter.

Something happened to Stephen Evans while he was in the Army, something never recorded. Or at least Mac imagined that it was something, although it may not have been any one thing, but perhaps just a long process of revulsion and disillusion. At any rate, Stephen Evans forever after showed a cold contemptuous distaste for uniforms and titles of rank and all the pageantry of war, which had, by the time he began writing his diaries, become so firmly a part of his character he never felt called upon to explain it.

He found a way out of the Army. Selma Evans recorded his marriage, in 1837, to Melissa Dabney of Richmond, the daughter of a tobacco manufacturer named Walter Jennings Dabney. A year later the couple had a son, Dabney, and a few months after that Stephen Evans resigned his commission and took off his uniform (from that dry notation Mac got a vivid flash of feeling: the exultation his great-great-grandfather must have felt as he looked down at the crumpled blue tunic and vowed that, whatever fate might hold for him, he would never again hold rank, wear uniform or sword). He came back to Richmond to work as commercial agent for a new venture his father-in-law and a group of others had started, a nail and bar iron factory on the narrow spit of land between the James River and the Kanawha Canal, from which it took its name: the Kanawha Iron and Nail Company.

Mac wondered what Stephen Evans thought of the company when he arrived in Richmond that summer and installed his wife and child in a small house on Fifth Street from which he could walk to the factory. It could not have been impressive, and when he began work there, he found himself little more than a glorified nail drummer. It is certain that both he and the stockholders of the new company wanted more; to them the little nail works was the seed of a larger factory. But for the next three years his efforts to boost sales all somehow went wrong, until by 1840 the nail works was staggering toward bankruptcy. Aunt Selma blamed his lackluster performance on circumstances, and there was something in that: he had come to Richmond in hard times, a year after panic had closed banks and factories and cut credit to the farmers and builders who might buy Kanawha nails. But Mac wondered. Because in the spring of 1840, when Stephen Evans and his father-in-law offered to buy the works and run it themselves, the purchase price was a fraction of what it might have been if there had been back orders and the prospect of new business and other types of iron work within reach.

After Stephen Evans took over the works (installing his wife's younger brother, Jennings Dabney, in his old job as agent and nail drummer), the prospects of the Kanawha Iron Works (as he named it) began to look decidedly better. Within a year Stephen Evans had been to Washington, where a Virginian now sat in the White House, and had spoken in the right ears and came back a confirmed Whig with a contract for fifteen thousand dollars' worth of Navy ordnance: cannon, an item of manufacture which Stephen Evans understood very well. And even while the carpenters were hammering on the new buildings where cannon would be cast, Stephen Evans was cajoling contracts for iron rails out of railroads in Virginia, North Carolina, and Tennessee, and drawing plans for a new building where locomotives and boilers would be made, and for another where iron-plated ships would be built.

Again, circumstance. How could anyone have known that President Harrison would drop dead and Tyler would inherit the White House? But it was certain, beyond doubt, that Stephen Evans had been thinking about the future of the works for some time before he acquired it; it was certain, too, that he had visited his father-in-law's tobacco factory and others like it, the little factories which dotted the "Tobacco Row" on the southwest side of Church Hill. Perhaps he had taken a guest there. The tobacco warehouses were a great attraction for tourists. Not just because it was slaves who rolled the cigars and cut the chewing plugs, although to many who thought the black by nature incapable of anything but field and house work this was wonder enough. What brought gaily dressed visitors to these factories, men fanning their faces with their hands, women breathing through scented handkerchiefs in the heady choking reek, was the chance that they might hear the slaves singing. If they were lucky, they might see an entire small factory force rolling and cutting in unison to a chanted psalm or hymn or hear an impromptu quartet sprinkling licorice extract on leaves for chewing plug while they sang a number complete with solos and self-taught harmony. That Stephen Evans had taken in the sight is evident by the fact that when the time came for him to staff the ordnance plant and the locomotive mills and the other new operations of his Kanawha Iron Works, he did it under a new system of his own devising.

In the early spring of 1840 Stephen Evans hired mechanics from New York, some veterans of works in Philadelphia and Massachusetts, others Germans or Englishmen and Welshmen new to this side of the Atlantic.

So much was customary. Richmond—indeed, the whole South—often found that it had to import its skilled labor, and the cost was often so high as to make chances slim for Southern products to compete with those of New England. But Stephen Evans signed his workers to an unusual contract at well above the prevailing wage. All they had to do to earn their wages was agree to work for five years with a slave apprentice, to whom they would teach their special skill—squeezing, puddle rolling, heating, or puddling—for that period. The terms, Aunt Selma noted, were "exceedingly generous, because Mr. Evans knew that, should he be compelled to discharge any of the men, the violent anti-Negro prejudice then prevalent among the laboring class might make it difficult or indeed dangerous for them to work at other mills if it were learned that they had taught their trades to Negroes."

Maybe it was simply that it took four and half years for the whites to figure out that the slaves they were training would be able to replace them when the contract expired; more likely it was simply that it took them until then to feel strong enough to try to stop it. When they were hired, they were grateful to get work at any terms. There were jobless men waiting to sign the Kanawha contract in place of any that were finicky. But by the time the contracts were expiring the situation had changed. The Supreme Court (Selma Evans recorded her grandfather's outrage) had decided that workingmen might lawfully strike and demand a closed shop. And times were good; the Kanawha works, like those elsewhere, were operating at capacity, enjoying profitable years, with orders backed up for bar iron, boilers, locomotives, iron cruisers, cannon. Perhaps they calculated that they could call the shots, that Stephen Evans could not find white labor to replace them, and that he would be unwilling to take a loss by replacing them with inexperienced slaves. They did not realize they were dealing with a man with a vision. Selma Evans explained:

> The events of late April and early May, 1846, at the Kanawha Works were a grim portent of what has now seemingly become commonplace in factories and mills. The Kanawha mechanics, under the influence of a group of foreign-born radicals, formed themselves into an association, which they grandly titled a Brotherhood of Mechanics. This group, or rather its ringleaders, proposed to dictate to Mr. Evans the conditions under which its members would consent to work at his factory. Following a boisterous meeting on the evening of April 30, they dispatched to him an imperious letter to the effect that they "could not consent to the employment of Negro Slaves in the position of puddlers, rollers, or heaters now or in the future." The note demanded that Mr. Evans agree to exclude Negroes from these posts in perpetuity. If he would not consent to these terms, the note curtly

132

concluded, "he should not fire the furnace Monday, for no iron would be rolled."

By contrast with the haughty tone of the mechanics' letter, Mr. Evans' response was the "soft answer" which befits a Christian gentleman. Addressed to "my late employees," it began by recounting from St. Matthew the parable of the laborers who agree to work for a penny and then remonstrate with the householder who gives the same pay to others who have done less. Mr. Evans used the Lord's saying: "Friend, I do thee no wrong: didst not thou agree with me for a penny? Take that thine is, and go thy way: I will give unto this last, even as unto thee. Is it not lawful for me to do what I will with mine own?"

He concluded by expressing his deep regret that "by attempting to dictate whom I may employ in my Works, you have discharged yourselves. You will oblige me by vacating my barracks immediately. Those who do so will receive full recompense for work to date."

But faced with the long-feared eruption of class antagonism, Mr. Evans was not foolish enough to rely on soft words and a clean conscience. Before dispatching the letter, he had visited with Governor Smith in the Mansion. The governor, who had been following the day's events with keen interest, agreed readily with Mr. Evans' suggestion that a battalion of militia should be called out. Citing Mr. Evans' military training, the governor suggested that the manufacturer, as he was most fully cognizant of the features of the barracks and the potential danger from the men, might wish to command the militiamen himself. Mr. Evans, after some coaxing, at last agreed only upon condition that he should not be required to wear any uniform or bear any title or badge of rank.

Accordingly, the following morning a traveler seated on Gamble's Hill might have seen the unlikely spectacle of militiamen, rifles at the ready, to all seeming about to invade an undefended iron works at the behest of a gentleman in beaver hat and broadcloth suit. Bloodshed was avoided, however, when the mechanics weighed the odds against them and prudently decided to accept Mr. Evans' offer. One by one they took their pay and with their families exited from the Works. The watchful riflemen escorted them to the depot of the Richmond, Fredericksburg, and Potomac Rail Road, which had at Mr. Evans' request prepared a special train to convey them north. They departed to the farewell cheers of a group of merrymakers exhorting them to "Remember us to the abolitionists!"

The alien gospel of conflict between classes had, not for the last time, found in Virginia's soil stony ground.

Stephen Evans was not a man given to public utterances, then or later. But after the strikers had left town, he must have known that he would have to speak loudly and well. The people with power in Virginia—like the powerful people of the rest of the South—did not understand factories or fully trust their owners. Now, in the strike, they had a reason, and the antebellum imagination, a giddy blend of guilt and fear which saw Nat

Turner and Denmark Vesey and Gabriel Prosser skulking always just beyond the edge of sight, would need no prompting to imagine, in the place of those courtly old-world artisans who had written Stephen Evans a mannerly letter, a band of rampaging slave mechanics, armed with hammered swords and hot irons and hungry for white blood. So he set out to calm them; for the only time in his life he tried to explain the vision those calm eyes saw.

Aunt Selma did not include the full text, but glued in the back of the old book was a handwritten sheet. The handwriting was Mac's father's; there was no date. Mac could not guess when his father had gone to a library and copied what he found there onto an outsized sheet of bond and carefully folded it in quarters and glued one quarter to the endpaper and put the book on his shelf to have with him always.

At the top, neatly centered, it read:

RICHMOND DAILY WHIG

May 3, 1846

Gentlemen,

It can scarcely have escaped the notice of any educated citizen of this city, that there have occurred in my Works of late momentous changes of a kind which may affect, not only the future of that enterprise, but of our City and our Commonwealth as well.

In brief, I have been forced to adopt a new system of labor in the Works and have placed Negro bondsmen, some belonging to the Works and others hired by me from individual owners, to work at skilled tasks in the manufacture of iron and iron products. This change is, of course, a matter of business, and fully within my prerogative as proprietor and operator of the Works. I have decided to address the community at large, only because I know that many of our leading men, here in Virginia and elsewhere in the South, have expressed the opinion, that industrial pursuits are not a fit and suitable use of slave property.

With this opinion I must respectfully disagree. For it is widely known and agreed, that the institution of African slavery is the only just and permanent foundation for Republican liberty. And it must also be seen, that the institution of slavery, judiciously applied to manufacture, forms the only infallible basis for material prosperity and domestic tranquillity.

That the African is suited, indeed peculiarly suited, to this type of labor, I can attest from personal experience. He possesses the imitative faculty; and, in the iron industry as in so many others, only a small degree of native intelligence is needed for the acquisition of the utmost skill in industrial operations, however delicate they may be.

Given the slave's suitability, it must be seen at once, that innumerable benefits flow from his use at these occupations. The events of the past week have shown us, what we can expect if we allow to grow within our borders a

134

class of skilled artisans alien to us by birth, education, and religion. My late mechanics, many of them foreign-born, entered into an unlawful combination for the purpose of excluding slave labor from my Works. It must be readily apparent that such a combination is a direct attack upon the institution of slave property and, if it does not originate directly from abolition, is at least pregnant with its evils.

Further reliance on artisans from beyond the borders of the South can lead only to more incidences such as that of the past week. But in the slave system the South has at hand the remedy for all such conflicts between capital and labor. Slavery gives capital a positive control over labor, even in manufactures using whites, as blacks can always be resorted to in times of need.

There are those, such as the Hon. James Taylor and my good friend Mr. Fitzhugh, who hold that we should staff our factories and mills with the white yeomanry of the South. To these gentlemen I reply that this is neither possible nor desirable. The poorer classes of our indigenous white population view factory labor with scorn; nor, in my experience, do they make good hands.

To those who hold, like Senator Hammond, that a Negro mechanic is half a freedman, I say, that it need not and shall not be so. To those masters who may hire to my Works their slaves, and to the community at large, I give a solemn pledge, that all bondsmen employed in my factories shall have adequate care and supervision. I shall prohibit the practice of boarding these Negroes in the community at large. I shall feed, clothe, and house them within the walls of my Works. I have already made arrangements with a white minister to see to their religious instruction. And I shall at all times ensure, that there is maintained at my Works a thorough system of security and a fair but firm discipline.

Lastly, I add a word to those who have warned for more than a decade that the South may be compelled in time to seek its fortunes outside the present federal union. Those who are determined to agitate for such a course, I hold, should above all others be eager to aid in steps which shall build our state's manufacturing capacity and render her in that degree independent of other regions.

Respectfully submitted,
Stephen R. Evans
President
Kanawha Iron Works

Weeks passed; from Virginia and farther South came messages of congratulations. No voice was raised against him. He must have breathed a sigh of relief.

Indeed, his whole life seemed now to relax, as if everything inside him had been waiting breathless for his plans to succeed or fail. Now he was established. After seven years of holding on at the house on Fifth Street, a house too small, too shabby for the master of the Kanawha, he belatedly moved to grander quarters on the west end of Grace Street, from which he would ride to work in a closed carriage. Mac wondered how Melissa Dabney Evans might have felt, after eight years of cramped quarters and making do and a husband who put every spare penny and most of himself into a factory she could not even enter, now finding herself with fourteen rooms with high ceilings and silk drapes and deep Persian carpets and solid mahogany furniture whose dark natural finish threw back the gleam of candles burning in silver candelabra, and padding through it servants with noiseless feet and hushed, deferential voices. Aunt Selma did not speculate. But she did record that, after seven years, Melissa Evans in 1847 gave birth to her second child, a daughter named Sarah after her husband's mother, and that less than a year later another daughter was born, this one named Martha.

Those must have been good years for Stephen Evans. Business was sound at the works. Shipbuilding was off, and he had, as usual, to fight for every dollar the Southern railroadmen would spend with him; they seemed to have a prejudice against iron products cast south of the Mason-Dixon line. But ordnance work was going well. The government needed cannon for the Mexican War, and even a Whig like Stephen Evans could get some tasty crumbs from the War Department table. Then, a few years later, the state of South Carolina decided to insure itself against the possibility that Senator Clay might fail to arrange a compromise. Stephen Evans cast for them sixty-four seacoast and siege cannon and shipped the last of them to Charleston in late 1851. He would see them again.

Aunt Selma told Mac what his great-great-grandfather had been doing in those years, but there was no one to tell him what Stephen Evans had thought. The journals were full of business and the day-to-day notes of a man with a factory and a family. But Mac wondered what Stephen Evans was thinking.

What did he think as he walked through his rolling mill by the canal and watched the slaves producing bar iron, the key to the success of his factory? They did not sing; their work was too loud and too dangerous for singing. There were puddlers, who melted pig iron and worked it into white-hot balls; squeezers and puddle rollers who pounded and rolled it into bars; heaters, who cut the bars into finished bar and rail iron. It was a principle of law that he could fill these jobs with whites or slaves, just as he chose, and with Godlike impartiality he chose for now to divide his labor force equally between the two.

Lining the canal beside the huge rolling mill were the ordnance factory, the locomotive shop, the carpenter shop, and behind them, on the riverbank, long, low wooden barracks: the old workers' quarters, surrounded by a high brick wall, and within the wall, too, a newer, smaller white-washed building: the slave chapel.

It was a seven-acre empire, employing nearly three hundred men, an empire such as few men on the American continent could boast. It began its day at five A.M., when the church bells of Richmond tolled to awaken house servants and the Kanawha drummer rolled his drums to bring the slaves out for breakfast. The forges were heated at seven and ran until five—in boom times later, and in those times even a slave mechanic might earn a bit of overtime, a piece of change he could spend in the commissary or drop in the box at the chapel. White foremen watched the slaves at work. White overseers guarded them at night. No slave could be disciplined without written permission from Stephen Evans; Evans required the use of the short, flexible leather switch, which did not lacerate the skin, and no offense drew more than thirty lashes. He watched each whipping himself and once discharged an overseer who showed too much enthusiasm for the work.

What did he think, Mac wondered, in the evenings, riding up Gamble's Hill and left on Grace Street in his carriage? Changing his shirt, most likely; whatever the calendar showed, it was always summer at the mill, and by day's end his linen would cling and crawl. After he had changed, he would have kissed his wife and bade good night to two sleepy daughers, clinging to the hands of their black nurse. Then perhaps he would speak gravely to his son, now twelve or so, old enough to have a future to think about. Perhaps he would ask him what he had learned from his tutor that morning, or perhaps they might even discuss the week's events and wonder aloud what would happen to the South and the Whig party with Calhoun and Zachary Taylor dead.

Then he would sit at a table as bright as a new drift of snow, and the servants would bear the dinner from the dumbwaiter to the table, and Mac rather imagined that what his great-great-grandfather would be thinking then was that his happiness and his prosperity were secure, that they would last him forever, that he was home free, that God's face was toward him and would never turn away.

But Virginia in midcentury was not the place for secure happiness. That place and time were such narrowly balanced mixtures of truth and illusion, safety and danger, permanence and mutability that his honor and happiness and prosperity were bubbles—passing fancies of the Almighty, gone before they had quite arrived. Stephen Evans believed, or Mac thought he must have believed in those years, that something belonged to him. He stood ready to learn the truth of the matter.

It began at the works, began, perhaps, when in his mind he overreached himself, when he came in his mind to believe that it had somehow been vouchsafed to him within his seven-acre empire to repeal the barriers that lay between black and white in the South of that decade. It began when an Irish foreman named Duffey brought to him a slave named Isaiah and asked Stephen Evans to have him whipped for refusing an order to fire his puddling furnace. When Stephen Evans asked the slave for verification, Isaiah replied that the furnace was unsafe, that had he fired it, he and others might have been burned or even killed. The slave spoke with such quiet rationality and lack of fear that Stephen Evans went with him and Duffey to examine the furnace and found that the slave was right.

He did not discipline Isaiah; he did not discipline the foreman. But from time to time, as he walked through the rolling mill, he stopped to talk to Isaiah. A few months after the incident he wrote in his journal that he had decided to buy Isaiah from his master. "He is in excellent health, and a very apt and ready boy. Indeed, for intelligence, piety, and natural sweetness of humor he is unmatched by any Negro of my experience." He had been hiring the slave from a planter in Chesterfield, for a rent of two hundred and twenty-five dollars a year. When he offered to buy, the owner asked for thirteen hundred dollars. It was more than he had paid for any slave before. But he paid it, for he had plans for Isaiah.

Mac wondered if he was perverting history when he supplied Stephen Evans with some of a father's emotions as he taught the young black the details of the ironmakers' trade. Were the barriers between the races so high that even inside himself—so deeply buried that even he did not truly suspect it—Stephen Evans might not have felt more for this slave than an owner's approbation? Perhaps, Mac thought, his great-great-grandfather had already sensed somehow that Dabney would never be the son he wanted. Perhaps, without knowing it himself, he was preparing another heir.

For whatever reason, Stephen Evans made Isaiah his first black foreman. He did not give him charge of white workers; anyone knew that would have been mortal folly. But, as it turned out, even giving slave a crew of slave mechanics was a mistake. It was more than Duffey, the white foreman who had first brought Isaiah to Stephen Evans, could stand: the slave he had brought to be whipped was now made, inside the factory at least, his own equal. There was no remedy at law. The law, Duffey must have known, belonged to Stephen Evans. Any protest would gain him nothing more than a northbound berth on the RF&P. So one evening (and here Mac had to rely on Isaiah's own account, which he gave later at his trial), Duffey met Isaiah at the door of the rolling mill. The two were the last to leave; Isaiah was now trusted to close up his furnaces and go back to the barracks alone. Duffey had waited for him. Now he cursed Isaiah and slapped him, and then he pulled out his bowie knife and told him to say his prayers.

And for all his piety and sweetness of disposition, Isaiah forfeited this chance to make peace with God. Instead, he grabbed a puddler's long hooked pole and beat Duffey to death with it in three blows. Then in an instant he was out the door and into the river and gone who knew where before the alarm went up.

It was bad, bad enough that Stephen Evans, though he never admitted it even to his journal, must have thought he might be undone. Suddenly the people around him were remembering that Gabriel Prosser had been a mechanic; Denmark Vesey as well. Now they had a slave foreman, who, not content with working equally with white men, must also murder one and make good his escape as well. Certain people were, moreover, not at all averse to seeing a Whig factory master embarrassed, or even to seeing him take a loss of much of what he owned. The *Enquirer*, rival of the *Whig*, pointed a finger: "The sanguinary report from the Kanawha workshops must give every householder in the city and environs pause, and lead him to wonder how secure his person, house and family may be with such a nest of turbulent black ruffians in the city's heart. Grave questions may be raised by those elected to safeguard our property and institutions."

Undone Stephen Evans almost certainly would be if he could not quiet the fuss before the General Assembly came to town that winter. No legislature in memory, of whatever party, had regarded factories as much more than an inconvenience. Now, given the chance, they might embark on an orgy of lawmaking which would at best leave him crippled, struggling along with a plant full of undependable Germans and Englishmen. They might, if they were feeling whimsical, do worse than that.

His only chance lay in capturing the slave himself, and soon, and quietly. His father-in-law and brother-in-law were all for bringing in slave hunters from the Deep South, with guns and chains and dogs. Stephen Evans refused. Something in him revolted at the idea of dogs; anyway, time enough for that. First he hired a detective. Mac read his name: C. D. Sprouse. The journal made no other mention of him, but Mac could see him. He would have been a small man, his clothes wrinkled about his frame like roofing tin, close-cropped countryman's hair over a bullethead, small, quick eyes. Sprouse had an office in Lumpkin Alley, near the jail and the Odd Fellows' Hall, and he had a quiet reputation as a man who could find runaway blacks or, that is, as a man who knew people who often knew where runaway blacks had run. He and Stephen Evans met by night, in the study of the house on Grace Street. Those meetings probably cost Evans plenty. But they were worth it, because one night Sprouse appeared (he must have come to the back door and sent his card in by a servant) with the name of a sawmill. The mill was near a tiny town in the Tidewater, and it was run by a man named Willys. Sprouse was ready to go there, with pistols and a set of leg irons, but Stephen Evans told him no. Isaiah was his slave; perhaps he blamed himself for what had happened. He decided to go alone.

The next day he took the train to Petersburg. Then, because the tracks did not connect, he spent a night in the Exchange Hotel. The journal recorded that he rose early and took a slow, smoky, rattling local to a place called Jeter's Crossing, arriving when the sun was beginning to fall in the sky. He pressed on, renting a horse from a depot idler who identified himself with the lordly title of Captain Davis. He rode for nearly an hour, following the directions to Willys' Mill:

The fields through which I rode were of a poor sort, coarse and sandy, where grew nothing but pines and broom-sedge, with here and there a berry-bush or a sassafras tree. I judge it had been used up and abandoned as little as five years before, for in many places the pines were dwarves, not exceeding five feet in height. Of wildlife there was little, save an occasional pack of wild hogs, scurrying about for all the world like hounds on a hunt. I had in truth begun to wonder if I had not mistaken the directions when the horse gave the reins a shake and I saw the creek to which I had been directed. This gave out into a clearing, at the end of which I discerned the mill. It was unpainted, and the sides seemed to lean toward the middle. I reflected that any mill which occupied itself supplying the farms of this area must perforce be a poor one; and indeed, though it was not yet three thirty o'clock, no sound came from within, and the whole gave an air of desolation, as if it had been, not simply shut for the day, but abandoned altogether. However, I rode closer, and soon noticed a singular individual whom I took to be the sawyer sitting motionless on the steps. He was hairless, and of such a gross degree of obesity that he reminded me of the heathen idols Chinamen are said to worship. He was dressed in the plainest, dirtiest homespun, and his moon face was topped with what appeared to be the crown of a straw hat from which the brim had been cut away. He did not seem to regard my approach, for he was staring at a small sausage in his hand with an expression of deepest reverence, so that I briefly entertained the notion that he was engaged in some sort of blasphemous prayer. At length I called to him, and he started and gave every evidence of terror, but rather than speak or flee, he remained sitting and contrived to stuff the sausage into his mouth all at one bite, as if he feared that I had made my ride for the single purpose of depriving him of dinner.

I saw that I would have to wait for my reply until the sausage was eaten, so I fanned myself with my hat, smiling the while to indicate that I was not come on a mission of sausage theft or any other bit of mischief.

At length, when I saw that it might be profitable for me to speak, I bade him good day and asked if he were Mr. Willys. He seemed to consider this a while, and replied, "Well, Colonel, this is my mill, yes, sir."

"Please do not call me Colonel," I replied, "as I am not one."

With this he doffed his extraordinary cap and bobbed his head. "Your pardon, Major," he said, "I'll not call you one more."

I declined to argue further over titles. I told him that I had come as a friend of a Negro named Isaiah, and that I had been given to understand that the Negro had been employed at this mill.

At this he became very warm and seemed disinclined to pursue the discussion. I hastened to assure him that I was not an agent of the state, nor did I purport to embroil him in legal trouble. "If the Negro lives nearby, you would render me a service to direct me thither, and I will gladly pay you for your trouble." He replied nothing directly, but said in a voice which betrayed agitation, "I am a law-abiding man, Major, and I don't know nothing about those as I hire but what they tell me."

"I am sure that is true," I replied. "Nor would I wish to discuss the matter with anyone in authority who might take a different view. But permit me to suggest that it is to your interest in more ways than one to satisfy me insofar as you are able."

Perhaps as a result of his hasty meal of sausage, my informant began to appear somewhat distressed, and said, "I don't know nothing about where anybody lives at all, Major, because I don't ask 'em. So I can't tell you nothing about that. But you are free to come tomorrow if you like, and if I was you, sir, I'd come about noontime."

"And will Isaiah be here then?" I inquired. To this he replied with a resounding belch, and mumbling, "Noontime, noontime, good day," he dashed into the mill and closed the door, leaving me to find my way back to the depot before the light failed.

Once there, I agreed with Capt. Davis that he would rent me the horse the following day, and upon learning that I would be remaining, he suggested that he and his wife would be delighted to have me as their guest for the sum of three dollars. To this I readily agreed, less because of any anticipation that his lodgings would prove memorable than because I knew how difficult it was to find a householder who would open his door to a stranger for any sum. The evening meal proved to be one I would not serve at my commissary, nothing more than cornbread, bacon, and thick black coffee. But my day's ride had awakened my appetite, and I ate all that I was given and wished it could have been more. We ate in silence. I do not remember that Mrs. Davis spoke once in my hearing, and the Captain himself bestirred only once, to ask me the going price of Negroes in the Richmond market. I replied that I had recently purchased several strong young males and paid in each case more than one thousand dollars. He gave a grunt, and opined that a man who had Negroes might make a tidy bit of money, but, alas, he had none to sell, to which I commiserated.

When I had bid them good night, I retired to my room, which was a narrow bare chamber lit by a single candle, containing a small bed and a low wooden table, and nothing else. After latching the door, I knelt at the foot of the bed and prayed to God that He might grant me success on the morrow. And as it had not failed to occur to me that I might run some personal danger, I commended myself to His keeping, now and forever, praying only that, if I should perish, He would keep my wife and children safe after I was gone. Then I crawled into the little cot, and contriving to curl myself into such a position as might serve for sleeping, I closed my eyes. As the mattress seemed to be stuffed with pine cones, I had virtually despaired of sleep, when there stole across my soul a deep sense of peace, and I felt a reassurance and comfort which I am convinced could have come only from above; and so I slept without dreaming the night through.

In the morning I was given breakfast which differed from dinner only in lacking bacon. Then I whiled away the morning sitting at the depot with Capt. Davis and other gentry of Jeter's Crossing, who spent their time making wagers on the trains that passed, guessing whether each would appear early or late. Capt. Davis, who always bet on late, was a consistent winner.

At length the sun grew high, and I confess to a bit of reluctance as I mounted Capt. Davis' horse, but there was no help for it, and I must go on. So I made the same bleak ride of the day before.

This time, on my arrival, the master of the mill was nowhere to be found. I rode into the silent clearing and looked about, but I could not see or hear any sign of human life. I waited thus a quarter hour, and had begun to reach the conclusion that Isaiah had escaped me, when a slight sound made me turn my head. I felt a thrill of fear as I descried a gigantic coal-black Negro of purely African type, such as I judged to have been at one time a field hand on a large plantation. That he was no longer in service was evidenced by his attire, consisting only of a pair of much-mended and torn homespun breeches and a suitcoat which seemed as it might have belonged not too long before to a well-dressed gentleman. His head and feet were bare, and from head and beard issued a profuse jungle of grayish woolly hair. He was watching me, motionless, and his expression and the rigidity of his limbs betokened instant readiness to flee.

We regarded each other silently for a few moments, though to me they seemed much longer. Then, putting his huge finger to his lips, he signaled me by gestures that I was to dismount and follow him. I hesitated, but then, remembering my prayers and their response, resolved to trust God in this matter. I tethered my horse and followed this silent Hannibal into the undergrowth.

We scarce had passed out of sight and hearing of the mill when the Negro whirled on me and I saw in his hand a large bowie. In that instant I gave my soul to heaven and counted myself as dead. But though he held the knife at my throat, he did me no harm, but signaled me not to move while he ran his hands under my jacket in a most familiar fashion. Then, having satisfied himself that I was unarmed, he replaced the knife in a most ingenious leather sheath inside his coat from which he showed me he could instantly retrieve it. Again laying a finger over his lips, he led me further.

I can conceive no notion of how much longer we went on, as we traveled a circuitous and confusing route and my thoughts were by this point in some disorder. But at length we came to the remains of a burnt-out cabin, which still retained three walls and a portion of roof. My guide pointed and indicated that I should enter this. Then he soundlessly backtracked on the path we had followed, turning his broad back to me without fear.

Warily I stepped over the threshold. It was obvious at first glance that no one was presently living inside. But when my eyes adjusted to the dimness, I saw Isaiah in the corner, seated on a stump. He rose and, to my surprise, greeted me warmly. I remarked how thin he had become. He smiled graciously and said, "I have been hunted, Mr. Evans, and I have suffered like an animal who is hunted."

I thanked him for seeing me, and remarked on the fright the large Negro had given me.

"Sam must be very careful," Isaiah said. "He has lived here for ten years or more, and no one has caught him in that time. I apologize if his familiarity upset you, but he will not do you any harm." He added that he, too, was happy to see me, and inquired after the works, and after his old mates at the rolling mill. I told him of the difficulty caused by his escape, at which he seemed genuinely penitent.

"I am sorry for the difficulty, truly," he said. "But I killed that man to save my own life, and when I realized that he was dead, and that I was the only witness, I knew I had to get away. I do not want to hang, Mr. Evans." Here he fixed me with his eyes, and they were of a curious expression, pleading and, at the same time, questioning.

"You will not hang," I told him. "The law recognizes that a slave may strike back at a white man in self-defense."

"I was the only witness," he said. "And no white man would speak up for a slave who had killed a white."

"I would, Isaiah, and I will," I told him. "I know what sort of man Duffey was. I believe you. And with me to speak in your behalf you will not hang."

"You would speak for me?" he said in amazed tones.

"Indeed I will," I told him, and then added the words I had come to say .
"I want you to come back to Richmond with me now, Isaiah," I said. "We will go back on the train, and there will be no pistols or chains on the trip. There is no posse with me, and you will come to no harm. But if you do not, they will hunt you down, sooner or later, if they must level half the state to do it, and when they find you, they will hang you without bothering about a trial. The white people feel very strongly in this matter; for you there is no escape. This is your one chance to live."

He jumped up, his eyes rolling in agitation, and made as if to run out of the shelter. "No, no!" he cried. "They will hang me! They will hang me!"

I took his elbow and looked him full in the face. "No, Isaiah, you shall not hang," I said. "I will speak for you at your trial, and they will listen. I had hoped once that you might earn your freedom, but now that will not be tolerated. But you shall be deported and freed. Liberia will be better than this swamp. And I give you my solemn promise that you will not be hanged."

"You give me your word?" he asked.

"I do," I said.

"And you will speak for me?" he asked.

"I will," I said.

He sat again on his stump and appeared for some time completely lost in his thoughts. Then he stood, and said, "Mr. Evans, you have always treated me fairly and well. I do not believe that you would try to trick me. I will go with you and trust your word that I will be deported."

We started at once out of the house. I looked about for the fearsome Sam, but Isaiah told me the big Negro would not come within sight, but would follow us back while maintaining his concealment. All the way back, I neither heard nor saw him, but I imagined his eyes on me, and recalled vividly the cunning arrangement by which he carried the bowie inside his coat.

However, we reached the mill without mishap. As I placed Isaiah on the horse before me and prepared to ride away, I heard the door of the mill open, and the rotund Mr. Willys appeared before me, dressed as before. He expressed pleasure that all had gone well, and reminded me that I had promised not to mention his name, and bowed to me and obstructed my way generally until I saw his intent and produced a banknote. He at once hid the money in his hat and returned to his mill. I reflected that he was assured of sausage for some weeks to come.

At the station my appearance with a strange Negro caused some comment, and worthy Capt. Davis grumbled a bit about overloading his horse. I paid him too a bit extra. But withal I was still glad when the train arrived. Once aboard we were no more remarkable than any other gentleman traveling with a servant. As the train to Suffolk pulled out, Isaiah stared out the window, seemingly lost in his own thoughts, while I silently raised my eyes to heaven and give thanks for my preservation that day. Then, marveling at my temerity before the Throne of Grace, I prayed that I might not be made a liar before this Negro, but that I might be permitted to keep the promises I had made that day.

Mac thought that Stephen Evans had probably intended to go to the trial, at the time he'd made his promise, anyway. But his father-in-law and brother-in-law would not hear of it. And once he looked at the matter rationally, Stephen Evans probably had to admit that they were right. There had been danger to the works; that danger had all but passed when Stephen Evans brought Isaiah back with him and turned him over to the sheriff. But the danger would return if the people saw the master of the Kanawha openly defending a slave who had killed a white man. It would frighten people, and outrage them as well, for they would be quick to conclude that slaves whose master defended them thus were very likely to do more killing and that the only way to be safe would be to move the slaves out of the city and break up his labor force.

He stayed in his office at the factory on the day Isaiah went before the Corporation Court. Five white judges found the slave guilty and sentenced him to hang. But Stephen Evans did not break faith completely: Isaiah did not hang. Mac wondered what flattery, or threats, or promises, or bribes, his great-great-grandfather had used on the governor (it was not long after this that Stephen Evans abandoned the drifting hulk of the Whig Party, and his great-great-grandson, schooled young in the cold logic of the *quid pro quo*, wondered if there had been a connection there). Whatever he did, it was powerful enough to make the governor willing to take the squall that came after he signed an order commuting the sentence to fifty lashes and deportation to Liberia. Stephen Evans went to Isaiah's cell to give him the news. The journal reported that Isaiah would not speak or look at him, by which he wrote he was "greatly saddened." So Isaiah passed out of his life.

He had been able, for the moment, to save the works. He could not do the same for his family. Less than two years after Isaiah left on a boat for Monrovia, in the summer of 1854, cholera cut its way through the city. Most of the deaths were in the valley of the Shockoe Creek, where the city's poor whites lived, but the disease came to the house on Grace Street, and it carried off Melissa Evans and her six-year-old daughter Martha. It left Stephen Evans with a sixteen-year-old son, Dabney (getting ready for his first year at the University, which he was to enter the fall after his mother died) and a seven-year-old daughter, Sarah, and a big house full of quiet black servants to cook his food and clean his clothes and care for his little girl, and silence and darkness in the rooms where his wife had walked.

It was after this that Stephen Evans began to write and talk about the end of the United States of America. When the change had come, neither Mac nor Aunt Selma nor anybody else knew for sure. Mac admitted that his position made hard economic sense. In a new Southern nation the Kanawha Iron Works would perforce be dominant. Stephen Evans was finding, in that sixth decade of the century, his back pushed further and further to the wall by the Northern ironmasters, who, for all that they might not have the cost-cutting advantage of slave labor, still had cheaper fuel and better ores and newer methods of smelting, rolling, and casting. A Southern nation would contrive to keep their products out. There would be a Southern army to equip with Kanawha cannon, a Southern navy in need of Kanawha steamers, Southern railroads whose Kanawha locomotives would pass over Kanawha rails. Others in those heady days perhaps saw a planters' commonwealth, a gaudy tropical slave empire stretching from Virginia to Guiana. Stephen Evans saw an empire of iron.

But neither biography nor journal could offer an answer to the question of how much of Stephen Evans' newfound ardor for disunion arose out of the defeats he had met at his works and in his home. There could, however, be no question that he embraced the cause of secession with quiet, methodical zeal. His move away from the Whig Party was complete by 1856. He supported Buchanan for president and Henry Wise for governor, and he and Wise became more than political allies. Wise was a loud, impetuous, irrepressible fire-eater, and he became Stephen Evans' friend and his tutor in the politics of disunion. For the next three years Stephen Evans traveled to the Southern businessmen's conventions as Wise's apostle, preaching the new gospel of secession and the Southern Empire.

But though his cause was headed for its profitless victory, Stephen Evans himself had another defeat to suffer. No picture remained of his son, Dabney Evans, as he had been in 1857. Mac could imagine him as a younger version of the father, with the lift of pride in his chin where Stephen Evans showed only a sober businessman's resolve. Certainly he must have lacked his father's pious, phlegmatic, calculating temperament; as a young brave in the freedom of the University he must have been energetic, mercurial, arrogant. He became the center of a crowd of flamboyant idlers—a type of extravagant wastrels which the University had been breeding since its inception, was still breeding in Lester Evans' time, and Mac's. They drank, and gambled on cards and dice and backgammon, and raced horses and fought cocks, and at night they visited the venerable bordellos of Albemarle County. There was in their giddy intense round of pleasures little time for the disciplines Stephen Evans must have hoped his son would acquire: prayer, the classics, mathematics, history, a sense of the world and a businessman's vision of his own place in it. But the father seems not to have been aware of his son's real course of studies until Dabney Evans sampled the last of a young gentleman's pleasure and had to come home.

It seems to have started over politics: so Stephen Evans, though he was and would remain distant from his son's life, played his part in the story. It was a dispute which began as the young men were drinking sour mash whiskey. A boy named Peter Boyd made a remark about traitors and turncoats—meaning, apparently, those who had left the Whig Party. The boy's father was a planter from Accomack, a "Know-Nothing"; the old man had lost his seat in the legislature in the Democratic sweep, and father and son were bitter. Dabney Evans asked sharply to whom the harsh words were meant to apply. Surely, he hoped, not to all those who had left the party to support Governor Wise? Yes, the other had answered, drunkenly belligerent; all were traitors, men who had cast off principle at the bidding of opportunity. Dabney Evans told him that his words were an insult to any number of honorable gentlemen, and most particularly to Dabney Evans' own father, and thus to Dabney Evans himself. He gave

Peter Boyd a chance to withdraw them and apologize. Peter Boyd didn't take the opportunity, and Dabney Evans demanded a chance to avenge himself and his father and perhaps the whole Democratic Party.

What they were planning to do was illegal, so they took a train across the North Carolina border. Mac would see them in a clearing not far from the depot, just out of sight of the road, four young men, shaking from excitement and the early-morning cold of March, not perhaps fully realizing that they were in earnest as the two principals paced away from each other, one of the seconds holding a carven case from which they had each taken an ivory-handled dueling pistol, not, that is, realizing they were in earnest until the flash of the pistol, the start of blood, until they saw and understood in a ringing silent timeless moment that Dabney Evans had shot and killed his classmate and drinking companion, Peter Boyd.

Dabney Evans came home to Grace Street in dishonor. There would be no legal steps taken against the son of a man like Stephen Evans, but the scandal made it impossible for the son to continue at the University. Mac imagined that Stephen Evans was perhaps just then discovering that between his son and himself there was now a gulf fixed, that he could not control him or keep him out of trouble in Richmond or anywhere else. That was the only reason Mac could imagine why Stephen Evans, with his feelings about armies and uniforms, should have sent his son in the fall of 1857 to finish his education at the Virginia Military Institute. For though they would dress him in a tunic and teach him to salute and pass smartly through the manual of arms, the whole martial charade his father despised so thoroughly, they would also watch him and keep him out of trouble. Watching his son day and night was something Stephen Evans, busy with his politics and his ironworks (being a secessionist didn't mean, apparently, that a businessman should not turn an honest profit by selling the U.S. armed forces rifles and cannon and shot and shell), had neither the time nor the inclination to do.

The son passed through the Institute and got his commission while his father worked to dismember the nation that gave it to him. On his graduation Stephen Evans spoke a few words to an old associate, former Governor John Floyd, now Buchanan's secretary of war, and his son was sent to Fort Fisher as an artilleryman. But there was apparently little communication between them. In those last few years before war Stephen Evans was busy. On the first day of December, 1859, he again conferred with a governor about a hanging; not, this time, the hanging of a slave but of a white man who sought to free slaves, not this time to urge mercy but to bid the governor carry out the sentence of the court in its full severity. He found his friend Henry Wise already resolute, so the next day John

Brown went to the gallows. A year later, as a Southern rights man, Stephen Evans spoke publicly for Breckinridge; even before the results of the election were final, he was receiving orders from Southern states for ordnance and ammunition to resist Abraham Lincoln and the Black Republican madmen.

South Carolina led the way. Two weeks after the convention in Charleston voted to secede, Stephen Evans got a telegram from Governor Pickens in Charleston. The Palmetto Republic needed some ammunition for the sixty-four cannon the Kanawha works had sold it ten years before, on the off chance that the federal government might be so foolish as to refuse an offer of orderly purchase of U.S. property in Charleston harbor: Fort Johnson, Fort Moultrie, Castle Pinckney, and Fort Sumter. Evans wired back at once: he could get shot and shell in a matter of weeks. "Prices same as to U.S. government." And to make sure the inexperienced gunners of the new nation used their Kanawha cannon to advantage, Stephen Evans would be delighted to accompany them south and supervise preparations for their use.

By the first week of March, 1861, Stephen Evans was in Charleston. This was the holy city of Southern defiance, the Jerusalem of secession, the capital of the entire region's imagination. But Mac's great-great-grandfather found it strangely shabby and tired. It seemed to have changed very little since he had served there in the Army more than twenty years before, save to grow poor and older, as if the culture of the great plantations could live only by sucking the life from their cities.

On the day he arrived he went to work touring the batteries. By now the seventy-man federal garrison had retreated to Sumter, leaving the other forts in the harbor to the secessionists, and the Carolina militia had been at work since Christmas erecting batteries against the last federal stronghold. Gangs of slaves had labored by torchlight to bolster the positions at Fort Moultrie and Fort Johnson. In addition they had erected new emplacements on James Island, Mount Pleasant, Cummings Point, and Sullivan's Island, and a group of enterprising desperadoes had even built a floating battery, a seagoing house of death which could be towed up to Sumter's gorge wall to fire its four siege cannon. Stephen Evans noted all this in his diary, with the dry professional detachment of a former artilleryman. He was impressed with the number of weapons the South Carolinians had brought to bear, but the secessionist artillerymen struck him as amateurs who needed professional supervision.

That night he stayed at the Charleston Hotel, one floor up from Governor Pickens's temporary quarters. The next night the governor sent an invitation to a dinner in honor of the commander sent by the new Confederate government to take charge of operations in the harbor. Stephen Evans found General Beauregard almost everything he disliked in a soldier (he noted with distaste that the little Creole used black dye on hair and mustaches), but the two agreed that the Carolinians had aimed too many of their guns at the fort itself; more should be deployed at the mouth of the harbor to forestall an attempt by warships to resupply the fort.

At dinner, Governor Pickens showed Stephen Evans a gift he had received from another Virginian, Edmund Ruffin—one of the pikes Brown's men had used in their raid against Harpers Ferry. "A sample of the favors designed for us by our Northern brethren," said a label provided by the old man. Evans handled the grisly thing gingerly, and said stiffly that Ruffin was a remarkable man who had done the South a great service in discovering how used-up soil could be restored. To his journal he confided that he considered Ruffin a malign old rogue with the temperament of a fanatic.

One of the ladies said she thought it unseemly for Ruffin to be stumping about Charleston urging an attack on Sumter; one so old should not be so eager to bring about suffering and bloodshed by the young.

Senator Chesnut politely replied that the lady need not worry about suffering and death. "The Yankees plainly have no stomach for a fight," he told her. "I myself will drink all the blood shed in gaining our independence."

Beauregard, a proper soldier and a polite guest, held his tongue. But Stephen Evans said mildly, "I hope you will not, Senator, for I fear it would be a long and bitter draft." Chesnut probably eyed the Virginian with some surprise, but he said nothing.

With Beauregard on duty, Stephen Evans concluded he could leave his guns and ammunition in good hands. But before he left Charleston, he had a call to make.

It was a windy March day, and rain blew into the open boat. Mac saw his great-great-grandfather standing up in the bow, stiffly enduring the rain in his sober merchants' garb, holding aloft a flag of truce as the oarsmen rowed him nearer to Fort Sumter.

When they reached the walls of the fort, issuing sheer out of the harbor as if it had been stuck there by God Himself, Stephen Evans sent a message to the commander, Major Robert Anderson. Did Major Anderson remember Cadet Evans, who had been his pupil in artillery at West Point two decades before? Anderson did; the two had known each other well, for as Stephen Evans noted, they were "brothers in Christian faith." Now Anderson insisted that Stephen Evans stay for dinner at the fort. It was a sketchy meal, eaten in a room so chill Stephen Evans could see his breath. For lighting the officers used a dab of oil in a coffee cup, with a wick floating on a sliver of cork. Afterward, Major Anderson and Stephen Evans knelt together in prayer, though what they prayed for—it could not have been peace or the future of the Union—Mac did not know. Then they walked on the esplanade and Major Anderson pointed across the harbor to the indefensible position he had surreptitiously abandoned in order to invest Sumter—Fort Moultrie, the guns of which, manned by secessionist volunteers, were now pointed at Sumter.

"There has been much criticism here of my decision to move," Anderson said. "But you can see that I was obligated to come to Sumter to protect the men in my command."

Stephen Evans replied somewhat stiffly that every soldier must follow his orders.

"Ah, Mr. Evans," Anderson said. "Very few soldiers have had such orders as mine. They are no orders, or next to none. I must do my best."

Then Stephen Evans bade his host good-bye. "God bless you," Major Anderson said. "I know we shall meet again, here or in another life. When we do, let us remember our friendship, and not the passions which have pulled our nation apart."

The next month, when Beauregard's men opened fire on Major Anderson, Stephen Evans raised the stars and bars over his factory. "If Virginia does not secede, I will take my Works and move them South," he wrote to the newspapers. Five days later Virginia had seceded, and Stephen Evans' first act was to write the governor a comprehensive schedule of those workers he needed exempted from military service if the factory were to serve the new nation efficiently. The governor agreed at once; it had occurred to him and others in authority that Stephen Evans was now the only man capable of supplying the Confederacy with ordnance and ammunition.

One of those Stephen Evans wanted exempt was his son, Dabney. The young man's training in artillery would be valuable at the works. This was plainly what the father had intended for his only son all along. Mac wondered if it had ever occurred to Stephen Evans that his son might not share that ambition; he thought probably not, for Stephen Evans seemed to have learned very late in life the father's bitter lesson, that his children are not himself. Mac could, if he looked long and hard at the opacity of the past, if he cleared his mind like a radio receiver scanning for faint signals from the stars, summon up his great-grandfather, twenty-two-year-old Dabney Evans, as he must have been then. How could Stephen Evans have imagined that the young man Mac saw, this hot-eyed, violent, mercurial scapegrace, would share his own fastidious disdain for the gaudy trinkets and lethal toys of war? How could he have thought that his son would be content to take off his U.S. Army uniform and don his father's sober broadcloth, to spend the greatest war his country would ever see behind a desk at the factory, ticking off on rolls of foolscap the mounting quantities of pig iron and coal received, or ordnance and iron trans-shipped? It defied belief, yet it was so. For Stephen Evans was outdone, seized with a father's blind disappointed rage, when his son without seeking permission or advice resigned his U.S. commission and signed on as a captain of infantry in a unit commanded by an artillery teacher he had studied with at VMI. Stephen Evans' journal recorded his outrage and disbelief. His son had thrown away a chance to serve the Confederacy and himself, to do well by doing good at the Kanawha Iron Works and, as if that were not enough, had not even sought the help his father would have been willing to give once convinced his son was determined to be a soldier, the influence which could have gained him a staff commission under a reliable, respected man: a Confederate officer of breeding and reputation, such as Governor Wise or Secretary Floyd. Instead, Dabney Evans had chosen to serve under a strange, ragged fellow. Stephen Evans had heard of him, a pious, silent man without money or family to speak of, a flinty psalm-singing Valley Presbyterian so lost in the love of Jesus and his own impossible dreams of glory the other instructors at the institute called him Tom Fool: Thomas J. Jackson. It was, Stephen Evans wrote, an insult by an ingrate son; worse than that, it was a mistake.

But he accepted it and settled in to fight the war from the foot of Gamble's Hill. While the blue and gray armies skirmished for Missouri and Arkansas and Kentucky, while Johnson and Lee dueled McClellan and Pope and Meade, Stephen Evans fought his own battles with incompetent mine owners and speculators for pig iron and copper and coking coal, with obstinate clerks and generals for exemptions and details of skilled labor, with purchasing agents and quartermasters for corn and pork and beef to feed his workers, with who ever might be Mr. Davis's current secretary of war for higher prices for ordnance and ammunition.

But though it was an uphill fight, in the first two years of the war Stephen Evans won some of his battles. His cannon saw action in the Confederate victory at Fredericksburg; his iron plate was used to armor a former U.S. Navy ship, raised from the James and rechristened CSS *Virginia*; his ship plate was fashioned into the first submarine the world had ever seen; his rifle factory fashioned the world's first machine gun, the Williams rifle. He expanded his plant and hired more slaves, and they poured out rail iron, bar iron, nails, shot, shell, Minié balls: Mac's great-great-grandfather, almost alone, it seemed, fueled the Confederate war machine.

In the first two years of war Stephen Evans approached his job with a businessman's calm. His diary was laconic, terse, containing chiefly notes on the prices of iron and slaves, the difficulties of rail transport, the progress of contract negotiations with the War Department. In those two years he saw many changes in his city. Much of it was transformed into prisons—prisons at Belle Isle and Chimborazo Hill for Union prisoners, prisons on Main Street for the government's political opponents. Much of the rest—schools, churches, private homes—became hospitals for the parade of wounded and dying from Lee's armies in the North. In the center of the city, in the old stream bed, which had before the war been considered unfit for use by any but the poor whites and free blacks, now appeared and disappeared the saloons and bordellos and gambling hells which catered to soldiers and Confederate officials and speculators, all operating under the benign protection of Mr. Davis's imported police, the plug-uglies.

The new nation was being squeezed by Union armies which were cutting it in half, and by navies blocking its ports, and by diplomatic and economic blundering which denied it the foreign exchange and diplomatic recognition it needed. It was squeezed from within by inflation, by scarcity and mismanagement which wrecked its currency and agriculture until Stephen Evans found he had to pay his factory's bills in barrels of nails and not its worthless paper money. It was squeezed by political fumbling and squabbling until men despaired of the ability of its neuritic, solitary president and drunken, secretive Congress to govern.

Still he sat for those two years at the foot of Gamble's Hill and ran his factory as well as he knew how, and it was not until the entry for July 11, 1863, that Mac read any indication of how his great-great-grandfather really felt. Stephen Evans had been reading the newspaper, piecing together news of what had happened in Mississippi and Pennsylvania the week before. Now he had realized what had really happened at 1 P.M. of July 3, when the Confederate batteries had opened fire in the barrage on Cemetery Ridge, Round Top, and Little Round Top.

"I reproach myself most bitterly," Stephen Evans wrote. "It is now apparent to me that the advance by Trimble, Pickett, and Pettigrew, and thus Genl. Lee's whole plan of battle, failed because our cannon could not provide a barrage of sufficient range. It is a most mortifying failure. Two years ago I told Mr. Davis that my Works were at the disposal of our country. Now it cannot be denied that, in the hour of maximum peril, they have not served her as she required. The loss in Pennsylvania is, despite what the Press may say, a grievous reverse; and coupled with the news of the evacuation of Vicksburg, it fills me with foreboding that our fight must now be hard and our hopes of success slim. I feel a grievous sorrow. I have prayed to God. I have told Him that I have failed Him and our cause. I pray only that God in his mercy and abounding Grace may forgive me, as at this moment I am unable to forgive myself."

Six days later there was another entry. It recorded the contents of a letter from Dabney Evans, the first letter Stephen Evans had received since his son had joined the Confederate Army. The two men, with the mad stubborn pride they would hand down to their children, had not spoken or written. During that time of silence Dabney Evans had fought at Gaines's Mill and Malvern Hill and in the Shenandoah Valley and at Lee's defeat at Antietam Creek and his victory at Fredericksburg and at another victory at Chancellorsville, where his unit attacked across the wilderness so swiftly and silently that Joe Hooker's troops had been surprised at their coffee and beans by the stampede of animals fleeing before the deadly charge—Chancellorsville, where blind chance had robbed them of their commander, that half-mad, ragged fanatic, General Jackson, whom nobody called Tom Fool anymore; his own men shot him in the twilight, mistaking him for a Union skirmisher.

Jackson died, but Dabney Evans fought on under his replacement, Bald Dick Ewell. He marched with Lee to Pennsylvania, and there on the third of July, only minutes before his father's cannon opened fire in that barrage, he fell on Culp's Hill with a Minié in his right arm, fell and was taken prisoner, sent to a Union prison hospital at Harrisburg, where a surgeon chopped off the arm and threw it away to rot.

Mac saw his great-grandfather as he lay on the camp bed dictating a letter to a volunteer nurse: hot-eyed still, to his great-grandson's imagination, but now pale and shrunken, the flesh almost transparent, as the body will be after it has sustained a sudden shock. Stephen Evans recorded the contents of the letter. They were dry and matter-of-fact instructions to be followed in the event of Dabney's death. Then there was a single line: "May God spare him. All is come to dust."

There were two more years of war ahead. Stephen Evans spent less and less of that time at his factory. This was because he had less and less to do. As the Union armies tightened their stranglehold on the Confederacy, shipments of iron from the furnaces in the Valley came less and less often. Union cavalry raiders burned the furnaces, one by one, and freed the slaves who worked them. Copper shipments from Ducktown, then lead shipments from Wytheville, ceased. There was no corn to feed his hands.

The Irish and German mechanics ran away to Union lines, and slave labor, at last stretched too thin, could not make up the difference. One by one, as if the Kanawha works were a small stage reflecting the decline of the Confederacy, the buildings which had bustled with activity fell silent. By 1865 Stephen Evans lived in a silent house, his son in a prison camp far away, his eighteen-year-old daughter Sarah off in Albemarle for her own safety. By day he went to a factory which was reduced to making nails and bullets: no rails, no cannon, no ship plate, no locomotives, only a great echoing factory standing ready for supplies that would never come.

He kept busy. Aunt Selma recorded the voyages of the SS *Melissa Dabney,* a sleek British-built blockade-runner owned jointly by Stephen Evans and his brother-in-law Jennings Dabney. She made twelve voyages to Nassau before war's end, carrying cotton Stephen Evans bought by selling his Confederate bonds and returning, Aunt Selma said, "laden with vitally needed supplies for the Kanawha Works and the Confederate government." What those supplies were she did not say.

The diary noted the events of those two years: the Confederates pushed out of Tennessee and Georgia and South Carolina, Grant's army bludgeoning Lee down the Peninsula until finally the gray troops hung on at Petersburg for nine savage months with the stunned strength of men who have already died and will not admit it. Until the diary's last entry:

April 3, 1865. I am writing these words in my study with my revolver at my elbow. By now the sun is risen, and it has cast a most unnatural dark red light across the page, as if it were shining through a sea of blood. This is the smoke of the city.

Since this time yesterday I have seen my city and all that remains to me in this life utterly destroyed. Now I am writing as much to calm my wits as from any apprehension that my words may prove of interest to any who come after me.

The events of the last twenty-four hours seem to stretch interminably behind me, as if I had lived a lifetime and more since that time. Yesterday was Sunday, and I rose, made my breakfast as well as I could from a glass of water and a hard cold pone, and went to Church. I had knelt in prayer and was listening to Dr. Minnegerode reciting the Great Thanksgiving when I discerned that a most unusual timbre had suddenly entered his diction, almost as an actor may sound when, though he may continue a speech, he has realized that he has forgotten his part and will shortly be compelled to stop. I looked up, and saw that Dr. Minnegerode's eyes were riveted to the back pew. Turning, I saw Mr. Davis quietly leaving the sanctum, and I felt in that moment a prick of fear; as if I sensed somehow without being told what was to follow. Dr. Minnegerode continued bravely with the liturgy, but soon the whole congregation was aboil, for no one failed to notice that the sexton was seeking out all those who held positions in the Congress and Cabinet and whispering to each a few words. One by one they left the service, until those of us who remained could hardly remember if we were in church or the railway depot.

Unaccountably, no message came for me. But though I was by now fully convinced that some disaster had occurred, I remained for the eucharist, as it is in times of disaster as no others that we ought to seek the help of God and the Grace of His Son. When I had drunk of the wine, I found myself suddenly pierced with a great desolation, and kneeling at the rail, I was racked with ragged, tearing sobs the like of which I have not experienced since childhood. Whence they came I know not, but I was unable to restrain them even when Dr. Minnegerode put a comforting hand on my shoulder. Indeed, this display of solicitude only made my tears flow the faster, so that I was obliged to leave the rail and the church.

Once in the street I regained my composure and hastened across Ninth Street to the Capitol, hoping to hear some news. There I was unable to locate anyone of the Cabinet, but I happened upon Sen. Hunter, who informed me that all were in conference with Mr. Davis at his house. As he spoke, he trembled ceaselessly, as he might be suffering from an ague, and his teeth rattled slightly as he spoke, which signs I took to be tokens, not of cowardice, but of the same grief and agitation which had overtaken me earlier. "It is all over for us here," he said. "Lee has abandoned Petersburg and the government is moving out. Grant will be here by noon tomorrow." He shook my hand and we parted as men do when they fear they shall not see each other again.

I went at once to the War Office on Franklin Street, for I hoped to talk with Secretary Breckinridge and gain assurance that my Works would not be fired by the retreating soldiers. He was nowhere to be found. Instead I encountered Mr. Jones, his clerk, who was burning papers in an iron stove. He told me that the Secretary was still with the President. I quickly penned a note entreating him to honor his earlier pledge to me on this matter, and went at once to the Works.

On entering the grounds I encountered a most profound silence, unusual even for a Sunday. I went at once to my office. When I entered, the blinds were drawn, and in the dimness I took the office for empty. After a few seconds I descried the figure of a man standing in a corner and regarding me fixedly. So unexpected was this apparition that I gave a small exclamation of alarm, but in a second I realized that it was Jennings. His expression did not alter when I spoke to him, so that I briefly took him for one dead or entranced. But at length he spoke, and his voice came as if from the tomb. "The city will burn," he said.

I told him at once of my visit to the War Department, and added that I felt we should take steps to organize the hands to repel any incendiaries or looters who might appear.

Again there was a pause while he stared into the air ahead of him. Then he said, "Oh, yes, you may take steps. You may organize. You may do anything you like, but it will avail you nothing."

"What do you mean?" I asked.

"Ring your gong," he said. "Summon the hands." He gave a laugh, such

155

that it entered my mind that he might be lunatic. I turned from the room and ran down into the courtyard, where I took the hammer and struck the gong to summon the hands. But though I rang long and loud, no reply met my summons but echoing silence. Not a hand, black or white, remained, nor were the overseers and guards at their posts. The Works was deserted.

I returned at once to the office and asked Jennings what had become of the force. "I told them they might go," he said.

I demanded with some heat how he could have acted so without permission from me or the civil authorities. He gave again that low, disturbing laugh.

"There are no civil authorities," he said. "If I had refused them permission, they would have gone at any rate, and might well have done me injury as they went."

I looked at him in silence, and he said angrily, "You are a fool, Stephen! Can't you see your Works is finished? Let us go now, as well."

"You may leave," I replied. "This is my place, and I shall stay here until the end."

He laughed again. "You are a fool," he repeated in a spiteful tone. "You will die here if you stay."

"Begone, coward," I told him, and like a silent shadow, he passed out of the door.

How long I remained in the office I know not. It was as if the same paralysis which had affected my brother-in-law now came upon me, for I fell to considering the situation, and its utterly desolate aspect had upon me a curiously hypnotic effect, so that in time I passed from myself into a curious blank region of icy despair. When I returned to my senses, it was full dark. Looking out my window, I could faintly descry a parade of tiny figures passing southward over the Mayo Bridge, and deduced it must be what remained of our army in flight before the federal troops.

Then, with a start, I saw from farther east a tongue of flame lap suddenly at the sky, and I realized with chill certainty that the tobacco warehouses were ablaze. Soon flames could be seen at several points to the east, and I became aware of the silence. Despite the general fire, no alarm bells were ringing, and this absence struck me as most sinister and frightening.

I raised the window and leaned out for a better view. I was at once aware of the stifling odor of burning tobacco, as if the city had become in burning a vast cigar, with fumes so strong I was soon forced to wet a handkerchief from the water jug and hold it before my nose and mouth.

Presently the silence I had remarked was broken by a jagged rumble which for a few moments I failed entirely to recognize as a maddened chorus of human voices. As the hullabaloo came closer, it gave evidence of such lawless savagery that the very marrow of my bones seemed transformed into slivers of ice. I believe I had until then entertained some notion of staying at the Works to prevent them from coming to harm, but when I heard those hellish screams, so like the cries of Red Indians, I felt my resolution waver.

Soon from the end of Arch Street there issued a singular stream of humanity, black and white, seemingly all drunk and mad and frenzied with the lust of destruction. Though there was no moon, I could see them plainly

156

by the light of the torches they carried, which gave to them the lurid appearance of demons dancing amid the flames of the Pit. In a trice they had surrounded the Armory. I heard the sound of splintering glass and saw flames licking the building. Without thought I hurled myself to the floor in terror, and in a few seconds there came a horrendous explosion. The force of the blast shattered my window and hurled the glass against the wall, and on my roof I heard a metallic drumming as shell fragments fell from the sky.

Suddenly I was stricken with terror such as I have never felt before. In a matter of seconds, without any decision on my part, I found myself outside the building in headlong flight through the main gate. Nor did I pause until I had gained the top of the hill, where I fell, exhausted, to the pavement in front of the Stove Works. My head drooped into the gutter, and for an instant I thought myself insane, for in the gutter was running, for what reason only God knows, a stream of pure corn whiskey, which I had tasted on my lips.

I gained my feet again and turned to look at the Works. The Armory was in full blaze, and the hot fragments had spread small blazes to the roofs of some of my buildings as well. The mob had gathered by the slave quarters, and were amusing themselves by lobbing firebrands over the walls. I saw the flames spreading, and acknowledged to myself that soon I should have no Works left but a heap of charred timbers and twisted metal.

When this fact was borne in upon me, I fell again to my knees, but in such deep despair that I could not pray or even lift my eyes to Heaven. In that moment I counted myself as one whom God hates and from whom He has turned His face. I am as a man dead, my life's work ruined, my posterity maimed and scattered, bereft of name, family, fortune, country and home. I am finished; I am destroyed.

157

TWO

In the two generations after Mac's great-great-grandfather there was little to set the Evans family apart—certainly nothing to mark them as a family destined for failure and dissolution. Stephen Evans had watched looters burn his factory and become a man destroyed in mind and spirit. When Dabney Evans returned to Richmond from the prison camp in Pennsylvania, he found the father he had loved and feared an ashen hulk, stunned by his loss into silence and gentle confusion. Though the old man had lived quietly another six years, a white-haired shadow by his son's fireside, the Stephen Evans who had built the Kanawha and dreamed of an empire of iron had died that day whiskey ran in the gutters.

But there was a surprise for Dabney Evans. His father was ruined, true, but he was not, appearances to the contrary, ruined financially. Indeed, Dabney Evans found himself the owner of quite a healthy fortune, a gift neither he nor anybody else had expected. Stephen R. Evans had planned for the consequences of defeat. He showed his son a sheaf of receipts from a London banking house, dated between August, 1863, and March, 1865, and totaling some £176,319—an enormous sum, even in the North. In shattered Virginia, its bonds and currency worthless, its slave capital liquidated, it was wealth beyond imagining. Dabney Evans, coming home in defeat, must have felt like a man who has inadvertently mut-

159

tered a magic word and found himself half buried in a shower of fairy gold.

The secret was his father's blockade-runner, the SS *Melissa Dabney,* its outgoing cargoes of cotton and incoming cargoes of "vitally needed supplies," in Aunt Selma's apposite phrase. Mac could imagine those supplies: corsets, cigars, silk dresses, French wines, opera hats—vitally needed by those few in the Confederacy who still had hard cash to pay for them, hard cash which had ended up in London, in Stephen Evans' personal account, as insurance against the awful prospect of defeat.

Surprised by wealth, Dabney Evans produced a surprise of his own. He had ridden to war a romantic scandal: tippler, duelist, rakehell. He returned without an arm and, as if there had been an amputation of the spirit as well, without the fiery temperament which had led him into disgrace. He settled into wealth as quietly as a seabird lighting on still surf. He gained his pardon, bought into a banking house, and throughout the long placid years that remained to him, few things in Virginia were built without bringing him profit: mines, textile mills, shipyards, railroads, hotels, whole cities—Richmond, Norfolk, Roanoke—rebuilt or built from nothing. All things conspired to make him wealthy, and he conspired with them, a quiet banker with an empty sleeve. He was friend to railroadmen, financiers, governors, senators; dutiful son to his dying father, he was husband, father, patron, friend, churchman, civic leader, in politics successively Conservative, Funder, Democrat, until, a few years before his death, he led the Virginia "Gold Bugs" out of the party in protest against the nomination of William Jennings Bryan. During McKinley's first term he closed his eyes and left life with polite haste, surrounded by family and tokens of fortune, justified before the God he professed, a wise servant who had multiplied his talents.

He married well and left two children: Selma, who had spent her long and contentious life elucidating minutiae of Evans family history, crowning her career with the biography of her grandfather, Stephen R. Evans; and Dabney Evans, Jr., for two decades diocesan Episcopal Bishop of Virginia.

Of Mac's grandfather there were few legends. He had built the house Mac grew up in, and in its study hung an oil portrait of the bishop in his robes. His face was a vague kindly avuncular version of the durable dark Evans features. On the bookshelves in the study were two musty books which Mac could not bring himself to open: *Christian Stewardship* by Dabney Evans, Jr., and *A Tree of Life: Sermons of the Rt. Rev. Dabney Evans Jr. 1920–1943.* Aside from these artifacts, Mac knew only one concrete fact about his grandfather: a story that, in his later years, the bishop had approached an RF&P conductor on a speeding train patting his coat pockets distractedly. "A terrible thing has happened," Mac's grandfather said. "I have lost my ticket." The conductor, noting the old man's clerical garb, had assured him that the railroad company would accept his word that he had bought a ticket. "You don't understand," the bishop had replied. "I don't know where I'm going."

Dabney Evans had never traveled far. He had spent a life in quiet piety as spiritual adviser to the people who by birth belonged to what in Virginia was to all intents and purposes the Established Church; he had preached its gospel of service, the parable of the talents, its God of Duty, who as years went on came more and more to resemble a slightly imperfect version of Robert E. Lee; he had planted his staff in the soil of Virginia and there had sprouted schools for the unlettered, kitchens for the unfortunate, maternity homes for the unwed; he had flung into the world like doves missions to the heathen in Africa, China, the South Seas; he had been gathered to his Lord's gray bosom two years after the Japanese attacked Pearl Harbor.

Even before his death he had become primarily known as the father of his only child, born 1899, Christian name to inspire him as a warrior of the church, second name to honor a small tribe of Indians the diocese had befriended: Joshua Tutelo Evans, later known as the Colonel, father of Lester Tutelo and MacIlwain Kuykendall Evans.

He seemed to his son Mac a man to whom a century had happened, like a streetcar accident or a shark attack. And as he studied his father's life, Mac might vow (as he knew his brother had) that it would not happen to him this way, that he would avoid the sudden wrenchings that had taken his father's life out of his control and sent it bouncing toward an end no-one foresaw, but Mac could find in the story no instruction on how to prevent it.

There were no books or diaries of his father's life. Mac had a few photographs, some letters, several documents, and a scrapbook of newspaper clippings. That was all, except for the testimony of those who had been there, had seen or known about the various parts of it.

There was the testimony of the man himself, living still—letters, infrequently tossed up by the tide of the international airmail. Mac got them on occasions: his birthdays, confirmation, graduation.

DEAR MACILWAIN [began the letter he had received after his graduation from Harvard]:
    I assume congratulations are in order—when last I heard your studies were progressing well. I am pleased to welcome you into the fraternity of

161

educated men! I can imagine that four years at Harvard have been challenging and exciting in the extreme—I envy you the hard work as well as the fun
and comradeship you must have known, the good friends you have surely
made. These friends are for life, son: as the poet advises, I urge you to
"grapple them to your bosom with hoops of steel."

Mary Owen writes that you plan to follow the law. As you know, I myself
studied at the University law school; and though my career in the law did
not lead me precisely where I once imagined it would, still, I would be less
than candid if I said I had found the legal profession anything but satisfying
and, at times, thrilling.

You, I know, are now enjoying Virginia's spring in the spring of your life,
but here in Puerto Morelos it is blustery and wet. June is our coldest month,
and after my decade and a half of residence here this seems only natural; it
is Virginia, not this country, which seems to me a faraway land with quaint
customs and odd weather!

Nevertheless, the cold and damp set my old bones to aching if I walk out
in them too long. Since my heart has now begun to make a nuisance of itself, the doctors have advised against travel if it can be avoided. I spend the
raw days before the fire with my Cervantes and my Shakespeare. *El Mer-
curio* is full of news about the elections here, but as I have fully retired from
politics I do not read the reports. My landlady, Srta. Krameyer, is full of
dire predictions of triumph by the "Reds," and she is convinced that only
divine intervention can turn the election to the Christian Democrats and
save the country from disaster. She must wonder why I am so silent during
her harangues. The fact is that even though I know she has lived in this city
since the age of seven, still there is something about Spanish spoken with
even a slight German accent which after all these years still sets my teeth on
edge.

Well, my servant Pedro has come to announce dinner and I must go. May
God bless you and keep you. I shall remember you in my prayers, and I
hope if you can spare a thought for an old gentleman who cares very much
for you that you will remember me in yours.

YOUR LOVING FATHER

Mac saved the letters and reread them periodically, searching closely
for hidden meanings, cryptograms, invisible ink; they contained nothing
more than the hackneyed sentiments, the flat phrases. They told him
nothing.

No more helpful was the testimony of his mother, who, when she
would consent to discuss his father at all, would only smile in her evasive,
ethereal way and say, "Your father was sadly misled. It's a terrible
waste," and then change the subject to automatic writing or the abuse of
power by the Supreme Court.

So Mac turned to the artifacts he had.

The first of these was a faded photograph. His grandfather's careful ecclesiastical handwriting noted on the back the time and place: Staunton, December 28, 1912. The picture showed the Rt. Rev. Dabney Evans, Jr., and his son Joshua posed stiffly with the President-elect of the United States, Thomas Woodrow Wilson. The occasion was Mr. Wilson's birthday visit to his boyhood Virginia home, a gala event in which the great progressive leader is reported to have proclaimed that "the men who serve will be the men who profit."

Such a sermon must have pleased Bishop Evans; in the picture he appeared smiling and content. His eyes were resting in the middle distance, as if contemplating comfortable vistas of striving and service. By contrast, the President-elect seemed withdrawn. Mac wondered if Mr. Wilson had been thinking about the bitter political squabbling which would surround his appearance that evening. Certainly he was feeling some strain, for although the picture showed him trying to smile, he was not having much success: one half of his upper lip had dutifully lifted away, exposing the teeth, but the other half remained obstinately in place, giving his face the look of a man at a dinner party who has found a cockroach in his soup bowl.

Between the two men, imprisoned in the crook of a paternal arm, was the boy who would be Mac's father. At thirteen he was already showing signs of the growth spurt that would make him the tallest of the Evans line, some inches more than six feet. The face was another version of the durable Evans features: coal-black hair and eyebrows, dark eyes, snub nose, firm, flat chin. But by contrast with the beaming vagueness of his father, Joshua T. Evans even then showed in his features that curious still intentness which characterized all his photographs. He was not looking at the camera, but up at the President-elect, gazing at his face with what might have been worship, or curiosity, or puzzlement, or any combination of the three.

That was what remained in the beginning of his father's life: boyhood in his father's episcopate, years at St. Cyprian's, the school his father had helped to found. The rest was gone.

Of his father's next decade there remained not even a picture. To Mac, his father's first war seemed almost like a fairy story; it was hard to believe that his own immediate forebear had marched to places with such magical names: Belleau Wood, Soissons, St.-Mihiel, Meuse-Argonne. But the fact was indisputable. Joshua T. Evans had fought as a corporal in the AEF, had come through the war alive to find himself on the loose in Europe.

Somehow Mac felt that that year in Europe was the key, and he felt

163

sure that if he could just find some photograph, some scrap of paper, someone who'd been there, if he could strap himself in a time machine, he would find the key to his father's life.

There had been some months in Valencia; whatever Joshua Evans had found there—whether it had been a woman, or a feeling of peace after a year of war, or just one moment of sunlight on the water—he had seemingly spent much of his life trying to find it again, indeed was perhaps still pursuing it on the seacoast of South America.

But that year was dark, gone forever. Mac had once thought of writing to his father and asking: *Was that it? Was that when it happened?*—but the flat phrases on the blue airmail stationery came back to mind, and he knew it would be no use; the old man his father had become would no longer recognize that anything had happened at all. It was a question with no answer.

After his year on the loose, Joshua Evans had read history for three years at King's College in Cambridge. Then he had come home to study law.

Mac knew about his life at the University law school and his years as a young lawyer, because there was a witness: Kenlow Anderson, who had met his father at the University and had been his friend all the days of his life. Judge Anderson had passed his years in Richmond, had never married, and each time Joshua Evans left on his adventures, it was Kenlow Anderson who looked after his property and family. Now that the Colonel was in South America, Judge Anderson looked after his children. So when Mac asked the judge about his father, Anderson had taken it as part of his duties as trustee to tell him what he remembered.

"Your father was a mess when he came to Charlottesville," Anderson told him. "I believe he thought the University was going to be like Cambridge. He was going to have a manservant bring him tea in the morning or whatever they do. Those boys at the University, I think they thought he came from Mars or somewhere. Don't misunderstand; you could tell he was as smart as a whip, right off; there wasn't any question about that. But he had some of the damnedest notions. He used to wear one of these little flat hats you see people driving sports cars with, and gray knickers, and he carried a walking stick, and he was always trying to get people to climb some mountain or other and look at birds and so forth. He used to walk around sort of stiff-legged with his hands in his pockets. I think he'd seen some British general do it. But he was so tall and thin, he looked like a whooping crane with the flux. And he was very serious all the time. Wanted to talk about God. Which was the least likely thing people in law school want to talk about.

"He had this damn guitar, too, he'd bought it in Spain, and he could play it pretty good. But when he sang, he could clear a room in no time flat. He didn't have any voice at all. He'd get some Hollins girl on a date, and he'd start singing her some Spanish ditty, and you'd watch her face, it was the funniest thing you ever saw. She wouldn't know what had hit her. It was like the mating call of a Mexican bullfrog. I remember one time he was at a party and some rich boy, St. A., offered him five hundred dollars for the guitar if he'd promise never to buy another one. Your father got pretty hot about it. We had to separate them. And the girl he was singing to made her escape in the confusion.

"But I liked him from the start. He was a tough guy, and like I said, we knew he was smart. I did some fast talking to get him into the Kappa Sigma house. A lot of those guys thought he was sort of a lunatic. But I told them they were going to be damn glad they had him when exam time rolled around. I still thought he was going to get blackballed, though, because there was one fellow who despised him. So the night we voted on bids, me and another fellow got this guy drunk as a lord. Then in the meeting we kept stalling until he passed out. Two of his friends carried him up to his room. We found out later he'd made them promise to ball your father, but by the time they got downstairs the voting was over.

"And inside of a month pretty much everybody liked him. Even that fellow who was going to ball him. He was just a decent guy, you couldn't help it. He was a little stiff sometimes, maybe a little slow to get a joke, but he never took himself very seriously, which is a great redeeming feature in anybody. And we worked on him some. I remember one time four of us went to dinner at the Hotel Roanoke, we were up there for some dance or other, I can't remember, but anyway four guys, and we ran up a pretty big check. But the three of us had worked it out in advance, and we snuck out. Except we hadn't told your father. He had to take the rap for all of us, and he couldn't pay it. The manager made him leave his gold watch. He was sore as hell for a day or two.

"He never seemed to need to work very hard. He was always trying to get people to play bridge or something when they should have been working. But he'd end up at the top of the class every damn time. At the end of the three years he'd won about everything you could win: president of the student body, most likely to succeed, Order of the Coif, Raven, Imp, the whole thing. It used to drive people crazy. People in law school really take that kind of thing seriously. You look back on it later, and you wonder how you could have gotten so caught up in all that mess. But at the time it seems like the most important thing in the world. There was one fellow in our class—I won't say his name, but he died just a few years ago. He worked like a damn dog to be first in the class. And every term your father beat him out without breaking a sweat. One winter this boy's father came to visit him, and the boy told him he was second in the class, and his father just said, 'Who's first?' And that boy tried to kill himself. His roommate found him hanging in the closet. They cut him down, and he was all right, but he quit law school and never came back.

"It caught up with your father later, though. He got out and he got the job we all wanted, with Powell, Valentine, and Reeves, and then he figured he didn't have to study for the bar exam. Now me, I was just a middling student, so I knew I had to work. But I think your father thought they wouldn't dare fail him. He sat around playing that damn guitar instead of studying, and they sure enough failed him. He was mad as hell about it. He figured everybody was laughing at him, which they were, a little. But it's no disgrace to fail the bar exam.

"The people at the firm smartened him up a little, too. They gave him his job all right—put him in charge of the file room. Old Mr. Valentine said he reckoned that would give him motivation to study for the retest. He passed it just fine the second time.

"Now I know you, young Pure-in-Heart. You probably think your father was a terrible conservative to take that job, and to serve in the House of Delegates and all the rest of it. But you have to remember it was all different then. The old man was governor. But he was a kind of liberal then himself. He was a reformer type. Hell, it was him single-handed that passed the antilynch law. That was the only one in the South for a long time. And he lit out after the phone company, too, and the gasoline crowd. I don't mean your father was a Don Quixote type back then. He was just like the rest of us, only smarter. But he was kind of liberal even then. They had this interracial committee—some white businessmen and so on, who met once a month with a group of colored preachers and political leaders. The idea was to prevent violence. They tell me it was your father who started the idea of putting the colored social relief agencies under the Community Chest. It took a couple of years and made some people pretty mad. But they did it.

"He was a pretty good legislator, too. Everybody said so. He was about the youngest man in there, and he was always talking about reforms that didn't have a chance. He wanted the state to borrow money to build roads, and that idea was very strongly frowned on by the old man and his crowd. And he kept trying to get them to pass some kind of civil service deal for state employees, which they didn't go for at all. You want to upset a politician, just try to take away his patronage.

"But even with all that, they thought highly of your father down there.

166

I have this feeling that the old man wanted him to join up with the machine. He kept inviting him to visit the apple farm and so on. And I don't know what your daddy thought about that. He might have done it; I guess that shocks you. But you see, he didn't have any great ambition to change the world back then. He was just his father's son. He wanted to do well by doing good, and you could do that if you worked with the old man. So sometimes I think he could have had all of that—governor, senator, what have you—if he hadn't got mixed up with Willie McKeever.

"Your father wasn't looking to defend a labor organizer at all. He had a pretty good career going for him, and he liked his life. He was still living at home, and he was banking the money he got from his practice, which had gotten to be considerable, him being in the legislature and all. He was saving his money because he'd started courting Elaine—your mother. I believe he'd met her at a debutante party; she was visiting Richmond from New York. She wasn't but seventeen then, but I'll tell you she would knock your eyes out. She was thin, and blond, and she had this aristocratic look, you know, upstate New York, that kind of thing. She was at Sarah Lawrence, and he would take the train to New York for the dances and all. I think he wanted her to marry him right away, but she wanted to finish college. She was a handful back then; when she made up her mind about something, it was worth your life to say no. So he waited. In the evenings we used to play bridge at the Confederate Club. He had a real flair for cards. And he was on the vestry at St. Paul's; all the old ladies loved him down there.

"What I'm getting at is that the last thing in the world he wanted was to get involved with the McKeever case. I guess he just didn't feel like he could turn it down.

"I'll be frank with you, son. I'm damn glad that Willie McKeever didn't write to me and ask me to defend him. It'd have been hard to refuse. We all knew Willie, and we liked him. He was the damnedest guy you ever saw. I think he was from Grundy or some such place, real Hatfield-McCoy territory, and he'd come to Charlottesville without a dime in his pocket or a brain in his head, just bound and determined to get rich.

"He had this sort of shiny green checked suit and a straw skimmer about two sizes too big for him, and seemed like every week he would be coming around the fraternity house with a new scheme to get rich. One time I remember he was selling genuine Havana cigars. The money was going to finance some kind of rebellion in Cuba. You know, *Cuba Libre*, that kind of nonsense. So we each bought a box. They were the foulest damn things you ever smelled. I ended up burying mine in Mad Bowl, I think. Then one time it was nine-day clocks, and he had some kind of miracle shoes, too, turned out to be like instant coffee: dissolved in water. But he was the kind of guy you couldn't stay mad at. He meant so well, and he was always so sincere, that we'd fuss at him and then we'd start feeling bad about it, and we'd end up buying the next thing.

"Willie finally got a dry-cleaning business going after we left Charlottesville. But when the Depression hit, he lost that pretty fast. That's when he went down to Dillardville and teamed up with his brother Jack.

"Now I will freely confess to you that I have no use at all for labor unions. I believe they have been the ruination of this country, and I don't care what you say, I believe the old man was right to try to keep them out of this state. They've bankrupted the damn railroads and just about anything else they got ahold of. But still and all, the situation at the mill down there was pretty awful from what they tell me. They were working women and children, fifty-five or sixty hours a week. They didn't pay much, and what they did pay was in scrip, which they got back at the company store. The company housing was not that bad, from what I hear—probably about as good as what those folks were used to. Still, I don't think I'd hanker to live in it.

"People had been after the millowners for years to clean them up some. I remember back in twenty-eight Bishop Cannon got a bunch of ministers to write letters to the press and all. Even your grandfather did. They said the owners were asking for trouble the way they ran things; but it didn't do any good. Those guys figured they were ordained by the Almighty, and not even reverend clergy could tell them a thing.

"Comes the Depression, and the owners decided to cut wages. That was where Jack McKeever came in. Jack was Willie's little brother, and he was a sure-enough Communist. Don't you make those faces at me. I don't mean a socialist or a liberal or a guy who subscribes to *The Nation*. I mean a guy with a party card in his pocket who took his orders from Moscow. I never met him, but your father told me he was a tough bastard. When he first got the union going down there, the company got a couple of guys to grab him. They drove him down to Edenton and beat the hell out of him and told him if he ever came back to Virginia, they would kill him. But he came back, with a couple of boys with guns to protect him.

"Then he got Willie in on it. I guess Willie thought he could become a union mogul or something, like John L. Lewis. Jack got the union out on strike and set Willie to work painting signs and writing leaflets and so on. Willie didn't know beans about politics, but he could work like the dickens when he wanted to.

"The company came through and moved the strikers out of their houses. Thought that'd break up the strike. So Jack and Willie got a

168

bunch of tents and set 'em up on the old fairgrounds. They moved out there, women, children, and all, cooking and hollering and singing. That just about ran those mill boys nuts. They called in the sheriff and told him to go out there and get 'em out. He said he wasn't going to do it, people might get hurt. So the next day there was a new sheriff, and they brought in a bunch of guys from out of town and swore 'em in as deputies, and about dawn the next day they hit the fairgrounds.

"God only knows who started shooting, I don't. I don't think anybody on either side told the truth at the trial, and then the newspapers went ahead and changed all around what they did say. But at the end of it there were six strikers dead, and two deputies, and the new sheriff was paralyzed from where somebody had gone upside his head with a pipe. And they grabbed Jack and Willie—just those two—and charged them with the whole business. First-degree murder.

"That took care of the strike, of course. The governor—it wasn't the old man, he was in the Senate by then—he got in the militia, and they broke it up pretty fast.

"That's when Willie McKeever wrote your daddy and asked him to represent him. He was scared to death. Jack had gotten down a couple of party lawyers from up North, and Willie had the idea they were going to get Jack off and let him go to the electric chair. Him not being a party man, I think he figured they didn't have any use for him except as some kind of martyr. I don't know if that was true or not, but I sure as hell wouldn't have wanted any party lawyer representing me.

"It was a hell of a decision for your father to make. It sure wasn't going to do him any good to get mixed up in that business down in Dillardville. There'd been a lot in the papers about it, and they made it sound about twice as bad as it really was. You'd been reading the Richmond papers, you'd have thought Stalin himself was down in Dillardville commanding the Red Army. It was going to be sticking his hand in the buzz saw to go down there.

"But your father had this religious streak. He prayed about it and so forth, and I guess he decided it was his Christian duty to go. He quoted the Bible: 'I was sick and in prison, and so forth, and ye visited me not, depart from me, ye cursed, into everlasting fire.' Plus I think maybe somebody at the firm sort of suggested to him that he shouldn't do it, and that got his back up. He was contrary. So he said yes.

"He called me after that first trial, and I asked how he'd done. 'I did fine,' he said. 'They're going to let me leave town.' That one had been a mistrial. Some damn fool commonwealth's attorney had been describing the shooting, and he'd brought in a life-size dummy of one of the depu-

169

ties, with fake blood and everything. One of the women on the jury took a look at it and had a nervous breakdown right there in the courtroom. They had to take her away in a straitjacket. So they recessed the trial for a week. He stayed down there to work on his defense.

"I don't think there was ever much chance of getting either of those boys off. The mill people had the town locked up tight, and after that fiasco with the dummy the governor sent down a special prosecutor to prevent any more foul-ups. And on top of all that, he told me he had the devil's own time with those party lawyers. They were defending Jack, and they insisted on putting him on the stand to talk about politics. Your father said they ought to just stick to the facts, but they were determined, so when the defense presented their case, they put him on.

"After Jack testified, the whole business turned into a turkey shoot. When Willie went on, the prosecutor asked him a bunch of questions like did he believe in God and the flag and baseball and pay-as-you-go financing for state highways. Poor old Willie tried to give them honest answers, and they whipsawed him. Your father told me the only thing that kept them out of the electric chair was the fact that every living soul in that courtroom knew they hadn't done it. So the jury gave them life in prison, plus ninety-nine years.

"They put in an appeal, but it seemed like the case was pretty much over, things were starting to die down, and your daddy had come out of it all right. People were starting to forget. But the party people had Jack out on bail, and he skipped out, and then the real shouting began. The FBI grabbed him about a week later in New Orleans, and they claimed he was trying to get on a ship to Russia. It hurt your daddy pretty bad, because people got it mixed up in their minds who was who and a lot of people thought your daddy had been Jack's lawyer, and they thought he'd helped Jack escape. There was some pretty ugly talk.

"Well, he knew he couldn't stay in the legislature. He was resigned to it; he told me he wasn't even going to run again, for a while anyway. But then old Mr. Valentine asked him to resign from the firm. I don't think he was ready for that. And when he started getting hints that he ought to quit the vestry, it really about broke his heart. I think that's when he started thinking about leaving.

"But he sweated it out for a couple more years, waiting for your mother to get out of school. Had his own office down on Third Street, and the labor people came to him, they respected him. Tobacco workers, textile workers, miners. But there wasn't any money in it back then, and if he hadn't been rich, he would have starved. But he stuck it out, and by the time your mother graduated old FDR was in the White House, and he

170

started fishing around for some kind of federal job. I don't know, I think he knew somebody who'd been at Cambridge with him, who'd gone on in the State Department, and this guy suggested the Consular Service: did he want a job in Spain? and he said hell, yeah.

"He married your mother in Binghamton; I was the best man. They sailed the next week, and that was the last I saw of him for four years or so."

If Mac was right—if his father had taken his bride to Spain looking for the same peace he had found there a decade before, he had picked the wrong place and the wrong time. There was no way to know what his life had been like in Seville: Lester had been born there, but he remembered almost nothing about his first three years; his mother would not discuss it.

But there was testimony—literally testimony—from his father. It was in a yellowing paperbound booklet: proceedings of a subcommittee of the House of Representatives in June, 1937. In small black government print Mac could read the statement of the witness, the Hon. Joshua Tutelo Evans, late United States Consul in Seville, Spain.

Mr. Chairman, members of the subcommittee [his father had begun], I am very grateful for this chance to appear here today in support of this measure, as I think it represents a chance for the Congress of the United States Government to rectify a serious mistake we have made in the past six months.

As you know, until two weeks ago, I was the U.S. Consul in Seville, Spain. I had served in that post a little more than three years, and I want to take this opportunity to say publicly that those three years were among the proudest and happiest I have ever spent. Having served this country as a soldier in time of war, I felt especially honored that I had been chosen to serve her abroad in peacetime as well. I would like to express my deep gratitude to the Consular Service and to Mr. Secretary Hull for this great opportunity, and to note for the record that I resigned from my post with deep regret.

But I have resigned from the Consular Service and returned to this country because I feel that the people of this country are making a great mistake in their current neutrality policy toward the situation in Spain. I feel also that many of our people and our leaders are currently laboring under a serious apprehension about the nature of the conflict in Spain at the present time. Among those leaders I must regretfully number the Secretary of State.

Let me say now that it is not my intention at present to argue that this country should abandon its policy of neutrality. It seems plain that the people of the United States want no part of this conflict, not even to the extent of allowing the lawful government of Spain to purchase arms in this country, as it has previously been its unquestioned right to do. The people have spoken and said, Let there be neutrality; very well, so be it. My contention is that the present neutrality legislation does not, in fact, ensure our neutrality. In fact, it does quite the reverse: it has made the United States the unwitting ally of the Fascist leader, General Franco, and the so-called Insurgents.

The difficulty with our present policy, as I see it, is that it regards the fighting in Spain as a civil war, and thus attempts to treat both sides equally by refusing them the right to buy arms or enter into loan and credit agreements from American companies.

But I have been in Spain, and I have studied the situation carefully, and I am firmly convinced that the present conflict is not, in fact, what we understand as a civil war at all, but something far more significant and dangerous to the peace of the world. It is my belief, backed by a year's observation, that the so-called Spanish Civil War is nothing less than a full-scale invasion of Spain by the Fascist powers, Germany and Italy.

This may seem a surprising, even impudent, statement at first. But I believe the American people have been confused by distorted press reports and erroneous statements by government officials. Again, I regret to say that I number Mr. Secretary Hull in the number of those making such statements. Indeed, it is largely because of the Secretary's statement on May 11 last that he saw, and I quote, no evidence of German and Italian military forces in Spain, end quote, that I am here today. I had thought that my reports from the Consulate in Seville abounded with such evidence, and it seemed to me that I should perhaps come home and make this evidence available to the general public.

Again, as an eyewitness to these events, I can assure you that from the very first moment of the so-called insurrection, before the first German or Italian soldier arrived, the Spanish generals have been completely dependent on foreign supplies and foreign troops. Seville was the first city of Spain proper to fall to the generals, and it is now a major headquarters and staging area for their military government. But even in Seville the uprising had little support, except among the adherents of the Spanish Fascist party, the Falange. Thus, when General Queipo de Llano first arrived in Seville, he knew his only chance to hold the city lay in bringing in the dreaded Moorish troops, who are not true Spaniards at all, but Africans. So desperate was he to bring these men from Africa that orders were given that when all space in the transport aeroplanes was filled, Moors were to be tied to the wings of the planes in order to transport them in greater numbers. I know this to be a fact, for two days after the uprising, I talked with a Moorish legionary in a cafe in Seville, and he showed me the rope marks still burned into his arms.

As soon as the fighting began, Ambassador Bowers gave orders that all Americans, including the dependents of diplomatic and consular officers, were to be evacuated, and this was done. As a husband and a father, I am glad that my wife and baby boy were safely at sea by the time the Legionaires arrived. Their conduct can only be described as atrocious. The conquest of Seville was carried out with inhuman enthusiasm. Whole quarters of the city were leveled with artillery. After entering the San Julian district, a suburb inhabited by poor workers, the Legionaries forced every adult male into the streets, without regard for their role in the fighting, and murdered them one by one with knives. In another part of the city, the

Moors entered houses from which they claimed there had been rifle fire; in these houses they spared neither man, woman, nor child.

By night, the Moors were encamped in the beautiful public gardens in the center of Seville, which in a matter of days they had transformed into a semicivilized makeshift Arab-style *casbah*. No one who saw the campfires which they made from the carefully tended bushes and shrubs, the long rows of teapots ceaselessly bubbling, the shameful scenes between Legionaires and prostitutes, often enacted in the open in broad daylight—no one who saw these things could doubt that Spain had been invaded by an army ignorant of European and Christian civilization.

Meanwhile, within weeks, a veritable flood of men and equipment from Italy and Germany began entering Spain. I was there, I saw it, I reported it. To cite one example, on August 9 of last year, less than three weeks after the invasion of Seville, there arrived in the city some ten Italian Savoia bombing planes, with twenty Italian pilots, and twenty-four German aircraft, eighteen bombers and six fighting planes, accompanied by a uniformed crew of thirty. In addition, on the same day, we noted the arrival of a squad of German soldiers with tanks and antiaircraft guns. These observations were duly reported to Washington, and should have been available to the Secretary when he made the statement to which I referred a moment ago.

In November of last year we witnessed the arrival in Seville of the so-called Condor Legion, which was and is nothing less than a German aerial expeditionary force, dispatched from Berlin with orders to subdue Spain.

The mind boggles at the size of this airborne armada. It is, I venture to say, the most fearsome flying circus ever assembled in the history of the world. There are four dozen bombing planes, and twelve fighter aircraft, all manned by uniformed German aviators, along with a reconnaissance unit and a detachment of seaplanes. In addition there are two German armored units, totalling some sixteen tanks between them. This does not include the so-called "North Sea Group," an artillery unit which is supplied by the German battleships *Deutschland* and *Admiral Scheer.*

Please let me repeat that this is not conjecture or hearsay. I saw it, and I know for a fact that it was reported to Washington. I also reported my conversation in early Decenber with Colonel Wolfram von Richtofen, a cousin of the great German air ace, who serves as the chief of staff to General Hugo von Sperrle, commandor of the Condor Legion, and who told me very candidly that Berlin had decided that the Spanish generals were not competent to prosecute the war and had sent General Sperrle to take tactical command!

These observations of mine, I respectfully submit to this subcommittee, are in fact evidence of German and Italian military forces in Spain. I will not dwell on those things which I did not see personally, except to say that I hope none of the members of the subcommittee is still in any doubt that the destruction of Guernica in April was a German operation from start to finish. And as for the German flotilla which bombarded Almería two weeks ago, I can only say that by that act Germany dropped her figleaf and stands revealed to the world as a naked aggressor.

I believe the evidence is overwhelming. The so-called Civil War in Spain is in fact a brutal Fascist war of conquest. German pledges of "non-intervention" are cynical lies. Therefore, if we must have neutrality, let us in fact be truly neutral. Let us embargo arms, loans, and credits to Germany and Italy as well as to the Republic of Spain. That is what this measure would do, and I support it wholeheartedly. I thank you for your indulgence.

Q. Thank you, Mr. Evans. I wonder if you will yield to questioning at this time.

A. Certainly, Mr. Chairman. I will be delighted to answer to the best of my ability.

Q. Mr. Evans, I wonder if you will tell us your reaction to the charge that the Republic of Spain is run by Communists and Soviet agents.

A. Well, Mr. Chairman, you must remember that I have not been in Republican territory since the uprising, but I would say that these charges in the Hearst papers and elsewhere appear to me to be without foundation. The Communists in Spain are a splinter group, much less numerous than they are in this country. In the *Cortes*, which is the Spanish Parliament, there are only seventeen Communist deputies out of a membership of nearly 500. At the time of the rising, the Spanish government had no diplomatic relations with the Soviet Union, and to the best of my knowledge ambassadors were not exchanged between these two countries until sometime this year. In addition—

Q. Mr. Evans.

A. Yes, Mr. Chairman?

Q. One moment, please.

A. Certainly, Mr. Chairman.

Q. Mr. Evans, counsel has informed me that Spain and the USSR established diplomatic relations in August of last year.

A. I regret the error, Mr. Chairman. As I said, I have not been in Republican territory since last July.

Q. Proceed.

A. As I am chiefly here to testify to what I have seen, I will simply say that President Azaña is a Republican liberal of impeccable reputation. Neither he nor Dr. Negrin, the Prime Minister, is a Communist.

Q. He is a Socialist.

A. I beg your pardon?

Q. He is a Socialist, is he not?

A. Dr. Negrin?

Q. Yes.

A. Yes, sir, I believe that is correct.

Q. But not a Communist.

A. No, sir.

Q. Do you believe there to be a difference?

A. There is a major difference. The two parties are quite distinct.

Q. Is it not a fact that in many parts of Spain the two parties have merged?

A. Not to my knowledge.

Q. It is not a fact?

A. It may be a fact. But I have not heard of any such merger.

Q. Mr. Evans, we have heard reports of widespread attacks on freedom of religion in Government-held territory. Do you have any information about this?

A. Again, I have not been in Government territory since the war began. But I will say that there was far more religious liberty in Seville before the uprising than there is now. During the months before the uprising, there were some churches destroyed. In my opinion, the vast majority of these attacks were the work of Fascist provocateurs. During the fighting in July, there were some churches destroyed—

Q. Eleven.

A. I beg your pardon?

Q. How many churches were destroyed?

175

A. I do not know the number.

Q. As an eyewitness, you do not know the number of churches destroyed?

A. No, sir. At the time I was occupied with evacuating American civilians.

Q. Would the number of churches be as high as eleven?

A. It might be.

Q. But you do not know?

A. As I said before, no sir.

Q. Reliable reports place the number at eleven.

A. If so, you have enlightened me, sir.

Q. That was my aim.

A. May I proceed?

Q. By all means.

A. My point is, that since the occupation of Seville, religious persecution has increased. Even some of the German diplomatic personnel have complained in my presence that the Spanish insurgents attempt to prevent them from holding Protestant services openly.

Q. What about the reports that priests and nuns had been attacked in the weeks before the Uprising?

A. I saw none of this. But since the occupation of Seville there have been so many summary executions that even members of the Spanish clergy have protested to General Queipo de Llano, to no avail.

Q. Mr. Evans, are you not concerned that by implementing these sanctions against Italy and Germany, we may find ourselves drawn into war with them?

A. In my opinion, the Fascist powers are not yet strong enough to risk a general war. But if we let them create a Fascist satrapy on Europe's southern flank, they will be emboldened to make new territorial demands, and the specter of a European war becomes very real. I believe we must draw the line against this aggression somewhere. I suggest we do it now, while the risk of war is comparatively small.

Q. Mr. Evans, I'm sure all the members of the subcommittee join in thanking you for coming here today to give us the benefit of your wisdom on this matter.

A. Mr. Chairman, like Socrates, I do not consider myself a wise man. But it has been a privilege to share with you the things I have seen and heard.

Q. Thank you, Mr. Evans.

A. Thank you, Mr. Chairman.

Then there was a scrapbook of newspaper clippings, painstakingly cut and pasted by Mac's mother; that was his father's next four years. The first was from the Richmond paper, now a journalistic collector's item: EVANS CHARGES HITLER, MUSSOLINI BEHIND SPANISH WAR BETWEEN THE STATES (the next edition had been hastily corrected, making the end of a sacred rule that the words "Civil War" could never appear in the Richmond papers).

The rest were from all over: the New York *Times*, the Boston *Globe*, the *Christian Science Monitor*, the *Herald Tribune*, the Washington *Times-Herald*, the Hartford *Courant*, the New York *American*, the Chicago *Tribune*, a jumble of strident voices reporting his father's speeches, meetings, petitions: JESUIT, CONSUL DEBATE SPANISH SITUATION; FORMER OFFICIAL HITS ARMS EMBARGO; BARCELONA TERROR-BOMBING SCORED; FRANCO VICTORY WOULD HASTEN WAR; PROTESTANT LAYMEN RESPOND TO SPANISH CLERGY; EVANS TO HEAD UMBRELLA GROUP FOR SPAIN; SPAIN RULERS NOT REDS, CONSUL CLAIMS; LAWYER'S COMMITTEE SEEKS EMBARGO END; STIMSON GROUP TO SEE HULL TODAY; U.S. "WAFFLING" ON EMBARGO SEEN; "REPUBLIC NOT BEATEN"—EVANS; "HUMANITARIAN" DRIVE SLATED FOR SPANISH REDS; EVANS "DISAPPOINTED" IN QUICK RECOGNITION OF FRANCO.

After the Spanish Republic had fallen there was another cause, another round of speeches, meetings, petitions, and headlines: CONSUL SEES EUROPEAN WAR; RUSSO-GERMAN TREATY SPELLS PEACE "DOOM"; GROUP BACKS AID FOR BRITAIN; TIME FOR NEUTRALITY PAST, EVANS ASSERTS; LINDBERGH STAND ASSAILED; PANEL SAYS NAZIS "PERIL CIVILIZATION"; ARMED SHIP BILL HAILED; LOBBY DRIVE PLANNED FOR DESTROYER DEAL; EVANS: AMERICA 1ST-ERS "TRAGICALLY MISLED"; JAPANESE "AGGRESSION" HIT; U.S. MUST ENTER WAR, SAYS FOREIGN POLICY LOBBY.

Then there was a photograph of his father, tall, thin, now bespectacled, his hair already showing glints of silver, in the uniform of a U.S. Army colonel. He was standing beside General Eisenhower. Eisenhower was

177

smiling, but on his father's face was the same intent look he had turned to Woodrow Wilson. Eisenhower had just awarded the colonel a Silver Star.

That was his father's second war.

"He didn't ever talk about it very much," Lester told Mac. "When he got back, I was eleven. You know how kids are, I thought he was the greatest man who ever lived, and I kept asking him questions, and he would never say a word. It about drove me out of my mind. I knew a couple of things. I knew he'd been in OSS, and I knew he'd been on Ike's staff, and all that, but if I ever asked him what he'd done for OSS, he used to put a finger to his lips and go 'Shhh,' like it was all still top secret.

"He did tell me one thing sort of by accident. We were talking about concentration camps—I'd seen pictures of them in *Life* or somewhere, and he said out of the blue that he'd seen one. I thought he meant Buchenwald or Dachau or one of those, but he said no, this one was in North Africa. That surprised me, but he wouldn't say any more about it. We didn't find out the rest of it till later.

"I guess a lot of that stuff really was secret at the time. But what I figure is that he really didn't want to talk about it anymore. He wanted to forget it. That's a funny thing about him, Mac. He was one of the smartest human beings you could ever hope to meet—hell, he probably still is. I mean, for sheer smart, I've never seen anyone to match him. But now it seems to me that he must have had a funny sort of innocent streak, because here he was, forty-odd years old, been all over the damn world and seen more lies and double-crossing and wars and murders and God knows what all than you or I are ever liable to, seen that full-scale frame-up down in Dillardville, which is all in the hell it was, and then gone off to Spain and spent a year or so cheek by jowl with the Nazis, then went off with Eisenhower and helped to conquer the world, for God's sake—and yet still I think, when he got back here, he had some idea that this was the good place, you know, the home of Jefferson and Madison and all that crap. Seemed like he believed what he'd read in the books. I never fought a war. Maybe in a war the only way you can keep yourself going is to make up some place in your head and believe that it exists, the good place, the place you're going back to. Maybe he started believing it.

"But anyway when he came back he seemed like he wanted to settle down with Mom and forget the whole business. You know, he and Mom hadn't been together for a long time. Not since she and I had gotten evacuated back in thirty-six. There'd been the war, and before that he'd been speechifying all over the country, and before that he'd stayed in Spain for a year without us. Mom had been kind of unhappy about it, I think. He'd been in Europe and she'd been stuck at home nursing Grandpa until he died and then looking out for me and the house and so on. I think it bothered her some. She was one tough lady in those days. Not like she is now. She had a lot on the ball, and doing a bunch of volunteer work and so on didn't suit her one bit. I don't think she ever liked Richmond very much, either, not deep down inside. She used to get kind of furious for what seemed like no good reason, and I think that's why.

"But they patched it up when he got back. I guess looking back on it, you might say they were fooling themselves. False dawn, sort of. Or maybe not, if things had happened different. I think they figured they'd finally gotten their lives set up the way they should be, and things weren't going to change. Maybe if they hadn't, it would have worked.

"But anyway then you came along, which surprised the hell out of everybody, me included. Mom was scared to death. She was thirty-five years old; she'd never expected another kid. It made everybody nervous. They put her to bed for a couple of months to keep her from miscarrying; it got pretty tense. But when you were born, they were both tickled as hell. It was funny, this middle-aged man all gaga over a baby. People in the park used to think he was your grandfather. I was, what, thirteen. I could have been jealous, I guess, but you were actually a pretty decent little baby. No visible defects, had some hair, didn't make much noise at all.

"So they were about walking on air. See, because while all that was going on he'd been building up a hell of a good law practice. I guess he was pretty much the top labor lawyer in the state. Which had begun to mean something, because it seemed like the unions were really busting loose then, or trying to. And those guys loved him. You'd have thought they'd been put off by him, you know, old family name, big house, Cambridge degree, former staff officer, but they ate it up. He'd have them out to the house and could see in their faces that they loved having a guy like that as their lawyer. They felt like they'd really arrived.

"It was all that union business that finally got him back into politics. He didn't have any idea about running for anything at first. But, what it was, the governor they had in there was a real cast-iron, four-way, revolving son of a bitch. I mean, not to mince words, what he was was a big fat red-neck—tolerably smart but mostly tough as nails and mean as a snake. He was fat as butter, his clothes always bagging off him. They say he was sitting in Capitol Square one Sunday feeding the birds and two soldiers came up to him and said they were between trains, did he know where they could get a drink on a Sunday? Which the answer was in Richmond back then you couldn't. See, they thought he was an old wino. Well, he said, sure, come on back to my house and hoist a couple, and they went back to the mansion and sat around and told dirty stories and

179

got crocked. Those boys missed their train, so he put 'em up in the guest bedroom. He was that kind of guy. Truth to tell, I don't think the old man and his crowd liked this guy any too much either, but they left him alone because he did such a good job for them.

"This guy was wild on the subject of unions. Hated 'em. Seemed like every time you turned around there was some new law about what you couldn't do if you were a union or what they could do to you. He'd call special sessions and all, and they'd pass 'em one after another. They banned unions of public workers, made it a criminal offense for public workers to strike, passed the Right-to-Work Law and so on and so on. The Colonel would go down to the legislature and lobby against them, and they'd pass 'em anyway every time. He'd come home mad as a hornet. He got so he hated those guys. He figured they were feeling their oats because FDR was dead, and I think that made him kind of sick.

"What really did it was when they busted the power company strike. They were all set to pull the men out of one of the generating plants, and everybody figured they'd have to try to keep it going with managerial types. The Colonel was the union's lawyer; he'd been working for them for a couple of months. The day before the strike the governor announced that he was drafting every member of the union into the state militia. It was a hell of a thing. I mean, we didn't even have a state militia, except on paper, since the war, and there sure as hell wasn't any law letting the governor draft anybody into that or anything else.

"I was with him when they called to tell him what had happened, and he was so mad I felt physically afraid. If the governor had been in that room, I believe he might have tried to strangle him with his bare hands. Because he knew damn well—they both knew—the union would win in the Supreme Court, but it didn't matter. They'd broken the strike, and by the time the ruling came down they'd had another special session and outlawed strikes at utility plants.

"I think that was when he decided he was going to run for governor. And let me tell you one thing. Don't ever let anybody tell you he was stupid to do it. People say he didn't have a chance, he was just tilting at windmills, and that's a bunch of crap. It's one thing to get beat, and it's another thing to be stupid. Turned out it didn't work, but he had a hell of a good chance.

"First thing he did was go all out for Harry Truman. The old man and the governor and them didn't like Truman, and they'd tried to pull this deal to keep him off the ballot: you know, unpledged electors. The people got kind of mad about that, so they dropped it. Then the Colonel stepped in and organized the state for Truman, and he went all over the state speaking for him. Truth to tell, I'm not sure he liked Truman all that much, but he kept that to himself, and he went around making speeches and getting his name in the papers, and he didn't say a word about running for governor.

"I don't think he even told Mom until fairly late in the game. She didn't like it one bit; here she was with a two-year-old baby, and he was off to the wars again. I don't know what he said to her. But I think that's when the real trouble started.

"He was lining his guys up very quietly. He met with a few labor people and some of the liberal types from the legislature, and they got pretty excited about it. It'd been a long time since anybody stood up to that crowd, and it seemed like the time was right. He looked like a pretty good candidate, too. So they gave him a list of names, people they really trusted. And he'd go into a town for Truman, and he'd look these guys up, and he'd talk to them about it. Just a few guys in each district, so not much of it would leak in the press. But they agreed to wait on the election results, because everybody figured if Truman took the state, he'd have a chance.

"Well, Truman carried Virginia by about thirty thousand votes. A lot of the people down in Southside voted for Strom Thurmond instead of Dewey. And the Colonel was ready. Because each of these guys who'd said he would support him, see, he made sure they were at the election party in Richmond. They all stayed the night, and the next morning he called a press conference and announced for governor, and all of those guys were there to stand up with him. So here was the guy who'd carried the state for Truman, running for governor, and right away he looks like a winner.

"You ought to remember that, Mac. You were there. You would have been almost two, I guess. You were all dressed up in a sailor suit, and Mom was holding you. She bitched like hell about it, but she brought you. They didn't have TV lights then, or you'd have started crying for sure.

"That campaign lasted for ten months. I guess each person has a time in his life when you sort of grow up, when you first realize what it feels like to be on your own, outside the place you grew up in. The Army's like that for a lot of people; for the Colonel I know it was. That campaign was like that for me. I was just fifteen then, and at first they made me stay in school, or anyway Mom did; he wanted to take me out for the semester, but she said absolutely not, so I only got out on weekends and vacations and so on. That was when they were going around trying to get people registered, which was hard as hell in those days. You had to pay the poll tax, which cost a poor man plenty, and even then the registrar was liable to give you a blank sheet of paper or 'lose' your form or ask you to recite

the Preamble to the State Constitution from memory and so on. I mean
this was for blacks and whites, too. If they didn't know you, they didn't
want you voting. So he was trying to fight that.

"A lot of people didn't even know where to go or how to try to register.
He was pretty smart about it. He made a bunch of records and bought
time on the radio stations; they played those records, and there was his
own voice telling people how they could register and why they ought to.
You know, he was one of the first people around here to really use radio
and so on. The machine crowd never needed to. Then he'd take ads in the
local papers telling people in each city where the registrar's office was and
when it was open. They got right many registered that way.

"Now, later on, the other side started saying we were paying people's
poll tax for them. That used to make him mad. He didn't hold with it; for
one thing, he said if you got started doing it, the other side could do it a lot
better, so it didn't pay. Like poison gas, he said. But I think there were
some people who figured, hell, the poll tax is just a cheat to do a man out
of his vote, so why not cheat and give the man back his vote? So I believe
there was some of that that went on, but nobody told him about it.

"But by the time the summer came and I started traveling with him all
the registration was closed. What he was doing then was trying to per-
suade the people who'd already registered. I drove the car while he
worked on his speeches. Let me tell you, Mac, that campaign was the
most fun I ever had. At first I was just out for a good time. Politics didn't
mean much to me then. And a lot of people wanted to be nice to me because I was the candidate's son. I got free liquor, as long as he didn't see
me. Hell, that was when I got laid the first time. We were staying at a
guy's house, and this guy and the Colonel had to go off to some kind of
secret meeting. And I was there with this guy's daughter—she was maybe
seventeen, right pretty, had sort of long red hair. So after they'd gone,
she said, 'Let's go swimming, I know a pond, we can walk there.' I said,
'Okay, why not?' Skinny-dipping sounded pretty racy to me. So we hid
our clothes in the woods and went and jumped off this dock. And about
five minutes later this pair of headlights came down the dirt road, and she
sang out, 'Oh, Jesus, it's the sheriff,' and quick we both swam up under
the dock. There was enough room to breathe if we sort of kept our chins
up. So I'm under there, and I kept seeing these headlines, CANDIDATE'S
SON SEIZED AS AMPHIBIOUS PERVERT.

"Pretty soon we heard this pair of boots walking on the dock, and then
they stopped right over our heads. The guy was flashing his flashlight over
the water and trying to decide if he'd seen anybody or not. We were under
the dock, keeping our chins up, trying not to breathe too loud, sort of hud-

dled together in fright. And scared as I was, I couldn't help noticing that that damn girl wasn't just pretty, she was built like a brick outhouse. She was one hell of a piece. And pretty soon she noticed that I was noticing.

"Well, women are something, Mac. Here we are in danger of a trip to the hoosegow, and she got this funny look in her face. I still remember, she had this red hair, and it was sort of floating on the water behind us. Before I knew what was happening, she had started sort of rubbing herself right up against me, and here I am trying to keep my head above the water and not make any noise, and she nearly drove me insane. She was loving every minute of it. And to show you how little I knew about things in general, the first thing I thought was, she's working for the old man. I really thought that, for a minute at least.

"But pretty soon I just thought I was going to die. If that red-neck sheriff had stayed one more minute, I'd have come right there in the water. Truth to tell, I didn't even hear him leave; she did. She said, 'Let's get out.' We climbed on the dock, and I was so hot we went at it right there. That sheriff had come back, he'd have had a real good charge to bust me for. You know, I still see that woman from time to time. Just to say hello, I mean. She married a doctor down there; they got a couple of kids.

"How the hell did I get off on that? You see what I'm saying; at first I didn't really care too much about the politics of it, I was having a good time. But it didn't take long for me to figure out that this campaign was something pretty amazing. He was really getting through to people. We'd come into these little towns, and they'd have a speaking in the town square. That's what they called it, a speaking. And he'd get up there, and he had this standard speech he'd do. He'd vary it a little for local issues, but to start with, he'd introduce himself, and then he'd say, 'I'm running for governor of Virginia because I fought for democracy in Europe, and I'm not willing to see a little band of men destroy it in this state. I'm running for governor because the so-called political machine in this state has tried to take away the rights we fought for in the last war. These men have taken our state away from us and put it under lock and key. They've taken our votes, they've taken our schools, they've taken our courts, they've taken our newspapers, and now they're telling us that if we don't shut up and take orders, they'll take our jobs and our homes and anything else they've got a mind to. Well, the American people wouldn't take that kind of talk from Hitler or Mussolini or Hirohito and we won't take it from any man in Virginia, be he chairman of the State Compensation Board or governor or senator or anything else! And he'd rip into the old man and the governor and old R. E. Lee Tevyepaugh, who was the head of the State Compensation Board.

"He'd been making speeches his whole life; he'd got to be pretty good at it. You could see those people looking at him and thinking about all that World War II stuff, and he made a hell of a good-looking candidate, he had that steel-gray hair, and glasses like FDR, and he wore a white ice-cream suit, and people would look at him, and they believed. I don't mean the rich folks, lawyers and doctors and bankers and businessmen and all. Most of them were against us, even some of his friends. They'd come and listen and stand in the back, you know, arms crossed, watching. No expression. But it was the ordinary people—small farmers and store checkers and mill workers and streetcar drivers and holy rollers and gas jockeys—they loved him. They thought he was terrific. They believed.

"I guess it was about the middle of July—about a month before the primary—that I began to figure out what was going on, and those next two weeks, Jesus Christ, Mac, I've been in politics for a while now, been in plenty of campaigns, and I'll tell you, I've never felt anything like that again. I don't believe I could live through it again. It was like—I don't know, it was like watching a man trying to lift the biggest damn rock in the world, and you know the son of a bitch can't do it, because no one can, and then by God he's doing it. It was like being drunk all the time. I suddenly realized that my father was going to be governor, and for a couple of weeks there I really thought the man was a sort of combination of Jefferson and FDR and God.

"And I got so excited I didn't really figure out what they were doing to us until it was all over. See, it was a three-way race. The old man and his guy, a congressman from the Seventh District, old Albemarle family, good-looking, good voice. But there was this other guy running who'd been mayor of, what, Newport News, Port Warwick, I don't know. He gave away ball-point pens. Kind of a crank, you know, but smart, and some of the old man's people were going to go for him, out of friendship, so he was going to get some votes. We figured he'd get enough so we'd get a plurality. There wasn't any runoff law then, so we'd have the nomination, which was the same as getting elected.

"But along about August first the Apple-Farmer figured out he was in trouble. If we'd won, he'd have been on the ropes. I won't say we could have finished him personally, but it'd have been for a real revolution in this state. So he started trying to turn it on us.

"First thing they did was get this third guy. Old Tevyepaugh, the Compensation Board guy, started making phone calls to his people, sheriffs and commonwealth's attorneys and so on. He let 'em know anybody who went with this guy was going to have a little trouble with his salary request. So that took about one weekend. Come Monday the poor bastard was buried in paper. Letters of regret. Withdrawing support. That was the end of him.

"But we still had a chance to beat them head to head. So they went to work on us. We were in Salem, I think, someplace like that. Big rally, and the Colonel was speaking, and in the back of the crowd were these two guys in some kind of field caps, American Legion, VFW, something like that, and carrying these little American flags. We didn't think anything of it. I thought they were there to support us. But the next day in the paper was an interview with one of these guys and he said he was making a gesture of protest against an unpatriotic candidate. By which he meant the Colonel.

"So from then on we had these bastards in beanies at every stop. They never said anything, just stood in back of the crowd with their little flags and put a little chill on all that World War Two stuff. I can't prove who put 'em up to it, but there's no doubt in my mind. Because within a week or so the Apple-Farmer himself opened up on us. Usually he stayed out of the primaries, but now he commenced making speeches. He said he had a duty to warn the state that the Colonel was unpatriotic. He said he was owned by the left-wing element of the CIO. There were maybe three thousand members of the CIO, tops, in the state back then.

"Well, we spent the last few days drying to defend ourselves. The Colonel went on radio and talked about his service in two wars. That's no way to be doing in politics; you need to stay on the attack.

"But we still would have made it if Pop Warfield hadn't called that press conference. He'd just been elected Republican state chairman the year before. He told the press it was an emergency situation, and he was asking all his fellow Republicans to vote in the Democratic primary to prevent the state government from falling into the hands of—I don't know, irresponsible elements or something.

"That's what sank us. We figured later about thirty thousand of those bastards crossed over, and we lost by twenty thousand or so. It hurt like hell. The night of the election I couldn't believe it. I felt like somebody had stabbed me right in the stomach, it hurt that bad. I went up to him and sort of threw my arms around him and cried and cried. I kept on saying, 'It's not fair, It's not fair.' And here he was comforting me. 'I know, son, I know,' he said. 'It's not fair at all.'

"Well, that was that.

"Next thing I knew he was asking me if I wanted to live in London. Some big job in the Marshall Plan. That sounded okay to all of us. They'd made life in Richmond pretty unpleasant for us after that. That crowd knew how to carry a grudge. They never forgot or forgave anything.

185

"So he decided to take the job. He and Mom were still not getting along too well, and I think they thought they could start over. We were all set to go. The job was pretty definite. All he needed was this FBI check, this new loyalty thing Truman had set up. Just a formality.

"I still remember the day those FBI guys came. The second time, I mean. He sent 'em away once because they wanted to talk about OSS and he said it was secret. They came back with clearance papers. It was a Saturday, right around New Year's. He was going to talk to 'em in the front room, and then we were going to dinner. I can't remember the occasion—Mom's birthday, I think. Yeah, that's right.

"When those guys left, he came out and went into the study in the back. I happened to be sitting there, and I saw his face. It was white. Here he'd gotten beat in the primary and so on, and he'd never really showed it, and it was like all of a sudden it had all caught up with him. I said, 'What's wrong?' He looked at me, I'm not sure he knew who I was. Then he sort of fumbled in his jacket and pulled out some money and said, 'Son, would you take your mother out to dinner for me? I have a little work to do.' He took off his suit coat and sort of draped it on the back of the chair, and he sat down right on it like he'd forgotten it was there. He pulled out a legal pad and started writing, and he didn't look up at me at all again. I stood there for a minute watching him write, and I heard a little voice inside saying, 'We're in trouble now.'"

Then Lester showed Mac a copy of what their father had been writing in such a hurry, so as not to forget any of it. It was a copy retyped by a patient stenographer on grainy yellow second sheets, the first item in a bulky untidy file his father had kept, headed "EVANS, J. T. (Fed. Loyalty Rev. Bd.)"

The paper was headed "Interview with Special Agents Buxton and Ghirardelli, Richmond, Va. Jan. 12, 1949." It was a dialogue between three characters named E, B, and G.

E. began it: Well, gentlemen, I am now satisfied about your clearances. I'm ready to proceed, and I regret the need for delay.

G. Believe me, Colonel, there's no offense taken. Most of the people we deal with are very sloppy about security. It's refreshing to meet someone who is security conscious.

B. You're ready to talk about OSS now?

E. Certainly, Mr. Buxton. As I told you before, I'm very eager to cooperate—

186

B. Yes, sir. You told us before.

E. Well, then, shall we begin?

G. You understand how this works, Colonel. This is a routine check; we make our report to the loyalty board, which then has to pass on your nomination.

E. Yes , I understand. But I'm not sure what in my background could be of interest to you. I have no skeletons in my closet.

B. You're a rare bird, then, Colonel.
(Laughter)

G. Let's just start very generally. Would you tell us where you served with OSS, Colonel?

E. Certainly. I was recruited by General Donovan early in 1942, and for the remainder of that year I worked out of his headquarters as a member of Mr. Dulles' staff. In January of 1943 I was posted to Fifth Army Headquarters in North Africa, where I remained until July, when I was transferred to General Eisenhower's headquarters in Algeria. In September of 1943 I was again transferred, this time to SHAEF Headquarters, London, where I was assigned to the OSS Labor Branch.

G. What were your duties at Fifth Army?

E. I was in command of the Fifth Army Climatological Survey Station in Spanish Morocco.

B. Look, Colonel, I don't understand why you refuse to level with us. We know you weren't a meteorologist. You're acting like a man with something to hide.

E. I assure you I have nothing to hide, Mr. Buxton, but the security habit is hard to break. I'm sure you understand.

B. We've showed your our clearance papers. Now—

G. Just a minute, Ed. We do understand, Colonel. Now, isn't it a fact that during this period you were actually commanding officer of Operation Matamoros?

E. Yes, of course. That is correct.

B. Will you please describe Operation Matamoros for us?

E. Yes, of course, I don't see why not. This was a plan to introduce a network of spies into Franco Spain, under OSS control.

G. For what purpose, Colonel?

E. Generals Donovan and Clark were afraid that Franco might enter the war on the side of the Axis. Our agents were to provide intelligence on that question and encourage resistance if Spain in fact did go to war.

G. You were in command of Matamoros from its inception, Colonel?

E. Yes.

G. And in that capacity you traveled to Mexico City in September, 1942?

E. Pursuant to orders, I did.

G. While there, did you meet with and recruit as agents two Spaniards named Armando Aguilar and Ramón Quiñónes?

E. Pursuant to orders, I recruited a task force of twelve agents. Those two were among them, yes.

B. These two men had been members of the Communist Party in Spain.

E. I'm not sure I understand. What is the question?

B. Did you know that these two men were Communists?

E. Certainly, Mr. Buxton. They were recruited for that reason.

G. How's that, Colonel?

E. Excuse me, do either of you gentlemen know Spain?

G. No, I've always wanted to travel there, but I never have.

E. You, Mr. Buxton?

B. No.

E. The Communist underground in Spain was well organized and very active after the Civil War. I recruited these men to make contacts with that underground. This was done with General Donovan's personal approval.

188

B. I see.

G. Did you in 1942 meet with and recruit an American citizen named Augusto Torres?

E. Yes.

B. Did you know that this individual was a member of the American Communist Party?

E. Certainly. Gus Torres was a veteran of the Lincoln Battalion, he was a skilled radio operator, and he knew Spain. He had contacts with the Communist underground. He turned out to be one of the most valuable men I had. And after he left Matamoros, I might add, he earned the Bronze Star for his work behind the lines.

G. I see.

B. While you were at this so-called weather station in Morocco, did you lead a covert attack against the French prison facility at Al Ayesha?

E. Yes, I did. I'm very proud of that operation.

B. You aided the escape of some seventeen convicts, isn't that right?

E. I hope you don't mind my asking, but did either of you gentlemen serve overseas?

G. Not me, Colonel. I was still in high school.

E. You, Mr. Buxton?

B. I was with the embassy in Paraguay.

E. Have either of you seen a concentration camp?

G. In the newsreels.

E. Well, gentlemen, Al Ayesha was a concentration camp, and it was a foul, stinking place. The men imprisoned there were not convicts in our sense of the word. They were not criminals. They were antifascist political prisoners. The French authorities penned them up under barbaric conditions and subjected them to the most appalling tortures. My task force liberated seventeen of these men, Spanish exiles who had agreed to serve in Matamoros.

B. This was done pursuant to orders, I assume?

E. No. I ordered it on my own authority as commanding officer of Matamoros.

B. It was reported to Fifth Army Headquarters?

E. No.

G. Why not, Colonel?

E. Fifth Army did not wish to come into open conflict with the French authorities. They were able to deny all knowledge of the operation and blame it on bandits.

B. So this operation was carried out solely on your own authority?

E. That is correct. You must remember that General Donovan gave his men wide leeway in making these kinds of tactical decisions.

B. Did you ever in conversation refer to Operation Matamoros as 'the sealed train'?

E. I'm sorry, I didn't understand you.

B. "The sealed train."

E. Not that I recall.

B. Did you use your command of Matamoros in an attempt to foment a Communist revolution in Spain?

E. I most certainly did not. What in heaven's name are you talking about?

G. Colonel—

E. The suggestion is laughable.

B. Isn't it a fact that your agents made an unauthorized landing on the Spanish coast after the naval authorities had specifically prohibited it?

E. Yes.

G. I see.

E. I'm not at all sure you do. The situation was this. Our first team of agents had been put ashore at Almería, with the full approval of the naval authorities. The landing in question was to supply this team.

B. With arms?

E. Some small arms, yes, and radio equipment. But at the last minute, for reasons unknown to me, the British Admiralty decided to forbid all covert landings on the Spanish coast. I believe there was some kind of diplomatic maneuver in progress. But I felt a deep personal responsibility to those men. Speaking for OSS, I had recruited them and promised them support, and I felt obligated to keep my promise. I hired a fishing boat, and we crossed to make the drop ourselves. But because of the delay, we missed the rendezvous, and my agents were spotted and arrested. That little piece of high-level blundering cost four lives.

G. I see.

B. Were you a member of the Communist Party in 1942?

E. I most certainly was not, Mr. Buxton. What is the meaning of that question?

G. Please bear with us, Colonel. You must understand that we have to follow up every lead in an investigation of this type.

E. To what lead do you refer?

B. Were you a member of a Communist cell including Armando Aguilar, Ramón Quiñónes, Agusto Torres, and others?

E. Certaily not. I have never been a member of the Communist Party at any time, nor have I attended a meeting of any cell. I find these questions highly insulting, and I demand to know who has been spreading these slanders about me.

G. I'm sorry, Colonel, I'm not at liberty to disclose that information.

B. That's right. For security reasons. You do understand that, don't you, Mr. Evans?

There was more in the file: notices of hearings, letters to lawyers, notes of appeal, letters of reference, denials of guilt, denials of appeal, denials of motion, denials of employment. They were the legal flesh of Mac's own first memories: memories of a house full of whispers, of conferences behind closed doors, of a tall man with a drawn white face, sitting hunched over piles of paper, a man who started at every sudden sound: his father.

But there was no paper to explain his last memory of that man: of a gentle pressure which woke him from sleep, and the man kneeling by his bed, saying, "Mac, listen, Mac, your daddy's got to go away now. I'm going away for a long time. You be a good boy now. Someday I'll be back. So you be good, you mind your mother."

Then two dry lips which in memory felt and rustled like paper touched his forehead, and his own lips were saying, *Me too, Daddy, take me, too,* but that was already in sleep again, speaking in a dream, so that in the morning he thought it had all been a dream, but then his mother had told him his father was gone. Gone to South America, and not coming back.

THREE

★

As it turned out, it was Lester who raised Mac. After his father left, Mac lived with his mother in the big house. He remembered her: a short, slight woman with gray-blond hair and a precise, musical way of talking. Her voice floated like a flock of multicolored balloons. Even at seven years old. Mac could tell she was restless. They stayed in Richmond, but as Mac remembered those years his mother was always on her way somewhere, or just back from somewhere, or working on something. She traveled to meetings and conventions, wrote articles for certain magazines and journals. She lived less and less in Richmond.

When Mac was nine, she asked him how he would like to have a new daddy. Even at that age, Mac was judicious; it would, he said, depend on the new daddy in question. This turned out to be a tall man, who to Mac seemed older than anyone he had ever seen, with a shiny bald head and a funny way of talking: he rolled his *Rs* and said *V* for *W*. His mother said that was because Emil had been born in Hungary. But he lived in Florida now, where he made parts for jet planes; he was very rich. Mother had met him at a convention. How would Mac like to have Emil for a new daddy and live in Florida? Mac thought that on the whole he wouldn't like either.

That was where Lester came in. It was his last year in law school: he was engaged to be married the coming June. Mac hadn't known Lester very well: he was a sardonic presence at Christmas. He and Mother had not seemed to get along very well together, although nothing was said. Now Lester asked Mac if he would like to stay in Richmond with him; Mac said yes, mostly because he didn't want to go to Florida and make parts for jet airplanes. "Okay," Lester said. "Let's sell it to the old ones." Which Lester did by pointing out that Mom's new life would leave her little time for Mac anyway; after all, she was now national vice-chairman of Americans for Preparedness, Inc., and hard at work on a book of her own, wasn't she? Pretty soon she'd have a full lecture schedule, and between that and writing and lobbying in Washington for bigger defense expenditures she would probably find the boy too much to handle at home. He'd end up in boarding school anyway (Mac didn't want to go to boarding school, but he said nothing. He was leaving it up to Lester). So why not let him stay up here, with Lester and his wife, where he could continue at St. Cyprian's? It would be like boarding school—Mac could come down to see her and Emil every summer and vacation. And if it turned out that they had time for him in Florida, fine: he could move then; this would be temporary anyway. Emil thought it was a good sound idea; Mother seemed a little more doubtful, but finally she agreed.

He spent that first summer, and every summer until he was fifteen or so, in Florida with his mother. Mac enjoyed those trips. He got to stay up late, waiting for the train in the big cool echo of the railroad station. Then Lester would hoist him aboard the train, into a cool damp old Pullman car, and give the porter five dollars to watch out for him. He slept in a roomette, between snowy sheets crackling with starch, and woke to the sight of Florida's palmetto jungle slipping past the frosty window. The porter led him to the diner, where from the ten-dollar bill Lester had pinned in his pocket he could pick whatever he wanted to eat; he always had French toast, because it came dusted with powdery sugar. There was a rose in a special vase in the middle of the table; the vase was designed so the train's motion would not knock it over. The waiter would give Mac a cup of coffee if he wanted, with plenty of milk and sugar, and he drank the hot drink in the cool railroad car and watched the steamy landscape slipping by. In Jacksonville he bought magazines, checking his watch constantly, fearful lest the train leave him behind. Then as morning wore into afternoon, he sat upright on the upholstered seat in his roomette, a small boy in a short-pants suit and a white shirt and clip-on bow tie, reading *Amazing Stories* and *Children's Digest* and *Popular Mechanics*, until the porter came and fetched him. His mother met him in Emil's shiny car, which she drove herself at first. Then later she let the chauffeur drive and waited in the back, motor idling, airconditioner running, while the driver fetched Mac and his bags. They drove back to Emil's house, which was not like any house Mac had ever seen: it was set back from a private beach, surrounded by spiky plants called Spanish bayonets which would go right through your eye into the brain if you ran into one. The house was long and low, one story, half of glass, half of pink stucco, which swirled like ice cream melting in the sun. In back was a swimming pool and patio.

The house was full of silence. Emil, who had retired and thus really did not have to go to work anymore to make parts for jet airplanes, spent each day in white pajamas and bedroom slippers, with a glass in his hand, watching television with an earplug in his ear so no one else could hear the sound. His mother worked at her desk or talked on the phone, her light, precise voice floating about the house. There was a girl to take care of Mac, hired from a local college. Each day she led him down to the private beach, where he spent hours scanning the horizon for sharks, dolphins, sea monsters, Russian ships. He would swim while the girl watched him, and once the undertow caught him and he nearly drowned, but she swam out to rescue him, and she brought him back in, holding him tightly against her body, slick and warm in the wet bathing suit, and Mac secretly thought it was great fun. Though she had asked him not to tell, he did anyway, because it had been so much fun. But his mother got angry and sent the girl away.

At night Mac played with a big red chestful of toys they had bought him or read his books. The nights were full of stars, more than he had ever seen in Richmond, and his mother gave him a star map, and Mac learned the constellations, Orion and his dog Sirius, Cassiopeia the W, the two Dippers, the tiny Pleiades, and Polaris and Aldebaran and Betelgeuse. At night he slept with the surf thrumming around him like the beating of a heart.

Every August he went home to Richmond, to Lester and his wife, Molly O. They sent him to St. Cyprian's every day. That first year, when he had gotten back, he had felt a sort of dry panic in the back of his throat which he hadn't been able to tell Lester about. It came when he went to the wooded playground and his classmates dug for sassafras root. They held it out for him to smell. It smelled good, but to him it looked no different from any other root. His classmates talked about sassafras and dogwood and honeysuckle, poison ivy, blackberries. Mac didn't know what they were. The other boys seemed to be connected to the land of Virginia, and Mac did not.

He didn't say anything to Lester until the dreams came, though. They came that winter, his first of living with Lester and Molly O. In the dream Mac was sitting alone on the big divan in the front room. He was sitting upright, worried about something, though not for quite a while, no matter how often he dreamed the dream, did he realize he was being attacked. It was the pools of shadow in the corners of the room, between the couches and cabinets and knickknack tables. Mac watched in terror as they darkened and flowed together until they surrounded the room, began growing until they covered the door and the furniture and the windows. Mac tried to cry out, but he could not speak, could not even move as the inky darkness grew around him in total silence. In terror, he had raised his eyes to the portrait of his grandfather, the bishop, because he had always thought that God lived behind that picture somehow, but then he saw that the shadows had covered the picture, and more than that, they had taken away the image so that only a mocking blank space remained, and then the shadows were closing in on him, and it was like the time he had drowned, but no fun at all because there was no one to rescue him, they were taking him away like the portrait, soon nothing would remain, or nothing had ever been there, he and the shadows would be one, he would be no one, he had never existed, he was nobody's child. Then he would wake up screaming in his bed.

Lester always came. The first time it happened, Mac choked out the dream to his brother, and Lester had soothed him back to sleep. "Don't worry, Mac, you are somebody. You're my brother, that's who you are. Nothing's going to get my brother." Night after night Lester came and held his hand, until finally the nightmares went away.

Lester did everything for Mac. They went together to buy clothes and shoes; they went to the doctor. Lester took Mac for walks by the river and explained to him about his mother. "Listen, bub," he said. "It isn't that she doesn't want you down there. It's just that you belong here, and she knows it. This is where you're from, this is where you ought to grow up, and you've got me and Molly O. to take care of you."

"Why do I belong here, Lester?" Mac asked him.

"Because this is where your daddy was born, and his father, and his father. Because your people have been here since this place has been here. It's your city, it's where you belong to live."

"But Daddy doesn't live here now," Mac objected.

"Mac, listen," Lester said, the corners of his mouth tightening a little. "Our daddy isn't here because he ran away. That's the worst thing you can do, run away. I don't want you to run away. You belong here."

"I won't run away, Lester," Mac said.

Mac had liked living with Lester and Molly O. It was not until much later that he thought that Lester might have needed him as much as he had needed Lester. They were the last two of their family living together in the big house.

They weren't alone. Mac loved Molly O., who was then what she was later: a gentle, calm woman with a quiet, warm laugh. Because Lester insisted on being responsible for Mac, Molly O. and Mac became, in time, co-conspirators. Lester felt that Mac was his responsibility, and he refused to pass it on to his bride. So the two of them conspired together on an equal basis as Mac grew up, planning surprises for Lester of one kind or another.

And Lester and Molly O. gathered about them a circle of friends their own age. It seemed natural to Mac that Lester would be the center of a group. It seemed natural that they should agree with Mac that things were more fun when Lester was around. The group went to the beach, or hunting, or fishing, or to parties: Lester was the organizer. He had a way of looking at Mac, or Molly O., or a friend, with his head cocked slightly to the side, his right eye squinting slightly, face deadpan. Then he would say the most outrageous things; he could reduce a whole room to helpless laughter without cracking a smile.

Every morning, when Mac went off to the third grade at St. Cyprian's, Lester went off to work. He was a lawyer with the same firm his father had worked for; it was bigger now and had expanded its name to Powell, Valentine, Snead, Carter & Andrews. Lester told Mac it was the biggest law firm in the state. He told Mac he'd gone there to have a chance to represent the best clients in the state: the power company, the phone company, the railroad, the Central Planters Bank. When Mac got a little older, one of the boys at school told him that his father had been fired from that firm. He asked Lester why he wanted to work somewhere that his father had been fired from.

"Well, bub, your friend didn't get it quite right," Lester said. "Our father wasn't fired from there. You see, when you work for a law firm, you agree to do what they say. Our father wanted to take a certain case, and the firm told him not to, and he did it anyway. So they asked him to leave."

"Isn't that the same as being fired?"

"No, not exactly."

"Why do you want to work somewhere that asked our daddy to leave?"

197

Lester thought for a moment. "Listen, bub," he said at last, "you're not old enough to appreciate it yet, but our father was a very famous man."

"He was?" Mac wondered how the pale scarecrow figure he remembered could have been famous.

"Yes, he was."

"What for?"

"For a lot of things. He was a lawyer, and a soldier, and he worked for General Eisenhower—"

"Daddy knew the President?"

"He wasn't President then, but yes, he got a medal from him and then he ran for governor."

"I knew that."

"Listen, bub, this is hard to explain, although I think when you get to be my age, you'll understand it. Sometimes it isn't easy to be the son of a famous man. Everybody expects you to be just like him and to do what he did, do you see?"

Mac nodded. "I think so."

"Sometimes if you want to have your own life and not just be known as somebody's son, you have to do something to show people that you're a different person from your father, so they'll treat you as an individual. Do you see?"

Mac thought about that for a moment. "But don't you want to be like our daddy?" he said. "Aren't you proud of what he did? Why do you want to be different?"

Mac was afraid he'd said something wrong because Lester's mouth tightened again, just for a minute; then it was all right again. But there was something wrong with his voice when he said, "Of course, I'm proud of him, Mac. It's not that. It isn't that." A pause while he searched for words. "You'll understand when you're older."

Actually, Mac didn't want to be like his father; he wanted to be like Lester. That was a hard job, though, because it was hard to understand just what Lester was like. Lester wanted him to go to St. Cyprian's, because he'd gone there and his father had gone there and his grandfather had founded it. But it seemed there were some lessons Lester didn't want Mac to learn. His teachers had explained to him that St. Cyprian's was a church school, which meant, thank God, that it wouldn't be integrated. Mac didn't quite understand what integration was, but he knew the school was against it. On the playground the other boys had taught him a chant. He came home and chanted it for Lester: "Two, four, six, eight, we don't want to integrate." Without warning Lester slapped him across the mouth; he tasted blood where a tooth had cut his lip. He was frightened; looking at Lester, he saw an angry stranger. That was the first time he realized that that anger was in his brother all the time, deep inside. From then on, though he still loved and idolized his brother, he had feared him a little, too.

Later, when Mac had cried and Molly O. had put disinfectant on his lip and said a few choice words to her husband, Lester explained to Mac why he was so angry. "Integration" meant that black children had to go to school with white children; it was a law, because the Supreme Court said so. But some people in Virginia didn't want black children in white schools; they hated black people, which was as wrong as it could be. One of those people was senator, and another was governor, and they had a plan to close down all the schools if they had to and not let anyone go to school. This was called Massive Resistance. Lester said that if it was allowed to succeed, it would be very bad for the country, like another Civil War. Lester told Mac that some people were working to try to stop it, and Lester was one of them. But it had to be done quietly. Mac had to promise not to say anything to anybody.

"Why does it have to be done so quietly?" Mac asked.

"Because if it gets out, it could make some people who are helping us have to stop," Lester said. "And I might have to stop."

"Why would you have to stop?"

"Because some people down at the firm would ask me to stop."

"Would they fire you like they fired our daddy?"

Again there was that sort of catch in Lester's voice. He didn't look at Mac as he said, "No, bub. It wouldn't come to that."

Massive Resistance didn't succeed. Mac remembered watching the governor on TV. The governor acted like a crazy person; he hammered the table with his fist and seemed about to cry. Lester said after the speech that the governor already knew he had no chance, that he was going to have to back down, which meant the plan would fail. Mac asked Lester if he'd stopped it, and Lester said that he had helped some, but a lot of people had worked on it, some of them publicly, and some, like him, quietly, and that it had paid off.

By the time Mac was twelve years old he understood why Lester had wanted to keep quiet during the Massive Resistance debate. Lester was going into politics. Oddly enough, Lester himself never explained this to Mac. Mac found it out when Lester's friend Deeb Grayson had moved to town. Deeb and Lester had been law school roommates. Deeb had finished first in the class, well ahead of Lester. But Deeb had turned down an offer from Powell, Valentine to go off adventuring; he had gotten some kind of job in Central America. The year after Massive Resistance died, Deeb had turned up back in town with a Central American wife and settled down to do as little work as possible. He had money; he didn't have to practice law. So he worked in a few charity drives and answered phones in a couple of political campaigns. Most people who knew him wondered what Deeb was doing with his life.

Mac liked Deeb and visited him often. Grayson was a short, elflike man with thick, tangled carrot-red hair and glasses perpetually askew. Mac enjoyed spending time with him because Deeb talked to him like an adult and because, unlike Lester, Deeb didn't seem to care very much about the appearances of things. Lester was perpetually concerned with doing things right; Deeb flouted convention with cheerful unconcern. He was slovenly, given to ancient corduroy trousers and suede shoes worn without socks; his apartment on West Avenue was a confusion of stark pre-Columbian statuary and steel-and-plastic furniture: on the walls were bizarre outsize abstract paintings and portraits of Juárez, U.S. Grant, and Trotsky.

Another reason Mac visited Deeb was that he found he enjoyed more than he would have thought possible looking at Deeb's wife, Angela. He thought she was the most exotic woman he'd ever seen: short, slender, tawny, with small breasts jutting upward and a mass of blue-black hair dropping past her slender waist. She was foreign, strange, desirable, silent. At night Mac lay in bed and thought of her before falling into wistful sleep.

But he would have come to see Deeb anyway, because he sensed that Deeb was as devoted to Lester as he was and because Deeb would explain things to him that Lester would not. It was from Deeb he learned that Lester planned to enter politics, although afterward it seemed so obvious that he wondered why he hadn't figured it out himself.

Deeb also explained that he was preparing for the time when Lester would be ready to run. Lester would know the time, and Deeb would be ready with the skills to run the campaign.

"I guess I always knew what was going on," Deeb told Mac as they sat in the cluttered living room. Mac was watching carefully, in case Angela should come out of the kitchen, but he was listening, too. "I had some half-baked idea about being a diplomat when we get a Democratic administration again, but that wasn't in the cards. I'm not cut out for it, and it's not the way I want to live my life. I knocked around Central America for a while before I figured out exactly what was going on. Let me see if I can explain it to you. You listening, Mac boy?''

Mac, thinking of Angela, started up with a guilty flush. "Oh, sure. Go ahead.''

"One time they sent me to interview this old fellow—Armando Calles was his name, I remember because he was Angela's great-uncle by marriage or something. The company wanted me to interview him, get his philosophy of government, because of all these local *caciques,* I guess you'd call them bosses, he'd lasted the longest.

"It turned out he didn't much want to talk, so he said—he was a portly old party with one of these Indian faces that don't give away a thing, damn, I'd hate to play poker with him, and a truly great mustache, one of the best I saw down there—he said in very elegant Spanish, 'My friend, I find it is useless to discuss these matters. However, if your time permits, it would be a pleasure for me to demonstrate to you the science of government as I practice it.' So I went with him on his rounds.

"Now we were way yonder to hell and gone back in the damn mountains, poorest place I'd ever seen. The people raised guinea pigs to eat, nobody had very much, even this fellow, and he was the richest man in the village. This old boy was not only the entire federal government for three villages—tax collector, health officer, law enforcement, you name it—he was also the entire economic structure—moneylender, landlord, owned the only store around, so on. He strapped a big old pistol on his hip, and we went walking.

"All he did all day was to go around taking things away from people they didn't want to give up and making them do things they didn't want to do, collecting taxes, so on and so forth. And he was the biggest crook I met down there, which is quite a statement, believe me. He had that poker face, and he went around making up laws as it suited him. It didn't seem to be any secret that he kept a good list and a bad list and the ones on the bad list were always having to pay a lot of fines for things the people on the good list never heard of. Here we are about thirty miles from the army, ten miles from any other policeman or anything: I was scared to death. Those Indians could have blown us away any time they wanted. But this guy Calles was as cool as you please. He stood there and committed the most outrageous larceny and never turned a hair. So when we got through, I asked him, real politely, of course, if he didn't worry about what they might do to him.

"He just shrugged. 'My young friend,' he said, 'this is a gift I have, from God I hope. They do as I say.'

" 'Why?' I asked him. 'Out of fear?'

" 'Oh, no,' he said. 'You see, if a man fears you, he will resent you, and soon he will try to destroy you. Any man will do that,' he said, 'but only a madman resents the wind or the rainy season or the tide. This is my gift. To these people I am a force of nature. I am inevitable.'

"Well, as you can imagine, that made a fairly strong impression on me. I'll tell you, Mac, you're over at St. Cyprian's, civics teachers are the biggest bullshitters in the world. You're probably learning about the law and the Constitution and checks and balances and a whole load of happy horseshit, and if you've got any brains, you'll ignore the whole business. Just remember that governments are made up of old boys like my wife's great-uncle Armando: as long as one of them appears inevitable, all the others are going to fall all over themselves explaining why the Constitution and the law and checks and balances and natural law and the theory of relativity justify this guy's every act. And as soon as he loses that gift of God or whatever, those same folks will be using that same bullshit to justify stepping on his head. You understand that, and the rest is just trimming.

"I thought about it a while, and then I decided to come back. I know you won't take this wrong, I've never been able to explain this to Lester, he takes himself a little too seriously—because what that old Indian had is what your brother's got. Inevitability. He's got more of it than anybody I ever met, whatever the hell it is. I haven't got it; you probably haven't got it either. I figure Lester is my big chance. With the right guidance, which I humbly think of as myself, he could go all the way. I don't know who to compare him to. But I'll make you a solemn prediction: old Lester's going to diddle a lot of people in the next few years, not that he's a bad guy, but that's politics. And barring something monstrous, most of them aren't going to resent it. You watch."

Deeb swigged his beer. Angela came out of the kitchen; Mac watched under hooded eyes. She and Deeb exchanged rapid-fire Spanish; then she wrinkled her nose with distaste and said in her musical, accented English, "That old thief? Why do you lose your time on him?"

Deeb laughed gently. "Because, innocent one," he said gravely, "he is an example of a very important political type."

"No, no," she said, making a graceful gesture of negation with her hands. "This is not true here. I have left my country to escape from these types."

"Well, *paloma*," Deeb said. His gravely humorous voice gave nothing away. "It would have been better to have left it for the sake of love, because you haven't escaped from them."

In the spring Mac turned fourteen, Lester told him he was going to run for the House of Delegates in the primary that August. He seemed a little taken aback, even annoyed, when Mac showed no surprise. Apparently he had not realized his little brother and his best friend had talked about him so much. In fact, Deeb and Mac had been over every stage of the campaign, and it went just as they thought. Deeb ran the campaign: got the press releases out and ordered bumper stickers and posters, set up the schedule, wrote the speeches. Lester made sure that Deeb had plenty of money, and the two of them brought Mac into it like an adult, asking his advice and sometimes following it. Mac organized the youth movement for Evans. He got teen-aged volunteers to stand in shopping centers and on street corners and to go door to door with literature until almost every house in the city had been visited once. Mac began learning from Deeb the things that make a campaign run: how to run a phone bank, how to organize a door-to-door canvass, how to write press releases or a direct-mail solicitation. Lester even let Mac help write a few speeches, and that was what Mac remembered best; seeing Lester before a group of businessmen saying words that he had helped write gave him the first heady rush of excitement, the godlike feeling of power he associated with politics from then on.

But it was neither Deeb nor Mac who won the election for Lester; he did it himself. It was not what he did or said during the campaign, although he knew what to do and say and he did both perfectly. It was what he had done in the years before. He led the ticket that year, which was more than even Deeb had expected. He led the ticket because he had put his coalition together perfectly. He had labor, because their bosses remembered his father, although he had not asked for open support, since that might prove embarrassing. He had the blacks, too, because they knew by now—Lester had made sure they found out—about what he'd done to fight the Massive Resisters. He had women and young people—more of them voted in that primary than in any off-year primary before—because he looked great and talked well at the women's clubs and colleges. He had the moneymen, too; not all of them, of course, because some could never forget that he was the Colonel's son. But there were many young bankers and investors and merchants who barely remembered the Colonel, and there were others who did remember but figured that the son had proved himself by working at Powell, Valentine and had shown that he understood business and its problems and, unlike his father, sympathized with it. Besides, there was something about Lester that made people forget the old grudges and quarrels. Lester Evans was different; he certainly wasn't a conservative, he was nothing like the Apple-

Farmer or his son Junior or Miles Brock, then working his way toward his first term as governor. But he wasn't like his father either, an idealist. He was a new breed, and with a new man in the White House and things changing all over, maybe Virginia needed to change, too, not too much, but enough to keep up. Everybody went with Lester that year, and he led the ticket.

Mac learned plenty about politics during that campaign, but he learned more about his brother. He had always known, ever since Lester had hit him in the mouth for chanting a racist slogan, that somewhere deep inside his brother there was an anger burning, something that he chose not to let out. Lester's plans worked beautifully, but all through the campaign he seemed more and more tense, solitary, irritable. Without warning he would lash out: at Deeb, or Mac, or someone else (though Mac noticed that Deeb was right: by and large they didn't resent it). His rage was surprising, violent, unjustified. During the campaign, for the most part, he kept it under control. But on the night the votes were counted, when it was obvious that all his work was paying off, it came out into the open at last.

Evans' headquarters was a tiny ground floor office in the Hotel Jefferson on Main Street. On election night Mac had set it up for a party: on the wall was a chalk board, marked off by precinct, to record the votes as they came in; in one corner was a keg of beer in a tub of ice, and plastic cups to drink out of; there was ice and setups, too, and red, white, and blue bunting strung around the ceiling. On the opposite wall of the precinct board was a poster of Lester, larger-than-life-size, looking off into the distance with genial interest. Underneath were block letters: "EVANS The Man for Tomorrow." A table of phones lined the back wall, where the precinct reports would be phoned in. Mac had worked most of the afternoon getting the room ready, after a morning at the polls giving out sample ballots with Lester's name in huge red type.

But when Lester came back from campaigning, he hardly glanced at the room. "Fine, fine," he said, and then passed straight back into the untidy back room, which had been Deeb's office during the campaign and now held an extra keg of beer, some cartons of ginger ale, boxes of unused bumper strips, and other detritus of a political campaign. Lester hurled himself into Deeb's chair, swiveling it to face the wall. From a compartment in Deeb's desk he pulled a half gallon bottle of Early Times, and he poured himself a healthy drink.

Mac was eager to talk about the election. "What do you think, Lester?" he asked. "How are we going to do?"

Lester fixed him with a baleful look that discouraged further questions. "Listen, bub, I need to think for a while, okay?"

"Sure, Lester," Mac said, and faded through the door.

Lester sat sprawled in that chair, looking always like a man who had just sat down for a moment's rest, for nearly five hours as the returns came in showing that he had won the election. He was sunk in a deep private silence which nobody—not Mac or Deeb or Molly O.—could penetrate. Deeb came into the back room hour by hour and read off the precinct returns. Once, just once, he tried to explain what the figures meant, but before he could get started, Lester stopped him with an upraised hand. "Can it, Deeb," he said. "I know those figures better than you do." Deeb left the room.

Lester was drinking. As the night wore on, the level in the bourbon bottle fell precipitously. He offered nobody else a drink.

Once Mac came in, full of the news of precincts falling like dominoes. Lester stopped him with a look. Then the two brothers regarded each other warmly but warily.

"Do you know what it is, Mac?" Lester said.

"It's a landslide!" Mac replied jubilantly.

"No, not really," Lester said judiciously. "Not a for-real landslide. Not this one. But it's a real all-American victory."

"No kidding," Mac said. "You're leading the ticket by three thousand votes—"

"Tell me this, bub," Lester said. "What do you think the Colonel is going to think about this?"

Mac was certain. "He'll be happy as hell."

"You reckon so?" Lester said. He appeared to consider that. "You want to call him in South America and find out what he thinks?"

"You mean on the phone?" Mac said.

"Yeah, sure, this phone here."

Mac stared at that instrument with a new respect. "You mean you can call South America on the phone?"

"Sure, why not? You want to call?"

The idea of talking across that gulf of distance to his father made Mac dizzy. "Right now? You mean, right here?"

"Yeah," said Lester crisply. "I suppose you're right. He's probably in bed anyway. But you think he'll be happy, huh?"

"Sure!" Mac said again. "Why not?"

"I got to think about that for a while, is what," Lester said. "Why don't you go out there and shake hands and so forth? I'll be out in a while.

You watch this door, and don't let anybody come back, except maybe Molly O. or Deeb, okay?'' Without waiting for an answer, he turned to studying the wall, raising the cup to his lips with studied precision. Mac went back to the party.

Then it got to be time for Lester to come out, and past time. In the front room, sipping beer and munching pretzels, were the people who had worked for him. There were well-dressed white ladies from the West End, and well-dressed black ladies from the East End, and union men and businessmen, and Mac's troops, the Evans Teens, with a miniskirted phalanx of Evanettes in plastic skimmers and blue dresses. Lester had to come out and thank these people, make them feel appreciated, because he would need them again and again. If they went home irritated or disappointed or hurt, they might not answer the phone the next time Deeb called them for help. So when it got to be past time for Lester to come out, Deeb signaled Mac with his eyes, and they met by the door to the back room.

"We've got to get him out here," Mac said.

"Maybe," Deeb said.

"What do you mean, Deeb?"

Deeb shook his head darkly. "I just hope he isn't so drunk he'll embarrass himself."

"Jesus," Mac said. The thought was stunning. He had never seen his brother show anything but iron self-control. The thought that Lester might not be in command of himself seemed profoundly threatening.

They went into the room. Lester was still sprawled in the chair like a man who had just finished a half-mile run, his eyes scanning the wall. He looked around at them without speaking.

"Uh, Lester," Deeb said hesitantly. "Are you—"

"What time is it, Deeb?" Lester asked.

"It's quarter past eleven," Mac volunteered quickly, glad to be of use in a task so easily done.

"It's time—" Deeb said.

"I guess it's time for me to go out and talk to these folks," Lester said as if Deeb had not spoken. From the pocket of his jacket he took a small white plastic squeeze bottle. Mac recognized it. They had become quite popular at St. Cyprian's: Lavoris mouthwash. Lester gave his mouth a couple of blasts of mouthwash, then started to rise from the chair. But before he got halfway up, his legs buckled, and he sat back down, a look of surprise on his face.

"Hmm," he said meditatively. "Been drinking a little more than I thought."

206

Deeb turned to Mac and whispered urgently, "You go get Molly O. and bring her back here." He gestured toward a coffee urn in the corner of the room. "I'll pour some of this into him, and—"

"Oh, come on, Deeb," Lester said. "There's no need for all that. Just give me a second here."

Mac and Deeb watched while Lester made another attempt to rise. He stood unsteadily, closed his eyes, and took a deep breath, massaging his face with his hand, and then suddenly, as if by magic, he was no longer a tired drunk, but a victorious politician, sober and sane and pulsating reassurance. Mac was awestruck, and Lester, who drunk or sober could tell what his little brother was thinking, threw him a smile and a private wink.

He went out into the front room and shook hands and made a little speech, giving the crowd just what it had come to see. He was funny and humble, and charming and serious, and when he was finished, he kissed Molly O. and held her while the crowd applauded them for being young and good-looking and in love and, most of all, for winning. Then he graciously thanked them and sent them home happy. As they filed out, he walked calmly to the back room with Deeb and Molly O. in his wake.

Mac was trapped by well-wishers who had been unable to shake Lester's hand and settled for his. By the time he had extricated himself and gotten to the door, Molly O. was coming out of the little room. "All right, Lester, all right," she was saying briskly. "It's your big night, and I'm not going to fight with you. You do what you want."

She gestured at Deeb, and he followed her through the door. She gripped his elbow. "Don't you let him get away from you," she said in an urgent half whisper. "And you be good and sure that he doesn't get himself arrested or written up in the paper. Don't you let him mess himself all up."

Deeb rolled his eyes at her helplessly. "I don't know how I can stop him," he said, waving his free hand helplessly.

"God damn you anyway, Deeb," Molly O. said. "Don't be a ninny all your life. You just stop him, that's all."

Deeb shot Mac a confused look that told him nothing. Molly O. followed his gaze and smiled at Mac. "Mac, honey, I guess you better go along, too. You watch out for your brother now."

Then she walked out of the headquarters before Mac could ask what he was supposed to be watching out for. Then he heard Lester's voice. "Where's Mac?" it cried loudly. "Where you at, bub?"

Mac went into the room. Lester was back in the chair, legs outflung, as if he had never gotten up. He was, once again, plainly drunk, but he was no longer sullen or apathetic.

He saw Mac and whooped for joy. "Baby brother!" he shouted. "Come here, you little bastard!" Mac walked over to the chair, and Lester grabbed him around the neck without rising, pulling Mac off-balance. "What do you say, bub?" he said. "We did it this time, didn't we? Damn right! We goin' do it some more. Here, have yourself a drink."

Mac took the bottle. He choked on the bourbon at first, then gulped a healthy swig. It burned, and Mac felt the pain and thought that this was what it meant to be grown up.

"Bub, you and me and old Deeb here are going to celebrate, what do you say?"

They piled into Deeb's car, Lester slumped in the shotgun seat, Mac in the back. They went to a dark smoky after-hours black nightclub where they were the only whites present; they went to a beer joint on the south side of the river where in a special room behind the bar the crew-cut country boys could bet five hundred dollars on one throw of the dice; they went to a cold, bare, echoing loft where Mac saw men dancing with men and women dancing with women and men dressed like women and women who looked like women but were men. Everywhere they went, Lester knew everyone; everywhere they went, a nod from Lester was enough to get the fourteen-year-old Mac admitted and served whiskey without a raised eyebrow from waiter or bartender. Mac looked at his brother and thought that even if he studied him for the rest of his life, he would never know him completely; he had never worshiped him more.

They finished the evening in a basement club on Broad Street where Mac sat riveted in his chair, unable to move or swallow, as a redheaded young woman danced across the stage and systematically removed her clothes, revealing what seemed to his inexperienced eyes the most beautiful body in the world, and then gyrated in a G-string, rotating before his bulging eyes a pair of breasts for which, if he had been asked at that moment, he would cheerfully have given his life.

After she left, Lester poked Mac in the arm and introduced yet another friend, perhaps the hundredth Mac had met that night, a drunken Rumanian psychiatrist hosting a group of his fellow countrymen, sailors whose ship was docked at the Deep Water Terminal on the James. "You're very intelligent, aren't you?" the alienist said with a toothy grin. Mac made no reply; he was in the process of discovering that both his legs had painful cramps in them.

The Republican seemed to come out of nowhere, materializing out of the smoke and confusion of the club. He stood before Lester, a burly, flat-topped, hard-eyed man bursting out of a blue jacket and tieless white shirt. A gold elephant gleamed in his lapel as he offered Lester his hand. "Aren't you Lester Evans?" he asked, smiling evenly below small, watchful eyes.

"Yes, I am," Lester said. He took the hand without rising. "Pleased to meet you, Mr.—"

"Congratulations to you," the man said. The two men continued to shake hands. "You figure you got the nomination so you got it made, I guess?"

Lester eyed the elephant pin discreetly, and said, "Sir, I don't mean to disparage your party—"

"You better not," the man said. "You better not." They stopped shaking hands but continued to clench palm to palm in a motionless intimacy. "We're going to stop your clock one of these days, rich boy."

"Is that a fact?" Lester said, withdrawing his hand. On his face was a conciliatory laugh, but it vanished as the man went on.

"Yes, it is a fact," he said. "We'll get you sooner or later. Maybe not this time, but we'll get you. We screwed your father, and we'll screw you."

Lester glared back at him, the affability gone. He was all cool fury. Mac gasped as his brother said, "The fuck you will." He bared his teeth in a contemptuous smile. "Who is going to do that? You? It's going to take more than a slack-gutted redneck salesclerk in a Robert Hall suit to handle me. It's going to take more than you got a chance of having, you penny-ante moron, you and your whole party of button makers couldn't lay a hand on me."

The man's face flushed, and he drew back a fist. Suddenly Lester had a ginger ale bottle in his hand, clutching the neck.

"Go on, try," Lester said, and he was almost whispering. "You'll be carrying your nuts in your wallet from now on."

The man looked dully down at Lester. "You chickenshit," he said. "Put down that bottle and fight like a man."

Deeb put his hand on Lester's elbow. "Come on, Lester, let it go, he's only a drunk—" he began, but Lester shook him off, and he fell silent.

Lester looked at the big man. "Your behavior is just what I would expect from a redneck who has only recently learned to walk upright," he said, each word icily precise. "A fight here would spoil the evening for the other guests at the club. However, if you would care to continue our discussion of the relative merits of our parties in the alley, it would be my pleasure to oblige you."

209

The man turned for the exit. Deeb tried again. "Listen, Lester," he said, "I'll get the bouncer, and we'll get rid of the guy."

Lester looked at him coldly. "Not a chance, Deeb," he said. "You come with me."

Heads turned as Lester, Deeb, and Mac followed the big man to the back entrance. By the time Deeb and Mac got to the alley Lester and the Republican were squared off.

Lester looked down at his jacket, fumbled with a button. "Don't want to mess this up," he said, his words suddenly slurred.

The other man looked stupidly at Lester. "Oh, yeah," he said. He began to take off his jacket, and Lester brought his hand straight up into the man's face with a blow that stunned him just long enough for Lester to catch him again, this time in the stomach with a solar-plexus punch that brought him to his knees, pop-eyed with amazement, trickling blood at the corner of his mouth.

Lester stood over him in cold anger. "Get up, you redneck bastard," he said harshly. "Get up, you cracker cunt!"

"Leave him alone, Lester," Deeb said. "You've already beaten him. What do you want?"

"You stay out of this, Deeb," Lester said, and turned back to the big man, who had by now staggered to his feet.

"Come on, cocksucker, swing," Lester said, and when the big man swung, Lester coolly and systematically beat him down again, until he was lying on the cobblestones with his eyes closed. Then Lester pulled back his foot to kick him in the head, and Mac remembered Molly O.'s warnings and broke out of his paralysis. "Stop, Lester," he shouted. Lester turned that furious face toward him again, but he went on, which was the first brave thing he'd ever done. "That's enough now. You're going to hurt him!"

Lester's eyes blazed for a minute, and then the fury died, and he was in control again. "Yeah, you're right," he said. He looked down at the man and then knelt over him. "You all right?" he asked. The big man nodded without speaking. Lester ran efficient hands along the man's chest. "Nothing broken," he said crisply. "But you're going to have a couple of black eyes. Here we go," he said, and putting an arm under the man's shoulders, he wrestled him to a sitting position. He took out his handkerchief and began wiping the blood off the man's face, but the man pushed his hand away and looked at him with sullen eyes. "Okay," Lester said. He took the man's own handkerchief from its jacket pocket and handed it to him. "Do it yourself."

The man took the handkerchief from him and began wiping his face, wincing at the pressure of the cloth on lacerated skin.

Lester stood up again and looked down at the man. "No hard feelings?" he said, offering a handshake. The other looked up at him in disbelief. "Okay, I don't blame you," Lester said, withdrawing the hand. "But let me tell you something anyway. You don't belong to go around making people angry in places like this, believe me, you don't. You're no bar fighter, and I knew that the minute I saw you. I hit you with your hands tied, and I'm sorry, but that was because you made me mad. Now you aren't hurt any, so let's just let it lay. You pull that stuff on the wrong guy some time, and you really will get hurt."

He turned and led the way; the three of them passed out of the club.

They drove home in silence, through the light-blue late-summer dawn. As they turned into Axe Trail Road, Lester spied an early-morning paper boy pedaling along on his bicycle. He motioned Deeb to stop the car. "Excuse me, young fellow," he said, poking his head out the car window. "Could you possibly sell to me and my associates an extra copy of this morning's paper, containing latest up-to-the-minute returns of yesterday's crucial Democratic primary?"

The boy looked at Lester in puzzlement, then shook his head.

"What's that you say?" Lester said. "No, is it?"

"No, sir," the boy said. "I ain't got any extras."

"Ah," Lester said. He considered this briefly, then added, "Well, then, fuck you, you freckly-faced little son of a bitch." He pulled his head in the window. "Drive on, Mr. Grayson," he said. "Pray drive us home."

After that first election it was obvious to Mac, and to the community at large, that Lester would be governor someday. Not right away, he was too young, and besides everybody knew that next time around the Apple-Farmer was going to give the nod to Miles Brock, who'd been stalking the State House for nearly fifteen years. Even the time after that would be too soon; Lester would still be too young. But there was time enough, of that everyone was sure; Lester Evans would be governor, and a young governor, too. After he was governor, there would be time to think about something else: the U.S. Senate perhaps, or even . . . but no one, certainly not Mac or Deeb, quite dared to say it aloud. But it was the unspoken thought: President of the United States. And why not? He was young, and rich, and good-looking—a lot like the president who had just been elected. And he had it, whatever it was—that "inevitability" Deeb had talked about. People didn't call it "inevitability," though; when the Richmond newspapers discovered Lester, they wrote about "charm" or "magic." Lester scorned such a notion. "Some damn fool reporter asked me today if there was an 'Evans magic'—I about laughed in his face. Stupidest idea I ever heard of."

"What did you tell him?" Mac asked.

"I don't know—something about having good people work for me. But it's just so much crap, there's no magic in politics, I know that much. All it is is, you plan everything, and I mean *everything*, you stay cool and you keep your balance. The British Secret Service used to say, 'Never complain, never explain, never apologize.' That's it. That's all."

Maybe not, Mac thought; but even if there was no magic, the ability to convince so many others was magic enough. At any rate, Lester seemed bound for glory, and it seemed to Mac that nothing could stop Lester but Lester himself.

Only Molly O., Mac, and Deeb really saw that irrational strain of anger deep inside Lester that surfaced from time to time without warning. Mac thought to himself that it was there because his older brother was somehow doing violence to himself—was following his careful plan which was designed to take him to the State Senate and then the governorship, but which was also making him into a carefully designed personality he had chosen for himself years before. Lester was like a square peg forcing himself into a round hole, even though he had to scrape bits and pieces of himself to fit, and Mac thought his brother must feel angry and frustrated and resentful at himself and the world because the process was so painful.

There were dark whispers among those who knew him slightly or not at all. Mac heard them in the schoolyard at St. Cyprian's—the flapping tongues whispered that Lester Evans was a drunkard, and a philanderer, and a liver of the low life, and that he might be worse, though what that might be no one could quite say. At first, Mac tried to suppress the gossip with his fists—a policy which earned him quite a collection of bruises, for at fourteen and fifteen he was already tall, but gangly and uncoordinated. He could not talk to Lester about it, or to Molly O. (she, after all, in the popular version of the tales, was the wronged one, the innocent who might or might not know of her husband's trespasses), or to Judge Anderson, who would have rendered Mac inarticulate with embarrassment and been left tongue-tied himself.

He turned to Deeb, who took the whole business in stride, pushing his glasses up into his unruly mass of hair. "You and I both know that Lester gets a little wild sometimes, he's been like that since law school. Lester is too cagey to do anything permanent to himself or anybody else, no matter

212

how drunk he is. And the press in this state is too damn timid to print anything like this. No lie: Lester could walk down Broad Street playing a
trombone naked with a ribbon around his prick, and these boys wouldn't
print it. So long as your profligate brother keeps himself out of the
clutches of the police—which at his meanest, drunkest moment he is believe me capable of doing—we've got nothing to worry about.

"Truth to tell, this stuff not only doesn't hurt us, it helps us a little. The
first time we ran people tried to use it against him that he was young and
rich and good-looking, but it didn't work. Hell, that's half of what elected
him. Lester's bigger than life, like the Kennedy brothers, sort of. So if
people hear he plays around, what the hell? That's what everyone'd do if
they were him."

So Mac learned to ignore the rumors about Lester as he went through
his last four years at St. Cyprian's. In fact, he tried to ignore Lester altogether while he was at school, which was hard to do, because even though
Lester had graduated a decade before, his memory was still vivid there,
so much so that some of the older teachers habitually called Mac by his
brother's name. Lester had been a true star in the narrow firmament of
the school—valedictorian, student council president, citizenship award
winner, football captain—and in the years since he had left he had become a sort of myth which the headmaster and the faculty used to prove
to themselves that their school really did turn out leaders imbued with the
ideal of service. Mac always felt as if Lester were behind his back or
might suddenly appear out of a classroom door, fifteen years younger,
crew-cut, wearing a white C letter sweater, carrying a bundle of books
and walking with the schoolboy athlete's rolling swagger: a living incite-
ment to his younger brother to shape up and honor the family name.

It seemed plausible; if time could be rolled back anywhere, it would be
St. Cyprian's. When he finally graduated, Mac would be amazed to realize that in his thirteen years there he had progressed only two or three
hundred yards through space, from the tiny one-story kindergarten at the
campus' east end to the squat two-story brick upper school at the west
edge. The school, its whitewashed classroom buildings and ramshackle
wooden lunchroom and enormous new gymnasium and drafty old chapel,
had seemed as large as the universe itself; his thirteen years he had
thought a journey of epic proportions, like the wanderings of Odysseus or
the Long March to Yenan.

It was a tiny, sealed, very special world, ruled by the memory of its
long-dead founder, Mac's grandfather, and living by his motto: "We can't
all be scholars, but we can all be gentlemen." It would be hard to come

out of St. Cyprian's a scholar of any kind; the curriculum was flaccid: a "classical" education with only halfhearted training in Latin and none at all in Greek; math through calculus, but only for a few students; science courses unchanged in content since the discovery of atomic energy; rigorous grammatical training but no training in how to use the language learned; American history, which concentrated largely on a detailed recitation of the horrors of Reconstruction and a careful exegesis on the constitutional rationale for the doctrines of nullification and interposition. There were a few good teachers, who fought the school's prevailing mediocrity. But when Mac reached Harvard, he found that he had almost no idea of how to solve a differential equation, research and write a scholarly paper, study for an exam, or read and criticize a book.

He did have a few odd lumps and bits of memory: the names of all the major battles fought by the Army of Northern Virginia; the eight steps used by Communists to gain secret control of democratic governments everywhere; the fact that Socrates said "The unexamined life is not worth living"; the full original borders of the colony of Virginia; the powers granted to the federal government by the Articles of Confederation; the five major accomplishments of the emperor Han Wu Ti; and his chemistry teacher's explanation of how to tree a raccoon.

From their first day in kindergarten until graduation, however, St. Cyprian's did teach its students to be gentlemen, as that term was defined in Virginia: special creatures for whom there may once have been a place in the universe, nineteenth-century petty squires who lived close to the land without living off it, gentlemen farmers, hunters, horsemen, fishermen who made their livings by dabbling in law or medicine or finance or real estate, rejoicing in their station in nature and society; the middle class of the great chain of being. The St. Cyprian's gentleman would never lie to, steal from, or cheat his social equal, was unfailingly polite to ladies and helpful to idiots, maintained a proper uncomprehending reverence for the Episcopal Church, a suspicious but unshakable allegiance to the national government of the United States, a judicious fealty to the Apple-Farmer and his political organization, and a moist-eyed worship for the memory of General Robert E. Lee.

But the world the St. Cyprian's gentleman belonged to, if in fact it had ever existed, was long gone; as Mac was growing up, the little squires were finding less and less room to live their gentlemen's lives, even in Virginia. The land for their farms was being bought up for housing tracts and giant corporate farms, the rivers for their crabbing and catfishing were choking in filth, the village they lived in was becoming a skyscraper-and-freeway metropolis. The gentleman in the corporate state was an economic unit like every other unit, his courtesy to ladies and love for a dead general and a dying political machine no more useful to him than an advanced degree in alchemy or a patent of nobility signed by the czar of Russia.

Even by his freshman year Mac had figured out that he wanted out of the school and the little world it believed in. For the next four years he had fought Lester over a succession of plans for escape: first to public school, then to a private school in Vermont, then to schools in Switzerland, England, Wyoming, and Florida. Each time Lester refused to consider it.

"No, God damn it," Lester said. "You are not running away to some fancy school somewhere, and I don't give a damn if it's in Geneva or Laramie or Ur of the Chaldees. That's what the Colonel did. He ran away. This is where you belong. This is your town. These are our people, and running away is wrong. This family is not going to do that anymore."

"You've got it all backwards, Lester," Mac said. "I'm not running away, nobody's chasing me. Can't you see I'm not the Colonel? Nobody's giving me a hard time. I just want to go."

Lester smiled. "I know you probably think I'm a real SOB about this, but try to understand what I'm saying," he said. "Our family belongs here; this has always been our home. Hell, we helped to build this damn city from the beginning. But we've almost been driven out of here, and by God, we ought to hold onto our place here. Believe me, Mac: if you go somewhere else, it'll never be the same. You'll never have another hometown like this one. So give it a chance."

Finally, it dawned on Mac that Lester was asking him to stay, that his brother needed him there, so he had given up his plans to escape from St. Cyprian's.

But in his senior year he knew he had had enough. When Lester began talking to him about applying to the University, Mac let him have it. "It stops here. I've done my time now. Thirteen years is long enough. I'm not going to go to Charlottesville and carry one of those orange-and-blue umbrellas and go to football games and drink out of hip flasks. I'm bailing out. And if you don't like it, tough. I'll go to Judge Anderson and get the money myself. It's my own money, and you can't stop me, so you don't have anything to say about it."

Lester seemed to accept that. But even at seventeen Mac had learned from his brother the use of calculation and craft; he decided the lesson needed a little reinforcement, for he did not think his brother incapable of blocking him by some move he had not foreseen: it seemed to matter that much to Lester that his brother be a true Virginian in Lester's definition.

One spring night, while his applications were pending at Harvard, Columbia, Berkeley, Michigan, and also the University (because Lester had said, "Just in case you change your mind"), Mac sat alone on the veranda of the big house and coldly considered the best means of evading any trap Lester might set. The idea that came to him seemed foolproof.

Lester pulled him out of the school the next morning after prayers. He was so mad he could hardly speak, but there was no menace in his anger because Lester knew he had been beaten and made ridiculous. Finally, he had managed to make himself coherent enough to ask why—what had Mac been trying to accomplish by spray-painting a sickle and hammer on the bottom of the Westhampton Club swimming pool and then signing his name? What had been the point of getting himself summarily expelled from the club and making the board of governors so angry it had taken Lester's fastest talking to keep them from calling the police?

Mac loved his brother, but that day he enjoyed laughing in his face. "I just wanted to make sure you got the message that it'd be better for both of us if I went to college out of the state. This was just a little graphic object lesson." He had laughed again.

Lester was trembling with helpless rage, but Mac was not frightened. He even felt a start of guilt at having put his brother, for one of the only times in his life, in a position from which he couldn't find his own way out. Finally, Lester managed to say, "All right, you little turd, you're really a cute bastard, you know that. You're a real quiz kid. One of these days you're going to get a little too cute, and you are going to get it right up the ass. You wait, you just wait."

"All right, Lester, all right," Mac said. "You go now and hush it up good so it won't embarrass you, and don't worry about me. You won't have any more trouble, as long as you got the message this time."

So in June, when the headmaster of St. Cyprian's handed Mac a diploma and a four-color pamphlet entitled *How to Respect Your Country's Flag,* everybody knew he was going to Harvard in the fall.

That summer Lester ran for reelection, and Mac worked on the campaign, but it was an easy race, just a warm-up for two years hence when he would run for State Senate. Miles Brock got the nomination for governor, which surprised no one, and the Republicans nominated a fall guy, a big slow-talking farmer from Botetourt, up in the mountains, named Horace Hapgood. Nothing was in doubt, and by the time Mac began packing his bags in late August he felt pretty sure he knew not only the winners of those races but the percentage spreads as well.

He was going up north alone. Lester was still angry enough that he would suffer Mac in the campaign but wouldn't help him go to school; he couldn't even bring himself to come to Mac's room the night before to say

216

good-bye. Molly O. helped Mac pack, and when they were finished, she took him by the shoulder and said, "Mac, I'll miss you."

"I'll miss you, too, O.," Mac said, embarrassed.

"You be sure to come on back here when he needs you to," she said.

Mac smiled. "Oh, come on, Molly O., you know I'll be back for the campaigns," he said.

She shook his shoulder a little with an impatient movement. "I'm not talking about the damn campaigns, you goose," she said. "I mean when he needs you to."

FOUR

★

Mac met Stephanian his first day at Harvard; they had been assigned as roommates in Weld Hall, a freshman dorm where John Kennedy had lived during his Harvard days. Mac struggled up to the third floor bearing two suitcases and a rug; more impedimenta were waiting in a taxi below in the Yard. The door of the room was already ajar, and Mac entered to find a short young man in a corduroy jacket driving a nail into the wall. Beside him, on the brown wood Harvard-issue desk, was a photograph of a girl with long blond hair and clear blue eyes, dressed in a light-green summer dress.

The other strode forward and extended his hand with a smile. He had short curly black hair and horn-rim spectacles. "Hi," he said. "I'm Arnie Stephanian."

"Hello," Mac said, setting down the bags. "I'm Mac Evans. We're roommates, I guess."

"I guess," Stephanian said. He gestured about him. "I took this desk, but if you want it, we can always switch."

Mac shrugged. "No problem," he said, glancing around the room. "Does that fireplace really work?"

"Yes," Stephanian said. "At least, I think so."

The two were looking at each other curiously. "Well, am I what you were expecting?" Mac asked, knowing the other boy had spent as much

219

time speculating what the luck of the room draw would give him as Mac had.

"I guess," Stephanian said. "I didn't really make too many conditions on the roommate form."

"Me neither," Mac said. "What were yours?"

"Well, I said I didn't want anybody who was too neat," Arnie said. "You know—fussy."

Mac grinned. "No problem there," he said.

"Well, that was really all. That and no Southerners, I said."

There was a moment of silence.

"Well, Arnie," Mac said, stretching out a commiserating hand, "you been screwed." He suddenly remembered the waiting taxi and went to get his other bags.

It took a few weeks for them to forgive each other, but they were stuck together in the double room, sleeping in the same bedroom, and it made no sense to quarrel. It turned out Mac needed Stephanian.

Harvard made sense to Stephanian. He was a California boy, the grandson of an Armenian immigrant who had bought a farm in Fresno, the son of a doctor, a product of the California school system. He bestrode the campus that year in a corduroy jacket and unforgivable polka-dot bow tie, choosing courses, making friends, decisions, and plans, swimming through Harvard like a minnow in a clear summer stream.

Mac, meanwhile, was stumbling. In his mind he had imagined Harvard as the good place, a cultivated, quiet, dignified intellectual wonderland where he might on a given day meet Emerson in the library, or T. S. Eliot at lunch, or sip afternoon sherry with a party including Bach, Bertrand Russell, Franklin Roosevelt, and Buddha in a wood-paneled drawing room: a golden land where life and thought were made easy and people valued ideas, friends, conversation, gentility.

Walking across the Yard as fall came in, pushed and shoved by other freshmen, eating dinner with them in the Harvard Union, he found it wasn't so: his classmates eyed each other suspiciously, spoke in guarded riddles, kept their secrets jealously; each feared the others, begrudged them every talent or accomplishment, compared himself assiduously with everyone he met. The dinner conversation centered on SAT scores, prizes and honors, athletic records, sexual conquests. Mac had few of any of these; he held his peace.

Stephanian, on the other hand, talked. He had a serious, confidential tone which convinced most people, students and faculty alike, that he was doing them a favor by sharing his thoughts with them, but further that he was so humble and kind that he did not realize it was a favor. The room in Weld was filled each night with new friends Arnie had made that day; they sat and drank California wine and argued about democracy and socialism, the role of the professional man, the poverty program and its failures and successes, and the menace of communism in Asia, which was threatening to thwart America's progress toward its social goals. Mac sat uneasily in the corner and conversed with the group in his mind. *Hi, y'all, how you? How you doin'? Well, hush my mouth, well, fuck me blind. Well, screw me sightless. Y'all take care. Y'all come back. Yankee bastard, don't let the sun set on your head here.*

Mac's classes were polyglot: Southern history, English literature, history and culture of the Islamic world, introductory Russian. The latter met on Saturday, at eight thirty in the morning; Mac remembered that later as the first sign that all was not going as planned for him at Harvard. The second Saturday of the year, he awoke in his room to the sound of the Harvard band parading down Massachusetts Avenue to the football stadium:

"Gaudeamus igitur!

"Veritas non sequitur!

"Illegitimis non carborundum, ipso facto!"

He had missed his Russian class. There was a momentary panic. He felt himself faced with reprimand, opprobrium, disciplinary action. He would be sent home to Richmond in disgrace. Then a novel thought penetrated: he was at Harvard, not St. Cyprian's. There was no requirement that he go to class; no one cared if he went to class; he might never go to another class again. He smiled and shut his eyes and slept until lunchtime.

Stephanian introduced Mac to marijuana, the killer weed. That made sense to Arnie, too, for he had used it in California. It made him laugh. On Mac the effect was different; it calmed him and quieted him, relieved him of the cares of his life, much like a sharp blow from a padded mallet to the back of his head. He spent the evenings not doing the reading for the classes he wouldn't attend, diving in the still unquiet pool of drugs. Some nights Stephanian was visited by the girl in the picture on his wall: Constance, his high school girl friend. She had blue eyes and long straight blond hair. She had come to Boston University. Stephanian and Mac had a signal: if Arnie's tie was hanging on the bedroom doorknob, Mac was not to enter. Of course, the plan was to work the other way, but Mac's tie never ended up on the doorknob. The first time he came in and saw the tie, Mac felt a powerful impulse to take it, wrap it around his neck, and pull the ends until breath left his body and his eyeballs rolled across the tile floor like marbles. But he refrained and went next door to become stoned.

221

Still, by the end of the year Mac had lost three things: his virginity, his Southern accent, and his interest in school. The first left him after a drunken party on the floor below; he had met a girl, and they had stolen away to his bedroom. Drunkenly, proudly, he had draped his St. Cyprian's necktie across the doorknob. Her name was Cassie McGraw; she went to Radcliffe. There was much fumbling, until Mac admitted he was intact: then a clumsy accommodation was reached, which Mac told himself was at least moderately pleasurable, and she assured him it had felt fine. They fell asleep. He had called her again for months and saw her in the Yard, but they never dated again.

His accent he lost by design, alone in the common bathroom of Weld's third floor, late at night, his head buzzing with dope smoke. He stared at his mouth and carefully shaped the vowels as they were said in the North: A-E-I-O-U, precise and hard at the edges. Participles ended in unequivocal Gs. Second person singular and plural used identical pronouns. It was work, like learning a foreign tongue; he studied hard, because it seemed the only passport into the nightly discussions, led by Stephanian, of freedom, logic, knowledge, will. Coldly, he cleansed the mush from his mouth, and years later, when he yearned again for the soft Piedmont drawl of his brother and sister-in-law, it was gone forever.

His interest in school departed more slowly. He would watch Stephanian admiringly as he plowed through his reading assignments, reviewed lecture notes, prepared seminar presentations, indefatigably researched and wrote papers. But each time Mac himself sat down to do the same, he felt about him a yawning gulf of ignorance. In that first semester at Harvard it seemed to Mac that all knowledge was one seamless web, with no beginning and no end: he could not possibly understand his readings in Arab history without understanding ancient history, archaeology, linguistics, comparative religions, economics; he could not read a poem or essay without knowing literary history, English history, Anglo-Saxon, Middle English, prosody, Latin, Greek—the complexities were too great; the carpet of ignorance lay on him so thick and dark it could never be rolled back. He would steal out and leave Stephanian hard a-book and go next door to drink beer and get stoned with a drunken gentle boy from Georgia who spent his days watching soap operas and failed out at midsemester.

Mac himself stumbled through his exams and remained, though, if pressed, he could not have said why. A dark, rolling lethargy settled over him during the cold, wet Cambridge winter; he stopped going to class altogether, stopped going to meals, began living on vanilla milk shakes and beer and throwing up frequently. He spent his days on a big green couch the boy from Georgia had left behind, reading and rereading his favorite science fiction books. ("Were they truly intelligent?—By themselves, I mean? I don't know and I don't know how we can ever find out. If they were *not* truly intelligent, I hope I never live to see us tangle with anything at all like them which *is* intelligent. Because I know who will lose. Me You. The so-called human race.") He slept twelve, fourteen, sixteen hours a day. He read and reread the *Globe* Sunday comics.

Stephanian, to whom everything but Mac made sense, tried to help, but it didn't work. Mac looked at his clear, friendly, uncomprehendingly logical face and could not speak of how he felt: of what it meant to find himself among people who seemed all the more alien for all that they spoke the same language and claimed allegiance to the same history: Yankees for whom history was not a long graceful static undoing but a pageant of upheaval and progress; children and grandchildren of immigrants for whom there were no grand family portraits and legends of noble failure but only a history of persecution and servitude and a determination that it would not happen again.

Instead, Mac began to see how far he could push Stephanian, began telling him tales of life in a South which was a mixture of Tobacco Road and hell: of nights spent dodging Klan bullets, drinking Dr Pepper and moonshine whiskey, coonhunting with dogs named Trigger, Bullet, Dixie, and Stonewall; days spent hunkered down on street corners watching fat sheriffs strut slue-footed as they guarded the color line, of horsewhippings in the public square, drunken syphilitic insanity in high and low places, incest, miscegenation, repression, Gothic terror—watching Stephanian's face, waiting for the moment when disbelief would dawn and he would see the joke, the moment that never came. Stephanian swallowed it all, told his friends, until Mac found himself night after night with an audience of credulous youths who had never seen the South and would believe anything about it, lovely, gentle Radcliffe girls who put their hands on his shoulder and asked if he had never been frightened.

Then there was a spring night when he got drunk and tried to tell Stephanian the truth about his life in Virginia; it was the night he heard on the news that the Apple-Farmer was dead at last. It was as if the king, or the pope, or maybe God Himself were gone, and Mac felt free and alone and a little frightened; he had never quite believed it would happen. He needed to talk to someone. Lester and Molly O. didn't answer, so he went to Stephanian and boozily tried to tell him what this meant, not for the comic-book South he had built up over the months, but for the real Virginia. But it was too late. He looked at Stephanian and realized that he had done his work too well. Stephanian was listening to him as if to the confessions of Deputy Dawg. Mac left him and stumbled off to bed.

223

He never talked about it again, but so well had he sold his bill of goods that at the end of the year, when he was leaving, Stephanian came to him and said, "Mac, listen, take care of yourself down there," and Mac gripped his shoulder and looked him in the eyes, because Arnie expected it, and said, "I will, Arnie, I will."

He took a taxi to the airport and on the plane he laughed himself sick with desperate laughter, glad to be away from it all.

Mac remembered the summer as the best of his life. It was the summer Tobey Carrington and his sober followers made their move. Carrington ran for the U.S. Senate, against an old organization wheelhorse, a foot-washing disciple of the Apple-Farmer and evangelist of his parsimonious political gospel. There were two Senate races that year.

Governor Miles Brock, elected the year before as a staunch Democrat, had dutifully appointed Junior, the old man's son, to fill his father's seat. Junior would keep that seat, but without the old man—for no one, not even his closest friends, suggested that Junior was his father's equal or in fact anything but a pale carbon copy, a picture-postcard senator who lacked all traces of his father's intelligence and drive—the surviving senator was vulnerable. Lester and Deeb were putting everything they had into Carrington's campaign because they saw him as a forerunner of Lester; if he won, Lester would have smooth sailing; if he lost, the old machine crowd might thwart and strangle Lester as well.

Behind the old senator were gathered Junior, for what he was worth, and Miles Brock, ready to defend the machine which had required a lifetime of devotion and repaid it by making him governor; these two served as the rallying point for the old courthouse crowd.

But this time, Lester explained, their number was up. "It all came together at once," he told Mac at the beginning of the summer. "In the space of about two years the old man died, we got rid of the poll tax, and we broke the old apportionment system." Not for several years did Mac learn that this last victory, which destroyed the old man's system for drawing districts for Congress and legislature by giving votes to farms and mountains and little courthouse towns where the machine was strongest and stealing them from the cities, where it was weak—that the victory had nothing to do with Lester but belonged to a Norfolk lawyer named Thomas Jefferson Shadwell, who had battered at the state's shameless voting laws for years in any court which would give him a hearing and had won at last, succeeding in carving out a new State Senate seat for Norfolk, which Shadwell then ran for and won.

"But that doesn't mean they're going to go belly-up," Lester went on. "These guys are still tough, whether the old man's dead or not. If we run

224

a perfect campaign, we'll win, but not by much. And if we make a mistake, we'll lose.''

And a perfect campaign it was. Mac had come home from college tired, confused, all but paralyzed by self-doubt, but that campaign saved him. He worked twelve, sixteen, eighteen hours a day; to himself he compared the work to the labors of a monk, which brought peace because they were ordained useful and proper by the highest authority, and later, as the primary neared and the pace of the campaign increased until finally it seemed to be moving as fast as any human activity could move, with new pressures and events and crises no longer even every day but every hour and minute, Mac felt the mad peace of a marathon runner, isolated from the world, intent only on finishing his course.

Carrington won the primary, as Lester predicted, and by less than a thousand votes. By the end of the summer his victory in the election was assured.

Each night that summer Lester, Mac, and Molly O. ate dinner around the big dining-room table. To Mac they seemed like a family in a way they hadn't before he went away, perhaps had not been since his father had disappeared. The change was in Lester: he seemed more relaxed and happy than ever before, more at ease in his life and his work. Mac was not very surprised the week before he went back to Harvard when Molly O. told him she was pregnant.

He did let his jaw drop in requisite amazement.

"Don't gape like that, you goose," she said happily. "You knew we were going to have children sometime, didn't you?"

"Yes, sure, of course," said Mac, who had known no such thing. "But—"

"But it took us so long to get around to it you thought we had forgotten, didn't you?" Molly O. said, grinning even more broadly. "Don't you know your family breeds late in life? Look at yourself, your mama was a sight older than me when you were born. Tell you the truth, Mac, I think Lester was waiting to see how you turned out before he chanced having one of his own."

Mac felt himself blushing. "I haven't turned out yet," he said.

Molly O. reached up and hugged him. "You'll turn out fine," she said. "And so will this little one." She held him at arm's length, looking up at his face. "Oh, Mac, aren't you excited?"

Mac was. When he left for school, he was leaving behind a family in being, and he felt glad for Molly O., but most of all for Lester, who had achieved the ambition he had never been able to confess; he had kept the family from being driven apart and forced out, he had kept it going against the odds. *All things fall and are built again*, Mac thought, and perhaps the joy of the building could erase the pain of the fall.

That year Stephanian and Mac roomed together in Dunster House. Mac felt reasonably content. No more did he indulge in the confessions of Deputy Dawg; quietly he went to his classes and even, on occasion, studied. He had become a government major because government was the largest department at Harvard, one where he could most easily keep out of sight, and because he knew the subject, had grown up with it, could do the work without breaking a sweat. Stephanian was in a special elite major called social studies; he was reading Marx, Freud, Weber, Durkheim. That fall, as they sat around the fire, Stephanian's ruminations had a new topic, the war in Asia, which had now grown far larger and more bloody than any of them imagined possible a year before. Mac did not understand his roommate's cavils: he had studied communism at St. Cyprian's; did not history teach us that we must resist its aggressive policies with high-minded determination, skillfully applied minimum force? There was the lesson of Munich to consider, after all; the episode in Asia was another example of Chinese expansionism, of Mao's unchecked imperial ambitions which had led him to seize picturesque Tibet and ruthlessly attack peace-loving India. This was the time to resist, under a president of unquestionably good intentions, LBJ, a great liberal whose voting rights laws were working a true American revolution in Virginia and the South.

Perhaps, Stephanian said, perhaps. Certainly what Mac said made sense, and sense was what Stephanian valued more than anything else. But still, he said, he was troubled: how far should this country carry its commitment to democracy? Could we be the policeman of the world?

These arguments were unresolved one bright November day when Stephanian and he walked along Mount Auburn Street to the gates of Quincy House. Members of a new socialist organization, Students for a Democratic Society, were planning to confront the secretary of defense, who had come for a visit. They stood on the edges of the crowd as SDS speakers denounced the war through bullhorns; their voices, filtered through the tiny amplifiers, had a tinny, distant, ominous sound, a menacing immediacy which would later become familiar.

The garage door opened; members of the crowd tried to block the black limousine emerging. Then a shout: "Hey! It's a trick! He's over here!" and Mac and Stephanian found themselves running around the corner to find the secretary of defense, master of the most fearsome flying circus in the history of the world, attempting to sneak away in a borrowed station wagon.

He was surrounded by students; students were yelling, chanting, shaking fists; then, like an animal in a mud wallow, the car began rocking back and forth, and Mac realized the crowd was attempting to overturn the car. Then silence and angry cheering, and the secretary of defense clambered to the hood.

Autumn sunlight sparkled from his rimless glasses as the crowd screamed questions. McNamara waved his arms, cast about him as if looking for a friend. Mac looked at his closed, certain face, at the dull reflection of his flat, pomaded hair, and did not feel friendly.

"How many South Vietnamese civilians have we killed?" someone called to him. "Why doesn't the Defense Department release the figures?"

Mac was startled. It was a new notion. He had thought that the dead of this war were American soldiers and communists; why should civilians be dying? He moved forward to hear McNamara's answer.

McNamara waved his arms again. "Wait a minute, fellas," he said. He seemed to be smiling. "This is one I'm really interested in—"

"Don't you care?" A voice screamed from behind Mac.

McNamara's jaw tightened. The crowd screamed and hammered the car, and the secretary of defense flushed red and shook a fist. "Listen, you guys," he screamed. "I spent four of the happiest years of my life at Berkeley doing what you're doing here, and I was tougher than you guys then, and I'm tougher than you now! Do you hear that?" Then he jumped from the hood of the car, this tough man, this mighty warlord, and a phalanx of police hustled him back into the house, where he could escape through an underground tunnel.

Walking back to Dunster House, Mac said to Stephanian, "I wonder what the answer is?"

"What answer?" Stephanian said.

"How many civilians have been killed?"

Stephanian did not know the answer—a first in Mac's memory.

Stephanian began going to SDS meetings. Mac did not. As he usually did when troubled, he called Lester.

"Listen, kid," Lester said, his voice dispassionate. "Take my advice and don't get mixed up with all this antiwar stuff right now. The damn war's going to be over soon, and people really don't go for this agitation; they think it's unpatriotic. I don't know who's right about it, but hell, LBJ's the President and the people are behind him, especially around here."

That was the last time Mac talked to Lester before winter closed down around Cambridge. He didn't hear from anyone in Richmond until December, a week before Christmas vacation was to start.

227

It was a rainy morning. Mac was sitting curled like a cat in the round window of his high Dunster House room, watching the rain fall.

Stephanian had bundled up and stepped bravely off to class, but Mac was resolved not to go outside, not to class or to visit friends or for any reason at all. He could reach the dining hall by underground tunnel, and he needed nothing else. Should the building burn, he would burn with it; in fact, he had lit a fire in the fireplace, and as he looked at the ruthless raw day, he felt the urge to climb into the fireplace now and burn up, warm, rather than risk ever being as cold as the day outside threatened to make him.

The phone rang. Mac didn't move.

He suddenly felt for no reason at all that he should not answer it. If he did, somehow he knew he would end up out in the rain. But it rang again, and so, because he was a well-brought-up boy who had been taught to put money in parking meters and cross with the light and expect an answer to prayer, he picked up the receiver and said, "Hello?"

There was an instant of silence; the hush of the long-distance wire, with beneath it the tinny gabble of other, distant, conversations; a sudden chill at the pit of his stomach because he knew it, there was bad news on the way.

Then a feisty old voice said, "Mac, boy, is that you?"

"Who is this?" Mac said.

"This is Kenlow Anderson," the voice said in a measured, weary tone. "Mac, have you heard from Lester?"

"Hello, Judge," Mac said. "How are you?"

"Never mind that now," the judge said testily. "Have you heard from Lester?"

"No, not lately," Mac said. It seemed a strange question. Why should the judge need to call Cambridge to find a man who lived four miles from his house? "What's wrong? Where's Lester? Isn't he there?"

The old voice lifted itself up again. "Mac, we don't know where he is. And I reckon you'd better come on home. All hell has broken loose."

That was how Mac learned that Molly O. had lost her baby and nearly her life. He packed a bag and fought his way into the cold rain to a cab to the airport and then onto a plane to Richmond and then, because there was no one to meet him, into another taxi to the hospital, where Judge Anderson told him that his brother had betrayed his wife and his best friend and disappeared.

It was raining in Richmond too. Mac and the judge stood at the hospital window and looked down on Broad Street.

"Be damned if I can figure it out," Anderson said. "Think you know a person—think you know what they're like—'' He shook his head. He seemed older than Mac had ever noticed before; his jaw muscles had a slack, brittle look. "I don't know," he said again. "Your goddamn family, Mac, I swear I can't get a handle on them. I been trying now for forty years and they don't add up."

Judge Anderson told Mac about Molly O.'s miscarriage. Anderson didn't know whether Lester had left before or after she collapsed. But while Molly O. was in the hospital, skating on the thin ice of death, Lester was nowhere to be found.

Anderson had gotten a call from Deeb Grayson. Listening to the judge, Mac remembered the hours he had spent in Deeb's apartment, and he realized with a shock that he had not been the only one quietly watching Deeb's wife; Angela was gone, too. She had gone with Lester.

They didn't say anything about it to Molly O. It seemed somehow not their place, and if she didn't know, she would surely figure out quickly enough. Mac stood in her hospital room and watched her sleeping. She didn't look sick, just tired and worn, like a frayed carpet. He was chilled: if Molly O., having lost her baby and perhaps her husband and almost her life, looked just like everybody else, what did that say about the lives others led? He turned away and watched the rain falling.

When she woke, she smiled at Mac and said hello; she didn't ask about Lester. Mac marveled at her tact. They spoke briefly; he put his hand on her arm; then he went home.

In the darkness the big house was empty and quiet, like a drifting hulk. He passed through the front hall and into the new room Lester and Molly O. had added to the rear of the house. It had a high ceiling, deep carpeting, a long leather sofa, and a powerful stereo. Two sides were of glass, overlooking the stone terrace. Mac kept his dripping jacket wrapped around him. He dropped his suitcase in the middle of the rug and went to the tiny refrigerator behind the bar. He took out a half-full bottle of orange juice, sat on the couch, and dumbly watched the cold rain falling on the terrace.

What was his brother doing with Angela Grayson? Lester had spent his whole life becoming one thing, and now that the thing was almost in his grasp, he had run away. Where did he think he could go—he, who had warned Mac again and again never to run away, who had constructed a self which could not survive without place and tradition—did he think there was escape for him?

Who were you before your parents were born? Mac thought, sipping the orange juice. He went back to the bar and put the bottle away. What happens to the light when the refrigerator door closes?

He flipped on the mighty radio set. A smooth disc jockey murmured in his ear and spun a Perry Como record. The signal came through perfectly; the wind tossed the branches of the mimosa tree by the house, and Mac felt as if he were in a remote fastness—an inaccessible mountaintop, Arctic outpost, lonely weather ship—with only this radio signal to link him to civilization. The soggy wind blew against the windows; Mac imagined that the rain was blowing through, that there was no glass; he shivered. He turned off the radio and the lights and the electric heater and went back into the old part of the house, to the front room still cluttered with his mother's furniture. There he sat on the slick worn divan and watched the dim light play across his grandfather's painted face until, still wrapped in the wet jacket, he slept.

The telephone pulled him from a dark repetitive nightmare. He was still half asleep, and with a dreamer's instantaneous certainty he knew who it was. "Hello, Lester," he said, and waited.

Lester's voice was subdued and flat. "Is that you, bub?"

"Yeah, it's me," Mac said, and he felt his throat muscles ache as they stretched upright in a swan's arch, rigid with the effort of not saying, *Where are you? What are you doing? Why don't you come home? How can you do this to us? What is wrong with you?* He knew that those questions would drive Lester away, knew with a flash of paranoid twisted cunning that his brother had called to hear him say them, to be reviled so he could hang up.

"Mac?" the voice began again.

"I'm here," he said.

"How's Molly O.?"

"She's doing well, out of danger. She'll be home tomorrow or the next day."

Don't hang up, Mac begged Lester in his mind.

"What are people saying?" Lester asked.

"Don't know, really. Just got home."

"What's Molly O. saying?"

"Not much. She's been sleeping."

"She's all right, though?"

"Yes."

"Well, listen—"

"Yeah?"

"Will you tell her I didn't mean to hurt her?"

"No."

"No, what?"

"I'm not telling Molly O. anything," Mac said. There was no anger in his voice or in himself. "Far as I'm concerned, this call didn't happen. You got something to say to her, come on and say it yourself. Come on tomorrow or so, because you can figure the angles as well as I can. You're coming back sometime, either now or in six months at the outside. You've got no choice..Everything you spent your life working for is here, and you can't make it anywhere else. In six months you're going to want to come home, and you'll come home, but by then it'll be too late. You'll be the biggest damn fool on the East Coast. You'll spend the rest of your life doing title searches and playing cards at the Confederate Club and trying to pretend people aren't laughing at you. You come back this week, you're still in business. Wait any longer and you've fucked yourself good. So don't give me any messages. I'll see you in a couple of days."

Mac dared not ask questions; if he had gotten through to his brother, he had; questions would weaken his position, let him off the hook. "Goodbye, Lester," he said, and hung up.

Two days later Lester was home.

Sometimes, in his mind (for he and Lester never spoke of that phone call), Mac liked to imagine that what he had said had won Lester back: that he had, in some way, paid his brother back for raising him and caring for him and soothing his nightmares away years before. Other times he wondered if it had made any difference at all. Lester was no fool; he could calculate as well as Mac, and better. Wherever he had been (and Mac never found that out either, he never spoke of it again) he might simply have calculated the odds and looked at Angela and the choices he faced and come back. Mac never knew, never would know.

As for Deeb and Angela, Mac didn't see either of them again. Angela disappeared, and Deeb left town and dropped out of sight. Periodically he heard that one, or both, of them were back in South America or in New York, or on the West Coast, or members of various religious orders—but nobody knew. Mac faced the fact that Deeb, who had been his friend and teacher in ways Lester could not be, was gone forever. He wondered if he ought not somehow to take Deeb's side, even if only by hating his brother for him. Lester had done a hateful thing, had taken a man who loved him and punished him for the crime of being weaker than himself, had seduced and abandoned a woman for a momentary thrill and perhaps mostly to show that he was better than her husband: he had played with two lives as a child plays with a straw, weaving them through his fingers until he chose to snap them.

But Mac could not hate his brother. He could not trade his family for another man's hatred; that way lay madness. So he went back to school, and if he had prayed, if he had known how, he would have prayed, not for

231

Angela and Deeb, but for Lester and Molly O. Life had forced a choice on him, and he had chosen his side.

Lester's political career recovered quickly, and by the time Mac came home for the summer he had patched it together so well the cracks hardly showed. Except for losing Deeb, who had been his memory and his calculator and everything else except his conscience, Lester had not really lost anything. In any other state capital, the papers would have printed the story or have gotten the news out somehow, by hints or allusions. But the Richmond papers did not. The story passed, and the only result was sympathy for Lester because his wife had lost her baby.

There were whispers, of course, but they didn't hurt very much. They were confined to the West End, to people who had already made up their minds about Lester anyway; there were still two years before Lester made his bid for statewide office, lieutenant governor (even as he made these calculations, Mac realized with a guilty start that the voice in his head, figuring the angles and calculating the timing, was Deeb's).

Mac stayed at home in Richmond that summer because he thought he might be needed. He wasn't; it was a quiet summer in the big house, a pool of silence in which his brother and his sister-in-law moved gingerly around each other. But Mac sensed that it was not the silence of decay, of indifference, of two people walling themselves away from each other. Rather it was rebuilding; Lester and Molly O. were like acrobats mounting the high wire after a nasty spill, learning again how to balance themselves; each was learning how to live with the new person the other had become. And they were succeeding.

Five years later, when Lester was dead and he and Molly O. lived in proximity, she in the big house and he in the little one, Mac finally brought himself to ask her what she had been thinking and feeling then, how she had been able to forgive Lester for leaving her in that hospital for five days without a baby or a husband or anything to rely on but her own self and will.

"I think you were a lot more surprised about what happened than I was, Mac," she said. "I mean, you were shocked, but I wasn't. I wasn't so damned pleased about it, but it didn't make me want to die or anything, because I had always figured there was some heavy weather coming from Lester. People are like that. They're just no good at all, and anybody who expects to change that is a fool.

"A lot of people liked to cry and carry on about poor old Molly O., innocent little nineteen-year-old girl who got herself married to this monster and look what a hard time he gave her. They've cried about a river of crocodile tears for me. Not that I mind; that's their way of having fun.

But they're fools, too, if they think I married Lester not knowing something like that was coming.

"Half the reason I married your brother was orneriness anyway—no, really, you think I'm just old Molly O. who works for the Episcopal Church and never felt like raising hell, but you're wrong. I wasn't any different from any other girl that age. They like to shock their mothers. Most of us end up doing pretty much what our mothers did, but we want that little rebellion to look back on to convince us we were really hell raisers. Least that was the way it was back when I was that age.

"My parents didn't approve of Lester. Because his daddy had been such a very scary fellow. I don't think you ever met my grandmother, thank God. You two would have hated each other. She was one of these old country *grande dames,* mean and tough as she could be. I remember when she got the news who I was going to marry and she called me over to her house. I was scared half to death, I was always scared of her, if she was still alive I'd be scared of her now. I felt like I was about nine years old standing there. She didn't get up when I came in, she just sat there rocking in her chair, and after a minute she stopped and drew herself up on her cane and looked at me. I still remember. 'Mary Owen,' she said, 'you are my favorite grandchild, and I believe you are going to be a fine lady when you grow up. But I think you should know a few things about the family this young man comes from. His father,' she said, sort of shaking her chin, 'was a thoroughly disreputable man. I do not know whether he was a traitor to his country or not, although I would not for a moment doubt it, but I can tell you that he was unquestionably a traitor to his class. I won't have you marrying his son, do you hear? I will not have it!'

"I'm laughing now, but at the time I went into hysterics and I went to my mother and she went into hysterics and I believe Gramma even shed a few tears before the whole ruckus was over. Mom and Dad came to the wedding and were polite, and when Lester started making good, they got over it. But Gramma never did.

"But that was just part of it. The real thing was that even at nineteen I had the gumption to see that your brother needed me a lot more than he probably ever realized he did. I can't exactly explain it, but if it hadn't been for me, he could never have done the things he did, the good things, I mean. He would have fallen apart, or run away, gone somewhere else, something. But the things I thought I was rebelling against when I married him, those were the things he needed to get closer to. That's why he married me.

"Yes, things got sure enough unpleasant for a while, and it did become the fashion to weep for poor Molly O. But I knew when I married him that

233

there were bad times coming, sometime, somewhere: a man isn't worth marrying if he isn't going to give you some bad times. So I was ready for it, more or less. Unconsciously, you might say.

"Poor old Molly O. my behind!" She smiled, and there was a hint of grimness—a piratical turn—to the corners of her mouth. "Let me tell you, while all of that was going on, that bastard—as long as this is in the family, I can say that, Mac—he got as good as he gave from me. You better know it. I don't mean I nagged at him or anything; that always struck me as a sign of weakness, to be screaming and whining all the time. I mean this: after you went away to college, he began to get this notion that everything was lost and he was going to start all over. Get a divorce, escape somehow. He ran into a brick wall with me on that. I don't think he ever knew what hit him.

"Now your brother, his mind was such a complicated affair—it was like yours, Mac, honey, but more so—sometimes he didn't really know what was in it. Whereas me, I always do. And I'd been raised up to get married and stay that way no matter what, and not any suffering poor old me stuff, and besides which, I loved the bastard. And it seems to me you get about one chance to get hold of a life that is a life—whatever it is you want your life to be—and you get hold of it and if you let go, you're a perfect fool.

"So I wasn't about to let Lester go. He'd made a big enough mess without breaking up his marriage. I held on like crazy. And, Mac, believe me, if he'd lived, we'd have been married the rest of our lives. Oh, he would have raised a little more hell, but by the time all that mess was over he knew he'd never get away from me alive."

Mac left his brother and sister-in-law to their new lives and went back to Cambridge. That was the winter he learned despair; studied it as a priest studies the psalms, mastered it and was mastered by it until for a while it seemed that nothing remained of him at all.

His teacher was Hartmann: a music major from Indiana, a senior who lived across the hall from Mac and Stephanian. He was a pleasant young man with a Cheshire cat grin and amiable green eyes which bulged as if the air were slowly being squeezed from his lungs. In his room he kept a piano practice pad, and he filled the air night and day with mute music. There was about him the joyful frenzy of a moth in a killing jar, and Mac thought he was the wisest person he had ever met.

Later he was to marvel at this friendship with Hartmann, it had been so instantly deep and intense; it was, he thought later, perhaps because in those months, with life in Richmond falling to pieces and rising again in a new unknown shape, Mac somehow felt his own personality, the family and tradition and web of beliefs and ritual and lies, fracturing and splintering, until his bare self lay open and exposed, ready to be touched in parts which might never be seen again; Mac took Hartmann's cynical humorous despair into himself like a one-celled organism absorbing a new genetic core.

Every night, while Stephanian went to the library or to visit friends or to his SDS meetings, Mac sat with Hartmann and smoked hashish until the world swam before his eyes with the incomprehensible icy precision of a shark cutting through deep water. They talked of many things, and Mac took their conversations to himself and brooded, brooded as the winter came on.

Hartmann on love: "Every time two people touch each other it's an expression of power." Mac brooded: was it true? Nothing in his experience any longer spoke to the question. The idea revealed to him dark, bewildering catacombs, shadowy, rushing passageways of deceit and villainy underneath everything he thought of as life, so that each word or action squelched in an unseen primal sludge of mysterious disreputable motives. Mac found the most honorable response must be not to touch anyone or to be touched in turn lest, all unknowing, he might be party to dishonor.

Hartmann on the family: "I guess I can imagine having a family and a wife, and I can imagine coming home and eating dinner and wanting to ball her, but why should I? There is no way to have a family which isn't going to turn out like families now; all people do is tear each other and rip each other and call it love. People were not designed to live in the proximity of each other." Mac brooded: could he refute that? His father in South America, mother in Florida, neither speaking of the other, his brother and sister-in-law living alone in a silent big house, struggling to stay together, why he didn't know, couldn't figure out then, his baby nephew unborn. Why not? Why not keep his distance and never do evil to those he might have loved?

Hartmann was most eloquent on the future: there wasn't any. The human race had prepared its own suicide; indeed, humanity was already a suicide, the frenzied life of the planet just the activity of the body in that instant before the poison reaches the brain. Death was coming: the massive overkill, the die-off, the apocalypse. The planet would die from poison, from pesticides, from gas in the air, from oil in the sea, from nuclear bombs, from heat, from cold, from the hideous swarming of killer insects, from blood on the moon. Mac brooded. Didn't the thundering of blood in his ears, the soughing of breath in his lungs, the aches and pains of his body after a game of squash, the rumble of his stomach all belie the no-

235

tion that he himself—much less the race or the planet—could ever die? And in his head Hartmann's voice whispered, *No; your blood is full of DDT, your breath of noxious fumes, your joints ache from strontium-ninety decay, your stomach rumbles from poisons in your food and water, you are doomed, the race is doomed, the planet is doomed.* The apocalypse took on a clammy inevitability. Mac was from the South, and though he would have denied it, deep in his brain was a view of history as a mournful progression of dissolution and decay; to that vision the end of the world, chain-store, mass-produced, assembly-line death, seemed the predestined end of time, which had after all been slowly running down since a bright golden moment of perfection a century before. So Mac, as winter came in full, learned to think of himself as a guillotined head in whom sense has not yet died—a bright fragment which, dying, still saw and thought and felt.

Stephanian hated Hartmann, hated his gospel. One night the three of them sat in Hartmann's room, beside his practice pad, under a giant print of Bosch's "Garden of Earthly Delights," before the empty fireplace, and Mac and Hartmann talked and Stephanian listened. As the evening passed, Mac could see that it was getting to Stephanian, too, to whom things always made sense; he was being pulled down with them into a despair where it sometimes seemed impossible to do anything, even to tie their shoes or brush their teeth or open and close their mouths. But Stephanian would not go; at last, he jumped up and shook himself and said, "Listen, listen! So what if it's true? I'm still not going to commit suicide. You want to know why? You want to know why I don't commit suicide?" From the back of a chair he plucked his shiny brown aviator's jacket, grasped the fur collar, and thrust it beneath Hartmann's bulging eyes. "Look at this! My leather jacket! This jacket makes me happy! This jacket keeps me sane! And if you want to be happy, you'll just go and buy yourself a goddamn leather jacket like mine!" He stomped out the door, and they heard the angry clump of his hiking boots descending the stairwell to the world below.

Mac never respected Hartmann as much after that, for the next day he saw him at dinner wearing a new shiny aviator's jacket and a thoughtful expression.

Stephanian argued tirelessly with Mac, like water wearing at stone, but Mac told himself he was not moved. Of all the people he met at college, Mac loved and respected Stephanian the most, because it did make sense to him, but he could not seem to follow him. After the exchange with Hartmann, he and Mac sat in their own room and Stephanian tried to bring Mac into his world of order and purpose. They drank black cherry soda from cans; Stephanian's mother sent him a case a week from Fresno, on the theory that it might keep him from drinking. Mac found the sweet flavor particularly refreshing after a night of hash smoking across the hall.

Stephanian told Mac he had become a communist, and he told him why. They talked about the killing in Asia, and Stephanian, whose mind bristled with hideous facts and unimaginable figures, made him see and hear it; the hum of the mighty death birds, B-52s, taking off from Thailand to destroy fields, schools, hospitals, bridges, temples; the whir of the helicopters leaving base, the pop and crackle of small-arms fire as they lit on hot landing zones; the rustle of straw and thatch burning as the zippo squads moved through villages; the bright flash of napalm falling from the sky, the sizzle and the screams as it clung to flesh, burned down to bone; the shrieks of children hit by tiny bomblets; the wailing of mothers who had drunk water contaminated with defoliants and had birthed deformities: the suffering of a subcontinent burning and dying because America was there and refused to go away.

Mac looked at Stephanian and saw from his tired, intense, gentle face that he did not permit himself ever to forget these things, that they were as much a part of his daily life as snow in the Yard or meatball subs from Tommy's Lunch. He shuddered; he did not think he could bear such knowledge.

But Stephanian could bear it because he had found a way to make sense of it. He rummaged in his bureau and pulled out a bit of ribbon and tarnished metal. He showed it to Mac; the tarnished gold glowed dully on his palm. It showed Mount Ararat; beneath it were words which meant "For this land I would give my life." It was his grandfather's medal, which he had won for fighting the Turks. His grandfather had given it to him when Stephanian had come to tell him that he was a radical. His grandfather had been a revolutionary, and now his grandson was one, too, and he had given Stephanian the medal as a gesture of pride.

He kept the medal to remind himself that he had put his life on the line. "I really am," he told Mac. In his round spectacle lenses Mac saw reflected the ceiling light globe. "I really am willing to die to stop the war." Mac was left breathless, admiring, bewildered; his friend had crossed into a world he could not enter, and Mac envied him and feared him together.

Stephanian's vision of that war did not leave Mac, but when Stephanian went off to spend the summer organizing a demonstration in protest against the Democratic national convention, Mac stayed in Cambridge to make up a course in summer school he had failed his freshman year. He watched the Chicago convention on the big television in the Harvard *Crimson* building and was duly appalled.

Stephanian came back with a bloody nose, a limp, and an arrest record. He and Mac talked about the convention.

"You should have been there, Mac," Stephanian said. "It was really amazing out in the streets. For a while—just a little while—it was like being part of the Red Army. It really was what we've been trying to do; it was pulling ourselves inside out and seeing the world through new eyes."

Mac looked at his friend in wondering awe: even after being arrested and beaten, after seeing his Red Army clubbed off the streets, he still maintained his scholar's equanimity and his freedom fighter's optimism.

"They came down on you pretty hard, didn't they?" Mac said.

"That just means that next time we'll be ready to protect ourselves better."

"Watching it on TV," Mac said, "I don't know—"

"What?" Arnie said.

"I don't even know if I can make this clear to you, Arnie," Mac said. "You were in the streets, and I guess that was bad enough, but you didn't see what was going on inside the convention hall. I've been to conventions and mass meetings, and I swear to God I've never seen anything rigged like that one. They'd have been ashamed to do that kind of thing in Virginia twenty years ago."

"What are you talking about?" Stephanian said. "Of course it was rigged, so what?"

"So what? Arnie, don't you understand, the President of the United States rigged that convention, it was just like a damn banana republic, and you say so what? I know the cops were unbelievable, you got beat up, but you're the historian, can't you see, we've always had riots in this country, but my God! Now they've stolen the political process—"

"Process! Process!" Stephanian burst out. "Fuck you, Mac! You're a fool! You've been brought up with the damn process in your genes! Can't you see that it doesn't mean anything? It never fucking did! Fuck your process! I saw my friends, people I loved, brothers and sisters of mine, beaten down in the street, and you're talking about the process! Makes me sick, the goddamn process, don't talk to me about it anymore."

Things had cooled between Stephanian and Mac after that. That fall they were living apart, each in single rooms, for Mac was writing a senior thesis and needed privacy. His paper was called "The Effect of Voting Rights Legislation on Voting Patterns in the Virginia Democratic Primary." It was a statistical analysis of Tobey Carrington's victory, showing just how the Voting Rights Act and the Twenty-Fifth Amendment had freed voters never enfranchised before and made enough of a difference to put Carrington in office.

As Mac worked on his paper, Stephanian and the rest of SDS were campaigning to get Harvard's ROTC chapter thrown off campus. As he watched Stephanian organize Dunster House, Mac thought to himself that for a man who despised the political process, Stephanian would have made a terrific ward boss. In fact, the entire SDS chapter that year functioned beautifully throughout the first semester: by Christmas they had called on him so often, been so polite and persistent and logical, that they had Mac's signature on a petition, as well as hundreds of others; they had raised the issue in every forum in the university; they had, like a political candidate dominating the opposition, made their issue the only issue on the campus. And by spring, when the glittering immaculate men who ran Harvard made it clear that they didn't care what SDS thought, what Mac Evans thought or the student body or the faculty thought, they were going to keep ROTC because they were for the Army, they were for the war, Mac was surprised to find how angry it made him, how, suddenly, like Stephanian, it made him want to do something to get back at them.

One night, working in his room on note cards for his thesis, Mac heard singing and chanting in the distance. Soon Stephanian came and knocked at the door. Mac noticed his friend was flushed, breathing hard, his face wreathed in a smile that would not stop. He couldn't stop moving; he fidgeted around the room as he told Mac how they had marched through the Yard and the streets of Cambridge and finally up to the president's door, where a policeman had told them to stay away or he would break their fingers, and they'd marched in anyway, marched in and stuck a list of demands on the door with a knife, for the president to read at his leisure.

"This is it," Stephanian was saying, and Mac looked at him and felt excited, too, but also scared, because he didn't know what Stephanian was going to do or what they might do to him as a result.

"What are you going to do?" Mac said.

"I don't know," Stephanian said, jiggling about the room. "No, really, I don't. But listen, Mac—"

"Yeah?" The two were standing face to face, and Stephanian took Mac by the arm and bent his head as if to whisper, as a politician might, even though there was no one to listen. "There's a rally tomorrow at University Hall. Against ROTC. You ought to come. You really should."

"What's going to happen?" Mac asked again.

"I told you I don't know!" Stephanian snapped, with annoyance in his voice and a hint of something else, and then he was out the door.

It was a sunny day, spring cool, the ninth of April. Mac went to the rally. But it turned out not to be a rally, not exactly, for when Mac got there, the radicals were there with the bullhorns, their voices again tinny, distant, ominous, but as Mac arrived at the white building he saw them turn away from the crowd and enter University Hall, the home of the university's administration: saw first a few go inside, then more, then a big surge, among whom he saw his friend Stephanian passing through the doors.

"What's going on?" he asked someone else, a large, pudgy boy in a crimson Harvard windbreaker.

"I dunno," the other replied. "I think these bastards have taken over the building."

"Taken it over?"

"Yeah—like Columbia."

Then in a flurry Mac saw the dean of freshmen, a rigid, sour lump of Yankee outrage, carried down the steps by students. Behind him, another dean, a black man, was pushed out, throwing punches behind him at those who had hold of his shoulder. Mac went numb; this was what was happening: takeover. This was what Stephanian meant.

"WE HAVE OCCUPIED UNIVERSITY HALL," said a voice from an upstairs window. "WE WILL NOT LEAVE UNTIL THE UNIVERSITY MEETS OUR DEMANDS!" Mac looked up; it was Stephanian's face above the bullhorn.

At the thronged entrance to the building, students held their arms aloft, hands in fists. "Smash ROTC!" they chanted. "No expansion!"

"ALL OF YOU WHO ARE AGAINST THE WAR AND AGAINST HARVARD'S COMPLICITY SHOULD JOIN US!" Stephanian was shouting. "ALL OF YOU WHO OPPOSE HARVARD'S RACIST POLICIES IN ROXBURY AND CAMBRIDGE SHOULD JOIN US! WE HAVE OCCUPIED THIS BUILDING! WE WILL NOT LEAVE UNTIL HARVARD GIVES INTO OUR DEMANDS!"

"Smash ROTC! No expansion! Smash ROTC! No expansion!"

"OFFICERS TRAINED AT HARVARD ARE FIGHTING IN VIETNAM RIGHT NOW! THOUSANDS OF INNOCENT CIVILIANS HAVE BEEN MURDERED BY STUDENTS WHO STUDIED RIGHT HERE! THIS IS AN OUTRAGE, AND IF YOU WANT TO STOP IT, NOW IS THE TIME!"

"Smash ROTC! No expansion!"

"THE CORPORATION WOULDN'T LISTEN TO THE STUDENTS WHEN WE SAID WE WANT ROTC OFF CAMPUS! THEY WOULDN'T LISTEN TO THE FACULTY! THEY SAID THEY WERE GOING TO KEEP ROTC, THEY SAID ROTC WAS A GOOD THING! BY OCCUPYING THIS BUILDING WE WILL MAKE THEM LISTEN! WE WILL GET RID OF ROTC ONCE AND FOR ALL!"

"SMASH ROTC! NO EXPANSION!"

"NOW IS THE TIME TO ACT!"

"SMASH ROTC!"

"THE WHOLE WORLD IS WATCHING!"

"NO EXPANSION!"

Stephanian was speaking, and he was not speaking to the crowd or the deans and tutors clustered at the back of the crowd or the student reporters scribbling on their pads or the TV crew just setting up their equipment or the plainclothes policemen with their slicked-back hair and pointed shoes or the MIT students who were burning a scarecrow SDS. He was speaking to his friend Mac Evans, who had spent the year writing on file cards and reading his brother's letters about how he was going to be lieutenant governor of Virginia, who had done nothing during a year when a subcontinent had burned and the smoke and the screaming had been heard half a world away, who had stopped his ears and done nothing because his brother told him not to, because it was safer, because it was easier, because the voters didn't like it, because someone might be embarrassed, and Stephanian was not contemptuous of Mac, he was speaking to him: "THE PRESIDENT OF HARVARD SAYS WE'RE NOT GOING TO GET RID OF ROTC BECAUSE ROTC IS A GOOD THING! THE CORPORATION SAID THEY DON'T CARE WHAT THE FACULTY VOTES, THEY'RE GOING TO KEEP ROTC BECAUSE THEY SUPPORT THE WAR!" and the crowd was chanting "SMASH ROTC! NO EXPANSION!" and it was all for Mac, it was all because he had refused to face it before, now it wouldn't go away, this was the choice of his life, and he looked down at his feet because step by step they were carrying him up the gray stone steps, he looked at his elbow, which was pushing his way through the crowd, he looked at his own fist, which was waving in the air and it was his own voice chanting: "SMASH ROTC! NO EXPANSION!SMASHROTCNOEXPANSIONSMASHROTCNOEXPANSION," and he was doing it, he was stepping over the doorway, it had happened, it was too late, he was in it now, and he found himself crying, weeping real tears as he cooled his forehead on the iron rail of the stairway mounting to the second floor, tears of joy because he was in it, finally, he was in it now.

Years later, things remained of that night in the building that would never leave him: the sight of Stephanian standing on a tabletop in the great second-floor faculty room, addressing the meeting of those who had occupied the building: "I think it's pretty clear that anybody who smokes dope in this building is helping to provoke a bust, and whether they know it or not, they're objectively on the side of the administration, so let's not have any smoking in here," to a chorus of cheering and boos; he remembered someone giving him a bologna sandwich for dinner and a can of black cherry soda, which might have come from Stephanian's room. He remembered someone offering him a file, which to his amazement turned out to be about him, and he read: "*Although Evans is neither an outstanding student nor a student leader, he has an interesting background and good recommendations. In my opinion he can be expected to make a solid though not spectacular contribution in the area of the social sciences.*" And he remembered setting his file on fire, burning himself and his records and his cowardly shameful past, spectacular but not solid, to black ashes on the carpet.

He remembered an interminable meeting as night darkened over the Yard, crowds sitting in the faculty room discussing what to do if the police came, and meanwhile, through the crowd, endless rumors running that the police were coming now, or in an hour, or at midnight, or at dawn, and fear and uncertainty running until every nerve of his body was rubbed raw, his adrenal glands wide open and pumping. He could no longer sit still, and he left the meeting and went into the hall.

Sitting on the steps, he found Cassie McGraw, her red hair cut short and curly. It came to him suddenly that she was on the steps waiting for him, and so, it seemed, she was. He walked up to her, she stood, they embraced as real lovers do who have not seen each other for years, forcing flesh against flesh in hope that they may escape into the other, standing there for long minutes awkwardly entwined.

"I'm scared," she said.

"Me too," Mac said. Wordlessly they went up the stairs, went two floors above where there were no crowds in the hall. They held hands like junior high school sweethearts. Cassie pushed open a door, and they stepped into a dark office, and Cassie reached up to him, and they kissed, and soon they were on the floor together, each almost invisible to the other in the half-light from the floodlit Yard, and Mac pulled at her clothing and she at his, and he noticed that they were not alone in the room, that in

242

the corner was another couple, he could hear their breathing as it became sharper, but it was all right: it was as if the building were breathing around them, they were inside a living thing they had made, it was good, but then in one short instant of time something happened to them both, brought them to a stop. For Mac it was as if those shadowy passageways he had imagined earlier, the sewers of the human heart, stood again open before him, and he rolled away on the rug, and in his mind unbidden were the words "cruelty," "deceit," "dishonor," and in her dim face he could see them, too, in the half-light he could see terror in her eyes. He helped her to her feet, and she fled before him down the stairway while he stayed behind to close the door on the breathing, which went on, rhythmic, ecstatic, unaware.

In the cold dead hours of morning he and Stephanian stood at a window and looked out at the Yard. People had stayed to support those in the building; they were sitting huddled on the steps of University Hall or nervously pacing between the building and the basement of Memorial Church, where there was warmth and a place to sleep.

"What time is it?" Mac asked Stephanian.

"Don't know," Stephanian said. "Sometime after four."

"Damn," Mac said. "I don't think I've ever seen anything like this."

Stephanian noded gravely. "You were always interested in process," he said. "Take a look. This is the historical process."

Mac winced at the memory of their quarrel. "It doesn't feel like history," Mac said. "It feels more like we've jumped outside of history."

Stephanian nodded again. Even now, on the barricades, he kept his solemn, scholarly air. "I know that feeling," he said. "But you've got to see this as a part of history—a long historical struggle, with its beginnings a long time ago and its ending—who knows, maybe soon, but maybe a long time from now."

"God damn you, Stephanian," Mac said. "Would you fucking quit grinding your ax? How can you talk about the historical process? This is now, this is the biggest fucking thing I ever lived through, I don't want to talk about hundreds of years."

"I can understand that, Mac, I feel it, too: the immediacy. But you've got to think of it in historical terms, or you'll never understand it. Without an ideology you'll never make it in the long run. You end up a liberal or a fascist."

"Jesus!" Mac said. "Your goddamned grandfather in Armenia, I bet he never sat around horseshitting like this waiting for the Turks to come."

"Yeah," Stephanian said. "Look what happened to him: he's a lettuce farmer in Fresno."

243

"What should he be?" Mac asked. "Deputy minister of rural electrification in Soviet Armenia?"

"There would be worse fates."

"God, Stephanian, you really are a Stalinist, you know?"

"No, I'm not," Stephanian said, shaking his head slowly. "But I do believe in analysis. Without that, we'll all end up voting Republican someday."

"Oh, kiss my red ass," Mac said, and they both laughed.

That was when they first noticed headlights in the predawn darkness—long dark cars and buses full of police cutting across the grass of the Yard—and even as Mac realized that the bust was on, he had time to be outraged on behalf of the grass. Then the cops were out, lumpy in helmets and shields, carrying clubs and rams, and he heard screaming below him as they rushed the stone steps, and he saw one girl hurled from the top step to the flagstones beneath, and even up there, even in the dark, he saw blood running, he had never seen it before: not drops from bleeding cuts or nosebleeds but blood running down the steps as the cops threw the kids off the stairs and rammed down the doors. He heard the smashing at the doors, and it was only then that he became frightened, because before they had been outside, and he had been safe inside, but now he realized that men with guns and clubs were breaking down his doors; they were coming to do him harm.

"Have you got the legal aid number?" Stephanian asked softly.

Mac found his breath coming in gasps and jerks and could not speak. He nodded, and the nod went on until he was shaking up and down, shivering with fright, they were coming to get him, they were through the door, he heard screams from the first floor, and Stephanian was saying "let's get out of this room, away from the window," and he led Mac into the Hall. "Don't resist," Arnie kept saying, "don't give them any excuse," and then there was a blue steely shape at the head of the stairs, and it came for Stephanian and clubbed him and clubbed him again, and Mac heard Stephanian screaming, a high, narrow noise like an animal in an abattoir, and the cop chased him into the room they had come from, and there was a thump and Stephanian's screaming stopped.

Kids were screaming up and down the hall. Mac drew himself into a ball, thinking perhaps the cop would not see him, but he came out of the room and stood over Mac, a mile tall in blue and steel and glass, and poked him with his toe and said, "Get up, faggot," and Mac got up and raised his hands, and his eyes said, *please don't hit me, don't hit me with that club.* But it was all right, the cop put his hand gently on Mac's shoulder, and then to his chin, and Mac wondered if he had drooled there, if the policeman were wiping his chin, and as he wiped it, he moved it just so, like an artist with a model, and then he took his hand away. "Thank you," Mac started to say, but then he saw the club coming up, then his head burst and there was blood in his eyes and he was down and the club came again and he kept hearing in his mind the word "process," "process," "process," and the word chased him down a long tunnel of darkness and he was out.

"RICHMOND YOUTH SEIZED IN HARVARD FRACAS—*Senator's Brother Charged with Criminal Trespass.*" Mac read the clipping from the Richmond paper and tasted ashes in his mouth. Molly O. had clipped the article and sent it to him. Beneath the headline was his St. Cyprian's graduation picture, firm of chin, unsmiling, short-haired, clean-shaven: the all-Virginia boy. "MacIlwain K. Evans, the caption read, "son of prominent family one of 200 arrested in Harvard building seizure."

Enclosed also was a note, on Molly O.'s square blue-bordered monogrammed stationery: "Are you all right, Mac? You ought to call your brother—Love whatever, O." Until that note arrived, he had not once thought about his family or about Lester and his ambitions and what he might do to them. He had been carried bleeding to jail and arraigned for criminal trespass, for being in a building he felt now by rights belonged to him; had President Pusey or Dean Glimp ever shed blood to defend it? Then he had called his tutor and told him that "The Effect of Voting Rights Legislation on Voting Patterns in the Virginia Democratic Primary" was just never going to get written because the author was on strike, was no longer interested in liberal politics, and had too much to do anyway, marching, picketing, writing leaflets, working a silk-screen machine in Emerson Hall, near the statue of the great Transcendentalist himself, and Mac felt transcendent himself and he was never going back to his old life. His tutor had thanked him gruffly for his courtesy and had hung up; he had, no doubt, had such calls in plenty and found them wearisome.

Those two weeks Mac felt his body, like an electric wire, plugged into the revolution, humming with power from the freedom fighters of the world, one with the Vietcong and the Chinese and Cubans and Bolivians, possessed by the ghosts of Che and Liebknecht and Rosa Luxemburg and Emma Goldman and Debs, one with Ben Bella and Lumumba and Samora Machel, Jacobo Arbenz and Pancho Villa and the Chicago Eight and Dr. Cheddi Jagan, revolutionary dentist. He worked hours in the cluttered strike headquarters, printing a poster which said: STRIKE BECAUSE THEY

245

ARE TRYING TO SQUEEZE THE LIFE OUT OF YOU. But in truth Mac had never felt so alive, a live bullet whizzing through space, bound on a mission of liberation and truth. When he got that letter, he knew at once that it was over, that he was back to the earth of his family and his history and that for all that he might still want to be plugged in to the revolution, for all that he might seek it and tell himself he was and always would be, he would never feel that pure feeling again without an admixture of terror and cynicism and defeat: the legacy of his forebears. He crumpled the letter and went off to call his brother.

Lester was civil on the phone. "Listen, bub," he said, "I wish you would have called earlier. They've been after me to make a comment on this thing."

"Just say I did it and I'm a different human being from you," Mac suggested warily.

Lester cleared his throat. "That doesn't work so well around here."

"What *are* you going to do?"

"Some folks are after me to make a statement saying I don't approve."

"Of what?" Mac said.

"Of what you did."

"What—you mean me by name?"

Another pause. "Right."

"Don't you do that, Lester," Mac said, the words coming out in a rush. "Don't you go to that damn newspaper and talk me down."

"Look, Mac," Lester said, his voice sharpening, "I don't see where you belong to tell me what not to do about anything. I mean, I'm in a hell of a spot on this thing, this could give me real trouble—"

"Bull-fucking-shit," Mac said. "The only way you could lose the primary this year is for *you* to get arrested, and all that would do would be make it close."

"Got it all figured, don't you?"

"Lester," Mac said, and he was not arguing now, speaking softly, in a conciliatory tone.

"What?"

"You're mad at me, okay, be mad. But don't drag those newspapers into our family. Don't you let them do that to us."

Lester said nothing for a moment; the phone wire bleeped and bonked. Then he spoke, and Mac could tell he was really asking for political advice. "Yeah," he said. "I don't want to do that. But what the hell am I going to do?"

"I happen to think I did the right thing—"

"Don't give me that shit now!"

246

"No, I mean, leave that out of it for the moment."

"All right."

"If you got problems, I'm sorry. But here's what you can do. You could make a speech and say that you don't approve of unlawful means of protest, although you may sympathize with the frustration—"

"Sympathize, hell," Lester said. "I start sympathizing I'm a real dead duck—"

"You could say you're against the war, but—"

"I don't give a damn about the fucking war! I'm not about to get into all that! This is a state election—"

"All right, Lester," Mac said. In his mouth a bitter brass taste had risen when Lester said, "I don't give a damn." "You do what you think is right, you make a speech against student protest, but don't mention me, don't mention Harvard. You're a grown man, and you have a responsibility to our family, and I'm your family—"

"You didn't fucking call me before you went and got arrested!"

Mac was quiet for a minute. "Just do it this way," he said. "It'll work for you, and I promise I won't get arrested again."

"All right. I'll take that," Lester said quickly. "You're not going to get expelled now, are you?"

"Hell no, I got a clean record except for this."

"You going to graduate on time?"

"Yes, Lester."

"With honors?"

"Fuck you, Lester, no. Not with honors."

"All right," Lester said. "You stay out of jail and graduate, and I'll come up there and we'll talk then."

So the strike was over for Mac; he picketed here and there, but the heart was gone, and when May 1 came, he sent in his letter accepting the University of Virginia Law School because that was what he'd planned to do all along. He expected Stephanian to be angry, but he wasn't.

"That's right," he said. "We're going to need lawyers."

Mac wondered if he'd ever be one of Stephanian's "we" again. But he nodded and went quietly about passing his exams. He was waiting to see Lester at graduation. But before his brother came, he got another clipping: "NO APPEASEMENT" FOR STUDENT REBELS, EVANS URGES—*Lt. Gov. Hopeful Says State Must Act Quickly in Disturbances.* Lester had kept his bargain: nowhere did the article mention Mac or Harvard by name. But it made it clear that Lester Tutelo Evans, if he ever got to be governor of Virginia, would smash anybody on a college campus who got out of line, expel them, take away their scholarships, put them in jail on felony charges, attack without mercy these disturbers of the public peace. Mac read, and wiped his face; he felt his brother's spittle dripping off it.

So when he came, and they talked, the talk was one both would remember for the rest of their lives. They left Molly O. waiting at the hotel while they went to Mac's room for a quick drink, and the quick drink ended four hours later with Lester on his feet, fist clenched, face red, screaming at Mac, "Listen to me, you punk crazy! You are insane! You are dangerous! I don't want you around me! I don't want you in my house or my campaign and you better stay out of my sight! I don't want to have anything to do with you!" and Mac screaming back, "All right! Fuck you! I wouldn't work with you anyway, because you haven't got any goddamn guts, you don't have one-tenth the guts our father had, you got no spine at all, and you never took a fucking stand on principle in your life because you don't have any fucking principles!"

Mac had won that exchange; he could tell by the hurt in his brother's eyes that he had reached him, and he wanted to call it back, to say, *No, I didn't mean that,* but he couldn't. Lester smiled grimly and said, "Okay, bub, you and the Colonel, you got each other now. You both going to amount to the same thing. Good-bye to you both."

He heard the heels of his brother's shoes clump briskly down the stairwell and out of his life.

FIVE

★

Even then, with his degree safely granted and money in his pocket and his brother's curse ringing in his ears, Mac could not think of anywhere to go but back to Virginia. The next morning Mac woke in his room in Dunster House, looked at the mass of cardboard boxes, suitcases, and packing crates, and knew where they were going.

He looked out his round window at the Charles River. It was after ten o'clock. In the green courtyard the old men back for their fiftieth reunion were sitting in lawn chairs, their legs stuck stiffly before them, like a brigade of white flannel pandas. Beyond the iron gates, across Memorial Drive, the street people were parading by the river in their springtime undress. The young men and women, lithe and free, chased after Frisbees, tanned legs flashing. The riverbank was a world of infinite possibility, a magical realm where love and death, danger and mystery, were waiting for him. But he was enchanted, guarded by magical pandas. He breathed the springtime air through the round window, and as he drew in his breath, he felt in every part of him the dreary knowledge that, despite the spring and the revolution and Lester, nothing had changed for him; his future was coded in his genes. He would go home for the summer and then up to Charlottesville to the law school.

In Richmond he shared a house with a pair of Yippies who had an extra room. This was in the Fan, a stately grid of treelined streets and brick houses where Richmonds' hardy band of longhairs had settled.

Mac's roommates worked in a cheese shop on Grace Street. At night they talked about the revolution, which they imagined lowering on the horizon like a summer thunderhead, about to burst. Mac moved his things into a narrow upstairs room and went downtown to Shadwell for Governor headquarters.

He had heard of Tom Jeff Shadwell by then as the wildest political fighter the state had seen since his father's last campaign. He told himself that this campaign was an extension of the revolution he had begun in April, but he knew better. His brother had promised him a part in this year's campaign and then taken it back; Mac was still determined to have his part, and in a place where he could gall his brother.

Shadwell headquarters was the same dark jumbled warren the candidate would use four years later. Mac walked in and gave the receptionist his name and asked to speak to Mr. Cheatham.

He wondered at the time why Knocko and Tom Jeff welcomed him so warmly that day, gave him almost immediately a job writing speeches and press releases, with responsibility and the ear of the candidate. They needed all the help they could get, true enough: Shadwell that year was outgunned and outnumbered. But it was something else, something deeper even than the mere opportunism of having the brother of Lester T. Evans, the most popular politician in the state, on their team. Mac gradually realized that it went back twenty years, to his father's campaign; Colonel Joshua T. Evans was the man who had first caught Tom Jeff Shadwell, had taught him to rebel. Shadwell felt it an honor to have his son on board his campaign; it marked his passage into a special political Valhalla. It made him and the Colonel equals somehow.

Like the Colonel, Tom Jeff was fighting the odds. This was the Democratic primary that Senator Tobey Carrington and Lester T. Evans and the rest of the moderates hoped would give them control of the Democratic Party and thus of the state government. Tobey Carrington had handpicked the moderate candidate to succeed Miles Brock as governor: Tom Slaughter, his best friend at the University and his campaign manager when he had run for the Senate. Slaughter had a high forehead where his thin sandy hair had receded. His eyebrows rose precariously high in skeptical amusement, and his voice was wry and conciliatory. Everyone agreed that Tom Slaughter was a nice fellow.

Backing him up was Lester Evans, who was running for lieutenant governor in the same primary. Carrington and Lester and their friends had it figured out: all they had to do was win this primary, and they were in. The Republicans were going to nominate someone, of course, probably the same man who had run against Miles Brock, four years earlier, a man named Horace Hapgood who owned a cattle farm, but there was no need to fear that; the primary was all that counted.

Shadwell was the only obstacle in a political fix as sweet as any Mac had ever seen. Tom Jeff had put in his years in the General Assembly knocking raucously at the doors of power. He had screamed and yelled, and when they had killed his bills in committee and laughed him off the floor, he had sued the State Corporation Commission and the governor and the telephone company and the electric company and the Division of Motor Vehicles and the Board of Elections and two or three dozen others, had made a name for himself as a man who fought the powerful and afflicted the comfortable. Now he wanted to step up.

To Lester and Tobey Carrington and Tom Slaughter, Shadwell seemed like a maniac, trying to ruin their perfect deal. They were reasonable men, disposed to compromise, convinced that no problem or conflict could not be solved if men of goodwill were willing to sit down and talk it out. They could not hope to understand Shadwell, this loud political brawler, a pious Christian soldier to whom the world was divided into the working people and their enemies, between whom God had decreed a state of ceaseless warfare. Most puzzling to them was the fact that Shadwell could not see the clear benefit that would accrue to the state and its people when the reigns of power fell into their hands, the vast improvement that would follow after the years of the Apple-Farmer and his machine. They were puzzled and hurt and confused that Tom Jeff saw no difference between them and the old guard, contemptuously dismissed them as weak copies of the men they had been so circumspectly fighting for so long. Shadwell was against them all, all machines, whether they called themselves moderate or conservative or what have you, and so, to their eternal shock and dismay, he borrowed on his house and paid his primary filing fee and sailed into Tom Slaughter with bayonet fixed.

It was a long shot, and Shadwell knew it. Slaughter had Carrington and Lester Evans, money and recognition; Shadwell had nothing but his own voice and Knocko Cheatham. Not that those were not assets: Knocko that year was indefatigable, and Mac came quickly to admire him as a political virtuoso who could conjure up a countywide organization overnight out of two spinster sisters, a retired deputy sheriff, and a bus schedule. And Shadwell's voice served him brilliantly: the first television commercial Shadwell was able to afford that year showed the candidate peering

251

out of a moving helicopter while the unforgettable penetrating squeak of his voice, rising plain and clear above the whirring rotors, called down the vengeance of the Almighty on the enemies of the people.

Then they had Mac—a name and a background that might open some doors, get some money and attention and respect—but they didn't have anything else.

Mac first saw what life and politics were like for Tom Jeff Shadwell when he went with the candidate to Danville for the AFL-CIO convention that July. Shadwell needed labor support that year, needed its money and its skilled manpower. Without labor support he would be shouting into the wind, without a base or any measure of credibility. Like the blacks, the union leaders knew that Shadwell was one of their own, was on their side. He came from a union town, and he had fought with them in the legislature in support of their lost causes: a state minimum wage, repeal of the Right-to-Work Law, better workmen's compensation and unemployment benefits. The unions were not popular in the legislature. Year after year they had been defeated and ridiculed, and Tom Jeff had stood with them. They owed him their support, and in his underdog's chance for victory lay their only hope of getting a place of power in the state now or in the future.

But years of defeat had left them wary and timorous. Early that spring, when Tobey Carrington and Tom Slaughter had realized that Shadwell was going to insist on trying to interrupt the cadence of their measured march to victory, they had sent Lester Evans to talk to the AFL-CIO Executive Committee. Lester had laid matters out for them as only he could do: friendly and reasonable and kind, but firm. Lester Evans made it clear that he was a friend of labor. No one could doubt that. His father had walked with labor when it did not pay to do that, and he had paid a price for it. Now Lester had come as his father's son to tell the union bosses that Tobey Carrington and Tom Slaughter wanted to be friends of labor, too. He told them that these two would be good friends for labor to have and very dangerous enemies for labor to make. It would be suicidal folly for labor to waste its strength tilting at windmills with Tom Jeff Shadwell that year: sentimentally satisfying, perhaps, but, in the end, unwise.

But Lester assured them that Carrington and Slaughter understood labor's position: labor didn't want to appear to turn on one of its own. He even admitted that that made some sense. So all Carrington and Slaughter would ask was for labor to stay out of this race.

So the word had gone out that the AFL-CIO would be neutral in the gubernatorial primary. It would endorse Lester Evans, for old times' sake and because he didn't have any real opposition, but between Slaughter and Shadwell it would make no endorsement. Both were invited to address the convention, but that was all.

Tom Jeff and Knocko had talked and pleaded and bluffed and cajoled and threatened for weeks, but the fix was in. By the weekend of the convention Tom Slaughter was so certain of the outcome that he decided not to bother with his speech at the convention: a lot of the people who were behind him didn't care for unions very much, and he saw no reason to annoy them by appearing on TV at a conclave of trade unionists. He sent Lester to handle things.

So when Mac piled into the station wagon with Knocko and Tom Jeff (that year there was no Winnebago and no little plane, just the Shadwell family station wagon, with worn green upholstery and a Batman sticker on the rear window, put there for luck by Shadwell's son, Eddie), he figured Shadwell needed a miracle to keep himself alive, and Mac had not yet come to believe that Tom Jeff Shadwell could work miracles.

The delegates sat in rows of bleachers, and where roller derby queens whirled on weekends there was a wooden speaker's stand. Mac and Tom Jeff manned a hospitality booth at a corner of the hall, dispensing buttons and stickers, handshakes and free cups of Dr Pepper, while Knocko stalked the hall in search of some lever to break the convention open, unfix the fix. But though Cheatham was as feisty as ever, Mac sensed that he had given up hope. Tom Jeff, by contrast, was placid and cheerful as he stood behind the wooden table, his left arm curled around a small cardboard parcel, his right busy shaking hands and gesturing and serving cups of Dr Pepper. "Here you are, this is my official campaign drink, I call it Dr. Shadwell," he piped merrily. "Dr. Shadwell, you like him, he likes you."

He knew most of the delegates by name and city and local number and office, and he introduced each one to Mac, saying, "I'd like you to meet my associate, Mr. Mac Evans, Mac here is from Richmond, you may have heard of his father, Colonel Joshua Tutelo Evans."

Mac understood why Knocko and Tom Jeff had brought him along, and he didn't mind, but he still refused to go with Tom Jeff to the speaker's platform while his brother gave his speech. Knocko and Tom Jeff went off together, Tom Jeff still carrying the cardboard box under one arm. Mac stayed in the bleachers to watch Lester make his appearance.

It was hot and drowsy in the auditorium, with little hint of excitement. The delegates were about two-thirds white, a majority of them men, but male or female, black or white, giving off a certain air of toughness, as tough they had to be to survive in a state where the political system and the courts and the press were rigged against them. They seemed matter-of-

253

fact, almost bored; the fix was in, and they knew it. The bleachers were almost full, though: the union people wanted a good look at Lester Evans, who was going to be governor and maybe even more than that someday.

Lester looked good that night; he looked like a winner. He wore a pearl-gray summer suit and a light-blue shirt and off-yellow tie. They loved him. He had them before he opened his mouth, because he was young, because he was rich and handsome and did things the way he wanted to, because he was a winner, because he was his father's son. It was not even work for him.

"I'm so pleased to be here today," he said. "This is a great year in Virginia's history. This is a year when all our people can join together and work for progress. This is a year when the barriers which have divided us for so long—barriers of race and wealth and creed—can fall, and we can all join hands to seek what is in the public interest. I'm very grateful to be here today because I believe that working people must be an important part of our efforts to move Virginia forward, and I hope to enlist your help in this great crusade," he told them, and he told them a lot of other things which added up to nothing much except *hello* and *how are you* and *give me* and *thank you*. When he finished, they stood and applauded him. He thanked them and shook hands with Tom Jeff and left, and they gave him their support by acclamation.

Mac felt angry because it had been so easy for his brother, because Lester had done it again and gotten away with what he wanted without giving anything in return. He was angrier still because part of him felt a little brother's pride and envy, still thrilled to see his brother get away with it.

Then it was time for Tom Jeff, for whom it was always hard, and this time it was impossible. The AFL-CIO president spoke briefly; he said that before the convention voted on the executive board's recommendation that neither candidate for governor be endorsed in the primary, Senator Shadwell had asked to say a few words. Then he yielded the microphone to Tom Jeff with the serene confidence of a man who knows the fix is in.

If Lester's cool elegance was the mark of a winner, Shadwell was already beaten, Mac thought. He wore tan trousers and a checked coat with leather patches on the elbows. In the car Knocko had fingered the material and said, "Tom Jeff, this is a winter coat, you going to be sweating like a pig up there." Shadwell had just smiled, but now under the television lights his face showed a sheen of sweat. He blinked owlishly at the audience, and as the buzz of talk subsided, he put the cardboard box down by his feet and gave them a tentative smile and started in.

"Thank you, Brother Edmunds," he said to the president. "I reckon all

254

of you know it's always a pleasure and a delight for me to be at a convention of the AFL-CIO and to be among friends, the real true friends I've made in this great labor movement. Now I know that most candidates come here like my good friend Lester Evans to talk about what they stand for and what they believe and so on. And that's good, because there are a lot of politicians who have to come down here and stand under these lights"—he mopped his face with a big checked handkerchief—"because you've never seen them before and you don't know what they look like."

There was a low cynical rumble of laughter.

"My good friend who's running against me in this primary and his name escapes me, I'll think of it in a minute, you still don't know what he looks like." He made a shrugging motion with his short arms, a doll's dismissal. "But let that pass, let it go. For me, I'm just here to say howdy-do, because out in this crowd here I see some friends I've known for years, I see Shorty MacManus from the carpenters' union, and I see Ed Willys from the CWA down in my own part of the state—hi, Ed—and I see Evelyn Rosanelli, who's been working hard to organize the municipal workers up in Fairfax, and I see seven or eight others who were with me when we went down to the legislature five years ago—five years ago! Now that was before Miles Brock was governor or Tobey Carrington was a U.S. senator, and I don't even know if my good friend whose name still escapes me, I don't know if he was even in the country five years ago when you and I went down to the legislature and asked for a minimum wage law for working people in this state."

He stopped again to mop his forehead, and then he hitched up the tan trousers, which seemed perhaps a shade too small for him, as if he were a big boy who was still outgrowing his pants. Mac saw his foot reach out and tap the cardboard box ever so gently, as if reassuring himself that it was there, and then he went on. "It was five years ago, and more. It was a cold day in January when we went down there and asked for that minimum wage, and we didn't win it that time, and we still haven't won it, but we went down there and we fought for it and we made 'em sit up and take notice because we went there and they said to themselves, 'Who are these people? These are nothing but some honest union men and women and one little bitty old member of the House of Delegates, and we don't have to listen to them because we are the mighty, on our side are powers and thrones and dominions, angels and archangels ceaselessly crying, "Down with the union, down with the workingman," ' and so they stopped their ears, sat before us in pride of spirit, and we made 'em listen anyway! Do you remember? We made 'em listen, because we went down there and said, 'O Mighty Ones, we're here because ordinary working people need a

255

decent living wage so they can fill that dinner pail.' And we hauled out a big old metal dinner pail and we said, 'O Lords of the Legislature, we want to make that dinner pail ring!' and we hit that old dinner pail with a spoon and it went *ring!* It woke them right up! Do you remember?''

He had raised a big loud laugh with that one, and he beamed at them as he mopped his brow again. ''I remember, I remember like it was yesterday, and I'm proud as I can be of that old dinner pail, my friends. Sometimes at night when I lay awake and asked myself if I've ever been any earthly use to anybody in the four dozen years God has let me walk around, I remember, and I'm proud that of all the one-hundred and forty members of the state legislature I was the only one who would stand up on that day five years ago and make that dinner pail ring!''

He didn't pause now, he gripped the rostrum, and he looked at them hard and said, ''Well, friends, I am here today to prove to you that I am the same man I was five years ago, when I stood up with you and none of your new friends were anywhere to be found. I'm going to prove it to you! Look''—and he was pawing at his own clothing—''Look! Look! I've got on the same clothes I wore that day five years ago! Look!''—and piece by piece he showed them, as the sweat poured off his face because he was wearing five-year-old winter clothes—''Look! I've got on the same shoes! I've got on the same pants! I've got on the same shirt! I've got on the same jacket! The same tie! And look! Look!'' And in a flash he had the box up and had ripped it open and there was something shiny in his hand, and he said, ''LOOK! IT'S THE SAME DINNER PAIL! AND NOW I'M GOING TO MAKE THAT OLD DINNER PAIL RING!''

And he brought the spoon down and rang the old bucket and the room went wild: it was pandemonium, grown-up men tough as cowhide shedding tears and screaming *''Gawdamn, lookit that son of a bitch,''* people breaking chairs and yelling like lunatics and a rush at the speaker's stand. It was to hell with the executive board and Tom Jeff Shadwell getting the AFL-CIO endorsement, and it was the president in a back room with Shadwell begging to be allowed to keep his job, and Tom Jeff smiling because all of a sudden he had the convention in his pocket and saying, all right, the president could stay, but something had to be done about that executive committee, and here just happened to be a list of the ones who should go. It was the lame walking and the dumb speaking and the blind seeing and old dead stinking Lazarus risen out of his grave.

And that was the first miracle Mac ever saw Tom Jeff Shadwell perform.

After that he was a believer. There was still a month to go before the primary, and for that month Mac sat in the sweltering headquarters (in the corner of the back room was a new desk, which was there for the man from AFL-CIO headquarters, a squat hairless man who worked without discernible pause from the moment he entered the room until the campaign's end). Mac wrote speeches and press releases and form letters and radio spots and television copy, and as he did it, he believed that Shadwell was really going to make it.

He wasn't alone. In those four frenetic weeks it began to seem to more and more people that Shadwell, this madman with the funny name and the loud voice, might actually against all the odds win the nomination, with God only knew what to follow. The money began to come in, not a lot but enough so Shadwell could get himself back on television and radio in raucous sixty-second spots preaching against the insurance companies and the electric company and the other big boys ("Every year like clockwork the big boys are down at the legislature, my friends, and they cry out to the legislators, 'You hold the people down while we go through their pockets!' And every year like Old Faithful, Tom Jeff Shadwell rises to fight on behalf of the ordinary taxpayer of this state. So if you want a governor who'll fight against high taxes, high rates, and hanky-panky, vote for Tom Jeff Shadwell, because Tom Jeff Shadwell is always on the job!").

People began calling on the phone and showing up to canvass door to door and work the phone banks day and night. Finally, even Tom Slaughter saw what was going on, that he was losing, and he swallowed his pride and went to Miles Brock and Junior, the Apple-Farmer's son, and the three of them got together and went after Shadwell with everything they had: press conferences in the governor's office and slick four-color Sunday supplements paid for by sudden contributions from a lot of the Apple-Farmer's old friends (SLAUGHTER: THE RESPONSIBLE CHOICE, they said, above a picture of Slaughter with Miles Brock, Tobey Carrington, and Junior, the four looking as sober and serious as a superannuated high school debate team) and "Truth Squads" cruising the state in special buses, blithely giving the lie to statements Tom Jeff had never made. The Richmond newspapers began to go after Tom Jeff with an ax murderer's hebephrenic glee, but still up until the last day Mac believed that Shadwell could work this miracle.

But the magic failed and Slaughter won by five percentage points. As they watched the returns in Shadwell's room in the George Mason Hotel, Mac was shocked and astonished. He felt inside himself the bitter fury of a child who has been cheated. Tom Jeff saw his face and said, "Cheer up, Brother Evans, it's not the surrender at Appomattox; we didn't belong to win this one anyhow. Now the people know who we are, they got to re-

257

spect us. We'll come back another time. And anyway, look on the bright side: your brother's winning." Tom Jeff patted him on the shoulder and went down to thank his people. Then he went back to Norfolk for a while to bide his time and practice law.

Mac felt empty, drained, without even the will to think about what had happened or would happen to him. Two days after the election he got on a Pullman car and rose in its noisy comfort to stay with his mother and Emil in their pink stucco house. By day he lay on the beach and watched through his sunglasses as honey-blond girls walked by. The plastic-silky nap of their bright bathing suits snapped back and forth to the motion of their perfect buttocks, and Mac, waiting like a cold lump of winter for the sun to warm him, watched them pass and wanted to die.

At night it was as if he had died, so still was the pink house. Emil lay on his bed in his white silk pajamas and watched TV, his emphysematous breath rattling in laughter at inaudible jokes. Mac's mother sat upright at a huge mahogany desk and wrote letters to retired admirals and congressmen and psychic researchers and priestesses of Mu, and she warned Mac in her light voice which still floated up like a flock of balloons that the communists were everywhere, that the nation was menaced and he must warn his brother, because Lester would not listen to her.

After a week he could stand no more. As the sun went down one day he walked out of the house to U.S. 1 and stuck out his thumb at the southbound headlights. He got a ride with a Cuban refugee named Julio Ibarrurri, a twenty-year-old college dropout whose father had been a doctor in Havana before Castro. Julio didn't care about politics, though; he was a hardworking full-time hippie, just back from pulling thirty days in a Nova Scotia jail for trying to run out on a restaurant bill.

"Come on with me," Julio told Mac. His speech betrayed no accent; he talked like Peter Fonda. They went to a tiny restaurant and ate black beans and *chorizos* and fried bananas and drank Carta Blanca beer; then Julio ran into a friend who wrote nightclub reviews for a newspaper in Coral Gables.

"You two come with me," the critic said, making an expansive gesture in the air. "You are my guests. In Miami I pay for nothing. Everything you want is free."

So they went with him to watch the showgirls parade in sequins and feathers. Mac smoked one of the critics' smuggled Havanas and drank a Piña Colada. "Drink up," the critic said, his genial, acquisitive face solicitously close to Mac's. "They know me here. In Miami I pay for nothing."

When the show ended, the man turned to them and gestured again.

"What would you like?" he asked. "They know me here. Name it, and it's yours."

Mac wondered if he had enough corruption of soul to ask for one of the beautiful young women in feather costumes, and found to his dismay that he did not. Instead he said, "Is there a card game around here I can get into?"

The critic looked at him and shrugged, then spoke to the headwaiter, and Mac was led upstairs to play blackjack at a broad green felt table, and in three hours he lost two hundred dollars, until he realized he was playing to lose. So he stopped, and said good-bye to his friends, and went out along Collins Avenue to greet the dawn.

When the sun came out of the ocean, Mac watched its red light glancing off the waves. Despite all he had eaten and drunk, he felt empty; despite his frenetic night, he felt dead. He looked southward toward where he imagined Cuba must be, and a voice inside him said, *O my vision. O send me the luck of the sailor,* because it suddenly seemed to him that if only he could be like Stephanian, if only he could believe in the revolution, in the people, in history, if only he could muster the will to offer his life on the altar of history, if he could break free of his corrupt self, then surely at that moment he could set out and walk the ninety miles to Cuba, stepping lively across the glassy sea.

Then that vision collapsed, for he could not, he was not pure, but corrupt, and even his corruption was corrupt, layers of corruption and venality and fear down to the core of his being, so he yearned instead for the pure flame of destruction, imagined over the horizon a vast flotilla of ships bearing an army of freedom fighters, Cuban and Vietnamese and Chinese and Angolan and Eritrean, implacable steel-hard shock troops of history, ready to land on the peninsula and march north with fire and sword until the whole continent should be a mass of flame and not one corrupt stone should remain on another.

Then that vision left him, too, and he was tired and turned to go home.

The University of Virginia Law School was like a cool bath after Cambridge. Mac and his old St. Cyprian's classmate, the angular Justin Foote, shared a house in the country; for Mac it was a quiet anchor-hold, a place of withdrawal and retreat. That fall he took to rising early and walking the woods in the still dawn. He watched each tree and leaf, each drop of dew on each leaf, single and perfect and separate, sliding, like him, silent across the face of time.

He did well in his courses. He had grown up with lawyers and he found their genial skepticism and ironic self-serving rectitude a suit of clothing he could put on or take off at will. Others in law school found in the world of torts and contracts, the play of forces under the surface of the Constitution and common law, a secular faith to inspire their lives, but Mac had been vaccinated against it. He could not accept the lawyers' world as his own. Always inside himself he heard the voice of the other Mac, who had been born in his last spring at Harvard, a Mac who saw the world no more clearly, but differently, and who saw the law as a complex and elegant mask for brute theft and exploitation. Mac could not choose between the two; he chose neither.

In the evenings he and Foote sat before the television set with drinks and watched the news from Richmond. Mac felt sorry for poor, genial Tom Slaughter that fall: that savage primary fight had destroyed him, though he didn't know it. He had Tobey Carrington and Governor Miles Brock and Junior behind him and everyone else in the party except Tom Jeff Shadwell; Tom Jeff had gone back to Norfolk to wait for Slaughter's phone call, and Slaughter, whether out of fear or bitterness or pride, had never called. So Shadwell said nothing, took no part in the campaign, and the people who had voted for him remembered those flyers, SLAUGHTER: THE RESPONSIBLE CHOICE, and those "Truth Squads" lying their way across the state, and a lot of them decided they didn't much care if Tom Slaughter ever got to be governor. They voted for the Republican, the big, slow, handsome cattleman named Horace Hapgood, a man who had a few friends and no known enemies and whose chief political asset was that he looked as if he might want to do the right thing.

So Tom Slaughter found that he had won his primary and with it the honor of being the first man to lose the governorship to a Republican since Reconstruction, and like the Union troops, Tom Slaughter packed up and left Virginia.

Lester won, of course; it was inevitable. He won big, and everybody knew, the way they knew that the sun will rise in the east, that Mac's brother would be the next governor. Mac watched him on TV that January presiding over the State Senate. He looked good; he looked like a winner.

Mac himself gradually realized that he had given up on the world. That spring, when the United States invaded Cambodia and the students went wild, when even the University of Virginia was hit with picket lines and bullhorns, Mac went to the meetings and walked the line, but he felt no enthusiasm for it, wanted mostly to escape back into the cool bath of the law. He still felt that the war was wrong, the worst thing he had ever heard of or perhaps would ever hear of; but he was oppressed by a sense that the world which had produced the war was malignant and would never change, short of invasion by his imaginary army of freedom fighters, and he felt sure that if he tried to change it or get in its way, he would be twisted and broken like a man falling from a high place onto jagged rocks. So he hid in his country house through the summer, walking in the dawn and working in the library as a professor's research assistant.

That summer the TV news carried a hot story out of Richmond. A federal judge ordered the city and the two counties to consolidate their school districts, to bus black children from the city into the lily-white counties where the people had fled to escape from them. The white people were angry. In Henrico, where the laywers and doctors and insurance men lived, Republican territory, and Chesterfield, where farmers and carpenters and factory hands lived, Wallace country, there was shouting and marching and burning in effigy and here and there the fiery cross. As the summer ended, the big farm boy, Horace Hapgood, proved that he really did want to do the right thing. On the first day of school he took his fifteen-year-old daughter by the hand and walked her to a bus, and the cameras whirred and clicked, and then he said that this was the law, and he was as sorry as he could be if people didn't like it, but as governor he wasn't about to try to defy the law.

They screamed in Richmond, the white people, and all over the state where white people still cherished hopes of keeping the blacks down. In Richmond ten thousand people marched on the Capitol lawn and a hardshell preacher got up in front of the Capitol bell tower and called down God's wrath on the governor and allowed as how when he thought of how spineless the governor had been and how he had betrayed the people, well, this servant of the Lord thought maybe he could see his way clear at last to the idea of euthanasia. That made the network news, and Mac saw it with a gin and tonic in his hand, and it occurred to him that his brother Lester was being awfully quiet that fall.

It wasn't hard for the lieutenant governor to stay out of the news. Mac wondered what his brother was up to. Was he working quietly for the good? And what good would working quietly do, anyway? This was not Massive Resistance, which had been engineered by the men at the top and could be stopped by the legislature and the governor; this was revolt simmering among the ordinary people: the kind of anger and defiance that could end, if not stopped, with blood on the pavement. As fall turned to winter, as Mac studied his lawbooks and walked alone in the early mornings, Mac even considered writing or calling his brother to ask what he was doing, but he didn't, because he didn't want to open it up again and fight it out on the same issues they had fought about before.

So it was a surprise in the middle of March when Lester called. Actually, it was his secretary. "Mr. Mac Evans?" she said. "Hold for the lieutenant governor." Of course Lester would have his secretary place the call; it would be an item on his schedule, a part of his working day.

"Hello, bub," Lester's voice said after a minute.

"Hello, Lester," Mac said, and he found his voice was friendly. It felt good to be talking to Lester again.

There was a pause.

"You ought to see this office," Lester said. "Some fool in Halifax sent me a cuspidor engraved with the seal of the office."

"You taken up chewing?" Mac asked. He laughed to himself at the image of his brother, immaculate in his Brooks Brothers suit, cutting a plug as he wielded his gavel in the Senate.

"Naw," Lester said. "This fellow reckoned I ought to, if I wanted to be governor, though. But I believe I'm going to let it pass."

"How about Hapgood? Does he chew?"

"No, I'm happy to say. But just between you and me, I've seen him dip a little from time to time."

"Snuff?"

"Yup. Not on state occasions, though."

They both laughed at that. Then there was another pause.

"Mac," Lester said. "You busy next Saturday?"

"Why?"

"Want you to do me a favor."

"What's that?"

"Well," Lester said, with a hint of diffidence in his voice, "these fellows asked me to give the speech at the Shad Planking this year, and I want you to drive me down there if you got the time."

"The Shad Planking?" Mac said. "I don't know, Lester. Those folks might lynch me."

Mac had meant it as a joke, but Lester reacted defensively, with a touch of anger in his voice and something else that was almost pleading. "Jesus, Mac, come on," he said. "They won't revoke your liberal card if you go down there once. It won't hurt you." Then he regained his balance, and the anger and the pleading vanished. "Besides," he finished lightly, "it's something you ought to see once, like the dance of the herons or a public hanging."

So Mac agreed to drive Lester down to the Shad Planking, which was in the heart of the beast. It was almost a legend now in Virginia: a yearly gathering of white men in Southside—no blacks, no women allowed— where the shirt-sleeve politicians, the old Apple-Farmer confederates, gathered to look over the political leadership. Mac agreed to go because

262

he knew Lester must want him there for a reason, and he found that whatever happened between them, he could still not refuse his brother if Lester needed him.

The first thing he saw that day as he steered Lester's Riviera down the dirt road to the picnic ground was a line of white-shirted men standing in the pine woods pissing on trees. Then he parked the car in a row of Fleetwoods and Bel Airs and Country Squires with the tailgates let down to hold coolers of beer. Mac and Lester drank whiskey out of paper cups. They didn't talk much. Lester was in demand. Men came by, singly and in groups, to pay their respects and shake his hand, with the superstitious reverence politicians have more than others for the touch of a winner. Lester seemed at ease. He joked with the well-wishers, slurping Early Times out of the thick white cup, while Mac lounged uneasily against the warm hood of the car and watched the herons dance.

They were mostly middle-aged or beyond, with a sprinkling of younger men, sleek in spring double knits and fresh razor cuts. The young ones smiled; they wore the open, friendly looks of Jaycee vice-presidents, looks of enthusiastic, disinterested civic-mindedness. The older men wore the Apple-Farmer's brand, stingy, humorous faces, faces of men to whom partisanship, the struggle to keep one side in and the other out, had passed beyond a way of life and become a metaphysical principle, a unifying metaphor at the beating heart of the universe. They were a sea of white male faces, an implacable army of sameness, and Mac felt trapped and threatened as he walked their turf, heard their flinty tuneful laughter, shook their aged, horny hands.

He did not envy his brother when the time came to speak. Lester had to get up on the platform and face those four thousand unforgiving eyes. Seated on folding chairs behind him were what remained of the Apple-Farmer's general staff: Miles Brock, and Junior, and R.E. Lee Tevyepaugh, the same man who, as head of the Compensation Board, had been the subject of their father's attacks, and Bunny Triplett, the old speaker who had kept the legislature in line, his eyes filmed with cataract, but his mouth as rigid as ever.

Though the crowd had banged their hands together in applause when he was introduced, though they barked genially at his opening jokes, though they seemed at first to have forgotten, though Lester had spent ten years and more trying to make them forget, still by the time his speech had ended they knew they had heard a speech by the son of Colonel Joshua Tutelo Evans.

Because Lester did something he had never done before. He challenged them; he dared them; he took it up and threw it in their faces, with the cameras there to take it all down. He told them in essence: *You nearly did it before, when you tried to close the schools, you hurt this state and you hurt its people, and it's only now we've begun to get over that, and you won't do it again with this busing business, and the reason you won't is that we won't let you.*

That was what he said, underneath politeness and eloquence for the cameras and the reporters: "Virginia has suffered too long and too cruelly from its battles for lost causes and causes which should never have been won. For a generation our state has been divided by race and class because our leaders have insisted on fighting battles against the tide of history, a tide which knows no turning. To those today who would bid us make yet another stand which will not, cannot, and should not succeed, I am proud to join with Governor Hapgood and say, it will not be. We will obey the law, we will enforce the law, we will uphold the law, not because we like or dislike any particular law, or because we feel that we can profit or lose from any law, but because we are sworn on our oaths before heaven to uphold the law and because if we do not do so with a good will, we will have betrayed Virginia and the principles which keep her alive." Underneath the formal words the message was direct and intimate.

They got the message. Mac could tell from the twitching of the grim letter-slot mouths that they understood what the Colonel's son had said to them. Mac understood, too, and he understood how much it must have cost Lester to violate his nature this way, and he admired it, but he didn't understand why Lester had done it.

They rode silently in the Riviera back to Richmond. Lester hunched in the shotgun seat, chain-smoking. He seemed lost in thought, but at the top of the hour he switched on the radio in precise time to catch the local news. He was the lead item. When the broadcaster finished, he made a wordless sound, a grunt of emotionless satisfaction, and then turned back to the window.

"What do you think will happen now?" Mac asked.

Lester eyed him warily. "What, on account of this?"

"Yeah."

Lester considered. "That old crowd right now, they're stymied. They can't yell and scream too much, those guys down there today, they've got too much to lose. Some of these other guys, the Kluxer types and that euthanasia guy, they'll get on me some, but they don't cut one way or another."

"You could be right," Mac said. "God knows the Republicans can't hit you with it, Hapgood is their boy, after all. But somebody might get mad enough, and stay mad enough, to run against you in the primary."

Lester grunted again and turned to the window.

Mac felt as if he had driven the car into a brick wall. It had felt good to be talking politics with Lester again, and he knew it had felt good for Lester, too, because, after all, he had never been able to talk frankly with anybody but Mac and Deeb and maybe Molly O. Mac knew that Lester had brought him along to the Shad Planking that day because he wanted Mac to see him stand up and spit in their eyes like the Colonel's son. Mac admired him for it. But now Lester had shut him off. Lester was watching the road in hot silence, and Mac knew he was not invited to talk.

After a time Lester said, "You going to stay the night in Richmond?"

"I thought I would."

"Molly O. will be glad. She's been missing you some."

Which meant: *Me, too. We both have.*

"Yeah," Mac said. "Me, too."

They talked about law school all the way home.

The three of them ate dinner around the TV set, watching Lester on the evening news, with Lester's own running commentary on the treatment of the news and the use of the camera. It was good to be at home with them again, but as he sat with them sipping brandy after the news (Lester leaping up every few minutes to answer the phone, to say thank you to the ones who'd called to congratulate him and to curse right back at the ones who'd called to curse him), Mac had again that sense he'd felt on the ride home, of some imposed restraint, something they weren't telling him. Still, it was a good night, and when he went back to Charlottesville to study for his exams, the world seemed like a better place than when he had left.

That feeling lasted all through his exams, lasted until he got a letter from Molly O. (which meant Lester had given his consent for Mac to know) explaining what nobody knew yet: Lester was going to die.

It was one of those moments when the whole world seems to vibrate silently from the force of a great blow. Revolt of the cells. Anarchy in that perfect order and precise jeweled movement which was the brain of Lester Tutelo Evans. A quick coup, in silence, which Lester himself had discovered only a few months before, when he found his eyes blurring and went to the doctor for a pair of reading glasses. That was why he had needed a driver to the Shad Planking; the blurring in his eyes couldn't be cured by glasses.

It wasn't even cancer; it was just a great big benign tumor growing in his brain, in a place where they couldn't carve it out without leaving him more dead than alive. They were going to shoot it full of X rays, mostly for lack of anything better to do. But if that didn't work, as seemed in

265

truth likely, then it would keep benignly growing until it had made Lester blind and then killed him. And it was growing fast. Unless the X rays worked, and nobody really seemed to believe they would, Lester had only a few months to live.

In June, Lester went to New York for another round of radiation treatments. Mac went with them; he and Molly O. got hotel rooms, while Lester stayed at the clinic, a big echoing building with a lobby like a railroad depot. On the upstairs floors the nurses and doctors walked on crepe soles, wheeling patients through long halls barred with sooty light from old big windows. Even Lester's private room smelled of disinfectant soap and cigars. But it was a good clinic: the money that might have gone on new lighting and carpeting had been spent instead on the best staff available and the latest equipment, like the huge radiation machine Lester was going under.

Lester lay in bed in blue pajamas and smoked cigarettes. To Mac he didn't appear different; he was tanned and muscular and he still looked like a winner. But it turned out he wasn't going to be leaving the clinic after the treatments; the treatments had, to no one's great surprise, had no effect at all.

So Mac and Molly O. stayed on in their hotel rooms. In the mornings Molly O. went and read to Lester, whose eyes didn't work very well anymore. Mac slept late in his hotel room, and when he woke, he wrote letters to Stephanian or played solitaire in his pajamas at the narrow hotel desk. After lunch he went to visit Lester. He was there to spell Molly O., who would slip out and take a nap, but he was also there to talk to Lester about the things Lester didn't talk to Molly O. about.

Lester knew he was dying, and there was no concealment: in his matter-of-fact lawyer's way he read Mac his will. Judge Anderson was the executor. Molly O. got the house, but it would go to Mac or his children when she died, and she got Lester's share of the family money. The physical and financial business of leaving this life was simple, and Lester gave detailed instructions for his burial. Mac could tell he had researched it and knew how to put a body in the ground for as little as possible; the instructions were written to leave no space for an undertaker to pad the cost—this though Lester even chose his undertaker as a matter of patronage; he was the vice-mayor of Richmond and a longtime supporter.

But that took only a couple of days. During the rest of the afternoons, when Lester sat on the hospital bed and smoked cigarettes and his tumor grew and outside the hospital the world prepared to do without him, he talked about the same things that had occupied his life. Mac had wondered if Lester might not begin letting go of that tight tangled world of causality in which he had spent his life, begin seeking another world. But he did not.

If anything, in those last weeks as his vision gradually failed him, he seemed to see more clearly the Byzantine political world of alliance and betrayal in Virginia, three hundred miles to the south. Mac was there to listen and ask questions. It was the last service he could perform for his brother, and he did it willingly. After a few days he would have been unable to stop if he'd wanted to, because Lester was dazzling. He knew what would happen long before anyone else did.

"Nobody figured on this thing," he said. His voice was dispassionate, the voice of a master political technician who could step backward and look calmly at everything, including his own death, as a political phenomenon. "That was the one constant thing, that I'd be governor next time, and everybody had made their plans around it, Republicans, Democrats, everybody: they were planning for afterwards, not even thinking about this time. Now that's got to change, and I'll tell you, neither party is in any too good a shape. The Democrats are going to find they don't have any choice at all. They're stuck with your friend Shadwell, and they are just going to have to like it or lump it. Lots of them will lump it, too, and he won't have a Chinaman's chance unless he's got the sense to start pretty soon and get his own people in charge of the party. He does that, he'll have a shot, but it'll take some doing.

"I mean get some guy in as chairman—that maniac Cheatham, probably—and people on the National Committee and the State Central Committee. He's got to do that, and it'll take some doing. He's got to understand that the officeholders—the congressmen and the General Assembly guys and so on—haven't got any use for him and probably never will. He just can't trust 'em. Even if he gets control of the party, those guys will still be out to knife him if they get half a chance. The only way he can keep them in line is to convince everybody that he's going to win. They know they can't keep him from getting the nomination, and as long as he's a winner, they'll shut up. But if he starts showing weakness, the Brock people will go after these guys, and they'll bolt. They haven't got any party loyalty to speak of; they'll screw him if they think they can get away with it.

"Now the Republicans, my God, they're even more screwed. They haven't got anybody at all, there are a few people in the bull pen, but they're too young. So here's what's going to happen. A bunch of old farts who play poker every day down at the Confederate Club, and you know their names, are going to commence having nightmares about Tom Jeff Shadwell. Those guys think he's Lenin or somebody like that. And they'll start crying out piteously for someone to save them, which it will seem like there isn't anyone. So by and by a delegation will go down to see old Miles Brock, and they'll say, 'Miles, you must do this for Virginia, just as General Lee drew his sword to defend his state,' and he'll start to believe them. So these old guys will go out and start spreading money around, and they'll what amounts to buy the Republican Party for Miles Brock, they'll get him the nomination on a silver platter, and if poor old Hapgood doesn't like it, tough.

"That's when the fun will begin. It's going to be the election of the century, and I'd like to see it. Old Shadwell is tough and mean and about half crazy—I know you don't agree, Mac, but hell, you're about half crazy yourself. But he's good on top of it. He can run a damn campaign. And Brock doesn't realize it. He's going to think all he needs to do is walk around some and show himself and Shadwell will roll over and die. And unless he gets somebody who can pump him full of Geritol and tell him what to do, he'll lose. He can win it, but he's going to find there's only one way, and that's to get out and yell Bus and Nigger and Mongrel and all the rest of it just as loud as he can. And it'll be just as mean and nasty as anything you ever saw."

Then Lester was off on a catalogue of the state, by city and town and county and district, juggling names and places and dozens of different relationships until Mac's head was spinning. Lester could remember who was who and who hated who and who liked who and why and who had what on who and who knew he did and whether it mattered and who worked hard and who didn't and who told the truth and who didn't; and Lester saw what might happen so clearly that afterward Mac sometimes thought that what really did happen, and his own role in it, might simply be part of a long dying dream in his brother's imagination.

They never said good-bye. Once when Lester had been silent for a while, Mac haltingly told him that he would always regret not having worked on the campaign for lieutenant governor.

"Forget it," Lester said. "You learned a hell of a lot more from being with Shadwell that year." He drew on his cigarette in silence. "Truth to tell, I was just as glad to have you over there with him, because I figured you'd be worth more to me when I ran for governor. I knew we'd patch it up before then. And you know that would have really been something, Mac, running for governor. You and me, we could have done it, no sweat. And when we won, we'd have brought the Colonel back and there we'd be on the reviewing stand inauguration day, you and me and Molly O. and him, and if anybody didn't like it, they could just stick it up their ass."

At the end of the summer there were hushed visits from Horace Hapgood and Tobey Carrington and a few others. Mac saw now why Lester had chosen to stay in New York. There were plenty of people in politics who would have wanted to be seen on television walking tearfully from Lester Evans' bedside, reporting on his condition while the cameras rolled. Up here there weren't any cameras, so a lot of them didn't come. Those who still wanted to come had to get through Molly O., and if Lester didn't want to see a man, that man found Molly O. a brick wall. There weren't many people Lester wanted to say good-bye to.

The last visitor was his mother. She paced down the hall, her light ceaseless voice as incongruous in the hospital corridor as a flock of party balloons. Molly O. walked beside her, her face carefully expressionless, as her mother-in-law commiserated at length. Mrs. Nordzecky had become a visitor of the sick, and she knew her way around the world of tumors and the pharmacopeia of pain; she talked to Molly O. as one specialist to another. Then she went inside to see Lester.

When she came out, Mac was in the lounge at the end of the hall. He faced his mother as she walked to the elevator. He had nothing to ask her; he could not ask after Emil or after her fight to keep fluoride out of drinking water, because he knew that she would answer him, and he did not want to know. He studied her quietly: her once dark-blond hair was now a careful mixture of brown and gray, set tightly about her head like a helmet. She bore about her the air of inexhaustible viability, as if she might live forever; it was not vitality she gave off but simple mobility.

"How are you, Mac?" she said.

He shrugged.

She looked back at Lester's room with a practiced glance of sorrow. "Such a waste," she said. "Such a waste."

The innocuous words annoyed him somehow. "What do you mean by that?" he asked, thinking of a moment in March when Lester had stood on the platform in Wakefield. "That's silly. It's not a waste. It's not."

She looked at him with unreadable pity in her eyes.

"It's not," he said again. "He did more than either of us is ever likely to do."

The elevator came. "Write to me, Mac," she said, and was gone.

Then Lester was blind and in pain. He seemed to shrink in his bed, and his flesh was pale and milky. He didn't say much anymore because the doctors gave him drugs for the pain. They had other drugs, too, and equipment which could keep him going longer, slow down the dying, but Lester said not, he believed he'd go on and get it over with.

So on a steamy hot late August day, Lester Tutelo Evans, youngest lieutenant governor of Virginia in this century, died in the big private

269

room while his wife and brother sat by, though he couldn't see them or speak to them or hear them speak to him. His wife and brother buried him in Richmond, in the Evans family plot in Hollywood Cemetery, after a big funeral at St. Anselm's Episcopal Church and a eulogy by U.S. Senator Tobey Carrington and a long procession to the cemetery, long, gleaming limousines and powerful cars with lights blazing and air conditioners roaring, and a blizzard of newspaper editorials and a lot of tears.

Mac didn't shed any of those tears, and neither, as far as he could tell, did Molly O. She buried her husband with her head up and her chin square, made the arrangements, answered the phone calls, thanked the people who came without letting down for a minute. She had done her grieving before Lester died; she had had time to look it in the eye and take its measure. Mac watched her with awe and love and envy.

For himself, the weeks after the funeral were like living in a dark crooked box. Lester had brought him up and taught him about life. Mac had loved and hated and feared and adored him, and never in the years since his ninth birthday had he once pictured life without his brother. Molly O. had lost her husband. She had loved him and known him as well as he could be known, which, because she was sensitive and persistent and determined, was pretty well indeed. But Lester had been Mac's brother and foster father and teacher and oppressor all in one; he had made Mac a present of his identity, first by giving him someone to emulate and then later someone to rebel against, and now it seemed to Mac that for all that, he might never really have known Lester at all.

And most frightening of all was that as soon as he was buried, the Lester Evans who lived inside Mac's head, the internal Lester he had argued with and explained himself to a dozen times a day, began dying too; day by day, like a statue crumbling, it had broken up, until there were left only fragments, some dozens of jagged images, lifeless pictures with nothing to hold them together, until Mac saw that soon he would carry with him only a few distorted, contradictory, jumbled memories to remind him of his brother. He learned then that death is final, that it is truly an end: that even the immortality we may aspire to in the memory of those we love is an illusion, for if the living remember at all, they remember a person who never was.

After a while Mac came out of the box and into the Indian summer sunlight browning the leaves along Axe Trail Road. It was time to go back to law school, and Mac went. He lived in the little house where Foote was dividing his time between drugs and a thesis on James Branch Cabell, and he went to a few law classes, but he found less and less reason to go, less and less reason to get up in the morning. He began skipping classes, then stopped going to classes altogether, stopped going anywhere. He lay on his bed reading science fiction ("Were they truly intelligent? By themselves, that is? I don't know. . ."); he considered the majesty of the seasons as the leaves fell from the trees, and one day inside himself a leaf fell from a tree and twisted lazily through the air and vanished, and that was his career as a lawyer. The next day he called Knocko Cheatham and asked if it were true that Knocko and Tom Jeff were getting ready to make their push to take over the party, and Knocko said yes, it was true. Mac said he was ready to help, and Knocko asked if he could come to a meeting the next day, and Mac said yes.

Mac said good-bye to Justin Foote and drove his battered old car to Richmond; that afternoon he went to a meeting at the George Mason Hotel with Tom Jeff and Knocko and the same squat hairless man from the AFL-CIO and Theodore Thomas, who was there to help organize the black vote.

After the meeting Mac knew what he was going to be doing for the next six months or so. He went to Thalhimer's and bought three suits; then traded in the old car on a big smooth shiny blue Lincoln Continental. For the next six months he lived in the car, suits hanging in cleaner's bags on the hook behind the front seat, roaring from one end of the state to the other and back again, rallying Tom Jeff's troops to precinct meetings and county conventions and citywide mass meetings and district conventions, until the state convention in June. Tom Jeff didn't need to pass any miracles that year; this time the fix was in, and it was his fix, and everything went according to plan. Blood flowed, but it was the other side bleeding, Tobey Carrington's people and the old Shad Planking crowd, and Knocko wielded the knife. Knocko was made state chairman, and Shadwell people went to the National Committee, and even Mac, who'd never been chosen hall monitor, was elected by acclamation secretary of the party. After that convention Tom Jeff had the party, and the nomination, too, the next year.

First, though, the party took its lumps in the presidential election. Democrats lost big that year, so big that Tobey Carrington got beaten, too, which even Lester would never have expected. So when the year began, it was Tom Jeff, unchallenged, in command of the party. And on the other side was Miles Brock. That had turned out just as Lester predicted.

Mac that year was a man possessed. He woke and slept, ate and drank, with one purpose in mind. He told himself he wanted to win. But it was more than that.

He had become a man of one dimension, flat and sharp as a face on a playing card. Around him moved the material world, death and rebirth, murder, mystery, and love; he was oblivious to it. Available to him were the pleasure of sense, the endless recurrent configurations of the body, pleasure and pain; he did not seek them. Always waiting were treasures of the imagination, the ever-new flowerings of the mind, music, art, literature; to them he was deaf and blind. All about him a suffering world sought relief; in the nations of the world men and women cried out in the pain of injustice, torture, murder, robbery, war, the agony of drought, famine, hunger; he stopped his ears. He was a closed system, and deep in the river of his soul was a need turning like a prayer in a waterwheel, silent, ceaseless, imperceptible, powerful, a voice inside himself which even he could no longer hear, whispering day and night one word: Revenge. Revenge. Revenge. Revenge. Revenge.

Part Three

★

ONE

★

Tom Jeff Shadwell charged into the conference room of his campaign headquarters, head lowered, shaking with rage. In his hand was a copy of the morning newspaper, with which he seemed ready to attack anyone who got in his way. He stopped and looked quickly around the room, fixing each member of his staff sitting at the big table with his angry gaze.

Mac felt for a second like a junior high school student cowering before the principal; he noticed the others shifting in their seats, as if they felt the same way. But at the end of the long table Knocko slouched, insolently unabashed, and said, "We all saw it, Tom Jeff. Why don't you have a seat and we'll see what we can do about it?"

Shadwell flashed his spectacles at Knocko and then threw the paper on the table. Without speaking he sat in the seat at the head, holding his stubby body stiffly erect, palms flat on the dark mahogany finish. He paused for a moment, as if gathering his breath, like a messenger who has run miles to deliver bad news. Then he said, "You all seen it?"

Heads nodded around the table. It had been hard to miss the report of Miles Brock's Labor Day speech: the Richmond editors had given it loving attention in their layout: BROCK SAYS SHADWELL PROGRAM HAS "SOCIALIST" TINGE. Mac had read it and lost his appetite for breakfast. Now he was trying to make up for the missed meal with a sugar doughnut and coffee in a styrofoam cup.

His fingers were gritty with confectioners' sugar. He rubbed them with a napkin and watched the candidate, who was moving his head back and forth, scanning the faces of his campaign staff as if he suspected one of them of writing the story. Then after a minute he reached up with one hand and adjusted his glasses, and in the motion he seemed to relax a little.

"Lady and gentlemen," he said. "I have been fighting this crowd for twenty years, and more and more I got to admit they still have the power to surprise me."

Knocko gave a skeptical grunt. "Don't see what you find so surprising about all this socialist mess, Tom Jeff," he said, turning sideways in his chair and gesturing impatiently at the ceiling. "You knew they were going to play dirty, they always do. What's the point of getting all het up about it?"

Shadwell opened the newspaper in front of his face as if studying it intently. "On close examination I can see you are absolutely right, Cousin Knocko," he said. "There's nothing in this little sermon by Brother Brock that should bother you at all. Why I don't believe he even mentions your name once. He says some harsh words about me. So I'm a little hot under the collar. But don't bother yourself, cousin, you just relax and take it easy—"

"Can it, Tom Jeff," Knocko said.

Mac caught his breath as Shadwell's glasses flashed at Knocko. For a moment they glared at each other while the assembled staff, not daring to move their heads, flashed their eyes from one to the other like paralytics at a tennis match.

Then Shadwell laughed, and he gave his crooked smile. He shook his head in wonder at the everlasting daring of his campaign manager.

Knocko took advantage of the pause. "Now, you want to bellyache about what Brock said about you, we'll do it that way, fine. We're all on the payroll here, we'll listen. But if you'd rather, we'd be just as glad to try and figure some way of coming back on Brock. That's what you've assembled all these brains for."

Shadwell adjusted his glasses once more. His anger seemed somehow to have vanished into the air. He beamed at the group with the cheery air of a schoolboy who knows his lesson. "I think maybe you're right for once, Cousin Knocko," he said. "Seems like if we've got all these good people together, I ought to listen to them instead of making them listen to me. You all are going to be hearing enough of me from now on, I'm going to be on the TV and the radio and helicopters and billboards and everything else. So let's go on. Cousin, you're the campaign manager, why don't you read the invocation?"

276

Mac took another bite of sugar doughnut; white flakes fell across his shirt. Not for the first time he wondered about the relationship between the candidate and his campaign manager. Both were proud men, their hides toughened by years of political warfare; there was between them a roughhouse intimacy neither permitted anyone else, based on knowledge, respect, and, he sometimes thought, a smidgen of mistrust. Knocko seemed to serve as a lightning rod for Tom Jeff's anger, provoking it toward himself because he knew it would run through him harmlessly to the ground.

Besides Mac, Knocko, and Shadwell, the council of war numbered six: Ralph Bova, a hulking Southside real estate developer who had taken a year off from his business to handle fund raising for the campaign; Danny Watkins, a wiry ex-newspaperman from the Northern Neck whose bushy brown hair and freckled face, coupled with yellowed, twisted teeth, gave him the look of an aging, corrupt Huckleberry Finn; Rose Fishbein, a tiny shrewd Fairfax travel agent with blue-rinsed hair and penetrating eyes, who supervised the candidate's schedule and kept the headquarters running; Ed O'Brien, the fireplug-shaped COPE worker who had served as labor's liaison with Shadwell in his first campaign; Tony Soleri, an immaculately dressed, dramatically handsome Norfolk lawyer who operated the Shadwell field organization, supervising local committees in each district, county, and town; and J. B. Fitzhugh, the minority coordinator, a tidy young black man wearing exuberant gold aviator glasses and a painfully narrow rep tie.

Knocko took out a monogrammed handkerchief and hawked phlegm discreetly into it. "All right now," he said. "I'm not about to get upset about all this socialist who-shot-John from Brock. You want to know the truth, it's actually a pretty good sign, because it shows they're getting desperate and don't know what to do about it. You call a man a communist, that's pretty much of a last resort, and here it's only Labor Day. They know they're in trouble, and we know they're in trouble, if you've all read the poll results. Rose, did those get Xeroxed and handed around?"

She nodded crisply, saying, "There's a copy at each seat, and each one is marked with the seat number. Please sign your name under the seat number, and give your copy back to me before you leave. None of these copies can leave the room."

"Now, have you all seen it?" Knocko said.

Heads nodded around the table. Mac saw Danny Watkins, the press secretary, hastily reading through his stapled copy.

"This is really something," he said, his voice cheerful. "According to this thing, we're beating the tar out of him!"

277

"Thank you for that summary, Danny," Knocko said frostily. "I think the rest of you can understand now why we didn't bring the fellow who made this poll, Hudson or Dodson—"

"Knudsen," Tom Jeff said.

"Right, Knudsen, down from Washington to explain it to us. The thing speaks for itself. It's so clear even Danny here can read it." He fixed the press secretary with a baleful glare. Watkins laid the paper down hastily, his face flushing. "Okay," Knocko went on. "According to this, and I have no reason to doubt it, this guy Knudsen is good and he cost us plenty, we have Brock by a little under eight percentage points, which is pretty good for Labor Day. Now they don't have this poll, but they know they have problems, and that's where all this socialist nonsense is coming from. It's a desperation thing. So far we've made 'em dance to our tune, and what we've got to do now is stay on the offensive, not let them get their balance and not give them a chance to come back on us."

Watkins had picked up the stapled sheets again; his eyes caressed it like a miser's hands sifting through the gold. "This stuff is dynamite!" he said. "It'll get us page one all over the state, and the *Post*, too, probably. When can we release it?"

"We can't," Knocko said. "Let me make this clear: nobody releases this poll, nobody even mentions this poll. As far as we're concerned, this poll doesn't exist. I want that understood."

"Now hold on a minute, Knocko," Ralph Bova said. "That doesn't make a whole lot of sense to me." Fifteen years after he had left the University, the big realtor preserved the look of a football player. His face and frame were padded with a layer of flesh shading imperceptibly at the waist and hips into fat. His hair had rolled neatly back to the crown of his broad skull. When he talked, his wide, flat mouth and goggle eyes gave him the look of a giant sea bass striking at a hook.

"What do you mean?" Knocko asked sharply. The two men had never liked each other. Tom Jeff had brought Bova into the campaign because he could open doors to the affluent upper-middle class, the reasonable, cautious businessmen who had supported Tobey Carrington and Lester Evans, but these were the people Knocko most distrusted and disliked.

"In my opinion," Bova said, "and you know this, Governor, because I have expressed it to you in memo form, we have a few image weaknesses in this campaign. One of these weaknesses is that a lot of people like Tom Jeff Shadwell, and they think he's a good man, but they're not sure that he can be elected governor of Virginia. I wish Mr. Knudsen were here today because I think he'd bear me out in this. In order to get those people, we need a winner-type image, and I think it's worth discussing whether we

278

ought to give this poll to the press for that reason. What's your feeling on that, Governor?"

"Never mind me," Tom Jeff said quickly. "I'm not here to give my opinion right now. You all are the staff, I want to hear what you have to say. Then I'll make up my mind, do a little prayer and fasting. You all go on, pretend I'm not here."

Tony Soleri laughed. "If you weren't here, we could talk dirty," he said, flashing a grin like a klieg light in his suntanned face.

Tom Jeff was not amused. He shot Soleri a guarded glance, mouth drawn into a disapproving line. "Not as long as Miss Rose is here," he said. "You let your tongue wag around Miss Rose, she'll staple it to your epiglottis for you."

Facing Shadwell's glare and Rose Fishbein's stern regard, Soleri was abashed. "Sorry," he mumbled. "Just kidding."

"I'm not interested in all this persiflage," Knocko broke in. "We got a campaign to run. But I think releasing the poll is the worst idea since Nixon agreed to debate Kennedy. It's just asking for trouble."

"I agree one hundred percent," Ed O'Brien, the union man, said. "It is a mistake to tip our hand and let the other fellow see our strength. Let him wear himself out guessing." Mac looked at his impassive face, pale-blue, incurious eyes, and wondered how it would feel to face him across a bargaining table.

Bova rose to the bait. "No, from your point of view that's probably true, because you two are preaching to the converted," he said, placing a broad forefinger delicately on the polished tabletop for emphasis. "But I'm telling you there's a big constituency out there that really is not sure what it thinks about Tom Jeff Shadwell, and I mean no offense to you, Senator. That's another reason why I'm sorry Mr. Knudsen wasn't invited here today because in my opinion this poll shows it." He waved his copy of the poll at Knocko. "Look here! We're eight points ahead, sure—forty-two to thirty-four. That's twenty-four percent undecided, and it doesn't take George Gallup to figure out that that's a soft lead. Tom Jeff Shadwell and Miles Brock are the two best-known political figures in this state, with the possible exception of Junior, and if he's better known, it's only because a lot of people still think he's his father. You and Brock are tied in name recognition at eighty-five percent, which is about as high as you're ever going to get for anybody. That means at least half of that undecided vote really is undecided. People who just can't make up their minds. In my opinion, a lot of those people would like to vote for Tom Jeff, but they don't think he can win; they've been brainwashed by the newspapers to believe he is somehow not a serious candidate, again

279

meaning no offense, Senator. But if we release this poll, I think we've got a shot at a lot of these people."

Knocko snorted in disgust. "Right, and also if we release this poll, we'll be setting ourselves up for about six different types of grief. We release the poll, we're going to panic the Brock people, and a lot of fat cats are going to start crawling out of the woodwork to give him money and so forth. On top of that, pretty soon Brock will have a poll showing him only five points behind, and he'll release that, and then the whole thing'll be turned upside down: you know, 'Shadwell Lead Only Five PerCent,' 'Tom Jeff Slipping,' and so on. But if we keep our mouths shut, the press will begin to pick up that we're in the lead, which will win over those people who are worried that we can't win, and we don't have to give away a thing."

"You can say what you like, Knocko," Bova said. "But we have to do something about this image problem I'm talking about or we'll never get more than we have right now. This forty-two percent we got now is Tom Jeff's base; they're the ones we start with. The rest we got to convert and those people need—"

"What people you talking about, Ralph?" Knocko asked in a deceptively casual tone. He had twisted his body around in the chair, long legs stuck out to the side, and his eyes were focused dreamily on the ceiling. The fingers of his left hand drummed lightly on the table. He looked relaxed, but Mac could read the signs: he was ready to strike.

"The Carrington vote for one—" Bova began. Knocko jerked the hook, swiveling in his chair, open hand smacking loudly on the tabletop, his barber-pink face now crimson with contempt, crying scornfully, "The Carrington vote! The Carrington vote! There is no Carrington vote! That's the biggest political myth since the Alf Landon landslide! That guy had the shallowest base in the history of the electoral process, but you Slaughter people are always babbling about the Carrington vote as if it really existed. What you mean is the people you play bridge with; that's why you want to release this poll, so they'll leave off teasing you, that's the only image problem in this campaign!"

Tiny shock waves of rage seemed to dance in the air around Bova's head. Knocko's barb had hit home: *you Slaughter people.* Bova had supported Tom Slaughter four years before, and now, like a repentant heretic, he felt himself constantly accused by the eyes of the faithful. "I don't have to take that kind of talk from you, Cheatham," he bellowed. His voice, throaty and resonant, filled the conference room, making it a tetrahedron of solid sound.

His mouth was opening again when Tom Jeff said quietly, "Y'all can both cut this stuff out right now or take a hike."

The effect was immediate. The two men, braced as if to lunge at each other over the table, stopped like puppets whose strings have been cut. Shadwell added, "You all just sit back now. We've heard all we're going to hear from you two."

Knocko slouched back insolently in his chair, and Bova eased himself back like a man with a painful sunburn. Tom Jeff was watching them intently, like a badger peering from its hole at two mice it might or might not attack.

"I'm not going to put up with any more hoorah like this on my campaign," Tom Jeff said. "I want everybody at this table to write that in his hatband. This kind of stuff is bad for everybody but Miles Brock. This poll business is up to me now, and I've had all the advice I care about getting on it for a while. We're just going to go on to something else. Tony, you wanted to talk about this gun business in the Ninth, didn't you?"

"That's right, Senator."

"You going to keep it clean?" Tom Jeff asked, and Soleri paled a little beneath his tan before he realized he was being teased. There were a few laughs around the table, and the tension began to ease.

Soleri was worried about gun control. The Brock forces in the Ninth District were going to hit hard on the issue, and if they could convince the voters there that Tom Jeff was antigun, he was in for trouble in that district, where some families ate most of the winter on what they could shoot. In the Ninth District, the saying went, no man kicks another man's dog or gun without paying the price.

Soleri, O'Brien, and Knocko began a rambling discussion of ways to forestall Brock's offensive. Ralph Bova kept his own counsel. Mac's mind wandered back to the quarrel between Knocko and Ralph. The entire staff seemed to be infected with a strange anxiety, like travelers in a strange wood who sense that the path they are following may soon peter out. The results of the poll, which should have comforted them, seemed rather to make things worse. Tom Jeff Shadwell was an underdog: all this career he had been fighting the odds, coming from behind, trying to overcome the lack of money, lack of recognition, lack of support, lack of organization. This year it was different: suddenly the candidate was well known, well organized, not rich (a candidate like Tom Jeff would never be truly rich), but at least comfortably financed, with the Democratic Party, or what was left of it after Lester's death and Carrington's downfall and Brock's desertion, if not united behind him, at least not yet openly in re-

281

volt. Now the polls—and something else as well, that indefinable politicians' instinct—all agreed that Shadwell was the front-runner, and it seemed to Mac that the candidate and those who had been with him in his lonely struggles now felt confused and even a little ashamed. These men did not despise victory: they wanted to win the election, wanted it with a hope deferred which had made their hearts sick. But to be in the lead seemed somehow dangerous and dishonorable; it smacked of bullying.

Mac heard his name called. Tom Jeff had asked him a question, but he had lost all track of the discussion. Shadwell looked at him mercilessly, and Mac felt himself panicking. What did the candidate want? His mouth opened, but no sound emerged.

He felt Knocko thrust a small square of paper into his hand below the table. He grabbed it and read quickly, holding it out of sight: "TJ WANTS TV RE: GUNS—U DO?"

"Certainly, Senator," Mac said smoothly. On his right, Knocko seemed intensely interested in the monogram on his silk handkerchief. "I'll talk to Wink Moran at the agency this afternoon and get back to Rose about a shooting date. All right?"

"Sounds all right to me," Shadwell said. He looked at Mac doubtfully. "You all right, young Mac?" he asked. "I could have sworn you were asleep."

"I never sleep, Senator," Mac replied with a grin. He turned the note over in his fingers, out of sight, feeling extraordinarily pleased with himself.

Tom Jeff looked from Mac to Knocko and grunted. "Got a mind like his daddy's," he said absently.

As the meeting broke up, Mac fell in beside J. B. Fitzhugh, the minority coordinator. "Want some lunch?" he said, hoping to get a companion for lunch before Knocko could seize him: Cheatham would want to replay the meeting, point by point, with appropriate rancorous commentary.

Fitzhugh turned his bespectacled face to Mac. The huge gold frames gave him a constant air of surprise, as if he had just taken a great lungful of air. It seemed inappropriate when his voice emerged, not shouting in alarm, but in friendly, breathy tones. "Yeah, I'll get my coat," he said, then added quietly, "You know, if you and Knocko keeping passing notes in class, teacher might keep you after school."

Wink Moran, the advertising man, had an impressive mane of blond hair and a carefully trimmed blond beard. He was fond of bright striped or colored shirts and vigorous wide ties, which he wore with expensive, custom-tailored suits. Mac, however, remembered him from another incarnation: Moran had, about six years before, been editor of *Fandance,* Richmond's intermittent underground newspaper. But those palmy counterculture days were gone forever; now he was founder and leading light of Moran & MacDonald, an advertising agency. Like Moran's new wardrobe, M&M combined an eye for the big money with carefully hip exuberance. His office was in the front room of an old house on Grace Street, which the agency had renovated as its headquarters: white walls covered with enormous op art murals. A big contributor had recommended Moran to the Shadwell campaign; the man used the agency for his own business and seemed to think highly of it.

Moran did have a good line of patter. Mac sat beneath one of the op murals and explained his problem. The adman sat with his back to the window, and the afternoon light slanted in through the window behind him. It caught in his blond hair, and his head appeared to burn as he said, "This is a very challenging assignment. What you are asking me to do, in effect, is to fill a vacuum with television. But television itself creates a vacuum. It replaces the solid, comforting brown of the screen with a universe of doubt and surprise. The commercial is even more treacherous. It is in itself a surprise, a trick, perpetually appearing when we least expect it, interrupting our thoughts with information of a highly dubious and speculative nature. In order to fill a vacuum with television, what we must do is re-create the moment of trust, like the moment before birth, when the viewer, if you follow, looks at the set without *turning it on.*"

Mac's misgivings were borne out the next day when he received a script for approval:

VIDEO

                                    AUDIO

Screen is dark brown.

                                      Faint electronic music; no discernible theme.

Gradually an outline drawing appears: a Winchester rifle, drawn in white.

                                      Music stops.
                                      VOICE-OVER: "The gun.

Outline begins to rotate, until it is
pointing out toward the viewer.

> "A tool. Like fire. Or the
> wheel. . . ."

Mac knew Moran would not accept a rejection from him, but would go
over his head to his patron, thus causing delay and bad feeling. Accordingly, he scribbled a note: "Won't work. Candidate *must* appear in commercial," and signed it carefully, "Thos. J. Shadwell, esq."

Two days later a messenger brought a second draft:

VIDEO	*AUDIO*
Screen is dark brown.	
	Faint electronic music, no discernible theme.
Shadwell walks on from r., wearing dark gold suit, blue shirt, yellow tie. He is outlined against the background.	
	Music stops. SHADWELL: "Hi. I'm Tom Jeff Shadwell. I'm running for governor of Virginia. And I'd like to talk to you about a subject most people just whisper about . . . guns. That's right, guns. . . ."

Mac sent it back, appending another forgery: "This sounds like a de-
odorant commercial. I do *not* talk like this, TJS." Before Moran could try
again, Shadwell himself solved the problem. One night, as Mac lay in bed
in the little house, teasing himself before sleep by reading a science-
fiction novel ("The universe is not a riddle to be solved," the author
opined, "it is a mystery to be experienced"), Tom Jeff called him.

"Hello, hello, young Mac Evans?" Shadwell said, his voice leaping exuberantly along the telephone wire like a hare in a sunny meadow. "I
didn't get you out of bed, did I?"

"No, indeed, Senator," said Mac, yawning. "I never sleep, I told you
that."

"Good! Good! That's what I like to hear," Shadwell said. "I'm up here

284

in Winchester, you ought to see this motel, it's the lap of luxury, they got Magic Fingers massage and whirlpool showers and I don't know what all else."

"How are you doing up there?" Mac asked.

"We've got some awfully good people up here, they'll break your heart, they're working themselves sick, but this is enemy country, it's the old man's country and now it's Junior's, and we've just got to do the best we can. But I'll tell you, Miles Brock hasn't got any people up here like I do, these are wonderful people, they'll never quit—"

Mac cast his eyes desperately around the room for a bathrobe. It seemed somehow improper to be talking to the candidate in his underwear. At last he spotted a rumpled pair of trousers wedged behind the sofa. He struggled into them as Tom Jeff continued, "The reason I'm calling is this TV business. We could have a real problem with this gun nonsense if we spend too much time waiting around on this. Don't want to give old Brock a chance to get there first. We get there first, by the time he comes around with the soft voice of the serpent, won't be anybody listening. How you doing on it? You get things settled with that fellow with the fine haircut?"

Mac for some reason found himself buttoning a shirt over the trousers. "I've been having some problem with it, to tell you the truth," he said. "Wink wants to shoot it like some kind of aspirin commercial or something." He tucked the shirt into the trousers and sat down at the desk.

"We can't have that," Shadwell said. "I'm no pain reliever, I bring not peace but a sword. That fellow, I knew when I saw him, I said to myself, he's a fine-looking fellow, but we just don't speak the same language."

"I'll see what he's got for us tomorrow," Mac said.

"Naw, can't wait for that now," Shadwell interrupted. "I'm going to be in town Saturday, want to shoot it then. Tell him to get ready."

"The problem is, we don't have a script yet."

"Let that go. Tell you the truth, I got some ideas about that side of it myself. You know some place near Richmond we can borrow, some place with woods and trees and all that?"

"I can find one."

"Good. What we need is a little bit of woods, see, and they can just shoot me with one of those hunting hats and jackets, holding a shotgun, and I'll just talk a little about guns. I figure, we really want to get the idea across, that's the way to do it."

"It sure would, Senator," Mac said. The idea pleased him; if they could get it on TV fast, it would make Brock's charges, when they came, absurd; the ad would be visual proof most people would accept without

question. "It'll make a terrific TV spot, if you don't mind doing it."
"Why should I mind?" Shadwell said.

"I mean," Mac said lamely, instantly sorry he had spoken, "if you don't mind going on TV with a gun and all."

"Aw, now, what you mean is you think it's phony baloney, don't you?" Tom Jeff said. "Don't you worry about my integrity any. This gun business is nothing at all. It's one of these phony issues this crowd pulls out every four years to scare people with. There isn't one chance in a million that gun laws in this state will be changed because the people don't want 'em changed, and that's all right, that's the way it should be, because all power is vested in the people and magistrates are their servants and amenable to them. So we're just going to stick it to Miles Brock by stealing one of his lies before he can tell it, that's all. It doesn't bother me any, and it shouldn't bother you, young Mac."

"Okay," Mac said. "I'm with you all the way. I think it's a good idea."
I want to win this one, he thought.

Across the buzzing wire, Shadwell seemed disappointed that Mac wouldn't argue. "Okay," he said. "All right. Now you tell that fellow to get his camera and not to bother to write anything for me to say. I'll just say what comes to mind. Don't want to be reading any of that katzenjammer he writes."

"Right," Mac said. He made a note on a piece of paper. "What else?"

"Get a place to shoot and get me one of those checkered hunting jackets, I wear a size forty-four, I'm a big man. My daddy was, too. Chest like a barrel. And one of those funny-looking hats hunters wear, you know, with the flaps, look like North Korean generals."

"Right," Mac said.

"And get me a shotgun. I mean borrow one. We don't need a shotgun sitting around the headquarters."

"Right," Mac said.

"I'll look good in all this stuff. Maybe I'll take up hunting."

"You're already a hunter, Senator. You hunt two-legged quarry."

Shadwell laughed quietly. "That's fisher, young fellow, not hunter," he said. "Well, now that's settled, I got to go, get my beauty sleep. I don't get five hours of sleep a night, my complexion's going to get all splotchy and I'll lose that women's vote."

"Good night, Senator," Mac said.

"You sleep well now," Shadwell said. "You young folks need a lot of sleep. One other thing, though."

"What's that?"

"You going to be signing my name any more, you got to do a better job on the *J.* I write my *J* a little bigger, with a big old loop." Mac heard him laughing softly again, then the connection broke.

Mac hung up the phone. His digital clock clicked off a minute: 12:46. He slipped his feet into a pair of loafers and decided to go for a walk. He was only mildly surprised to find that the candidate's phone call had left him fully dressed and wide awake.

Moran protested bitterly at Shadwell's edict. "You are passing up a chance to make a uniquely deep penetration into the consciousness of the viewing public," he said. "A TV spot that would make advertising history."

"Sorry, Wink," Mac said. "Orders from on high." Then he called Hoke Spottswood, his old St. Cyprian's classmate, to ask if they could use his family's farm in Opechancanough County. The idea seemed to make Spottswood nervous; he was afraid his father, a rabid conservative entrepreneur, would find out.

"Where's your father now?" Mac said.

"Taiwan."

"And when will he be back?"

"Three weeks."

"And how many acres do you own?"

"Two hundred or so."

"Then, barring high-altitude overflights by Chinese Nationalist aircraft, how is your father going to know?"

"My father has ways."

"I thought you told me this land belongs to you."

"That's just a tax thing. If my father finds out, he'll go through the roof."

"Spottswood, you have no elan, no vital force," Mac said. The idea of the elder Spottswood's wrath, in fact, appealed to Mac, first, because it would be futile, since he could do nothing to Tom Jeff for coming on land at the invitation of its legal owner, and, second, because it would in any case fall on his hapless son. "Dare to be great, Spottswood!" Mac went on in an urgent whisper. "The angel of opportunity is knocking at your skylight! If we win this election, we won't forget our friends."

"I don't know."

He was wavering; Mac drove in for the kill. "Besides, it costs you nothing."

As he had suspected, the chance of getting anything, even something as nebulous as friendship, at no cost was irresistible to Spottswood. So, the following Saturday, the candidate and Wink Moran's film crew clanked in caravan down the dirt road on Spottswood's farm. Mac and Tom Jeff rode ahead in the Continental. Behind them Wink Moran brooded in a maroon Maserati, and behind that came an upright van with the camera crew and equipment, lumbering along like a child's pet elephant.

It was a bright, still Indian summer day. "Don't get too many close-ups of these trees here," Shadwell warned Moran. "If hunters see all these green leaves, they're going to know that Tom Jeff is hunting out of season."

"Don't worry, Tom Jeff," Moran said. "We'll shoot you next to this pine tree."

"I heard of being hung from a pine tree, but now they're going to shoot me at one," Shadwell grumbled, but he consented to being led to the spot Moran indicated. He took off his jacket. Mac offered him the new red checked jacket and square hunting hat, but Shadwell waved him away. "You just hold on to that stuff until they're ready to shoot," he said. "They see Tom Jeff with sweat pouring of his face, they'll suspect I'm up to some devilment. You better pull that off, too," he added, pointing to a tag on the jacket: GARMENT CARE INSTRUCTIONS. "And for the love of mercy make sure that shotgun is not loaded. I might murder us all."

Mac had checked the gun once before, but now he broke it across his forearm and checked each barrel again. It was a beautiful weapon, practically new, with dark bluish barrels and an intricately carved stock. It had been Lester's; he had bought it because he believed every Virginian should know how to hunt, had hunted enough to be able to trade hunting stories if need be, and then, thoroughly bored, had put the gun away forever. Mac had not told Tom Jeff whose weapon he would be using today.

The cameraman, a silent, round man who hummed incessantly, bustled up to Shadwell, light meter in hand. The sound technician was making adjustments on a console. She held a padded directional microphone under her left arm like a spear. Mac noticed that she was young and extraordinarily beautiful, with short brown-and-gold hair which even on this windless day managed somehow to look magnificently windblown. Her eyes were huge, a clear light blue, with a small mole beside the left one. Her body, twisted above the sound equipment, was slender and lithe.

Mac wanted to speak to her, and he watched for his chance. Moran had set up a folding canvas chair. Now he bent over to take something out of his attache case, and Mac saw the girl's right hand dart toward the adman, index and little fingers extended: devil's horns. He slipped over to her and whispered, "You mad at Wink?"

She showed no surprise but looked up at him and gave a sigh which might have set all the leaves in the forest dancing. "He's been a great disappointment to me," she said.

Tom Jeff was wiping his face with a handkerchief. The cameraman came up to him and began applying powder makeup. "Brother Moran, let's get this show on the road," he said between pats with the puff. "What you doing over there anyway?"

Moran was hunched over in his chair, throwing pennies on the ground. He held up an imperious hand, as if to silence Tom Jeff. "I Ching," he said.

"What's that?" Tom Jeff said, mouth open in irritated surprise. "You think you're itching, you ought to put some of this makeup on."

Wink looked at him blankly, like a man awakened from sleep. He held up a small, thick book with a gray cover. "*I Ching*," he repeated. "You know, *The Book of Changes.*"

Tom Jeff squinted at the book. "Changes?" he said. "Be some changes made if we don't get this thing cracking here," he grumbled, but Moran plunged on with his divination.

He opened the book and scanned the page rapidly. "It would be the duty of the official to keep in touch with the people," he read aloud.

"I don't need any Book of Changes to tell me that," Shadwell said.

Moran flipped to another page, scanned, then read again. "The superior man encourages the people at their work and exhorts them to help one another." He put the book down and stared blankly at the air, his mind obviously miles away.

"All right, now," Tom Jeff cried suddenly. "Let's go! No more social hour! I'm not about to sit here sweating while you seek nirvana. Wake up! Let's get shooting!"

Moran came alive. He tried to give Tom Jeff directions, but Shadwell cut him off. "Never mind all that," Tom Jeff said, "you just hold the camera in a medium close-up while I come around the tree. I'm going to talk for twenty-two seconds, and you zoom in slowly to a full close-up in the last seven." He was speaking directly to the cameraman, who nodded. Moran threw his arms in the air disgustedly.

"Mac, you quit romancing the help and give me those hunting duds." Flushing, Mac tore his gaze away from the lovely girl and helped Shadwell into the jacket. Then Shadwell clapped the hunting hat on his head, broke the shotgun across his arm, and stepped behind the tree. "Cue me," he said.

Moran declined to watch the proceedings. He seemed to be studying the sky. But he called, "Camera—action," in a loud voice.

Tom Jeff stepped from behind the tree and began talking immediately. "I am opposed to any measure that will interfere with the right of Virginia hunters to keep and use firearms, and as governor I will fight for that right. The people of Virginia know that I mean what I say." He snapped the shotgun together; it jutted skyward next to his face as the camera began to close in. "The right to keep and use firearms is an important part of life here in southwest Virginia. The people know that Tom Jeff Shadwell will fight for all their rights."

"Cut," Moran said.

"That was beautiful," the cameraman said. The sound girl nodded her head. Moran kept his own counsel.

At Shadwell's insistence, they ran three more takes. "I haven't got the time to do this again another day. And besides, Brother Moran's coins might fall wrong, and then we'd all be in the soup."

When it was over, Tom Jeff thrust the shotgun at Mac warily. "Put this thing under lock and key," he said.

"Right," Mac said. He broke the gun, then took the hat and jacket. Shadwell mopped his face.

"Would you mind catching a ride back to town with Wink?" Mac said. "I need to stay around here."

"Merciful heaven," Shadwell said. "You abandoning me, Mac? I can't ride with that man, he's liable to want to read my palm."

"I'm sorry, Tom Jeff," Mac said. "It's just that I have a date down here in an hour or so."

Shadwell broke into his crooked grin. "A date?" he chortled, poking Mac's elbow. "By all means, go to it. I'm not about to interfere with a young fellow's love life. That's no way to get elected. No, sir, there's no sacrifice I won't make to keep my staff happy."

Moran walked up to them. "We're about ready to go, Mr. Shadwell," he said. His face was gathered in lines of tragic dissatisfaction.

"Will you give the senator a ride home, Wink?" Mac asked.

"Certainly," Moran said with alacrity. "I'd be glad to. I'd like to talk to you about a few things anyway, Mr. Shadwell."

Tom Jeff's eyes rolled in panic between Moran and the long, low sports car. Then he saw the camera crew's truck and his face relaxed.

"That's mighty nice of you, Brother Moran," he said. "But you know I have a terrible back problem, it's been bothering me for years, and I think my doctor would order me not to ride in that beautiful machine of yours, it's just too low. I'd best ride in the truck yonder. I wish I could come with you, that's a mighty fine car." He walked quickly to the truck; in his walk was a stiffness Mac had never seen before.

The last Mac saw of him, Shadwell was sitting beside the cameraman, who was driving. The sound girl peered from a back window, her pale-blue eyes fixed on Moran. Again she stabbed the devil's horns at his unsuspecting back.

"Will you let us see a print Tuesday?" Mac asked.

290

"All right, all right, all right," Moran said angrily. He leaped into the Maserati and vanished down the road in a clatter of gravel.

Alexandra lived far down a gravel road, in a tiny cottage perched on the edge of a wooded slope leading down to a creek. The big blue Continental seemed to dwarf the house, and Mac was not sure he had found the right place. But the mailbox said OLMSTED in gold aluminum stick-on letters, and he walked up to the door and knocked.

There was no answer, so he called her name and listened; then he heard a voice, indistinct, behind the house. He walked around and found her on a stone terrace, perched on a stool, legs folded, her back to him as she watched the sun setting. She was cutting up an apple and putting the pieces in a bowl. Below her the little creek chuckled quietly, and above its noise he heard her voice, singing:

> Sukey Tawdry, Jenny Diver,
> Polly Peacham, Lucy Brown,
> Oh! the *line* forms, on the *right,* dear,
> Now that Mackie's back in town.

"Hello," he called, smiling. "It's Mack the Knife himself."

She started briefly, then regained her composure. "Sneak!" she said in an unresentful tone. "I was not singing about you anyway. It was some other Mac."

"Of course," Mac said. "And I'm not a sneak. You didn't answer your door."

"You're early," she said. She got up off the stool and set the bowl down on the low stone wall around the terrace. She was wearing blue jeans, a tight brown tank top which outlined her breasts, and dark soft ballet slippers. Her long black hair framed her dark face, and the dark teardrop glasses set off her eyes. "You look swell," Mac said, and immediately felt silly. Where had that word come from?

But she didn't seem to notice. "Thanks," she said gravely, and gave a sketchy curtsy, so the hair fell forward across her face. "You look extremely . . . what is the word I want?"

Handsome? Dashing? Mac thought. *Sexy?*

"Professional," she said after deliberation. "You look like you're here to sell me something."

Mac looked down at his double-knit suit, blue shirt, yellow checked tie. "Come on," he said. "These are just my working clothes. I was down here anyway, so I didn't go home and change."

"Mack the Knife," she said. "Keen-eyed political operative."

291

Mac felt suddenly ashamed and tongue-tied. "Lay off," he said. "What should I wear, a dashiki?" He draped his coat self-consciously over the wall and sat beside it.

"Don't be so sensitive," she said. "I'm not making fun of you."

"Ah," Mac said.

"Or maybe just a little," she added gravely, as if ethically bound to set the record straight. "Would you like some beer?"

"Yeah, I guess so," Mac said. She walked past him into the kitchen. Mac watched her pass, marveling again at the intricate economy with which her legs and hips moved.

The dinner she had promised, it turned out, was a complicated, strenuously healthful salad, with apples and radishes and pine nuts sprinkled over all. Mac stirred his indecisively. "Are you a vegetarian?" he asked.

She was sitting cross-legged on the wall, between him and the last rays of sunset. Around them the evening was warm, but the land seemed to be glowing, radiating heat into the air, and Mac guessed the temperature would drop quickly when it was full dark.

"Sometimes," she said. "I assume you're not."

"Tell the truth, no," Mac said. "I consider myself a carnivore."

"Oh, if you don't like the salad, I can make you something else. Do you like liver?"

Mac realized he had given offense. "No, I was just kidding," he said, stuffing his mouth full of the salad, which to his surprise tasted good. "This is fine. I'm not real hungry, it was so hot today and all, don't worry about a thing." He munched desperately and then tried to change the subject. "What do you hear from your family?"

This seemed to make her unhappy. "Not a blessed thing," she said mournfully. "I don't hear from anybody. I'm beginning to feel as if I've been forgotten here at the end of this dirt road."

"Ah, well," Mac said. They ate for a while in silence.

After dinner she served him brandy in a tiny snifter. Something in the drink, or the night, or in her seemed to touch some secret spot inside him; he felt himself relaxing so suddenly it seemed to make a noise, a groaning as of a tired old spring unwinding. He lay full-length beside her on the stone wall, eyes closed. "This is terrific," he said. "I really like this little house, it's so quiet."

She said nothing for a while; the creek gurgled. "This dumb little house," she said finally. "People really like it as long as they don't have to live in it."

"Are you kidding?" Mac said without opening his eyes. "It beats my little house all to pieces."

"Maybe," she said skeptically. "But I'm sick of little houses. Little places for one person. I don't like living alone."

The statement sounded odd to Mac, like *I don't like breathing.* "I don't know," he said in a tone intended to console. "It's pretty convenient, you don't have to worry about the other person, you can come and go as you please."

The creek chattered to itself. Then she said in a soft voice, "There are other things in life besides coming and going as you please."

"Name three," Mac said.

"Not being lonely all the time," she said.

Belatedly Mac realized he was being, as usual, a clod. He opened his eyes and raised his head to look at her. "You are not feeling particularly good tonight, are you?" he said.

She had clenched her hands on her lap; now she looked at them and wordlessly nodded.

Mac sat up beside her. Suddenly he felt like a man who has taken a first-aid course years before and suddenly finds himself called on to use his knowledge. Could he remember? Had he ever known? Slowly he reached out a hand and rested it, gingerly, a safecracker's hand, lightly on the nape of her neck.

Whether he was giving comfort or seeking attention he did not know, but whatever, she gave forward like a teetering rock, her head sliding, not onto his shoulder but forward into her hands, the long black hair falling on either side of her face, parting neatly over the neck, where Mac's hand rested, still tentatively but firmer.

She said nothing. She appeared to be crying; no, she *was* crying. His hand, as if developing its own volition, began to wander through her hair like a herdsman through his flock. He saw, above the collar of her tank top, the bunched dancer's muscles of her neck, covered with the tanned skin; it seemed to glisten like gold or silk, something infinitely precious.

"Is there," Mac said, before his tongue stuck in his throat so that he had to begin again, "is there anything I can do?"

She turned her head and looked at him through her hair. "Will you stay here tonight?" she said after a minute. "Will you stay with me?"

Qualifications rushed through Mac's panicky mind: *Yes, but I, not to-night, yes, but not right away, yes, but I have to go home now, yes, but I can't help you, yes, but somebody else, yes, but I've got to run, I left my dachshund on the stove.* But somehow he cut them off, drew breath, and light-headed, like a man taking the oath of an office he never dreamed he'd hold, said, simply, "Yes."

She smiled faintly and brushed back the black hair. Hand moving, arm, breast lifting slightly beneath the silky black cloth: her gesture ravished Mac suddenly like a sword piercing his heart. He had, for once in his life, said the right thing, he thought.

The little house was one small room, with a tiny bathroom and kitchen tacked on the side. The ceiling slanted up to a point above wide wooden beams. She slept on a couch which folded out neatly into a double bed with a green spread; there was room for Mac. They lay together, still dressed; Mac felt wooden as she turned her face to his. He knew what he was waiting for: that sudden doorway opening into the sewers of the heart, the rushing pathways of dishonor, that blend of fear and distrust and self-hatred which had sent him running out of the little office at Harvard so many years before, had kept him since then aloof and celibate. By the time he realized it was not coming he had passed beyond fear and hesitancy. Soon he lay naked beside her. He moved to join with her, his long, straight, ample body with her full, intricate, curved one, and he felt clumsy and unsure, but she did not seem to mind, and they moved together for a time, and the sewers did not open, there was no sound but pure water rushing below in the creek bed when finally they were still, and the soft susurrations of their breath mingling. She nestled on his shoulder and slept. Mac fought against sleep, for his hands were exploring her body and her fine skin warmed him like a banked fire; he felt himself thaw, felt again inside him the stirring branches of that tree of life.

As he drifted toward sleep, a light rain began to fall, and wind rushed in the branches of the trees about the little house. Mac lay in the green bed, beneath the cedar beams and pine rafters, and breathed in gently the scent of her hair, which somehow seemed in that moment to promise him a world, a universe, of rescue, comfort, peace.

TWO

Miles Brock bestrode the state like Godzilla, uttering menaces. The Antichrist had come, his name was Shadwell; terror, chaos, civil war loomed. No man's life or property was safe.

This had a curious effect on Mac. He saw on television, heard on radio, read in the Richmond newspapers about this queerly unfamiliar Tom Jeff Shadwell, not the candidate he had come to respect, but an unpredictable, half-mad demagogue, sower of dissension, snake-oil salesman, confidence man, whose accession to power would mark forever the end of responsible state government, bankrupt the schools, drag the dead gibbering from their graves, shatter the universe. It made Mac angry, but it also somehow attenuated him, as if calling into question his own reality. The campaign seized hold of him, swelled increasingly to dominate the world.

On intermittent nights he would sneak away to Alexandra's house. The stone patio, the foldout couch still offered peace and rescue, but both of them knew that Mac had to wrench himself, make an effort, to reach them. He habitually promised himself to sneak away early, to reach Alexandra's for a dinner of pine nuts, or a walk in the woods, or to see her dance with an amateur group she had found in Opechancanough, or even just to sit with her and watch television or talk. But invariably there were crises, deadlines, bureaucratic snarls, failures of communication—he was kept busy straightening them out past eight, past nine, past ten. He would arrive in the country exhausted, still in his office wear. Walking from the big car to the tiny house, he felt for all the world like a commuter back from the city.

He sat in a tense lump on the patio, jacket off, tie loosened. He would try to talk about the campaign. It was automatic, like breathing; if he did not stop himself, he would talk politics. But it was, for better or worse, no use. He could not make her feel the importance of what he was doing. Virginia was not her state; its history was not her history. She looked at Shadwell and Brock and saw a loud, funny little man fighting a grim, pompous big man; good and evil did not apply. So Mac stopped talking about it, which meant he stopped talking.

Besides being a dancer, she was skilled in massage. She had studied it in college. She walked on his back and rubbed at his neck. His shoulder muscles appalled her. "I don't usually get to work on any that are this tense," she explained. "If I could relax them, I would be the Michelangelo of massage." He sat on the stool while she perched behind him on the wall, vainly rubbing at the knots. He rested his head between her breasts and sipped beer, and because it seemed ungracious to sit there in silence, he began asking her about herself.

Her father had been a doctor in Winston-Salem, a dour, distrustful man, obstinate, contrary, and proud; he had quarreled with the neighbors, other doctors, the AMA, the newspapers. In the end he had accumulated a long list of enemies. When he fell ill, even with only a slight cold or flu, other doctors took up a collection and sent massive, lugubrious floral gifts, with notes wishing him a long recovery. She and her brothers had grown up fearing the smell of flowers, the smell of illness and enmity.

Even when well, Dr. Olmsted had been distant and elusive. Night after night he sat in his office at the back of his house, while a big grandfather clock ticked away the evening, drinking moodily and contemplating private vistas of betrayal and revenge. Five years before, death had claimed him.

"He had a motto he taught all the children and made us repeat," she said.

He held a beer bottle between his knees; the cold and moisture seeped through his porous knit trousers. "What was it?" he asked.

" 'People are no damn good,' " she said placidly, fingers massaging.

"What?" Mac sat upright in astonishment. "Are you serious?"

"Sure," she said. "We used to get a nickel to repeat it for company."

"Jesus," Mac said. "What was your mother doing during all this?"

"She used to answer him back some," she said. "But after a while she decided he was right. After all, she was married to him, and I think she thought he was living proof of it."

"That's a terrible thing to teach a little kid," Mac said.

"Why?" she asked, still laughing gently. "You have proof it isn't true?"

"Oh, hell, no," Mac said. "All I mean is, I guess, a kid ought to have a chance to figure it out for himself."

He settled back against her breasts; her fingers began again. Mac sipped his beer. The TV commercial, pried loose at last in acceptable form from Moran, had been on the air in the Ninth District for more than a week, but it was still too early to tell what effect it was having. There were newer headaches to contend with. Brock supporters were scurrying around the state like a squadron of trained mice, nibbling at Shadwell on a dozen issues, misrepresenting his positions, inventing statements, making threats: nibble, nibble, Shadwell wants to raise the property tax; nibble, nibble, Shadwell wants to raise the auto titling tax; nibble, nibble, Shadwell is against the police and for the criminal; nibble, nibble, Shadwell wants to make men and women equal by abolishing separate toilets in public buildings; nibble, nibble, Shadwell is planning to abolish the highway department and make everybody join a union and wear a number and he wants to bus everybody's children halfway across the state.

Mac sat up. It was hard to be in the lead. It was harder to hit back against Brock. What they needed was an issue, something like the food tax, but newer, stronger, to put Brock back on the defensive. Of course, Shadwell was still ahead, and though Tom Jeff had decided not to release his poll, everybody knew it. Mac could sense that the lead was still holding. Unless Brock pushed much harder, he would not be able to overcome Shadwell's advantage. So far, he had not proved to be a very formidable campaigner; he was tired and old, and the people could tell. Maybe, just maybe, things would be all right.

He leaned back again meditatively, but he did not encounter Alexandra's massaging fingers. Instead, he fell backward until his back met the rough stone wall and he found himself lying, elbows asprawl, uneasily hung between stool and wall. He heard a laugh; when he turned his head, he saw Alexandra through the screen door, pulling a beer from the refrigerator.

Mac was nettled. "Laugh, Pagliacci," he grumbled, sinking to the floor. Then he began to rise with exaggerated stiffness. "What do you do next—exploding cigars, electric hand buzzers?"

"You dunce," she said with some asperity. "If you are so out of it you can't tell whether I'm there or not, serves you right to fall down."

He brushed at his trousers. His beer had tipped over, splashing them. She peered at him through the door, brushing the thick hair out of her face. In the motion Mac sensed a certain nervousness; behind her glasses her eyes regarded him warily. He looked down at himself, dusty and splattered, and laughed; then he opened the screen door and stepped toward her.

Her body tensed, hands out in a karate pose. "Don't you knock me down," she said.

"I would certainly never do that," Mac said. Very slowly, he took her face in his left hand and kissed her; their lips met, her eyes closed; with his right hand he poured his beer down her back.

"You creep!" she cried, leaping like a startled deer. They began to laugh and stood there for a moment, laughing across the kitchen, very pleased with each other. Then she darted into the bathroom to change her shirt.

They slept naked, washed by moonlight through the trees, beneath the green bedspread. Mac did not dream; his sleep was heavy and dark. He was awakened by a fist in the face.

She was seized by nightmare, thrashing about her, crying out softly. He grabbed her shoulders and shook her quietly, calling her name. Her eyes came open and caught the moonlight; she lay still on the pillow, her sides heaving like a racehorse after a steeplechase.

"Are you okay?" Mac asked. Her gaze caught and held him, and a slight chill of fear passed through him. He was in bed with a stranger; the eyes were cold and malevolent. Something had entered into her while she slept.

"Yeah," she said in a whisper, and at the sound of her voice his fears vanished. She lay quiet on her stomach, facing him, relaxed now and quiet.

"Were you dreaming?" Mac said.

"Yeah," she said again.

He waited for her to speak, but she lay still. Her eyes still watched him, warily, speculatively.

He rubbed her back. Touching her still gave him the same pleasure it had at first; it was like stroking fine fur, rich silk; his fingers tingled with pleasure.

"I was in India," she said slowly. "Some city."

"Benares?"

298

"Maybe. I don't know. It doesn't matter," she said. "Just a city. It was crowded as hell. I was looking for someone, and I couldn't get through."

"Who was it?" he asked. "Was it Willie?"

"Maybe," she said, shooting him a piercing look. "Maybe not. I can't remember, because I could never get to him."

Mac stroked her hair. "Well, listen, it's okay," he said. "You're not in India. You're here. That's all over."

"Is it?" she asked, and in her eyes was that same speculative look. "I hope so, but I'm not too sure."

"What do you mean?"

Her eyes reflected the moon like silver searchlights. "Well, Mac, you know, you come out here at night, you leave early in the morning, sometimes I wonder if you're real at all. It's like having a demon lover or something."

"Listen," Mac said, "I'm no demon."

"Maybe not," she said, a bit stubbornly. "But I am getting awfully sick of being involved with men who are—"

"Who are what?"

She turned over on her back. "I would love it sometime if a man were in love with me. All the men I get involved with seem to be in love with death."

I'm in love with you, Mac wanted to say, but his tongue tangled, and instead, he said, "That—that's not true. It isn't."

She said nothing. In her eyes he read her father's motto.

"What can I say, Alexandra?" he said finally.

"Nothing right now," she said. "Go to sleep."

Back at the headquarters, in his tiny alcove off Knocko's cluttered office, the memory seemed somehow unreal to him, as if he were remembering a previous incarnation; so distant did Alexandra and her house seem that when Knocko began Mac didn't even know what he was talking about.

"MacIlwain, my boy," Knocko said, lolling back in his chair, cigar between his teeth, white sleeves rolled up to his elbows, "it has long been my considered opinion that you are a tireless worker, a prodigiously talented young fanatic, and, in addition, a scholar and"—here he delicately flicked from his cigar an inch-long ash, dropping it into the trash basket, upraised pinkie symbolizing his contempt for the next word and all it implied—"a gentleman. But I am, I confess, surprised to discover that you are also a great lover."

Mac looked blankly at the pink, beaming face swimming in a globe of

299

smoke. At that moment he genuinely did not know what Knocko was talking about.

"It's all very well for you to sit there in innocent glory," Knocko said. "But I know you are slipping away at night to rendezvous with a beautiful girl."

How could he know? Maybe he'd called the house. "Did you hear from Molly O.?"

Knocko's laugh boomed against the walls. "No, indeed," he said. "I have my own sources, Mac. I get around here and there on this earth, up and down on it. To me is given knowledge of many things."

Mac faced the full force of Knocko's unabashed, saturnine gaze. "Okay," he said, shrugging uncomfortably. "What about it?"

"Nothing but my deepest congratulations," Knocko said, inclining his head in sardonic salute. "I like to see young people having a good time in the days of their youth. Yes, sir. *Carpe diem,* old buddy. Go at it." He puffed philosophically on the cigar, then held it stiff-armed away from him, exhaling the smoke through grinning teeth. "Of course, from my own point of view it's too bad. Makes you a worse po-li-ti-co. Fellow gets all set, shacking up with some girl he's crazy about, first thing you know, his work goes to hell. I like my staff lean and hungry, because then they want to win, they're desperate to win, because they figure that then they'll get money, power, women, so forth. But I can see your point of view, believe me. Liberal in Virginia waits to win an election to get laid, he gets pretty damn horny."

Mac looked away in embarrassment. "Jesus, Knocko, let it drop, will you?"

"Drop?" Knocko said. "Nothing drops around here. Not even a sparrow drops without me knowing about it. I see all and know all. I'm watching you in my crystal ball."

But Knocko was worrying for nothing. Mac pressed on with his work as vigorously as ever. He was the switch-hitter of the campaign staff; he divided his time between helping Danny Watkins with the press work and researching and speech writing for Shadwell. As researcher, he even found himself with an assistant, a peppery gray-haired former social worker named Lola Kreznik. Mac admired her unflagging energy, but even the two of them found they couldn't keep up with the research needed to keep the campaign going.

They had to guard the candidate's speeches against factual errors: one misstatement would provoke a statement from the Brock headquarters signed by a banker or a Republican state senator or a corporate executive

300

or a retired Army general, expressing sorrowful regret that Tom Jeff Shadwell had once again chosen the low road of demagogic distortion. Besides, Shadwell himself was a stickler for facts, and his formidable wrath could be loosed against any speech writer who let an error creep into his speech. On top of that, the two of them had to sift and comb Brock's statements for his mistakes and lies—and there were many of these. They then had to produce information of his term as governor to use against them. This involved hours of wading through newspaper morgues and blowing dust off the meager records of the Virginia General Assembly, combing archives and files at the State Library, often only to find that the information had been lost, or had never been written down, or was simply useless. Then there were newspaper advertisements, leaflets, circulars, position papers, and financial disclosures to be written. And always there were emergencies, situations where charges had to be refuted immediately, in detail, and for good.

Mac found himself in awe of the candidate's memory for dates and names. One day in mid-September the headquarters received a panicky phone call from a Shadwell chairman in a county in Southside; the local Brock supporters had begun whispering vague charges that Shadwell had used undue influence to prevent a local veterinarian from losing his state license. The story had been leaked to the county newspaper, which wanted a statement by Shadwell by that afternoon, because of deadline.

Mac reached Tom Jeff in Lynchburg, at a lunch meeting with the local Farm Bureau, and asked him, hoping he might have some vague memory of the incident to furnish the basis of a rebuttal.

Shadwell did not even pause to think. "Dr. DePaul," he said crisply. "Absolutely right. I wrote a letter to the Board of Veterinary Examiners, it must be seven years ago last March. They wanted to railroad him out of business, or I guess not really but just to scare him some, and it was a silly business. The commonwealth's attorney's godmother's dog died, and she got hysterical and started screaming about it, and this old commonwealth's attorney, I believe his name was Harrison, he was well connected at the Capitol, and he said something to somebody, just to get his godmother off his back, and the first thing you know some cluckhead was making an inquiry. Nobody'd even made a formal charge. Silly nonsense, but this fellow was scared and he asked me to help. All this stuff is on file in my law office, you call Nancy Andrews, she's my secretary, and tell her to get the 'Veterinarians' Association' file and Telex it to you, because as I recall they sent the man a written apology and he sent me a copy. You got a pencil? Here's your statement: 'I know Dr. DePaul as an

301

outstanding veterinarian and a public-spirited citizen, and it was a privilege to help defend his reputation against baseless and malicious attack. His professional standing among his peers is unquestioned, and I deeply regret that my opponent has chosen to attempt to harm an innocent citizen in an attempt to get at me.' I could say more, but it ain't right to get this guy all embroiled in the campaign. It's a cheap trick them trying it, but it's going to end up hurting them more than us. Okay? Now let me go, Mac, because I'm sowing the seed on thorny ground here, got a lot of cultivation to do."

As September passed into October, Mac found himself caught up with all the others in a desperate hunger for any scrap of information about how the campaign was going: not the daily gossip about politicians; the headquarters was aswirl with that, reports of who was supporting whom and who had double-crossed whom. What they all wanted was some shred of information about how the campaign appeared to the people who would decide it, the ordinary voters to whom the contest was a distant confusion, like the rumble of thunder beyond the horizon. For the people who had spent a year or more of their lives in a universe with politics at the center, the mass of mankind had become as alien as Martians. They studied news of the average voter as an astronomer studies a star which he can barely see and never touch.

Danny Watkins was an assiduous gleaner of this type of gossip; he regularly burst into the headquarters, his aging urchin's face agleam with self-important excitement, to report that his auto mechanic or television repairman had said that Shadwell seemed like a good man or that his nephew's scoutmaster was going to vote for Shadwell because "that other fellow is a crook." Such items would float around the office for days, acquiring new forms, until within a week someone would tell Watkins himself his own story, but by now so changed that the press secretary would accept it as a new story, and the cycle would begin again.

On a day early in October, Mac woke early in his little house, where he had slept alone after working later than usual. It was a warm sunny day; the night before, there had been a pleasant autumnal snap in the air, and the fall winds had rustled in the trees like memories troubling the edge of sleep. Mac walked out into the yard. A squirrel crouched at the foot of a tree, an acorn in its claws. Mac advanced on it, arms rotating windmill-fashion. The little animal darted up the tree. "You furry coward!" Mac shouted. "Stay down here and fight like a rodent!"

He walked up to the big house and drank coffee on the patio with Molly

O. Of late he noticed a certain approving gleam in his sister-in-law's eye; it had begun when he started staying out at Alexandra's. Or perhaps it was simply that she no longer seemed to watch him so closely. She had relaxed around him as if he had been a problem she had worried about but was now, suddenly, just another human being.

This morning she kept Mac amused by describing the goings-on at the offices of the Episcopal Diocese of Virginia, where she worked as administrative assistant to the bishop. A young priest in Arlington had given an interview to a local weekly newspaper warning that "satanic cults" were on the rise and that the demoniacs were desecrating churches by performing the Black Mass; he had casually mentioned that he personally had performed "more than two dozen" exorcisms of people troubled by evil spirits.

"Now we've got people calling up at all hours wanting to be exorcised," she said. "The bishop is as mad as he can be. He called that boy in and read him the riot act. I heard him when the fellow came into his office. He smiled this very small smile and said, 'Here's my little Gadarene swine,' and I thought to myself, *Great God, I sure am glad I'm not that fellow right about now.*"

Mac nibbled at an English muffin.

"Mac," Molly O. said, stirring her coffee. Her voice was tentative, almost shy. "Why don't you bring your girlfriend out here some night for dinner or something? I'd like to meet her. If you want to, I mean."

Mac looked out across the yard. A cream-colored cat had wandered into the yard. It was crouched now at the base of the dogwood tree, pressing itself into the earth as if trying to take refuge there. After a minute Mac saw why: a barn swallow, like a tiny dive-bomber, was buzzing the cat again and again.

"Just a thought," Molly O. said.

We always manage to embarrass each other, Mac thought. Across the yard, the cat moved off in stately haste, as if fleeing from marauding birds were the farthest thing from its mind. "It might be fun," Mac said. "I'll see if I get the time." He poured them both more coffee; they drank in silence.

He drank another cup of coffee at headquarters with State Senator C. Rodgers Putnam. Putnam was Mac's assignment for the morning. He was a wealthy, ambitious legislator from northern Virginia. He had been born and raised in Philadelphia, and his looks and manner were, in some indefinable way, not of Virginia nor indeed of the South. He was a long, lean aristocrat, and his measured, self-assured speech and reserved face were tokens of a generous self-confidence which no native politician could ever match, as if in the ancestral memory there remained a vision of defeat and penury, which instilled a certain wary parsimony at the back of every word or action, however generous.

Putnam had the face of a well-barbered, suntanned bloodhound. His voice resonated with moral authority, and on television he had the air of a plenipotentiary from the Almighty bearing important news. This was why Tom Jeff had asked him to come to Richmond to hold a press conference designed to counter the attacks Brock had been making since Labor Day. "Senator Rodgers Putnam is just the man to tie the tin can on Miles Brock's tail," Shadwell said. "Get him on the TV shaking his head in sorrow, and they'll read old Brock right out of the congregation."

Danny Watkins, the press secretary, was in Newport News with the candidate, and Mac had agreed to handle Putnam's press conference. Now his teeth made a semicircle in the styrofoam cup as he checked over Putnam's draft statement.

"May I suggest a change here, Senator?" Mac said, extricating the cup and setting it on the conference table.

"Certainly, certainly." Putnam looked at him, one eyebrow rising in delicate inquiry. Mac found himself admiring Putnam's impeccable exterior: his dry, friendly reserve, his elegant manners and unobtrusively splendid clothes.

"I just thought we might change this phrase here," Mac said. He read from the statement: " 'I've known Senator Shadwell for years, and he is a Christian gentleman.' Somehow that seems a little"—Mac groped for the word to express his meaning without offending Putnam—"ponderous."

"I'm not sure I understand."

"It just sort of sounds more like the kind of thing Brock's people would say. It's—I don't know, it's what people used to say about Franco in the thirties."

Putnam was now frankly puzzled. Mac reflected that even this cultivated, literate patrician somehow failed to understand why Mac would think of Franco in this connection, as if the name belonged to a history which had less than nothing to do with the world he was living in now.

"I'm still not sure I understand you fully," Putnam said. His face was an agreeable mask. "But if you think it should be changed, by all means go ahead."

"Thank you, Senator," Mac said, inking out the phrase with a felt-tipped pen. "Otherwise this looks fine. I'll get the secretary to type it up and run it off."

* * *

The press conference was set for 11 A.M., to give the Norfolk and Roanoke TV crews time to fly film back to their home stations. Mac and Putnam walked up Tenth Street at a leisurely pace toward the Capitol. Mac clutched the file of mimeographed statements under one arm; in the other he carried a small cassette tape recorder, to keep his own record of what was said. Putnam, his hands clasped behind his back, surveyed the green slope of Capitol Square like a squire overlooking his demesne.

The little park began at Capital Street and sloped sharply down to Bank Street. On the west was Ninth Street, a bustling thoroughfare which led south to a wide new bridge over the James and north to City Hall and the complex of buildings housing the city and federal governments, school board, and police department. In the northeast corner of Capitol Square, behind a low white brick wall, was the governor's mansion, a surprisingly unassuming place to be the object of so much striving. Behind the mansion was the narrow downhill curve of Governor Street, and on the far side were small upright houses, now occupied by state offices; in Mac's great-great-grandfather's time the street had held the offices of lawyers and slave factors.

The Capitol itself reared up magnificently out of the grounds, its broad white steps facing south toward the river. Few people used the front stairs, which passed under a set of massive pillars into an opulent marble portico. Instead, Capitol regulars like Mac and Senator Putnam used the west entrance, ground-level double doors. Adjacent to them was an asphalt driveway circling the massive monument to George Washington. This was a huge pillar topped by an equestrian statue of the Liberator; his eyes gazed east-southeast, while his hand gestured vaguely west and south. By Capitol tradition, Washington was looking at the legislature and pointing at the penitentiary. Tradition also taught that Washington had wanted to be buried beneath the statue and that his widow quietly forbade it. If so, she acted wisely, for the pillar had collected an agglomeration of statuary over the years which would have made it an unbecoming tomb. Around the base were life-size standing statues of Meriwether Lewis, John Marshall, Patrick Henry, George Mason, Thomas Nelson, and Thomas Jefferson. And at the feet of each of these men was a smaller figure of Liberty, also facing outward, seated on a throne of cannon and shot; each of these statues bore an inscription which, taken together, formed a peculiarly Virginian recipe for a healthy state: Justice, Colonial Times, Bill of Rights, Independence, Finance, and Revolution.

Jefferson himself had designed the Capitol building, a fact which helped to explain why Virginia's contemporary leaders chose to slink in by the side door, for however much the parade of governors and legislators relished invoking the name and spirit of the exuberant mad master of Monticello, however boldly they might wrap themselves in his mantle, not one in a hundred felt himself to be anything but a pygmy, one of a race of pygmies dancing about the catafalques of giants.

Even inside the building they were dwarfed; once Mac and Senator Putnam passed through the west door, under the somnolent eye of a Capitol policeman in a glassed-in alcove, they passed along a checkered black and white marble hall, under a ceiling which seemed high as the sky, past great oaken doors. The ceilings reflected sound in an unceasing echo, as if hurling back at each speaker all the words that had been said before him.

The first floor was largely given over to committee hearing rooms and other public congregating places; on the second floor were the legislative chambers for the Senate and House of Delegates; on the third floor Governor Hapgood and his staff passed their last months in office in powerless silent grandeur, walking on thick carpets through doors meant for giants to sit at polished empty desks beneath portraits of their predecessors.

The press conference was on the ground floor; Mac and Senator Putnam followed the corridor to the central lobby, where the Seal of Virginia was set into the floor, then turned right, past Chicken's, the snack bar. At the end of the hall were the twin doors of the press room, one, forbiddingly closed, marked PRESS, the other, wide open, marked RADIO-TV.

From behind the first door came the rhythmic chatter of Teletype machines. In the press room, Mac knew, the senior members of the print press corps would be quietly playing cards in an endless round of a peculiar game called mullet gin. Mullet had been invented by the press corps decades before and was played nowhere else in the world but in that one room. The rules were intricate, confusing, and closely held; somewhere in the downtown area was an aging lobbyist who was their guardian, officially voted Commissioner of Mullet by the other players. Mac was not privy to the rules; he knew only that each hand in the game referred somehow to happenings in Virginia political history, some lost to living memory, others fresh and new. Once he had come into the press room on business and watched a hand; one of the players had announced grandly, "I've got an H. Rap Brown," and laid on the table a hand composed entirely of spades.

There had been a time, not too many years before, when the major qualifications a young white man needed to succeed as a political reporter were a grasp of the rules of mullet and a firm sense of the party line. Day after day the cards were shuffled and reshuffled, dealt and redealt, and

306

stories came in the intervals between hands. The players would receive a summons from the governor or the speaker of the House or another of the three or four men who had jealously held the power in the days when the Apple-Farmer was still running the state; there would be a few minutes behind closed doors, and the next day the story would appear, written as the governor or speaker or chairman wanted it, because mullet players were not invited to the conferences unless they could be trusted to do the job correctly, to write what they were expected to write. Moreover, each player knew that his managing editor, who might himself be a veteran of the mullet game, would put the story right even if it were written wrong and then ask why it hadn't been written right to begin with.

The mullet game had been losing importance since Miles Brock left office, but it went on, as exclusive as ever: members were carefully differentiated from nonmembers. The correspondents for the two Richmond papers, the Norfolk papers, and the AP and UPI could play, provided they had amassed enough seniority; also included were those who had moved into editorships or political jobs with the state or jobs as lobbyists and political operatives: once a mullet player, always a mullet player. To the rest of the world, the game was a bit less closed than the deliberations of the College of Cardinals.

The mullet players kept their door scornfully shut, and Mac had always suspected that this was intended less to exclude the general public—who might, after all, conceivably have something newsworthy to say—than to keep out the radio and television reporters, whom the mullet players regarded as journalistic untouchables, less than human: empty-headed, mellow-voiced electronic dilettantes whose appalling popularity had done so much to rob the mullet game of its rightful role in state government.

Mac and Senator Putnam went into the Radio-TV room. The press conference was to be held in its small back chamber, where the cameras could be set up easily. The front room, as usual, looked as if it had just been the scene of a simultaneous hurricane and martial arts championship: papers and documents littered the tables and floors, stained by the remains of a half dozen unfinished cartons of coffee and canned soft drinks. The huge round wastebasket was stuffed to overflowing; every inch of vertical space, walls and doors, was covered with official notices, scribbled messages, printed comic mottoes, and sarcastically captioned photographs of state officials, office seekers, and reporters. The room's four corners were crammed with cameras, microphones, tripods, light units, and sound equipment. One wall of the room was taken by a pair of semi-enclosed soundproofed booths used for transmitting sound recordings over the telephones; these were the property of local stations. On the opposite wall was a long, low counter with four telephones.

One of these phones was shrilling with the plaintive sound of a child abandoned in a freight car. Next to it, reclining in a swivel chair, two-tone shoes balanced squarely on the counter, was Ed Hackett, a reporter for a local TV station. Hackett wore a lemon-yellow double-breasted sports jacket, lapels and pockets outlined in lime-green trim, a yellow bow tie with red polka dots, a shirt two shades of blue in a checkered pattern, deep-blue corduroy bell-bottom trousers, and the aforementioned shoes. His face added to the motif: it was a deep freckled red, crowned with a carefully styled mop of alarming red hair; it had perky college-boy features behind large, oval tortoiseshell glasses.

The phone rang again, but Hackett neither woke nor stirred. Mac jolted his elbow. "Hey, Ed," he said. "Aren't you going to answer your phone?"

Hackett's eyes half opened. "It's not my phone," he said briefly, and closed his eyes again. The phone rang once more; Hackett opened his eyes and gave it a savage cross-eyed stare; as if on command, it rang no more.

Mac noticed Senator Putnam moving about the room cautiously, with a faint look of distaste. The senator had stepped into the sticky stain left by a spilled soft drink; as he walked, his shoes made a faintly audible pop. Mac wheeled one of the swivel chairs over and offered it to Putnam. The senator took out a handkerchief and carefully wiped seat, arms, and back before sitting.

"I'll round up the other kiddies," Mac said. "Would you like a cup of coffee while you're waiting?"

"Gracious, no," Putnam replied incisively. "If I drink any more coffee today, I am liable to begin to percolate myself."

Hackett laughed loudly, leaning back in his chair. "That's a good one," he said, pulling a notebook from his pocket. "Mind if I write it down?" down?"

"By all means," Putnam replied with painful bonhomie.

Mac found most of the other reporters in Chicken's; as he herded them back toward the room, a few stragglers appeared, followed by cameramen laden like bearers trailing after big-game hunters. Last of all, Mac respectfully interrupted the mullet game, and the print reporters came en masse.

Putnam sat patiently behind the small table during the clatter and confusion, as cameramen took light readings and set up batteries of bulbs and reporters arranged tape recorders and microphones on the table before him. The reporters pushed and elbowed one another for the best vantage point in the tiny room. Mac handed out copies of the statement and advised the TV reporters when they should start sound filming to catch the most important parts of the statement without wasting expensive film. When everyone seemed ready, he nodded to Senator Putnam. After a few false starts, all the equipment was finally working, and Putnam got under way.

Tom Jeff was right; Senator Putnam was very good. Even under the harsh lights, he did not sweat; his skin looked rather like dry, firm living Naugahyde. When the lights went on, he seemed to draw himself up to a great height, like a magician donning his tall pointed hat; his words carried an air of unearthly truth.

Putnam pronounced himself deeply disappointed in Miles Brock, a man who had held the highest office the people of Virginia could grant and who now was seemingly intent on covering himself with shame in a desperate effort to stave off defeat by the Democratic nominee, Senator Thomas Jefferson Shadwell. Brock had made serious charges against Senator Shadwell, and he had caused his agents to make others even more serious; there was every reason to believe that more were on the way. Putnam himself did not propose to aid Brock's forces at their slanderous work by repeating the charges one by one. Suffice to say that they impugned every facet of Shadwell's character: his intelligence, his integrity, his manhood, and the present and future health of his immortal soul.

As an American, a Virginian, and a public official, Senator C. Rodgers Putnam was deeply grieved that Miles Brock should himself utter and cause to be uttered in his name such pathetically palpable untruths and by so doing besmirch the name of a man who had shown himself to be a loving husband and father, devout and active churchman, able and incorruptible public servant. . . .

Mac watched the reporters to see how it was going over. The reporter for Richmond's morning paper sat with his legs crossed on an equipment locker, his long gray face properly judicious as he studied the printed text, marking corrections with a Bic pen. Beside him sat his colleague from the afternoon paper, a great stone idol of a man, arms crossed on his chest, face impassive, jaws methodically chewing gum. Hackett, busy with stop watch, was intent on getting a sound segment of the proper length, and his face showed neither thought nor comprehension. Beside him crouched the AP bureau chief, natty in three-piece shagreen, taking notes furiously, intent on filing his lead ahead of UPI, whose representative, a sebaceous youth with a wispy beard, leaned nonchalantly against the wall.

A young black man, representing a Roanoke TV station, seemed absorbed by Putnam's performance; his face periodically showed the ghost of a grin, as of a connoisseur appreciating a particularly fine performance. Next to him was a blond young man, representing a Richmond radio station, who seemed lost, like a man who has come in the middle of a complicated ritual and cannot find his place. At the back of the room was Nell Weld, the political correspondent of the Washington *Post,* who had come down because Putnam was from northern Virginia: a sage-looking middle-aged woman in severe gray tailored tweeds. Beside her crouched a fat young man whom Mac did not recognize, dressed in a khaki uniform shirt and a flashy tie, eyes bulging behind thick round gold glasses.

Putnam finished his statement, and the room became a tangle of arms and hands, voices clamoring for recognition. They seemed today a bit more rapacious than usual; a bad sign, Mac thought.

Putnam recognized the lean, judicious mullet player from Richmond's morning paper, who regarded him over semicircular reading glasses. "Senator," he said in a speculative drawl, "was it your own idea to come down here today, or were you asked to come by Senator Shadwell?"

Putnam shot him a faintly disappointed look, like an exacting schoolteacher reproving a slow pupil. "Sir, as you know, I am an announced supporter of Senator Shadwell. The statement in your hand is printed on Shadwell campaign stationery, and Mr. Evans here is a member of the Shadwell campaign staff. I think you can draw your own conclusions." He pointed at the UPI reporter, who was tugging at his wispy beard as he gestured urgently with his free hand. "Yes, sir?"

"Do you think these charges are hurting the Shadwell campaign?" the young man asked.

"They are certainly not designed to help us," Putnam said. "But I do believe the people of Virginia will see them for what they are and ignore them ."

"Senator!" Hackett's deep television bass cut through the air like a sonic boom. He signaled his cameraman; the lights came back on. The sound camera was turning.

"What about Governor Brock's charges that Shadwell is an advocate of socialist-style government?"

"Hogwash," Putnam said. His mouth closed like a falling window sash.

Hackett waited, camera grinding, for Putnam to say more. After a few

310

seconds he gave up and said, "But isn't it a fact that Shadwell favors big-government programs and a planned economy?"

Putnam was playing it beautifully, Mac thought, turning Hackett's sound camera around on him. Now he said briskly, "Mr. Hackett, Tom Jeff Shadwell stands for the right of ordinary people to make an honest living and pay their fair share of taxes. If there is an advocate of big government in this campaign, it is the Republican candidate, who stands for the interests of big business and big contributors."

Hackett would not give an inch. "But hasn't Shadwell accepted the support of big labor and the out-of-state union bosses?"

Mac saw Putnam glance away from the camera. It was too bad; on TV he might appear shifty or uncertain. "Senator Shadwell has labor support, and I personally hope he gets more. I think working people recognize that Tom Jeff Shadwell is working to make jobs, to insure all of our people a fair break in state services, to end the food tax, which is inherently unfair to the ordinary wage earner, and to curb abuses by the giant utilities and the insurance companies which are costing the taxpayers millions every year. I think that is why the unions have supported him."

"What about Governor Brock's charges that Shadwell has made a deal with union bosses to sabotage Virginia's Right-to-Work Law?"

"Once again, Mr. Hackett, that is hogwash."

Hackett seemed prepared to pursue the subject further, but the AP reporter turned and spoke toward his boom microphone: "Can it, Ed." The camera ground to a halt. Mac wondered why Hackett was being so aggressive.

"Do you think Shadwell has peaked too soon, Senator?" the AP writer now asked, still balanced in his sprinter's crouch.

"I do not think Senator Shadwell has peaked at all," Putnam said. "I believe he is still drawing away from his opponent and will continue to do so."

"Is it true that Shadwell's polls show Brock only two points behind?" the *Post* writer asked.

"I know of no such poll, Nell," Putnam said.

"Perhaps young Mr. Evans here can answer that," the morning paper correspondent said, with a flick of his shoulder at Mac. All heads turned toward him.

"It is not true, Nell," Mac said.

"What do they show, then?" she asked.

"I can't make any comment on that," Mac said.

"Do they show Shadwell ahead of Brock?" she persisted.

"No comment," Mac said.

"Come on, Mac," said Hackett in an exasperated boom. "What's the big secret?"

"This is Senator Putnam's press conference," Mac said. "Don't waste his time on me."

But there were no further questions for Putnam, and the press conference dissolved lunchward.

Ed Hackett bustled toward the door, but the fat young man in the khaki shirt stopped him. "What are you doing, Ed?" he asked. "Auditioning for the *Fulton Lewis TV Hour?*"

"Oh, come on, Pete," Hackett replied with a smile as bright as his bow-tie. "You know me. I'm just trying to get good TV!"

The young man shook his head at Hackett's retreating form. "The sad thing is, it's true," he said to Mac. "We haven't met. I'm Peter Grasp, from the *Sentinel.*"

"Oh, yes," Mac said. "Peter T. Grasp. Huntington told me about you. I've read your stuff, it's pretty good."

Grasp's pudgy face beamed. "Thanks," he said. "I'm having a good time. It's a little like shooting at a B-52 with a bow and arrow, but it's good for the soul."

"The Vietnamese used to shoot down helicopters with bows and arrows," Mac said. "Keep it up."

Putnam came up to Mac. "Senator," Mac said, "do you know Peter Grasp, boy crusader? He works for Gravelier Huntington's paper, the *Sentinel.*"

"Hello, Mr. Grasp," Putnam said.

"We've met before," Grasp said. "I came up and interviewed you at your house about three months ago."

"I remember it well," Putnam said impassively. "As I recall, you ate all the jelly eggs in the bowl on my desk."

Grasp's fat face flushed, and he busied himself polishing his glasses on the gaudy necktie. "I skipped my breakfast to get there on time," he said.

"I suppose jelly eggs are an acceptable form of press subsidy," Putnam said. "Nice to see you again."

"So long," Mac said. Then he had a thought. "Are you going to the party tonight?"

"The anniversary thing?" Grasp said. "I sure am. It's a command performance for the staff."

"See you there then."

* * *

312

Mac had hoped Putnam would take him to lunch; he imagined the senator's taste in restaurants would be expensive and good. But Putnam professed himself tired and went back to the George Mason to shower and change for the drive home. As they parted, he gave Mac a cool but personable handshake, suitable for thanking a talented underling. Mac bought a W-T Burger at the White Tower on Tenth Street, then walked back to the headquarters.

The afternoon crawled by, a welter of minutiae. Mac was working on two speeches for the next week, and in addition Ralph Bova had asked him to review the invitation list of a fund-raising party for the upcoming weekend and suggest volunteers to help serve refreshments. Knocko was in Norfolk with Ed O'Brien for a COPE strategy session: every inquiry that would have come to Cheatham ended up on Mac's desk. Although he lacked authority to decide them, he could advise on whether the matter was worth calling Knocko long distance.

Lola Kreznik, meanwhile, had worked herself into a blind rage at Danny Watkins; the press secretary, with characteristic tact, had responded by calling her a "dumb kneejerk liberal broad." Mac had difficulty preventing her from bashing Watkins with her loose-leaf notebook and storming out of the headquarters, never to return.

By four o'clock Mac's head throbbed; though he was the youngest member of the staff, he felt like a combination slave overseer and playground monitor. Alexandra's phone call, when it came, seemed like one more annoyance.

"Is this my demon lover?" her voice said from the phone.

"Who—what?" Mac said, momentarily disoriented. Then he recognized the allusion. "Oh, hi, Alexandra," he said.

"How are you doing?" she said.

Mac wondered if she had called to chat; she had never called him at the headquarters before. "Pretty busy," he said. As if to illustrate, he ran his hands over the pile of papers on his desk.

"Too busy to talk?"

Mac realized he might have blundered. "No, no, I have a minute," he said. "What's on your mind?"

She whistled softly into the phone. "Gee, thanks," she said. "I feel like a pharmaceutical salesman or something."

"I'm sorry," he said. "I'm a little rattled. Bad day, you know."

"Sure enough," she said. "I'm having one myself."

"What's wrong?"

"Hell, it's nothing, I guess, I mean, maybe I shouldn't bother you."

313

"No, really, I'm sorry I was obnoxious,'" he said quickly. "Is everything okay?"

"No, not terribly," she said. "I had a rough time at school. The principal is really on my back about this field trip."

"What field trip?"

"Don't you remember, I told you about it, I wanted to take my kids to see some of the battlefields?"

"Of course," said Mac, not remembering at all.

She went on to recount her troubles with the bureaucracy. Mac fidgeted with his papers, only half listening. "Plus," she finished, "I'm overdrawn at the damn bank and I came home and there was a letter from Willie."

Mac thought of Willie's long, lean face, of his pinwheeling, unreadable eyes. "Bad news?"

"Not exactly," she said. "It's just confusing."

"How so?"

"He wants to come down here and stay with me, or so he says, anyway, and I guess I have to decide how I feel about things, I mean get things worked out."

Mac felt a quick stab of panic in his stomach. He did not want to decide things or be called on to work anything out. He had looked to her as an escape from pressures and decisions; he did not want to face them here, too.

"We ought to talk about it, I guess," he said hesitantly.

"No kidding," she said.

"You're still planning to go to this party with me tonight, aren't you?"

"Yeah," she said.

"We can talk about it there."

"Meaning you're too busy now?"

"Oh, you know," he said vaguely. "It's hard. I'm distracted here."

"I don't suppose you could get away early?" she said. "It'd be kind of a nice change to see you in the daylight."

"Gee, I'd really like to," he said, with a careful note of sincerity in his voice. "But I'm stacked up like the devil here, and Knocko's out of town and Lola and Danny are fighting—"

"I get it," she said. "We'll talk tonight."

"Right," he said quickly. "Definitely tonight."

But as it turned out, Mac was not ready for decisions even by party time. The stab of panic had become a full-scale throb of fear and indecision by the time Alexandra came by to pick him up. She was, he thought, looking very lovely, in a long blue cotton dress cut low to show off the

314

tanned tops of her breasts. She accepted his compliment noncommittally; they rode in silence to the party, which was being held at Huntington's family home, not far from the Evans house.

Mac streaked for the bar. He did not intend to avoid her questions all night, he told himself, just to postpone them for the moment, at least until he could relax with a couple of drinks. She stood at his side, watching him curiously, as he surveyed the party.

It was being held in the backyard. Hoke Spottswood, wearing a tall white chef's hat, was enthusiastically charring hamburgers on a big iron grill, his livid freckles lit from below by the glow of the charcoal. Unseasonable mosquitoes swarmed around the bar. The guests stood between two carefully tended sourwood trees, drinking from plastic cocktail glasses and slapping absently at their arms.

The party was designed to build goodwill for Huntington's paper, the *Sentinel*; it marked its fourth anniversary. Huntington continued to cultivate the paper and pour large amounts of cash into it. Mac had long suspected that his old classmate hoped to use it as the beginning of a political career. It was a slickly produced, splashy sheet, given to periodic exposés of the Opechancanough County sheriff's department, violent attacks on Miles Brock, pages of shopping tips, and gleefully derisive stories about beauty pageants and meetings of the Richmond City Council.

Many of those invited to the party were wealthy liberals, actual or potential investors in the paper, and among them were merchants who might advertise, ad agency personnel, and corporate public relations people.

Mac at once became pleasantly tight and wandered among the guests shaking hands and exchanging bits of conversation, which he remembered in a senseless string of phrases spoken and overheard:

"—gaining on Shadwell—"

"—like *New York* magazine but not so flashy—"

"—most expensive election ever—"

"—aimed at the typical young couple in the Fan—"

"—good basketball team this year—"

"—don't always agree, but by God, this town needs another paper—"

"—appreciate all you've done for us—"

"—did some damage with this busing issue—"

"—remember your brother very well—"

"—understand he's raised over one million—"

"—never finished law school—"

"—beautiful girl in the blue dress—"

The evening seemed enchanted, and Mac wished it would never end, although he admitted to himself that the party was not so wonderful. It was simply that he wished to avoid making decisions. But the party began to thin out, and at length he came back to Alexandra and said, "Let's go over here and get out of the noise."

He took her by the arm and led her across the yard, toward an alcove sheltered from view by two large shrubs, with a stone bench, where they could talk privately. Mac, a little tipsy, walked with head high, feeling himself somehow like a nobleman walking to the gallows.

But when they came to the bench, they found the fat reporter, Peter Grasp. He was lying full-length on the bench, with a cocktail glass on his hand. Seated on the grass beside him was a tall young woman with long brown hair and an elegant thin body.

"Hail, Evans," Grasp said, waving his glass. "More refugees from the sticky love feast."

Alexandra bucked in his grasp, as if to leave, but Mac, feeling somehow rescued, held her firmly. "Hello, Peter," he said. "I wondered where you were."

"We are the staff," said the young woman in soft, ironic tones. "We don't feel at ease with the truly important people."

"You'll love us, then," Mac said. "We're truly unimportant."

Introductions all around were, of course, then in order. The thin woman was named Irene. Mac reasoned that it would be rude to walk away quickly, so he sat on the grass. Alexandra reluctantly sat beside him.

They fell to chatting. Peter, it developed, was a graduate of Columbia, and though a few years younger than Mac, he was also a graduate of the radical movement, and he knew its attendant mythos well. He was a fund of trivia: names, demonstrations, slogans, demands. Mac felt himself carried back to his senior year, those heady days when he had felt himself at one with the world revolution.

"Do you remember the chants?" Peter said, his pudgy features alight. "I know all of them."

Quietly he began:

> Hey, hey, LBJ, how many kids did you kill today?

Then, a bit louder:

> GE-er, profiteer, keeps the people down,
> Warmaker, strikebreaker, run him out of town!

And with even more feeling:

> Chairman Mao, live like him!
> Dare to struggle, dare to win!

"This one's my favorite," he said, now in a true frenzy, and leaped up from the bench, face contorted like a baby's, beating his arms in the air, chanting:

> Viet-nam is winning!
> And that's just the beginning!
> We'll win in Guatemala!
> The U.S. goes tomorrow!

Mac was delighted; he joined in for the familiar chorus:

POWER—POWER—POWER TO THE PEOPLE!

But before they could finish, the boxwood bush behind them began shaking indignantly, and after a moment's struggle Huntington burst into the clearing, tie and collar askew, shirttail out. "What the hell are you trying to do?" he asked Peter. "These are very important advertisers and investors here. Do you want them to think we're running a nest of communists?"

"Heavens, no," Irene said, still with the haughty tone. "Never that."

"Why don't you all come out of hiding and give me a hand here?" Huntington said.

"Why, certainly," she said. "Would you like me to serve drinks? Or perhaps entertain with an exotic dance?"

"Don't try yourself," Huntington said. The two reporters shambled reluctantly back toward the party. Huntington looked at Mac and remarked vaguely, "Those two—those two—they'll push me too far some day." Then he left them alone.

But it seemed the time for talking had past. Alexandra was wrapped in an angry fog. Mac tried to get her attention; he was sobering up, and suddenly felt tired and lonely. If she wanted a decision, then perhaps he could make one.

But she would not listen. "I've got to get home," she said. "School tomorrow. Do you want a ride?"

"Come on, Alexandra," he said. "I'm sorry—"

"I think maybe you and that fat guy should run home through the street with sticks and rocks, like the Weathermen," she said.

"West End Weathermen," he said, with an ironic smile. But she would not respond. "All right," he said. "Let's go."

She would not speak on the way home. When she let him out, she said, "I think maybe I'm going to have to decide things for myself, without any help."

"I'm sorry about tonight—"

She massaged her temples wearily. "It's all right," she said. "You're busy and all the rest of it. When you have some time free to talk about it, call me."

"We could talk about it now."

She waved one hand at him. "Not now, Mac," she said. "I'm a little tired of you right now."

"All right, fine," he said, angry himself. He jumped out of the car. "See you later," he said and closed the door.

In the hour before dawn, Mac was awakened by the buzzer. He had been dreaming of Alexandra; as he stumbled to the phone, he felt somehow certain it was she, and he felt pleased and relieved that she had called, that all was not lost. But it was not her voice, but that of an indifferent Western Union operator, who read the following telegram, addressed to him:

YOUR FATHER JOSHUA TUTELO EVANS GIVEN REFUGE IN US EMBASSY AND WILL BE EVACUATED ON EMBASSY FLIGHT TO MIAMI ETA NOON TOMORROW STOP AS NEXT OF KIN PLEASE MAKE ARRANGEMENTS FOR TRAVEL FROM THAT POINT STOP JONAS CATESBY US VICE-CONSUL.

THREE

★

Mac was waiting in the airport at twilight the next day. He had spent the morning on the telephone, making arrangements with a travel agent to meet the embassy flight, see to his father's comfort, and get him to a plane for Richmond. The agent had called back in the early afternoon: the Colonel was safely aboard, and the airline would see that he made his connection in Atlanta to a plane for Richmond. That was due very soon, and Mac was sitting in a hard plastic seat apparently designed for chimpanzees, wondering what to expect.

It was as if he had inherited Lester's memory, for somehow he found himself imagining not the pale shadow he remembered from his own childhood, but the mighty warrior of Lester's recollection: a tall man in a white suit, erect and fearless, who had spoken from the courthouse steps and called down God's wrath on the faithless mighty. The notion made him embarrassed before himself. He checked his watch and looked at the airport clocks. One, above the entrance marked SOUTH CONCOURSE, seemed to have stopped midway between 2:39 and 2:40. The other agreed with Mac's watch. His father's plane was ten minutes late.

He rose and walked into the back hall of the terminal, to the row of ticket counters and car rental booths. The listings board had been changed; his father's flight was now marked DELAYED.

"Excuse me," he said to the man behind the counter, who was leaning forward, arms folded on the counter. He was dressed in shirt sleeves and thin black knit tie; pulled low across his forehead was a black peaked pilot's cap, with a round airline emblem where the pilot's wings would have gone. The man inclined his head toward Mac but did not speak. He raised his eyebrows to signify partial attention. "The flight from Atlanta," Mac said. "How late do you expect it to be?"

The man's head lazily turned toward the arrival board, as if to verify that such a flight existed. He remained in his careless pose, flung forward against the counter as if frozen there in the midst of performing some acrobatic trick. "Sorry, sir, we don't know just yet," he said. "Otherwise we would post the information."

"Can you tell me if the plane has left Atlanta?"

"Yes, sir," the man said. "It's been delayed in flight, and we're expecting a report on it very soon."

"Then is there any way for me to check and be sure a passenger got aboard in Atlanta?"

"What, do you mean a specific passenger?" asked the man, unmoving.

"That's right."

"No, I'm afraid we don't have that information."

"Who does have it?"

"Sir, we couldn't give it out even if we had it. Airline regulations."

Mac nodded. He found himself seized with a desire to make the man move from his careless pose, by whatever means necessary. His face wide-eyed, innocent, he pointed at the peaked cap. "Gee, are you really a pilot?" he asked in awed tones.

The man coughed nervously. "No, I'm not," he said.

"In training?"

"No," the man said curtly.

"Golly, too bad. What was it, bad eyes?"

The man stood up and began busily shuffling papers on the counter. "We'll be making an announcement as soon as we know anything about your flight."

"Thank you," Mac said, victorious. He walked away.

In the airport gift shop was a sign: CRAFTS OF VIRGINIA. Under it, Mac was offered his choice of pens, lapel buttons, mugs, flags, T-shirts, neckties, and wall plaques, all emblazoned with a red heart and, in white, the slogan: VIRGINIA IS FOR LOVERS. Mac opted for the Washington *Post* and went back to his chimpanzee chair.

The front page of the *Post* was dominated by news of the revolution in South America from which his father was fleeing. Reports were vague and fragmentary. The president was dead, allegedly a suicide. Others denied this claim and accused the army of murder. The presidential palace had been bombed, attacked by rockets, breached by tanks. The military had assumed all power and declared a state of siege, dissolved the legislature, imposed strict press censorship, and proclaimed a curfew. Mass roundups of the dead leader's supporters were under way; extraordinary powers had been given to police and soldiers, and a soccer stadium in the capital had been placed at their disposal for mass detentions. There were unconfirmed reports of drumhead courts-martial, summary executions, wanton shooting. Witnesses claimed to have seen headless bodies floating downriver; there were denials. Other rumors hinted at renewed fighting, civil war. A loyal general was said to be leading resistance in the interior, his forces at division strength or above. There were crisp denials. Refugees in neutral embassies charged U.S. involvement in the planning of the coup. There were heated denials.

Mac studied the pictures: the smoking, ruined palace, the files of tanks. Inset was a picture of the dead man: a fleshy, square-jawed face, with dark spectacle rims above a small prideful mustache. Next to it was a blurred photo of the general who had led the coup. All that could be seen was a protuberant nose and a peaked cap worn low—precisely, in fact, at the angle of the ticket seller's pilot's cap. Mac gaped in surprise. He had known nothing of this, he had heard no warnings that it impended. He had thought his father safely ensconced in quiet exile, facing only the Pacific Ocean and death. How had Mac let reality get away from him, until it could explode into chaos and butchery without the slightest warning? How had his father wandered into the midst of it—hadn't he been living miles from the capital, in a sleepy fishing village named Puerto Morelos? Why had he needed rescue, sanctuary, evacuation?

Mac glanced down the page: BUSING "ISSUE" DOMINATES VA. CAMPAIGN, read the headline. There were photos of Tom Jeff and Miles Brock and a story by Nell Weld, the *Post*'s Virginia political writer.

With only four weeks left until the election, the potentially explosive issue of court-ordered busing of school children for purposes of integration has come to dominate the hotly contested race for the governorship of Virginia.

The busing issue has become crucial even though supporters of both candidates—liberal State Senator Thomas Jefferson Shadwell, the Democratic nominee, and conservative former Governor Miles J. Brock, a former Democrat now turned Republican—admit that there is almost nothing the governor of Virginia can do to affect current court-ordered busing programs.

321

Brock, whose well-financed campaign appeared to be faltering earlier in the fall, has now begun a massive "blitz" of television, radio, and newspaper advertisements designed to link Shadwell with the highly unpopular busing orders.

And in the past two weeks, Brock has drawn cheers from audiences in Virginia's conservative Southside by proclaiming the gubernatorial election "a referendum on liberal utopian busing schemes."

Brock further claims that a Republican vote next month will "send a message to Washington and the courts that our children here in Virginia will not be used as pawns in a game of sociological chess."

Shadwell publicly dismisses the busing issue as "a load of phony baloney." The colorful Democrat, a self-avowed "populist," says that the real issue of the campaign is his plan to abolish the state's four percent sales tax on food and nonprescription drugs.

Shadwell strategists, however, admit privately that Brock's latest charges have slowed the momentum of their campaign. Some observers feel that Brock may be cutting into Shadwell's lead, which only three weeks ago was conceded by both sides to be substantial.

Mac looked up. Against the wall was a row of black plastic seats with small pay-TV sets built into the arms. A florid, bored businessman was slumped in one of them; he had spent a quarter to buy himself the evening news. Mac could hear Ed Hackett's voice indistinctly intoning the latest reports. What "Shadwell strategist" would admit that Brock was putting them on the defensive? Surely not Knocko; Mac's boss did not recognize the idea of defensiveness. Ralph Bova, perhaps: he might be trying to turn the campaign away from the food tax issue, to convince Tom Jeff to go after the "Carrington vote," if such a thing existed.

Mac sat up, and his back fetched painfully against the upper lip of the chimp chair. The announcement was repeated over the anechoic public address system; "Flight Six Twenty-two from Atlanta has arrived and will be landing shortly at Gate Six on the North Concourse."

He threw down the paper; he found himself short of breath, and his heart was pounding; he had felt like this at Harvard, waiting for the police to arrive. His father would be landing soon.

But at first it seemed that there had been a mistake. The plane landed and emptied of passengers: business executives, faces glowing from their inflight cocktails, and shaggy young people, carrying backpacks—the two classes which can fly, the young and those on expense accounts. There was no old man, no one who could have been his father, warrior or shadow. Mac had visions of his father abandoned in the Atlanta airport.

But then through the plate glass windows he saw the plane extrude a long ramp from its tail. Down it passed stewardesses and a man in flight attendant's uniform. They walked slowly, and Mac at first thought they

322

were carrying something between them. It was not until they reached the pavement that Mac saw that they were wheeling another person in a chair, bundled and indistinct. Then a breathy voice whispered his name directly in his ear, or so it seemed; but when he whirled, he realized it was the PA, whispering, "Mr. MacIlwain K. Evans, please come to Gate Six. Mr. Evans, please come to Gate Six." Mac realized they were wheeling in his father.

As the wheelchair passed through the terminal doors, Mac saw him, and he was neither ghost nor warrior, but a gaunt old man, shrunken inside a blanket, with pale white hair and two days' growth of gray tufted whiskers, wearing on his head a blue wool watch cap much too large for him, looking through steel-rimmed spectacles with tired red eyes in a drawn pale face, his long features collapsed on themselves, the stubbly cheeks drawn tight over his jaw. Mac could not move or speak. This shrunken gray person was his father, a tired old man.

Mac stood paralyzed until one of the stewardesses came up to him. "Are you Mr. Evans?" she said, and Mac nodded. He knelt by the chair and looked at his father. "Colonel?" he asked hesitantly. "Father? Are you all right?"

The old man's eyes turned slowly toward him. Then his voice, miraculously as Mac remembered it, cultivated and polite, but now with a hint of effort in the words: "Mac? Is that you, son?"

He nodded.

"Yes," his father said softly. "I'm all right." An arm emerged from the blanket and gestured toward the airline people. "These ladies have been kind. But I find I am very tired. Have you a car?"

"Yes, sir," Mac said. "I'll drive you home."

"Thank you, son." The arm huddled back under the blanket.

Mac looked at the stewardess behind the shell chair. She was blond, and he noticed a network of fine wrinkles at the corners of her eyes. Her nameplate read "Mrs. White."

"Will you stay with him while I get the car?"

She nodded. "Yes, of course."

"Fine," Mac said. "I have to make a call, too. I'll meet you in front."

On his way out, Mac stepped into a round glass phone booth and called Molly O. "He's here," he said. "Will you call your uncle Harry and ask him to meet us at the house?"

"Why?" Molly O. asked. "Is he sick?"

"I don't think so," Mac said carefully. "I just think he's tired, and I'd like to be sure he's all right." He could not say to her what he really thought: that he had looked into his father's face like a man who discovers he can read a foreign language. He had read death in his father's face. "Listen, O., I'll talk to you when we get there," he said, and went to get the car.

Molly O.'s uncle, Harry Randolph, was a pale man, with fine, clear skin, thin hair, and thin lips. In his private life he was almost reclusive, a stamp collector and connoisseur of Civil War relics, who shunned parties and spoke little. But as a doctor he was brisk and self-assured. He wasted no time getting Mac's father into bed, commandeering a pair of Mac's pajamas. The old man did not resist. He was tired; on the way home in Mac's big car he had spoken only once. As they turned onto the interstate, he had asked, "What is this?"

Mac had marveled again at his father's voice: its clear, firm tone and aristocratic Piedmont drawl. "It's a Lincoln Continental," Mac said, feeling a moment's proprietary pride in the sleek rich car.

"No, son," the Colonel had said. "I mean this highway."

Mac was chagrined. "Oh," he said. "This is Interstate Sixty-four. It was built only a few years ago."

"Ah," his father said, and did not speak again until they entered the driveway of the big house. Then he looked into the square gray facade, the white pillars and the veranda, and shook his head gently like a man waking from a dream.

"It's still here," he said.

"Yes," Mac replied, and in that moment the fact amazed him, too.

They went inside, his father leaning on Mac's arm. Harry Randolph took charge, slowly helping the old man upstairs and bundling him into the four-poster bed, the master bed, which had been there when he left twenty years earlier.

Mac and Molly O. waited in the front room. It was dark outside, and a gusty October wind was blowing. The trees rattled their branches against the windows, and rain began falling. Molly O. expertly built a fire in the fireplace. Mac poured himself a glass of bourbon; Molly O. drank wine. After half an hour, when the rain was pouring and the fire was blazing, Harry Randolph came down, carrying his black satchel and his professional face. Molly O. gave him a drink and he sat before the fire.

"He's sleeping now, or will be," he said. "I gave him a very mild sedative. On the whole I'd say he's come through it pretty well, for a man of his age. If the papers are to be believed, this was a pretty bloody situation down there, as I suppose these things have to be. I gather he was quite lucky to get to the American embassy with no problems.

"Now I'm sure you understand this is all relative. He is an old man, and he has had a great shock. On top of that, he has a history of some heart trouble. From what I gather, he has had episodes of angina over the past two or three years, and perhaps even some arrhythmia, although it's hard for me to be sure about that because he's not entirely sure about it, and of course his records are unavailable." He smiled a thin-lipped, rueful smile.

"From what he says, it seems he did have one of these episodes yesterday, and I questioned him rather closely on it. He says it was quite mild, and he took the nitroglycerin pill which his doctor down there had prescribed, which is just right, by the way, and the pain passed. His heart sounds all right now, for the moment, anyway."

He drained his glass and held it out to Molly O. She mixed another drink and handed it back. "But although there is no real crisis, he is exhausted, and he's had a shock. He's in a very emotional state, and unless he rests up and calms down, I can't rule out the possibility of a heart attack of some kind, and even a small attack would be very dangerous for a man of his age. I did suggest to him a few days in a hospital, just to be on the safe side, but the idea seems to upset him terribly, which is what we are trying to avoid, so I dropped it. If he would rest better here, then that's where he should be."

He turned to Molly O. "Mary Owen, I imagine you'll be seeing to him."

"No, I will," Mac said.

Both of them turned to him in some surprise. "Molly O. has her job," Mac said. "He's my father, and I'll take care of him until—while he's recovering."

"Ah?" Dr. Randolph said, delicately. "I thought you had . . . political responsibilities, Mac."

"I have family responsibilities too," Mac said. Then, because he could not resist twisting the knife, he added, "Anyway, things are going so well Tom Jeff won't need me to win."

The doctor looked shyly into his glass, rolling it between his hands in embarrassment. Behind him Mac saw Molly O. lift a hand to conceal her mischievous grin.

"Ah, be that as it may," Harry Randolph said. "I think you'd be wise to get a nurse, for a few days or weeks, to see to his meals and medication and so on. He has his nitroglycerin tablets in case of another angina episode, and I'm prescribing a new drug which I imagine his doctors down there didn't know about. It's also a nitrate compound, but long-lasting, so I want him to take it four times a day. If you like, I'll stop by the pharmacy and have them run it out here."

Mac nodded. "That would be very thoughtful," he said. "Can you arrange for the nurse, too?"

"I don't see why not," the doctor said. "In fact, I can try to get hold of someone tonight. But let me finish with this. I don't want him to have any exercise. He can come downstairs once a day, no more, and I want him to spend most of his time in bed, for the next few days, at least. I'll prescribe a sedative, too. I want him to have plenty of sleep."

"What about visitors?" Mac asked.

"Gracious, yes," Randolph said. "If you mean his friends, people he knows, yes. But no press, no politics, no speechifying, not until he's stronger. I'm very serious about that."

"You don't have to worry about that," Mac said.

"All right," Harry Randolph said. He stood up to go. "I'll get by every day or so, and the nurse will be here. You two call me if there's any problem."

Molly O. brought him his coat; he rewarded her with a brief avuncular kiss. "Good-bye, Mary Owen," he said.

"Thank you for coming," Mac said as they shook hands.

"Nothing, nothing," Harry Randolph said with his thin smile. "In a way he's family, I guess, and besides, he's a pretty illustrious patient to have. Good night."

After he left, Molly O. looked at Mac, the mischievous grin again playing across her face. "Mac, you're so mean," she chided him gently. "Why do you want to pick on poor old Uncle Harry?"

"Poor Uncle Harry, my ass," Mac snorted.

"All right for you, Mac," she said. "You want something to eat?"

"Yes," Mac said, a little surprised to find himself hungry. "Let me go make a phone call."

Rain was drumming at the window of the little back room. Mac dialed headquarters and got Knocko.

"I won't be in for a while," he said quickly, hoping to forestall an argument, "my dad's pretty sick."

"What are you talking about?" Knocko replied. "Not coming in? Buster, we need you down here—did you see that piece of shit in the *Post*? We got problems down here."

"Knocko, it's my father," Mac began.

"Yeah, and I guess if you hang around there, you can cure him by the laying on of hands."

"Jesus, Knocko, will you cut it out?"

"How about in the afternoons?"

Mac sighed. "Is Tom Jeff there?"

"He's here somewhere," Knocko said. "But he's busy."

"Busy doing what?"

"I'm not sure—"

326

"Tell him I need to talk to him, will you?"

There was a brusque click as Knocko shifted the call to "hold." After a minute, Shadwell came on, sounding a bit irritated. "Mac, is that you?" he said. "You've got Cousin Knocko all in a snit. What's all this striving after wind?"

Mac quickly explained the situation. At once Tom Jeff's voice changed. "You stay with your daddy," he said. "Don't worry about a thing until he's out of danger. Isn't anything more important than that."

"Thanks, Governor," Mac said.

Tom Jeff laughed. "Don't get ahead of yourself," he said. "These folks at the Washington *Post* don't think I'm going to be governor. But you tell your daddy I said hello, and tell him I said I'm glad he's back."

"Will do," Mac said.

There was a pause; Mac heard Knocko's voice in the background. "Knocko says he needs to talk to you again," Tom Jeff said.

"No time right now," Mac said quickly. "I hear my father calling. Tell him I'll call him tomorrow."

"Bye now."

Mac went off to eat with Molly O.

The next morning was splendid, as if Virginia were putting on a display for the Colonel's return. The air was crisp and clean, the sky was cloudless, the temperature mild. The nurse arrived early, a fleshy, friendly woman named Miss Ross. She settled her round suitcase in a bedroom and went instantly to work fixing the Colonel's breakfast. While his father ate, Mac drove the Continental to a men's store at Willow Lawn and bought pajamas, slippers, and a dark silk bathrobe; the Colonel had come home with empty hands.

In the late morning, with Mac at his elbow and the nurse looking on anxiously, the Colonel paced laboriously down the big stairway and out to the veranda. The rest seemed to have done him good; his face was no longer so pale, and his eyes seemed brighter. He had borrowed Mac's electric razor, and his hair was neatly combed. Inside Mac a cautious hope stirred; perhaps he had been tricked, perhaps death's hand had not touched his father. Mac was no prophet, he could not tell.

They settled themselves around the table on the terrace. Miss Ross brought a pot of tea and seemed determined to stay and drink it with them. Mac drew her aside and whispered, "Excuse me, Miss Ross, but I haven't seen my father in twenty years. I wonder if—ah—" And being politely bred, he found himself simply coughing and rotating his eyes toward the house.

327

She gave him a vague but benign look. Mac wondered if Harry Randolph had had time to brief her on the patient. "Yes, of course," she said. "I didn't realize. I'll be inside if you need me."

The Colonel took milk and sugar. Mac's tongue flew inside his mouth like a moth trapped in a streetlight. "Did you sleep well?" he asked at last.

"Yes, thank you, son, I did." The Colonel set down the china cup in the saucer and wiped his mouth. About both his speech and his movements there was a thrifty precision his son suddenly found entirely admirable. "I had forgotten what a comfortable bed that is." He picked up his cup and looked into it, as if reading leaves. From deep in his throat came an exclamation: the smallest, driest of laughs. "Perhaps that's because when last I slept there it was not so comfortable."

His father turned to him, his eyes sharp over the small steel spectacle rims. "Do you hear from your mother?" he said.

"No, not often," Mac said. "I saw her—ah—two years ago."

"At your brother's funeral, I presume?"

"Yes."

His father fidgeted with the robe. It was a dull, rich blue. But beneath it the pajamas were snowy and dazzling; once again, the Colonel's son had clad him in white. "Yes, yes," his father said. "I was sorry to miss that. My doctor in Puerto Morelos, you know, assured me that the trip would kill me." Again came that ironic, nearly inaudible laugh. "Apparently he was wrong."

Mac hastily poured more tea.

"The truth is, son," the Colonel continued in his cultured, exact voice, "I never expected to see this place again. I thought I'd left it forever."

"Ah," Mac said, his tongue leaping about again. He brought it to heel. "I'm—ah—I'm glad you're back."

"You're very kind, son," his father said. "Most young people would resent having an invalid parent dropped on them from the sky, I imagine, disrupting their lives."

Mac thought briefly of Alexandra. *Who has a life?* he thought.

"So she came to the funeral, did she?"

"Who?" Mac was still thinking of Alexandra. He would call her if he got the time.

"Your mother," the Colonel said casually.

"Yes."

"Did she have her aeronautical Slav in tow?"

"Why, no," Mac said. He was embarrassed by his father's jealousy. "Emil doesn't travel anymore. He's Hungarian, actually."

His father waved an impatient hand to indicate that he knew that perfectly well. "That's a lovely dogwood," he said, nodding at the young tree by the entrance to the driveway.

"Yes, very nice," Mac agreed hastily. "You should see it in bloom."

"I hope I shall," his father said.

"Sure, of course," Mac said. "Molly O. planted it."

"I rather suspected as much," his father said. "Neither of my sons seems to have turned out to be the tree-planting type."

There was a silence.

"Son, there's a favor I want you to do for me," the Colonel said, sitting suddenly erect in the chair.

"Yes, of course, what is it?" Mac began idiotically searching his pockets, as if what his father wanted might already be there unrecognized.

"There is a man named Pablo Bahamonde Sánchez, a Catholic priest. He's a Paraguayan. He saved my life during the fighting, and I was later told he was arrested. I'd like to know. I'd appreciate it very much if you could call these new authorities—call their embassy in Washington, there has probably already been a shift there. As soon as I feel up to it, I'm going to make a protest about the way he was treated."

"Right," Mac said, glad to fall into the role of an aide. He scribbled the name on a scrap of paper. "Sánchez."

"No, son," his father said sharply, then reeled off the name in crisp Spanish. "The full surname is Bahamonde Sánchez." He spelled it out. "Two words."

"Right," Mac said again. "Pablo." He put the paper in his wallet. "How did he save your life?"

There was no answer. Mac looked up. His father had abandoned his erect posture and now slumped in the metal chair, once again a tired old man.

"Are you all right?" Mac asked quickly. "Do you want to go upstairs?"

"No. Not yet." He paused, then spoke, again with an effort. "I enjoy your company, son, but I find that talking tires me. Would you care to read to me?"

"Of course, of course," Mac said.

At his father's direction, Mac haltingly read from *The Tempest*. He made it through the second scene:

> Thou best know'st
> What torment I did find thee in; thy groans
> Did make wolves howl, and penetrate the breasts
> Of ever-angry bears; it was a torment
> To lay upon the damn'd, which Sycorax

329

Could not again undo; it was mine art,
When I arrived and heard thee, that made gape
The pine and let thee out.

His father motioned impatiently for him to stop. "You aren't familiar with this play?" he asked mildly.

Mac shook his head sheepishly.

"You should study Shakespeare, Mac," the Colonel said. "Poetry is a great source of comfort in life. Do you know Spanish?"

"No," Mac said.

"Ah," his father said, and gave a startling melancholy shrug: a gesture imported directly from South America, a graceful Latin sign of resignation. Again the Colonel broke into rapid Spanish. "*Llorando de los ojos, como nunca visteis tal, como la uña de la carne, es el dolor al separar.*" He cocked his head at his son, as if hoping that his recitation might have shattered the barrier of noncomprehension. Mac sadly flashed back at the Colonel his own Latin shrug; his father smiled slightly, as if in recognition.

Miss Ross appeared briskly with lunch and a midday pill. The Colonel asked to be helped upstairs to eat. Mac left him in the bedroom with his tray and went to the study to call the embassy.

After holding for half an hour, he reached a cultured sibilant voice. "May I, ah, help you?" it asked in a broad, melodious tones. "I am Miguel Sanjurjo, acting, ah, consul general."

"Yes," said Mac, who was not totally unschooled in the ways of bureaucrats. "This is MacIlwain K. Evans, special assistant to Senator Shadwell of Virginia."

"Ah, yes?" the voice said on a noncommittal but rising note.

"I've been asked to inquire of your office about a Father Pablo Bahamonde Sanchez, who was arrested in your capital sometime day before yesterday."

"The name once more, please?"

Mac summoned the memory of his father's crisp accent. "Ba-ha-monde Sánchez," he said.

"I see," the voice said. "The Christian name once more, please?"

"Pablo."

"His occupation?" The word was rhymed elegantly with "fashion."

"He is a Catholic priest."

"A priest," the voice said lightly. "May I inquire if this individual is a native of our country?"

"I believe he is not," Mac said. "It's my understanding that he is from Paraguay."

330

"Señor, you will of course understand that since our revolution there has been much, ah, confusion in the capital."

"Surely there are records—"

"Yes, certainly," the voice went on firmly. "All formalities are being strictly observed, and our government has promised to respect, ah, human rights. But it has been necessary for our authorities to detain a number of foreigners who have come to our country for, ah, ulterior motives, if you comprehend."

"But surely a Catholic priest—"

"Subversion takes on many disguises, Señor Evans. Even at times the priest."

"But you will inquire."

"Most assuredly. But as I say, the confusion—there will be a delay, you understand."

"Yes, of course," Mac said. "When may I call you?"

"No, no that will not be necessary," the other said quickly. "For an aide to a senator, it will be a privilege to call you the very moment I receive word. Your number, please?"

Mac gave the home number and area code. "You are not in Washington?"

"No," Mac said. "Senator Shadwell is a candidate for governor of Virginia."

"I see."

They said good-bye with cordial hostility. Mac read *The Tempest* all afternoon while his father slept; no call came.

He and Molly O. had dinner upstairs, with the Colonel; then the two of them watched television while the Colonel slept. Late that night Mac moved his clothes from the little house to the guest bedroom and slept in the room next to his father's.

The next day was still warm; they sat again on the terrace. After a cup of tea the Colonel asked Mac to tell him about Lester. Mac haltingly recounted his brother's career, ending with the speech at the Shad Planking; the Colonel listened, on his face that still intensity Mac had seen in his photographs. When Mac was finished, the Colonel was silent for a moment.

"What a curious young man Lester did turn out to be," he said at last.

Mac tested the phrase. He felt obscurely that he should defend his brother against it, but there was no reasonable way to deny it. "He was a very complicated person," he said.

"Yes, indeed," the Colonel said. "He was always that. I remember him as a little boy. He seemed more like a little grown-up than a child. He

331

was very quiet, and even then nobody was ever quite sure what he was thinking. I've always felt rather guilty about dragging your brother with me around the state like that, making him drive the car and so on. It can't have been a very good experience for him."

Into Mac's mind there flashed suddenly the image of his brother trapped naked under a pier with a seventeen-year-old redhead. He found himself chuckling aloud.

His father looked at him curiously. "Have I amused you?"

Mac hastily composed his features. "No. It's just that Lester told me about that campaign. He remembered it very fondly. It meant a lot to him."

The Colonel did not seem consoled. "Perhaps that's what I meant. I got the boy hooked on politics. I don't imagine that was a favor to him at all."

"I don't know," Mac said. "Lester loved politics. He was good at it, too."

"So I gather," the Colonel said. "But then, he was like the athlete who dies young. 'Smart lad, to slip betimes away, from fields where glory does not stay.'" He looked at his son with wry inquiry. "You do know Housman?"

"Yes, indeed," said Mac, relieved to pass at least this simple test.

"Yes," the Colonel said enigmatically. "Lester never knew the bad side of it. He never lost an election, I believe?"

"No," Mac said.

"I thought not. So he never knew that feeling when old friends desert you and those you trusted betray you. I don't imagine he ever saw a member of his own family cross the street to avoid speaking to him."

"No, I guess not."

"Perhaps he died in time then," the Colonel said. "That seems rather cold, doesn't it? You loved your brother, didn't you?"

Mac nodded.

"Lester was a lucky man," the Colonel said. "A loving brother, a lovely wife. But if he'd lived, if he'd stayed in politics—who knows? he might have lost . . . everything."

There was a silence; both of them were looking inward, at memories the other did not share. After a time the Colonel spoke softly, as if to himself. "You know, son, I was in the House of Delegates for four years. I had a good friend there, a very intelligent and faithful man, his name was—that's unimportant. He used to fight for what was right, and that was no easy task then. He would introduce his bills in committee, and the chairmen would always thank him. They were always very courteous. They'd say something like, 'We'll be glad to give this bill due consideration,' and of course before the session was over, they'd have chopped every one to ribbons. And finally one day when someone told him that his bill would get 'due consideration,' he let all his frustrations out. He reared up, eyes flashing, and he stuck out his finger, and he said, 'Yes, Mr. Chairman, I know the consideration you'll give this bill. It's the consideration of the fisherman for the shad, Mr. Chairman,' he said. 'When the fisherman catches a shad and brings it into the boat, the poor fish flips and flops and tires to escape. And the fisherman speaks so politely to the shad, he says, "Lie still, little shad! I'm not going to hurt you. I'm going to treat you well, I'm not going to do a thing to you except cut your tail off. And I'm not going to do a thing more to you except cut your head off. And after that I'm not going to do a thing to you except cut all your bones out!" 'And he pounded on the committee table and said, 'That's the consideration I expect from you, Mr. Chairman. The shad treatment, Mr. Chairman, the shad treatment! And I may have to take it, but I will fry in hell before I'll say thank you!'

"The shad treatment. We thought it was very witty at the time. It became a sort of catchword, and you know, when I came back from the war, the expression was still in use down at the Capitol, even though my friend had been dead for ten years or so. For all I know they may still use it. But it took me twenty years to realize that it wasn't something that only applied to legislation. It's what happens to people who stay in politics too long. They are dismantled, taken apart, piece by piece. And that's—" His broke voice broke off, so that his son had to complete the sentence silently: *That's what happened to me.*

The wind rustled the trees, and shadows played on the Colonel's pale old face. Squirrels chattered in the treetops, and a few leaves blew unheeded onto his lap robe.

"Father?" Mac said.

"Yes, son."

Mac took a deep breath, like a man about to dive from a high cliff. "You don't have to answer this," he said carefully. "But—well, when you—why did you?" He tried again. "Why did you leave?"

Mac's father stared ahead as if he had not heard. Then, as if waking from a spell, he began brushing at the leaves on his lap: a tired old man dabbing peevishly at himself. "MacIlwain, would you please fetch Miss Ross?" he said hoarsely.

Wordlessly Mac's father hobbled upstairs for lunch and a nap.

That night after dinner Judge Anderson came to visit the Colonel. Mac had wondered earlier why the judge had not been by, but his father had not mentioned it, so Mac had said nothing. Now Anderson seemed nervous. He adjusted his clothes like a bridegroom and did not respond to Mac's political sallies. Mac led him upstairs to the master bedroom. His father was sitting up under the blankets, eyes half-closed. "You have a visitor," Mac said.

The Colonel did not move. "Hello, Kenlow," he said at last.

Anderson ducked his head with a curious bashful motion Mac had never seen him use before. "Hello, Joshua," he said. He sat down stiffly in a chair, hands folded in his lap. Mac stole out the door and left the two old friends alone together, blinking at each other, unmoving as statues in the dim bedroom.

When Anderson came down, he was not loquacious. "What does the doctor say?" he asked.

"Apparently he's had heart trouble, and there's some danger," Mac said. "But he seems to be getting better."

"Better," Anderson said, shaking his head doubtfully. He turned to Molly O. "You take care of him now," he told her sternly.

"Don't tell me," she said. "Tell Mac. He's making me go off to work while he and Miss Ross take care of him."

Anderson looked at Mac as if seeing him for the first time. "That right?" he said. "You mean you've left off crusading—"

"Don't you get on me, too, Judge," Mac said.

Anderson looked at him solicitously. "I wasn't trying to tease you, Mac," he said. "I'm just surprised. Your damn family's always surprising me." He buttoned his coat. "I'd best get home and sleep. I'm an old man, too."

"Come back, Judge," Mac said. "I know he wants to see you again."

The judge shot him an odd questioning glance. "You do, eh? Just how do you know that?" he asked.

Speechless, Mac watched him go.

The next day was cold and rainy, and the Colonel stayed in bed. Mac built a fire and read to him again. This time it was Shakespeare's sonnets, and Mac did better:

> Is it for fear to wet a widow's eye
> That thou consum'st thyself in single life?
> Oh! If thou issueless shalt hap to die,
> The world will wail thee, like a hapless wife;
> The world will be thy widow, and still weep
> That thou no form of thee has left behind,
> When every private widow well may keep
> By children's eyes her husband's shape in mind.

334

He heard his father sigh and looked up to see him gazing out the window, oblivious. After a minute the Colonel turned back to Mac. "I'm sorry, son," he said. "My mind was wandering."

"What were you looking at?" Mac asked.

"Nothing in particular, I suppose," he said. "This is a beautiful house."

"Yes," Mac said. "It is."

"I guess I must have lived here, off and on, for thirty years or so," his father said. "This is where I grew up. But when I came back this time, it was like coming to a foreign country. I don't really think of this as home. It's a very curious feeling."

"Where did you—did you think of Puerto Morelos as home?"

"Yes. And no. Mostly no, I suppose."

"Well, then—"

"Where was home?"

Mac nodded.

His father's eyes were far away. "Here's another poem," he said. " 'Traversed by blood and metal, triumphant and blue,' " he quoted softly. "The man who wrote that is dying now, I understand. But anyway, that was Spain. We were—driven out of Spain. Then I was driven out of here. Now it seems I've been driven back."

Once again, the question danced at the tip of Mac's tongue. *How did they drive you out? Why did you leave?* But before he could speak, the Colonel said, "Did you get any news of Father Bahamonde?"

Mac fell at once into the aide's role. "I called the embassy. They promised to inquire." He mocked the diplomat's elegant accent: "There is much confusion, they say. There may be, ah, delays."

His father did not smile. Mac saw him sitting erect in the bed, a frail old man bundled against the cold, but in his posture, the set of his jaw, and the sudden flash of his tired eyes, he could see for a startling moment the imperious white-clad soldier he had heard about. "You must call them back and keep calling," the Colonel said. "If I can help the man, I must; he saved my life at the risk of his own."

"How?" Mac said. "How, Father?"

"It's a long story, son," his father said. But he seemed willing to tell it, in his own way. "You know, MacIlwain, I was brought up in a very . . . Protestant . . . home. My father was a good man in many ways— in most ways—but he had very little use for the Church of Rome. And I grew up feeling the same way. Certainly what I saw of the church in Spain did not change my mind, as you can perhaps imagine."

"Yes," Mac said. "I've read about that war."

"You have?" his father said. Mac basked in his look, which seemed to

335

suggest that perhaps Mac was not after all a complete intellectual loss. "At any rate, it wasn't until I met Father Bahamonde that I even suspected there was another side to the church. He was a refugee, as you know—from Paraguay. He had been very active there, working with the Indians. He was tortured for his pains. When I met him, he was working in one of the *poblaciones*—shantytowns on the outskirts of the capital, truly awful slums. His people, his parishioners, were called the *rotos*, broken ones, the very poor. And he was a good man, not at all like the priests I met in Spain." The Colonel's lip curled in remembered contempt. "To most of them, it was a work of supererogation to go about with the firing squads and offer absolution to those being shot.

"I had come to the capital for a funeral—my lawyer, the man who had introduced me to Father Bahamonde. Do you know, it was my first trip to the capital in three years or more? I had a terrible time getting there—the truckers were all on strike, and they had strewn booby traps across the road, little spiked things called *miguelitos*, designed to puncture the tires. Also my driver was very frightened that we might be stopped and beaten, but we saw none of that.

"I stayed the night in a hotel, because there was no room in Father Bahamonde's house; he lived very simply. But on the morning of the funeral, very early, he came to my room. I was not awake when he knocked. I could hear him puffing outside the the the door. '*Coronel!*' he was saying. '*Coronel*, open up! The fleet has returned to harbor!'

"I was rather sleepy and stupid, and I had not been following politics; I didn't know what he was talking about. But I let him in, and he said, 'The fascists have begun a *golpe*. We are in danger. You must dress quickly.' I slipped on some clothes—the same clothes I had on when I arrived here. He would not let me pack a bag. He said there was no time.

"When we left the hotel, I saw what he meant. There was a convoy of armored cars passing at the corner. He held me back until they had gone. Then we went out, and he took me to the embassy, which I would never have found on my own. We heard aircraft overhead, and I became a trifle disoriented. You know, son, for a few seconds I honestly thought I was back in Seville; it all seemed to be happening again, as if those thirty-five years had not passed. But we got to the embassy, very much out of breath, and then the marine guards would not let us in. I must have been a sight in my old clothes, sweater on inside out, but still, we were in danger, and they had no business keeping us out. Father Bahamonde did not speak much English, so I tried my best; I drew myself up and said, 'I am Colonel Joshua Tutelo Evans, former U.S. consul, and as an American citizen I demand sanctuary for myself and this man, who is a political refugee. There's a revolution under way.' Which I shouldn't have had to explain to him, since by this time you could hear small-arms fire from the center of town, but marines have never been the brightest of men. Finally, one of them telephoned into the embassy for a civilian, who took our names and went back inside, and after quite a long time he came back out and said I might come in but that Father Bahamonde would have to go elsewhere: asylum was refused. And that was shocking! Shocking!''

Mac looked up in sudden alarm: his father, cheeks red with rage, was panting like a spent racehorse. Mac began to make soothing noises, but his father cut him off. "Son," he said, his eyes narrowing, the word bitten off, "do you know what Father Bahamonde said to me to convince me to go in without him?"

"No," Mac said. He edged toward the bed, then stopped; he had been moving to hold his father, but he could not, could not even touch him.

"He said, 'You must go in, *Coronel*. They will be looking for you. They know who you are.'" The Colonel reached out a hand and clutched at his son's shirt. "Son, I have not been in politics of any sort for twenty years. *How did they know who I was?*"

Mac looked at his father; his hands were dancing in a kind of ague, his mouth twitched. He pushed the electric button to summon Miss Ross.

She seemed able to comfort the patient with sedatives and kind words. Soon the Colonel dozed. "No harm done, I think," she reported cheerfully. "We should keep him quiet for a while. I'll stay with him until the doctor comes." She picked up an Ellery Queen mystery from the hall table. "You run along now," she said.

Harry Randolph duly arrived and listened to the patient's heart. "The situation hasn't changed," he said. "He would be safer in a hospital, but he won't go, and there's no percentage in forcing him. He could have an attack tomorrow, or he could live to be a hundred. But don't you talk politics to him anymore, Mac." He fixed Mac with accusing conservative eyes.

"All right, Doctor," Mac said. "If Molly O. will stay with him a few days, I'll go back to work tomorrow."

"I suppose that's best." Randolph sniffed. "Call me if there's any change."

His father's hundredth birthday, it seemed, was not to be. Late that night, as Molly O. and Mac were watching TV doctors perform miracles, they heard him cry out, a long, low, desperate cry like a wounded animal; it died away and then started again, stretched out until it seemed to Mac to contain all that followed: running to the bedroom to find the nurse, grim

337

but calm, telephoning an ambulance even as she prepared an injection; his father, face distended in pain, crying hoarsely to someone, *"Infamia! Infamia!"* then, more softly as the morphine took hold. *"Yo soy el consul de los Estados Unidos,"* as brisk muscular orderlies bore him into the night. Contained in that cry was Harry Randolph in the hospital hallway, lips thinner than ever, telling them, "He's had a very serious coronary. We have him in intensive care, but it's a very bad situation, and we won't know if he's out of danger for a couple of days."

Mac and Molly O. sat in a lounge at the end of the hallway as night inched toward gray dawn. Eight stories below them shone a particolored round fountain, ceaselessly changing hue. Molly O. talked. She had grown up on a farm in one of the wet counties of the Northern Neck, now she told him about her childhood, fishing and boating and crabbing with nets. Mac gave thanks for the sound of her voice; he found after a time that she was holding his hand.

Night became day. The fountain below went out, and Molly O. stopped talking. Down the hall, at the nurses' station, interns and nurses came and went on quiet soles. The duty nurse, who had promised to notify them of change, said nothing. Mac's eyelids ground shut: he slept an upright and anxious sleep.

FOUR

★

At midmorning a nurse came to tell them that the Colonel was awake. Each of them was allowed a visit: ten minutes, no more.

Mac went first. His father was in a tiny cubicle opening off a central area from which a nurse could supervise it and five others. Blue-masked and gowned, she sat enthroned amid electronic equipment, watching electric dots leap and squiggle across green screens, recording each movement of each patient's heart, lungs, blood, brain.

When Mac saw his father, he knew death was holding him in its palm, as a child will hold a butterfly, ready at any moment to crush it or let it fly. The Colonel's flesh was gray, with faint livid whorls; his eyelids were blue over sunken eyes. His breath was shallow, loud and precarious as an elevated railway, and he lay back against the bed in awful stillness, as if flattened against the sheets by a great weight.

Mac knelt. His father's eyes opened, and Mac saw death there, too: they were the eyes of a robbery victim, one from whom all hope of rescue and escape have been stolen.

"MacIlwain," his father said, each syllable distinct, the voice like wind in distant pine trees.

"Yes, Father," Mac whispered. "Here I am."

"Don't forget," his father said, and drew a laborious breath. "Father Bahamonde."

"Don't worry. Please, Father, don't worry. I won't forget. I promise."

339

His father's hand moved in acknowledgment. "Another thing, son."

"Yes, Father?"

"You asked me a question once."

Mac could not at first imagine what his father meant; then he said quickly, "Oh, that. Please, Father, don't worry about it, it doesn't matter now, really—"

His father's hand moved again, then his lips. "Later," he said. "Later."

"Yes?"

"Ask Kenlow, son. He knows."

His father's eyes closed. Mac tiptoed out.

Molly O. was led in next. Mac stood in the hall; his legs shook from fatigue and fear. When he began walking down the hall, he found himself suddenly face to face with the same balding young reporter who had traveled with Tom Jeff and him through the Ninth District in August.

"What are you doing here?" Mac demanded.

The man extended a hand. "Covering your dad," he said. "You've just seen him, haven't you? How is he?"

Mac did not move or speak. The other man withdrew his hand and shifted nervously. "I'm not going to talk to you for publication," Mac said.

"Hell, Mac, I need something on the record, you know that."

"Then get it from the hospital," Mac said.

The man tried again. "Not for attribution, is it true he was arrested during the fighting down there?"

"Get away from me," Mac said, and brushed past him. Then he turned back, forefinger outstretched. "And you stay away from my sister-in-law, too, buster, or you'll answer to me."

The reporter's eyes goggled in surprise, but before he could speak, a nurse bore down on them in silent, pale-blue fury. "Please keep your voice down," she hissed at Mac.

"Sorry," Mac whispered. "Can you see that this jackal is kept out of my father's room?"

She sensibly said nothing but watched the two men until they separated.

When Molly O. came out, Mac was astonished. She was close to tears. He took her elbow and led her down the hall to the lounge; his eyes scanned like radar, searching for the reporter. "Are you all right, O.?"

She nodded. Her face was tired and drawn. "Oh, God, Mac," she said. He found he was hugging her, a brother's hug—the first they had shared in many years. Then she said softly, "Too much death."

"You go home and sleep now," he said. "I'll be all right for a while."

That morning and evening Mac waited alone outside his father's room. Armed with ten dollars' worth of change, he entered the phone booth in the hall and called the embassy again.

There was a long, frosty wait until the cultured voice of Sanjurjo came on the line. "Ah, yes, Señor Evans," it said in bored tones. "I am curious. What is the nature of your interest in this Father Bahamonde Sánchez?"

Mac knew better than to give anything away. "We are responding to a constituent request," he said. "Have you found anything out?"

"Yes, Señor Evans, I have received a report," Sanjurjo said. "I am very much afraid your Senator Shadwell is being used by, ah, constituents who may be involved in some, ah, unsavory political dealings. I fear that associations of this kind will do him no good."

"I'm sure the senator will appreciate your advice," Mac said evenly. "Can you tell me the contents of your report?"

"Very well, sir. I regret to report that your Father Bahamonde was implicated in a planned communist uprising in my country. As, ah, you know, it was this danger of insurrection which made it necessary for our military authorities to assume temporary power.

"This Bahamonde, a foreigner, was involved with a group known as the Movement of the Revolutionary Left. We believe his involvement may have been innocent. At any rate, it was necessary for the authorities to detain him briefly in the National Stadium. He was released pending trial. However, I regret to tell you that his, ah, comrades apparently feared he would betray them, and he has been a victim of a communist execution squad."

"What?" Mac said. "Killed by communists?"

"That is the report I have," Sanjurjo said. "His body was found in a suburb of our capital, tied hand and foot, and shot through the head. Near his body was found the emblem of this terrorist group, which I mentioned."

"I thought the communists had all been arrested," Mac said.

"Alas, it is not so easy as perhaps your newspapers suggest to control these terrorists," Sanjurjo said with elegant melancholy. "Some secret death squads remain on, ah, the loose, and apparently this priest has become their victim. It is unfortunate that the Reds treat their, ah, sympathizers so, but perhaps a priest should have been more careful in his associations."

"I see," Mac said. "Has the body been identified?"

"Yes," the other replied cheerfully. "There is no doubt about it. Now

341

perhaps, as a courtesy, you would oblige me by telling me where this inquiry originated?''

"As I told you," Mac said. "Constituent request. Can you send me a copy of your report?''

"I regret that I cannot," Sanjurjo said. "These are our regulations. At any rate, it would of course be in, ah, Spanish.''

"I'd still like to have a copy," Mac persisted.

"What a pity," Sanjurjo said. "I must refuse.''

"Very well," Mac said, pulling a pencil from his pocket. "Let me write down what you've given me. You say he was murdered by this—what was the name?''

"Movement of the Revolutionary Left.''

"And his body was found where?''

"I regret I do not have that precise information. In a suburb of the capital.''

"I see. And he had been shot by terrorists.''

"That is correct.''

"That is your story.''

"That is the report I have received.''

"All right," Mac said, snapping shut his pen. "Last chance. You're sure that's how he died?''

"Certainly," Sanjurjo said. "Why do you ask?''

"I simply wanted to give you a chance to change your story. 'Shot by terrorists.' I thought you might want to change it to 'hanged himself in his cell.' ''

"What are you suggesting?''

"Or perhaps he fell on the steps of the police station and suffered a skull fracture? Or perhaps he took a secret cyanide pellet provided by the KGB? Or was shot trying to escape—that's always a good one.''

"Señor Evans," Sanjurjo said, voice rising, "I must protest these imputations. They are an insult to my country and my honor. They are unjustified and discourteous.''

"Señor Sanjurjo," Mac said. "I suggest we have nothing more to say to one another.''

"Very well," Sanjurjo said. "Good-bye, sir.''

They waited in shifts in the lounge, while behind the door the Colonel's life threw dancing beams of light before the nurse's eyes. It began to seem that death did not want Mac's father just now. Four days after his attack, Harry Randolph told them he was moving the Colonel out of intensive care and into a private room. "This crisis is past," the doctor said. "He's an old man and I can't promise a thing, but if he takes care and rests and gets his strength back, we may be able to let him go home in a week or two. If not, well, he'll be here where we can watch him. To be very frank, I doubt he could survive another major coronary right now. So take it easy around him, no visitors except family and a few friends, and we'll keep our fingers crossed."

The new room was light and warm, its furnishings shiny and white. On the bedside were flowers brought by Molly O., rich purple and bright yellow, with nothing in them to hint of grief or suffering or loss. When they had led Mac in, his father rested easy on the bed, his face still pale, with new lines cut by pain, but the invisible crushing hand was gone, and he breathed quietly. Mac convinced himself: nothing in this room spoke of death, nothing. It was a gateway to life and strength, surely—a placid old age for his father, his son to care for him and love him and learn from him.

But the Colonel's thoughts were elsewhere. At his father's direction, Mac read to him from St. Paul: "Now if Christ be preached that he rose from the dead, how say some among you that there is no resurrection of the dead? But if there is no resurrection of the dead, then is Christ not risen: and if Christ is not risen, then is our preaching vain, and your faith is also vain."

"A pretty problem, is it not?" the Colonel interrupted. On his face was again his sketchy smile. "What is your opinion, son?"

Mac thought hastily. "Well, Father," he said, "I don't really have an opinion."

The Colonel peered sharply at his son, as if suspecting that Mac might somehow be an impostor. "Well, I imagine agnosticism has its advantages at your age," he said. "They will recede, however. I myself am in the opposite condition—I am of many opinions at once." He shrugged again his incongruous Latin shrug. "Perhaps agnosticism would be preferable to that."

"Shall I read more?" Mac asked.

"Not now," he said. His eyes scanned ceiling and walls. "You never knew your grandfather, son—my father. He died while I was in service. He had his limitations, to be sure, as have we all. But he was a very faithful man. He knew his own beliefs. A trait which he regrettably did not pass on."

"Father?" Mac felt awkward. "Would you like to see a minister?"

To his surprise, his father smiled a real smile, broad and faintly cynical.

343

Mac suddenly saw a ghost of what his father must have been like decades before. Even this pale shadow struck Mac like an electric shock, so that he involuntarily smiled back, and father and son for the first time found themselves laughing together.

"Oh, me, no," his father said, patting his chest with his hand. "I've never been much of one for confession. My father, I think, believed that a gentleman kept his sins between himself and God. As a matter of delicacy, really—to avoid embarrassing another gentleman with his confession." He chuckled faintly. "And of course, it seemed unlikely to him that a gentleman would need a great deal of forgiveness."

Mac laughed again. "So true," he said. "They taught us that at St. Cyprian's, too."

They sat awhile in warm silence.

"Would you like any visitors?" Mac said. "Would you like to see the judge again?"

"If Kenlow comes, let him in," the Colonel. "If not, I'll see him when I come home."

"Of course, of course," Mac said quickly. Then he paused, again embarrassed. "How about Mom?"

"What, have her fly up here in her custom-built Balkan bomber?" his father snapped, "What a waste of fuel that would be."

"Oh," Mac said, rebuked.

"How about you, son? Now that I seem to be mending, I don't imagine you'll want to keep watch here quite as constantly as before."

"To tell the truth, I was thinking that if you—if you are feeling better, I thought I might go back to work—oh, tomorrow or the next day. I'd still come by here every day, of course—"

"By all means go back to your campaign," his father said. "It isn't right for the strength of the young to wait upon the weakness of the old. I'll be fine."

"And I'll be by to see you—"

"Of course," his father said. "I shall look forward to it. But you work hard for Senator—what was his name?"

"Shadwell," Mac said. "Thomas Jefferson Shadwell." He felt a sudden prick of memory. "In fact, he knows you. He worked on your campaign. He asked me to remember him to you."

"Shadwell?" his father asked. "Where is his home?"

"Norfolk."

Recognition dawned. "Ah, of course! Tommy Shadwell, we called him then. A very energetic young fellow. You say he's running for governor?"

"Yes," Mac said.

"How is he doing?"

"I think he's probably going to win."

"Is he?" his father said. He seemed half pleased, half puzzled. "Tommy Shadwell. There's one surprise more, isn't it?"

"I guess," Mac said. "I guess so."

He came back that afternoon for another visit, but his father was tired and seemed unwilling to talk. The Colonel asked only one question. "Have you heard any word about Father Bahamonde?"

"No," Mac lied quickly. There would be time to tell his father later.

"Son," the Colonel said sleepily, "do not forget this."

"I won't," Mac said. *How could I?* he thought to himself. In his brain was a picture he had never seen, of a priest he had never met, dead in a gutter in a city he had never visited. Where had they shot him: in the head, the stomach, the heart? Had he been tortured? And for what? "I won't forget, Father."

He left the Colonel dozing and walked to the eighth-floor corridor, restless, unwilling to go home. The calls of the loudspeaker drifted softly in the still air: "Dr. McColl, Dr. McColl, please come to emergency." "Dr. Bourgholtzer, please call the page center, Dr. Bourgholtzer."

He stepped into the phone booth and dialed headquarters to warn Knocko of his impending return. The Phone rang and rang while the gentle voice paged Dr. Purdy, Dr. Faso, Dr. Rand. Then Danny Watkins answered.

Knocko wasn't there. "I'll tell him you're coming back," Watkins said. "How's the old man?"

"He seems to be getting better," Mac said. "How's the campaign?"

"We got our problems, but I got to think we're going to win," Watkins said. "There are no flies on Tom Jeff Shadwell. Lemme play you this radio spot."

"What's that, something Wink Moran did?"

"Hell, no, we got rid of him. This is terrific. It's for black radio stations." Mac heard him fumbling with a tape machine while the loudspeaker asked for Dr. Fink.

Then the sound came through, a young black woman speaking, polite but cynical: "I was just a little girl when someone tried to close down the schools in my town, but I remember. His name was Miles Brock. I know because he's running for governor again, and I don't think he's changed a bit. You know what he said last week? Just listen." Then another voice, an actor, but so like Brock's voice Mac was startled: "I have never regretted the role I played during the time of so-called Massive Resistance, because I feel we gained valuable time for Virginia to adjust to the problem of school integration. I have always felt that the Supreme Court acted hastily and unwisely when it handed down the 1954 decision."

Then the girl's voice came back again. "Thanks a heap, Miles!" she said bitterly. Then, after a pause, she said deliberately, "Now, I don't know about you, but I still remember. I'm going to vote for Tom Jeff Shadwell." Then another black voice, male, shouted exuberantly, "Paid for by a whole heap of black folks for the election of Tom Jeff Shadwell, J. Randolph Hopkins, Treasurer!"

Mac stuffed his fist in his mouth to keep his laughter from disturbing the patients. "That's wonderful," he said when he regained his breath. "Did Brock really say that?"

"You bet he did," Watkins said. "We got another one here somewhere, let me get it." The phone fell silent.

"Code Blue, eight-sixteen," the loudspeaker said politely and calmly. Mac felt a twinge of memory: eight-sixteen. Where had he—he remembered. That was his father's room number, wasn't it? Or was it eight-fifteen? "Code Blue, eight-sixteen," the polite voice said again.

"Just a minute, Danny," Mac said. Then he dropped the receiver, for out of the elevator came five blue-clad figures wheeling a tray of equipment, and they were not walking crisply, as most people did in the hospital, they were running, in step, down the hall to his father's room, which Mac, running behind, could see, as the door slammed in his face, was 816.

"I'm sorry, you can't go in there just now," said a voice at his elbow.

He turned: a tiny nurse. "That's my father," he said. "My father's room, eight-sixteen. What is it? What's wrong?"

"I'm sorry," she said. "The patient has had an attack. That's the coronary unit in there."

"What? What are they doing?" he asked wildly, reaching for the doorknob.

She stopped him firmly. "You really must stay out here. I'm sorry. They are doing everything they can. Please, just wait here."

Afterward, when they had come out and Mac had seen the sheet over his father's face, they talked at him: their mouths had moved—the emergency doctor, the nurse, Harry Randolph puffing from his dash from home. But Mac hadn't heard them, because all he could hear, until it drove him outside in terror, was that gentle, disembodied voice, which had so calmly announced his father's impending death, asking now with the same horrible politeness for Dr. Henson, Dr. Pettit, Dr. Mann.

*　*　*

There were death's chores to be done that night. Mac knew the easy ones; he had learned them from Lester. A funeral home to be chosen. Unlike Lester, the Colonel gave no patronage in death—Mac's selection was politically neutral. Funeral arrangements to be made. Mac chose a small church in the East End of town, a place where his father's type of faithfulness belonged. That much was easy.

But here were special arrangements to be made after his father's death; Mac realized he would have to make them, whether he wanted to or not, because a life depended on it, his own. He had the phone number in his wallet; he had put it there while his father was in the intensive care unit.

The phone rang four times. Then a stately black voice answered. "Mr. Williams, please," Mac said politely. "MacIlwain Evans calling."

Then a white voice. "Hello, MacIlwain, what a pleasure to hear from you." Mac could picture the speaker. He had met him more times than he cared to remember: short, slim, with the broad shoulders of a wrestler, the muscles of a middle-aged athlete; set on the bullneck a full face, dark black hair, thick pink-rimmed spectacles; incongruously, a dandy, and Mac pictured him in velvet smoking jacket and thick carpet slippers, at ease among his possessions, the most startling of which was his voice, which was so rich, so archaic, so perfectly patrician it seemed an heirloom handed down through generations.

"Mr. Williams, my father died tonight."

The voice was all sympathy. "I'm so very sorry to hear that, Mac. I had known he was ill, of course."

"Mr. Williams my father was an old man. He'd been out of politics for nearly twenty-five years. Do you see what I'm saying?"

"I'm not entirely sure I do, son."

I'm not your son, Mac wanted to shout. "My point is there would be no damage to you in letting his death go without comment."

"Son, I'll have to run an obituary," Williams said in a tone of reason sweet as marzipan.

"I understand that," Mac said. "I'm talking about your editorial page."

"Yes, I see," Williams said.

Mac held his breath; much hung in the balance.

"Mac, I knew your father quite well at one time," Williams said. "In many respects he was a very fine gentleman. Now I know I'm not well thought of in the circles in which you move, but truly, son, truly I have no desire to rake up the dead past and hurt you or anyone else."

Slowly Mac's breath began to escape, like air hissing from a tire. Perhaps his worry had been for nothing.

347

"There is one thing, though," Williams said.

Mac's breath hissed in again. "Yes, sir?" he said sharply, almost whispering.

"Mac, you and I are on different sides, but I'm sure we both appreciate how terribly important this election is."

"Yes, sir."

"Well, son, to be frank, I could not afford to pass up any ammunition against your Mr. Shadwell, if you understand."

"I'm sorry, sir. What do you mean?"

"The funeral. You see, son, if your Mr. Shadwell comes to the funeral, then I'll have to assume that you have chosen to make it a political occasion, and I would be remiss in my own responsibilities if I did not respond."

Mac was silent a long time. Then he said softly, "I see." Again he fought for control of his tongue, until he could say, "He won't be there, Mr. Williams. You have my word on that."

"Thank you, Mac. I appreciate that. I'll also just send one of my boys to the cemetery. I'm sure you'll be courteous to him." The voice gave a chuckle which could have been wrapped and put in a museum. "Mac, it's always good to hear from you. Please give Mary Owen my sympathy as well."

"Good-bye, Mr. Williams," Mac said.

He quickly dialed Shadwell headquarters. The candidate was in Richmond, as it turned out, at the George Mason. Mac called him there and baldly told him the situation.

The phone was quiet a terribly long time. Then Tom Jeff's voice burst out, "It ain't right!" and there was in it no humor or joy, only pain and rage. "It just ain't right!"

"No, Tom Jeff, it's not," Mac said. "Maybe someday things will be different."

"Mac," Tom Jeff said, "let's stand up and take their best shot, let's not bow down."

"Tom Jeff, that'll hurt you, and it'll hurt me, too. You know that." *And there's another reason*, he thought.

"Mac, you know"—the voice broke for a minute—"I loved your father."

"I know that, Tom Jeff," Mac said. "And so did he. He spoke of you warmly."

"Mac, do you not want me to come to the funeral?"

It was hard to say it, but he had no choice. "I'm afraid not, Tom Jeff."

"All right, then," Shadwell said, his voice distant as the moon.

As he hung up the phone, Mac sighed, sighed with shame and violation, but also with relief, because he had vowed to himself that if they had for any reason whatsoever done this final outrage, run one of their sniggering editorials about his father, taken a final coward's kick at his corpse, then Mac would do what he had to do: would take Lester's shotgun with the carved handle and go to the newspaper office in the light of day and shoot someone. Now that did not have to be.

He came out of the study into the front hall, where Molly O. was standing in black. On a table by the door was a silver serving bowl, now holding a cluster of visiting cards. She gestured at it. "Mac, do you want to see these people?"

"No," he said crisply. "If you'd just keep taking them, I'd be very grateful."

"Of course," she said. "I'm glad to help." She fidgeted with the collar of her trim black dress. Mac looked at his clothes: brown corduroys, gray sweater, red shirt. "I guess I'm not dressed right," he said.

"Don't worry about that," she said, shooing him with her hands. "Nobody needs to see you anyway."

"Has the judge been by yet?"

"No," she said. "He called to say he was on his way."

"When he comes, I'd like to see him," Mac said. "Right away."

"Yes, of course," she said, giving him a curious look. "Certainly."

When Anderson opened the study door, Mac was sitting in the dark. "Are you all right in here?" the judge said, flipping a switch.

"Yes," Mac said. He squinted at Anderson in the light. The judge put his hat and coat down on the desk. Mac's eyes followed his movement. It was the same desk at which his father had sat to transcribe his FBI interview a quarter century before.

The Judge regarded him with wary affection. "Mac, if it's about the will or anything, it's all in order, I don't have it with me, but there's no problem—"

"No," Mac said. "It's not the will."

The Judge bent slightly, as if to touch Mac then seemed to think better of it. "What is it, Mac, boy? Can I help you in any way?"

"Judge," Mac said, looking at him without expression, "why did my father run away? Why did he go to South America?"

Anderson stopped still, like an electric device with a pulled plug. "Why do you ask me that, Mac?" he said.

349

"Because my father told me to."

The judge jerked as if the power had suddenly surged. He shook his head; his eyes were far away. "Joshua," he said, as if the Colonel were in the room.

"Why, Judge? Please tell me. Do you know?"

"Yes, Mac, I do," Anderson said. "Do you mind if I sit down?"

"No, please."

The judge settled his body like a man sitting in the electric chair. "Mac, I hoped I'd never have to tell you this. But you have a right to know, and I guess Joshua had a right to make me be the one to tell you." He drew in his breath; it rattled, as Mac's father's had, but more faintly.

"You see," Anderson said. "Your father's trouble came, as you know, and went on and on, it like to never stopped. And after a few years, some people—never mind who they were, that's not important—but some friends of the old man's, very good friends—asked me to come see them, which I did, and they asked me to give your father a message, which I did."

"What message?"

"By this time, as you know, your father had been before a couple of these committees, closed sessions—of course they leaked out the press, enough to make your father look bad—but anyway, he'd testified under oath. And you and I both know the man never lied in his life, he was no more a communist than Foster Dulles, but that didn't seem to matter much at the time. The thing went on and on, got worse and worse. These people told me that your father was going to be indicted by a federal grand jury."

"Indicted? For what?"

"Perjury." Anderson raised a hand to forestall Mac's protest. "I know, I know, he was innocent. As far as I was concerned, that was the whole point; this was the chance he'd been waiting for, to have the whole thing out in open court."

"That was the message? That he was going to be indicted?"

The judge coughed into his fist. "No, not entirely. You see, these people—"

"Who were they? Bunny Triplett? Lee Tevyepaugh?"

"Mac, I'm not going to tell you, and I promise you'll never guess."

"What was the message?"

"They said that if Joshua—if your father would just sort of quietly leave the country, the whole business would be forgotten. Or he could stay and go on trial, either one."

"So you told him."

"Yes, I did."

"And he ran away."

"Mac, believe me, I didn't expect him to do that. I thought he'd be pleased. I really did. It was what he'd been wanting all along: a chance to defend himself in open court."

"Why did he run then?" Mac looked at the judge, not accusing, but asking, or even pleading. "Why? I mean—did he—was he—"

Anderson cut off the word. "Don't you ever even think that, Mac. Never. Let me tell you, your father never told a lie or did a dishonorable thing in his life, never. It was not that."

"Then why?"

"Mac, boy, they had worn him down. He felt ashamed, and alone, and his marriage was breaking up, and he just couldn't face it. I didn't realize how he felt, because in all my life I'd never been on the wrong side of power. I didn't realize how that can eat at you. It taught me a lesson, and later I got to be sorry I didn't tell those people to go to hell. It could have been a bluff or God knows what. That crowd was always scared of your father, they wanted him gone. And I don't believe it was my place to carry their messages."

"But you did."

"Yes, Mac, I did."

"And so you got to be a judge."

Anderson looked at him; in his face there was no anger, only weariness and shame, as if, out of his duty to his dead friend's family, he permitted even this insult to pass. "It wasn't that way," he said quietly. "Everything in life doesn't have to be a deal. I used to get very provoked with your brother because he always thought everything had to be a deal. There wasn't any deal. I would have been a judge anyway."

Mac looked down at the carpet and felt the judge's hand resting lightly on his shoulder. "Son, I made a mistake, that's all. Don't judge too harshly. Someday you'll do wrong to somebody you love, I promise. And you'll have to live with that for the rest of your life." The hand withdrew; footsteps crossed the rug; the door opened. "Mac," Anderson said, "I'll—" His voice gave out like a guttering candle, started up again. "If you need me, call me." The door creaked, and he was gone.

There was a blank time which seemed short but was probably long. Then Molly O. came in. In the half-light her eyes were wide with surprise. "Mac," she said, "do you want to take a phone call from Miles Brock?"

"What the—" Mac said, and jerked the receiver from the study phone.

"Hello?"

It was only when he heard the voice say, "Hello, Mac, is that you?" and heard the tidewater drawl deep and thick as ever he heard it, in person or on TV, that Mac remembered Danny Watkins' actor and realized this must be a crazy joke. "What is this?" he barked angrily; then, more softly, because, after all, Watkins might not know yet that his father had died, "Danny, is that you?"

"Excuse me," the voice said, puzzled, but still unmistakable. "Is this MacIlwain Evans?"

"Yes. Who is this?"

"I'm sorry, Mac," the voice explained in a tone so reasonable and innocent that Mac knew what was coming next. "I thought that Mary Owen had explained. This is Miles Brock."

And so it was. "Oh," Mac said lamely. "Hello, Governor Brock."

"Mac," Brock said. "I'm sorry to disturb you tonight, but I wanted you to know how very sorry I was to hear about your father's death and to give you my sympathy, both our sympathies, myself and my wife's."

Because Mac had been well brought up, schooled in manners and delicacy, his mouth moved now without his volition and said smoothly, "Thank you, Governor, you're very kind."

"Mac, you and I have our differences, but that's just politics. I've known your family for years, your mother is so lovely and energetic, and your brother was a very able and attractive young man, and your father was always a fine man, in my opinion, always. His death is a great sadness to me."

"Thank you," Mac began.

"I was so sorry during his trouble," Brock continued. "Between you and me, I never for a minute believed a word of what was said."

Mac found himself speechless; Brock went on, "That's all, Mac, I won't take your time, I just wanted to let you know you were in my thoughts and my prayers."

"Thank you for calling, Governor."

"Good night, Mac."

He put down the phone. Molly O. was in the new room, stretched out shoeless on the shaggy couch, eyes closed. He stood nearby, face pressed lightly to the plate-glass window. Outside the wind was tossing the bare tree limbs as a dancer tosses her hair. Fine cold clouds scudded across the sky. Inside Mac there were still no tears: only a rushing whir, a tornado whirling around a center that was empty and cold and dead.

FIVE

★

By the time Mac got back to headquarters he didn't need anybody to tell him that the Shadwell campaign was in trouble. In the days since his father's death he had read the newspapers and watched TV. Seeing Brock's speeches and advertisements, he had caught the faint scent of a Republican surge. Knocko had called on the day of the funeral, asking him—even, in his stubborn way, begging him—to come to a staff meeting the following Monday. "Don't come in until then," Cheatham had said. "I know you're tired and upset. It'd be good for the campaign if you were fresh and alert."

Headquarters, which had been boisterous and chaotic, was now a place of shadows and whispers. The hallway leading back to Knocko's office was a boulevard of tightly closed doors, guardians of secret despair. Only J. B. Fitzhugh, the minority coordinator, was in the open when Mac walked in that Monday. "Oh, man, I'm glad you're back," Fitzhugh said.

"Things as bad as they look?" Mac asked.

Fitzhugh's voice dropped to a whisper. "Listen, I don't even know how bad they are," he said. "I'm still finding out. See you at the meeting." He slipped away down the silent hall.

Mac found Danny Watkins sitting in his office, chortling merrily at something in the Roanoke newspaper. "Listen to this," he called out as if Mac had not been away. "Brock made a speech in Vinton about the food tax, listen to what he said. 'This plan of my opponent's is but a shopworn liberal panacea masquerading as tax reform,' and the reason he gives is that, and I quote, 'Under my opponent's proposal, the poor will be taxed for their clothing, while the rich man's lobster goes untaxed.'" Watkins gave his cackling laugh. "What a crock! I'm going to draft a statement for Tom Jeff and see if I can't stick that lobster up his ass." He began rummaging in his desk for paper.

"Danny, where's Knocko?" Mac asked.

"I don't know," Watkins answered absently. "Off with this pollster guy getting ready for the meeting." He slipped paper into his typewriter. Deepest concentration marked his face, and from one corner of his mouth a determined tongue protruded.

"What is this meeting all about anyway?" Mac said.

Watkins waved away the interruption with a belittling hand. "I don't know, some kind of big pep talk about how hard we've all got to work. Typical end-of-the-campaign horseshit." He began typing rapidly. Mac left him to his work.

One by one the staff trooped into the meeting room. There was an air of ritual solemnity as they fiddled with legal pads and poured cups of water. By the time Knocko entered, all were in place except Watkins. "Tony," Knocko said to Soleri, sitting near the door, "would you go remind that thimblewit Watkins? He's forgotten again."

A minute later Soleri returned with Watkins in tow. The press secretary was sheepishly tucking in his shirttail.

After a minute Tom Jeff and Rose Fishbein swept in. With them was the pollster from Washington: a gaunt man with a clipped fringe of hair around a shiny bald pate. The flesh of his face was creased in emphatic folds.

"All right," Shadwell said. "No need to waste time. We're here to get bad news, so let's read it and weep. Rose, will you do the honors?"

"Yes, Senator," she said. "Now once again, this is information which is not to leave this room. Like last time, I've numbered each copy with the seat number. When you get your copy, please sign directly below that number. At the end of this meeting I will collect all of these copies."

She circled the table, handing out thin stapled sheaves of paper. Tom Jeff eased himself gently into the head seat, his face unreadable. Next to him the pollster stood at ease, like a professor about to begin a lecture. Mac studied the faces as staff members took their copies. Ralph Bova nodded his big head gravely, as if seeing in print something he had known all his life. Tony Soleri, flawlessly dressed and tanned as ever, winced as if he had been kicked in a tender spot. Ed O'Brien, the labor man, read it with incurious eyes; his bargainer's face gave nothing away. Knocko, at the end of the table, did not deign to look at his copy; legs outstretched, he studied the ceiling, stroking the photocopied sheets like a man patting a lapdog.

To Mac's right, J. B. Fitzhugh shook his head and laughed, a soft, mournful sound, at the evil and injustice of this world. Mac took his copy and read the tabulated figures quickly, then busily began signing his full name under the seat number, 7: "MacIlwain Kuykendall Evans, esq.," he wrote in large cursive script. To his left was Lola Kreznik, his former assistant, who had in his absence been promoted to head researcher. "I don't see what's so terrible about this," she whispered softly to Mac, even as, on her left, Watkins began a startled "Jee-eez—" before catching Tom Jeff's glare and trailing off.

"You didn't see the last poll," Mac whispered quickly back.

In fact, considered baldly, the tabulated figures did not seem so unfavorable:

	%
BROCK	44.8
SHADWELL	47.2
UNDEC.	8
	100.0

Tom Jeff still had a lead of nearly two and a half percentage points. But compared with the first poll, the figures showed that in about six weeks, Brock had narrowed the gap from almost eight points; this meant that his campaign had taken on a frightening momentum, which, unless the situation were changed, could be expected to carry him past Shadwell by election day. Even now, the lead to which Shadwell had clung was within the poll's standard deviation—was, thus, almost no lead at all. The poll meant that Tom Jeff, who on Labor Day had seemed almost unbeatable, was going to lose unless something drastic was done.

"All right," Tom Jeff said after a minute. "I don't want any gnashing of teeth at this point. Mr. Knudsen here has come down from Washington to explain the situation, and when he's finished, we'll decide what to do about it." He gestured to the pollster. "Professor, if you please."

Knudsen dipped his head gravely. "As you can plainly see," he began, "these figures indicate that Brock has effected substantial erosion in Senator Shadwell's lead, and the momentum of the situation is such that, unless new factors are introduced, it is virtually certain that Brock will pass Shadwell on or before election day. My own projection is that, at the present rate of change, he will pass in ten days, on the Wednesday before the election, and then go ahead significantly by the time of the actual voting.''

Knudsen put on a pair of square brown reading glasses and consulted a note card in his hand. ''The reason for this is that the Brock campaign has in the past twenty-five days begun to do an extremely effective job of communications. Before then it was really quite shoddy work, not systematized, somewhat lackadaisical. But since the second or third week in September they have begun to take a very effective approach and produced a well-coordinated and professional campaign, particularly in the fields of television and newspaper advertising.'' He gave a professional's nod of the head, impersonal obeisance to quality workmanship. ''In addition, they have obtained intensive funding, while the Shadwell campaign has had to remain within previously established budgetary limits. The net effect has been that, in terms of volume of information, the Brock campaign has reversed the previous situation and taken a dominant position.''

Mac looked around the table. Knocko was still studying the ceiling. Ralph Bova was assiduously making notes. Ed O'Brien's eyes were closed, but his posture was attentive, like that of a bird dog on point. Knudsen's voice had a crisp self-assurance, an experienced calm that reassured his listeners even as it delivered bad news. He would have made a good lawyer, Mac thought.

''The object of this information barrage,'' Knudsen continued, ''has been primarily to transmit negative information about Senator Shadwell, rather than to build a positive image of Miles Brock. It has been well done, and its effect in most areas has been a perceptible blurring of the generally positive Shadwell image in the minds of a significant portion of the public, and the creation of a suspicion that Senator Shadwell is a somewhat untrustworthy person with a volatile and opportunistic political posture.

''The major issue utilized, of course, has been the question of so-called forced busing of school children. Through the use of television and newspaper advertisements, the opposition has fostered a double impression: first, that Senator Shadwell has in the past been a proponent of forced busing, again so called, and secondly that he has in his current campaign made an inept attempt to change his public stance for opportunistic reasons. May I have a cup of water, please?''

Tom Jeff quickly gave the pollster his own. Knudsen drank, then adjusted his reading glasses. Mac looked at Lola Kreznik. Her peppery grandmother's face was tight with anger. Gently he patted her shoulder. ''Don't you pat me!'' she snapped softly.

"All right, all right," Mac said, withdrawing the offending hand. "I'm not Miles Brock."

Knudsen cleared his throat and glared at Mac. "The campaign has been effective because the issue involved is a visceral one and affects the emotions of many voters who are in fact not directly involved in busing-type situations. In addition, it has hit directly at the positive image of Senator Shadwell as a man who tells the truth and stands by his word. This image has heretofore been a major asset and continues to work to Senator Shadwell's advantage, although to a significantly reduced degree.

"In addition to his statewide focus on the busing issue, there have been regionally tailored campaigns attacking Senator Shadwell's credibility on other issues. Gun control has been used extensively in the western part of the state, for example. But most of these have been extremely effective newspaper advertisements featuring attacks on what I call intangible issues. In northern Virginia, for example, they have concentrated on something called responsibility. In some of the less sophisticated areas of the state there has been an attempt to portray Senator Shadwell as somehow unchristian or morally lax. The latter campaign has xenophobic and anti-Semitic overtones and sometimes features veiled or overt attacks on Shadwell contributors who are of the Jewish faith."

Tom Jeff's hand hit flat on the table, with a report like a cannon. "Ain't *right*," he said. "It's a disgrace. It ain't right."

"That is the substance of my presentation," Knudsen continued mildly. "The conclusion is obvious. Unless the Shadwell campaign takes bold steps in the next ten days, a Brock victory is almost certain."

There was more than a moment of silence. Finally, Danny Watkins spoke up. "Well, Mr. Knudsen, what should we do?"

The pollster looked pained, as if Watkins had committed a breach of etiquette, like picking his nose with a dessert fork.

Tom Jeff answered for him. "Mr. Knudsen is a specialist, Danny," he said with gravid courtesy. "He makes surveys and interprets them, and that's all, right, Mr. Knudsen?"

The pollster nodded.

"We got to decide what to do ourselves," Shadwell said. He looked at them, and Mac could see inside him the anger smoldering like a brush fire. "Who's got an idea?" he asked.

Ralph Bova was ready. "Senator, if I may?" he said.

Tom Jeff nodded.

Bova goggled briefly at his notes. "Senator, since we all agree that we are facing very serious trouble, I'm going to make a suggestion that a few weeks ago we wouldn't have considered. I'm not doing this out of any great enthusiasm for the idea, but because I believe we have to get Tom Jeff Shadwell elected at almost any cost."

"That's a right pretty speech," Tom Jeff said. "What's the suggestion?"

"The Neighborhood Schools Defense Committee is meeting in Richmond this week."

Shadwell nodded.

"I have been talking with some of the people involved in that meeting, more or less confidentially," Bova said. "This Wednesday, the day after tomorrow, they're planning to call on both candidates to support an amendment to the Constitution against busing. It's a setup for Brock. But what if you went to that meeting and announced your support for the amendment? You'd steal Brock's headlines. It would tie them in knots and shoot this whole antibusing campaign. We'd be off the hook and we could go back on the offensive."

Tom Jeff's mouth was open to answer, but J. B. Fitzhugh's voice cut him off. The quiet, tidy young black man was plainly furious. "What?" he cried. "What kind of nonsense is that? I cannot believe what you are saying, Ralph. Do you want to kiss the black vote good-bye? 'Cause that's what you're talking about."

"Come on, J.B.," Bova said. His wide flat mouth gaped in irritation. "We won't lose the black vote. The blacks are going to vote for Tom Jeff Shadwell—"

"Why is that, white man?" Fitzhugh said. He was shaking with anger. "Because we got no other place to go? Is that it? Well, let me tell you something. Tom Jeff asked me if black folks would keep a low profile in this campaign, and we did it. But we're not going to dig any foxholes. You can't push us that far. Black people will not swallow any talk about amending the Constitution, because that means repealing the Brown case and everything else, and you and I know it and black voters know it too. They're not as dumb as you think they are, brother!"

"All right, that's enough out of both of you," Shadwell said abruptly. "Ralph, forget that idea. It sounds like phony baloney to me. I don't like it, don't believe in it, don't want to mess with it. You understand?"

Bova flushed. "But, Senator . . ." he began, and Mac felt Fitzhugh beside him tensing again.

But Ed O'Brien broke in. "Forget it, Ralph," the union man said without rancor. "There's no way that could do us anything but harm, anyway."

"What do you mean?" Bova said. "Listen—"

"No," O'Brien said impassively. "You listen. You just heard the man say they hurt us because they made out that we changed our position on busing, and now you want to change our position some more."

"We haven't changed our position any," Tom Jeff said quickly.

"What is it then?" Bova said. "I'll be blessed if I know it."

Shadwell's head turned to him with a snap. "Ralph, you're trying me," he said softly, and Bova, the big football player, blanched. "You ought to know my position. The people of this state are overwhelmingly opposed to busing, and as governor I will not propose or support any laws designed to cause more busing or permit consolidation of schools. But as governor I will not attempt in any way to interfere with any ruling of any court. Now that's what it's been, that's what it is, that's what it will be, you understand?"

Bova nodded.

Knocko had by now brought himself upright in his chair, facing the group. "All this busing stuff is missing the point, anyway," he said now. "I've been listening closely to what Mr. Knudsen had to say, and it seems to me that there may be a weakness in the Brock surge and we might be able to use it against them."

He paused, so plainly prolonging the silence for effect that Shadwell said irritably, "Spare us the dramatics, Cousin Knocko."

"All right," Knocko said. "From what I hear, the Brock people got so far behind that they decided the only way to win was to tear us down. It's like in chess. They've gambled that they can trap us. But I think they may have left their king unguarded."

"What do you mean?" Shadwell said. But behind him Mac saw Knudsen's bald head nodding in agreement.

"I mean they haven't spent any of this loot on building up their own man. They just assumed that people know he was Governor Brock and let it go at that. Am I right, Mr. Knudsen?"

"I think the point is well taken," Knudsen said. He looked at Knocko like a professor assessing a particularly apt graduate student. "As I'm sure you know, Governor Brock's recognition factor is very high: eighty-five percent of the voting age population knows who he is, and a high percentage of that group has a positive image of Brock, expressed in such terms as 'he was a good Governor,' or 'he did a lot of good for the schools,' and so on. But of that group a significant percentage were either out of state, or in military service, or too young to remember Brock in his term of office. And another substantial group has only vague memories of Brock as governor, although they were in fact of voting age and in the state at the time. We did a few in-depth interviews, and the number of subjects who could enumerate one or more of Brock's actual accomplishments was in fact remarkably small."

"Do you see what I'm getting at?" Knocko said urgently. "We've been talking about the food tax and getting on him about that, but we've let the rest go, we've been so bogged down in defending ourselves on this busing mess." He hammered his fist on the table. "Well, I say let's pull this— this"—with a visible effort Cheatham controlled his foul tongue—"double-talking so-and-so off his white horse! Let's go after him tooth and claw, take his record and rip it to bits, and we'll make him so mad he'll start defending himself. We can do it! We can turn this thing around. We've got to get mean, that's all, get mean!"

"Wait a minute," Ralph Bova said. "If we get to questioning the man's integrity, we might alienate—"

"What, the Carrington vote?" Knocko began, but Tom Jeff cut them both off.

"We won't say anything that's not the truth," the candidate said, and Mac could see from his face that Tom Jeff, who only a few minutes before had seemed lethargic, almost hopeless, had come alive; his eyes showed that he saw the possibility of another miracle. Everyone in the room seemed to notice; Mac felt the mood lifting, like a high-speed elevator racing upward.

"I believe Cousin Knocko may be on to something pretty good here," Shadwell said. "We haven't got much left to use at this point in the campaign. Don't have money. Don't have any organization. We got the party people, but half of them are out fishing, and a lot of the rest are just waiting for an excuse to bolt. Don't have a lot of corporate lawyers and former governors to go around speaking for us." Tom Jeff began to gesture with his arms, his peculiar blunt motions somehow sketching a vision of hope against all the odds. "All we got is one thing," he said. "We got truth on our side. And that still could turn out to be enough. Because everything that is evil hates the light. Let's just turn the light on Brother Miles Brock, and I don't mean make a few tough speeches, I mean let's make a big noise about it." The hands, palms outward, fingers to heaven, framed the vision Tom Jeff was seeing. "Ten Days of Truth! How about that? What do you think?"

Knocko seemed a bit nettled at the rapidity with which Tom Jeff had appropriated his idea. "What are you talking about, Tom Jeff?" he asked.

"Ten Days of Truth," Shadwell said again, as if the idea were self-evident. Shadwell began to tick off points one by one on his stubby fingers. "See, first, we have a statewide rally, get it on TV. Next Sunday night.

We're going to count down till the election. Sunday is ten."

"What, do you mean a televised rally?" Ralph Bova asked, his flat mouth open in amazement.

"Indeed I do."

"Statewide?"

"Yes, sir, statewide."

"Senator, we haven't got that kind of money, we can't do it."

"That isn't what I want to hear from you, Ralph," Tom Jeff said. He gestured toward the big man with forefinger extended. "I want the faith that can move mountains! I don't want much from you, Ralph, just a little stroll on the water, one week, that's all. You got to believe, or we might as well quit now. Do you believe? Do you?"

Flushing slowly, wordless, Bova nodded his ponderous head.

"All right, then," Shadwell said. "You get me to dinner with ten or fifteen of our best friends and I'll get the money out of them; I can do it. Ed, will your friends at COPE help us out?"

"Yes," O'Brien said. "And we can set up some fund raisers in Washington to shake some national funds loose, too, if we've got a plan to show them."

"We've got a plan," Shadwell said firmly. "You talk to Ralph after this is over. Second, I want a speech every day between Sunday and the election, in which we talk about the truth about Miles Brock, and I want facts in each one that'll make people listen. Each day a different subject, one day schools, the next day roads, the next day guns, what have you. I want factual stuff, no katzenjammer. Lola, can you and Danny deliver that?"

Watkins seemed panicked by the prospect, but Lola Kreznik nodded her gray head firmly. "You bet, Tom Jeff," she said. "We can get enough for a hundred days of truth."

"That's it!" Tom Jeff cried, gesturing at her with delight. "That's faith! That's what I like to hear! Rose, you work with them on scheduling, so I can give these speeches where it'll hurt the guy most.

"Third, I want a special issue of *True Facts* in every county weekly a week from Thursday, as a supplement, and it's going to be mean stuff. By which I mean it's going to go after Miles Brock and nail the guy, no apologies. Polite, but tough."

"I can do that, Senator," Mac said.

Tom Jeff looked at him in surprise. "Why, thank you, young Mac, but Danny and Lola can get this."

Mac was surprised and a little hurt. *True Facts* had been his paper from the beginning, and now he had lost it. He sulked quietly while Shadwell instructed Soleri to put his field organization to work getting buses for the rally Sunday night and told Watkins to call a press conference the next day to announce the rally. Then he heard his name called. "Mac," Shadwell said, "what I want you to do is organize this rally, find us a place, work out the TV coverage. Will you do it?"

Mac, caught off guard, said the first thing that came to mind. "Do I have to work with Wink Moran?" he said.

Like a balloon blown too full, the tense mood of the room exploded in laughter. Mac blushed red as Shadwell laughed until tears came. "Young Mac," the candidate said over and over, "once bitten, twice shy." He dabbed his eyes with a handkerchief. "No, Thomas, have no doubts. We got rid of old Wink. We got somebody for you to work with you're going to like, a real pretty girl."

"Woman," said Lola Kreznik grimly.

Shadwell was taken aback. "What's that?" he said. "Well, excuse me, Ms. Kreznik. Woman." He smiled again. "Anyway, she's no Wink Moran."

Everyone laughed once more. Mac looked at the faces of the group, which had seemed close despair not half an hour ago. Now they were happy and relaxed, eager to work, hopeful. Mac felt a foolish grin on his own face, and he suddenly believed that Tom Jeff Shadwell could win, would win, must win, despite anything the dour Knudsen, sitting bemused in the corner, might say or think: that Shadwell could work miracles, and another one was in progress.

"All right now," Tom Jeff was burbling. "Are we ready for Ten Days of Truth? Are we ready to stop this double-talking? All right, then!" And, astonishingly, he burst into squeaky song, as he stood to leave the room, his arms beating time:

> Glory, Glory Hallelujah!
> Glory, Glory Hallelujah!
> Glory, Glory Hallelujah!
> His truth is marching on!

Mac walked out with J. B. Fitzhugh, who seemed to have forgotten his anger of a moment before. He shook his head, and soft laughter burst irrepressibly out of his mouth. "Somebody better tell Tom Jeff that's a Yankee nigger song," he said softly to Mac, "or old Brock'll start using that against him, too."

Mac had a month's work to do in six days. It was already late afternoon, and he had to find an auditorium for the rally and clear the place and time with Bova, so the big man could begin buying time from local stations and arrange for transmission of the broadcast over television lines. Mac picked Charlottesville, because it was in the circulation area of both the Richmond papers and the Washington *Post*. He asked for the use of a high school auditorium. At first there was a problem: the superintendent of schools would not give his approval without a vote of the school board, which would not meet until after "Truth Sunday." Mac bucked the problem up to Knocko, who retreated into his office with a telephone. Forty minutes later Mac got clearance. "Charlottesville's a good Democratic town," Cheatham said.

Mac met over dinner with the new TV director. As advertised, she was no Wink Moran. Her name was Hope Pinnell. She was tall, slim, and elegantly dressed, but her face was a jarring note. Stubborn blemishes dotted her cheeks, although Mac hardly noticed them at first; dominating her face were her eyes, so raw and intense he could not bear their direct gaze for more than a few seconds at a time.

They ate in the courtyard of a new restaurant on Cary Street, outdoors in the cool dusk. The waitresses were uniformed in short tartan skirts and black tank tops with plunging necklines. Mac barely noticed; he felt weighed down with responsibility, squeezed by the shortness of time. Hope Pinnell, for her part, noticed nothing but the matter at hand. She drank white wine and scribbled on endless note cards as they talked about the program.

"Do you want to make this a fund raiser, too?" she asked. "You could have local people on the phones in the cities where it's being shown to take pledges."

"I hadn't thought of it," Mac said. "I'll ask Bova. I don't know if we have the people to man those phones."

"It's probably not a good idea, anyway," she said, noting a question mark on her card. "It gets in the way of the message." Her words rushed from her mouth, doing violence to each other in their haste. "Now what I would suggest is an appeal for cash at the end, superimposed on the screen, with an address for mailing it in. That had good results in the last presidential campaign."

"Jesus," Mac said. "We sure don't want to remind people of that campaign. That poor dumb bastard didn't get but thirty-some percent of the vote in Virginia."

"I worked for that poor dumb bastard," she said primly.

"So did I," Mac said, looking up, away from her eyes, over the courtyard wall. At either corner of the square outdoor dining area the management had hung blue fluorescent lights to attract insects. They flew toward the light and were crisped by tiny electrified wires; each insect, dying, made an audible snap. "That doesn't mean I have to believe he wasn't a poor dumb bastard."

"We haven't got time to argue. Take my word for it that the technique works—that is, it does if the program itself is good." She reached across the table and put a hand on his arm. "Listen, Mr. Evans."

"God, call me Mac."

"Fine, Mac," she said, brushing the issue away. "But listen, you know what's going on—tell me. Am I going to get a decent budget for this program? I can do it in six days, but I need the money to do it right. Are they going to give it to me?" Her look might have accompanied a question like *Do you really love me?* or *Is there a God?*

"Listen, Hope, to be real frank, I kind of doubt it. We're down to our last nickel, from what I hear about half the staff hasn't been paid in two weeks, we're going to be lucky to get this thing on the air at all. You're going to have to do it for rock bottom. I'm sorry."

"Oh, *hell*," she said, throwing her napkin down. "Why can't I ever work for anyone with money? I never get to show what I can *do*."

Mac tried to console her. "You're burdened with a conscience," he said. "It usually works out that one group has principles and the other has money."

"No, damn it, I don't have any principles," she said. "It would be different if I did. It's just that I can't get *along* with Republicans."

Mac raised his glass in salute. "Those sound like principles of the most basic sort."

She laughed; he felt he had accomplished a heroic feat.

They spent that evening working out a minimum budget. The next morning Ralph Bova cut it nearly in half. "You all must think you're working for Brock," he said. "We haven't got this kind of money."

To Mac's surprise, Hope took it stoically. "All right," she said briskly. "I'll get back to you this afternoon." She gathered up her note cards and strode purposefully off, leaning forward slightly as if walking against a high gale.

"Damn," Mac said. "I wouldn't want to be in her way."

"Is that right?" Bova said without interest, his eyes already darting over another paper from the high stack on his desk. "Well, you're in mine now. Go get busy."

Mac went with Tom Jeff and Danny Watkins to the press conference to announce the "Ten Days of Truth." They had rented a meeting room in the George Mason Hotel, with a tasteful blue backdrop for the color cameras and the candidate's name emblazoned on the podium. Shadwell looked sober and earnest; he had combed his hair back slick and straight, like a schoolboy out to make a good impression. He read the prepared text: it promised to name names, give dates, figures, and places. "The Ten Days of Truth will be a revelation for the people of Virginia: a message of truth about my opponent, who has sought so long and hard to deceive them."

Ed Hackett asked the first question. "Senator, the Neighborhood Schools Defense Committee is planning to ask the two candidates for governor to support a constitutional amendment banning forced busing. Will you support such an amendment?"

Watkins, standing next to Mac in the back, winced. "Duck it," he whispered prayerfully.

The question was easy to evade; Tom Jeff could simply say he would wait for the request and promise an answer then.

But such was not Tom Jeff Shadwell's style. "No," he said.

"There goes our headline," Watkins whispered as the reporters noted furiously and the cameras clicked.

That afternoon Mac, Watkins, and Lola Kreznik went over the material for the "Ten Days." Mac was stunned by the transformation in his former assistant. In his absence she had acquired bookkeeping expertise and the passion of an IRS auditor. She had spent hours in dusty archives and newspaper morgues, adding up figures and deciphering documents. Now she laid out her truth.

"Item one," she said. "An average of thirty-four million dollars of state funds kept in interest-free accounts for the four years of Brock's term. Now every government has to keep some money in interest-free accounts, so they can get at it quick. They call it maintaining liquidity. But this thirty-odd million was not necessary for that; Hapgood got by with a lot less. At the rates of interest then prevailing, this cost the state more than three million in lost interest. Item two, on retirement, Brock becomes a director of a bank holding company. There's no evidence that the state played favorites with the banks; everybody got a piece. They weren't favoring one bank over another; it was favoring banks in general over the ordinary taxpayer, which established Brock as a friend of bankers, which leads us to item three: direct contributions from directors and major shareholders in banks and bank holding companies to the Brock campaign, at the last reported disclosure, totaled eighty-seven thousand five hundred and sixteen dollars. They want their friend back in office. I think that ought to carry Tom Jeff through one day of truth."

"Hell's bells," Watkins said, eyes popping. "This stuff is fantastic."

She gave a brief prideful smile. "I've only begun," she said. "Item, the

State Department of Taxation in the four years of the Brock administration neglected to collect all the corporate taxes owed to the states. This is not tax evasion by the companies; it's negligence by the revenue people. The amount isn't that much compared with what the companies did pay, and there's no reason to believe this was done deliberately or that Brock ordered it done. It was just sloppiness. But on the other hand, the amount is more than I'm liable to pay the state in a lifetime, and if I didn't bother to pay them some year you can imagine how quick I'd end up on the Women's Farm. Now item five, when he leaves office, Brock is appointed director or consultant to four major corporations—all of which have underpaid during his administration. Now there's no reason to think he wanted that done, but on the other hand, he wasn't going to bust a gut to make sure the corporations did pay, either, because he's a friend of the corporations. We can't nail down how much he's making for these corporate jobs, but his total income, exclusive of his law practice, is probably in excess of one-hundred thousand.''

"That'll be a hard one to handle," Watkins said.

"Yeah, but it's terrific," Mac said. "Uncollected taxes! You know that's going to tear them up."

"There's more," Lola said. "Listen!" she said, pointing at the cardboard box at her feet. "I have really nailed this guy!" She dropped her wintry calm facade, and hopped in her chair like a nervous gray-haired teen-ager. "I love it!" she said. "I love it! I can nail him up six ways and still have a hammer I haven't used yet! I love it!"

As she went on through her list, what surprised Mac was that nothing she had found was corruption in the classic sense. There was no evidence of favoritism, payoffs, illicit pledges, or criminal exchanges. These were the time-honored practices of the Apple-Farmer's political machine, ways to keep business and businessmen happy and healthy, and after all, what else was government for? Mac had no doubt that Miles Brock would be outraged when Tom Jeff suggested that there was anything wrong with treating the state's funds in so cavalier a fashion, and when Shadwell objected to his taking jobs and money from those he had benefited while in office, Brock would surely be shocked and even wounded. For if as governor he had, as he saw it, done well by doing good, what else did God intend for us in this life? Mac remembered the voice on the phone; it seemed to him that Miles Brock probably did in fact think there was something vicious and heathen and unchristian about Tom Jeff Shadwell to deny a man the just fruits of his labors in the house of his fathers.

Later that afternoon Mac was in the conference room with Tony Soleri working on logistical plans to get busloads of Shadwell supporters from all over the state to the Charlottesville rally. Because the auditorium was small, only a few from each district would be needed, but Shadwell wanted representatives from all areas of the state to symbolize the importance of the occasion. They had to be recruited, transported, and fed; Mac and Soleri were discovering how tricky this could be when Watkins burst through the door.

"The bastards have shut us out of the A.M. cycle altogether," the press secretary said, waving a piece of teletype paper.

"What are you talking about, Danny?" Mac said.

"Tom Slaughter endorsed Brock."

"What?" Soleri said, grabbing the paper. "Let me see that." he read silently and whistled. " 'To prevent the integrity of Virginia government from falling prey to an irresponsible demagogue,' " he quoted. "Mother of Mercy."

"He really did it," Mac said, reading over Soleri's shoulder. "He bolted the party. He couldn't keep his mouth shut."

"Nope," Watkins said.

"Does the candidate know?"

"Yes, sir," Watkins said. "He just dictated his statement. Would you care to hear it?"

Soleri was still reading the wire report in horrified fascination. Mac nodded.

"Okay, get this," Watkins said. He read expressionlessly from his notebook. " 'Virginians should remember that Mr. Slaughter has spent the last four years living out of the state as an executive of a giant textile mill. It appears that Mr. Slaughter has spent too much time in the mill. His statement shows that some of the cotton has found its way between his ears.' "

They were silent for a minute, reverent before such a profound mutual hatred.

"Damn," Soleri said.

"Double damn," Mac said.

"He'll lose the linthead vote," Soleri said.

"No," Mac said. "They don't mind seeing the boss catch some flack."

"I got to get this out to the press." Watkins turned to go.

"Have you told Knocko yet?" Mac asked.

"Hell, no," Watkins said. "You do it. I value my life too highly."

Knocko was in his office when Mac brought him the news. He exploded, his cheeks flashing crimson, eyes spiraling with hatred. "That bastard!" he bellowed. "That belly-crawling, party-bolting lickspittle son of a bitch!" His mouth gaped in fury, and his hand grabbed at the air. "God

367

damn it! God damn it, I'll tell you, if we win this one that bald-headed piss-ant better not show his face in this state for four years, I'll tell you that! I'll bust him, I'll have his ass on the fucking road gang!"

"Jesus, Knocko, cool it, you're talking crazy," Mac said. He looked around wildly; after a second he realized he was looking for a button to summon the nurse. Knocko's fury had reminded him somehow of his father.

Knocko settled back into his chair in a semblance of calm. Mac could see his mind, that dark, mistrustful maze, turning over slowly. "This is it," he said. "It's part of a plan. All these bastards are going to bolt now— all the congressmen and about half of the General Assembly. The Brock people mean it to be the *coup de grace*. We got to do something."

Mac, still elated from his session with Lola Kreznik, said, "Listen, wait'll we start this truth stuff, that'll knock 'em back some—"

Knocko silenced him with a scornful wave of his hand. "Truth," he grunted scornfully. "What the fuck is truth? You tell the truth, and they'll nail you to the wall every time." He reached in his desk for a cigar, wet it with his tongue, bit the end off delicately, and lit it. The ritual seemed to calm him. His eyes, behind the smoke, were distant and thoughtful. "You run along and play now, Mac," he said. "I got to think of something."

Mac went home late that night, dead tired and tense. The light was on in the front room; he knocked on the french windows, and Molly O. let him in. She was doing needlework and watching the late movie.

"What is this?" Mac said.

"*Attack of the Bat People*," she said, wrinkling her nose slightly. "It's really awful. I was just waiting up for you."

"That's nice of you," he said. He sprawled on the couch; the soft upholstery caressed his back muscles. "I am beat."

"Want something to eat?"

"No," he said. He felt a weariness that dulled hunger, an emotional fatigue which left him limp, unfeeling. On the screen a young couple were crouching in a cave; their torch was flickering and would soon go out.

"Your mother called tonight," Molly O. said.

On the screen the man suddenly brushed his neck; he had been bitten by a bat.

"Did she say why she didn't come to the funeral?" Mac asked. "Was the Balkan Bomber being repaired? What would you call it, ground dock?"

"I gather Emil's been real sick. He had a stroke."

"What? When?"

368

"About a month ago. He can't feed himself or anything else. She's been staying with him."

Mac thought of himself and his mother, six hundred miles apart, keeping watch over the deathbeds of old men.

"You know, Mac, I think you're mean to your mother," Molly O. said, looking intently at her needlework. "She's had a rough time in a lot of ways."

Because Mac saw the justice of her words, they wearied him. "Let's not go into that now," he said.

"All right," Molly O. said placidly. On the TV screen, the young couple had been rescued. But something odd had happened to the man; he bravely hid his worry from his wife.

"Mac, honey," Molly O. said, "you know I don't like to pry. But are you doing all right? Do you feel okay?"

"Yes, I guess so," he said. "Tell you the truth, I'm too tired to tell."

"Excuse me again," she said. "But what happened to that girl you were seeing? Did you have a fight with her?"

Mac gave a start; it was almost as if he had forgotten Alexandra or, more properly, as if the hustle of events, death and burial and now the desperate hurry of the campaign, had blocked his memory of what she was beginning to mean to him. What had that been? "I guess we did, sort of," he said. "And then, with the Colonel coming back and all, there wasn't any time."

"She sure sounded nice," Molly O. said.

Mac had an image of her, in her blue jeans and leotard, doing her dancer's exercises on the flagstone patio one early morning. Her black hair moved back and forth as she lifted her graceful thighs. Then he thought of pouring beer on her back and smiled. "Yeah," he said. "She was. Or is, I guess."

"If you like her, you're a perfect fool to let her get away like this."

"Maybe so," Mac said. "I guess I should call her." Then he felt a great weight on his shoulders: the days ahead. "But hell, I've got so much to do between now and Saturday, and then I've got to go up to Charlottesville. I haven't got any time at all."

"Perfect fool," she said again softly.

"Maybe so," Mac said. He heaved himself to his feet. The young husband had grown fangs. "I'm a tired fool, too. I'll see you tomorrow.'

Mac had no time for anything all week. There were newspaper ads to get out, advertising the rally on local channels from Norfolk to Abingdon. There was the special issue of *True Facts,* which had to be ready by Sunday: Mac helped Lola Kreznik and Danny Watkins whenever he had a chance. There were dozens of details to be arranged with Soleri and his field organizers. There was the final script to finish with Hope Pinnell. Mac's phone rang constantly, day and night; he ate seldom, slept less.

Knocko, by contrast, seemed wrapped in impenetrable suspicious gloom. All was happening as he predicted: one by one, the state's five Democratic congressmen bolted the party and endorsed Brock, and their treachery stole the headlines from Tom Jeff as he stumped the state announcing the countdown until the Ten Days that would shake the state. Knocko muttered of revenge and retaliation, but as each day passed, he seemed less disposed to do anything concrete. The campaign was by now almost running itself; rarely was Knocko called on for a decision. The others avoided him; like a carrier of the plague, he was surrounded by a globe of inviolate space. He began to disappear from the headquarters for long periods of time, without leaving a number where he could be called.

Mac wondered if Cheatham's nerve could have failed him. It did not seem possible. Knocko was a fighter, and he had been in battle all his life, had taken the measure of betrayal and bitterness, the nasty surprises of a political campaign. Something was up, Mac sensed.

On Thursday night he and Hope Pinnell were finishing the script in the conference room. They had redone it four times in three days; now they were both warily satisfied.

"All right, all right," she said fiercely, her penetrating eyes aglow. "I don't care about the budget, it's good, the talent is good, the ideas are good, it's going to be good, good, good! Oh, I hope somebody from the network is watching!"

Mac felt an ironic touch of affection for her. "Yes," he agreed enthusiastically. "Then maybe you can get to be associate producer of *Return of the Bat People.*"

She bit her lip. "All right, go ahead and laugh," she said. "Everybody's got to have an ambition."

"You know, even if you make it to the network, it's just going to be like working for Republicans—hundreds of Republicans."

"The *hell* with you anyway!" She thumped the table with her fist. "Someday I'll spit on your dreams, too."

"You can't," Mac said, by way of apology. "I haven't got any."

J. B. Fitzhugh poked his head tentatively into the room. "Am I disturbing you all?" he asked delicately, as if fearful of interrupting a love scene.

"No, indeed," Mac said. "We were just finishing up."

"In that case, Mac, can I see you for a half hour or so?"

"Sure." Mac gathered up his papers and his copy of the script. "Hope, I'll see you in Charlottesville tomorrow."

Fitzhugh led him down the hall to the candidate's office. "What is it?" Mac asked.

"Need your advice on a little problem," Fitzhugh said. "Tell the truth, a pretty big problem." He pushed open the door. Tom Jeff was behind the desk, eyes closed, moon face in exhausted repose, hands folded over his belly. Beside him, Knocko lounged on the desk, puffing furiously at a badly gnawed cigar butt.

Knocko nodded. Shadwell did not move. "How are you, Senator?" Mac said.

"I believe my staff is trying to kill me," Tom Jeff said without opening his eyes. "Get me elected governor even though dead, and then have me stuffed and put me in the big chair, and they'd do whatever was right. Believe it would work. Believe my staff would make a better governor than I would."

Knocko gestured at Fitzhugh with his glistening cigar end. "We haven't got much time, J.B.," he said. "What's on your mind?"

Fitzhugh sat on a metal folding chair, his back straight, watching the candidate through his enormous gold glasses. "I'm sorry to bring you down here when you ought to be sleeping, Senator, but we have a fairly serious problem with the black vote."

Shadwell did not move or speak, but his eyes were open.

"In the last two weeks or so the Brock people have been very active, putting pressure on a lot of our people, especially in this district and in Southside. They know they can't get any support or endorsements— we've got the black organizations locked up—but they're trying to get some key people to stay home on election day, not do anything to get out the vote. That could cut our margins pretty seriously in places. I believe some money has changed hands."

"Can you prove that?" Shadwell asked.

"No. But I've gotten the word that unless a couple of these organizations get some money—expense money—then a few of these people will stay home. And that will be trouble."

"You mean bribe money?" Shadwell said.

"No, Senator," Fitzhugh said. "This would be legal—contributions to the organizations, no need for secrecy, you can disclose it at the next disclosure. What happens to the money after that, I don't know. I haven't seen the books."

"How much do they want?" Knocko asked.

"Not much, really—about five or six thousand," Fitzhugh said.

"And can you get it to the people it should go to?"

"Yes," he said. "I can handle it all. As I say, it's legal, so checks are no problem—"

"No," Shadwell said, closing his eyes again.

"All right, cash then," Fitzhugh said. "Or money order, that doesn't matter, the point is—"

"I mean no deal," Shadwell said. "I'm not paying a red cent."

"What!" Knocko exclaimed. "What do you mean?"

Still the candidate did not open his eyes. "I mean it doesn't matter how legal it is; it's buying votes, which I am not going to do."

"Senator," Fitzhugh pleaded, "if these people really do go back on us, we could lose—I don't even know, five thousand votes, maybe more. Black folks won't turn out without somebody to remind them. We need these people."

"If you need 'em, you get 'em," Shadwell said. "That's what I pay you for. Twist some arms. Make some threats. You're a smart guy. Don't come around me asking to buy votes. I'm not going to do it. I don't believe in it. It ain't right, and it doesn't pay, and if we do it, the other side will do more of it, and there's no end to it. It's like poison gas. It's wrong."

"I don't believe you, Tom Jeff!" Knocko was almost shouting. "Do you *want* to lose this election, is that it? Do you not *want* to be governor? Because you are sure as hell acting like it. What you are acting like is a pussy, and pardon my French, but I got to tell you the truth."

The candidate's eyes snapped open again. He looked at Knocko with no evident expression. "God damn you to hell, Knocko," he said, and because Mac had never heard Shadwell use those words, it suddenly struck him that they were a very powerful and frightening curse. Knocko, too, seemed for once struck dumb.

"You've been with me too long to think you can do me like this," Tom Jeff went on. "You know damn well I'm not running for governor because I want to sleep in that goose-feather bed up there in the mansion. I can sleep fine on my Posturepedic in Norfolk and nary a nightmare for twenty-five years. And when this is over, win, lose, draw, I'm going to be sleeping good still, wherever I am. And if you want to be talking trashy at me like that, then I don't want you around me. You get on out of my office and stay out of my sight for a while. Go on, get!"

He pointed the way, until Knocko realized he meant it; then Cheatham was gone in a flash, the door slamming behind him like a coffin lid, with a hollow boom.

Mac's heart was hammering. Tom Jeff was looking at him. "What do you think, Mac?" he asked quietly.

"Who, me?" Mac's voice was faint.

"Yes, you."

"What, about these contributions?"

"Right."

"Well, uh, I—well, Tom Jeff, it's legal. We need those votes. We want to win. I say pay it."

"You do, huh?" Shadwell gave him a disappointed look, and Mac knew what was coming next: *your daddy wouldn't,* and the unspoken reproach stung so hard that Shadwell must have read it in his face, for instead, he simply closed his eyes and said, "Three ayes, one nay. The nays have it. Thanks for your advice. Now, if you all will excuse me, I'm going to get some sleep." Slowly, painfully, the dumpy little man rose to go.

"Can I drive you to your hotel?" Fitzhugh asked.

"Thanks, J.B.," Tom Jeff said. "I'd be obliged."

"I'll come, too," Mac said. They went out together, and behind them the door boomed again, hollow in the empty darkness.

SIX

The next morning Mac drove the Continental to Charlottesville, along the interstate through Goochland, Fluvanna, Louisa, and Albemarle. The trees seemed to be dressed especially for him in reds and orange and yellow. The sun was bright, and the air was cool, and Mac had the road to himself in the big smooth car. He felt his mood lighten; the hand pressing him down seemed to lift. He turned on the radio for some music. But instead, what he heard was Horace Hapgood's drawling, slow voice, intoning, "I believe the election of Governor Brock is crucial to the future of our state and our people. I regret to say that his opponent has revealed himself during this campaign as no more than a carnival barker, a huckster, a political confidence man."

Mac snapped off the radio and cursed inventively through five miles of scenery. Hapgood had been quiet for most of the campaign; most people felt he still clung to his ideals and resented Brock's antibusing crusade. But now they had gotten to him, too. The noose was tightening; they were isolating Tom Jeff, getting ready for the kill.

At the auditorium all was chaos. Mac had ordered a trailer with three telephones. These were ringing when he got there, and they rang without stopping for the next two days. He answered them, and listened to Hope Pinnell screaming about defective equipment and bad lighting, and rewrote the script when one band canceled and another had to be found at the last minute. But despite the confusion, the rally gradually took shape.

375

For all her air of tense disorder, Hope Pinnell was a good organizer, decisive and confident. She directed the cameraman, sound people, and electricians with crisp self-assurance. Tony Soleri's people came through: the buses were ready, the outdoor kitchen was ready to serve a good political meal—fried chicken, creamed potatoes, black-eyed peas, and biscuits—before the show. Mac recruited members of the University's Young Democrat Club to handle security and make sure no one got in without an invitation: believers only were invited to witness this miracle.

On Sunday, as the clock crawled toward 8 P.M., the rest of the campaign staff filtered in. Lola and Danny brought four thousand copies of *True Facts:* the new "Days of Truth" issue, hot off the press. Danny got advance copies of the candidate's speech ready for the reporters. At dinnertime the candidate himself arrived, looking tired but bouncy and determined, to greet the faithful and eat with them off plastic trays. Mac could not eat, his stomach galloped and bucked. He drank coffee and watched Hope Pinnell brief the performers and speakers.

The show would open with a bluegrass band playing a medley of mountain songs; the MC, a slick, handsome TV actor from northern Virginia, would introduce the four speakers. There was a retired tobacco farmer from Lunenberg County, a young woman from the Reston City Council, a black businessman from Suffolk, and a student from Virginia Tech. Each had written a speech explaining why he or she would vote for Tom Jeff; each speech (cleared in advance with Mac and Hope) ended with the words "and that's the truth!" Between speeches there would be songs from a gospel choir. Then Tom Jeff would speak, and the announcer, off camera, would ask for contributions. Hope seemed confident in her equipment and her script, but Mac was in a haze of tension and fear as seven o'clock became seven thirty and the faithful began gathering in the auditorium, then seven forty-five as the MC warmed them up, told jokes and instructed them to clap on cue. The candidate came in and sat in the wings, speech under his arm; behind him, in chiaroscuro in the play of light from the stage, appeared Knocko, his face curiously expressionless.

Then it was seconds, not minutes, and the band struck it up, banjos and fiddles and fat old bass fiddle thumping through the first bars of "Wabash Cannonball," and the crowd, as instructed, was clapping in time, and the walls shook and the floor rocked. Then the red light was on, Hope Pinnell's finger flashed down, and the MC bent his elegant head over the offstage microphone and crooned in his deepest, richest voice: "And now LIVE! from Charlottesville's Meriwether Lewis High School, it's the Tom Jeff Shadwell Hour of Truth, with music by the Roanoke River Boys and the Blessed Redeemer A.M.E. Zion Church Gospel Crusaders! So reach for the phone, call your friends and neighbors to watch, and then sit back and let the good times roll!''

The band began to sing "Oh, listen to the jingle, the rumble and the roar," and Mac started to relax. His job was done. He looked out at the crowd, which seemed to be enjoying itself. To his surprise he saw, in the jumble of equipment in the orchestra pit, the same strange, wild, beautiful girl who had—how long ago?—shot devil's horns at the departed Wink Moran. Mac had no time to take in the fact, however; he felt a tap on his shoulder, and turned to find Danny Watkins, his freckled young-old face puzzled. "Phone call for you in the trailer," Watkins whispered.

"What the hell?" Mac whispered back. "I can't come now. Take the number, will you?"

Watkins leaned closer. "It's Tobey Carrington," he whispered. "He says it's urgent."

The trailer was dark and chilly. The doorway let in a rectangle of light, and faint echoes of the music drifted back from the stage door. Mac settled into a metal chair and lifted the receiver. "Hello, Senator?" he said doubtfully.

The calm, reasonable voice was nearly a whisper. "Mac, is that you?"

"Yes, sir," Mac said. "Is something wrong?"

"Yes, Mac, I'm afraid so," Carrington said. *Oh, Jesus,* Mac thought. *He's endorsing Brock,* too. But then Carrington said, his voice even lower, "Mac, is this phone secure?"

Mac's eyes darted around the empty trailer as if seeking eavesdroppers. "Uh—well—sure, I mean, I guess so," he said. "What do you mean?"

"Never mind," Carrington said. "Is there a pay phone around there somewhere?"

"I guess so," Mac said. "Yes, yes, in fact, there is one downstairs in the hall."

"Will you call me back at this number?" Carrington gave a Richmond exchange.

"Sure," Mac said, mystified. "Can I call you in an hour or so?"

"You call me back right away," Carrington said. His voice promised dire consequences.

"Yes, sir," Mac said.

The downstairs hall smelled of high school: sweat socks and bad food. Mac couldn't find the light switch; he dialed in the dark. Carrington answered on the first ring.

"All right, Senator," Mac said.

"Okay," Carrington said. "Son, do you remember when you came to

377

see me and I told you I didn't want to get involved in this damn election?"

He is going to do it, Mac thought, his stomach plunging. "Yes, sir?" he asked cautiously.

"Why couldn't you just leave it at that?" Carrington's words were angry and tired and sad.

"What do you mean?" Mac said.

"You know what I mean," Carrington said, still sad, but angrier.

"No, sir, I do not," Mac said, polite but crisp, as a little anger rose in him, too, at having been pulled away from his rally and sent downstairs to play games in the dark. "I wish you'd tell me. I've got a live TV show going on, and I'm supposed to be upstairs, and I don't have any more time, so please tell me."

"You really don't know?"

"No, sir, I do not."

He heard Carrington take a deep breath, like a pearl diver going over the side. "Listen carefully. Yesterday, a man came to see me, a friend. Or was a friend. He said to me that Shadwell wanted my endorsement worse than ever. He said he wanted it enough to be willing to make a deal."

"A deal? What kind of deal?"

"Just listen. He said if I would do it, then when Shadwell got to be governor, he would guarantee me the presidency of the University when the job falls open in two years."

"What?" Mac said, or screamed. "What are you talking about?"

"That's what the man said."

"What man? Who?"

"Never mind that."

"Is he in this campaign?"

"Let's say he's a friend of your campaign. He told me to let him know tonight."

"Senator, I don't know what you're talking about, but let me tell you, Tom Jeff Shadwell does not make deals. I have never seen him do it, not anything like this. He doesn't believe in it, and he certainly would never make such an offer or give his approval."

"I would have thought so, too," Carrington said. "Until yesterday. But this fellow sounded mighty sure of himself."

"Who was it?"

"Never mind," Carrington said again. "The point is, if this is true, I'm mad as hell. I love that University, and this kind of stuff makes me sick to my stomach. Maybe you can get some kind of explanation for me. But I'll

378

tell you, unless I can get assurance that this offer did not come from Shadwell, I am prepared to go to the Brock people tomorrow with this. I won't like it, but I'll have to. You know what that will mean."

"Sweet suffering Jesus," Mac said. He could see it: the "Days of Truth" would be days of disaster; it would mean landslide, ruin, the end of Tom Jeff Shadwell and those who believed in him. "Senator, can I call you back?"

"I'll be at this number. Call me soon." Carrington hung up.

Mac held the receiver as the hall whirled around him. Upstairs he heard the music; it struck painfully against his ears. How could this happen? Could Shadwell have—the thought was absurd. Could Brock somehow have engineered it, organized a last dirty trick to get the one endorsement he lacked? Perhaps—but how to prove it? Would Carrington believe that? Could Mac tell Tom Jeff? *It might kill him,* he thought. *Or me, if it's true.* But it was not, could not be true.

He stood in cold despair until, when hopelessness had cleared his mind of thought, he saw suddenly in memory's eye a familiar face, half in light, half in shadow, with a curious look which seemed in retrospect suddenly not so much expressionless as expectant, tense; the face of a gambler who has bet all on one turn of the cards. Mac felt a sudden wild suspicion, felt it first in his feet, which were moving before his brain had fully realized where he was going, and why.

Onstage the tobacco farmer was speaking. "My name is Jeremiah Willys, and I am a retired tobacco farmer from Kenbridge, Virginia," he said in a combative voice, as though expecting someone to contradict him. "Senator Tom Jeff Shadwell is my friend. He's the friend of every retired person in this state. He's the best friend we ever had in the General Assembly. When Miles Brock was the governor, he wanted to dip into the pension fund for state employees and lend it at low interest to his friends at the banks. Tom Jeff Shadwell fought against that. When Governor Brock vetoed a bill to give tax relief to the elderly, Tom Jeff Shadwell said it was wrong. When Governor Brock stuck a tax on our food and medicine, Tom Jeff Shadwell voted no. Now every retired person with a fixed income knows how unfair it is to tax medicine and food. And when Tom Jeff Shadwell gets to be governor, he's going to get that tax taken off. When he gets to be governor, retired people and people on fixed incomes are going to have a friend in high places. And that's the truth."

The gospel choir began to sing "Jesus is my savior, I shall not be moved." From the pit beneath the footlights, Hope Pinnell caught Mac's eye. She smiled, and her thumb and forefinger joined in a triumphant cir-

379

cle. Mac did not respond. His eyes darted among the figures lurking backstage. Shadwell still sat grimly, wrapped in determined silence. Next to him was Danny Watkins. Mac bent close to his ear.

"Where's Knocko?" he whispered.

Watkins cast his eyes at the rear entrance. "Trailer," he mouthed.

"Why?" Mac whispered.

Watkins shrugged.

Waiting for a phone call, Mac thought.

Cheatham was sitting in full darkness. Mac found him by the glow of his cigar.

"Knocko," he said.

"Not now, Mac."

"Now or never," he said. "Did you have somebody offer Tobey Carrington a deal? Did you tell them to offer him president of the University?"

The red circle of Knocko's cigar dipped gracefully, like a firefly at dusk. Mac heard him exhale.

"Listen, sonny," he said in a voice as cold as Mac had ever heard, "if you want to stay in this campaign, you'll butt out of this."

"What do you mean?" Mac was struck with a terrible doubt; it hit him in the knees. "Do you mean—does Tom Jeff know about this?"

"Drop it, Mac," Knocko said, implacable, terrifying. "You don't want to know."

Again Mac wondered: *could it be?* But he remembered Thursday night and summoned his faith. It could not, it was not possible. Knocko was lying.

"Knocko," he said, "I have a phone number here where Tobey Carrington is staying. Now what I'm going to do is give that number to Tom Jeff and have him call it now. Not later. Not after his speech. Now. Then we'll see."

The cigar glowed in silence; Mac flipped the light switch and saw what he had hoped for: Knocko's face, always pink, confident, composed, was pale, and Mac knew he had won. He had called Knocko's bluff.

"You poor dumb bastard," Mac felt, and even as he spoke, he felt astonished that he should be speaking this way to Knocko, who had been his boss and his teacher and sometimes his friend. "You thought you could pull this off, buy this endorsement, get back in favor again, win the election, and not even tell him about it till afterwards, didn't you? Or maybe you weren't ever going to tell him. Maybe you would work it so Carrington would get the job anyway. Or maybe you'd double-cross everybody and not do anything for Carrington at all. How could he object, after all? What could he do, sue you? Jesus, listen to me." Mac was suddenly overcome with sick self-loathing. "It's disgusting. I'm talking like you. Makes me sick. And you know, that's how come you didn't get away with it. You taught me too well, I can think just like you. Makes me sick to my stomach."

Cheatham, in the metal chair, seemed to sag, like a fighter who has taken a gut punch and can't keep his knees from folding. His lips moved, but he did not speak.

"Knocko, old pal, you have bet too much on one turn of the cards, and you have lost," Mac said. "Now why don't you do everybody a favor and get in your car and go home, okay? Now, not later. Get in bed and get sick and don't say anything to anybody, run a fever until election day. Do you understand me?"

Knocko nodded.

"All right," Mac said. "Now you've probably lost us this election, but I'm going to fix it up if I can. Don't be here when I get back."

The phone rang six panicky times before Carrington answered. "I have traced that offer," Mac said. "It was not made by Tom Jeff Shadwell, he was not aware of it, he would not approve it, he knows nothing about it. The individual responsible has left the campaign as of tonight."

"Who was it?" Carrington asked suspiciously.

"Listen, Senator," Mac said, "You held out on me, and I'm going to hold out on you. But if you don't believe me, just watch your newspaper."

"Do I have this assurance from Tom Jeff Shadwell himself?"

"No, sir. You have it from me."

"I think maybe I should talk to Shadwell myself."

Mac prayed for the gift of tongues. "Senator Carrington," he said, "if I tell Tom Jeff right now, it will break his heart. It might literally do him physical damage. He's got his back to the wall; he's bleeding in a dozen places; he's exhausted. If he hears this, it will cost him the election. Do you want to do that?"

"Well," Carrington said doubtfully.

"You knew my father, you knew my brother, you know me," Mac said. "I give you my sworn word that this offer did not come from Tom Jeff or represent the Shadwell campaign. I swear to you before heaven, as a gentleman, a Democrat, and a human being. Isn't that enough for you?"

After a silence of years, Carrington said, "I guess it is, Mac, I guess so." His tone had changed; it was gentler, more thoughtful. "You know, when I was in the legislature, they wanted my vote to close the schools. They came around and said if I'd vote their way, they'd make me governor. I turned them down, but I didn't call any press conferences about it. I guess I can let this go, too."

Mac exhaled: a breath that seemed to travel from his toenails up through his whole body. "Senator, thank you," he said.

"Thank you, too," Carrington said. "I guess. You know, whoever did this might have outsmarted himself. Because if you-all had come back again and asked me nice, I just might have gone along."

Mac was suddenly exasperated. "Oh, come on, Tobey!" he snapped, then stopped short, fearful of undoing what he had accomplished.

But Carrington only laughed gently. "Maybe you're right," he said. "I guess I was turning the knife a little. Good night, Mac. Take care."

"You too, Senator." The line buzzed, empty, broken.

By the time Mac got backstage again Tom Jeff was finishing his speech, spotlighted on the dark stage. "Yes, my friends!" he cried, flinging his arms at them. "They are trembling in the Confederate Club tonight! They are peering through the windows with frightened eyes and stirring pots of boiling oil! They're scared, friends, scared of you and me and of this great crusade for truth and honesty in state government we have begun. They've called on all their mightiest servants for protection, and against us they have arrayed one governor, two senators, and ten congressmen, and against us they have hurled their mightest champion, Miles Brock, and terrible is his fury and mighty is his wrath, my friends, and he is girt about with the armor of confusion and his sword is the sword of darkness and he has come among us to sow chaos and despair."

Then he lowered his arms and leaned forward confidentially, and his voice was gentler, "But we will withstand him, you and I, we will be faithful. We will turn away his falsehoods with truth." He held up a copy of the special issue of *True Facts*. "Here is our sword and buckler, friends, and it is the truth, simple truth, the plain light of the truth that will strip away this man's deceitful armor and hold him up to the world as he really is!" He waved it at them, pointing, as he called the litany: "Brock the school closer! Brock the food taxer! Brock the big money boy! Brock the fund juggler, delight of the corporations! Brock the darling of the boardroom and the scourge of the ordinary man and woman! Here it is! Here is the truth! And in the next ten days we will be all across this state, from Accomack to Abingdon and Roanoke to Richmond, and we will say to the people of Virginia, here is the truth! We will say, Virginia, you shall know the truth, and the truth shall make you free!"

Then, as the crowd stood and screamed, the stage lights came on, and through the screaming Mac heard the gospel choir start to sing:

382

THE SHAD TREATMENT

Oh, Happy Day!
Oh, Happy Day!
When Jesus washed,
He washed my sins away!

The cameras panned on the crowd as the music flowed on. The MC, offstage, murmured his pitch for funds as the monitor showed a slide, the address of the Richmond headquarters. The red light went off; it was over.

Mac leaned carefully back against the wall. His arms and legs were shaking; his teeth were chattering. People clustered around to congratulate him; he had forgotten that it was his rally, he had organized it. He could not speak. Finally, Shadwell himself took his arm. The candidate looked drawn, stretched like silly putty, but his smile was triumphant. "Thank you, young Mac, you did a grand job."

Mac, still shaking, said only, "Think nothing of it, Governor, nothing at all. Don't give it another thought."

The Ten Days of Truth swept by so fast Mac could hardly breathe. On Monday Mac and Ralph Bova split Knock's duties between them. Bova did not seem curious about Knocko's departure, but he was glad to be rid of his rival. Tom Jeff himself, as if possessed of some preternatural perceptions, seemed hardly surprised. "Something's been eating at Cousin Knocko for a while," he said. "Guess he couldn't take it anymore." He flew off to Front Royal to deliver another of Lola Kreznik's speeches. Mac issued a press release saying that Knocko was sick.

On Tuesday the first of the letters came in, perhaps twenty in all. Most were hand-addressed, in cheap drugstore envelopes; some contained notes or cards, others nothing, no return address. All had money, sometimes a five- or ten-dollar bill, sometimes coins, even one book of trading stamps. Mac took them to Bova.

"How much you figure is there?" Bova asked.

"Seventy-five dollars," Mac said. "Hundred at the outside."

"Hell, that's peanuts," Bova grumbled. "Just a big headache to disclose. I don't know whose bright idea that money business was, anyway. It's too late to do us any good."

"Ralph," Mac said, " I know this is hard for you, but try not to think of this as money."

"What do you mean?"

"These are people who saw the special and got turned on. These are people we got through to, see? If we keep getting these, it tells us that something's going on."

Bova looked at the envelope thoughtfully. "Maybe you're right," he said.

On Tuesday there were fifty letters; on Wednesday more than a hundred. On Wednesday, too, Miles Brock held a press conference with Junior, the Apple-Farmer's son and hereditary successor in the U.S. Senate, by his side. The pair were the picture of outrage as they protested against the "Truth" campaign. "These are smears, pure and simple," Junior said, in the pure and simple style that characterized all his public utterances.

On Thursday there were seventy-five letters. On Thursday, the Richmond paper attacked, a shrill whine in its editorial voice. SHADWELL'S SMEAR TACTICS, the headline read. Mac didn't read further. On Friday there were fifty letters. On Friday, Miles Brock trotted out a distinguished panel of bankers, lawyers, and brokers to defend his handling of state funds. "We got to the bastard," Danny Watkins said. "We're making him play our game."

By Saturday there were only twenty-odd letters. In all, less than a thousand dollars had come in. But by Saturday they knew it was anybody's race, knew it from the reports from Tony Soleri's field organizers. Something was happening out there; the people were stirring, like a great beast shifting in its sleep.

Sunday and Monday Mac spent helping Soleri and Ed O'Brien arrange machinery to get the voters to the polls: phone banks, car pools, poll watchers, precinct captains. From a distance they heard their candidate's voice, preaching over radio and TV, calling down wrath on his enemies. The headquarters was like a house on a hill, swept by winds from all points of the compass; there were rumors of triumph and treachery, moments of despair and, seconds later, hope. By Monday night, when Mac closed his eyes, no one knew what might happen, but all felt profoundly stirred, touched by something remote, mysterious, huge.

He pulled his gummed eyelids open to the sound of Molly's O.'s buzzer. It was just past six o'clock. Mac looked out the window and saw a faint light in a cloudless sky. Election day would be fine weather. He stumbled to the phone.

"Have you seen it?" Danny Watkins' voice was rapid, shrill. "Have you seen what those bastards have done now?"

"Wha—what?" Mac said, still groggy.

"The Richmond papers? Those bastards! Those pimps!"

"What are you talking about, Danny?" Mac said. He caught sight of himself in the mirror on the wall. The face that looked back was pale, tired, unshaven, and frightened. "What have they done?"

"Their lead editorial! Want to hear it?"

Mac steeled himself. "I guess so," he said.

"It's called 'SHADWELL'S TAXES,'" Watkins said. Mac heard the rest in snatches. "For all his raving about honesty in government, Senator Shadwell's record has some curious gaps. . . . Information recently obtained by this newspaper shows that of $1,643.52 in dividend income he received from Virginia corporations during the last four years, the 'apostle of integrity' himself paid not one red cent in Virginia income taxes . . . unmasks the shoddy charade of 'Truth Days' . . . reject this hypocritical charlatan. . . .'"

"What?" Mac said. "What does it mean?"

"It's the big lie!" Watkins screamed. "Of course he didn't pay taxes on that income. You know why? It's fucking tax-exempt! Nobody else paid any taxes on it either! You know where they got those figures? From Tom Jeff's tax returns! We released 'em two months ago! And they wait until election day! Oh, Jesus, God in heaven!"

"This could hurt us."

"You bet your toupee it could hurt us," Watkins said. "Listen. The candidate's in Norfolk. He knows about it. He's going to vote at seven and then fly up here. We got a press conference at nine at the airport. Now you and I have got to get some reporters out of bed and get 'em to it. If we get the TV people there, this guy Hackett, his station has a noon news program we can make."

"I'm supposed to work the polls."

"Fuck the polls! This is life or death! Here's your list—got a pencil?"

"Hell, no," Mac said. "I haven't even got my trousers on." He went to get both.

The press conference was in a deserted passenger lounge at the airport. The radio people were there; they could broadcast denials every hour. There was a reporter from the afternoon paper, and Ed Hackett and his camera crew. Tom Jeff was tired and so angry he could hardly talk. "This is the foulest slander of an unspeakable campaign!" he cried, and then, eyes brimming with tears, he grabbed a copy of the paper and tore it to shreds while the cameras rolled.

"Great TV," Watkins whispered.

"Are you planning to sue the paper for libel?" asked one of the radio reporters, a blond youth in a red suit.

Again Tom Jeff struggled for words. "There will be an announcement at the appropriate time," he said. "Proper action will be taken."

Ed Hackett now cued his cameraman again; the TV lights came on. "Senator Shadwell, isn't this just the same tactics you have been applying yourself against Governor Brock?"

385

"Oh, God," Watkins said, and like a squirrel, he jumped over a crouching photographer and stationed himself in front of Hackett's camera, thereby depriving Hackett of the footage of a lifetime, for Tom Jeff's brow darkened and on his face was an unspeakable rage.

"God damn it!" Hackett cried, grabbing Watkins by the elbow. "Get out of the way!" But the little press secretary would not be moved; so Hackett's camera failed to record the Democratic candidate for governor pointing a furious finger and screaming, "Hackett, you born fool, if you had one brain to rub against another—"

"Thank you, Senator!" Mac cried loudly. He grasped Shadwell by the arm and dragged him down the hall to the men's room. "They won't follow you in here," he said. "Wait until I tell you to come out. Splash some water on your face." He guarded the door and found himself facing the blond radio reporter. From a distance he heard Watkins and Hackett screaming imprecations at each other.

"Are you Mac Evans?" the reporter said.

"Yes," Mac said.

"I'm Teddy Smith."

They briefly shook hands. "You'll have to use another bathroom," Mac said.

"That's all right," the reporter said. Behind him Hackett swept by furiously, a hapless cameraman in tow. In his wake floated Watkins' voice, crying, "After the polls close, buddy! Anywhere you say!"

"Is he going to sue for libel?" the reporter asked again.

"Jesus, pal, I don't know," Mac said. "Not now, okay?"

"If you hear anything, will you let me know?" he proffered a card. "Teddy Smith."

"Yeah, sure, fine," Mac said, pocketing the card. "Later."

They took the candidate, shaken and silent, to his room at the George Mason; his family would join him there later. The campaign had booked the hotel's rooftop ballroom for the election night party, celebration or wake.

"You lie down now, Tom Jeff," Watkins said.

"Believe I will," Tom Jeff said. His bounce and drive, that furious animal vitality which had carried him through this campaign and a lifetime of challenging the mighty, still showed, but dimly, like a lamp whose oil was almost gone. "Don't reckon they'll write that one up as my finest hour," he said, rubbing his face.

"Don't worry, Governor," Watkins said. "That picture of you ripping up that newspaper's going to win the election for you."

"If it does, it'll be because my staff saved me again." The candidate summoned a smile, a sunny beneficent beam that warmed Mac's heart. "Reckon it'd be better if you all did have me stuffed, after all."

Ralph Bova met them at the headquarters door. "I didn't know you were the campaign manager, Mac," the big man said, his mouth gaping angrily.

"What are you talking about now?" Mac said.

"Haven't you heard on the radio about how you're going to make a statement and all?"

"No! No! I don't know what you're talking about," Mac said. "I've just been at a press conference that made Pickett's charge look like a Sunday school picnic, and I haven't got time to listen to you tell riddles."

"It'll be on again in twenty minutes, listen to it then," he said. "What did happen at the airport anyway?"

"Read about it in the papers," Mac said, walking back to his office.

At the hour he tuned in the news. "Democratic gubernatorial nominee Thomas Jefferson Shadwell struck back this morning at charges by a local newspaper that he had failed to pay his state income taxes on stock dividends at a hastily called press conference at Richmond's Byrd Airport. Teddy Smith files this report."

Smith's voice cut in. "At the early-morning press conference, a visibly shaken, angry Shadwell called the report, quote, the foulest slander in this unspeakable campaign, unquote. He tore a copy of the editorial to shreds, and both candidate and aides exchanged heated words with a local television reporter. But Shadwell also dropped broad hints that he may bring charges of libel against the newpaper. Shadwell campaign manager Mac Evans has promised a statement later in the day."

The announcer began an account of Brock's day, which seemed in the telling considerably less frenetic. "What the hell?" Mac was saying as Ralph Bova burst through the door.

"Now do you see what I'm talking about?" Bova shouted.

"Yeah," Mac said, reaching for the phone. "Sit down, Ralph, I'm going to clear this up right now." A switchboard operator answered. "Teddy Smith, please," Mac said.

Smith's casual voice came on the line. "Hi, Mac. Got your statement yet?"

"No," Mac said. "Are you taping this?"

"I can," Smith said.

"Don't," Mac said. "You aren't going to want to remember it. Now listen. Item one, I didn't promise you a statement. Item two, I am not the campaign manager. Item three, you are the dumbest shit God ever made.

Item four, I am going to get your job, and if I have my way, I'll run your ass right out of journalism. Got that?'' He hung up the receiver with a bang. "I think that takes care of that, don't you think, Ralph?''

Bova seemed to be looking at him oddly. "My God,'' he said. "You must have had some dustup out at the airport.''

"Yes,'' Mac said.

"You feeling all right?''

"Of course not, Ralph. I feel like shit. So does everybody else.''

"Mac,'' Bova said, in the tone of voice customarily reserved for small children and the insane, "why don't you hang it up for the day?''

"I got to work the polls,'' Mac said.

"Forget that,'' Bova said. "Just forget it. You go out to the polls, you're liable to ax-murder somebody.''

"Don't be silly,'' Mac said. He rose and walked toward the door, but for some reason the floor rose up and hit him in the face. He studied the linoleum tile pattern carefully, as if trying to memorize it.

Bova bent over him. "Are you all right?'' the big man said.

"Certainly,'' Mac replied equably, not moving. "But you know, Ralph, I'm beginning to think you're right. I'm going to go on home.''

After seven more hours of dull dreamless sleep, Mac's head buzzed and crackled like an old radio on a stormy night as he entered the Shadwell election party. One wall of the long rooftop ballroom was a picture window; it looked over the city's east end, Church Hill, at whose crest St. John's Church, where Patrick Henry is reported to have asked for liberty or death, slumbered among decaying one and two-story tenements. A new white building, floodlit, floated eerily on the hillside: a radio studio. The other long wall of the room was covered with a chalkboard, marked off in spaces for each of the state's thousand-odd voting precincts. Soleri was presiding over a bank of phones, and teenaged volunteers stood ready to chalk up results as they arrived; as yet, none was posted.

At one end of the ballroom was a makeshift bar, with beer kegs, cartons of soda pop, and piles of styrofoam cups. Opposite it was the stage dominated by a photo of the candidate in profile. SHADWELL, said the legend. *The Truth Shall Make You Free.* A bluegrass band was tuning up; Mac remembered them from the "Hour of Truth" rally—how long ago? A week? Ten days? A year?

It was still only seven thirty. The room was almost deserted. Mac saw Danny Watkins and Lola Kreznik bent over the afternoon paper, figuring the relative voter turnout.

388

When completed, it appeared to be a distinctly mixed picture. The turn-out had been heavy in Tidewater, Shadwell's home area, and relatively light in the Shenandoah Valley and the Valley of Virginia, the western areas which had been the traditional backbone of the Republican Party; so much was good. But turnout in the Richmond area, which seemed like-ly to be hostile to Tom Jeff, was also heavy, as it was in Danville, another conservative stronghold; this was a bad sign. Early reports indicated that black voters were not turning out heavily, except in Tidewater; that was also bad. The turnout in northern Virginia, heavily populated, affluent, and politically volatile, was light; that was a mixed omen, probably good. And in the Ninth, that harsh mountainous enigma, the voters had turned out in record numbers, far more than ever before, promising a late count, and what that meant nobody pretended to know.

"Where are the gentlemen of the press?" Mac asked, gesturing toward the empty press tables.

"And ladies," Lola snapped.

"Eating, if they got any sense," Watkins said. "This is a waste of time right now. No news. We got a long night coming up." His voice lowered deferentially. "We have with us tonight a representative of the National Broadcasting Corporation."

"No kidding?"

Their heads nodded in unison.

"Goodness," Mac said. "We must be having an election down here af-ter all."

"Reckon so," Danny said.

"Speaking of gentlemen of the press," Lola said, with a malicious twinkle in her eye, "here comes your friend Teddy Smith."

"Oh, God," Mac said. "I'd better go apologize to him."

Smith was wearing the same red suit and blank look. "I'm sorry about this morning," Mac said. "I was—you know—overwrought."

"It's all right," Smith said, frozen-faced. They shook hands briefly. Danny Watkins came up behind them.

"Hello, Teddy," Watkins said. "I'm sorry to hear about your trouble."

"Thanks," Smith said gravely.

"What trouble?" Mac said.

"Didn't you hear on the radio?" Watkins said. "Their traffic copter crashed."

"You're kidding."

"Wish I was," Smith said. "Scott McCarthy and the pilot, both killed."

"Plus two children," Watkins said. "It landed on their house."

Mac shivered. Once again reality had snuck up on him. He pictured the house, the children, the whirling rotors: death from above.

One of the phones rang. The room fell silent as Soleri, immaculate and calm, wrote something on a piece of paper and read it back. Then he hung up and picked up the microphone. "Ladies and gentlemen, your attention please," he said, smiling broadly. The small crowed of loyalists drifting in from dinner fell silent. "The first official return of the gubernatorial election is in." He prolonged the suspense, cleared his throat, pulled out a pair of reading glasses, and said, "From precinct number twenty-six in Richmond's East End, we have, for Governor Miles Brock . . . one hundred and twenty-seven." He paused to allow a few boos and groans. "For Senator Thomas Jefferson Shadwell . . . three hundred and forty-nine."

There was absurdly wild applause. With a flourish, Soleri handed the paper to a volunteer page. Mac walked over to the table.

"That's good news, at least," he said.

Soleri's smile had vanished. "Good news, my ass," he snapped. "We should have had three eighty-five out of twenty-six easy." Another phone rang. "Here we go."

After that things moved faster. Precinct by precinct, returns came in, each one indecipherable but together gradually adding up to the truth, whatever that would be. The press tables filled. TV cameramen began filming background and color shots. The bluegrass band played, and Soleri read the returns over the PA between songs. Supporters, workers, and sightseers poured out of the elevators.

By nine o'clock Mac had begun thinking about victory. The returns were pointing to an upset: with a little more than half the votes in, Tom Jeff held a narrow twenty-thousand-vote lead. He was carrying Tidewater, his home base, by a wide margin; the rest of the black-dirt country was going for Brock, but it was hard to tell how wide the margin would be. In northern Virginia, the two candidates traded the lead minute by minute: Mac guessed the area would go for Brock, but not by much. The Valley was, of course, coming in for Brock, but, it seemed, his margin there might be less than expected as well. The Third District, the Richmond area, was going for Brock, although Shadwell seemed to be carrying the city itself; the two counties were Brock country, but, again, the margin was hard to predict. And from the Ninth, where the votes were marked on paper ballots and counted by hand, there was no word.

At nine fifteen Danny Watkins ran up to Mac and grabbed his lapel, nearly bowling him over in his excitement. "I just talked to the guy from NBC," he said. "He says New York is going to project us the winner inside half an hour!"

"What?" Mac said. Looking up, he could see the rumor pass through the crowd like a ripple in a pond: at its center stood the network reporter, eyes cast down modestly, exquisitely tailored, gleamingly coiffed.

"It's true," Watkins said. "We won. I swear to God, we won!"

Unaccountably Mac found that Ralph Bova had thrown a mammoth arm around his shoulders. "Mac, old buddy, I do believe we have done it, yes, sir," Bova said. "I believe this is trending. We got it all, we got the Wallace vote and we got the Carrington vote, and there is a damn Carrington vote, I don't care what Knocko Cheatham—"

He broke off. Looking up, Mac saw why. As if he had been summoned by the utterance of his name, passing out of the elevator and into the ballroom came none other than Knocko himself, looking good, tanned, and rested and enormously self-assured, wearing a new suit and smoking a big cigar, and stopping here and there on his way toward them to accept a congratulatory handshake.

"What the hell?" Mac said.

Knocko came up to them puffing merrily; he seemed to be considering offering his hand, then decided not to, settling rather for a condescending but friendly nod.

"Hello," he said. "How're you boys?"

Mac glared at him. "Thought you were sick," he said.

"I'm feeling a lot better," Knocko said. "Had to be here at the finish." He nodded again, then wandered off, stopping in the crowd to buttonhole a crony here and there.

"Damn," Mac said.

"What was wrong with him anyway?" Watkins said.

"I couldn't begin to tell you," Mac said.

"I'm going to wake the candidate," Watkins said.

Some superstition in Mac's soul resisted. "Not yet," he said. "Wait till they do it."

"Maybe you're right," Watkins said. He wandered away, saying over his shoulder, "I think we got it won, though!"

Tony Soleri beckoned to Mac. "Could you get me a beer?" he asked. "My throat is killing me."

"Sure," Mac said. "Heard the news?"

Soleri nodded. "Damn if I can figure it out," he said.

"What do you mean?"

"Look," the field organizer said, ticking off points on his fingers. "We carried Virginia Beach. That.doesn't make sense. I figured we'd lose Buckingham, two to one, but we're carrying it, and that doesn't make sense. We carried Port Warwick, of course, but we carried it by sixty-five percent. Which is great, because it means we're winning by a landslide. Only we aren't winning by a landslide. We're getting killed in this district, and I'm afraid the worst is yet to come. I just can't figure this election out. If I was the damn computer, I wouldn't project."

And in fact, half an hour later, they heard that the projection had been "delayed." The network reporter stole away from center stage. The crowd quieted and thinned. The first beer kegs gave out. The band took a break.

The returns came in from the Third District, worse than expected. For the first time, Brock took the lead. The room was abuzz with whispers; in Mac's nostrils was a mixture of fatigue, uncertainty, and fear.

"It's the Ninth," Bova was saying. "It's all down to that now. We got to win big."

"Twenty-thousand-vote majority in the Ninth," Mac whispered: it was half memory, half prayer.

"What? Who said that?"

"Somebody said it a long time ago," Mac said.

Watkins came by. "Talked to the candidate," he said. "He says get the band playing. Sort of like the *Titanic.*"

"Why don't you shut your fucking mouth?" Bova was waving a fist at the little press secretary.

"Take it easy," Mac said quickly. "It was only a joke."

"Don't need no fucking jokes," Bova muttered. "Need some votes."
Watkins passed on toward the stage.

Soon the Gospel Crusaders began to sing: "Joshua fit the battle of Jericho, Jericho, Jericho." Mac found an overstuffed chair and watched the totals mount.

"Psst," said a voice. He turned his head. Knocko appeared to be actually lurking behind a potted palm. The image was ludicrous; Mac had to laugh.

"Your nose still out of joint?"

"Knocko, why don't you leave me alone?" Mac said.

Knocko stared at him with a look in which were blended fear and pride and mistrust and resentment. Mac had another glimpse into the tangled dark labyrinth of Knocko's mind; he saw that Knocko was rewriting the events of the last two weeks and convincing himself that his version, whatever it might be, must be the truth. "What are you so pissed off for?" Knocko said. "You got your way. We played it clean, the way gentlemen do. We're probably going to lose it, too."

"Knocko," Mac said evenly, "you are so fucked up you can't see straight."

"Hell, Mac," Knocko began, and Mac knew what he was about to say: *I brought you into this campaign, you worked for me, aren't you my friend?* He wondered how many friends Knocko had in this world, and suddenly a part of him wanted to say, *Yes, I'm still your friend;* it felt cold and lonely to be cutting Knocko off like this. But Mac remembered Cheatham's cigar dipping in the darkened trailer, the cold fury in his voice as he tried to bluff Mac into believing that Tom Jeff Shadwell had made a deal.

Mac stared him down. Knocko turned away, but he could not resist the last word. "See you tomorrow, in the office," he said vaguely. "There'll be a lot to do."

By a little after one A.M. it was obvious that Tom Jeff was going to carry the Ninth. All the work and hope and sweat he had poured into the hills and hollows of the district had paid off that much. But he was not going to carry it by enough to offset Brock's enormous margin from the Third District, where Tom Jeff had gotten a little less than forty percent of the vote. The sweep of Tidewater and the victory in the Ninth helped cut that killing margin, but not by enough. Bova, Soleri, Danny Watkins, Lola Kreznik, and Mac were all kneeling by the phone table, figuring on napkins, envelopes, and tablecloths; all came up with the same figure. No matter what happened in the forty-odd precincts remaining unreported, Tom Jeff Shadwell would end up 11,000 votes shy of victory. The number seemed absurdly small in an election in which more than a million people had voted: barely one percent. They figured and refigured, adding the same numbers over and over in the vain hope that somehow they would find those votes unnoticed in one or another of the districts, that their arithmetic would be faulty, that unnoticed counties would report; hoping for a miracle.

But nothing changed: the eleven thousand votes Tom Jeff needed were not there. He would not be governor; he had lost.

When this fact had sunk in, Ralph Bova began to moan softly. "Fuck it, fuck it, fuck it, fuck it," he said softly, pounding the table with a fist.

"Somebody's got to tell the candidate," Soleri said.

Nobody spoke.

"I'll go," Mac said finally.

They watched him go. He felt their eyes as he passed across the silent, crowded room.

* * *

Shadwell was watching TV with his wife, Peggy, and his son, Ed. Peggy Shadwell was a short, stout woman with a wide face creased from smiling. Neither of them was smiling now, but they did not look particularly sad, either; an alert, well-dressed middle-aged couple, sitting in hotel chairs, holding hands.

Ed was fifteen. He was sitting on the floor, leaning against one of the beds, watching TV. His face, a thinner, darker version of his mother's, was curving downward in tragic lines. Mac looked at him and thought of his brother, feeling his father's defeat in his stomach like a sharp sword.

"Tom Jeff—" Mac began, then stopped, embarrassed and grieved.

"Come on in, Mac," Peggy Shadwell said. "Sit down with us for a minute. It's gotten to be right lonely down here with this TV set."

Mac sat on the precise corner of the double bed. The TV was showing a war movie: Jack Webb was training young men to be marines. Every fifteen minutes the local station cut in with returns. Mac had seen them upstairs in the roof garden. But the TV returns were behind Soleri's figures; Mac realized Tom Jeff might not know.

"Senator," he began, "we've been going over the figures—"

"I know what you're going to say, young Mac," Shadwell said. "I've figured it out all by myself, me and Peggy here."

They sat a while longer without speaking. Jack Webb addressed the boots: "What are you, men?" "Marines, sir!" "I-can't-hear-you!" "MARINES, SIR!"

Mac's tongue again fluttered in his mouth. "Came close," he said lamely.

"Yes, sir," Tom Jeff said. "We gave 'em a scare. I guess if you can't beat these guys, it's better to scare 'em."

Silence again.

"Of course," Tom Jeff said, "what I've really wanted all along is to beat 'em. Didn't want to come close."

"You hush, Poppa," Peggy Shadwell said, her chin lifted combatively. "You'll beat 'em yet."

"Listen to that, young Mac," Tom Jeff said with a faint smile. "Momma's got more faith than I do. Bless you, Momma." He sat up straight and breathed in. "Come on, let's go see the folks." They stood. Ed Shadwell seemed unsteady on his feet; his eyes sparkled. "Steady up, Ed," Tom Jeff said, laying his arm lightly on his son's shoulders. "Why don't you look proud? Here one-half million people voted for your father. That's right many. We've got to go thank 'em." Ed was his father's son; he smiled. Mac gave him his handkerchief; he wiped his eyes and blew his nose, and the family party was ready.

In the ballroom they passed silently through the mourning crowd. Tom Jeff took the microphone and spoke into the silence. "I guess I have something to say to you all and to the people watching TV," he said. "But before I do, I want to ask the Gospel Crusaders to give us a song, and I want the people who've been with me in this campaign to come on up and sing with us, because they've meant so much to us, like another family—Ed and Ralph and Tony and Danny and Lola and Hope and J.B. and Mac—come on up here and stand by me now." One by one they came. Mac stood beside Peggy Shadwell; she linked her arm in his. Then Tom Jeff said, "Now if the Gospel Crusaders, who've sung for us so often, will sing once more before we go home, just once more, I'd like to hear 'O Happy Day,' because this is a happy day, when so many friends can be together and work together and one-half million people can stand up and vote and say, yes, we want a governor who's honest and hardworking. God bless you all."

The choir began to sing, so softly Mac could hardly hear it:

> O Happy Day!!
> O Happy Day!!
> When Jesus washed
> He washed my sins away.

Then everyone was singing, swaying with the music, and they were all crying, even big Ralph Bova weeping like a child; only Mac, it seemed, was tearless in the crowd. He felt Peggy Shadwell's arm in his; hers was warm, his was cold.

Then it was over, and Tom Jeff was gone and the lights were going out. He found himself at the elevator with Danny Watkins.

"What are you going to do?" Mac said.

"With my life?" Watkins said. "Don't know."

"I mean tonight."

"What are you thinking of?"

"Let's get pretty drunk."

SEVEN

★

"All along you're telling yourself, I'm not like these other guys, I'm not going to end up a hack like these guys," Danny Watkins's voice seemed to be saying.

Eight o'clock sunlight was slanting through the venetian blinds in Knocko's old office. Mac blinked and wondered how long he'd been awake or if he had slept. Watkins' voice flowed on around him. "You're in it to change the world," the press secretary was saying. If Mac's attention wandered, his words lost all meaning, and he might have been listening to a gigantic, aggrieved duck. " 'You shall know the truth, and the truth shall make you free,' that business," Watkins went on. "And what the hell, the city editor seems like a decent guy, he likes you, and he won the Pulitzer Prize once, a long time ago, so you figure you'll stay for a while, maybe learn something from him, you know, change the world."

Watkins paused. They were drinking bourbon from enormous Sweetheart cups. Mac read the side of his: "———Syrup Line," it said, and then above that, "———Milk Line." He put it to his lips; ice cubes clinked against his teeth. He was feeling good. The only sign that he had not slept was a deep muscular ache around his chest. It was the way he had felt two days after the police had beaten him up.

"So what the hell," Watkins was saying. "You go to work, and if you're really lucky, you get to expose some poor bureaucrat; if you're *real* lucky, you cost him his job, some guy, say, who's been getting kickbacks from landlords, something like that. You ruin the guy, and that's terrific, that makes your week. It makes you so goddamn happy you start feeling like the paper is your home, and it comes as a shock the first time they kill one of your stories. They never come right out and say, 'This guy is the publisher's brother-in-law.' They say, 'We can't print this, it's not *news*,' don't you know? That's really weird, the way that bothers you. Not *news*. I don't know what it might be, say, a story about an old man, a dentist, maybe, who's fighting the city to keep from being thrown out of his office because they want to build a parking garage there. Now, the reason it's not news, the real reason, is that the fellow who wants to build the parking garage is the publisher's brother-in-law. But you think it's because it isn't *news,* and that bothers you, because you thought it was news, and if it isn't, there must be something wrong with you, don't you know?''

Mac felt his jacket wadded between his back and the seat of the chair. The air was light with morning's promise; the sunlight through the blinds made pale bars on the wall above his head. He might have been sitting there listening to Danny Watkins's voice forever; he might sit here an eternity still.

"So you start being really tough on yourself. You go around all the time asking, 'Is it news? Is it news?' because you don't want to get a story killed again. So the next time some poor old bastard needs help, you're wondering, is it news? And when it comes up to the city editor, and he *doesn't* kill it, you're kind of torn up about it. You wanted him to kill it, don't you know? Because then you'd have something definite. But as it is, you're fighting shadows."

Watkins swilled his drink. Mac poured himself more from the bottle on the desk. He held the bottle to the sunlight; it glowed darkly. The corn god: whose head had been cut off this time? He studied the liquid in the Sweetheart cup, thinking of the fields of corn that went each year to distilleries, corn that people could eat. Take a drink and starve a child, he had read in the *New York Times Magazine*. He raised the cup; the liquor was strong and raw. Good-bye, little fella.

Somewhere a telephone shrilled insistently. Mac's peripheral vision caught sight of a blinking light on his desk phone. He turned his chair away from the flash and faced Watkins, who was by now fully reclined on the couch, like a psychiatric patient, paper cup balanced on his chest, eyes meditatively focused on the ceiling, saying, "Time passes quickly when you're having a good time, ha-ha. You get married, get a house, car payments, house payments, and all right, maybe my wife turned out to be a no-good lesbian, but that's another story. I married her in good faith, and you'll just have to take my word for that. But you see my point. Pretty soon you need the job, or a job anyway, and you're worrying all the time about what is news, so you won't get stories killed again. You don't like to waste your time, because it's begun to get you, all this pounding the pavement. Your back, your feet. It's one thing if you can go home and have a woman there to rub your back, I suppose, but what if your wife is a goddamn bull dyke, out every night at the bowling alley?''

The phone rang again. Watkins poured whiskey from the cup into his mouth, wetting his collar and chin in the process. He appeared not to notice.

The phone rang. Steps raced down the empty hall, and Knocko burst into the office, his face baleful and contorted, eyes red with lack of sleep, hangover, rage. A half-smoked cigar, extinct, jutted from his grimacing mouth, and in his hand was a twelve-ounce Coca-Cola.

He surveyed the room with a lordly glance; he seemed somehow to be taking possession of it once again, like a king returning from the Crusades. He gave Mac a commanding glance. "Don't you answer the phone anymore?" he asked.

"Why don't you get it, Knocko?" he said defiantly. "I don't work for you anymore, and besides, I'm off duty."

Knocko's red eyes transmitted inchoate threats. "Yeah, I forgot, you're a big shot now. I heard on the radio how you were campaign manager and all." He stepped behind his desk and picked up the phone. "Yeah?" He cocked his head to listen. "I don't think he's taking any calls this morning." He listened again, eyes narrowing in disbelief. "Are you serious?" The phone buzzed; from Knocko's face it appeared the speaker was. He shook his head in disgust. "I don't mean any offense to you, Teddy," he said, "but you haven't got one chance in hell of getting a statement about that today. You call him in a week or two. . . ." The buzzing broke in. "Oh, yeah?" Knocko said. Then, "I can't help you. You guys figure it out. The man just lost an election, he's had about four hours of sleep in the past week, he is not about to do it, and I'm not about to ask him." He listened again. "All right, then, that's it."

He set down the phone and gazed at Mac and Watkins with vaguely hostile aplomb, lifted the Coke bottle and methodically drank off half its contents, then pounded his chest until an enormous burp emerged.

"Mexican breakfast," he said. "Best thing for a hangover I know." He sat at his desk, then glanced across its surface as if looking for papers he might have left there the day before. Mac marveled at Cheatham's ability to forgive himself and forget his past. It was as if he had never left. He appeared sublimely unconscious of his position.

"Who was on the phone?" Mac asked, for lack of anything better to say.

Knocko belched again, then wiped his mouth on a monogrammed hand-kerchief. "Bastards at the radio station," he said. "I swear, those people are about as dumb as you can get. Call up at nine o'clock the day after the election and want Tom Jeff to come down to their studio and make a state-ment about that jackass copter jockey who got killed yesterday." He reached over and fiddled with the radio. Suddenly the room was filled with the liquid, resonant, utterly vacant voice of Ed Hackett.

"All of us in broadcasting knew Scott McCarthy well. We considered him a warm friend and a respected colleague. He was scrupulous, careful and dedicated. In this world of formula reporting and cut-and-dried jour-nalism, Scott remained an individual dedicated to his craft. Off the air, he didn't say much; he was no big talker or name-dropper. But all of us who had the privilege of knowing him or working with him knew that here was a heart as big as all outdoors, a quick mind, a gentle spirit—a young man with a future."

The electronic words swirled around the room like a school of bright tropical fish in a gloomy lagoon. In the doorway they seemed to resolve themselves into the tidy figure of J. B. Fitzhugh, head cocked to catch the voice, eyes scornful behind his huge gold spectacles.

"Damn," Fitzhugh said. "That helicopter killed two black children. I haven't heard a word about them on the radio."

Knocko flipped the radio off. "They're going to be broadcasting all day about this guy," he said. He finished the Coke and belched roundly once more. "Mr. Evans," he said, "do you think you might be favorably dis-posed toward doing some work around this place?"

"Fuck you, Knocko," Mac said. "What the hell is there to do around here? And how would you know about it anyway?"

Knocko did not flare back; instead, he looked vaguely around the room, muttering, "There's a lot to do. I know. I have my sources."

"If I was you, I wouldn't do very much of importance today, old bud-dy," Mac said. "You aren't official at this point."

"Yeah," Knocko said. "I keep forgetting you're the bigshot campaign manager, not me."

"Stuff it," Mac said, rising. "I'm off duty today. I'm leaving."

"Fine, have a good time," said Knocko with precarious equanimity. "But take this lump out of my office."

From the couch came a snore. Danny Watkins was asleep, his Sweet-heart cup still poised on his chest, hands folded beneath it as if in death.

"Right," Mac said. "Give me a hand, will you, J.B.? We'll put him in his own office."

As the two wrestled Watkins out the door, Mac saw Knocko scrabble futilely in a desk drawer. "What happened to my cigars?" he said.

"I smoked 'em," Mac answered. "They were good, too."

As the door closed, Mac saw Knocko glaring at him; his eyes stared from inside a wilderness of hatred, betrayal, and defeat.

Mac and Fitzhugh left Watkins to sleep it off and went to the White Tower for breakfast. Mac expected to feel unsteady on his feet, but instead, he felt preternaturally stable, as if he were somehow connected to the center of the earth. Main Street was bustling with well-dressed figures: sober gray bankers and brokers in suitable dark suits, young lawyers and executives resplendent in tidy mustaches and double knits, the first hint of corpulence collecting at jowls and beltline, tiny stenographers flashing Elaine Powers-perfect legs beneath short, flounced skirts, aged black messengers scuttling back and forth bearing legal folders and canvas bags. Across the street, on the steps of the old Post Office building, a group of young men lounged uneasily before the Army induction center: Today's Army had joined them, and soon a bus would come and carry them off to a place where they would learn vital skills to assure them of good jobs in later life. In front of the Central Planters Bank, an armored truck, motor idling, was taking on bags of money. A uniformed guard lounged against the building, cradling a shotgun, studying the passersby as if selecting a target. A group of construction workers were hammering and sawing at an old iron-front building, calling sexual invitations to passing women.

At the door of the restaurant Fitzhugh paused before a mechanical newspaper dispenser. Through the plastic window Mac saw the banner headline: BROCK NARROWLY DEFEATS SHADWELL TO WIN HISTORIC SECOND TERM *Huge District Sweep Gives Governor Winning Margin.*

"Don't mess with that garbage," Mac said.

"No, man, I want to see," Fitzhugh said. He brought a paper, and they passed inside.

The restaurant was a maze of shiny angles and reflecting surfaces. Mac sat at the Formica table, neatly pinned at the vortex of a universe of optical and geometric paradox. He addressed himself to eggs, sausage, potatoes, toast, and coffee, while Fitzhugh glumly studied the front page.

The whiskey had whetted Mac's appetite; after breakfast he would

401

want more to drink. He felt set apart from the busy jostle on the street outside, as if flowing through a different stream of time. Suddenly, after nearly two years of ceaseless activity, there was now nothing to do, nowhere to go, no tomorrow or yesterday, no night or day; he was a spinning mote, a particle at entropy. Utter freedom beckoned him on every side, vast, empty, silent. He felt no grief or anger, but emptiness, and a sort of vast godlike detachment.

He cleaned his plate and looked up, unsatisfied, at Fitzhugh, who was still reading the paper while his breakfast cooled untouched on the table before him. Mac sneaked a slice of toast from his plate and munched it surreptitiously. "You know, strangely enough, who I feel sorry for in all of this?" he asked.

"Who's that?" Fitzhugh said without looking up.

"Miles Brock."

Fitzhugh dipped the paper and looked at him suspiciously.

"What I mean is, the poor bastard's got to go on now and be governor and so on," Mac went on. "I really don't think he'd counted on that. He just wanted to beat Tom Jeff and go on home. He doesn't want to be gov-.ernor."

"Bunch of shit," Fitzhugh said. "What's wrong with you, man? A man wins, you don't feel sorry for him. When he loses, you feel sorry for him. Hell, I don't feel sorry for that bastard. Bunch of shit."

Mac shrugged. "Maybe so," he said. He wondered why he did not feel what had happened as Fitzhugh did, why he felt this separation, not only from the stream of life outside on the street, but even from those to whom he should feel closest. He shared no victories, no defeats.

Fitzhugh picked up his fork and leaned forward. He seemed to consider his plate briefly, then he called irritably, "Waitress!"

A short stout black woman appeared. "Yes, sir?"

"What are you thinking about?" Fitzhugh demanded. "I ordered toast and you only brought me one piece."

She looked blankly at Fitzhugh, then at the plate. Mac busied himself finishing his coffee.

"I'm sorry," said the woman. "I'll fetch you another."

"Yeah, and get me some more coffee, too, this cup is cold," Fitzhugh said.

"Me, too, please," Mac said, wiping his mouth. The waitress bustled away again.

Fitzhugh began to eat with mechanical ferocity, mumbling between bites, "Hell of a thing, bring a man only one piece of toast." Mac took the newspaper. AT THE SHADWELL HEADQUARTERS, FROM ELATION TO

GLOOM, read a headline. Above was a picture of Tom Jeff leading the singing. Mac's head appeared, a smear of newsprint. He turned quickly past the election reports and editorial columns to the vital news of the day.

Squat Oriental communists had trapped a beautiful American spy. Stripped to filmy black underwear, she was about to be subjected to obscure dialectical tortures when a yellow-haired Air Force colonel appeared and put her captors to rout. Muttered one of the fleeing guerrillas, "The imperialist fights like a demon!" His superior reproved him. "We no longer believe in demons, comrade." "Perhaps," replied the first, "it is time to revise our doctrine on this point." "Bite your tongue and run!"

An alligator was trying to teach a puppy to talk; after much coaxing, the dog responded, "Poltergeists are one of a number of spontaneously manifested supernatural phenomena." A lantern-jawed policeman flew above the surface of the moon in a magnetic space platform, while a sign warned: "The nation that controls magnetism will control the universe!" A householder attempted to repel two maniacal club-wielding salesmen. A bald deaf-mute juggled ice-cream cones. Yokels boggled at yodeling yogis. Clams spoke; frogs danced. The sheeted dead gibbered in the streets.

"What time you got?" Fitzhugh said.

Mac glanced at his skin diver's watch. "About ten or so," he said. The date window was, as usual, two days behind; for his watch, the election had not happened.

Fitzhugh drained his coffee cup. "Let's go on up and get a drink, what do you say?"

"Right!" Mac said. "Just my thought! What's open this early?"

"I reckon they won't throw us out of the two oh eight," Fitzhugh said. He shot Mac a speculative look.

The 208 was a black private club. "That's a good idea," Mac said. "I haven't been there in years."

"You been there?" Fitzhugh was momentarily puzzled. "Oh, yeah, your brother belonged, didn't he?"

Everywhere, Mac thought. He nodded.

Fitzhugh drove a sleek Belair, with leather seats and deep pile carpet. On the way across town he played the radio over the rear stereo speakers. The halting mountain accents of Horace Hapgood began in midsentence: "—a quiet man, but a man I instinctively liked from the first. We first met, I believe, during my first campaign for governor some eight years ago. He followed me across the state one week, and as I recall, he didn't say much, didn't ask a lot of questions, but to the best of my knowledge his reports were always fair and honest, and let me say that in my experience our Virginia press corps is almost never anything but fair and honest. I remembered his friendship and professional manner for years, and like a lot of people in Richmond, I have relied on his traffic reports, although of course I myself do not commute, my wife and I live in the mansion with our two sons, Buzz and—''

"Dumb jackass," Fitzhugh said, snapping the switch.

"I don't know," Mac said vaguely. "Poor old Horace. He generally tried to do the right thing."

"Maybe so, maybe so," Fitzhugh said grudgingly. "He sure as hell didn't have to pimp for Miles Brock the way he did."

"Yeah, that's true," Mac said. "Wonder why he did it? He was cutting his own throat."

"Don't mind if he cuts his own throat," Fitzhugh said. "It's my throat I'm mad about."

They crossed Broad Street. To white Richmond, Broad had a right side and a wrong side: a white side and a black side. North of Broad was Jackson Ward, the city's venerable black ghetto and the heart of black Richmond's social structure. Its rectangular grid of streets was lined with small upright brick and frame houses, churches, office buildings, barbershops, shine parlors, rib houses, boxing and karate gyms, groceries, and pool halls. In this area were the offices of the black civil rights and criminal lawyers, the city's black newspaper, the *Afro-American,* and its only black bank, the Consolidated Bank and Trust Company. Nearby was Booker's Hotel, where black lawyers and bankers and businessmen and politicians met for lunch or for political meetings. Farther west, across the street from the Fat Boy Drive-In, stood or rather danced the statue of one of Richmond's prominent black sons, Bill Robinson, known on the screen as Bojangles. Farther to the north was the campus of Virginia Union University, a private black institution which numbered among its graduates preachers, lawyers, doctors, carpenters, waiters, and African Cabinet ministers.

The city fathers of Richmond and their hired planners reserved for this area the peculiar fury of the powerful for the structures of the powerless. Scarcely a year passed without the unveiling of another civic improvement plan which would incidentally involve the destruction of this or that quarter of the ward; the blacks fought against the pressure with mixed success. The Richmond-Petersburg Turnpike snaked through the ward, and at the eastern edge, where black families had once lived, squatted a red and brown bowl: the Richmond Coliseum.

The streets were busy this morning. Unemployed men lounged in front

404

of a pool parlor. Women walked briskly to market. Insurance and rent collectors rang doorbells, clutching account books. A young man in a shiny robe emerged from the Capital City gym and crossed the street; next door a furtive white man pushed open the opaque doors of Wong's Oriental Massage Parlor.

"What the hell is an Oriental massage?" Mac asked.

Fitzhugh laughed. "Man, if you don't know by now, don't mess with it." As they drove on, he patted the car's dashboard and sighed. "I guess I got to get rid of this land yacht if I want to go back to school. Get me a Vega or something. School board in Suffolk County won't go too much for a science teacher cruising in a big old car like this." He eased into an alley and parked behind a gray stone building. "Would have been just right for a governor's aide, though."

In the shadowed early-morning quiet of the 208, billiard balls kissed in the next room beneath the susurrant murmur of the player's voices. Mac contemplated the face of J. Randolph Hopkins, civil rights lawyer, and in its wrinkles and folds contemplated time, fate, and history. Fitzhugh traded badinage. "You not practicing today, Mr. Hopkins?"

"Not today, Brother Fitzhugh," the older man replied. "Today's a legal holiday, declared by me." He poured them a drink from his private bottle; the 208 could not afford a bartender. They gravely drank, and Mac studied Hopkins's face.

Randolph Hopkins had been in every civil rights case in Virginia since before the Brown case. He had run for Congress and lost, had been arrested once for contempt of a white judge and threatened with disbarment, had been nominated by the black bar association for state and federal judgeships he had no hope of getting. He had shown the flag for thirty-odd years, fighting the racist system in Virginia, and his face showed every moment of it. A constellation of lines drew down from his eyes and mouth, molding his face into a brown mask, not of grief or resignation but of a determination which had looked long and hard at despair. He looked back and Mac with skeptical, ironic eyes, nodded his head in salute. They drank.

The sun shone obliquely through venetian blinds. They sat in a high-backed wooden booth in a corner of a wooden room, feet resting on a gritty linoleum floor, elbows on the tattered tabletop, while the unseen billiards players murmured and shot, shot and murmured.

The morning seemed timeless. Black men gathered in the room to drink bitter glasses of regret. Theodore Thomas, the athletic cocky legistator, came in: he had been reelected, but even so he seemed defeated. He

405

walked like a linebacker who has pulled a muscle, legs rigid, thighs painfully apart. He waved off congratulations, shaking his head in disgust. "Goddamn! I'm ashamed to be in politics today!" he said. "Goddamn! It was this district that did it. These white redneck bastards would step over their grandmothers to kick a black man. They trying to turn the clock back."

"Trying, hell," Hopkins said. "They been doing it, they doing it now, they going to keep on doing it."

"That's right, Mr. Hopkins," Thomas said.

"They got their leader now, they going to get back the death penalty, they going to go after the Voting Rights Act."

"That's right, Mr. Hopkins," Thomas said.

"Those brothers in the penitentiary might as well just cut their own throats now, save the state the expense of doing it when Brock gets in."

"I should hope to shout," Thomas said. "I mean, I don't want to face that damn legislature this year. Those old bastards are going to be out for blood."

"Backsliding," Fitzhugh said.

"That's right," Thomas said.

"Looks to me like y'all doing the backsliding," a voice said. A tall black man loomed over them, broad-shouldered, gray-haired, clothed in sober black.

"Reverend Davis," Thomas said. "Sit down and backslide with us." The taller man sat down ramrod straight on the bench, arms folded before him on the tabletop.

Thomas indicated the bottle with a diffident gesture. "Don't imagine we could tempt you with a drink, Reverend," he said.

"You may not," the minister said, and glared around the table with disapproving eyes.

There was an awkward pause.

"Do you know Mac Evans, Reverend?" Fitzhugh said.

"Indeed I do," Davis said, nodding briefly at Mac. "I knew his brother as well."

"How are you, Reverend Davis?" Mac said. They shook hands. "What brings you up from Petersburg today?"

"Purgation," the minister said, and his mouth snapped shut briskly.

"Say what, Reverend?" Thomas said.

"Purgation," Davis repeated. "I have come to purge the temple. I have come to name the lickspittles and fools who have brought us to the current pass." From the inside pocket of his dark suit jacket he brought a thick sheaf of papers. "I have here records of names, dates, and amounts. I know who took money from whom."

"Took money to do what?" Mac asked. He noticed that the others all seemed to know already; they had averted their eyes as if at an embarrassing or stupid remark.

The minister drew back and regarded him like a teacher looking at a stupid or refractory child. "To do nothing, of course," he said.

Randolph Hopkins was seized with a fit of dry, wheezy laughter. Mac feared the civil rights lawyer might choke, but at length he drew breath and smiled a tight-lipped grin. "White folks get paid not to grow cotton, young fellow, you know that," he said. "Black folks get paid not to vote." He chuckled again, softly.

"You laughing, Mr. Hopkins?" Davis said indignantly. "I would expect more from one of your years. You've been in our movement too long to be laughing at this kind of going on."

"I've been in the movement too long not to laugh, Reverend," Hopkins said. On his face was his ironic smile, but his voice was compassionate.

"Come time to stop laughing," Davis said, unappeased. "I'm not laughing now. I'm not laughing anymore. I'm going to purge these money changers. I'm going to scourge them with whips and drive them before me like the wind. I've got all the information right here."

"You got the information, Reverend?" Hopkins said. "That's fine. Now you tell me what you're going to do with it."

"At the proper time," Davis said.

"Who you think wants it?"

"At the proper time."

"There ain't any proper time," Hopkins said with a touch of scorn. "Don't you know that by now? There hasn't ever been any proper time for black people in this state, it ain't the proper time now, ain't coming any proper time. You think that stuff is going to do any good? What you going to do with it? You going to the attorney general? He's a white man. He cares a lot more about Governor Brock than he does about you. You going to the newspapers? What do they care about it? Nobody's going to mess with Miles Brock because somebody who works for him gave some money to some nigger politicians, don't you know that?"

"Maybe not, maybe not," the minister said between clenched teeth. "But if white folks don't care, black folks better care. We better turn on these traitors and drive them from us, that's all. We'd best pluck them out root and branch and cast them into the fire. I'm going to do it. I'm going to see to it. I don't need your help, if you'd rather sit around and weep. I'll do it myself."

The two men stared at each other without expression; after a second moment Hopkins grinned again and raised his hand in salute. "Reverend, I wish you good luck." In the words there was a mixture of irony and respect.

"Don't need luck," the minister said, rising. He patted his jacket where the papers nestled. "I'm armed with truth. I leave you gentlemen to your tippling."

They watched him go. "Lord save us from more truth," Hopkins said as his feet clumped down the stairs.

"He's liable to pull down the temple on top of all of us," Thomas said, laughing ruefully.

"Maybe so," Hopkins said thoughtfully. "But it wasn't much of a temple in the first place. Am I right?"

"Amen."

"Amen," said Fitzhugh.

"Amen to that," said Mac.

Afterward, when he pieced together that long day, Mac found it difficult to understand how he had ended up at sundown in the Ladies' Bar of the Confederate Club, the one place he had vowed to stay away from. The day, the city, perhaps the whole campaign or his whole life or even all of human history—all seemed some vast conspiracy, a maze or machine designed to force him to that one spot at that time, to that corner of the universe which was the epicenter of all he hated and hated him, all he had fought against and been defeated by.

He could reconstruct his journey across town. He had said good-bye to Randolph Hopkins and J. B. Fitzhugh in the early afternoon. He remembered standing on the corner of Broad street, in the center of the shopping district, and he remembered being attacked there by a fearful knowledge. At the corner, he pressed the green button and waited for the WALK signal; but when the sign flashed permission to proceed, Mac found himself rooted to the spot by a sudden vision of this crossroads, this grid of streets he was moving across, the heaving anthill that was his home. He knew every inch of this street, to his left the Greyhound terminal, beyond that a tired hamburger restaurant, beyond that a row of men's shops catering to blacks, beyond that the Army & Navy store where at the age of fourteen he had bought a black leather motorcycle jacket twinkling with gold stars and thus earned a tongue-lashing from the headmaster of St. Cyprian's for making a mockery of the school's dress code. Farther down, on the other side of the street, were the two great department stores, Thalhimer's and Miller & Rhoads—the latter a name he had misunderstood as a child, thinking it "Million Roads," imagining it as a marvelous bazaar where all ways met and caravans came from all corners of the world.

All of it . . . all of it now was his, from the tobacco warehouses, the poisonous chemical plants, the office buildings, the old churches and tenements of Church Hill, the market stalls in Shockoe Valley, the Capitol building, Jackson Ward, the wide avenue leading westward, past statues of Confederate heroes, all of it belonged to him, bound to him by the generations, by more than blood, more than history, by a bond more intimate than slavery; for a moment he saw it all and it was his as the earth is the Lord's, it was sprung root and branch from him as he from it, and without it he could not survive, nor without him could it exist, and he had but to clap his hands and it and he would disappear forever.

Then unaccountably he found himself surrounded by a flock of young Chinese women in white smocks, all of them walking across Broad Street together, and the fearful knowledge left him, and he was just a somewhat tipsy stroller on a sunny November day.

Somehow, after that, he made his way to the offices of the *Sentinel*, Gravelier Huntington's newspaper, though how and exactly when remained a mystery. He had probably been looking for the two reporters he had met at Huntington's party the month before: the corpulent Peter Grasp and the elegant Irene (though it seemed perhaps in retrospect that he had been looking for Irene not for herself but for another image—full, intricate dancer's body, long dark hair, quizzical face: Alexandra, as if he were hoping she might somehow appear unbidden before him). But whatever his motives, after his seizure on Broad Street he next remembered himself at the front desk of the *Sentinel* asking for Peter or Irene or both; a coolly efficient black receptionist bit off each word like a piece of thread as she replied, "I am sorry but they are no longer employed here."

Summoned then by a seemingly invisible buzzer was Huntington, Mac's old classmate himself, from his office in the back; Mac, wearing confusion on his chin like breakfast eggs, suffered himself to be greeted effusively and led back through a corridor to the publisher's office. The paper was housed in a narrow converted town house; it seemed as cramped and squeezed as a space capsule. Huntington's office featured a commanding view of the alley; next to it was the furnace room. On the door was a plaque unaccountably reading "Charles Foster Kane, Publisher." In the office, stretched out on a threadbare couch, was Hoke Spottswood, whom Mac had not seen since Shadwell had borrowed his farm to make his TV commercial. Hoke waved a livid hand in greeting, did not rise.

Huntington positioned himself adroitly behind the oversized executive desk and gestured Mac into a canvas chair before it. The room took on the air of a formal interview, with Spottswood acting as Huntington's chorus. Mac eased the chair till its back was to the wall; he faced perpendicular to the desk, watching both of them, ready, if need be, to flee out the door, though even as he did so he realized the notion was absurd: what reason could there be to flee from his old St. Cyprian's classmates?

"What happened to Peter and Irene?" he asked Huntington. In that moment he was mildly surprised to find a cigarette between his fingers. He had not smoked in years: where had it come from? Even more surprising was the bulge in his left coat pocket of an almost-full pack of (as he read from the blue printing on the cigarette in his hand) Marlboros. Made, he remembered, from the Richmond recipe.

Huntington produced a red plastic lighter and tossed it at Mac, who caught it and fumbled it alight. This operation kept him busy while Huntington explained, "We had a difference of opinion about news judgment—"

"Who did?" Mac was suddenly confused, holding the cigarette gingerly in his hand, undecided what to do with it.

"You asked about Peter Grasp and Irene Sorrento," Huntington explained patiently.

Mac took a deep smoker's drag, expecting his lungs to revolt in a painful spasm of coughing. They did not. Instead, his lungs, bloodstream, and brain turned out joyfully to greet the smoke like a delegation of dignitaries leading a tickertape parade. "Was her name Sorrento?"

"Yes," Huntington said.

"Still is," Spottswood said.

"Thanks, Hoke," Mac said. "What happened to them? Did they quit?"

"I'm trying to explain that," Huntington said. "We had a difference of opinion about policy, and it seemed to me that they were no longer wholeheartedly behind the concept of the *Sentinel.*"

"You mean you fired them?"

"I prefer not to use that term." From the couch Spottswood gave a smothered giggle.

Mac puffed the cigarette again, then stared at it in fascination. It was a surprise visitor, and it seemed that it might have come to stay. "I don't understand," he said. "Who's going to put out your paper?"

"Frankly, we find we don't have much difficulty in acquiring skilled personnel," Huntington said. His voice took on the reverential tone he reserved for discussions of business. "The newspaper industry is in a depressed state at the present time. Competent people are willing to work hard for the *Sentinel* much more readily than a few years ago. We already have a dozen good applications on file."

The room was filling with smoke. Huntington's words seemed to buzz around Mac's face like gnats. He waved his hands in front of his face to clear them away.

"Of course," Huntington was saying, "I intend to give them good references for further employment."

"How's that?" Mac said. "If they were good at their jobs, why did you fire them?"

"As I say, I'm not sure they were wholeheartedly behind the concept of the *Sentinel* as I see it. They had no business experience, and I don't think they understood the pressures on a small operation like this one. We're a marginal operation in many ways, and we have to be very careful not to strike a shrill or unnecessarily negative tone if we don't want to alienate our advertisers."

"Yeah," Spottswood said. "And besides, they were real wise-mouths, always giving us a hard time."

"I see," Mac said.

"We're currently putting out the paper with free-lance contributions," Huntington said. "Have you seen our latest issue?" He extended a copy: OPECHANCANOUGH SHERIFF STALLS ON REFORM, the headline read.

"No, thanks," Mac said hastily. "I'm not reading newspapers today."

Huntington's face was solitious. "The campaign, you mean?"

"That's right," Mac said.

"It must be painful to lose an election that close," Huntington said.

Mac shrugged. "Close, not close," he said. "Losing is what hurts, not by how much."

"Don't you think Shadwell blew the election?" Spottswood said.

Mac turned to look at him. "What do you mean by that?" he asked.

Hoke was about to say more, but Huntington stopped him with an upraised hand, like a stationmaster flagging a freight. "I'm not sure that's the most tactful way to put it," he said mildly, "but Hoke and I both think this district could have been organized better than it was."

"Well, what do *you* mean?" Mac said with elaborate formal irony.

Huntington's hands made a gesture of diffidence; they scrabbled at a globe of air, lifted and dropped it. "The campaign was defeatist, in my opinion," he said. "Shadwell let the Richmond newspapers go unanswered, and this was a mistake. We both feel pretty clear about that. He should have blanketed the district with replies to the charges."

"Ah, come off it," Mac said. He felt his lips lift from his teeth in defensive contempt. "Answers to charges never neutralize the charges, any fool knows that."

"You're correct, of course," Huntington said. "But a vigorous answer would have reversed the moral tide and thus helped make it respectable to support Shadwell. The daily papers built up a lynch-mob psychology, and I think people were terrorized. By election day they felt very hesitant about admitting it in public."

Mac watched the cigarette burning down toward his fingers. The smoke flew toward his eyes and stung; in his eyelids gritted fragments of impatience and disgust. "Tell me, E.G.," he said, "if you knew how to stop all this, why did you wait until after the election to bring it up?"

"I didn't think it was my place to do so," he said.

"What did you think, you dipshit? Did you think Tom Jeff would call you up some night and ask for your advice?"

Huntington was silent. Suddenly Mac, who earlier had detached from defeat, experienced a flash of anger at those who were not involved in it—those like Huntington who had stood back and watched and had not been involved. "Ah-h-h," he said, and then, as much to change the subject as anything else, he asked, "Have you got anything to drink around here?"

That moment, as Huntington reached into his desk and pulled out a bottle of blackberry wine, had tipped them toward the Confederate Club. Mac couldn't say why, except that when Huntington handed him a conical water-cooler cup full of the wine, he experienced a sudden overpowering urge for a real drink, which he must have voiced loudly. For as he remembered the afternoon, it seemed that the efficient black receptionist had been sent down the block to buy Mac some cold bottles of beer. He remembered her bringing the beer, and he drank it while his old schoolmates drank noisome dark syrup out of conical cups. The wine seemed to evoke fond memories of days gone by: they sat reminiscing about St. Cyprian's until Mac, between them, beer bottle held between his thighs, began to feel like a scapegrace nephew who had fallen into the clutches of a pair of dotty aunts and must endure an afternoon of the past.

Periodically the intercom buzzer sounded, the receptionist entered with another beer; outside in the alley the shadows advanced, until by the time they emerged into the street it was full autumn twilight. They were bound for the Confederate Club, although Mac could not remember who had decided that, or how: Huntington, it had developed, was a member, and they were all invited as his guests. Mac knew they were going for a drink, and he had suggested the drink, but if he had suggested that they go to the Confederate Club, it seemed later, then he must truly have been deranged—indeed, could be considered deranged merely for having agreed to go. This very thought flashed through his mind as he walked with his two old classmates under the green awning of the upstairs entrance to the club, the Ladies' Entrance—and it was perhaps this name which prevented him from turning back in that last moment of sanity. Would it not, he felt, be an act of grossest cowardice to shrink from the Ladies' Entrance? Would he not be shamed before his classmates? After all, he was an Evans, and an Evans might run from a burning factory or a perjury indictment, true, but never from the Ladies' Entrance. He breathed deeply, squared his shoulders, and passed through the glass doors. His two classmates, again like aged aunts, followed slowly behind.

EIGHT

★

In fact, they had chosen the Ladies's Entrance simply because it led to the quieter and more elegant of the club's two bars. Downstairs was the male domain, the pool and exercise rooms, the barbershop and sauna and the Men's Bar where the members gathered to drink beer and watch football games on TV. On the second floor was a quiet carpeted series of rooms where members brought their wives to sip drinks around small tables. On the third floor were the dining rooms, where members and guests could dine on crab stew, fried oysters, Smithfield ham, and spoon bread.

A black headwaiter in a tuxedo led them through a succession of anterooms furnished in dark wood paneling and hung with huge gilt-framed mirrors and dim oil portraits of departed members and great Virginians. Mac had begun to feel that they might walk forever between images of themselves when their escort murmured, "The Lee Room. Will this be satisfactory, Mr. Huntington?" By means of magic hand movements he hustled them into wooden armchairs around a small octagonal table. "Your waiter will be with you directly," the headwaiter's voice seemed still to be saying even as his broad back, accompanied through the maze of rooms by its invisible enantiomorphic escort, retreated from them.

Mac felt a certain confusion of time and place. Unobtrusively he reconnoitered. On the table before them was a five-sided glass ashtray, nestled in a dark circular wooden holder. In the precise geometrical center of the

415

ashtray was a fresh matchbook, its cover an appropriately subdued shade of gray, upon which in flowing white script was a modest announcement: "The Confederate Club." The tabletop itself was dark, nonreflecting, leatherlike, bordered on its eight sides by a rim of varnished wood. The chairs were of light brown or tan wood, with semicircular backs which formed armrests as well. Above each chair was the face of one of Mac's classmates: Huntington's complacent and inquisitive, exuding the air of a genial host, Spottswood's suspicious, fidgety, his eyes darting from one corner of the room to another as if expecting to spot a hired assassin lying in wait for him.

In midair appeared a black hand at the end of a white sleeve, clutching a pewter bowl of peanuts. It set them down beside the ashtray with unemphatic decisiveness, so that when the hand withdrew, it at once became impossible for Mac to be sure that the bowl had not in fact been there all along. He craned his neck to get a better view of the composition made by bowl and ashtray on the dark dull surface and felt Spottswood's bony elbow in his ribs.

"What do you want to drink?" Huntington's voice said in the opposite ear.

Mac saw that the black hand in white sleeve belonged to a black waiter in a white coat, who towered above him now, tall, scornful, faintly familiar. "Double bourbon on the rocks, please," Mac said.

The waiter—where had Mac seen him before?—nodded, started to turn away.

"Excuse me," Mac said. The man inclined his head. "What's your house brand?"

"Virginia Gentleman, sir," the waiter replied.

"Aha!" Mac said. He felt an absurd grin come bubbling out of him. The waiter, ironic, deferential, did not return it. "That will be fine," Mac said. The waiter walked away, his feet popping faintly on the carpet.

Mac addressed himself to the peanut bowl. He took a handful of nuts and began throwing them into his mouth. "You'll be fascinated to learn," he said to the table at large, "that St. Augustine considered what we're doing a cardinal example—almost, in fact, a paradigm—of human depravity."

"What's that, drinking?" Huntington said.

"Certainly not," Mac said, drawing himself up scornfully. "A moment's thought would convince you that the fathers of the church could not possibly have been opposed to drinking per se. How could they? Was not the central mystery of their faith a piece of ritual magic involving wine? The wine was changed into blood at a crucial moment, but it began, nonetheless, as wine. Then there is the marriage at Cana to consider, where the Savior Himself changed water into wine—"

"What are you talking about, then? Huntington said.

"About St. Augustine," Mac said reasonably.

Huntington seemed exasperated. "I understand that," he said. "But what is the example of human depravity?"

Mac was carefully dislodging salty fragments from his teeth with a thumbnail. "Eating peanuts, of course," he said indistinctly.

"Eating peanuts?" Spottswood's suspicious face swam into view; midway to his mouth was a hand holding peanuts.

"Why peanuts?" Huntington joined in.

"Well, not actually peanuts *qua* peanuts," Mac said. "Although of course such ritual prohibitions were not unknown at the time of the early Church. There is the obvious example of Jewish dietary law, and the Pythagoreans, who were forbidden to eat beans. Before his conversion to Christianity, Augustine himself was a Manichaean, who were forbidden to eat fruit—or perhaps they were required to eat fruit, I can't quite recall just now."

"But what about peanuts?" Huntington demanded.

"You see my point. I'm in fact not even sure that peanuts were known in the Old World at that time. But it's the concept that matters. Augustine would have been equally opposed to, let's say, potato chips."

"Do you mean the ancient Romans had potato chips?" Spottswood said.

"They may have, but I don't know."

"Mac," Huntington said, "what are you talking about?"

"Augustine was opposed to drunkenness, you see."

"Yes?" Spottswood said.

"And he felt that the proof of the drunkard's depravity was the fact that he used salty foods to create thirst when he was not thirsty, solely so he could drink to quench the thirst he had thus artifically created."

There was a brief silence while they considered this concept.

"What do you think Augustine would have thought of you, Mac?" Huntington said.

"Very little, I imagine," Mac replied vaguely, casting his eye about for the waiter and the drinks. "There would be the language difference, for one thing, and on top of that is the fact that my knowledge of his writings is limited to the item I just quoted to you."

As if in conscious defiance of the spirit of Augustine, the other two now

417

began to eat peanuts frantically. Huntington even appeared to be throwing them at Spottswood, and as he did so, he made small explosive sounds, as if the peanuts were tiny bombs.

Mac ignored this display. He had once again found in his pocket the cigarette pack. He extricated one and lit it with the Confederate-gray matchbook.

"I do remember one other thing," he said like a movie gangster, with the cigarette in the corner of his mouth. The smoke whirled about his face. The others did not seem to be listening; it was hard to tell in the dim light, but he went on ruminatively, "In his *Confessions,* he tells the story about one of his friends whose name escapes me, who was more or less addicted to the gladiatorial games, *retiarius* versus swordsman, blood on the sand, which incidentally is where our own word 'arena' comes from, thrill of victory, agony of so on and so on." The smoke crawled acridly up his nose. He took the cigarette out of his mouth and held it gingerly upright between thumb and forefinger, like an Axis general.

"But he became a Christian, you see, and resolved to give up going to the games." With his free hand he waved the smoke away from his face. "This worked well enough for a few years, until one day in the street he was accosted by a gang of rowdies, his former companions at the arena." He felt a tap on his shoulder; his train of thought at once derailed, smashing into an abutment, hopelessly wrecked. He swiveled in his chair and saw above him the ruined old face of Kenlow Anderson.

"Hello, Judge," he said, standing; he tried to extend his hand, but it seemed to be holding a cigarette; he dropped it, still lit, into the ashtray. Mac saw that the judge's face was disapproving and stern, but his first words were light in tone. "Never expected to find you here, Mac," he said.

"Why not?" Mac asked. He gestured expansively at Huntington. "I am the guest of a member."

Huntington politely rose, and Mac said, "Judge, this is Gravelier Huntington, publisher of the *Sentinel.* Judge Kenlow Anderson, late of the Circuit Court."

"How do you do," the judge said, his face twitching disapproval of the *Sentinel.* Huntington, unabashed, introduced Spottswood. There followed an interval of general handshaking, from which Mac stood aloof.

"This is a mighty strange place to find you," Anderson said again, looking at him intently.

Mac shrugged.

The judge placed an avuncular hand on Mac's arm. "I'm just on my way out, Mac. Why don't you walk with me?" Anderson turned to the other two and inclined his head in stiff apology. "I'll keep young Evans here for a minute, gentlemen, and then he can return to the revelry." Clutching Mac's elbow, the judge steered him through the maze of mirrored anterooms to the central hall. At one side was a small green elevator door. The judge picked up his hat and coat from a rack, then pressed the down button.

"What are you doing here?" he asked again as they waited for the car.

"Everybody's got to be somewhere, Judge," Mac said.

The tiny car came, and they stepped inside a space which was small, dim, and green. The judge hit a button, and the elevator began laboriously moving down to the ground floor.

"Where are we going, to take a sauna?" Mac asked.

"No," the judge replied, absently patting his coat pockets. "I have my car in the side parking lot. Hope I can find the keys." The elevator ground to a halt, and the door slid open with a wheeze.

Instantly Mac felt himself assaulted by light: every surface on the ground floor was polished, reflective: the tile floors and walls, the glass doors of the spa, the barbershop with its gleaming mirror and glittering steel chair, the long shiny bar rail inside the glass door of the Men's Bar. Mac squinted, shutting out the glare.

"Listen, Mac," the judge was saying. They stood awkwardly in the middle of the hall, in front of the door leading to the tunnel to the parking lot. "I know you must feel pretty rocky right now." The judge was avoiding Mac's eyes as he patted him stiffly on the shoulder. "But your man didn't lose by much. You came pretty damn close. That's something to think about."

Mac looked at him in disbelief. "Judge, why are you consoling me?" he said. "I would have thought you'd be delighted that Brock won. Isn't that what you wanted?"

The judge shook his head slightly in exasperation. "That's not what I'm talking about, he said. "I'm not talking politics now. I'm worried about you, that's all."

Mac treated the judge to a sarcastic smile. "This wouldn't be the tiniest touch of guilt speaking, would it, Judge? A little remorse at the methods of your old friends? A slight case of bad conscience?"

"Oh, God damn you for a fool anyway, Mac Evans," Anderson burst out, his face twisting harshly in irritation and hurt. He looked Mac full in the face. "Look at yourself, will you? Half drunk, you look like a slob, babbling nonsense in a place you don't belong—why don't you go home and get some sleep and quit making a display of yourself?"

Mac watched him in silence. He could feel the same sarcastic grin playing on his lips. Unbidden, his tongue spoke. "Thank you for your advice, Your Honor," it said coldly. "Our family has always found it useful in the past."

Expressionlessly the judge whirled on his heel and passed through the glass doors, down the long stone tunnel to the parking lot, leaving Mac, the angry smile slowly turning foolish and rueful, poised as if to fight the empty air, fanned by the breeze as the door swung shut.

After a minute, he turned away. Around were faint murmurings. In the Men's Bar the television played quietly. From the door to the spa came the quiet whir as someone shuffled a deck of cards, the clink of poker chips as the players threw their ante on the felt. Mac felt a stirring in his bowels; he passed down the hall to his right, away from the Men's Bar, and entered the vast spotless bathroom.

Here the light was nearly intolerable: it glinted from scrubbed tiles, spotless white floor-length urinals, polished shiny piping, dazzling mirrors. Mac stumbled to the urinal, undid his trousers, and relieved himself. He felt a deep panic: a fear that if he closed his eyes the world might fly apart in jagged fragments and whirl him obliquely into violent cold darkness. He stood upright, like a soldier on parade. The silver handle was cold in his hand. The urinal flushed. Still at attention, muscles rigid with the effort of pressing back, shoulders, stomach into a comforting web of right angles, he zipped his trousers, then turned crisply and marched to the washbasin, where he scalded his hands red. *Out,* a voice inside him was saying. *I've got to get out of here.* He straightened his tie and looked at himself in the mirror. The image nodded sober agreement. *Right,* he thought. *One drink and out. Home we go.*

The hallway was still too bright. He stood for a moment, searching for the way back to the elevator; a high piping accented voice took him between the shoulder blades, burbling, "Well, well, well, young Mr. Evans, how do you do!" with such unexpected, wholly inappropriate glee that he jumped clean off the ground in surprise. Heart pounding, he turned and saw in the doorway of the spa a tiny, elflike old man, with thin white hair and thick glasses: the Confederate Club masseur, whose name, he recalled, was Mr. White.

The merry Australian bore down upon him like a ship under sail, hand extended. He was dressed in a blue raincoat and a checked hat adorned with a jaunty yellow feather. Under his left arm was a folded copy of the *Racing Form.* He beamed at Mac, smiling a gap-toothed smile and saying, "This is indeed a pleasant surprise, Mr. Evans. I've not seen you now for—how long has it been, would you say?"

"Five years, Mr. White," Mac said. Occasionally, in his days at St. Cyprian's, Mac had come with Lester to the club on Saturday mornings to swim in the pool and enjoy the luxury of a massage. The little man had aged since then; one side of his face had sagged, shifting downward like a rock formation settling, and long white hairs protruded from his nose. But he seemed as garrulous and cheerful as ever, and his eyes, behind the lenses, were bright and mischievous.

"That long, has it really now?" White said, shaking his head in disbelieving regret. "Terrible, isn't it, the way time passes us by, so quickly. What is it the poet says: 'One thing is certain, that life flies; one thing is certain, and the rest is lies,' if memory serves."

"Yes, it does," Mac said vaguely, grasping the masseur's elbow in a friendly gesture chiefly intended to quiet a slight agitation he was perceiving in the hallway: a peristaltic tremor in floor, ceiling, and walls. "The years have been kind to you, Mr. White. Do you still have the ear of the mighty?"

White was seized with laughter at this sally. "Oh-ho-ho, the ear of the mighty," he said, doubling over slightly, so that Mac was forced to release his elbow. "You remember my little joke, do you?"

"Indeed so, Mr. White," Mac said.

"Yes, indeed, Mr. Evans," White said, straightening up and wiping tears from his eyes. "I have always said, Mr. Evans, that in my job here I have the shoulders of the mighty, and while I have hold of them I have ruddy well got the ear of the mighty as well! Right, right?"

"Absolutely, Mr. White," Mac said. "So they still come to you, do they?"

"Yes, indeed, yes, indeed, Mr. Evans. The governor, you know, comes to me regularly for relaxation from the cares of state."

"And do you give him the benefit of your views?"

"Ruddy right I do, Mr. Evans. He listens very attentively. I may say, though"—and here the masseur, settling his hat more firmly on his small head, took Mac by the elbow and began to guide him toward the outside door, talking without a break—"Although, I may say, what I call my period of influence appears to be drawing to a close, so to speak. Since Mr. Brock has never been one of my clients, and confidentially, Mr. Evans, though I don't generally discuss the members"—here he stopped dead and gave such a furtive glance up and down the hallway that Mac almost laughed aloud, he seemed suddenly so much like a musical comedy pickpocket or confidence man—"it is my opinion that Mr. Brock would not be disposed to hear my views in any event, am I not right?"

Mac nodded. "I'm afraid so, Mr. White. In fact, I think you've hit the nail on the head."

"What matter?" White shrugged elaborately as they resumed their progress down the glittering hall. "Politicians come and go. What is it that the poet says? 'Think, in this batter'd caravanserai whose doorways are alternate night and day, how Sultan after Sultan with his pomp abode his hour or two and went his way,' if memory serves."

"Memory serves you well, Mr. White," Mac said.

"You are kind, Mr. Evans," the masseur said. "But you do see my point," he continued, stopping again to raise a didactic forefinger. "These politicians with their perquisites of office and their bright pride of spirit, what are they, after all, but expressions, puppets if you will, of certain forces, economic and social forces which they can no more control than the tides or the seasons? Eh? Am I not right?" He looked at Mac inquiringly.

"Why, Mr. White, I never took you for a student of the dialectic."

"Indeed," the Australian said. He gave his head a mournful shake, eyes cast down at the tile floor. "I regret to say that recent events have forced me to abandon the philosophical posture I have maintained for more than two decades."

Mac felt at a loss. "I'm sorry to hear it," he said lamely, as if a relative, not a world view, had died.

"Ah," White said with a shrug. "Bitter necessity, Mr. Evans, which it is fruitless to mourn. You see, sir, like many another who fought against facism during the Second World War, I became an optimist. It seemed to me that if the nations of the world could join hands to destroy this social monster, if you will, then it would be a simple matter to achieve world peace and social justice, don't you see? Simply a question of cooperation, of evolution. I was naive and optimistic, and I was wrong. Today, we see everywhere"—and he made a gesture which took in the hallway, the club, the world—"the struggle for simple justice and self-determination is thwarted by the forces of monopoly capital. We see it here in Virginia, we see it in Southeast Asia, we see it in Latin America, everywhere. Mr. Evans," he said, slapping his forefinger into the opposite palm for emphasis, "a rational man cannot ignore facts! And that is why, Mr. Evans, I am no longer a philosophical anarchist, as when last we met. No, sir. I have regretfully become a Marxist!"

"I must admit, I'm a little surprised to hear that, Mr. White."

The little man relaxed a little. "Yes, sir," he said. "The governor said much the same thing when I broke the news to him. Much the same thing.

But I will say he's taken it like a gentleman and still listens as respectfully as ever to my advice. Though, of course, what can he do? He's only a cog in the great economic machine, like you or I. Well, cheery-bye," and Mac found that they had somehow arrived at the glass door. He and the masseur shook hands again. "See you on the barricades," White said, and passed through the door and down the long tunnel.

Mac found his way with difficulty back to the elevator and through the mirrored maze of rooms, until he turned a corner and unexpectedly came upon Spottswood and Huntington, sitting for all the world as if they were where he had left them, though to Mac they seemed to have moved, or perhaps the whole room had moved, for this was unmistakably the table he had left, with empty peanut dish and ashtray, in the midst of which was the still-burning end of his own cigarette, and there, in front of his empty seat, neatly centered on a Confederate Club cocktail napkin, gleaming in the corn god's amber splendor, was what was unmistakably his own drink.

He sat. His classmates were discussing business. "Unless our profit picture improves rapidly, we will be forced to go into the capital market under very disadvantageous circumstances," Huntington was saying.

"Or retrench," Spottswood suggested with a helpful air.

"Well, you're correct, of course," Huntington said thoughtfully. "But I'm not sure how far we can retrench further without causing substantial deterioration of the product."

"Ahem," Mac said modestly.

The other two looked at him with mild interest.

"Shall we drink a toast?" he asked.

"We've started without you," Huntington said, gesturing at his glass, which was half full of white wine.

"So I see," Mac said, then added, "Egad, Spottswood, what's that you're drinking?"

"This is a Tequila Sunrise," Spottswood said, with a proprietary gesture at his multicolored glass.

"I may be sick," Mac muttered.

Huntington forestalled that originally rhetorical but suddenly somehow very real possibility by saying politely, "Will you propose a toast, then?"

Mac raised his glass. Suddenly his brain, which until that instant had been rattling with words, his own and Tom Jeff's and his father's and Mr. White's, went blank: he had nothing to say. He stalled by taking a deep breath, such as a man might in fact take before beginning a very eloquent and self-assured toast, and lifted his glass a little higher, his eyes follow-

423

ing it upward until with the suddenness of dawn he found himself bathed in the still, gray, patient, saintly gaze, the quiet, virginal radiance of the eyes of General Robert E. Lee, CSA. The Lee Room! Of course! It did not seem blasphemous to Mac to imagine that this apparition, neatly framed on the opposite wall, might have been sent or ordained by heaven to provide precisely the material for this toast. With his free hand he covered his heart and said reverently, "Gentlemen, a toast to General Robert E. Lee."

The others nodded quickly and made as if to drink, but Mac stopped them with a pontifical wave of the hand. "A man," he said, "who turned his coat and threw in his towel with as much dignity as possible under the circumstances."

This was coming out all wrong. Mac again motioned for silence, inhaled deeply, and began again. "Beloved son of the estimable if inept speculator, 'Light-Fingers' Harry Lee, who—" Again it had come out all wrong, as if some demon had seized his tongue. Yet, it occurred to him, perhaps it was no demon, but a revelation, from heaven or the unconscious mind, whichever might be applicable. He felt a stirring in his brain, a sound of rushing winds and meshing gears, and as he breathed in to begin again, "who—" it hit him like a dull blow to the back of the head that he had never understood Lee, never put the facts of his life together as his contemporary experience and modern political training uniquely fitted him to do. "—who—" For if he looked at certain facts in the light of modern logic, did they not now assume a certain awful clarity which should have been obvious at once?

He looked at the kindly portrait with a wild surmise. Consider the irony if here was depicted, not the patron saint of the old South, but the father of modern espionage, not, as he seemed, a stylish but rather backward-looking military tactician but rather, it could now be argued, a true pioneer in the fields of treason and betrayal?

Mac nearly staggered under the weight of his new knowledge, for did not, he asked himself reasonably, all of Lee's subsequent career revolve around the celebrated interview with Francis P. Blair in 1861—April, wasn't it?—in which Lee had been offered the command of the Union Army? And did not it seem possible, no, likely, no, irrefutable, that in fact Lee had not, as legend holds, in fact declined this command at all, but actually *accepted it*? Was it not now possible to see behind the previously random blunderings of the two armies, blue and gray, the fine hand of R. E. Lee, double-crosser, double-dealer, double agent?

"—who—"

Mac was awestruck at Lee's cunning and guile: first, the expedition to western Virginia for the Confederacy, where he had allowed the Union to snatch off the western half of the state, adroitly shifting the blame for the disaster to those Southern patriots, Floyd and Wise. Then the fortuitous—or had it been fortuitous, or perhaps part of the conspiracy?—bullet which had wounded Johnston, giving Lee command of both armies simultaneously. Mac saw the audacious duplicity of Lee here, the bargain he must have struck with Lincoln: to lose the war quickly. And yet, once irrevocably committed to his treasonous course, would he not surely have realized that history would then regard him as a blundering incompetent—a verdict which, with his exquisite sense of honor, he could not abide? Hence, the triple-cross: he would, as instructed, lose the war, but slowly, with style, until he was sure that it would be he and not McClellan or Pope or Meade or Grant whom history would honor as the master tactician and gallant leader.

"—and—"

Proof? Proof? The pages of history abounded with it! Why was McClellan allowed to escape unharmed after the Seven Days' Battles? Were we seriously expected to believe the explanation of late troop movements and tactical "blunders"? And why at Second Manassas did Lee permit Longstreet to delay his attack and then himself delay in advancing after the victory the next day, giving Pope time to slip into the fortifications around Washington? Why would Hooker, a fine general himself, no doubt, named by his men "Fighting Joe," have blundered so grievously at Chancellorsville, if not under secret orders from Lee? And Longstreet— that poor, bewildered man now appeared in a much different light, a loyal officer deliberately misled by his commander about his orders at Gettysburg, until the poor man's justifiable confusion caused another fatal delay there!

"—when—"

It occured to Mac that history even recorded how Lee's secret messages had been passed across the lines, for on September 7, 1862, McClellan's men found—"by chance," we are told—Lee's battle orders wrapped around a bundle of cigars. Was this not in fact simply the only recorded instance of Lee's regular message drop (an explanation which would in itself help to explain the enormous demand within the Confederacy for fine Havana cigars)?

"—if—"

More proof? More proof? It was historical fact, was it not, that certain papers were hastily burned at the Confederate War Department on the night of the evacuation of Richmond: Why? Might they not have been evidence of a conspiracy, perhaps involving collusion, overt or tacit, between the traitor Lee and his friend and former comrade-in-arms, Jefferson Finis Davis? Why, after the surrender, was Lee allowed to keep his sword? Why was Lee so quick to urge his soldiers to accept defeat (if defeat it was)? Why was the treason indictment against him quietly allowed to drop? Why was his application for a pardon so conveniently "lost"? Might it not have been because it would have raised embarrassing questions on the floor of Congress?

"—thus—"

QED! QED! Mac was thinking when he became again aware of himself, glass upraised, in the Lee Room of Richmond exclusive Confederate Club. In fact, he realized, he had been standing precisely there for an undetermined length of time, and he further realized that he was not at all sure that he had not been speaking some or all of his thoughts aloud. Perhaps it was imagination that his classmates were looking at him strangely, Spottswood with narrow mouth agape and Huntington with head cocked in what might be called presumptuous concern. It might also be imagination that the small room had fallen deathly quiet and that the parties at other tables were watching him as well. And didn't he seem to remember noticing even in mid-fugue one old man stamp angrily out of the room? Or had he imagined that? His head swam, and he said hastily, "Gentlemen, I give you Robert E. Lee," and sat, drinking quickly from his glass a healing draft.

After a minute, Huntington intruded a discreet cough into the silence at the table. "Well, Mac," he said, "I guess it's time to get on home."

"Yes, indeed," Spottswood said.

Mac was about to agree when he felt a tap on the shoulder again. He turned to find yourself looking into the obscurely familiar face of the waiter: triangular face, liquid eyes, deferential, opaque, leaning forward to whisper, "Telephone message for you, Mr. Evans. Judge Anderson says he must see you downstairs right away."

"Wha—" Mac began, but the waiter padded away. He turned and thrust a tangle of bills at Huntington. "Here, you pay up and I'll meet you outside."

"Right, right," Huntington agreed quickly.

Mac passed quickly through the mirrored maze of rooms. But the elevator seemed slower than before, and he put his forehead against the green wall and allowed his mouth to hang open, his breath coming in quick gasps. He was prepared to apologize to the judge, to General Lee, to the world. He felt leaden and ready for sleep.

The shiny hall was darker; the lights from the barbershop and spa were gone. The rattle of cards had stopped. Mac looked amid the shadows, but found no judge.

Then there was a slight sound behind him, and an old voice, like nails on slate, said, "I am holding a gun on you, son, so put your hands up and turn around slowly."

By the end of the eternity it took him to turn around, it came somehow as no surprise that there should in fact be a gun, a short-barreled revolver pointed at his navel, black and deadly, held in the hand of an old, scrawny man he had never seen before—or perhaps he had; those yellow, malignant eyes seemed to strike a chord in his memory; the Lee Room? Had he walked past Mac?

It did not seem important, with the gun barrel yawning in front of him, because there was nothing between him and a bullet except the finger of this man, who was saying, "Now you just put your hands down and walk through that door real slowly, in front of me, and you remember that I would dearly love to shoot you, so if you would please make one funny move I'd be obliged." Then, when Mac simply looked at him stupidly, the man gestured savagely with his free hand and hissed, "Move, you little shit!"

Mac pushed open the swinging door and entered the tunnel to the parking lot, and the man followed close behind him. As the door swung shut, Mac heard the TV set from the Men's Bar, a bright voice shouting, "Your new car!" as if Mac Evans were not facing death. Then there was no sound but their footsteps on the brick floor, and the man's (who was he? what was happening?) wheezing breath, and the quieter sound of Mac's own breathing, infinitely precious because it was his and might stop suddenly. Mac walked carefully, trying not to stumble; he felt half dressed, as if the rear of his clothing had been cut away, leaving him bare, back, buttocks, legs, naked to the bullet waiting at the end of that barrel. He wondered if the old Bolsheviks had felt this way, pacing down corridors waiting for bullets, and the thought angered him, because it was absurd to spend his last minutes in this life thinking about the old Bolsheviks: when had they ever thought of him?

"Excuse me, sir," he said, between teeth that seemed to be chattering, "I think you have the wrong person."

"Shut your mouth," came the old voice behind him. "You don't think I know who you are, Evans? Keep walking."

Which he did, for some reason counting his steps; thirteen more and they were out of the tunnel, in the deserted parking lot. The air had turned cold and above them was a gibbous moon in a clear sky; soon it would be full, the hunter's moon, second brightest of the year.

"Keep walking," the voice said. They came up behind a black Mercedes, and the voice said, "Stop and don't move."

Then from around the car came a brown bulky shape, and Mac's heart

427

leaped: a policeman! He was saved! He was about to cry out when the policeman, a white man of middle years, still trim in his brown uniform, no doubt off duty, hired by the club to watch its parking lot, stopped, looked at them, and nodded pleasantly at Mac's captor, saying "Good evening, Mr. Jarvis, what you got here?"

Mac listened in dumb amazement as the old man said, "Roscoe, I got me a hippie here who's been mouthing off and making a scene, talking dirty about General Robert E. Lee. Thinks it's funny to cast aspersions."

The policeman looked at Mac gravely, like a grade-school teacher at a naughty boy. "You don't mean it," he said finally. "That's dreadful. What are we going to do about it, Mr. Jarvis?"

"Got to teach these hippie bastards some respect," the voice said. "You know what to do."

The cop came up to Mac and looked him up and down scornfully, thumbs hooked in his belt. Then, as if to himself, he said, "Right," and there was a quick glint of silver beyond the edge of Mac's vision and then a bewilderment of stars, a ribbon of light in the sky and Lester lifted him higher and said, "Look, bub, that's the Milky Way," and he wanted to say, *I'm scared, Lester,* but his voice went out and then Lester went out and the stars went out, and Mac was going out, but he couldn't go out, a voice was telling him to go out, there was a way out, he could come out, and another voice said, "He's coming out of it, Mr. Jarvis," and he tasted blood in his mouth. The cop was lifting him from the pavement and saying, "Son, I want you to apologize to Mr. Jarvis."

"Yes, sir," Mac said thickly. "I apologize, Mr. Jarvis."

"All right, Roscoe," Mr. Jarvis said. "Let him go."

The cop put Mac's head on the pavement and he saw a pair of wingtip shoes in front of his face. From somewhere above them Jarvis's voice said in measured tones, "My name is E. K. Jarvis, Junior, and I live in Omega, Virginia. I know who you are and I knew your family and there wasn't one of them worth a goddamn. Your father was a fool and a communist and your brother was a clown and a coward, and you look like an idiot to me and maybe a faggot to boot, and if you want to dispute any of this you come on down to Omega and I'll be happy to give you more of the same." The shoes moved out of Mac's vision and Jarvis said, "Good evening, Roscoe," and there was a rich rustle of banknotes passing. Then a car door slammed, and the Mercedes started up and drove away.

Mac waited, motionless. The cop's footsteps moved away; he heard him whistling through his teeth: "The Darktown Strutter's Ball." Ever so carefully, Mac levered himself off the pavement and stumbled off to find his classmates.

They must have taken him home: when next he came to himself, he was walking through the back lawn of the big house, in the silver moonlight, past Molly O.'s rose garden, toward his little house. Inside he stripped off his jacket, tie, and shirt, then wiped the bloodstains from his face. A little water on his face, and he was as good as new, although he didn't seem to feel that way. He didn't feel anything, except a kind of aching emptiness, and when he picked up the phone, he didn't know who he was trying to call.

It was long distance to Opechancanough County. Four rings, five; he had despaired of her when suddenly she answered, her voice just as he remembered it, quizzical, cool, slightly breathless, and inside himself there was an unexpected breathless leap as she said, "Hello?"

"Hello, Alexandra?"

"Who is this?" she said. "Mac?"

"Yes," he said. "Yeah, it's me."

There was silence, not friendly or unfriendly.

"I was expecting you to call," she said. "You never did."

"Yeah," he said. "I know. I'm sorry. But you know, with my father dying and all—"

"What? Your father died?"

"Yeah. Last month."

"Oh, God, I'm sorry," she said. "Did you go down there?"

"Where?"

"South America."

"What? No," Mac said, surprised. "He came back. Didn't you see it? It was in the papers and all."

"Mac, I'm so sorry," she said. "I don't read the papers. I didn't know."

"It's okay," he said. "Then the election, you know—"

"I heard about that. I'm sorry," she said. "I seem to have a lot to be sorry about."

"Forget it," he said. "I'm sorry I didn't call you. I should have found the time."

He waited, but she said nothing.

"Listen," he said finally. "I'd like—I really need to see you." More silence. "Could, ah, could you come up here?"

"Mac, I am sorry I didn't know," she said again. "I can't."

"Tomorrow, then?"

"No, Mac, listen, I can't. Steamboat's here."

"What?"

"Yes, Mac, we're getting married."

Words stuck in his throat. Had he said something? He did not know, but the connection was broken, and he was looking at the receiver, and from its gaping mouth came the droning dial tone, a malevolent empty hum: BADNEWSCOMINGBADNEWSCOMINGBADNEWSCOMING until he could stand it no more and he brought the receiver up over his head and then down, smashed it against the cradle again and again until it broke into two jagged pieces. He threw the phone across the room, and then he was outside in the thick grass, shirtless, barefoot, behind his little house, by the azalea bush, in the silver moonlight. And in the moonlight he looked down at himself as if from a height, as if for the first time, and saw himself plainly then: a fool. Suddenly sobbing, he threw himself down, face pressed to earth, and he was crying at last, and the tears he had not shed before, for his brother and his father and for Tom Jeff Shadwell and for hope lost and innocence betrayed and most of all for himself, wet the dewy grass.

Part Four

★

Now his feet sound in the cool hush of the railroad station, and its high ceiling gives back the echo. He clutches his suitcase and looks down the nave of the building, vaulted and high as a cathedral's. It is almost deserted. On the west wall, chiseled in stone for posterity, is an enormous legend: THE UNION NEWS COMPANY. But beneath it, the newsstand is defunct, locked forever. Next to the dead newsstand are the double doors to the lunch counter, but inside them, the soda fountain has been replaced by a row of vending machines. On the east wall, at the ticket counter, one lonely ticket seller drowses in his enclosure. Beyond that, in the north hall of the depot, are the doors to the tracks.

He is almost alone in the station, he and the ticket seller. In one corner of the huge room, he can see another traveler slumped on a wooden bench, seemingly asleep: a middle-aged black woman, thin and bony, with hard high cheekbones and straightened hair . Her feet rest on a cloth suitcase, and her head laps over shoulder, mouth open, eyes closed.

Mac remembers it from his childhood, a bustling crossroads alive and mysterious, the newsstand bulging with glossy magazines and strange crisp newspapers: *Police Gazette* (HITLER ALIVE IN ANTARCTICA?), *Swank, True Confessions,* the *Daily Mirror,* the *Herald Tribune,* the *Journal-American.* He remembers crowds of travelers waiting on the benches in sleepy clumps, long lines at the ticket windows, the intermittent blare of loudspeakers echoing, the sizzle of eggs in the lunch counter, the sta-

433

tionmaster, jangling keys with the self-importance of St. Peter himself, taking tickets at the gate.

For him as a child it was freedom, adventure, romance; now it is dying. He stands in the desolation, and the vaulted ceilings echo back at him: *gone, gone, no more, no more.* Under one arm he has a copy of the afternoon paper and a bundle of magazines: *Esquire, Reader's Digest, Rolling Stone, Analog.* With his free hand he hefts his suitcase; his hand is sweaty on the plastic handle. His feet, in crepe-soled traveling shoes, pad on the marble as he walks to the ticket window.

It was December, the first really cold day of the year; Mac and Tom Jeff drove to the cemetery in the blue Continental. The sky was clear and clean, frosty blue, etched with fine white clouds. Mac steered the big car uneasily through the narrow roads of the cemetery, up the hill by the river. Hollywood Cemetery was the finest neighborhood in the kingdom of the dead—one hundred and thirty acres, set among rolling hills and shaded by holly, magnolia, willow, oak, and fir. Everything in it conspired against the fearful anonymity of death: even its narrow streets were named and marked with signs: "Hillside Ave.," "Midvale Ave.," "Davis Circle," "Confederate Ave." The jumbled profusion of its marble monuments—angels and crosses, soaring obelisks, neoclassic mausoleums—the iron railings separating family plots, the tidy, well-tended trees and shrubbery, all gave testimony to the mute self-confidence of its dead.

At the far north end stood a stone pyramid some fifty feet tall, memorializing the Confederate dead. Near it was a wrought-iron gazebo, where for nearly a century the politicians had come on Memorial Day to eulogize the fallen. They no longer came; a new generation had arisen which seemed unable either to remember or to forget. But the dead, modest and tidy, remained.

At their head lay General George E. Pickett, whose charge at Gettysburg had brought so many of them here; beneath him, in tight military ranks, they rolled down the hillside, their numbers overflowing its bounds: eighteen thousand of them, "the bloody fruits," the inscription read, "of Williamsburg, Seven Pines, Mechanicsville, Gaines' Mill, Savage's Station, Frazier's Farm, Malvern Hill, Sharpsburg, Gettysburg, Fort Harrison, Yellow Tavern, Drewry's Bluff. . . ."

At the far south end of Hollywood, unregenerate to the last, lay Jefferson F. Davis, beneath a stone which fittingly proclaimed him "the most consistent of American statesmen." Between Pickett and Davis, the cemetery's two poles, rested a galaxy of Virginia dead: General J.E.B. Stuart, Ellen Glasgow, James Branch Cabell, six governors of Virginia, and two presidents of the United States.

It was to "Presidents' Circle" that Mac and Tom Jeff drove that morning in the big shiny car. But they were not visiting the wrought-iron-and-marble tomb of James Monroe or the tall smooth obelisk marking John Tyler's grave. Near the two presidential graves was a crowded plot dominated by a square upright marble monument:

STEPHEN R. EVANS

Master of the Kanawha Iron Works

"Lord, thou deliveredst unto me five talents; behold, I have gained beside them five talents more."

As a child Mac had thrilled to think that his family could be buried near two presidents. But since then he had realized that Dabney Evans had not selected his family plot because it was near Tyler and Monroe, but because "Presidents' Circle," high atop a bluff, had a commanding down-river view of the James. Stephen Evans was buried overlooking the rocky shallow river, facing toward that narrow spit of land which had been the site of the Kanawha Iron Works.

As in all else, Dabney Evans had planned well in matters of death. There had been room in the plot for himself and his wife, his spinster daughter, his son and daughter-in-law, his great-grandson, and now his grandson.

It was to this most recent grave that Mac and Tom Jeff went, Tom Jeff holding stiffly in two hands a bowl of flowers: red roses and white carnations. The earth of this grave was a bare dull red; in the spring, attendants would plant ivy over the rectangular outline and tend it through the long years to come; a small dark marker at the front of the plot announced that all within it were to be given perpetual care. Above the red outline was a new headstone, made to Mac's specifications:

COL. JOSHUA TUTELO EVANS, AUS

Soldier and Patriot

"Why should it be thought a thing incredible with you, that God can raise the dead?"

Tom Jeff placed his flowers on the grave, and they stood a moment looking at the stone. Sunlight glinted on the river: the water rushed past the rocks in a confusion of blue and white, and from this distance there was nothing to mark the water as dirty, though dirty it was; farther downstream it was poison. To the east the big trucks rolled south over the Lee

435

Bridge, and farther on the towers of the city stood against the sky. On the lonely bluff the silence grew. Mac tried to break it. "Looks like there won't be room left for me," he said, indicating the crowded plot. "I guess I'll have to break new ground when I go to get buried."

Tom Jeff smiled faintly at the feeble joke, made no reply. A gusty wind blew off the river, ruffling his hair; it fell in his face, and more than ever he had the look of an aging schoolboy standing before the principal. "You know, Mac," he said, "your father was a great one for poetry. He was always reading Shakespeare and Dante Alighieri and so on. He had a quote for every occasion, most amazing memory I ever knew."

"I know," Mac said. "I read to him a few times."

"He was always after us to read poems, too," Tom Jeff went on. "So finally I tried it. I went down to the library and got a big book of poems and read right through it. But you know, I only remember two or three of 'em, and those are about politics. There's one this fellow wrote about Governor Altgeld, do you know it? It's called 'The Eagle That Is Forgotten.'"

"No," Mac said.

Again somehow like a schoolboy, Shadwell put his his hands behind his back, stuck out his stubborn chin, and recited:

> A hundred white eagles have risen, the sons of your sons,
> The zeal in their wings is a zeal that your dreaming began,
> The valor that wore out your soul in the service of man.

Tom Jeff's eyes suddenly were full of tears, and in the cold wind Mac found his own were stinging. He looked at the grave, embarrassed, then back at Tom Jeff, who was wiping his eyes with a red bandanna handkerchief. "Sleep softly, eagle forgotten," he said, then shook his head ruefully. "Mac," he said, then again, "Mac, I should have been at that funeral."

Mac could find nothing to say, "Come on, Tom Jeff, let's get back to town." He led the way to the warmth of the big car, and Tom Jeff followed after a minute.

They ate lunch that day in the same restaurant where Mac and Hope Pinnell had planned the "Hour of Truth" TV special. The courtyard was closed for the winter; they sat in the sunken indoor dining room. Mac enjoyed watching heads turn as they passed back to the table; even in defeat he found pride in being seen with Tom Jeff. Their waitress was a small blonde with a pneumatic figure which just suited the clinging uniforms. She looked at Tom Jeff with big eyes, her mouth an O of amazement, and seemed about to speak; but Shadwell was silent, glum, uninviting, and she thought better of it. Mac ordered a big salad and a cup of soup; Shadwell settled on flounder.

They ate quietly. "How do you keep your weight down?" Shadwell asked Mac as he looked at the salad. "It's just not fair, your whole family's always been so slim and good-looking, and I'm always on a diet." But the pleasantry died away, and the silence went on so long Mac became alarmed; it seemed that the drive and vitality which had kept Shadwell going were gone, vanished, extinguished by a cloud of gloom and despair.

"Tom Jeff," Mac said at last, hesitantly. "Are you feeling all right?"

Shadwell looked at him without speaking, and his thick spectacles flashed in the dim light. Then he mustered a smile and a shrug, flapping his arms in his unforgettable broken-winged gesture. "I reckon so, young Mac, good enough for the time being," he said. "I don't much care to read the papers these days, I'm sure you understand."

Mac nodded grimly. He had seen the morning paper too. It was not the lead story—BROCK PROMISES TOUGH CRIME PROGRAM—but the one below it, on the bottom of the page, with a beaming photograph of Knocko: DEMO. CHIEF SAYS SHADWELL CAMPAIGN LACKED "FOCUS." In the article, Knocko made clear that the election had been lost because the candidate had failed to follow his advice, and he added parenthetically that he considered Tom Jeff's political career over.

"Listen," Mac said awkwardly. "Don't worry about Knocko. He's just mad because he screwed up so bad in the campaign."

Tom Jeff considered this slowly. "You may be right, young Mac," he said. "I'm not sure I understand it, myself. Cousin Knocko's playing his own game now, and there are wheels turning, and wheels in wheels, you can be sure about that. He's deep. Sometimes I think he's too deep for me."

Mac felt suddenly that he should tell Tom Jeff about that meeting in the trailer behind Meriwether Lewis High School; but the words stuck in his throat. He still could not speak of it; perhaps later. But the unspoken words were a guilty burden to him.

Shadwell gave him a speculative look. "By the way," he said, "why don't you go on and tell me now what went on with you and Knocko that night? You got to do it sometime."

Mac looked at his coffee cup and sighed. The moment had caught up with him. "Walk out with me, Tom Jeff," he said. "Let's talk where we can't be overheard."

In the street he told the story baldly, looking away from Tom Jeff like a man who is setting off an explosion. But the blast did not come; when

437

Mac looked up, Shadwell's face was not angry and hard, as he had expected, but pale. Shadwell rocked on his heels, as if recoiling from a blow, and passed a hand across his face.

"Damn, damn, goddamn," he said. It was the second time Mac had heard him curse. Then he shook his head, in denial, and sighed. "Mac," he said, "I went into politics—what was it—about twenty-five years ago, and never once in that time have I ever wanted something just to have it. I've spent that long out of my life trying to put an end to this kind of katzenjammer. I don't believe in it, Mac, I don't. It's wrong." He reached a hand to Mac's shoulder, as if to steady himself, but in the touch and the look Mac sensed something else: a plea for reassurance. "You believe that, don't you, Mac?"

"Yes, Tom Jeff," Mac said at once. "I do. Of course I do."

Shadwell withdrew his hand and passed it over his face again. "Young Mac's got faith," he said. "Momma's got faith. Lola and Danny and Ed got faith. Looks like Tom Jeff's going to have to keep the faith."

Suddenly Mac, who had been afraid of rousing Tom Jeff's anger against himself, saw that his story had touched Shadwell more deeply than that. He remembered his father's voice: "Lie still, little shad!" The knives were working on Tom Jeff. Mac averted his face.

"Yes, sir," Tom Jeff said after a minute. "Going to keep my faith. Don't care about Knocko Cheatham or anybody else."

"Don't worry about Knocko," Mac said. "You're better off without him anyway."

"That's right," Tom Jeff said, as if convincing himself. "I've got plenty of other friends. I don't care what Knocko Cheatham says in the newspaper, I'm not dead yet." Mac looked at him, and saw in his chin the shadow of his magnificent combativeness. "I might just run again. You going to come back and help out, young Mac?"

Mac knew the answer, but he could not say it. "Maybe so, Tom Jeff," he said.

"Looks like I'm going to need a new campaign manager."

"You don't need me for that, Tom Jeff. Ralph Bova will do a good job for you."

"Ralph's a good man, no question about that," Shadwell said ruminatively. "But if we go again, we're going to need every good man we can get. Virginia's a tough state, you know that better than anybody."

Mac shrugged uncomfortably. "I don't know," he said. "I'll have to see. But I really do have to get away, maybe I'll be back."

"I guess I can understand why a young man would want to see the world," Shadwell said. "I'd love to take some time off myself. I got to practice law, though. But it sounds like fun, young Mac. Just don't forget us here in Virginia." He clasped Mac's elbow and said again, "Don't forget us."

"Don't worry about that, Tom Jeff," Mac said. Then, as he turned to the car, a dim memory surfaced inside him, and he turned back. "Listen, Tom Jeff," he said. "Tobey Carrington gave me a message for you."

"What's that?" Shadwell said; interest flickered on his face.

"He said for you to call him up. He wants to get together."

"Is that right?" Shadwell seemed to mull over the possibility. "That's right interesting. I wonder why? We've never been great friends or anything."

"Maybe it's time you got to be," Mac said. "You belong to be, after all, you're both good lawyers, honest men, good legislators. . . ."

Tom Jeff laughed and cut him off. "Don't cast all that in stone yet, now," he said. "We're both losers, too."

"You go see Tobey Carrington," Mac said fiercely. "Tell him I said he's got some things to tell you."

Shadwell seemed mildly surprised, but he nodded tentatively. "I guess I will," he said. "You say so. You give pretty good advice."

"I have to pack. Are you sure I can't give you a ride to the hotel?"

"No, I think I'll walk," said Tom Jeff, patting his sides and breathing deeply. "Do me good, make me slim and good-looking like you."

"All right," Mac said. "Take care."

They shook hands. ' 'I will," Tom Jeff said. "You too."

Sitting in the car, Mac watched Shadwell walking down the sidewalk, back straight, head up, and suddenly he felt a mixture of love and fear for this courageous dumpy man, and he almost cried out: *Be careful, Tom Jeff! Don't let the shad knives get to you! Be careful!*

But of course he said nothing, and Tom Jeff did not look back; instead, Mac watched him pass down the block and turn northward toward the George Mason. Then he was gone.

In the echoing station he checks his watch: there are a few minutes left until train time. He walks quickly to the small passageway next to the defunct lunch counter, to a row of phone booths. He can dial direct to Opechancanough County. As the numbers click through the switching machinery, he smooths his hair and straightens his tie. But it is for nothing; the phone rings unanswered, seven times, eight, nine. He holds it for a moment against his shoulder; perhaps it is just as well, for what, after all, could he say? *Good luck*, perhaps, *best wishes*. Inside himself he discovers that he would like to say that to her, to them both; would mean it. A

439

wedding seems a fit end, somehow, and even if it is not his own, somehow he feels a participant, as if he had helped plant the tree of life. Once more he wishes that it may flourish and grow.

Then he is out again in the main hall. He sits at one of the curved wooden benches and unfolds his paper. His eye is caught by a small headline: BLACK CLERIC SCORES BROCK; SEEKS "RECKONING." He sees again the tall angular frame, the rigid angry face, of the Reverend Mr. Alonso Davis, bound on his mission of purgation. To him also he silently wishes luck.

Then the reverberating voice, like the voice of God, calls train time. He rises and folds the paper. Nearby a squat trash can bids him FIGHT LITTER! He puts the newspaper there and, hefting his suitcase, walks toward the gate.

"You have to take more than that," Molly O . had said adamantly, tipping her head toward Mac's single suitcase.

"Why?" Mac said blandly. He did not tell her what he was thinking: *I wish I could take less. I wish I could leave my name, my past. I want to see the world with empty hands.*

"You just ought to," she said. For the fourth time, not so much because she did not understand as because she did not want to stop talking or say good-bye, she repeated, "I don't see why you want to go back to Boston anyway. You never liked it so much when you were there before."

And for the fourth time, not impatiently, because he recognized that behind her seeming querulousness was a genuine concern and even some dismay at being left alone, Mac repeated, "I'm not going to stay in Boston, O., I'm going to visit Arnie for a while, look around, you know."

"Where will you go then?"

"I don't know, South America maybe, Spain, Africa. Maybe I'll see the places my father saw. Or maybe someplace new."

"I don't see why you don't just stay at home and keep out of trouble."

Mac laughed, and fingered the crown of his skull. There were two scars there now. "I'm not sure that's the right way for me to stay out of trouble," he said.

"What do you want me to do with your car?"

Mac laughed again. He reached in his pocket, pulled out the keys to the Continental, and flipped them to her. She caught them awkwardly. "Here," Mac said. "Make a rose planter out of the damn thing. Grow John F. Kennedys in it."

"No, Mac, seriously."

"I'm serious," he said. "Sell it. Junk it. Give it to the poor. I don't real-

440

ly give a damn. I don't care if I never see it again. Why don't you have the judge take care of it? He's got my power of attorney."

She looked at him with shy speculation. "Did you and the judge make it up?"

"Yes," he said shortly. "I went and saw him." They had come to an understanding, after their stiff natures. The judge had once more accepted responsibility for the affairs of an Evans, and when he left, there had been a spark of wary warmth; not as if they had forgotten what lay between them, but rather as if each recognized that they still needed each other for reasons neither could express.

Mac looked at Molly O. She was home from work, and she was wearing a red-and-brown dress and blue sweater. To him she looked familiar, warm, dependable, and kind, and he loved her. "I guess I better get going," he said.

"Let me drive you to the station," she said. "It's no problem, really."

But Mac was looking foward to his solitude in the sounding railroad cathedral. "Thanks," Mac said. "It's all right. I'll get myself there."

"Okay then," she said vaguely. "I guess. Okay." She moved toward him uncertainly, and he reached down to her. They embraced awkwardly, and she kissed him on the cheek. "Take care, she said.

Mac turned his face to the window to hide his tearing eyes. In the December dusk, a cold wind stirred the pine needles, and a few dead leaves flew along the frosty ground. The dogwood tree was bare. "I'll miss you, Molly O.," he said.

"Me, too," she said behind him. "And if you get weary traveling, you come on home. I'll be here. I'm not going anywhere."

"I know," he said, still watching the wintry yard.

In the half-deserted passenger car he settles in a window seat, piling magazines and jacket on its companion to make a cozy nest. He reclines, stretches his legs, and closes his eyes. Around him are the faint smells of a passenger train, stale air, cigars, moisture, sweat. They are a nostalgic perfume, and he breathes deeply in contentment. He remembers Lester putting him aboard a Pullman car. "Now you be good, bub," his brother said, handing him five crisp one-dollar bills. "Don't you go up to the club car and use this money to buy whiskey and women, you hear me?" "I won't, Lester," Mac, eight years old, replied.

Around him he hears the other passengers stirring in their seats. They are mostly black, northbound. Now he hears a faint black voice raised suddenly in anger: "Goddamn redneck don't ask no questions! Last time I go back to Alabama alive. . . ." Then another voice: "Hush now, shh. . . ." He opens his eyes and leafs through a magazine: "NUCLEAR POWER: *Menace or Miracle?*" He flips: "Campus Comedy." He flips: "Humor in Uniform."

With a welcome lurch, the train starts; he is on his way. Outside it is full dark, and a cold rain falls against the window. But inside the car he feels warm and dry, facing the long trip up the Eastern seaboard. He thinks of Stephanian's voice on the telephone, voluble, professorial, excited, sketching great plans of what Mac will do: schemes for research and agitation that will bring revolution, reform, socialism, the just city. He wonders where he will go, what he will do, and the wondering make him smile.

"Excuse me," says a polite voice. "May I borrow your *Reader's Digest?*"

He looks around. It is the thin, birdlike black woman he saw sleeping in the terminal; she is awake now, in the seat across the aisle, watching him with head cocked, eyes bright.

"Certainly." He hands her the magazine.

"Thank you," she says primly, watching him still with that bright inquisitive stare. They regard each other without speaking.

"Where are you going?" he says at last, to be polite.

"Philadelphia," she replies.

There is another pause.

"Is that your home?"

"Yes, indeed," she says decisively. "I've lived there for twenty-three years."

"Ah," he says. "What do you do there?"

"I'm in education."

"I see," he says. He looks down at the magazine in his hand but feels those sharp eyes watching him still. He surrenders to them again. "Are you a teacher?"

"No, I'm a vice-principal."

"High school?"

"No, elementary."

"Ah." That line of conversation seems exhausted, but still she watches him. "Are you from Richmond?" he says.

"Yes, indeed," she says pridefully. "From Richmond is exactly right. I hate to go back there. I tell people I'm from Richmond, and being from Richmond suits me fine. I don't want to be there. I only went back for my grandmother's funeral."

"Oh," Mac says. "I'm sorry."

She waves aside his sympathy with a crisp motion of one hand.

"You're very kind," she says. "But Gramma was ninety-six years old. She died in her sleep. I'd like to go exactly that way when my time comes."

"Ah," Mac says.

"What do you do?" She is fiercely polite, and seems determined to keep the conversation going.

He gestures vaguely. "I'm . . . at liberty," he says. "Off to see the world."

"My goodness." She seems fascinated and dismayed. "That's quite an assignment."

"Yes," Mac says. "I've got plenty of time."

From the front of the car appears a black conductor; he gestures at the passengers like a minister blessing his flock. "Brothers and sisters, your tickets, if you please!"

Mac holds his up for inspection. Then there is a pause while the conductor attends to the vice-principal's. Mac takes the opportunity to bunch up his jacket and wedge it against the window, reclining on it, ostentatiously sleepy.

"You tired?" the bright voice calls.

"Yes, ma'am," he says, without opening his eyes.

"Well, I'll read your magazine."

"Fine, fine."

She falls silent. Mac, to his surprise, finds real sleep stealing across him, as if his body were seeking to redeem his lie. He sighs deeply. He is swaying gently as the train rocks along, and the motion is soothing. He thinks briefly of the people he is leaving behind him: Molly O., briskly living her life, riding and working and keeping her own counsel; Knocko off on a new paranoid crusade, lost in incomprehensible plans for revenge and vindication; Tom Jeff determinedly preparing to fight for the right again and (if need be) again and again and again; Tobey Carrington among the pines in Tabbville, at peace with himself.

. . . And then suddenly, as easily as he might draw a breath, he is out, he is free, for him it is over. He leaves behind the graves of his brother and his father, their unsettled score of victories and defeats, debts, promises, and betrayals. All is behind him: the gleaming state Capitol, the bright lobby of the George Mason, St. Cyprian's School, the Confederate Club. Rocking gently in the train, he has left all these behind as a moth leaves its cocoon, he is poised now on the lip of the future, and he feels quiet and confident and good. Before him lies the bright phenomenal world, all that had been hidden behind metaphors of vengeance and victory, and he is ready now, at last, to let go, to enter it. Into his mind unbidden comes the thought that nothing lasts forever, not family or family curse or ancient wrong or even earth itself. The thought is comforting. The world, seen thus anew, flashes in his mind's eye, a bright globe, the line of nightfall cutting the Atlantic. He will study it with diligence, he will work out his salvation, he thinks, and then, like night off the ocean, in the swaying train, northbound, away from home, sleep comes.